The Politics of Music
in the Third Reich

American University Studies

Series IX
History

Vol. 49

PETER LANG
New York • Bern • Frankfurt am Main • Paris

Michael Meyer

The Politics of Music
in the Third Reich

PETER LANG
New York • Bern • Frankfurt am Main • Paris

Library of Congress Cataloging-in-Publication Data

Meyer, Michael,
   The politics of music in the Third Reich / Michael
Meyer.
      p. cm — (American university studies. Series IX,
History ; vol. 49)
      1. Music—Germany—20th century—History and
criticism.   2. National socialism and music.   I. Title.
II. Series.
ML275.5.M49   1991   780'.943'09043—dc20   89-8216
ISBN 0-8203-0805-0   CIP
ISSN 0740-0462   MN

© Peter Lang Publishing, Inc., New York 1991

Printed in the United States of America.

ACKNOWLEDGEMENTS

This book is an outgrowth of a dissertation completed in 1970 at UCLA under the guidance of the late Eugene N. Anderson. Since then I have benefitted from the help of several individuals and institutions. I should like to express my gratitude to all:

California State University, Northridge for several grants, two sabbaticals and publication support; the History Department at CSUN which made the talents available of Marcia Dunnicliffe for typing the manuscripts and Amy Althoff for typing corrections; Robert Olsen who produced the camera-ready copy; and the American Philosophical Society for a grant in 1977.

The library staff at CSUN and UCLA; Musikwissenschaftliches Seminar, University of Heidelberg; Bundestagsbibliothek, Schumannhaus and University of Bonn; Musikhochschule and Staatsbibliothek in West Berlin.

The archival staff at the Berlin Document Center and the Akademie der Künste, Berlin; Bundesarchiv Koblenz; Institut für Zeitgeschichte and Bayrisches Staatsarchiv in Munich.

Individuals who contributed discussion, correspondence and/or interview: Ingeborg Jahn, *Frankfurter Rundschau*; Fritz Sänger, and Joachim Heinz, *Frankfurter Zeitung*; Dr. Elke Fröhlich, Institut für Zeitgeschichte, Munich; the emigres Rudy Brook, Richard Dresdner and Karl Ulrich Schnabel, Los Angeles; Dr. Uwe Roehl, Alfred Etzold and Wolfgang Steeger, Norddeutscher Rundfunk, Hamburg; Dr. Jürgen-Philip Furtwängler, Bergedorf; Peter Dannenberg and Joachim Wenzel, Hamburgische Staatsoper; Dr. Günter Schab, *Düsseldorfer Nachrichten*; Dr. Walter Huder and Hannelore Pitscher, Akademie der Künste, Berlin.

My colleagues Alan Dirrim and Vern Bullough for critical reading of early drafts; and Harry Robin and my wife Miriam for editing the manuscript. My final thanks to Michael J. Flamini of Peter Lang Publishing for the final editing and guiding the book to completion.

Pacific Palisades,   Michael Meyer
October, 1990

CONTENTS

LIST OF ILLUSTRATIONS

Children and HJ in villages near Magdeburg (Photos: Karl Meyer, "Herr Linse", *Magdeburger General-Anzeiger;* author's archives).

Facsimile: *Unsre Fahne flattert uns voran* (author's archives).

Franz Sedte and Hermann Blume (Bildarchiv Preussischer Kulturbesitz, Berlin).

HJ in Finland (Ullstein Bilderdienst, Berlin).

Facsimile: Horst-Wessel Song, (*Horst Wessel Marschalbum,* Frz. Eher Nachf., 1933; author's archives).

German Soldiers (Photo: Karl Meyer; author's archives).

SA concert (Ullstein Bilderdienst, Berlin).

Franz Adam (Bildarchiv Preussischer Kulturbesitz, Berlin).

Hans Hinkel and Hans v. Benda (Bundesarchiv, Koblenz).

Hitler and Bruckner bust (Ullstein Bilderdienst, Berlin).

Hitler at window (Bildarchiv, Preussischer Kulturbesitz, Berlin).

Joseph Goebbels (Ullstein Bilderdienst, Berlin).

Furtwängler and Strauss (Bildarchiv Preussischer Kulturbesitz, Berlin).

Peter Raabe (Peter Raabe, *Die Musik im Dritten Reich,* Gustav Bosse Verlag, 1935; author's archives).

Hitler and Rosenberg (Ullstein Bilderdienst, Berlin).

Facsimile: Elly Ney, drawn by Walter Rath (Stadtarchiv Bonn).

Wilhelm Brückner-Rüggenberg (Ullstein Bilderdienst, Berlin).

Hitler in audience (Ullstein Bilderdienst, Berlin).

Wilhelm Furtwängler (Bundesarchiv, Koblenz).

Hans Hinkel (Bundesarchiv, Koblenz).

Kurt Singer (Bildarchiv Preussischer Kulturbesitz, Berlin).

Jonny, Entartete Musik exhibit poster (Bildarchiv Preussischer Kulturbesitz, Berlin).

Arnold Schönberg (Bildarchiv Preussischer Kulturbesitz, Berlin).

Kurt Weill (Bildarchiv Preussischer Kulturbesitz, Berlin).

Wilhelm Furtwängler at HJ concert (Bundesarchiv, Koblenz).

Wilhelm Furtwängler and Yehudi Menuhin (Ullstein Bilderdienst).

Chart: Reich Music Chamber

GLOSSARY OF SELECT TERMS AND ABBREVIATIONS

AD	Arbeitsdienst, Labor Service
ADM	Arbeitsgemeinschaft Deutscher Musikkritiker, Study Group of German Music Critics
ADMV	Allgemeiner deutscher Musikverein, General German Music Society
AMRMK	Amtliche Mitteilungen der Reichsmusikkammer, Official Bulletin of the Reich Music Chamber
Amt für Konzertwesen	Office of Concert Management
Anschluss	annexation
AO	Auslandsorganisation der NSDAP, Foreign Countries Organization of the NSDAP
Arbeitersängerbund	Workers Choral Association
arteigen	native
artfremd	alien
BA	Bundesarchiv Koblenz, Federal Archives
BDC	Berlin Document Center
Blut und Boden	blood and soil
DAF	Deutsche Arbeitsfront, German Labor Front
DAS	Deutscher Arbeiter-Sängerbund, German Workers Choral Association
Deutsche Christen	German Christians
Deutsche Musikgesellschaft	German Musicological Society
Deutscher Gemeindetag	Organization of German Municipalities
Deutscher Musikalienverleger Verein	German Association of Music Publishers
Deutsches Tonkünstlerfest	German Music Festival
Deutschland Erwache	Germany awake
DM	*Die Musik*
DSB	Deutscher Sängerbund, German Choral Association
DSBZ	*Deutsche Sängerbundszeitung*
E-Musik	ernste Musik, serious (classical) music
entartete Musik	degenerate music
Entjudung	the purging of Jews
Fachschaft	professional organization

Gau	district, administrative district, region
Gauleiter	regional commander, leader
Gesamtkunstwerk	total or unified work of art (Wagner)
Gleichschaltung	coordination
GMD	Generalmusikdirektor, general music director
Grossdeutschland	Greater Germany
Hauptkulturamt	Central Culture Office
Hauptprüfungs-ausschuss	Official Review Board
HJ	Hitler-Jugend, Hitler Youth
Horst-Wessel-Lied	the SA song commemorating the early Nazi martyr sung on festive occasions
IfZ	Institut für Zeitgeschichte, Institute for Contemporary History, Munich
JKB	Jüdischer Kulturbund, Jewish Cultural League
KdF	Kraft durch Freude, Strength through Joy
KfdK	Kampfbund für deutsche Kultur, Fighting League for German Culture
Land, Länder	region(s), province(s), state(s)
Landeskirche	regional church
Landeskulturwalter	Supervisor of Regional Cultural Affairs
Landesleiter	Regional Leader
Landesmusikerschaft	Regional Association of Professional Musicians
Landesorchester	Regional Orchestra
Landesstelle	Regional Office
MiJV	*Musik in Jugend und Volk*
Musikpolitik	politics of music
Nachtkritik	Evening Review
NS	National Sozialistisch, National Socialist
NSBO	NS-Betriebsorganisation, NS Labor Cell Organization
NSDAP	Nationalsozialische Deutsche Arbeiterpartei, National Socialist German Workers Party
NSDStB	Nationalsozialistischer Deutscher Studentenbund, National Socialist German Student Association
NSKG	NS-Kulturgemeinde, NS Cultural Community
NSRSO	NS-Reichssinfonieorchester, NS Reich Symphony Orchestra
Obersturmführer	Schutzstaffel (SS) chief commander
Ortsmusikerschaft	Local Organization of Professional Musicians
Ortsmusikerschafts-leiter	Leader of the Local Organization of Professional Musicians

PAdK	Preussische Akademie der Künste, Prussian Academie of the Arts
Pg	Parteigenosse, party member
Preussisches Ministerium für Wissenschaft, Kunst und Volksbildung	Prussian Education Ministry
RDS	Reichsverband deutscher Schriftsteller, Reich Association of German writers
RDTM	Reichsverband deutscher Tonkünstler und Musiklehrer, Reich Association of German Musicians and Music Educators
Reichskartell der deutschen Musikerschaft	Reich Cartel of German Musicians
Reichskulturrat	Reich Culture Council
Reichskultursenat	Reich Culture Senate
Reichskulturwalter	Reich Culture Supervisor
Reichsleiter	Reich Leader
Reichsleitung	Reich Directorate of the National Socialist Party
Reichsmusikprüfstelle	Reich Music Censorship Office
Reichspropagandaleiter	Reich Propaganda Leader
Reichsrundfunkgesellschaft	Reich Broadcasting Company
Reichssendeleiter	Reich Director of Radio Broadcasting
Reichsverband der deutschen Musikalienhändler	Reich Association of German Music Dealers
Reichsverband der Jüdischen Kulturbünde	Reich Association of the Jewish Cultural Leagues
RFM	Reichsfilmkammer, Reich Film Chamber
RJF	Reichsjugendführung, Reich Youth Leadership
RKK	Reichskulturkammer, Reich Culture Chamber
RKKG	Reichskulturkammergesetz, Reich Culture Chamber Law
RMK	Reichsmusikkammer, Reich Music Chamber
RMS	Reichsmusikerschaft, Reich Organization of Musicians within the Reich Music Chamber

RMT	Reichsmusiktage, Reich Music Festival
RMVP	Reichsministrium für Volksaufklärung und Propaganda, Reich Ministry for Popular Enlightenment and Propaganda
RPK	Reichspressekammer, Reich Press Chamber
RVDZV	Reichsverband der Deutschen Zeitungsverleger, Reich Association of German Newspaper Publishers
SA	Sturmabteilung (der NSDAP), Storm troopers
SD	Sicherheitsdienst (der SS), Security Service (of the SS)
SS	Schutzstaffel, Hitler's black-shirted security force
Staatssekretar	Undersecretary
Städtischer Musikbeauftragter	City Music Representative (supervisor)
Stagma	Staatlich genehmigte Gesellschaft zur Verwertung musikalischer Urheberrechte, Official Copyright Review Board
Stählerne Romantik	steel romanticism
Ständestaat	state of estates
Thing Theater	Assembly theatre
U-Musik	Unterhaltungsmusik, entertainment music
Untersturmführer	Schutzstaffel (SS) deputy commander
VB	*Völkischer Beobachter*
VDA	Verein Deutscher Zeitungsverleger, Society of German Newspaper Publishers
völkisch	national, in the sense of pure German
Volksempfänger	radio set
Volksgemeinschaft	national community, community of the people
Volksoper	people's opera, national opera
Wunschkonzert	concert by request
ZfM	*Zeitschrift für Musik*

Wilheom Furtwängler conducting a "Recreational Concert" at the Machine Tool Factory R. Stock & Co., Berlin-Marienfelde, December 1939.

Introduction

The history of the Third Reich has been written by numerous historians and specialists from many disciplines. Yet, rather than having exhausted the subject, the stupendous amount of information, interpretation and theory continue to grow. Karl Dietrich Bracher's *The German Dictatorship* (1969) synthesized archival records, memoir literature, previous research and theoretical positions, but even this magisterial work did not put the corpse to rest. The live historiographical tradition feeds on itself—ever-expanding in formulations, challenges, confirmations and, again reformulations which variously reflect new insights based on old and new sources, but— significantly—also on contemporary attitudes. Germany's caustic 1980s debate over the significance and uniqueness of Nazism and holocaust, known as the *Historikerstreit*, bears witness to the intensity of the ongoing scholarly and popular interest in the Nazi past, though manifestly in the light of current issues and concerns.[1]

Most analysts agree that the Third Reich deviated markedly from the general behavior patterns of western society. Shocked by the radicalism of the terror state, the regimentation of the population, thought and culture, and the aggressive attitudes and actions which led to the horrors of world war and unprecedented genocide, the authors have attempted to understand the inexplicable. How was it possible for the Nazi dictatorship to rise in the country which had boasted of its share of bourgeois propriety and rich achievement in culture? What were the mechanisms by which the behavior of German society was made to coincide with brutal Nazi policies? And what were the consequences of those fateful years for today's Germany and for western civilization? Transcendent theory and global interpretation of those twelve years will continue to evolve. Some areas of Nazi totalitarian control still merit examination because they have not received the same attention as others—almost blank spots until recently, in an otherwise well-charted map.

Music is one such blank area—surprising, not only because of the apparently insatiable public interest in Nazi affairs, but also in view of music's celebrated tradition in Germany, its international prominence—perhaps even preeminence, a considerable memoir literature of its distinguished representatives who had either practiced their craft in Nazi Germany or abroad during emigration and, then, also the requirement of publication in an imperialist academic establishment whose designs would appear to tolerate no bounds—certainly not in such intriguing terrain which continues to hold more than academic interest. How is it that, for so long, music and musicians have escaped all the questions addressed to the totality of the Nazi experience? One invariably asks whether the "culture producers" who betrayed enthusiastic support for the "Third Reich" did indeed genuinely identify with Nazi cultural policies or—in view of the incredible unemployment rate among musicians (far exceeding that of the population at large)—whether they simply took advantage of new opportunities at the expense of Jews and others purged at the onset of the regime. If the latter, to what degree were they aware of their contribution to a cultural facade for the terror state, for the cynical manipulators and perpetrators of unspeakable crimes? Terror and fear adds another dimension which is stressed in nearly all recollections and is legitimate in view of the many people who fell victim to the regime. Motives and rationales most certainly were contradictory in the case of many, and varied among individuals.

How are we to explain the blank spot? In part, music's escape from its "brown" (Nazi) past mirrors selective German amnesia in general—a tendency of disassociation from the defeated terror state and its ideology—either genuinely or out of fear of Allied retribution or for both reasons. Preoccupied with survival during the years that immediately followed, the "rubble years,"[2] at least 120,000 professional musicians joined their countrymen in erasing traces of the past twelve years through denial, distortion, omission, lying and destruction of compromising records in the context of the denazification proceedings to which musicians, like so many other Germans, were subjected before being permitted to resume professional activities.[3] Having donned brown uniforms in the context of a massive purge of personnel in 1933, in acknowledgment of one historic change, many musicians altered their colors again, against the background of yet another purge, to signify a second major historical turn in 1945.

Denazification clarified ideological lines as people testified for each other, denounced others, and closed ranks against those found guilty. Purged of a segment of its obviously brown contingent, the music establishment—presumably denazified and "reeducated"—stood ready to contribute to the construction of a new "free" and democratic society in the West, a socialist "people's republic" in the East. Soon, in the context of the Cold War and the need for new solidarity declarations, the more Nazi-tainted members of the profession were reemployed and could even, in the case of those in the west, draw on the anti-bolshevist slogans of their Nazi past.

In addition to conditions and denazification procedures experienced by all professionals in the cultural sector, musicians and musicologists made reference to and benefited from distinct features and traditions of their medium. Live music, for instance, could not be recreated as testimony, while recordings and especially tapes were not widely distributed then. Secondly, pure music was understood to be the most abstract and, thus, "apolitical" art, one that symbolized the claimed situation of its practitioners. Compromising scores, texts and dedications—which were illegal to begin with—were destroyed and generally omitted from postwar biographies, autobiographies and music encyclopedias—testifying to the solidarity of musicians, musicologists, editors and teachers. Music has historically lagged behind the literary and other artistic stylistic developments which reflect and address contemporary social and political issues more obviously and concretely. Musicologists traditionally have confined themselves to music-immanent analysis rather than study the historical context of music, musicians and related political engagement. They have concerned themselves, least of all, with the idea of socio-economic determinants or structures that might be gleaned from musical forms and material. Consequently, for nearly a generation after the so-called "zero hour," musicologists have failed to probe the policies of music in the Third Reich. There has been no investigation in empirical terms as to who did what, when and where; in what capacity, quality and quantity; and for whom, under what circumstances and through whose support. There has been no social-theory-informed manner of decoding the musical material as to its negative, affirmative or possibly even fascist quality; what it can reveal about the moral, social or neutral role of the artist, indeed, about instrumental compared to *l'art pour l'art*; and what it might contribute to our understanding of fascism (or national socialism) in general.

Impressed by the gap in scholarship of both the Third Reich and music, as a doctoral candidate in history with a background and interest in music, I decided in 1966 to study Nazi music policy in a dissertation completed in 1970. During the research phase I discovered the 1963 work of Joseph Wulf, who had published his pioneering examination of archival records in *Musik im Dritten Reich*. His documentation was helpful in writing my dissertation, which has led to the present book. Meanwhile, musicologists and other interested scholars in Germany, too, have broken the conspiracy of silence about the role of musicians and musicologists in the history of Nazi culture. A music-specific *Historikerstreit* has intruded upon the pristine world of musicology. The student and related movements of the late-60s and 70s have played a crucial role in breaking taboos and rudely confronted the "brown past" of music and musicians, at symposia and in the journals. Defenders of an assumed apolitical world of music and musicology are now challenged by social-theory-informed scholars who insist on the decisive economic and political determinants even of musical life—if not obvious at all times, clearly visible in the unmediated world of Nazi totalitarianism and terror. Fred K. Prieberg, a non-academic music historian, confirmed the exposure of Nazi involvement of hundreds of musicians, musicologists, journalists and institutions in the, to date, most comprehensive political music history, *Musik im NS-Staat* (1982). The distinguished Society for the Study of Music finally agendized "Music of the 1930s" at its 1981 Congress, though still without naming the "actual" topic, as noted by Hans-Günter Klein in an introduction to *Musik und Musikpolitik im faschistischen Deutschland* (1984), coedited by him and Hanns-Werner Heister. Concerned not to perpetuate the evocative labels coined by the Nazis for themselves (e.g. "National Socialism"—traditionally offensive to Socialists for its usurpation of their own movement; "Seizure of Power"—instead preferring to stress the machinations of power brokers that brought Hitler to power and, thus, to identify fascism as an extension of capitalism; "Third Reich"—rejected, as too glorious and devoid of any reference to its regressive and evil qualities; etc.), the editors took the exact title and, indeed, the theoretical presuppositions and organizational framework from a both learned and sectarian Hanns Eisler essay of 1935.[4] In reformulating the Marxist anti-fascist tradition of Eisler who retained confidence in a proletarian music culture of which he was an outstanding practitioner, and that of the rather different Theodor W. Adorno whose jaundiced view of all "administered" music—not only the fascist totalitarian but also the Soviet variety, as well as that of the manipulated consumer culture of western democracies—the Heister-Klein collaboration has contributed to a broadening of our topic to include the historical and social foundations of music and music politics in the Third Reich (fascist Germany), while adding new insights specifically about entertainment, everyday life and Nazi pageantry. It is within this expanded framework that I examine Nazi music policy, its organization, ideology and impact. By introducing those elements of the totalitarian state and its ideology which deal with music, this study will demonstrate that musicians were not only victims of totalitarian measures but also accomplices to it.

The relationship between music and National Socialism in the first year of the Third Reich will be explored in Chapter I in the context of the Nazi "revolution," descriptive incidents, journalistic coverage, and personnel and other changes at musical institutions. Sharing the fate of other artists and intellectuals, cultural and educational leaders, churches, and the press, musicians responded to the Nazi revolution variously in their resistances and accommodations. Many outstanding exponents of all branches of German music life either resisted Nazi totalitarianism, resigned, emigrated, or suffered various degrees of pressures and purges. Other noted composers, performers, music directors, educators, critics, and musicologists, however, availed themselves for defining German music and music policy for the new state in accordance with Nazi principles and to integrating musical life with the ceremony and the organization of the Nazi state. Musicians thereby contributed to the Nazi effort of cultivating an image favorable to culture. Through their role in the administration of music, periodic solidarity proclamations, supportive articles and books, dedications of compositions, and festive performances, musicians joined party ideologists and organizers in the confirmation and justification of totalitarian design and practice. This development played a crucial role in the legitimization of Nazi power in the cultural sphere. Musicians spoke and wrote a new language consistent with Nazi principles, which was standardized by the regimented press, Nazi organizers, musician collaborators, and even the victims of purges, who had to defend themselves in the idiom used to condemn them. This study concentrates on the relationship between National Socialism and music, that is, on the conditions of music in a totalitarian society. However, it is not to be thought of as an attempt to encompass the entire musical life in the Third Reich, or as a comprehensive musicological statement on music culture, its developments, outstanding individuals, compositions, and performances. Incidents and material are selected exclusively in demonstration of music's situation in a totalitarian society.

The review of 1933 offers a confusing picture of the Nazi leadership and the musical profession alike, probing in an atmosphere of experimentation and adjustment. By the end of the year, however, the coordination of sentiment and institutions with National Socialism, the making and unmaking of careers, and finally the proliferation of official decrees, produced a national organization of music which extended into the far reaches of the land and beyond its borders into conquered territories a few years later. The national Reich Music Chamber, *Reichsmusikkammer* (RMK), an organization within Joseph Goebbels' ubiquitous Propaganda Ministry (RMVP), was the crowning achievement of the organizers who would direct musical affairs for the duration of the Third Reich. Its operations, policy statements, internal problems, and conflicts with rival Nazi organizations are the subject of Chapter II, crucial to an understanding of the Nazi administration of music. The propagandistic role assigned to music and musicology will be the subject of Chapter III. Music contributed to the operation of the Nazi state as an embellishment and important component of Nazi ritual, while musicology established Nazi myths and symbols as conceptual constructs reinforcing and promoting ideology. The realms of totalitarian politics and functional art were therefore complementary. Art was no longer permitted to develop in response to its intrinsic tensions. Ironically, both German institutions and some leading musical personalities had found aspects of Nazism congenial, a paradoxical situation that leads to the last chapter, which offers a portrait of the musician in a totalitarian society in all its complexities. When the conductor Wilhelm Furtwängler, the most representative authority in German music life and the final subject of Chapter IV, rose to defend his realm against totalitarian invasion, the demise of Germany's conservative tradition in music was manifest. His stand illustrates the bankruptcy of the anachronistic elites which had resisted modernization in politics and music during the Weimar Republic and then attempted to do the same in the Third Reich.

The Nazi control of German music and the complementary effort of the music community to participate in what was then termed "the regeneration of the German people and culture" suggest at first glance a departure from traditional governmental attitudes toward music and from the way most German musicians had viewed their social and political obligations. German music of the old order was composed and performed within the sheltered position of the authoritarian political structures of a disunited country. Tied to aristocratic households, states, or cities with life-long contracts, German musicians enjoyed the necessary financial security for devoting their full time to music. In this atmosphere of seclusion and quiet they created that absolute music which, according to the pianist Artur Schnabel, was "perhaps the most exclusive medium for the spiritual exaltation of the active individual in an intimate, private sphere of personal experience."[5] Furtwängler boasted that this music had developed into "the most joyful, clearest, and most profound manifestation of the German spirit, the last original and artistic achievement of all modern peoples."[6] Non-verbal and spiritual, this music could be heard in demonstration of German idealism, with its characteristic emphasis on inwardness which lent itself to social authoritarianism—not, it would seem, to public-mindedness. *Machtgeschützte Innerlichkeit*, Thomas Mann called this socio-political reality, and developed the story of *Dr. Faustus* during the war in illustration of music's mirror image of the German situation.

In addition to the idealistic tradition and the paternalism of the ruling elites which supported cultural activity, the system of German disunity had contributed to music's exclusiveness, and, for that very reason, its excellence and proliferation. Whereas culture was centered in the capitals of other countries, Germany and German culture were decentralized so that the united Germany inherited from previously sovereign political entities a cultural network of excellent stages, orchestras, operas, and choruses, many of which could rival music in Berlin. Bismarck's unification of Germany in 1871 and Austria's political humiliation did not restrict musical life. On the contrary, the surviving benevolent authoritarianism of the day contributed to the maintenance of the autonomous development of music. The persistence of traditional institutions and social structure guaranteed stability and protected culture. Patterns of intersocial relationships and the role of cultural institutions within the social fabric were not even significantly disturbed by the "late, rapid, and thorough" German version of the Industrial Revolution,[7] as the great bourgeoisie had not developed into a self-conscious and socially and politically independent class. It strongly identified with traditional culture, whose leadership it accepted in demonstration of its own attitude toward professional excellence. Opera continued to attract great audiences, therefore, being an art form through which the achievement-conscious bourgeoisie could celebrate itself in an aristocratic setting. Chamber music established itself firmly in the bourgeois home and on the concert stage; instruments were improved and became more accessible throughout society, while conservatories spread and trained more and better musicians.

Aspects of this tradition of excellence, autonomy, benevolent support, and the spread of an active music culture were alive in 1933 when the Nazi revolution threatened, above all, music's autonomy and excellence. The memoir literature of those musicians who were either prevented from working in the Third Reich or unable to adjust to its demands indeed suggests a story of an unprepared musical profession virtually raped by a sinister force dedicated to the extirpation of the best in Western culture. It is the story of an external power thrusting itself upon an inward-directed, socially conservative eighteenth-century-like music community whose political innocence, these musicians felt, ought to have secured extraterritorial immunity from the Nazis. In reality, the eighteenth-century exclusiveness was but a feature of a far more complex and involved music community in the twentieth century. In spite of their truly remarkable lack of political awareness and interest, musicians had become affected by sweeping historical changes which were not, to be sure, of their own making. Centralizing forces which culminated in a national market and political unification were reflected in the cultural nationalism whose leaders—even in the early nineteenth century - advertised musical offerings as profound revelation of the national spirit. Some musicians were flattered, while others such as Weber and Wagner, actually became celebrated articulators of what amounted to a nationalistic cult of the musician. However, gradual historical transformation and its intellectual reflections had no immediate and pervasive impact on the provincial and even obscure musical order. Furtwängler complained in a noted essay of 1937 that, even when the work of German musicians had become popular between the last years of Haydn and the time of Beethoven, "they still had not entered the national consciousness to the degree of the contemporary literature of Goethe and Schiller."[8] Aside from the social and political reasons for music's exclusiveness and relative obscurity, Furtwängler blamed Goethe himself, who had dominated German intellectual life and influenced aesthetic judgment. Although the contemporary of outstanding German composers, the

great cosmopolitan and representative of German particularism did not realize
the magnitude of their achievement—in spite of his interest in German folk
music which he shared with Herder and later nationalists. Shortly thereafter,
however, in 1834 the musician Robert Schumann founded a journal, *Neue
Zeitschrift für Musik*, with which he broadened public taste; but Richard
Wagner was the first who had gained the prestige necessary to affect public
opinion in favor of music.[9] Although created from within the old feudal-
absolutist order of German disunity—a condition essentially anathema to German nationalism—and tied to it, music was identified by nationalists like
Wagner as the most revealing product of a national culture which transcended
the political disunity of Germany before 1871. Thereafter, music so understood,
contributed to an image of true spiritual unity which thus lent itself to pointing out the shortcomings of the real and limited German empire created and
shaped by Bismarck's *Realpolitik*. Music became then an accomplice to projecting the cultural ideals which the Nazis would eventually appropriate.

During the latter third of the nineteenth century music was thus no longer
an exclusive domain, simply an adornment of good society, acknowledged
for its profundity, spirituality, and/or entertainment value. It had become
inextricably tied to the ideological milieu which also produced National
Socialism via the cultural nationalists who had opposed Bismarck.[10] The entry of German music as a superior artistic achievement into national consciousness coincided with the victory of German arms and the creation of
the Reich, whose export articles included Wagner's music, thus reinforcing
Germany's claim to cultural superiority. Wagner and the Reich complemented
one another. This means that the thesis of the innocence of German music
relative to the Nazi dictatorship tells only part of the story. Wagner's music,
like his hero Lohengrin, had become involved in the world. It had come to
offer complete escape, no longer alone in its abstract or autonomous sense—a
potential of all music—but also in a suggestive programmatic way, contributing
to national awareness and advertising national ideals.[11] Increasingly subjected to ideological design, an important component of music had developed
features which could readily complement the ambitions of totalitarian leadership in the twentieth century.

Although the conjunction of music and ideology in Wagner illustrates the
same aspects of German society which constitute the intellectual background
of National Socialism, the latter was also rooted in a reality that was essentially hostile to the social structure which had sustained music. Elitism and
authoritarianism were challenged by the democratic-socialist movement, the
other ingredient of National Socialism which lent expression to the needs
and expectations of the masses of modern society. The industrial state had
moved progressively toward the establishment of new classes and the col-

lectivization of the individual, a process symbolized in the world of music by the decline of the *lied* and the rise of the large orchestra. To bewildered traditionalists, the modern condition stood for increasing economic complexity and insecurity, instability of the capitalist order, and the pervasive cultural discontent of the *fin de siècle*—the background for the rise of dictatorial-authoritarian mass movements and the ultimate capitulation of the free individual to the totalitarian state. However, prior to 1933 the concrete changes in the position of musicians (in the revolutionary attempts of 1919, for instance) were not yet apparent. The conductor Bruno Walter wrote that after November 9, 1918 he was offered the sole directorship of the prerevolutionary Royal Theatre of Munich, then called the National Theatre. Royal officials were removed, but the old staff and employees generally remained. Walter had to struggle against attempts by his political superiors to interfere in his affairs, since he believed that heads of political departments should have no real artistic influence, but he succeeded. The Theatre survived again when the Republic of Councils, under Kurt Eisner, was suppressed by the Bavarian and Prussian Free Corps in 1919.[12] All in all, his theatre weathered revolutionary change from right and left. The pre-republican rulers of German states had permitted the preservation of this musical hierarchy of authority that guaranteed the orderly survival of music, independent of political change. Indeed, it illustrates the perpetuation of the feudal order, the *Ständestaat*, its habits and attitudes in Germany into the early twentieth century.

Music's ability to maintain its autonomy and excellence was not so much due to the tenacity of its leaders, but rather to the culture and the non-totalitarian ambitions of Germany's leaders prior to 1933 who did not tie musical affairs to their political fortunes. If they were interested in music, they appreciated good music, so that when the old order finally fell victim to the violence of World War I and revolution, music again survived as an expression of traditional culture with which new elites could still identify. Moreover, the position of music had actually been enhanced by the political developments, by national unification, industrialization, and the democratization which reinforced national consciousness and a sense of appreciation of a common musical heritage. Although the cultural network of the past had survived political unification, centralizing tendencies within the musical community were also realized through economic and organizational necessity and in common recognition and practice of a tradition. Music was now firmly established on a national basis, nationally acknowledged, and praised as a special German art. Through the various performing groups, the radio, phonograph, touring orchestras, choruses, soloists, and academies, all of Germany succumbed to the accepted forms of music. The uniformity of programs, standardization of instruments, and the professionalism of the musicians in response to commercial demands contributed more than anything else to centralization. Furthermore, a musical elite was recognized nationally. Touring conductors, soloists, and groups brought the highest standards to all corners of the land, while the German elite was integrated into an active international exchange program. Concert agencies and managements operated on a national level, while the festival and concert societies, financed privately or by state or municipal government, offered a range from traditional to progressive music,[13] and the great conductors like Wilhelm Furtwängler, Bruno Walter, and Otto Klemperer held posts in various cities. Already before the advent of National Socialism, the musician in Germany had become a German musician.

Centralization, economic concentration, and autonomy of musical authority contributed to the tremendous musical activity following World War I, for which Germany, defeated in war and punished by international treaty, provided a bewildering background. The teeming masses of the big cities participated in the desire for living in the present as new forms of entertainment became available. The music critic Adolf Weissmann wrote his book *Die Entgötterung der Musik* at this time, warning that tradition was threatened by the radio, car, airplane, sports, film, and American jazz. To Weissmann entertainment and music were symptomatic of disruptive forces tearing at the social order, yet somehow established institutions of the arts flourished; music was sheltered, thoroughly organized, and well attended. Every town maintained its orchestra and stage, and musicians found employment, although they were affected by the rampant inflation. Bruno Walter related that upon arriving from America he was engaged by the Berlin Philharmonic during the first period of inflation in 1923.

> The first rehearsal took a thoroughly normal course up to a certain point. During the intermission, the representatives of the orchestra informed me that the musicians were just then being paid their salaries and they asked me to understand that they would at once have to make some kind of purchase; if they waited to do so two hours later, the purchasing power of their money would in the meantime have shrunk. Naturally, I yielded and contented myself with the rehearsals which were to follow. I no longer know in what queer merchandise the money was invested, though I believe a musician told me he had bought bags of salt. The experience in the orchestra furnished a particular striking example of the currency's galloping consumption.[14]

A semblance of stability was reached during the Stresemann years between 1924 and 1929, a period which witnessed new economic productivity and cultural bourgeoning and was called a virtual Periclean Age by Germany's foremost theatre critic Alfred Kerr. "But it was a precarious glory," wrote Peter Gay, indeed, "a dance on the edge of a volcano." Beneath prosperity and besides "the exuberant creativity and experimentation . . . was anxiety, fear, a rising sense of doom." What to us clearly amounted to the strains which produced the republic's "tragic death—part murder, part wasting sickness, part suicide," was reflected in music's acute conflict between its institutional, tradition-bound, and practical needs, on the one hand, and the artist's claims to creative autonomy, on the other.[15] "Music life is no life for music," universalized Theodor Adorno, as he captured the contradiction between the creative process and institutionalization of music.[16] Nonetheless, the resulting tension did not have only negative consequences, since it contributed to the celebrated radical music of the time. The variety of compositions, ranging from Richard Strauss, Hans Pfitzner, Max Reger, and Gustav Mahler to Arnold Schönberg and even Paul Hindemith, testifies to the greatness of that age of creativity which extended into the period of the Weimar Republic, indeed to its very end.

Central to all controversy was Berlin which had strengthened its position with the abolition of the courts, while Munich, Stuttgart, Dresden, etc, had declined in importance. Boasting four opera houses which offered works of a great variety of composers: Richard Strauss, Hans Pfitzner, Igor Stravinsky, Arnold Schönberg, Paul Hindemith, Manuel de Falla, Ernst Krenek, Franz Schreker, Erich Korngold, Eugene d' Albert, Alban Berg, etc., Berlin attracted star singers, performers, chamber groups, and conductors. Here the public witnessed experimentation in literature, art, the theatre, film, and music. An international elite flourished around musical salons, especially of Peter Landecker, the owner of Berlin's Philharmonic Hall, and Louise Wolff of the Wolff & Sachs concert agency, which were open to political and artistic circles. The various musical factions were represented by many critics and journals, all contributing to the ferment of the period. Berlin had indeed become the most liberal and active cultural center of Europe. It was also characterized by the growth of political, industrial, and financial bureaucracies that had gained preeminence over the various bureaucracies of the provinces. It was now the center of business, politics, and increasingly of official representation. Music, with its roughly 13,000 professional practitioners (or nearly 15 percent of the nation's musicians) in the creative sense and as an official institution, centered here.[17] The impact of National Socialism on music can consequently best be studied at such prestigious institutions as the Prussian Academy of the Arts in Berlin. Yet, Berlin's position was not popular throughout Germany. Its international flavor, turbulence, gayety, sophistication, decadence, and avant-garde artistic expressions offended the provinces.

It was the capital of the Republic, owing status and character to the world war and the Republic, while its population was politically identified with the republican-democratic faction and communism. Berlin's success suggested disrespect for the past, a reputation shared by modernist music. Notwithstanding its controversial status, and precisely because of it, Berlin lends itself to representative analysis. As the artists of the Weimar period, like the writer Karl Zuckmayer, flocked to Berlin, which "was worth more than a mass," so the Nazis realized after Hitler's failed putsch in Munich—"the fiasco of the year 1923," in the words of Joseph Goebbels—that the capital "represented the centre of all political, intellectual, economic, and cultural forces of the country."[18]

The ultimate crisis of the Weimar state emerged with the economic troubles of 1930. Music's financial difficulties were illustrated in the demise of the Berlin Philharmonic, whose fifty-year tradition of complete independence and self-sufficiency ended in 1932. It became a limited-liability company, with the orchestra itself, the city, the Prussian state, the Republic, and the Broadcasting System represented on the governing board—a transitional position, it now appears, to its official incorporation into the Reich bureaucracy in October 1933. While general unemployment was 28.9 percent in June 1933, that of musicians stood at nearly double that rate. The economic pinch made for the unstable political tempers of those in search of security. By and large, musicians stood by the Republic, the new embodiment of authority and order. Yet political discord had attained radical proportions even in "the years of hope" under Stresemann. Arthur Schnabel recalled friction with nationalistic instructors at the Berlin State Academy of Music; Bruno Walter noted the same in Munich. Antisemitic and nationalist sentiment had been reflected in the Wagner cult, perpetuated most notably by the talented composer Hans Pfitzner, who had sounded alarm over the crisis in music with his publications, *Futuristengefahr* and *Neue Ästhetic der musikalischen Impotenz*. In a moment of agitation, he even had allowed himself to threaten Franz Werfel, the liberal writer, with the astonishing outburst, "Germany will yet win, Hitler will show you."[19] The Nazi movement too had been active and organized in 1928 in the Fighting League for German Culture—*Kampfbund für deutsche Kultur* (KfdK) which was to be rewarded for its efforts after 1933. The right wing in general had complained of Jewish-Marxist control of cultural institutions, education, and the press, concentrating its attack in the world of official music on Leo Kestenberg of the Ministry of Education, Franz Schreker, the director of Berlin's State Academy of Music, and the latter's assistant, the musicologist Georg Schünemann, a non-Jew. Yes, German culture included prominent Jews, but not in the numbers and of the power suggested in anti-Semitic propaganda.

Apart from the well-known Jewish Ullstein, Mosse and Sonneman-Simon enterprises, little Jewish capital was invested in the German newspaper trade—the largest at the time in the world.[20] As to music, a professional census taken in June, 1933 listed 1915 confessional Jews among the 93,857 career musicians whose main income derived from musical work—a percentage of 2.04 which, in view of Jewish emmigration since the Nazi assumption of power, Prieberg allows at the most to be doubled for the period of the late Weimar Republic.[21] These Jewish musicians and audiences shared with their persecutors traditional views of their art, largely late romantic and folkloristic as revealed in the programs of segregated Jewish cultural organizations in 1933.[22]

It now seems clear that the sense of security gained during the Stresemann years had obscured the fact that Weimar Germany was a crisis state. Those who felt spiritually and intellectually isolated yearned for cultural identity. The Nazis thrived in this atmosphere of cultural crisis, reinforcing discontent through propaganda and being repared to offer solutions. Their ideology leaned on the tradition of the "conservative revolution," the militant conservative reaction to all liberal-democratic, secular, and industrial developments, which among a number of political off-shoots produced the *völkisch* movement of mystical nationalism with its apotheosis of the German people as the repository of all genuine creativity. Native and affirmative art was invariably upheld against the critical, modernist, international, uprooted, "soulless" products of the alien force of a "materialistic" civilization. While Hitler thus reacted to political disaster, the educated elites either had embraced the same ideology which looked for charismatic leadership against the Republic, escaped into self-congratulatory denunciation of bourgeois hypocrisy, or withdrew into their private occupational domains and lost the sense of urgency altogether. The latter choice was to give grounds to the memoir literature with its expression of shock over the radicalism of Nazi totalitarianism. Furtwängler, for one, completely misunderstood the nature of modern totalitarianism for which he was not prepared. As first conductor in Leipzig, Berlin, and Vienna, and rooted securely in a tradition of great conductors, he reigned supreme in a musical world which, to him, enjoyed a life of its own. He simply was not political in a period which was eminently so.[23] By 1933 the forces which had contributed to the creation of the framework of the liberal state were dissipated, so that when that state in its specific German historical setting was unable to cope with the problems of modern mass society, the musician after 1933, too, was forced to become political through his integration into mass organizations.

In spite of the genuine horror expressed by the victims of fascism and the obvious break with tradition of the Nazi revolution, music was no innocent art, nor was it an innocent institution. The crisis of society and the state was mirrored in the turmoil, agitation, and violent polemics in the world of music. The articulation of attitudes, moreover, had been colored by political opinion, at least as far back as the time of Richard Wagner's artistry and penmanship. Wagner's nationalism and racism had contributed to an attitude in Germany which confused social with musical achievement. Erich Valentine's 1939 biography of Hans Pfitzner traced the origin of both cultural and political parties to Wagner's time—a period of social disintegration and the ascendancy of the individual over totality and community, a process Wagner had wanted to reverse by advancing the revivalist notion of a German Reich.[24] The Wagnerian ideal was promoted most vociferously by Pfitzner, who represented the "conservative revolution" in *völkisch* terms in the context of the twentieth century debate on music, according to which musicians were to participate in the creation of a "new Germany." Focusing as they did upon the intersection of National Socialism and German music, upon their merger in the Nazi policy toward the organization of music in the Third Reich, as well as upon the Nazi understanding of music in history and society and of its own mission in cultural terms, we find Wagner and Pfitzner most akin to formal Nazi thought, almost identical in terminology, and above all, representative of the acute sense of crisis which preceded the Nazi assumption of power.[25]

Musicians of all political and musicological persuasions reacted to the so-called crisis in music. Progressives like the then young thinker and critic, Theodor W. Adorno of the famous Frankfurt Institute for Social Research, feared for the autonomous rights of music, including its critical capacity, and the musician. Wilhelm Furtwängler and fellow conservatives worried over a meaningful relationship between music and the community and about the survival of a spiritual quality in art. Nationalists like Hans Pfitzner showed concern for the nation and increasingly for the German race as the base of German music, a position sharpened by the Nazi musicologist Richard Eichenauer. Pfitzner and friends of the "conservative revolution" wanted to save the nation through a purified music and, conversely, music through a revitalized nation, the characteristic predicament of the Germanic cultural critics.[26] Against the background of crisis, the debate raged in the press, at the academies, and in private—opponents still talked to each other—continuing into the Third Reich, when the universal crisis led to political and social changes, to dictatorial controls that were to render this musical debate meaningless, with even idealistic nationalism, in the final analysis, among the losers. Pfitzner realized this, obstinately refusing to join the Party or to sign solidarity proclamations after 1933.

Notwithstanding the disillusionment of idealists, the Nazis appropriated the literature of cultural nationalism and racism in music to give direction to and offer justification for their policies toward music. However, a clear distinction was made between the cultural criticism of the period from 1871 to 1933 and the positive program of the Third Reich.[27] The nineteenth century was basically liberal, said Alfred Rosenberg, the chief ideologist of the Party, and the cultural criticism of the prophets of National Socialism bears testimony to the former ethos of freedom of speech. The twentieth century, on the other hand, he argued, belonged to National Socialism, which resolved conflict, neutralized all opposition, and true to its name established a new synthesis. Prophecy was replaced by a new order as Germans, and specifically German musicians, were ready to submit to an updated version of traditional authoritarianism, which in the twentieth century, also challenged traditional liberties and professional authorities. Representative of the apolitical, inner-directed Germans and their habit of accommodation to established authority, German musicians accepted the fait accompli of the Nazi revolution and were then forced to become involved in public demonstration of a political ethos—a radical departure from their earlier status and habits. Thomas Mann had prophesied something along these lines before his own conversion to liberal republican ideals when, in 1911, he referred to the fateful course of the German people in crisis: They "ought to be made to decide between Goethe and Wagner. Both won't do. But, I fear they would say Wagner."[28]

ENDNOTES

[1]See Richard J. Evans, "The New Nationalism and the Old History: Perspectives on the West German *Historikerstreit,*" *The Journal of Modern History* (December 1987), 761-797; *Historikerstreit: Die Dokumentation der Kontroverse um die Einzigartigkeit der national-sozialistischen Judenvernichtung* (Munich, 1987). This recent controversy relates to major themes and issues in the historiography of National Socialism and the Third Reich, most notably the "structuralism" (or "functionalism")—versus —"intentionalism" debate over the nature of the Nazi regime and Hitler's role. The structuralists, led by Hans Mommsen, Martin Broszat and Tim Mason stress a "polycracy" of conflicting authorities in Nazi Germany and the weakness of Hitler's role and of the other leaders in the shaping of policy; they note forces of chance, the logic of social change, and the Nazis reacting to circumstances. The intentionalists, on the other hand Klaus Hildebrand, Walter Hofer and such holocaust historians as Gerald Reitlinger and Raul Hilberg, as well as classical political historians like Alan Bullock and Karl Dietrich Bracher—stress Hitler's program, set in *Mein Kampf,* which he essentially implemented. See Gerhard Hirschfeld, et al., *Der "Führerstaat": Mythos und Realität* (Stuttgart, 1981)—a collection of essays which address the controversy; and Ian Kershaw, *The Nazi Dictatorship: Problems and Perspectives of Interpretation* (London, 1985).
    Today's practicing scholars try to blend the two positions. Although this book on the politics of music reflects "intentionalism" in its examination of intellectual antecedents, cultural traditions and ideological guidelines, it also tends in the "functionalist" direction in view

of the manifest subordination of music policy to power politics and Goebbels' pragmatism and the equally evident rivalry among Nazi leaders and contradictions in the reality of Nazi music politics.

[2]Hermann Glaser, *The Rubble Years: The Cultural Roots of Postwar Germany* (New York, 1986).

[3]Fred K. Prieberg, "Nach dem Endsieg oder Musiker-Mimikry," in Hanns-Werner Heister and Hans-Günter Klein (eds.), *Musik und Musikpolitik im faschistischen Deutschland* (Frankfurt a.M., 1984), 297-305. See also Constantine FitzGibbon, *Denazification* (New York, 1969). Criticism of denazification came early. See John H. Herz, "The Fiasco of Denazification in Germany," *Political Science Quarterly* (1948), 569-594; Ernst von Salomon, *Der Fragebogen* (Hamburg, 1951)—a mockery of denazification and the questionnaire as well as an argument against individual and collective German guilt by a former right wing activist.

[4]Hanns Eisler, "Musik und Musikpolitik im faschistischen Deutschland," *Musik und Politik 1924-1948* (Berlin/DDR, 1973), 334-357.

[5]Artur Schnabel, *My Life and Music* (New York, 1963), 5.

[6]Wilhelm Furtwängler, *Vermächtnis: Nachgelassene Schriften* (Wiesbaden, 1956), 10.

[7]Ralf Dahrendorf, *Gesellschaft und Demokratie in Deutschland* (Munich, 1966), 47.

[8]Furtwängler, *Vermächtnis*, 89.

[9]Ibid., 90. Furtwängler added, though, that Wagner was "too busy with himself" to exert that influence. Nietzsche, he felt, was too much a Wagnerian to have a proper understanding of absolute, particularly, classical music, but his comments made a strong impact on the musical taste of the German public, despite their "literary pretension" and the obvious "dilletantism which they expressed." Other important German commentators, such as Stefan George, continued to misunderstand and abuse music into our own period, according to Furtwängler.

[10]This nationalistic opposition to Bismarck—though much discussed—ought not to be exaggerated. The romantic national opposition to the great nation builder tended to overlook its dependency on the latter's achievement. Robert M. Berdahl has reminded us that German unification was rooted in socio-economic conditions and interests, not in poetic ideas ("New Thoughts on German Nationalism," *American Historical Review*, February 1972), thus, confirming relegation of the poets to the sphere of superstructure. Later romantics simply wanted more than reason of state had been able to secure, a foreshadowing of Nazi policy and practice.

[11]Wagner had tried to express grandiose visions, in spite of strictures of traditional defenders of absolute music—led by Eduard Hanslick, who would not allow that music could be descriptive, purposive or negative. (*Vom Musikalisch-Schönen*, Leipzig, 1854). Schnabel commented that "it is a miracle to what a degree Wagner has helped the illusion that it can be all that." (*My Life*, 18).

[12]Bruno Walter, *Theme and Variations* (London, 1948), 251-256.

[13]See Adolf Weissmann, *Berlin als Musikstadt* (Berlin and Leipzig, 1911), specifically on the changing situation of music from aristocratic protection to professional societies.

[14]Walter, 277.

[15]On the "Periclean Age," see Peter Gay, *Weimar Culture: The Outsider as Insider* (New York, 1970), XIV; Curt Riess, *Furtwängler: Musik und Politik* (Bern, 1953), 73; the remaining quotes from Gay.

[16]"Musikleben," *Einleitung in die Musiksoziologie: Zwölf theoretische Vorlesungen* (Munich, 1968), 130. In a way the modern trend in music was a response to the general social, political and technological conditions of our time. Adorno argued that radical music reacted against the commercial exploitation of the traditional idiom and that atonality was a reaction to the mechanization of modern art. See also Walter Benjamin, "L'oeuvre d'art à l'époche de sa reproduction mécanisée," *Zeitschrift für Sozialforschung* (1936).

[17]Fred K. Prieberg, *Musik im NS-Staat* (Frankfurt a.M., 1982), 51.

[18]Carl Zuckmayer, *Als wär's ein Stück von mir: Erinnerungen* (Vienna, 1966), 311; Joseph Goebbels, *Kampf um Berlin*, 6th ed. (Munich, 1934), 11. The excitement and vitality of artistic life in Berlin is captured in much literature dealing with the Weimar period, in the memoirs and biographies of musicians and of other artists and intellectuals. For some generalizations see Golo Mann, *Deutsche Geschichte des neunzehnten und zwanzigsten Jahrhunderts* (Frankfurt a.M., 1964), 692-699; Gay, *Weimar Culture*; Otto Friedrich, *Before the Deluge: A Portrait of Berlin in the 1920's* (New York, 1972), an account of a noted American journalist; and Fred Hildenbrand, *...ich soll dich grüssen von Berlin: 1922-1932* (Munich, 1975), an account of the feuilleton editor of the *Berliner Tageblatt*.

[19]Alma Mahler-Werfel, *And the Bridge is Love* (Amsterdam, 1940), 200.

[20]Oron J. Hale, *The Captive Press in the Third Reich* (Princeton, 1964), 2-3. See also Modris Ecksteins, *The Limits of Reason: The German Democratic Press and the Collapse of the Weimar Republic* (London, 1975), which describes the involvement of Jewish publishing houses with liberal political parties and the vulnerability of both to the depression and radical politics.

[21]Prieberg, *Musik*, 47-48.

[22]Ibid., 93. See also Peter Gay who comes to the same conclusion about Jewish aesthetics in "Encounter with Modernism: German Jews in Wilhelminian Germany," *Freud, Jews and Other Germans: Masters and Victims in Modernist Culture* (Oxford, 1978), 101. Rejecting the notion of Jewish distinctiveness in high culture, Gay stipulates the need for a historical and sociological study, "that of stupid Jews," 99.

[23]Riess, 114-115.

[24]Erich Valentin, *Hans Pfitzner: Werk und Gestalt eines Deutschen* (Regensburg, 1939), 71. See also Jacques Barzun, *Darwin, Marx, Wagner* (New York, 1958); Winfried Zillig, *Von Wagner bis Strauss: Wegbereiter der Neuen Musik* (Munich, 1966).

[25]Pfitzner's difficulties after 1933 did not negate his status as important progenitor of the Nazi policy. His biography suggests the same atmosphere evoked in Fritz Stern's classic study of Lagarde,

Langbehn and Moeller van den Bruck, *The Politics of Cultural Despair: A Study in the Rise of the Germanic Ideology* (New York, 1965). The intrinsic development and the integrity of Wagner and Pfitzner are not considered here.

[26]See Theodor W. Adorno's entire oeuvre; Hans Pfitzner, *Gesammelte Schriften* (Augsburg, 1926); Richard Wagner, *Gesammelte Schriften und Dichtungen* (Berlin and Leipzig, 1911), particularly, "Das Judentum in der Musik," "Oper und Drama," and "Was ist deutsch?"; on Furtwängler his own work, the *Vermächtnis*, especially the essay of 1937, "Die Frage nach dem deutschen in der Kunst"; on race and music, Richard Eichenauer, *Musik und Rasse* (Munich, 1937); and for a comparison of all positions, Michael Meyer, "Music on the Eve of the Third Reich," in Michael N. Dobkowsky and Isidor Wallimann (eds.), *Towards the Holocaust: The Social and Economic Collapse of the Weimar Republic* (Westport and London, 1983). About the "conservative revolution," see Klemens von Klemperer, *Germany's New Conservatism: Its History and Dilemma in the Twentieth Century* (Princeton, 1957); and Armin Mohler, *Die Konservative Revolution in Deutschland, 1918-1932* (Stuttgart, 1952).

[27]See Jeffrey Herf, *Reactionary Modernism: Technology, Culture and Politics in Weimar and the Third Reich* (Cambridge and New York, 1984), which suggests the paradox of the German reconciliation of technology and unreason (and culture) and, thus, the incorporation of "modern technology into the cultural system of modern German nationalism, without diminishing the latter's romantic and antirational aspects." (2)

[28]Quoted in Joseph Wulf, *Musik im Dritten Reich* (Gütersloh, 1966), 5. The same conclusion was reached during the war by Peter Viereck in *Metapolitics: The Roots of the Nazi Mind* (New York, 1941). See Mann's assessment of National Socialism and its depressing impact on Germany in, *An Exchange of Letters* (New York, 1937) and *Order of the Day* (New York, 1942).

1933: Nazi Power, Purges and Revolutionary Promise

The Nazi assumption of power in January 1933, though not inevitable, signaled not an alien experiment, but was rooted in a dynamically interrelated combination of political, socio-economic and intellectual-ideological circumstances.[1] Links between nineteenth-century *völkisch* cultural ideals and artistic expressions with Nazi music policy were especially clear. What had begun in the Romantic age as a *völkisch* intellectual and artistic opposition to formal academic standards until its turn later in the nineteenth century in favor of affirmative art and sentiment against radical negativism and as the positive projection of a militant and expansionist national community— the *Volksgemeinschaft*, had broadened into a comprehensive political ideology, reflecting, justifying and sustaining the Nazi drive to power.[2] *Völkisch* and like-minded intellectuals and artists welcomed the events of January 1933 as the necessary precondition for national and, especially, cultural reconstruction in realization of their dreams about rooted and meaningful art, an expression of the national community it would thus help revitalize—which of course is not to suggest that Nazi power was rooted in aesthetics. The thinkers and artists who had articulated *völkisch* ideals were not involved in the machinations which brought Hitler to power, while the military, business and political power brokers who figured prominently in those fateful events were otherwise preoccupied. However, the star of those days, as of the next twelve years, consistently presented himself as both programmatic thinker and politician. His genuine love and respect for the foremost embodiment of *völkisch* ideals, the great artist-polemicist Richard Wagner and his celebrated music dramas—with the heroes of which he was identified in myth-making efforts, such as Leni Riefenstahl's cinematic *Triumph of the Will*—is thoroughly documented. Adolf Hitler indeed bridged the worlds of "blood and soil" and "blood and iron," of myth and deed. A practitioner of *Realpolitik* of the highest order, he impressed the world with his ability to turn the table quickly on those reactionaries who had thought to manipulate him, and by the consolidation of his power, reassuring the culture-ideologists who stood to benefit by his success.

The "national revolution" had begun, as "authority and responsibility" became the passwords which captivated a generation in demonstration of the Nazi "leadership" principle. Nazi leaders committed themselves passionately to cultural reconstruction and full employment—after ruthless suppression of Jews and dissenters—and to a new order within which the arts and politics would reinforce each other's shared ideals. The Nazis offered hope and left no room for wavering; they formulated clear *völkisch* principles and followed with decisive action. In view of the background of crisis and insecurity, debilitating unemployment and cultural pessimism, *völkisch* musicians were not alone in their eagerness to demonstrate solidarity with the new regime. Bewildered by the rapid political transformation and caught up in the revolutionary elan of early 1933, the musical establishment at large wanted to participate in and extend the slogan of "national renewal" to the musical realm. Accustomed to state support and traditionally respectful of the authorities in return, Germany's professional musicians welcomed official pronouncements in behalf of culture and the honored role promised music in the projection of a reintegrated, revitalized and corporatively organized national community. They were pleased by Hitler's reassurances that National Socialism differed significantly from traditional parties, the latter "considering the day of assumption of political power a high point of their desires....indeed of their existence." The establishment of the herewith pronounced totalitarian state constituted only the beginning of a higher mission.[3] Goebbels echoed these sentiments variously with references to political success, the penetration of all life by the revolution, and the forthcoming transformation of society. This revolutionary reality, he noted in a major speech inaugurating the Reich Culture Chamber—*Reichskulturkammer* (RKK) on November 15, 1933, would be shaped by a new heroic spirit which would bind all Germans—especially its artists—to the national community (the *Volk*) and lend purpose to art. In this address he coined a frequently quoted expression which reflected the elan of the moment, synthesized the romantic-*völkisch* past with the Nazi present, and endeavored to elicit a creative response from the cultural community: *Stählerne Romantik* (romanticism of steel, which suggested both toughness of mind and idealist commitment)—a term eagerly picked up by cultural organizers, music journalists and educators who applied it to the definitions of a new German music.[4]

In practice, many musicians looked forward to the state to increase its financial support of the arts and the creation of more jobs, not surprising in view of the disastrous economic situation and the incredibly high unemployment for musicians at 46%, for singers and voice teachers at 43.5%, as compared to 28.9% for all workers—reported 16 June 1933.[5] The totalitarian pretentions of the Nazi state thus complemented the musicians' authoritarian habits and their need for security and recognition. Music pledged itself to contribute to the creation of a cultural facade for the terror state, certainly not seen in these terms by musicians who participated in 1933, but clearly evident to those who did not.

Yet not all activity in behalf of the new order was due exclusively to opportunism. Many beneficiaries had been genuine Nazi supporters, either as relatively non-political *völkisch* sympathizers or as militant members of Nazi cultural organizations, such as the national Fighting League for German Culture—*Kampfbund für deutsche Kultur* (KfdK)—with its strong music chapter that included a chorus, an orchestra under the direction of the violinist Gustav Havemann—a major force in Nazi music organization and purges—several other ensembles and a general membership of prominent composers, practicing musicians, music educators and journalists. Support for the new order also issued from conservative members of the musical establishment who had been appalled by modern musical developments; they were rooted instead in the tradition of representational art that confirmed and elevated the social order it served. These musicians rejected expressions of critical art in the form of explicit texts (like those of Brecht) and in the dissonances produced at modern music festivals like Donaueschingen. Alienated and fearful about music's condition, they welcomed or at least acquiesced in the Nazi attacks on the radicals. Consequently, usurpation in *völkisch* and traditionalist circles was hardly necessary as the Nazis identified with so much of the musical tradition and honored masters like Wagner and Pfitzner who—albeit in distorted form—were elevated to serve as inspiration and symbols of National Socialism and its cultural policies. Especially Pfitzner's alarmist reaction, in the twenties, to the disintegration of tonality—the dissonances, twelve-tone theory, and alien jazz—accorded with less-stridently expressed conservative sentiment. When Pfitzner attributed this "musical chaos"—a symbol of threats to civilization itself—to an active anti-German internationalist conspiracy, he spoke for many as he anticipated important features of National Socialism. His conservative defense of traditional harmony (the triad), melody, and melodic inspiration (*Einfall*)—were all claimed as characteristically German; and his attack upon a plethora of subversive forces drawn from music and politics—especially atonality and jazz as expressions of international bolshevism, Americanism and Jewry—were simply reformulated in racial terms with little violence to the original. The school teacher, *Untersturmführer* Richard Eichenauer attributed atonal modern music as such to Jews who "are following a law of their race." Chief party ideologist Alfred Rosenberg felt that "atonality contradicts the rhythm of the blood," and Hans Severus Ziegler applied Pfitzner's ideas as conceptual constructs for the "degenerate music" exhibit in 1938.[6] From the ideas of Pfitzner and likeminded *völkisch* thinkers, Nazi music policy, the leadership principle, totalitarian controls and an integrated population were derived and thus sanctioned.

The quest for a genuine national culture appeared within reach in 1933, a promise acknowledged in June 1933 by one of the key Nazi music organizers, Peter Raabe, a well-known conductor who would become President of the Reich Music Chamber—*Reichsmusikkammer* (RMK) in 1935, as he spoke of the failure of previous governments to "constitutionally and administratively plan for the security of German culture."[7] Pfitzner biographer Erich Valentin dramatically called the period between 1871 and 1933 the "German passion."[8]

From the time of its inception the Nazi movement had indeed stressed national unity and posed as reconciler of conflicting classes and ideologies. The auxiliary tradition of pageantry of marching columns, flags and music presented the united front of the responsible and inspiring leader and the obedient and enthusiastically led people. Musicians contributed marches, Nazi fighting songs, Führer cantatas, oratorios and the like to these elaborate rituals. Yet, the myth-making also involved serious music at the State Opera, the Philharmonic and other formal centers for the more solemn ceremonies of state. For instance, on March 21, 1933, known as the "day of Potsdam," the official inauguration of the Reich took place, truly a day of victory for the Nazis. Uniformed men, flags and festivals indicated that the new order was indeed launched in a positive spirit. Ludwig Neubeck's choral work, *Deutschland* was composed for the occasion and was heard on radio;[9] and Germany's celebrated conductor Wilhelm Furtwängler had been asked by Hitler personally to conduct *Die Meistersinger* that evening at the Berlin State Opera. Among the specially invited state officials and dignitaries, Furtwängler's Jewish secretary Berta Geissmar attended. "I was given a seat in my usual box. The fact that I went shows how little I realized how matters really stood."[10]

Geissmar was not alone in not knowing how things stood. While the Nazi leadership assumed positions of power, representation and legality, the KfdK with SA support instituted terror in the musical world in what Gustav Bosse at the *Zeitschrift für Musik* (ZfM) termed an unofficial "revolution of the street."[11] In the early months of the new regime concerts of Jews and other unacceptable musicians and music were disrupted. The opera stages of Berlin had been the victims of vicious attacks in the Nazi press before January 30, 1933 for their alleged promotion of Jews and Jewish music, jazz and other expressions of "alien" entertainment: atonality, Marxist and otherwise critical rather than affirmative or representational music. In February and March the newspaper attacks were reinforced by action, as the SA invaded the City Opera. SA men also manhandled music director—*Generalmusikdirektor* (GMD) Fritz Busch in Dresden during a rehearsal whereupon the actor Alexis Posse, a Nazi organizer and ombudsman, declared the distinguished conductor incompatible with the new order. When Busch agreed to conduct the next day anyway, he was shouted down by party members—*Parteigenossen* (Pg's) who had bought up tickets for the event and for that purpose. His assistant, the conductor and composer Kurt Striegler, who was present "by chance" took over at the request of the mob, while Busch managed to escape by the back door. The maligned Busch left Germany for Argentina, where he was joined by Carl Ebert, director of the Berlin City Opera who had also been bullied from office by the SA, while Striegler continued to demonstrate support for the new order and Alexis Posse was promoted. The personnel at the Dresden State Opera was so thoroughly intimidated that only four people voted to accept Busch back even after his reinstatement had been recommended by Göring himself, who presided over Prussian stages at the time. The KfdK was puzzled by Göring's intervention and more so when its members learned of Nazi support for a German opera in Argentina under the leadership of Busch and Carl Ebert and contributions of defamed singers from Germany. The Busch incident illustrated the combination of threats, disruption, dismissal of one and promotion of others, self-coordination, and the intimidation of a humbled profession, yet, also the facade of official propriety—a malicious cat-and-mouse game not even understood by Nazi foot soldiers. Hundreds of incidents unfolded. As a Jew and musical innovator, GMD Otto Klemperer had attracted the special enmity of the KfdK with a new *Tannhäuser* production in early February in commemoration of the fiftieth anniversary of Wagner's death—termed a "parody," an "offense." Then, a Klemperer concert was cancelled "for reasons of public safety," after an anonymous caller had threatened disruption. Similarly, the KfdK organized opposition to Bruno Walter, and the Reich commissioner for Saxony prevented a concert with the famous *Gewandhaus* orchestra in Leipzig. A mob stood ready to enforce the order against the man who had led the orchestra for four years. Walter then asked his agency Wolff & Sachs, which was also on the KfdK hit list, to request police protection for a concert with the Berlin Philharmonic Orchestra. Rather than approving this, State Secretary Walter Funk of the Reich Ministry for Popular Enlightenment and Propaganda (RMVP) recommended an "Aryan" substitute, Richard Strauss, who happened to be in town and accepted after some hesitation and urgent requests, on the condition—rather remarkable for him—that his fee be donated to the orchestra which was suffering financially at the time. Denunciations, boycotts and dismissals spread throughout the country. While the seasoned Strauss experienced some discomfort, younger men have left no signs of compunction to launch careers. The young Herbert von Karajan, for instance, who had joined the party in Austria in early April, 1933 and then again in Germany (May 1, 1933) rose to the position of GMD in Aachen in 1935—and the rest is history. The assistant director of the Rhenish Music Academy in Cologne, Richard Trunk—Pg since 1931 and composer of the popular Nazi piece, *Feier der neuen Front* ("Festival of the New Front") in four movements entitled, "Hitler," "The Führer's Guard," "O, Land," and "Horst Wessel" (text by Hitler Youth Leader Baldur von Schirach) was elevated to director of his institution, again illustrating career opportunities for the young and talented to whom the organizers looked for fulfillment of *völkisch*-Nazi ideals.[12]

Characteristic features of the Third Reich emerged in this early conjunction of official pomp and terror, to both of which, music—it is clear—contributed. Musicians denounced colleagues, competed for vacant jobs, assumed positions in Nazi cultural organizations which carried out the purges and then contributed compositions, performances and solidarity proclamations. While the world was about to behold the resurgent might of the German state and army, the cultural realm developed respect and admiration for its apparent unity, state support and vitality. Meanwhile, fifty concentration camps had been built in Germany where opponents of the regime—including musicians—were interned and abused, and, as we learned from an actor who managed to get out, music was performed in those camps by the prisoners for the edification of the guards. Later, in the Reich's expanded system of concentration and extermination camps, prisoners would again perform for their oppressors, and also for new arrivals as another form of deception, of facade.[13]

The aura of normalcy, to which the instrumentalized sounds of music also contributed, accorded with Hitler's "legal revolution," emphasized by the Decree of the Reich President for the Protection of People and State (February 28), the Enabling Law (March 23) and the various *Gleichschaltung* Laws (which coordinated all organizations with the new regime). Most immediately the Law for the Reestablishment of the Professional Civil Service (April 7)—with its denial of jobs for "non-Aryans," communists and others "who cannot be trusted to support the national state without reservation"—intensified the bloodletting within musical ranks which, in the language of the official Pfundtner-Neubert "realized for the first time the racial demands of National Socialism and the program of the entire German people."[14] This law of April reassured beneficiaries of Nazi patronage and revealed to anxious victims the true nature of the regime. The "revolution of the street" had been manipulated by the state all along and prepared for the legal action to follow. Bureaucrats now issued questionnaires to members of institutions; dismissal notices followed in an orderly fashion—a well-documented process. Yet even the earlier, seemingly random actions of the KfdK and the SA had suggested governmental collusion and, to concerned observers, pointed to the emerging struggle between previously autonomous institutions and the totalitarian ambitions of the new state as the press, churches and educational institutions reacted with regard to musicians in their charge. When, in the very first days of the Third Reich Heinrich Mann was pressed into leaving his position as president of the prestigious Prussian Academy of Writers, the entire Prussian Academy of the Arts (PAdK), the world of the arts, scholarship and education, churches and the press suddenly recognized the threat to their common tradition and political interest. All the major newspapers of Berlin and Germany covered the Mann affair, while members of the Academy engaged in heated discussion. The threat to the Academy was clearly demonstrated when Bernhard Rust, the new Reich Commissioner and Minister of Education, according to the *Berliner Tageblatt* (February 16, 1933), threatened to close it down in case Mann and Käthe Kollwitz remained members. While the *Montag Morgen* (February 20) reported the deep concern of republican circles, Wilhelm Stapel in *Deutsches Volkstum* celebrated the victory of the new order:

When Heinrich Mann was expelled from the Academy, it would have been morally encumbent upon those who had elected him as their president, to resign from the Academy in protest. We scorn these gentlemen for having decided to treat this case in an unpolitical manner and to remain in the Academy. They left their chosen one in the lurch. You are fine republicans.[15]

The PAdK ceased to be independent. Academic freedom in its traditional role was denounced officially and also by outstanding members of the academic community: Martin Heidegger noted that "the much-praised academic freedom is tossed out of the German university because this freedom was not genuine."[16] Thus the seeker of the authentic life justified the Nazi action. The new collectivism in turn appropriated profound existentialist thought. Fritz Rostosky wrote in *Neue Literatur*:

The individual must be absorbed by the community with his soul in order to fulfill his innermost calling...To do what is in his power...makes a man free, in spite of having taken orders. He is free because he wants to obey."[17]

Then, after April 7, an official wave of purges swept Germany's musical institutions. At the music section of the PAdK the Professors Arnold Schönberg and Franz Schreker received dismissal notices. Thus, the founder of the twelve-tone system, the acknowledged leader of contemporary musical thought, found it impossible to make a living in Germany. Schönberg left the country, fought over breech of contract and the fee imposed on emigres (the *Reichsfluchtsteuer*)—also contested by Klemperer upon his departure for Vienna—returned to the Jewish faith in a synagogue in Paris and settled in Los Angeles. He was a giant to his admirers, but to the Nazis, Schönberg the Jew and "destroyer of tonality," represented music's crisis per se, the embodiment of all the anathemas within the realm of serious music, what Pfitzner had identified as "the aesthetics of musical impotence." If in the eyes of later historians his departure signified a serious gap in the landscape of German music, the Nazis viewed his expulsion as a necessary precondition for musical reconstruction along *völkisch* lines. Thus, the promise of a revitalized national community and culture was legally formulated and implemented organizationally, while contradictions were rationalized and excessive ruthlessness dismissed as necessary and temporary. Meanwhile, musicians did not call the shots; as powerless accomplices, their commitments intensified. Shameful compromises with ethical standards became more glaring and the totalitarian controls rendered reconsideration increasingly difficult.

Gleichschaltung of the Press: An Area that Counted

The Nazi revolution was reflected in the press, an important source for the historian of Nazi music politics, both for what was reported and as a model of the totalitarian controls of a vital information system. Due to the significance it shared with films and radio as propaganda tools, the press was subjected to immediate "legal" *Gleichschaltung* (coordination), including the characteristic extra-legal measures as Nazis at all levels enjoyed their moment of triumph, settled accounts with enemies and began "reconstruction." Circulation of the party press from the authoritative *Völkischer Beobachter* (central organ of the party) and papers of various national organizations and bureaus, down to the regional papers—the *Gau* locals, increased tremendously in 1933. They profited by party membership growth, government support and the confiscation of Socialist and Communist plants after the *Reichstag* fire, the March 5 election, and the "Law for the Confiscation of Property of the

Enemies of the State and People." This intensified anxiety among the middle class independents who were also threatened with closures and takeovers by Nazi rivals and government spokesmen. Publishers were pressured to either collaborate or close shop. Their powerful national association, the *Verein Deutscher Zeitungsverleger* (VDZV, later RVDZV), like that of the editors, the *Reichsverband der deutschen Presse* (RVDP) cooperated, issued solidarity proclamations, reorganized in accordance with Nazi wishes from April through June, and Nazi leaders assumed controlling positions. Hitler's confidant and personal banker and publisher, Max Amann—Reich Leader for the Press and the powerful director of the Eher Verlag, the giant Nazi publishing company—was chosen chairman of the reconstituted VDZV, while the executive directorship went to his trusted and talented lieutenant Rolf Rienhardt who, "cloaked with Amann's authority, was the most powerful figure in the German publishing industry."[18] Similarly, the RVDP was taken over. Elected chairman on April 30, 1933, Hitler's press chief Otto Dietrich immediately instituted ruthless purges of Jews and Marxists. Simultaneously, the party leadership occasionally tried to promote a more moderate image. Hitler even spoke of his need for a free and critical press[19] in order to reassure a worried profession, the public and the international community; but more threatening speeches by Goebbels and Dietrich countered the impression with hints at further purges, more rigid controls and threats to private property, thereby reinforcing fears.

The anxiety was well-founded. In fact, the Nazi state under the leadership of Goebbels and Amann via the Eher Verlag moved with determination and dispatch toward total operational control and ultimate ownership. The ease of immediate *Gleichschaltung* can be explained, in part, by Nazi organizational skills, ruthlessness and deception, but also by their understanding and exploitation of the press's structural weakness, special needs and problems: above all the depressing economic and political crisis that had produced the Third Reich which was mirrored in publishing and translated into the depressed moods of individuals; the decentralization of the existing press—the world's largest—of varied political orientation, largely family-owned and including many "special interests"; and the enmity between publishers and editors associations, which prevented concerted action against the Nazi threat. As editors had asked for state protection from the private publishers in the past, and a proposal had been drafted in 1924 to regulate the editor-publisher relationship, Goebbels simply revived this in the form of a new Editor's Law (October 4, 1933) which, in effect, substituted the state for the publishers who meanwhile had become organized as a *Fachschaft* within the newly-created Amann-led Reich Press Chamber—*Reichspressekammer* (RPK) by the Reich Culture Chamber Law—*Reichskulturkammergesetz* (RKKG) of September 22.

Legally, organizationally and functionally, the old enemies—editors and publishers—operated and received orders within the Goebbels ministry; the editors, in fact, were subject to instruction for what and how to publish at the daily so-called Press Conferences and other informational press gatherings at the Propaganda Ministry (RMVP).[20] Having traditionally been understood to perform a public function and subject to censorship under emergency decrees in republican times, Nazi measures, in part, were interpreted as being rooted in precedent and legality.[21]

There is no doubt that Hitler and the *Reichsleitung* (Reich Directorate of the Nazi party) were in complete control of *Gleichschaltung* of the press all along. What appeared as local and inter-departmental competition—though very real—was skillfully managed, above all by RMVP Minister Goebbels in concert and competition with Reich Press Leader Amann and Press Chief Dietrich—an example of a unique form of checks and balances within a totalitarian society. Legal control was based on the RKKG of September 22 and its implementation ordinances, which mandated membership for professionals in the press and publishing, and was enforced by a questionnaire and interview administered by local RPK offices in collaboration with secret police agencies which validated Aryan status and political reliability. Goebbels retained final authority in all personnel matters, including review of requests for exceptional treatment.

By the end of 1934 the mechanism for effective control of the "captive press" was in place. Personnel lists were finalized early in 1936.[22] The business aspect, too, had been relegated to the RPK via the Eher Verlag. Amann gradually absorbed directly or through subsidiaries the bulk of German publishing—both the former independents, with the exception of local papers of limited circulation, and the Gau press—thus nationalizing the press under what had become Germany's biggest trust. The extent of "probably the largest confiscation of private property" in the Third Reich[23] was disguised by the retention of old firm names and not generally known - one reason, perhaps, why historians of Nazi culture have paid relatively little attention to the impact of this powerful instrument of the Nazi state on the arts and art commentary.[24] In addition to the regular RMVP press conferences, as of mid-1936 a special weekly "culture-political" press conference was instituted which, again, amounted to briefings and instruction sessions. Music critics, then called commentators, had become members of the RPK rather than the RMK, a circumstance rendering appreciation of the much tighter control and outright nationalization of the press essential to an understanding of Nazi music politics.

Instrumental Music Journalism

The music journals were captured by the revolution as well, reflecting the *Gleichschaltung* of the press in general and covering the changes taking place in the world of music, as a number of journals went out of existence, while *völkish*-oriented ones were established at an increased pace. A reading of terminology and ideological considerations alone, however, does not reveal significant change in music journalism inasmuch as the "new ideas" had been proclaimed before by Pfitzner, for instance, or reviewed in the Austrian monthly for modern music, the *Anbruch*, which had brought out its January issue of 1931 under the title of "politization." With great foresight Hans Heinsheimer had written about the approaching Third Reich, noting the "secret terror" even then, and referring to the countless incidents in Germany involving the forceful suppression of modern, so-called "decadent" and "racially alien" forms of art.[25] In the December 1932 issue of Germany's progressive music journal, *Melos*, Karl Wörner had taken a dim view of trends which, in the form of modern political and cultural campaigns and slogans, caused, among other things, the closing down of the world-famous Bauhaus in Dessau before 1933. He had noted that, significantly, the moderate parties of the City Parliament had voted this action and that fear had already affected middle-class sentiment. In Berlin the Bauhaus still operated under the leadership of Mies van der Rohe; yet everywhere reaction launched its attack on modern art in newspapers, journals, magazines, pamphlets, books, and election propaganda. Wörner's article on "Culture Bolshevism" captured the slogan of the day in its title, reflecting the great debate in other art journals. *Kunst für Alle* and *Form* featured articles which dealt with the Nazi conception of "Building Bolshevism," a term used to refer to the Bauhaus and its art. Progressive journals also took issue with the increasing amount of racist literature and language in matters of the arts. Schultze-Naumburg, for instance, had described one of Barlach's sculptures as a "physically and spiritually deeply degenerate version of mongoloid blood."[26] Although the author of this latter article ridiculed Schultze-Naumburg's race literature, he noted that not only the NSDAP had been active shortly before 1933, but also that broad sectors of the arts and the public had already been intimidated into some form of collaboration. *Melos* stood for all that which the Nazis were to replace. It was the object of the coordinated attack in the music profession soon after the takeover and, under pressure, the image of the journal changed markedly. In one article of the *Zeitschrift für Musik*, that successor journal to Robert Schumann's *Neue Zeitschrift für Musik*—long since dedicated to the dissemination of the German standpoint in artistic matters under the leadership of Dr.

Alfred Heuss—the editor claimed that indeed the ZfM had contributed with repeated attacks on that "Melos-joke sheet" of Professor Mersmann to the silencing of that journal. At this time, in May, Mersmann was dismissed from his post as chief editor. The name of the journal was changed to Neues Musikblatt, appearing as such from August 1934 to November of 1946. Mersmann also was pressed to leave his post at the German Broadcasting System[27] being condemned in various ZfM articles, as in the one above and in the May issue, for his "propagation of atonal music."[28] Although Melos no longer existed, Mersmann was able to publish a book, Eine Deutsche Musikgeschichte (1934), which received devastating reviews in the coordinated press.

The Austrian journal and the committed German progressive ones maintained their integrity. The viewpoint of these journals had been anathema to Nazism in its movement phase, and had to be suppressed as a consequence of the political takeover. Strictly impartial in ideological matters and therefore less in focus during those critical days, purely professional journals also reflected change, although at a slower pace. The Yearbook of the Peters Music Library of the year 1933, published in 1934 by Kurt Traut, Leipzig, did not differ from any former edition. Attendance figures at the library and the number of volumes checked out were normal. However, even in this politically remote domain of a distinguished institution, the respected Dr. Alfred Jeremias was replaced as curator by a leader of the Cultural-Political Department of the NSDAP, F. A. Hauptmann.[29]

The seemingly harmless field of musicology, too, had been drawn into the sphere of ideological concern before 1933. The change of early 1933 was therefore less obvious in the professional journals. The noted musicologist Willibald Gurlitt, founder of the musicological Seminar at the University of Freiburg, welcomed the new order in a revealing article about "the German quality in music"—not altogether surprising in view of Gurlitt's earlier restorational and völkisch commitments. Like Pfitzner he had deplored the disintegrating influence of alien elements (jazz, Americanization, "colored" musicians, etc.) in German music in the 1920s. While the non-Nazi Gurlitt fought for the baroque organ against modern deviations and concentrated on music of the Reformation era which he related to the events of 1933, his student Josef Müller-Blattau—one of the most productive scholars during the Third Reich and a Pg since May 1933—devoted his successful career to the identification of German qualities in music with an emphasis on pre-historic Germanic origins and the folk song whose influence on modern art music he demonstrated in his numerous publications. When Gurlitt was retired from his university post in 1937 because of a Jewish spouse, Müller-Blattau—who also lectured extensively on the Horst-Wessel-song and whose voice has been preserved on recordings of folk- and HJ songs—succeeded his mentor.[30]

The February, March, April, and May issues of the scholarly journal, *Zeitschrift für Musikwissenschaft*, published by the *Deutsche Musikgesellschaft* (German Music Society) still under the editorship of the renowned Alfred Einstein, appeared in traditional form and content. The *völkisch* viewpoint had been presented before and then carried over into the Third Reich, particularly in articles about old Germanic music and various features of music which were traced to Germanic origins and characteristics. Interestingly, one article of A. Z. Idelsohn of Cincinnati, entitled "German Elements in Old German Synagogue Songs," in the June-July issue, addressed Jewish music in the manner of the new order. Idelsohn maintained that "through tonality racial characteristics emerge." He believed that such traditional children songs as *Fuchs, Du hast die Gans gestohlen*, contain a melody line which is sung by Germanic peoples in a Major key, while Slavs, Basques, Armenians, Portuguese, and East-European Jews sing the line in a Minor key—views which accorded with Nazi orthodoxy—although he did acknowledge that Jewish songs were influenced by the German environment, thus changing from the Doric to Germanic Major. Jews had also incorporated German songs into their liturgy, some of the significant changes taking place between the twelfth and fifteenth centuries. The journal printed brief news of events throughout Germany, touching on the Stein-Schünemann affair—Fritz Stein, a beneficiary and leading contributor to Nazi organization, replacing Georg Schünemann (a thorn in Nazi eyes) as director of the Berlin Music Academy; and the advancement of Dr. Friedrich Blume, distinguished scholar and increasingly an authority on the relationship between race and music, who succeeded the promoted Stein in his former position at Kiel. The Minister of Education, Dr. Bernhard Rust, also promoted Blume to Professor in the Philosophical Faculty at Berlin University.[31] Otherwise scholarly articles and news-bulletins implied the persistence of normal conditions. Then in January 1934, after failure of the journal to be published in the fall and winter months, an issue appeared that concentrated upon reporting the change in the political and social context of Germany with its effects on the scholarly world. "The *Deutsche Musikgesellschaft* understood the call for national unity and solidarity quite well."[32] Change was recorded and "the sense of scholarly isolation" and the mania for "esoteric publication" were "rejected," wrote Arnold Schering. By then, Max Schneider had replaced the editor Alfred Einstein, who emigrated to the U.S. Schneider, on the other hand, remained active in the politicized musicological society and contributed to the erection of the scholarly facade for the Nazi state.

Progressive journals were immediately affected, while neutral ones were temporarily safe. Most interesting was the reflection of general trends in those established journals which survived. The most representative and influential journal, *Die Musik* (DM), which traditionally contained contributions of the most prominent editors of both conservative and progressive persuasions, published all governmental decrees which applied to music. Dismissals, resignations, and emigrations became routine features of the publication after March 1933. In late 1932 progressives still had entertained the faith in the ultimate success of modern music and progressive aesthetics, and in the belief that a new era would witness acceptance of new music like that accorded to revolutionary creativity in former times.[33] The programs of late 1932 and early 1933 in German concert halls, on great stages, in music societies, etc., were covered, reflecting the rich and varied German music culture in spite of the increasingly vicious dialogue between modernists, traditionalists, and *völkisch* musicians. The developing crisis provoked disputes over aesthetics and the proper relationship between the musician and society. Then, in the critical months under review here, the journal gradually changed content. The failure to attract the normal number of foreign visitors to the Munich Music Festival was attributed to insecurity, international problems and the general crisis within the music community. However, in March 1933, the Nazi state and ideology still found no significant coverage in *DM*, while such "inadmissible" musicians as Arnold Schönberg, Georg Schünemann, Simon Goldberg, Otto Klemperer, Carl Ebert, Josef Schuster, Adolf Busch, etc., were warmly praised, and Klemperer—the victim of the above-mentioned boycott action—received congratulations upon his award of the Goethe-Prize from President Hindenburg. German concert life and music journalism still reflected the totality of Germany's acceptance of traditional and contemporary music.[34]

In April, however, the Revolution was expressed explicitly in announcements of an increasing number of resignations and dismissals. Several music directors of noted stages—including those discussed above—were listed: Carl Ebert of the City Opera of Berlin, Reucker of the State Opera of Dresden, Hartung of the Provincial Theatre of Darmstadt, and Maisch of the National Theatre of Mannheim; the list was longer. Also a number of noted conductors were publicly asked by political authority to cease work: Hermann Scherchen, Bruno Walter, Heinz Unger, and Joseph Rosenstock. In the same issue Bernhard Rust announced that elections would be held in the PAdK. Announcements of this kind, symptoms of change and anxiety, were balanced by the traditional form and presentation of the journal. Paul Bekker wrote the feature article on opera, attacking that musical form as an outmoded and antiquated expression. He praised Wagner as an innovator and upholder of great artistic freedom directed against the bourgeoisie because that class already at that time was no longer revolutionary.[35] Although the journal still exuded an independent spirit, its readers were caught up in the daily experience of the Nazi revolution in all aspects of public life. Inasmuch as an alarming number of musicians retired from professional life, while Pg's were promoted, the reader had to conclude that music had been drawn into the revolution. However, the May issue of *DM* still presented its traditional format—being dedicated to Brahms and mentioning Mendelssohn and Heine favorably. Even the celebrated exchange of letters between Furtwängler and Goebbels—one in defense of music's autonomy, the other on totalitarian and *völkisch* claims—was reported in responsible journalistic style. A slight change appeared in terminology, one which increasingly was to characterize the impact of National Socialism on music and journalism. The constant reference to *Umschwung* (revolutionary change) expressed the general intention of authors of several articles—the self-coordination of sentiment. This issue reported the threat to Bruno Walter, director of the Gewandhaus orchestra in Leipzig, his dismissal, and Richard Strauss's acceptance of the offer to conduct in his place. It also covered the introduction to prominence of the Fighting League of German Culture (KfdK) that Alfred Rosenberg and Hans Hinkel had moved to the center of cultural activity. The journal noted that Rust had ordered the KfdK to perform at the Reger Festival. This issue of the journal mirrored the confusion of the time: Schnabel, still performing in Germany, received a favorable review.[36] Along with Rust, Hinkel, the KfdK and Schnabel appeared the old cultural critic of the twenties, Hans Pfitzner, who sounded the traditional Germanic note, "Only Germans know the concept of profundity in music." The issue contained more about the revolution in practice. It included a note on the hundredth anniversary of the Music Division of the PAdK, March 31, its distinguished President Max von Schilling officiating amidst the furor over Heinrich Mann's and Käthe Kollwitz's dismissals and Ernst Barlach's threat to resign from the Division of Plastic Arts over the question of political and artistic freedom.[37]

During the days of the Weimar Republic, music criticism above all other musical domains represented the cultural establishment in the eyes of traditional cultural critics and the Nazis, though not exclusively by them. Back in December 1932 Eberhard Preussner of *Melos* had taken issue with some critics, referring in that context to a concert in which Gieseking had substituted Chopin for the announced Debussy and Ravel; yet critic Paul Zschorlich of the *Deutsche Zeitung* had raved about Gieseking's superb rendition of the French masters (November 8, 1932). It was obvious that Zschorlich either had been absent or was incompetent.[38] At this crucial moment of change, *DM* published a statement concerning the founding on April 11 of an official organization, the Study Group of Berlin Music Critics, headed by Dr. Fritz Stege—member of the KfdK since 1929, music critic of the *VB* and one of the most important formulators of Nazi music politics and a trend setter in terminology. Membership in the new organization was predicated on "national sentiment and Aryan ancestry"—a significant first step toward *Gleichschaltung* of music criticism. All thus defined critics were to be included through strict national organization.[39] Under Rosenberg's patronage and Stege's leadership an extensive organization headed by KfdK and Pg's was in place nationwide by June 1933.

The new party offices and organizations complemented the lengthy list of dismissals which in May included more well-known music directors: Gsell of Dortmund, Hartmann of Breslau, Hartmann of Chemnitz, Hofmüller of Cologne, Felsing of Schwerin, Kehm of Stuttgart, Klitsch of Kassel, Krüger of Freiburg, Schönfeld of Koblenz, Turnau of Frankfurt, and Waag of Karlsruhe, and the following conductors retired from their positions: Engel of Dresden, Horenstein of Düsseldorf, Jalowetz of Cologne, Klemperer of Berlin, Lindemann of Augsburg, Prätorius of Weimer, Steinberg of Frankfurt, and Szenkar of Cologne. At the Music Academy at Cologne, the active Nazi music commentator Walter Abendroth and Pg Richard Trunk (see above) were new appointees, while its director, the composer Walter Braunfels was dismissed. Likewise, the new regime installed new music directors: Otto Krauss at the City Theater in Stuttgart, Alexander Spring at the City Theater in Cologne, Dr. Prasch at the Provincial Theater Darmstadt and Fritz Mecklenburg at the City Theater Schwerin.[40]

DM enjoyed a tremendous influence in spite of its relatively small distribution of 3,300 copies, and its reputation was impeccable; its writers were well-known and prominent members of the music establishment. In noting the practical manifestations of the "new spirit" at a time of ill-defined standards and generalized ideological confusion, the journal provided its readers in a still unbiased manner with an accurate account of the impact of the new state on music.

Things changed radically with the June 1933 issue, which was published under the title of "The New Germany." The "new tone" was unmistakable, since Goebbels himself addressed the reader with an introduction: "If art wants to shape its time, it has to confront its problems. German art of the next decades will be heroic, hard as steel, and romantic, sentimental and factual, national with great pathos, and it will be binding and demanding—or it will not be."[41]

The Goebbels proclamation introduced the first edition of *DM* totally dedicated to the Nazi revolution. The noted composer Paul Graener, another *völkisch*-oriented and active pre-1933 Pg, took to task the existing music culture in Germany. The sad state of music was self-evident, he said, because "the people are not singing along." A systematic attack was here launched, unanswered, in the hitherto liberal journal against progressives, the progressive position in music and intellectuals in general. Ideology was now presented with authority in the debate on opera and absolute music. The reference to the political revolution, to the care of the new regime for culture and to the consequent reaction from within the community of sympathetic musicians demonstrated clearly that open debate on the arts in modern society had come to an end. The ideologists of the right settled accounts with alleged ideologists of the left, that is, modernists in music, in a way which must have shocked even the traditional and idealistic cultural critics of the conservative right in music. Indeed, the new men directed their fervor against the entire pre-1933 era as having been dominated by progressive and otherwise totally unacceptable elements in music. While the anti-modernist and pessimistic culture critic of the past hundred years in Germany and the Nazi policy makers of 1933 spoke an identical language, the meaning and significance of their respective pronouncements differed, took place under distinct conditions, and led to a change in perspective. The pessimism and complaining note of Pfitzner in the 1920's seemed, for one, out of place in the environment proclaimed by Graener in June 1933: "Colleagues, it is wonderful that we can now serve the people with our ability to create. Long live German art."[42]

The excitement of the Nazi revolution had found its way into the pages of *DM*, but, so had the hope and mandate for a new art music—the ultimate goal and test of the revolution in music—that would be worthy of the masters of the past and reflect and magnify National Socialism, its achievements and aspirations and thus help shape the new national community of *völkisch* projection. Seduced by jobs and flattery—if not genuinely inspired or terrorized—musicians responded enthusiastically with solidarity proclamations and supportive ideological formulations, applications for party membership and organizational positions for the profession, educational and youth institutions, the party and state. They contributed their talents to folk and political festivities and groped for definitions of what might constitute German music apropriate for the great historical moment—not simply music produced and performed in Germany, but one that revealed an inner German essence. When Goebbels asked for "art for and of the whole people," musicians provided the expert analysis of affirmative contemporary music. Finding that inner essence elusive, however, they described music of the great classical-romantic past instead. The Dresden music director—*Generalmusikdirektor* (GMD) Werner Ladwig illustrated by example the expert's support of the enterprise. *DM* published his evocation of German masters who had engaged in the noble effort of communicating with the people in the past. One such master was—who else, but—Wagner, who tirelessly had endeavored to construct a bridge between the people and art, thereby being a model for a new type of leader in the arts who might again create a new "people's opera"[43]—a National Socialist musical drama.

Bridges were to be built but, admittedly, in terms of the past. The composer Max Trapp, distinguished member of the PAdK since 1929 who was also active in the KfdK, wrote an "Appeal to the Creative" in the same issue as Ladwig. With this anti-intellectual attack on modern forms of music—reminiscent of the more substantial anti-modernist strictures of the past—the conservative orthodoxy of melody, i.e., its priority in the elemental makeup of proper composition, was reintroduced. Trapp had already written along these lines during the age of "Marxist corruption," when a "strange race" had undermined German effort. It was evident that *DM* had become the platform for the official music policy, and, significantly, for noted German musicians, who found no difficulty in adjusting to the new situation. The sanctity of traditional melody, the need for a people's opera, definitions of "native" and "racially alien" music appeared in article after article. Trapp unabashedly urged composers to break with the immediate esoteric past. "We will now conform in music" because "the people have to participate." In the spirit of revolutionary enthusiasm he confessed his traditionalism, but only in the sense that tradition had to be the basis of all new music. The Third Reich would foster creativity if tradition were properly respected.[44]

The composer, conductor, and recipient of the Mendelssohn prize, Hans Bullerian also actively participated as a member of the KfdK. Already in early February, 1933 he had demonstrated his solidarity with the new regime by protesting the performance of a student's modernistic composition at the Berlin Academy of Music. After his colleague, the composer Paul Graener, had complained about conditions at the academy and specifically the quality of the composition in point, with the loud comment: "Ladies and Gentlemen. Members of this German academy of music dare to impose this pitiful stammering on you as German art. I protest as a German artist,"[45] he and other members of the KfdK left the auditorium. In February, the views of Bullerian were printed in the *VB* and the *ZfM*. In June, Bullerian contributed an article to *DM* on "German Concert Life and its Renewal." "Now that the revolution is over, we want to serve the German state." He rejected the former era of "literati theoreticians of the new music," whose leader, Adolf Weissmann, was representative of "intellect and wit [meant as an insult]." ..."And then came January 30, 1933. This revolution will be as far-reaching in music as in the fields of politics and among the people."

Bullerian represented those musicians for whom the revolution and the subsequent turmoil created career opportunities. Political loyalty was rewarded with commissions, jobs and performance on the German Radio Station, whose new musical program director, Max Donisch, discovered and promoted Bullerian and other, mostly younger, KfdK composers. Bullerian's enthusiasm harmonized with the editorial policy of the recently coordinated journal. Aside from his ideological paraphrasing of official viewpoints, he endeared himself by using his articles to flatter major culture organizers, attributing to these men the accomplishment of all essential groundwork for the revolution in culture even before 1933. For instance, we learn from Bullerian, that Professor Gustav Havemann, a prominent violinist and leading KfdK activist, had discussed in early 1932 with such noteworthy functionaries as Siegfried Burgstaller the incorporation of the German music profession into the cultural reconstruction program of the NSDAP. Consultation with the political culture organization of the NSDAP had produced the agreement that indeed the KfdK would be most instrumental in executing future musical policy. Hans Hinkel had emerged as leader on a broader scale, always ready to listen to new ideas and to allow for the advancement of dedicated young members in this expanding organization. Minister Rust, however, was held to be the most important link between the KfdK—his proteges being placed in all significant organizations—and the total area of organized artistic life in Germany. Bullerian's article paid tribute to the successful movements in politics, and he contributed enthusiastically to what appeared to him as the creation of a new nation within which the arts would be able to develop again from folk sources.[46]

Another ambitious climber in the days of the new regime was Dr. Fritz Stein, Professor at the University of Kiel, who through support of the KfdK received an appointment as provisional director of the Music Academy in Berlin after the former director, Dr. Georg Schünemann, was relieved of his duties. The above-mentioned disruption of the performance of a student's work at the Academy had been instrumental in the transference of position.[47] Fritz Stein offered a speech of acceptance at the Music Academy May 2 in which he praised commissioner Hinkel, his benefactor, and DM printed the speech in its June issue. Stein emphasized his own accomplishments within the guidelines of the new regime and in the "spirit of the new Germany, which aims its policy toward implementation of cultural commitments through nationalistic education." He promised to participate in this endeavor and to act in his new capacity at the Academy in the spirit of the "leadership principle," meaning with authority and responsibility. "We want to raise not only artists but German artists." He indicated that henceforth at the institution of music education, in addition to ability and accomplishment political sentiment would count.[48]

All articles of this edition reflected the new times and the new rhetoric. One review of "German Music Education and its New Form," focused on

education of the young as a means of affecting cultural renewal—a priority
suggesting, apart from its obvious revolutionary merits, the practical nature
of Nazi policy, since the new state could easily control teachers at institutions of learning. The turnover of personnel clearly indicated implementation of policy. Other articles addressed ideological questions, to which the
völkisch romantics could contribute. One treatment of "New Approaches to
the German Song" applauded Hitler for awarding an annual prize for the composition of the best new German folk song, while another article, "Nationalization of German Music," appealed to musicians to establish contact again "with
the blood of the people, now that music has been saved from international
contamination."[49]

The important issue of June 1933 also contained the official bulletin section, entitled "Under the Sign of Change," where dismissals and appointments
were listed, while featuring the most prominent of the "inadmissable" conductors, Bruno Walter and Otto Klemperer. "Non-Aryans" were reportedly
organized with their own periodicals and journals, and Furtwängler was
quoted as voicing dismay over conditions in music. He questioned the motives
of new elements in music who would threaten persons like Klemperer and
Walter. Walter himself took to the pen, upholding the German tradition of
autonomous arts, which he believed to be in danger: "I have never belonged
to a political party. My life and action are dedicated to my art alone."[50] The
bulletin contained a long list of dismissals again, some cases being repeated.
The Strauss substitution for Walter at Leipzig was mentioned; Fritz Busch
no longer had a position at Dresden, Karl Böhm taking over for him there—
one step in the talented young conductor's extraordinary career in the Third
Reich, which included glowing public loyalty, declarations for Hitler and the
Hitler salute at one time upon entering the stage of the Great Concert Hall
in Vienna in late March 1938—a gesture not required of conductors as per
specific RMVP instructions to the RMK, September 28, 1936—cited by Prieberg
in connection with Böhm's post-war denial;[51] and the Stein-Schünemann affair at the Berlin Music Academy was again noted. Various teachers at the
equivalent academy at Frankfurt were dismissed, while Bernhard Sekles and
various colleagues were dismissed from the famous Hochsche Conservatory.
In Berlin, the well-known instructors, Oskar Daniel, Leonid Kreutzer, Bruno
Eisner, Immanual Feuermann, Strelitzer, Borries, Charlotte Pfeffer, and
Fanny Warburg had to resign. The theatre managers, Paul Legband of Erfurt
and Hans Meissner of Stettin; the music directors, Walter Beck of the City
Theater of Magdeburg and Josef Krips of the Karlsruhe Provincial Theater;
and Bruno Seidler-Winkler, conductor of the Berlin radio orchestra
(*Funkstunde*) also were dismissed. Furthermore, the bulletin contained at-
tacks on Klemperer, Thomas and Heinrich Mann.[52] In most cases replace-

ments were recruited from the national KfdK and other Nazi organizations.[53]
The success of the ideological campaign of the coordinated and coordinating officials was illustrated through the announcement printed in this issue on jazz, which had been eliminated from all musical performance in Bamberg, Frankfurt a.m. and Passau—having been banned from Berlin radio before. This logical translation of music ideology into policy, implemented through political decree, the bulletin reported, was to be extended to the whole Reich.[54] The *Deutsche Kultur-Wacht* reported that hostility to jazz had been a feature of Nazi ideology and organized policy before the great *Umschwung*. Reich Minister Frick had already abolished jazz in Thuringia by government decree in his drive of 1930 to purify the arts of all alien elements.[55] The bulletin contained other items, for instance, about Adolf Busch, who left Germany in protest over "actions against Jews and his brother Fritz Busch." The country was also asked to object to the foreign boycott of German music in France and Poland. In spite of opposition, however, Furtwängler's concert in Paris was reported a success. In Cologne, the reaction prevented employment of foreign musicians, justified on grounds of limited job openings and the 15,700 unemployed German musicians listed for 1932. Again, KfdK activist Fritz Stege's new nationwide Study Group of Berlin Music Critics with its extensive provincial organizational network supported all government policies. This group was joined by the famous *Bruno Kittelsche Chorus*, the *Deutscher Arbeitersängerverband* (German Workers Choral Organization), the *Westdeutscher Musiklehrerverband* (West German Music Teacher Association of Cologne), the *Deutscher Musikerverband* (German Musicians Association), and the *Arbeitsgemeinschaft zur Pflege und Förderung evangelischer Kirchenmusik* (Study group for the cultivation and promotion of Protestant Church music)—all in order to become part of the new "national people's community."[56]

The bulletin of *DM* covered the tremendous activity in behalf of the Nazi policy toward music, the party's elan, the *Gleichschaltung* measures which complemented and implemented theory and ideological formulations. It spelled out, in detail, the reforms within the musical community, the blending of *völkisch* idealism and Nazi ruthlessness—suggested in Goebbel's well known phrase of "romanticism of steel"—which increasingly pointed toward centralization of musical life and its administration. The policy statements, news items and reform projects revealed the trend toward the creation of the Reich Music Chamber (RMK) by the Reich Culture Chamber Law (RKKG) of September 22, 1933.

The management and policy of *DM* was typically affected by the transformation and Nazification, as the KfdK member Johannes Günther became its editor that year. Later, in April 1934, the journal announced that it had become an outlet for the Reich Youth Leadership—*Reichsjugendführung* (RJF), and in June 1934 it became the official organ of the increasingly active and official National Socialist (NS) Cultural Community—*NS Kulturgemeinde* (NSKG), after it had absorbed Rosenberg's KfdK and continued the latter's agitation for extreme ideological measures and the realization of *völkisch* ideals in protest against Goebbels' more pragmatic policies. Its authoritative member Friedrich W. Herzog, who enjoyed connections to Goebbels' circles as well, assumed the editorship at that time and became its publisher in April, 1936, until replaced by another Nazi music journalist in that capacity, Herbert Gerigk who was active at the Party Directorate and the Rosenberg Bureau and co-edited the later *Dictionary of Jews in Music.*

Die Musik illustrated regimentation of the press in general. The editors received specific instructions to communicate government policy and contribute to the "rebuilding of national life." In this centrally coordinated effort, the Nazi state collided with the tradition of German exclusiveness and the respected and autonomous expert. Goebbels took the lead in this pervasive shift, exhorting musicians and their public not merely to create from within, as was traditional, but to participate in national life as active members of the people.[57] All music journals, party papers, documentary films, newsreels, the radio and music-related institutions in education and the churches presented a united front in shaping the new culture, and in making musicians and the masses aware of incidents created by Nazis and tendentiously reported in the routine application of Nazi procedure.

When the composer Paul Graener, pre-1933 KfdK member, created the above-mentioned incident at the Berlin Music Academy, the *VB* immediately took up the matter on February 10, 1933, expanding the context to denounce the acting director of the institution, Dr. Georg Schünemann, for tolerating this kind of "modern nonsense," for representing "the Marxist regime," and misunderstanding the meaning of "German art." In the ensuing dispute, Schünemann lost his position and membership in the prestigious Senate of the PAdK. The case involved ideological standards in music, change of personnel, and a ruthlessly executed policy. Yet, members of the music establishment still defended Schünemann on the basis of competence, a nonpolitical past, proven Aryan descent, recent membership in the NSDAP Civil Service Study Group, and an excellent record as director of the Music Academy— "no non-Aryan having received a position" at the institution during his term of office which began in July, 1932. The points cited in Schünemann's behalf resulted in partial rehabilitation. It must be noted, however, that leading officials of the PAdK who were responsible for the letters commending Schünemann addressed to Education Minister Rust had to conform to the rhetoric of the Nazi revolution. Revolutionary jargon shaped both attack and defense. Race, politics and other features of the ideology reflected in the terminology had become the basis of judgment in the area of music.[58]

Various activities were condemned in otherwise sympathetic journals. As noted above, the editor of the *ZfM*, Gustav Bosse, cautioned his readers against excesses of what he, too, called "the revolution of the street," advocating, instead, the Nazi principle of "leadership responsibility." Disapproval was carefully presented on the basis of the new values and in the new language. Hoping for a renaissance of German music, Bosse "deplored the importation of educators of alien blood" and "noted with grief that countless leading positions in our leading musical life were occupied by aliens—Jews." He was looking forward to the effort of the new government to "eliminate this extra-German pressure" and to create conditions in which "the German will to leadership can be exercised" and "pure German culture may thrive again." Central to his conformism was the crucial line, "Indeed, we all can benefit from 'coordination of sentiment'. . . However, we have to stop a situation in which anybody can denounce a rival on the basis of earlier disagreement, threatening position and bread." He deplored the smaller "special revolutions," removed from central control, citing celebrated cases in music. Although Fritz Busch had been attacked by members of the SA, Bosse defended him, emphasizing his qualities as conductor. "It would seem that defamation of an artist of the stature of Fritz Busch, which led to his dismissal, would be an impossibility in Germany." Furthermore, he traced the dismissal of GMD Walter Beck of Magdeburg to groundless denunciations. Again in this case, Bosse defended a victim by noting the absence of politics from his life. "He belonged to that group of our musicians who did not belong to any political party."[59] Bosse deplored that the provisional mayor of Magdeburg never agreed to meet with Beck, especially since Beck had emphasized German compositions in his programs.

Other victims of organized terror, dismissal and unofficial pressures, like the noted music educator Fritz Jöde, were given space in Bosse's journal for defending themselves, in addition to which other musicians did come to the aid of less fortunate individuals in spite of the dangers implied in such action. This type of deviation became less and less feasible as consequences became clearer. In the end, only men of Furtwängler's stature dared defend fellow musicians. Although withdrawal from public involvement was possible for the little man, it was more profitable to engage in polemics on behalf of the new regime. Disagreement was presented under the mantle of the official ideology which, to be sure, reflected some of the assumptions of other opinions. In the context of 1933 this meant that it was possible to play the official ideology against organizational and propagandistic calculation.

It was also apparent that musicians were willing to become activists on behalf of National Socialism by exploiting situations which had rendered others defenseless. Nobody could feel entirely secure. Graener, though a member of the KfdK and future Vice-President of the RMK, had to defend himself against the accusation of being half-Jewish. Hans Hinkel, commissioner in the Education Ministry, KfdK leader, powerful cultural organizer and in charge of Jewish culture, personally had to attest to the Aryan status of Graener before his opera *Friedemann Bach* could be performed in Saxony[60]—even though the libretto of the opera was written by Rudolph Lothar, a Jew.

These incidents were reported in the style of the revolution. Religious and moral pathos were applied, while reference to combat, to actual fighting in the area of culture conveyed the unique flavor in other instances.[61] KfdK member Fritz Stege, major contributor to the *VB* and the *ZfM*, the later organ of the RMK, tried to maintain his good connections with all important Nazi organizations, even with the feuding Reich leaders, Rosenberg and Goebbels. The style of his reports on the music scene in early 1933 typified the times and reflected the state of war of Goebbels' creation. "Music in Berlin," he wrote, "is subjected to the National revolution...Nationalists are conquering the city. The City Opera has fallen, the State Opera is still resisting lightly, although the position of GMD Otto Klemperer is shaken so badly that he is barely holding his own, according to reports of KfdK leader and State commissioner Hans Hinkel." The article maintained the same tone throughout:

> Bruno Walter is a casualty, likewise Heinz Unger, the latter having resigned his post as President of the Society for the Friends of Music after having been informed by the Philharmonic Orchestra that he no longer can count on permanent employment as conductor. Under the leadership of Prof. Gustav Havemann the conquest of musical organizations commenced . . . The Marxist Workers Choral Society has been conquered . . . . Final victory has been won over the Association of German Music Critics. . . .[62]

The tenor of Stege's journalism set the tone. The Nazi composer, musicologist, and commentator Walter Abendroth[63] filled the *Berliner Lokal-Anzeiger* and other papers and journals, books, and party pamphlets with similar Nazi jargon. His article, "Purified *Tannhäuser*," written after Klemperer's dismissal from the Prussian State Opera at Berlin, the famous *Lindenoper*, exuded malicious joy: "So there. The general protest evoked by the Klemperer-Fehling *Tannhäuser*—assassination in public and press—excepting some papers noted for the lack of interest in the cultivation of German culture—has not been spent in vain. Finally, justice is done to the opera, in the spirit of the master."[64] Paul Schwers extended his critique beyond Fehling and

Klemperer, asking for the head of the director of Prussian stages, Heinz Tietjen, "on a silver platter." The composer and musicologist Friedrich Welter picked up the tone in his article, "Concern for German Music—A Confession," describing culture of the former years as "sin against the spirit." Welter saw in the national revolution a break with outrageous conditions in Germany's political and cultural life, especially in music, denouncing the immediate past and its leading spokesman in the spirit of official ideology.[65]

Political decisions pertaining to music, execution of policy, and the helter-skelter reality in musical institutions were depicted throughout the professional press in uniform terms, thereby conveying the idea that coordination was centrally controlled. After Bruno Walter's Leipzig concert had been cancelled, in March, Goebbels himself moved to prevent the Walter concert in Berlin via the office of Walter Funk. It is significant that in Saxon affairs, Goebbels' personal intervention had not been necessary, as eager officials had volunteered *Gleichschaltung*. On the other hand, in Berlin, Hinkel had to intercede in opposition to Walter. Following the concert, performed under the baton of substitute Richard Strauss, Hinkel explained, "We never prevented this concert, nor did we forbid Bruno Walter, whose real name is Schlesinger, to conduct. However, it was impossible to offer the necessary protection."[66]

The attacks on musicians paralleled dismissals. Jewish members of the State Opera at Berlin were dismissed, along with GMD Otto Klemperer, the conductor Fritz Zweig, the singers Tilly de Garmo and Lotte Schöne and the tenor Noè. An exception was made in the case of GMD Leo Blech in view of his twenty-five years of service dating back to Kaiser Wilhelm. The contracts of the two bassos, Emanuel List and Alexander Kipnis, also were temporarily honored.[67] The latter retentions had to be related to the special powers of Furtwängler, who had received a guarantee that racial legislation would not be applied to members of his orchestra, and since Göring was most anxious to retain the services of Furtwängler, repeated exceptions were made. In early 1933 the new tone, style and tension characterized the uneasy state of maneuvering. Furtwängler held his own to some degree, but his activity was overshadowed by the total effect of the verbal revolution and the purges. The *Deutsche Kultur-Wacht* attacked the noted tenor Richard Tauber as son of "the hundred percent Jewish theater manager Tauber" and denounced his "non-German way of singing." Said to have capitalized on the low standards and the confusion after World War I, in the pose of the prototype of German singing, his career was phenomenal, "until one day, even before the National Socialist revolution, the people awoke in its healthy instinct, tired of Tauber's singing and howling [*tauberische Singerei und Säuselei*]."[68] Articles of this sort were the norm, and hundreds more could be quoted to convey the mood.

Gleichschaltung of the Academy

The task of establishing meaningful control over music and the policy of propagating the world view and attitudes of National Socialism of necessity involved a carefully planned and thoroughly pursued approach to education. National Socialism had styled itself a movement of the young, capturing anti-establishment sentiment and the traditional suspicion of the elder generation. Although policy embraced the educational structure of the whole Reich, the monumental effort had to be compromised by virtue of major difficulties that arose from the federal structure of German education. The individual states represented different developments in education, and centralization could not immediately produce a unified school system. Thus, the initial attempts at restructuring education and filling the curriculum with National Socialist content were carried out by Rust in Prussia, while changes were effected consistently in the other states only after the passage of the law of coordination between states and the Reich, January 30, 1934. In Prussia, courses on racial anthropology and other ideological courses were offered. German literature, music, history and physical education received top priority with the use of new textbooks as well as traditional *völkisch* and racist literature.

The PadK was subjected to Nazi intimidation immediately after January 30, 1933 as we have seen. The administration of the institution at that time was responsible to Rust's Ministry. Dr. Wolfgang von Staa of the Prussian and Reich Education Ministry became the official legal and administrative expert of the Academic Senate in July 1933, therewith constituting a direct line of communication between the Academy and Minister Rust, although it managed to preserve the functioning of its internal structure. As the most distinguished representation of the arts in Germany it served as a convenient tool in the process of coordination of higher education and for propaganda purposes.

In the affair concerning membership of Heinrich Mann and Käthe Kollwitz, Academy President Max von Schillings—a musician—discussed the situation with the members in question, eliciting a declaration from both to resign voluntarily. This step saved the Academy from open confrontation. Heinrich Mann noted that the constitution of the Academy contained no clause whatsoever restricting political expression of academic members, and that this tradition of liberty had been respected by all political sectors of the membership in Republican times, but the Academy bowed.[69] After the stormy general session of the Berlin membership, in which a number of members declared solidarity with the first victims of purification, while others accepted the principle of coordination in the interest of self-preservation, President von

Schillings engaged in sweeping measures in support of the national revolution. On March 31, 1933, the Music Division of the Academy celebrated its
one-hundredth anniversary, calling on von Schillings to conduct the music
for it. He also lent himself in the same capacity to the City Opera at Berlin
in honor of Hitler's birthday. As president of the Academy and as honorary
president of the prominent music educators' organization, *Reichsverband
Deutscher Tonkünstler und Musiklehrer* (RDTM), an organization of 10,000
members and 200 local chapters, von Schillings became one of the most
important men in the process of *Gleichschaltung* and *Entjudung* (Jewish
purges). The Academy preserved itself to some degree, but the RDTM received
a new administration which was integrated into the *Reichskartell berufstätiger
Musiker*, Havemann's organization of professional musicians, which constituted the provisional basis of the later Music Chamber (RMK).[70]

Membership in the Music Department of the Academy at Berlin began
to conform to the typical Nazi documentation, listing name (Graener, Paul),
authentic descent (Aryan), descent of spouse (Aryan), comments (Pg.- Party
member). Proof of ancestry was listed under "comments," variously referring to the authority of the questionnaire, the expert of the Office of
Genealogical Research of the Interior Ministry, or the Education Ministry. All
members of the Academy filled out the questionnaires which were forwarded
to the Ministry of the Interior. Notices of dismissal were based on recommendation of the Interior, pronounced by the Education Ministry and carried out
by the Academy. The volume of correspondence between these offices
attested to the priority of the questionnaire. In May 1933, Arnold Schönberg
was first given a leave of absence in writing. Von Schillings and Amersdorffer
signed the letter on the basis of Rust's decree of May 17. On September 18,
1933, Schönberg was informed by the Academy that he was dismissed from
his post at the Academy in consequence of the minister's order, reference
Paragraph 3 of the Civil Service Law (April 7). As noted above, he never accepted the fact of termination of contract. Since leading musicians from all
over Germany belonged to the Academy, Nazi influence here led to consequences which illustrate the serious effects on music in general. Minutes of
meetings of the general membership and the Senate of the Academy in Berlin
reveal the centrality of the April 7 law, in consequence of which the Aryan-
status of members as a precondition for membership and the right to teach
was discussed at a meeting of the Music Department (June 16), which was
attended by President Schumann and Amersdorffer, Graener, Juan, Kahn,
Kempff, Moser, von Reznicek, Seiffert, Tiessen, Trapp, Stein, and von Wolfurt.
A membership list was made with all relevant information insofar as it was
available. The question of race was again discussed in meetings of July 1 and
4. It was noted that the Academy had offered its assistance to the Race Of-

fice of the Interior when that office requested advice concerning questionable members.

The Academy itself initiated proceedings against several fellow members. Amersdorffer asked Minister Rust whether it would be appropriate to retain Professor Franz Schreker, in view of the latter's open sympathy for the new order and conservative position in musical matters. Schreker's repeated letters to von Schillings testify to the level of desperation reached by persecuted individuals, documented in moving terms by Gösta Neuwirth in his book *Franz Schreker*. Within two weeks of the request, Rust, in a letter of May 17, 1933, authorized termination of the appointment of Schreker.

The Academy offered assistance in other countries and to take avantage of international connections in cases which were time-consuming and costly. Amersdorffer wrote, "naturally the Academy is ready to assume the cost of checking out the ancestry of members working abroad." When asked to check up on the Italian composer, Ermanno Federico Wolf-Ferrari, Amersdorffer cautioned against this in deference to Italian authorities. Moreover, it was known that his wife was "Aryan." Foreigners with business in the Reich were subjected to the questionnaire as well. As a composer of works published in Germany, Béla Bartók was questioned "are you of German blood, are you racially related or non-Aryan?" [71]

Individual cases were reviewed by the Academy, always in close touch with the relevant political office. All decisions were based on thorough research which in each case went back many generations. Musical progressives were especially subject to scrutiny. In July, Hindemith, Juan, Tiessen, and Trapp were declared Aryan. Also newly-elected members, Max Butting and Ottorino Resphigi were acceptable on grounds of racial legislation. Professor Heinz Tiessen's political past was reviewed and Amersdorffer recommended the composer's retention on the basis of his Aryan status. His Marxist tendencies were attributed to youthful errors. Having led the *Junger Chor* (Young Chorus) of the *Arbeitersängerbund* (Workers Choral Association), which was dissolved May 25, he in fact had demonstrated his idealism, it was argued, wanting to bring music to the people. Tiessen admitted that he had committed a grave error in composing the *Aufmarsch*, using texts which were now unacceptable. It is striking what sophistry Amersdorffer and others who managed to survive had to employ in order to defend the "idealist" of those times. The former Schönberg student, Alban Berg, was declared unacceptable for his music, though. On the other hand, the race expert of the Interior also informed the Academy that the composer Julius Weismann was Aryan.

Some individuals benefited from the persecution of those in suspected categories. A most interesting case in point was that of Walter Braunfels, an

Academy member since 1925 and composer and director of the State Academy of Music at Cologne. The secretary of the Music Department of the Berlin Academy, Kurt von Wolfurt wrote Gustav Hermann Unger—Pg since 1931 and active at the Cologne Academy since 1925, but significantly also leader of the Music Division in the KfdK and music editor of a journal, *Deutsches Volkstum*—asking him to provide some information regarding Braunfels. Unger responded that Braunfels was the son of a Jewish father, and in fact Braunfels admitted this, that he was dismissed from his post in Cologne immediately after the "national revolution" (see the Trunk substitution above) and was presently living in Bad Godesberg. Then, Unger added, "I have been recommended to substitute for Braunfels as special advisor to the government." Yet, according to Paragraph 3, Sec. 2, veterans were not subjected to the non-Aryan clause and Braunfels attempted to remain a member of the Academy on the basis of service in World War I, during which he had been wounded. Schumann answered that Minister Rust decided that having fought at the front had no relevance in matters pertaining to the Academy. This verdict was reached in consultation with the Ministerial Chancellor's Secretariat.

The relationship between the Berlin Academy, other German music academies, the Education and Interior Ministries, and musicians was clearly spelled out. Those who survived the purges and were listed in the membership roster as Aryan and acceptable on political terms, were constantly reminded that they lived in a revolutionary society. On November 3, 1933, members of the departments of Plastic Arts and Music were asked to sign a loyalty oath to Adolf Hitler. The document read:

Those artists and musicians united in the PAdK affirm their loyalty and adherence in deep gratitude for the memorable words with which you acknowledged in Nuremberg and Munich the significance of the arts for the nation and state. As upholders of the creative arts and music, we are aware of the tremendous responsibility we shoulder in the effort of fulfilling our cultural mission to the people and state—and especially we are prepared to assume our responsibilities in anticipation of the day when all Germans will stand by the side of their Führer unanimously.

The note was signed by Amersdorffer, August Kraus, as President of the Department of Plastic Arts, and George Alfred Schumann, President of the Music Department and regular members were informed of the content and encouraged to follow suit. Yet this appeal to solidarity of the coordinated arts led to a controversy. Joseph Haas, Professor at the State Academy of

Music at Munich and member of the Prussian Academy since 1930, wrote a most revealing letter to Schumann, shortly before the declaration was to be signed.

> Herr Dr. von Hausegger (Director of the Munich Academy), Professor Reuss (Director of the Trapp Music School in Berlin and Munich), and I are happy to sign the loyalty proclamation which the Academy of the Arts intends to send to Adolf Hitler. Herr Dr. Hans Pfitzner... wants to sign only when he knows its content. He could not possibly sign something, the content of which he did not know. My interjection that the Academy of the Arts would presumably write no nonsense to Adolf Hitler was of no avail.

The *völkisch* aestheticist could be difficult, although he was celebrated throughout as prophetic forerunner of the new order.

The PAdK was the most illustrious educational institution to be thoroughly coordinated, but others were included in the process. The events at the Berlin Music Academy involving Graener, Schünemann (both Academy members) and Stein reflected the general trend and the same legal and policy principles noted above. Although Schünemann was not Jewish, the Nazi justification for the great purge was based on alleged Jewish control of all education until the time of change in 1933. Music academies were run by Jews, wrote Hans Fleischer in *Deutsche Kultur-Wacht*, July 2, 1933. Changes in personnel were affected throughout the world of music academies and conservatories in the manner of the Graener-Schünemann affair, followed by the administrative controls as applied to the PAdK. In many instances, the KfdK was involved in personnel turnover; Stein had the support of this Nazi organization in his bid for the post in Berlin. Fighting Leaguer Havemann had promised Stein that "the foreign Jew, Professor Leonid Kreutzer" would be replaced by Professor Carl Adolf Martienssen of the Leipzig Conservatory and "the foreign Jew, Emanuel Feuermann" by Professor Paul Grummer of the Cologne Music Academy and Adolf Steiner. Indeed, Kreutzer and Feuermann were dismissed, and Martienssen, Grummer, and Steiner were hired in 1933, 1934, 1939, respectively. The two men furthermore agreed that retention of Professor Jöde, Professor of choral conducting and folk music education at the State Academy for Church and School music at Berlin since 1923, would no longer be possible and that all positions in German music education had to be reviewed.[72]

The effort of *Gleichschaltung* in music education on political and racial grounds focused on two personalities in particular—Leo Kestenberg, a pianist who had become secretary for musical affairs at the Prussian Ministry of

Education in 1918 and emigrated in 1933, and Fritz Jöde. The two names, symbols of music education in the Weimar Republic, were denounced as such throughout the Third Reich. Countless dismissals of musicians at musical institutions of learning were justified on the grounds that the original appointment could be traced to Leo Kestenberg. As early as March 4, 1933, Walter Abendroth, writing in the *Berliner Lokal-Anzeiger* on "Music in the New State," referred to the "spiritual and cultural renewal of the German people" as a precondition for the "national regeneration of our state." In elaborating upon the place of German music in German history and society he emphasized the need for broad purges of "racially alien elements." Most representative of alien blood in a position of power was Leo Kestenberg, who had contributed to "systematic disintegration and non-productivity . . ., as a result of irreligiosity and internationalist uprootedness . . . This soulless postwar music was supported by the state and taught at the schools." Kestenberg had helped to lower standards and contributed to the decline of "patriotic authority" through the elimination of religious and national songs in the music education at schools. This Marxist subversion of German culture allegedly had produced indignation in the public, which was shocked by the new generation subjected to this kind of education and ready to denounce traditional German values and musical treasures of the past. "The entire musical culture was threatened in its existence and its material constitution because of lack of interested competent young blood." Abendroth typified the pointed manner of denunciation when he noted

that too few people realized that these manifestations of decline were the result of tenacious effort . . .The soul of this strenuous subversion of the conviction of our youth was Fritz Jöde, most zealous follower of Kestenberg.

His program attacked the "bourgeois music culture" of the past . . . Kestenberg's and Jöde's joint accomplishments, under the guise of musical reconstruction, of actually undermining our cultural foundation to the point of misleading the young and devastating our racial soul were tremendous. Their names will symbolically remind us of an epoch of deepest spiritual impoverishment of creative, active and receptive musical life.[73]

According to Siegfried Günther, in an article on music education in the *ZfM*, music educators had the obligation instead "to make youth aware of its roots in folk, soil, blood, and nature." Günther inveighed against the formalism and compartmentalization of education in the preceding era and demanded instead that music education contribute to the education of the whole person.[74] Thus, Jöde became a live controversy, while Kestenberg, having no choice as a Jew, left his post and country. The June issue of the *ZfM* featured the "Fritz Jöde" controversy in a sequence of articles, introduced by some comments of Gustav Bosse. Jöde's enemies received space under the heading of "Declaration against Jöde," with contributions by Karl Hasse of Tübingen, Otto zur Nedden of Tübingen, and Fritz Stege of Berlin, followed by a list of signatories which covered one whole page, including Fritz Brust, Max Donisch, Carl Ehrenberg, Hans Gansser (a composer of popular Nazi fighting songs), Bruno Kittel, Hermann Matzke, Hans Pfitzner, Heinz Pringsheim, Paul Schwers, Walter Trienes, Richard Trunk and other names that figured prominently in Nazi music politics. Then Hans Joachim Moser, Bernard Scheidler, the student Helmut Bräutigam, and Jöde himself wrote in behalf of the subject. All in all, twenty pages were allotted to the dispute, and every author based his line of argument on *völkisch* principles. As in the case with most victims of National Socialism, Jöde pleaded his cause in the language of the day, pointing out his contributions to the organization of German folk music and education over a long period. His efforts were rooted in "the soil of the German folk tune, Christian faith, . . . and German thought." He welcomed the new "*völkisch* movement and offered his whole hearted support" because its service, like his own, was dedicated to the German people.[75]

In this, as in other cases, the victim spoke the language of the oppressor. Abendroth and the coordinated press set the tone for all who were heard in militant *völkisch* tones, although the motive can frequently be ascribed to opportunism, political advantage, and personal rivalry. When Jöde finally lost his position at the Academy for Church and School Music in early 1935, he was replaced by Heinrich Spitta, a composer who was committed to the new order. The cultural critics of earlier times had already attacked Kestenberg and Jöde. The parallel views of traditional critics and Nazi critics suggest the invaluable function of moralist voices in behalf of calculated policy, representative of broad public support. Mobilizing and manipulating public opinion, the Nazi elite utilized the voice of traditional resentment against the powers of the former era; it was ready to embark upon its own policy, through its own musical journalists who also tended to practical business. In education, the Nazi ideology was also implemented by a decree of Rust on June 16, 1933, "enforcing the law of April 25, 1922 against crowded conditions in German schools and academies." "Non-Aryan" students were to be listed separately upon entering a German university, so that their numbers would be known. A commission was to establish the percentage of "non-Aryan" students. If enrollment in any department amounted to more than one and one-half percent "non-Aryans," no others were to be admitted. Certainly five percent should be the upper level of "non-Aryan" enrollment anywhere. Every student immediately had to furnish proof of "Aryan ancestry." This Ministerial decree was also addressed to art academies, with the PAdK being asked to comply with these standards.[76]

Gleichschaltung of Church Music

Even though National Socialism was fundamentally anti-religious and its power was predicated on conflict with the churches with whom it competed for ultimate public loyalty, in practice the regime betrayed some sensitivity to people's religious identification and habits which were—to be sure— manipulated and contributed to compromises. *Gleichschaltung*, as such, implied the channeling rather than the brute suppression of traditional institutions and customs—nowhere more revealingly expressed than in the church-state relationship in spite of revolutionary rhetoric, violations of religious principles, some forceful adjustments and consistently ruthless purges of Jews and political opponents. Compromise came relatively easy in church music by virtue of shared roots, assumptions, habits and attitudes. Fundamentally, both KfdK and church musicians were largely committed to musical convention and hostile to modern musical forms of expression. (Church music had indeed atrophied, since the death of Reger in 1918, in isolation from secular musical development.) Both groups relied on programmatic music in their respective rituals, addressed communities of believers, and intended to stimulate devotional responses. Moreover, the Nazis were eager to appropriate the form and spiritual-emotional features of sacred music—naturally, devoid of its textual content—and some of its auxiliary trappings and means of performance, such as the organ, in order to reach Christians who were accustomed to these musical offerings, neutralize Church opposition, reassure church musicians about jobs, and impart their own *völkisch* message by this proven and familiar means. Nazi organ concerts, worldly oratorios, consecration rituals and devotional exercises were derived from sacred traditions, thus illustrating Nazi pragmatism and the skilfull manipulation of coordinated people and institutions, but also risking disappointment among their own anti-religious radicals and leaving room for pockets of spiritual opposition. In fact, not all went smoothly as the Nazis continually offended religious sensibilities by variously censoring confessional texts, purging personnel, and confining religious musical offerings to the churches since the party planned and instituted its own instruction and indoctrination programs, especially for German youth. The oratorio was problematic since it had entered the concert hall and radio programs—a trend to be reversed as the sacred was to be replaced by worldly oratorios. Arguments also arose over Nazi policy to revise classical texts consistent with *völkisch* views. Religious works of Bach and Handel were especially controversial (the latter's *Judas Maccabaeus* becoming, in one instance, *The General* plus new text)—although most of these corrections took place after 1933.

Notwithstanding problems and conflicts, church music was subjected to *Gleichschaltung* since the church itself went through a period of crisis and adjustment to the reality of National Socialism. Protestant churches were especially integrated into the new Germany via the numerous Nazi cells among the faithful. The new political regime pressed churches into line, while the so-called *Deutsche Christen* (German Christians) undermined church autonomy from within. The "Aryan-paragraph" of the Career Civil Service Law was applied in the old Prussian Evangelical Church as well as to churches in other states, to the clergy and other church officials as stipulated in the Church Law of September 6, 1933.

In 1933 Hitler tried to "deconfessionalize public life"[77] by eliminating the political role of Catholicism through an agreement with the Vatican and that of Protestantism by means of the creation of a German Evangelical Reich Church, the latter embracing the more than two dozen Evangelical *Landeskirchen* (State churches) in a tightly centralized organization.[78] The Concordat with the Vatican of July 20, 1933, enabled Hitler to achieve the first objective with surprising speed.

Meanwhile the German Christians within Protestantism proclaimed solidarity with the principles of National Socialism, speaking of the creation of an all-encompassing "German Christian National Church". German Christians proclaimed the slogan of "one Volk, one God—one Reich, one Church," in the spirit of Third Reich slogans. They demanded the application of the Aryan-clause in the *Landeskirche* and the consequent creation of a separate Jewish-Christian church for all "racially alien Protestant Christians." "We profess to participate in the creation of a militant and truly *völkisch* Church, in completion of the German Reformation of Martin Luther, which alone does justice to the total demands of the National Socialist State."[79] The Church musicians who identified with the German Christians organized in the KfdK, publishing their own journal, *Kirchenmusik im Dritten Reich* (Church Music in the Third Reich) the cover of which was adorned by swastika and cross.

German Christians were vehemently opposed by Martin Niemöller's *Pfarrer-Notbund* (Emergency Association of Pastors), the basis of the later Confessional Church, which announced a defensive struggle against the Career Civil Service Law, especially its Aryan-clause and against the "non-evangelical leadership concept";[80] and finally separated itself in May, 1933 from the collaborating church.

It was then that church music was coordinated. In June 1933, the *ZfM* published a statement by Dr. Karl Straube, famous Thomaskantor in Leipzig and friend of Furtwängler, which was signed by thirty-eight other Church musicians, testifying to the coordination of Church music, at least in spirit and terminology. "National regeneration has moved the Church again into the focus of the people," Straube wrote.

> We who have been working for the regeneration of Church music and the study of organ music, witness with joy the return of the people to Church music today. We profess our faith in the community-rooted power of all Church music . . . born in the struggle against disintegrating forces of liberalism and individualism. We acknowledge the *völkisch* basis of Church music . . . We reject a German Evangelical Church music which is not indigenous, which is born of a cosmo-political spirit."[81]

A sympathy declaration was signed by an additional group of twenty-nine leading Church musicians in Hamburg, Schleswig-Holstein and Lübeck, and presented to the prominent leaders of German organists holding a convention in Berlin, May 17 and 18. Other signatures were requested.[82]

In language and spirit these declarations demonstrated that everything was being coordinated in an effort to reduce autonomous institutions and organizations to abject compliance and identification with the principles of National Socialism; particularly in the institution as powerful as the Church and a definite rival for ultimate loyalty. When Professor Hasse was asked to submit an expert opinion concerning the degree of coordination of Protestant church music, he wrote to State commissioner Hans Hinkel on the KfdK letterhead that "the best Church musicians are not yet members of the organization of German Christians." Indeed, he denounced members of Church musical organizations who had joined in solidarity proclamations with National Socialism in order to sabotage efforts of the German Christians. Whether the totalitarian state cared beyond the actual *völkisch* conception, production, and consumption of spiritual music in the churches of both groups remains an open question. Yet, Hasse's suspicion has indeed been confirmed in more recent studies on church resistance to the Third Reich. For instance, Oskar Söhngen interpreted Straube's manifesto as a clever device for stealing a march on the German Christians, of appropriating the ideological position of National Socialism, and thereby leaving the minority radicals without grounds for existence.[83] The music director at the University of Tübingen, Karl Hasse, on the other hand, wanted the effort of German Christians properly honored for its political significance. As the author of numerous music-political essays in defense of National Socialism in the areas of education and Church music, he had experience in denouncing enemies and in appealing to State authority in his behalf. He was one of the main opponents of Jöde, for instance, contributing to his dismissal with letters written to Hinkel. At this time he retaliated against a follower of Jöde who had wanted to save Jöde by identifying him with interests of National Socialism. Hasse asked Hinkel "whether Berlin could not intervene in this matter with some force." [84] As a dedicated supporter of the Nazi cause, and suspicious of the recent mass support of the movement within music circles in Church and education, he broadened his expert musical and political advice to the regime and members of the KfdK by publishing his thoughts in a feature article of the July 1933 issue of the ZfM. The title, "German Christians' Church Music and Organ Movement," suggests the political nature of a committed musician who supported the German Christians against the traditional Orgelbewegung (organ movement)[85] for the same reasons cited in the letter to Hinkel. The acrimonious polemic had been introduced by a member of the Organ Movement in the June issue of the same journal. Herbert Schulze of Leipzig had traced the illustrious history of the movement to innovations associated with such names as Albert Schweitzer and Hans Henny Jahnn, the latter having set new standards at the 1925 convention at Hamburg and Lübeck. He claimed that various organists and organ builder associations had already attempted to discredit his movement before 1933. These well-organized opponents now supported the German Christians who appealed to all evangelical Christians of German descent and threatened the autonomy of the traditional movement by demonstrations and proclamations, as if "only they qualify for leadership in the craft"—a claim rejected by the organ movement. Organists and builders, said Schulze, had to be alerted to the threat to their professional, confessional, patriotic, and ethical freedom. Hasse was one of those warned against. Indeed, Hasse had attacked the proclamation of the organ movement as too vague, general, and lacking a detailed account of the commitments of individuals, and had singled out one of the leaders of the movement, Hans Henny Jahnn, noted organ builder, music publisher and important member of the German organ advisory board, as cultural bolshevik.[86] Jahnn was forced to emigrate as early as 1933.

In the meantime, the Protestant (Evangelische) Press organization had become an organ of the German Christians. Having been responsible for news pertaining to Church music during the past ten years, the organization was suitable for the coordination of Church music with the principles of National Socialism. Fritz Stein, who recommended the organization to Hinkel in the interest of the KfdK, made himself available to establish the proper contact between Church music and the KdfK. Indeed, Stein was one of the driving spirits behind the coordination of Church music. He corresponded with Carl Hasse, Hinkel and other party authorities in order to "normalize" music in the Church again. Although he agreed with the ideological standpoint of Hasse, he was more interested in organizational matters, congratulating the moralist but urging a practical approach to all problems.[87]

Complete control of music in the realm of the Church was not readily established. Apart from the attempts of various organizations and individuals to benefit themselves at the expense of previously autonomous institutions, centralization under Nazi control also lagged. Hinkel, in a letter to the appointed *Reichsbischof* Müller, (the prominent bishop responsible for the application of the "Aryan-clause" in the Protestant Church organization,) complained about organizational difficulties, specifically in the matter of Church music, which could be overcome only through "an immediate and unequivocal statement of the Church leadership." He recommended recognition of the *Reichsbund für Deutsche Kirchenmusik* (Reich Union of German Church Musicians), whose honorary president was Karl Straube, as the instrument of a new collective organization of Church musicians, inasmuch as valuable and constructive elements were already united therein. He further commended the person of the Union President, Fritz Stein, also Reich Leader of the KfdK music division, who would assure friendly cooperation between the Church and party and state organizations.[88] This important letter reflected the difficulties, the clever manipulation and utilization of existing organizations, and the success of opportunists like Stein in a transitional period. Stein could speak of "pious Church musicians" in an ironic note to Hinkel, while representing that group before Church and state leadership. Such were the times, in which the ideologist maneuvered, while maintaining the *völkisch* faith in moral and cultural regeneration. Stein was really more representative and significant than Hasse, although both were invaluable in the establishment of totalitarian control over music.

Centralized Control and Manipulated Ideals

Before the end of the year and the creation of the RMK, musical life had settled into recognizable patterns. Though not as vital to the regime for propaganda purposes as were the press, film and radio, music, as we have seen, was regimented and involved far more people than any other category of the arts and the media. The incidents involving celebrities and ideological formulations described above were not isolated, but in concert with numerous similar developments throughout the country. This suggested a tremendous degree of self-coordination and careful governmental attention to musical life. Revolutionary claims yielded results in personnel, organization, and propaganda, the latter reflected in control mechanisms and standardized concepts, language and revolutionary gestures. And, even though leading organizers and commentators argued in the journals, while their Nazi leaders, in the manner of feudal lords, competed with each other and for alternative suggestions for the realization of that militant *Volksgemeinschaft*, the sum total of activity in this first year of the Nazi state resulted in music's *Gleichschaltung* in its essential features.

Meanwhile, commissioners were dispatched to all musical institutions throughout the Reich. Some were political only, while others, like the one appointed to supervise affairs at the Berlin Philharmonic, were highly cultured and, to a degree, qualified for their new posts. In the early stages of coordination, initiative frequently originated within the organizations to be coordinated. Nazi cells were founded in musical organizations as in other institutions throughout Germany, most notably in labor circles. Here, Nazi cells operated through a national organization, the National Socialist Labor Cell Organization—*NS-Betriebsorganisation* (NSBO). Also the "Strength Through Joy"—*Kraft durch Freude* (KdF) of the German Labor Front—*Deutsche Arbeitsfront* (DAF) organization claimed, in May 1934, to have successfully established music cells in all labor units in Germany.[89] Similar cells existed among students, other youth organizations, and the professions. The politization of music on a national level facilitated the effort of the RMK to institute itself at the local level. The music community had been softened and rendered receptive to national organization and control.

Berlin's standards of denunciation and purges spread to the provinces; to the profession at large. From Hannover, Karl Gerke sent a letter to Gustav Havemann that included the statement, "We have had our differences with Ladscheck (the concertmaster of the Hannover City Stage), because my son belongs to the NSDAP." In an additional note he testified that "Ladscheck had called members of the NSDAP pigs and idiots." Furthermore, Ladscheck was accused of having said, "If the son of Gerke were to have dealings with them (members of the NSDAP), he could rot away in the gutter. In any event, he (Ladscheck) would kick him (Gerke's son) out, if he were to appear with the party insignia." [90] Gerke addressed himself to the right authority, for Havemann had the reputation of viciously denouncing and persecuting victims. Three days following the receipt of Gerke's letter, Havemann informed Hinkel of the letter and note, recommending the dismissal of Ladscheck.[91]

Dr. Leo Franke wrote to State Commissioner Hans Hinkel, that

the two biggest "German" concert agencies of Wolff & Sachs and Schiff have preferred Jewish and foreign artists . . . Through their blood-sucking procedures many promising and highly talented German instrumental soloists and singers were cheated . . . I propose the creation of a central organization for German concert life in coordination with the KfdK . . . I would like to take over artistic management of the new organization.[92]

At the Weimar Music Academy Paul Elgers, the instructor of a violin class and of the orchestra, had lost his job as a result of differences with the principal of the institution, Professor Bruno Hinze-Reinhold. In order to regain his former position Elgers addressed a letter to the office of the KfdK musical section of Dr. Fritz Stege, since the principal was

finally leaving the institution this October, besides which other changes will be affected in the faculty of the Weimar Music Education Institute in consequence of the Naational Socialist cultural purges . . . The KfdK, which is so successful in its attempts to invigorate German music life and place industrious German artists in positions commensurate with their interests in furthering German renewal, . . . could be a great help to me, by supporting my application to Weimar . . .I am at your disposal, ready to supply factual evidence about my artistic activity and my former, sad, Weimar experience with Mr. Hinze-Reinhold.[93]

As the provinces aligned themselves with the rhetoric of the revolution in Berlin, rival musicians were brought to the attention of the new political authorities; some were denounced and purged, others gained jobs and promotions. Thus a lesser musician could hope to gain the vacated position. Provincial musicians displayed amazing knowledge of the new centers of power and official policies. In this way unemployed and unhappy musicians offered their services to fill Nazi needs for musical and organizational positions in their efforts of reconstruction.

In this transitional phase of constructing the Nazi order in music, Goebbels and other Nazi leaders shared with provincial musicians, and not only malcontents, a partnership of mutual benefit. Goebbels, Hermann Unger wrote, regarded active music in the provinces as the real source of the nation's strength. Therefore, he supported the national organization of male choirs, the *Deutscher Sängerbund* (DSB), which was active in all corners of the country. When it convened in Dortmund in June 1933, Goebbels spoke of accomplishments in the area of organized singing, congratulating Dr. Glassmeier, the Westfalian archivist and *völkisch* expert of the organization, and the newly appointed manager of the West German Radio, as the "keeper of educational values of the people." He further cited the patriotic program of the Cologne Male Choral Organization in honor of Hitler's birthday that had culminated in Richard Trunk's new choral cycle, *Du mein Deutschland*

("You, my Germany"). Goebbels related all individual demonstrations of this kind to the new forces at work throughout Germany, mobilizing national sentiment. New associations were formed incorporating old ones, "all crying out for a purge of our music life of racially alien and disintegrating forces and tendencies." He called attention to "the ability of the new political leadership to provide clear guidelines for the people." DSB President Georg Brauner of Berlin claimed that his organization had always served German people's culture, and was now most willing to contribute to the reconstruction of that culture in a new Germany. This "largest folk music organization in Germany" had been the "keeper of the most precious possession of the people—the song." [94] In accordance with the principle of centralization, the DSB did indeed absorb other organizations, defunct as a consequence of political change. The *Deutscher Arbeitersängerbund* (DAS)—(German Workers Choral Association), for instance, and other previously non-nationalist groups were integrated into the larger organization, the KfdK assisting here too, with Havemann in charge. Havemann also became the founding president of the ambitious Reich Association of German Musicians—*Reichskartell der deutschen Musikerschaft*, which absorbed numerous smaller organizations of professional musicians, such as the Reich Association of German Orchestra Musicians, Reich Association of German Professional Musicians, German Music Association, Conductor's Union, Berlin Piano Club, thus including professional organizations of orchestra ensembles and free-lance musicians. To this first national group was added the above-mentioned group of educators and the Union of German Concert and Performance Artists[95]—before it would become the foundation of the truly national RMK within the RMVP at the end of the year.

Fritz Stege's Study Group of German Music Critics, connected to the office of Rosenberg and the KfdK, also had national ambitions, while a rival organization of critics was founded within the Reich Association of German Writers led by Johannes Günther and F. W. Herzog in behalf of Goebbels' exclusive claim to represent all music criticism. The Stege group prospered, held meetings and established local offices and leadership: North-West Germany (Oldenburg, Hannover) was led by Dr. Curt Zimmerman (KfdK), music critic of the *Bremer Nachrichten*; Schleswig-Holstein by Siegfried Scheffler (NSDAP) of the *Hamburger Nachrichten;* Rhineland by Professor Hermann Unger (NSDAP); Saxony by Dr. Alfred Heuss, co-founder of the existing Organization of German Music Critics (KfdK); Braunschweig by Dr. Franz Rühlmann (NSDAP) of the *Braunschweiger Landeszeitung;* Silesia by Dr. Hermann Matzke (KfdK), publisher of the *Zeitschrift für Instrumentenbau;* Hesse by Willy Renner, music expert at the local KfdK chapter at Frankfurt a.m.; Mecklenburg by Dr. Erich Reipschlager of Rostock; Baden by F. W. Herzog (NSDAP), who worked in both organizations and served as publisher-chief editor of

Die Musik; and Bavaria by Wilhelm Matthes of the *Fränkischer Kurier* of Nuremberg. These organizations at the local level were asked to stake out exclusive claims. In Silesia Matzke was able to establish a functioning organization by June 1933. The national organization noted that in the future non-members would not be considered representative of the new Germany.[96] The fight with Goebbels would have to be resolved, but to the practicing music critic, the profession was being coordinated by and within the National Socialist state.

A Reich Union of German Radio Critics was also founded in June under the leadership of Hans Joachim Weinbrenner of the RMVP and Karl W. Sonntag, the Manager of the NSDAP Radio, Gau Berlin. Control of this organization directly through Goebbels revealed the close relationship of all cultural and media activity and the RMVP. With four million listeners already in 1932 and steadily increasing during the Third Reich, the radio in Goebbels' view was the most modern and important means of influencing the masses. His Reich Radio Producer (*Reichssendeleiter*), Eugen Hadamovsky, and the director of musical programs, Max Donisch, balanced traditional offerings with principles of the NS revolution. Meanwhile, the Reich Radio Chamber appealed to all Germans in October, 1933 to tune in—to become a *Volksempfänger* as a patriotic duty.[97] Film, film music and film criticism were also coordinated with National Socialism under the watchful eyes and ears of Goebbels and his Reich Film Chamber. The totalitarian state had invaded all cultural and media expressions, criticism, reception and the business end of this monumental enterprise in manipulated sound, images and information. This had already been accomplished by 1933.

In celebration of Hitler's forty-fourth birthday, the German radio presented an "hour of the nation" program, which included Wagnerian music and dialogue from *Siegfried*, such as "Nothung, Nothung. Sword of wonder. Why didst thou break?" An article united the fate of Hitler and Wagner, recalling the prophetic gesture before 1933 by H.S. Chamberlain; Bayreuth was listed as a Nazi shrine, and music was singled out as the most German art.[98] Removed from the practical aims and vital problems of the Nazi elite in 1933, music could be flattered and defined in pure ideological terms, and its preservation became a sacred obligation of the state. "All German music should be judged by the ethical standards which contributed to its being," wrote the music educator, Walter Kühn, who was also a choral conductor and an editor of a music education journal. Subject to attacks of the intellectuals in historical movements, from the Renaissance and Enlightenment through recent modernism threatening the elimination of mystery from the world, the German spirit resisted, its essence being rooted in the blood . . . The racially determined metaphysical German nature escaped . . . into an area of expression which, far removed from conceptualization and intellectual development, was receptive to this characteristic: music. Thus, music was destined through a racial determinism to become the specific art of the Germanic people.[99]

Music as holy of holies, the profound expression of the German spirit, the essence of German creativity! To the believers in the promise of 1933 the promotion of music remained the justification of the Nazi revolution and collaboration, the excuse for the "unfortunate but necessary and temporary" cleansing measures. Indeed, the elimination of Jews, as of all expressions of "cultural bolshevism," was consistent with *völkisch* understanding of a revitalized music culture. The gradual nature of the campaign was manifest in the June 1933 issue of the *ZfM* wherein moderate statements by musicians on "modern music" later to be rejected were still published. Hindemith, representative of the "modern" element, was featured positively in an article, "Paul Hindemith and German Music" by Walter Berten. While Strauss, Reger, Pfitzner, and the younger Hindemith, Karl Marx, and Kurt Thomas were all called "modern," Schönberg, Toch, von Webern, Alban Berg, Honneger, and Krenek were called "transitional figures" in an article by Claus Neumann, "Modern Music—A Yes' or No'?" Younger composers and some traditional modernists were still listed as contributors to the *Deutsche Tonkünstlerfest* (German music festival) of the venerable General German Music Society—*Allgemeiner Deutscher Musikverein* (ADMV) which convened in Dortmund, June 18 through 22. The composers offered analyses of their own works: Walter Braunfels, Clemens Freiherr von Franckenstein, Ottmar Gerster, Paul Gross, Karl Höller, Werner Egk, Hans Brehme, Josef Lechthaler, Willhelm Petersen, Hubert Pfeiffer, Hans Pfitzner, Franz Phillip, Hermann Reutter, Emil Nikolaus Freiherr von Reznicek, Helmut Saller, Peter Schacht, Hans Joachim Therstappen, Anton von Webern, Frank Wohlfahrt. A few pages later, however, the editors added a note: While the issue was being prepared, changes in the program for the music festival had been suggested. Wolfgang von Bartels, Max Trapp, and Hermann Unger added compositions to the program, while the *Scottish Fantasie* of Walter Braunfels and Anton von Webern's Six Orchestra Pieces were withdrawn.

Thus proceeded *Gleichschaltung*. More difficult, to be sure, was the definition of what constituted German music, if something other was meant beyond what Germans composed and performed in Germany. Throughout 1933 scholars, musical practitioners, music journalists, educators and propagandists collaborated in this definitional enterprise. *Völkisch* musicologists endeavored to correlate basic racial characteristics with musical expression. Although this was difficult relative to highly complex art music, which involved too many stylistic features, the folk song in its purity might reveal those basic qualities and thus became the musical object of research, ideological manipulation—music's contribution to the blood and soil myth and the inspiration for Germany's young composers.

Scholarly authenticity is of course not easy to assess in the atmosphere of regimentation, the absence of free empirical research, and sloganeering. The topic has interested musicologists and ethnomusicologists before, during, and after the Third Reich, and we know of the challenge to pierce mediating layers of cultural change, ideological manipulation, and market forces, in addition to the values of the research, to gain access to pure folk forms in an industrial society that has evolved considerably from its traditional norms. To the KfdK and like- minded formulators, however, the correlation between musical and racial types was not an issue to be explored but an axiom to be utilized in clarifying and evaluating music and to be propagated, especially in education. Walter Kühn wrote much about folk music, corresponding racial characteristics, the state of music education and, in one case, on "German Music in the Context of the Reconstruction of German Culture" (1933). Reviewed in the ZfM as a most characteristic statement on music education and in support of raising community consciousness, his readers learned that

(1) German music education is rooted in the Christian Weltanschauung; (2) German music education in school, family, and at home is to create a German people's community; (3) German music education is to represent the German conception of music; (4) Methodology is to be based on German principles of education; (5) Its basis is the German folk and home song in simple form; (6) Only pure musical form is to be offered to German youth.[100]

In the same issue, Professor Frank Bennedik of Hanover deplored in an article on "The Folk Song as Source of Musical Education" that ninety percent of school graduates were not familiar with German music. Although most pupils had taken five hundred hours of music in eight years of school, they were not familiar with German folk songs. This situation had to change since good music education and the song were deemed basic to national education. In this way National Socialism managed to cultivate an aspect of music culture with which the community at large identified. The folk song had enjoyed popularity before National Socialism and it has outlived the Third Reich. The national rising of the German people in 1933 was said to have originated in the hearts of the people, always accompanied by songs. Unlike all the products of the decadent modern world, "the true folk song is not artifically created," wrote the Nazi composer Hermann Blume, "It originated somewhere, like a spring on a quiet mountain top." The future *SS Untersturmführer* was awarded second prize in the newly instituted folk song contest. He noted that generally a folk song was not produced by professionals, adding modestly,

> If I won the German folk song competition with my song, *Kamerad Horst Wessel*, then I must give credit to deep rootedness in soil and the people, rather than to my gift as composer. The rhythm of the song was determined by the spirit of Adolf Hitler . . . Its content was derived from Horst Wessel, whom I imagined before me at the head of those heroes who gave their lives for the patriotic cause. The soft and melancholy undercurrent of my song is the mournful expression of my grief over his inability to be here in order to celebrate the victory.[101]

A Singing Ideological Posture

In 1933 the folk, soldier, and political songs became the basis of a national song literature, published in numerous collections through traditional and party organizations, thus giving rise to new melodies in contemporary situations and encompassing the whole people. All kinds of new songs were produced, year after year: marches, festive songs, light and serious ones, for the new organizations and the armed forces. It was a good beginning for composers of limited ability who were commissioned, won prizes, gained employment—and were honored and appreciated. All forms of music—including serious art music—were affected by this popular movement. Finally, in 1936, a new journal was founded to assess the development; *Deutsche Musikkultur*, published collaboratively by Peter Raabe, Fritz Stein, Christhard Mahrenholz, Heinrich Besseler, Josef Müller-Blattau and Wilhelm Ehemann, was totally dedicated to the *völkisch* interpretation of music, and to "the build-up of the German folk song research and its cultivation."[102] The romantic vision of the singing village community had thus been transferred to the Third Reich.[103] But also "big city folk music" had found a voice.[104] National Socialism had to permeate the city culture in spite of its peasant cult and the numerous folk song publications attested to the effort to indoctrinate an existing city-based civilization. Folk singing was to involve everyone.[105]

The promise of *völkisch* idealism was indeed realized in "the singing nation," especially among the national youth, as millions of Germans were organized into active music making, group singing and listening. Giving free reign and encouragement to dedicated youth organizers, music educators and promoters, the Nazi state was eminently successful in (1) involving the nation and its youth in this collectivist music culture, (2) propagating *völkisch*-Nazi principles in an enthusiastic, pleasurable, accessible and repetitive manner, and (3) benefiting from an activity which elevated the spirit and thus distracted from political unpleasantness, the hardships of daily reality and, later, from war.[106] The RJF, the Education Ministry, the KdF, etc. joined established and new choral societies like the giant coordinated DSB in the promotion of folk and Nazi fighting songs—a unique and popular medium for indoctrinating the nation.

This active music culture captivated youth—especially for the *Hitlerjugend* (HJ)—for collective identity, experience (even if only imaginary) and action, skilfully channeling youthful and populist idealism and anti-bourgeois and anti-institutional sentiment, and liberally incorporating existing musical groups, educational programs, and ideas of the republican youth, church and labor movements. The Nazi cult succeeded upon the fertile ground of an inherited nationalistic folk, youth and song culture, identified strongly with the famous, though then defamed pioneer of the German youth movement in music, Fritz Jöde, whose Music Schools for Youth and People (*Musiksschulen für Jugend und Volk*) were appropriated by the HJ for the training of musicians and music educators. Jöde's student, the prominent HJ music educator, Wolfgang Stumme, expanded significantly the music teacher training program of music academies in order to supply the music schools with needed personnel when he became head of the Music Division of the Cultural Office of the Reich Youth Leadership (RJF) in 1935. Stumme supported, with his considerable energy and commitment to National Socialism the long-range goals of the Cultural Office chief, Karl Cerff, a man who also had choral experience and appreciated the value of participatory music. Other competent and dedicated music pedagogues, composers and musicians were recruited for the youth music schools—eighty in number by 1939—and for conducting the music educational camps and national conferences, the *Reichsmusiktage* of the RJF for which performances and master classes were offered by outstanding artists like Edwin Fischer, Georg Kulenkampff and Elly Ney, the latter noted for her enthusiastic support of National Socialism.[107] In concert and competition with Rust's Education Ministry, the KdF, RMK and other organizations, the RJF was most aggressive and successful in creating a vast network of music educational institutions which employed over 1000 music educators by 1939 and a growing body of practicing musicians and singers in HJ formations. Here composers like Wolfgang Fortner converted to National Socialism and offered acclaimed compositions, while Hans Baumann became perhaps the best known composer of HJ songs. Financial support as well as other forms of assistance were institutionally assured by the National Radio which also offered opportunities for airing HJ concerts and staff positions to its organizers by numerous municipalities, and such organizations as the German Labor Front (DAF) and its recreational "Strength Through Joy" organization (KdF), while the essential organizational and support base, of course, rested in the RJF.[108]

Traditional scholarship, other than music pedagogy, has not paid much critical attention to this successful part of Nazi music culture. Critical sociology of the student movement from the late-fifties on, preoccupied with fascist manipulation of popular culture, with exposing fascists and collaborators, and unmasking false consciousness, generally has not even moved beyond basic reference to it in negative intellectual/ideological terms. There has been a failure to address music as music, the subjective aesthetic experience, the very emotional state of those singing, making music and listening which actually helps explain Nazi appeal in its time.[109] The influence of Adorno and Eisler has shaped an attitude which intelligently decodes but simultaneously is patronizing and unsympathetic toward much behavior, belief and activity when not in accord with their definition of progressive thinking and commitment. Attributing the emotional pull of the "inauthentic" folk songs and even more "derivative" and "demagogic" Nazi fighting songs to manipulation and false consciousness, emancipatory sociology has assigned the singing masses to fascism. Challenging the production of folk songs in the Third Reich, Eisler wrote as early as 1935 that folk songs are rooted in a traditional, agrarian-patriarchic society and came to an end with the rise of modern industrialism, being replaced by the "revolutionary fighting song of the proletariat."[110] Therefore, the folk song as cultivated by National Socialism in our time is inauthentic, a reflection of regressive ideology which, too, denies class reality by positing an equally inauthentic organic Volksgemeinschaft. The denigration of fascist music experience—of overused harmonies, the triad, obvious cadences, the romantic rising of a second voice found also in traditional folk songs and the classic-romantic repertoire—has left this realm of capturing the emotional needs and desires for the familiar, for roots, integration, identity and common purpose to the fascists (fascism, of course, related to fascination, spell-binding, etc.). It was precisely the use of traditional form and content (apart from the decidedly political texts) which in combination with Nazi elan proved so appealing and useful. Fred Prieberg has reprinted an interview conducted by J. Prieberg-Mohrmann with the Alsacian painter Toni Ungerer (born 1931) who referred to the seductive Nazi songs as a drug which, still many years later (before the time of the interview in 1981), he would sing in order to help him overcome the blues. Noting the reliability of the therapy, he related the medicinal quality of these uplifting Nazi songs, which had a hold of his brain for twenty to thirty years, to heroin's staying power in the blood[111]—attesting to the power of music without which National Socialism as we know it would not have been thinkable. Here the fighting community was realized, as the imaginary order evoked in songs merged with the reality of internal unity and subordination, on the one hand, and outward posturing of heroism and domination, on the other—the great contradiction and appeal of National Socialism.

The elite formations of SA and SS also appropriated much of Nazi literature in song form. Most song collections of the party and the elite organizations were republished after 1933, but already in that year of change, the *völkisch* and specifically Nazi traditions were voiced by "singing columns." In 1933 the political fighting song was defined by Martin Wähler (not dissimilar to Eisler) in the *Mitteldeutsche Blätter für Volkskunde*, 1933, as "contemporary folk song."[112] He explained in another article that most songs of the National Socialists give "direction to the execution of programs, to the establishment of domination. The means is as revolutionary as the goal." He then illustrated with "a National Socialist song of the time of struggle": "We are Hitler's brown army, heia, hoho/we eliminate big shots. . ." Later it was expanded to: "Thus, the storm columns are ready for racial combat,/We will only be free/when the Jews are bleeding;/Let's hear no more of negotiations,/which are of no use anyway./With our Adolf Hitler/we are ready to attack with courage."[113]

Thus the Nazis were trying to express the experience and the combative ideology of their movement in song, allowing German youth to re-experience the time of struggle which had always been pictured in terms of the brown columns conquering the nation to the accompaniment of the fighting song; so the revolutionary atmosphere was kept alive. In two issues of *Die Musik*, December 1936 and January 1937, musician-activist Hans Bajer reviewed the history of the SA song as a reflection of the movement before and after 1933 in articles entitled "Honor Pages in the Annals of the SA Song". Bajer made reference to the existing song publications of the NSDAP, introducing his article with Hitler's words which also appeared in the latest party publication: "Bold pride and sacred faith are the songs of a hopeful people." Thus were "described for all times the fighting and freedom songs of the movement." The fighting song was portrayed as encompassing more than the folk song, having been the "dearest comrade" of the SA. "The vigorous texts and steel rhythms embodied a power which incited to bravery and the will to sacrifice." These songs were said to reflect the times more truly than any other selection of songs, having been composed by activists. Indeed, the history of the songs paralleled the history of the movement.[114]

Bajer selected the most prominent and characteristic SA songs of the "first" SA song-book, *Was der Deutsche Singt* ("What Germans Sing"), contained in the official NSDAP publication, and of the *Horst Wessel Marschalbum* ("H.W. Marching album"). Each of the selections was reviewed in its historical development. For instance, the song, *Lied der Sturmabteilungen* ("Song of the Storm Troops"), received its first text version in 1920. Erich Tessmer had conceived the song for the well-known "Ehrhard Brigade." The text is typical: "They may fight us, we shall not go under/Comrade, give me your hand. . ./Swastika on the helmet, black-white-red band." The most characteristic line, identifying the singers, was: "We are called *Sturmabteilung* Hitler/We have been betrayed . . . /We remained true to the fatherland . . ." This refrain, the line of identification, was subjected to change as the song spread rapidly until it was appropriated by the party as national property, as *Bundeslied*, by *Bundesführer* Seldte (of the *Stahlhelm*) in June 1933. Various texts were written to suit each group as identification. The SA version was called "The Hitler Song": "Come, fighters, pick up your guns/This will not do, the fatherland is beckoning/victory or death. . ./Our sacred insignia shall never go under. . .", The refrain of the original version was added: "Swastika on the helmet, black-white-red band/We are called *Sturmabteilung* Hitler." These words were sung to the rhythm of an American soldier song "Blue eyes, we must part," composed by Theodor Morse in 1904. Tessmer altered the melody to suit the marching image of the SA in 1923, and in the new version it accompanied Hitler's group on November 9, 1923, as *Hakenkreutz am Stahlhelm* ("Swastika on the helmet"), thus, in the words of Bajer, making history. Tessmer lent himself to the typical hero-worship, being an actor, author-composer, and, most characteristically, an unknown member of his troop. He became known as an author only through *Stahlhelm*-research in 1933, and even then he never received a copyright for his work.[115]

Nazi idealism and individual heroism were illustrated in the songs. The "Fighting Song of National Socialists" was written in 1922 by Kleo Pleyer, a student at the German University at Prague who, as local Führer of a Nazi Student cell, had distinguished himself by appealing to the University Senate not to employ a Jew as rector. When Samuel Steinherz was appointed nonetheless, Pleyer called for a student strike. In that context he wrote his verse: "We are the army of the swastika, raise high the red flags./We want to prepare the road for freedom for German labor./We do not pact with Jews . . ./nor with our tyrants. . . : and applied these words to an existing folk melody, *Stimmt an mit hellem, hohem Klang* ("Tune in with light, high sound"). An original melody was never composed. The song was first published by the Sudeten-German NSDAP in 1923, remaining their own fighting song until 1933, by which time the organization was dissolved. The song traveled from Prague to Munich and throughout the Reich. Its first stanza was frequently used as party motto, for instance, in Gottfried Feder's "Program of the NSDAP", in 1927. Pleyer became an outstanding activist—Führer of the Nazi youth movement, lending himself as a party speaker, and between 1923 and 1933 he was a member of the Free Corps Oberland. In characteristic fashion, Pleyer was wounded in a fight with *Reichsbanner*-men and arrested. At present, wrote Bajer, he was teaching at the University of Berlin. Thus, the popular fighter-author found his way into the most respectable pages of *Die Musik*.

The conscious effort to make heroes out of SA-activist-authors frequently involved an encounter with Hitler. Bruno C. Schestak composed both text and melody to his popular *Heil Hitler Dir* ("Hail to you, Hitler"), having been inspired by a 1926 Hitler speech. The original march was called "Saxon March of the NSDAP," popularized by the SA from Plauen as "Germany Awake," introduced to Berlin as "We are the fighters of the NSDAP," and finally presented by the First SA band under Fuhsel's direction as

Hail to you, Hitler/Germany awaken from you nightmare./do not provide any space to alien Jews in your Reich./We want to fight for your awakening./Aryan blood shall not perish./We will throw out all hypocrites./Juda, leave our home./when the land is purified and clean,/we will be united and happy./We are fighters of the NSDAP./Faithfully German at heart, firm and tough in combat./We are dedicated to the swastika./Hail, to our leader, Hail to you, Hitler.

The author-composer had begun as concertmaster of the Dresden Philharmonic, and during the Third Reich he became conductor at Plauen. His song was adapted to the piano and used in schools and labor, educational and recreational organizations in the whole Reich.

Sentimentalism, ideological slogans and group identity combined in the creation of the fighting songs. Most of them were explained as reaction to some historical situation. Karl-Heinz Muschalla wrote his well-known "the Hitler Comrade," subtitled "Forward Over Graves," after having gone through the experience of witnessing burials of fallen comrades. In August 1925, *Frontbann*-member Werner Dolle "was shot by a Jew." He was carried by *Frontbann-Nord* of the SA-Berlin to his grave, the men singing one of the most established and beloved German songs, *Ich hatt' einen Kameraden* ("I had a comrade, you cannot find a better one./The drum sounded for combat, he walked at my side in step. . /A bullet came flying, is it meant for him or me?/It took him, he lies at my feet, a part of me, a part of me. . .")— music by Friedrich Silcher and text by Ludwig Uhland. For the occasion the traditional tune was sung in choral form. In the Third Reich the song was reserved for memorial ceremonies, played by bands in measured beat and softly, while all guests expressed the solemn mood by raised arms. Muschalla liked the song, but he wanted a special tune for the group. His melody derived from an old folk tune that he adapted to a new text which he composed in reaction to the death of a blacksmith apprentice, Renz, "killed by *Reichsbanner* hordes" in February 1926:

> As the golden evening sun sent its last rays/a regiment of Hitler entered a small town./Their songs sounded sad in the small, quiet town, since they carried a Hitler comrade to his grave./And they sent the last best wishes to the mother far, since her son fell proudly, the shot piercing his heart./Boldly, their flags were waving, when they put him to rest, and they swore eternal allegiance, true to the Hitler comrade./You did not fall in vain, they swore anew, three times they saluted, he remained faithful to Adolf Hitler.

Then followed the refrain: "As the golden evening sun sent its last rays, a regiment of Hitler entered a small town." The song became popular and was used in honor of fallen comrades.

Muschalla was the most active SA fighter and composer-author of many SA songs. The "Song of the Storm Troops" was conceived in the company of SA friends. Goebbels was present at an inn, playing the tune, "Freedom is not yet lost," at the piano. Muschalla picked this up and changed it to "Leave, misguided fellow Germans," intended as contradiction to the spirit of the "Internationale," the rhythm of which was used. The final version, the "Song of the Storm Troops" became:

> Leave the red front and reaction, fellow Germans./Join us in the common and unified fight for the victory of the German revolution./Join Hitler's storm columns, stand up for freedom and justice./ Already the struggle has begun for a new type of worker./National Socialism fights for freedom, work, and bread./National Socialism leads us out of misery.

The song was first heard in Bernau/Berlin in 1928 and appealed to millions. The melody was borrowed from a patriotic composition by Florian Majewski.

The conscious effort to undermine the strength of communists and socialists among the proletariat was expressed in songs of the SA, like those by Muschalla. Generally, the appeals to workers through musical creations originated in the Marxist-Nazi combat in the streets. As a mass movement the Nazis encompassed the proletariat, which was traditionally controlled by leftist political formations. Thus, Roman Hädelmayr wrote his "Young Workers of Vienna" out of the experience of combat with the Marxists. Again, the melody was not original, being derived from a folk song. Hädelmayr's Nazi career, too, lent itself to the hero-worship of the activist. He was a young fighter, born in 1907, having joined the NSDAP and SA as a sixteen-year old. In 1928 he headed the HJ in Vienna, met the sacrosanct Horst Wessel, and in 1929 his "Young Workers of Vienna", was received as "favorite song" at the Party Congress at Nuremberg. Again, in demonstration of the virtue of anonymity, modesty and identification of the individual with the group, Hädelmayr's authorship was not made known until 1933. This man, who had met Hitler personally in 1927, represented Nazism in Austria. In 1932 he received his doctorate in political science and in 1934 he joined the *Österreichischer Beobachter* as chief editor. He was arrested for subversive activity by Austrian authorities and convicted, providing Nazism with another martyr who would be avenged after the *Anschluss*.

"National Socialism began in Southern Germany," wrote Bajer, and it was only fitting that the first "storm song" came from the South, written by Dietrich Eckart of Munich and with music by Hans Gansser of Stuttgart. Eckart was the father of Nazi political poetry; Nazi literary authority Hellmuth Langen-bucher gave him much credit for having taken a stand when Nazi views were still unpopular. Hitler had proudly accepted the *Deutschland Erwache* from Eckart, which the latter had written in expression of his personal awakening on reading the notorious anti-Semitic pamphlet on the *Elders of Zion*. The SA thought of Eckart as one of theirs. He stood at the beginning of a new age of poetry, having placed his art at the service of the movement which was "the prerequisite for the total reconstruction of German life".[116] The words *Deutschland Erwache* merit a translation here, inasmuch as they were reprinted and recited throughout the Third Reich as an original German fighting song:

Storm, storm, storm!/Ring the bells from tower to tower!/Ring, so that sparks fly,/Judas appears to conquer the Reich,/Ring, so that the ropes will get red with blood./Everywhere burning, martyring, killing./Ring storm for the earth to tremble,/Under the thunder of delivering vengeance./Woe to the people who still dare dream,/Germany awake!

The second verse became most popular:

Storm, storm, storm!/Ring the bells from tower to tower!/Wake the men, old-timers, and boys,/Wake the sleepers from their rooms,/Ring the girls down the stairs./Ring the women away from the cribs./The air shall thunder and resound,/Rage, rage with thunder of vengeance,/Wake the dead from their graves,/Germany awake!

This was written in 1919 as a battle cry of the movement for Greater Germany. Numerous composers set these words to music. Eckart himself preferred the melody of Hans Gansser, who dedicated his version to Hitler in 1922. It was premiered at the first Reich Party Congress of the NSDAP on January 26, 1923 in Munich, Hitler himself participating in practice for the presentation. This foremost Nazi fighting song was to be heard at every future party congress on Hitler's personal order. As exclamation of the masses, *Deutschland Erwache* was heard at Nazi demonstrations, rivaled in popularity only by "Heil Hitler." In Nazi lore, the author, the "poet and martyr," was immortalized through the first words of *Mein Kampf*—a dedication to Dietrich Eckart.[117]

The dedication of songs to Hitler was standard practice in the Nazi movement, like the sentimental and patriotic "Freedom is not yet lost" by Robert Prutz—music by Gansser. Introduced to Berlin by Goebbels, the story of the song captured the political course of the movement. Like other Gansser songs, this one was suppressed by the authorities in 1927 and was henceforth sung only in secret by SA groups. Gansser had become a noted composer of Nazi songs and received praise as such from music authorities like Dr. Karl Grunsky of Stuttgart, Dr. Karl Hasse of Tübingen, and Bajer. His most popular songs were published in *Wir tragen deine Fahnen* ("We are carrying your flags"), by the Ernst Klett publishers, Stuttgart. Known as "the musician" among Hitler's fighters, having joined the party as early as 1923 and wearing party number, Pg. 10,844, Gansser also put to music some of the most noted poetry of the Nazi movement, like that of Gerhard Schumann, national book-prize winner in 1936, whose poem, *Dennoch*, expressed all the sentimentality, patriotism, manliness, and dedication of the SA spirit. Gansser added a melody to his *Für Deutschland soll es sein* ("For Germany"). He also used verse of the major Nazi poet, Heinrich Anacker, recipient of the first art prize of the NSDAP in 1936, who was called the "poet of the brown front." Although many composers added melodies to his work, Anacker, "whose words demand music," liked Gansser's version best, particularly that of, "When Hitler folk are marching," while Bajer's contribution rated second.

As to Heinrich Anacker, he had become a representative poet of the Third Reich and Erich Wintermeier put many of his texts to melody in a publication, *Singe mein Volk* ("Sing, My People"), containing thirty-seven texts plus folk melodies which were a basic expression of the SA tradition. The poet, who had met Hitler personally in 1922 and become a party member that year, was published by the Franz Eher Verlag; some of his other works were:

Die Trommel ("The Drum"), a collection of SA poems; *Die Fanfare*("The Fanfare"), poems of the German revolution; *Einkehr* ("Self examination"), non-political poems; and *Der Aufbau* ("The Build-up"), political poems. His poem *SA marschiert* ("SA is marching"), to which Herbert Hammer added the melody, was most popular: "We are marching through Greater Berlin./We are fighting for Adolf Hitler./Break the red front in two,/SA is marching/attention/clear the street/. . .we are fighting alone,/our lives are welded together by blood." Hammer did not select an original melody but, characteristically, an old melody, *Argonnerwald um Mitternacht* ("Argonne Forest at Midnight") was adopted. The completed version traveled through Germany, gaining national attention through Nazi publication. Bajer mentioned an encounter of a Nazi troop with communists in Leipzig, the Nazis moving to combat while singing the tune. At age eighteen, Hammer was inspired to join the party by a Goebbels speech, thus wearing the party number, 108,374. His exploits included a personal meeting with Hitler in 1932.

The melodies of the SA song literature were to a large extent borrowed, especially of those composed before 1933, the "time of struggle." Most of them were old German folk or soldier songs, others were foreign adaptations. Poelchau's *Hitlerleute* ("Hitler Folk"), for instance, was inspired by the fascists' *Giovinezza* of Italy. The German text, which began "In the struggle for the homeland, many Hitler folk died," retained the Italian melody. Premiered in the presence of Goebbels, it was immediately appropriated by Berlin storm troops as theirs. Polchau, who was born in St. Petersburg, Russia, joined the NS German Workers Youth Organization at age eighteen, the NSDAP and SA one year later. He became a fighter against communists in South-West Berlin, an atmosphere which inspired the composition of *Rot-Front-Bann*. More interesting yet was the borrowing of communist and socialist songs. *Das Lied vom nationalen Sozialismus* ("Song of National Socialism"), of which the author is unknown, was sung to the melody of the "Internationale." While communists were seduced with familiar melodies, lyrics were so selected as to contradict the "Internationale" directly: "National Socialism will be Germany's future."[118]

Meanwhile, the SA song literature was performed by the SA and other organizations. On order of Goebbels, Herbert Malenaar had founded an SA *Sprechchor* ("Speaking Chorus"), called *Deutscher Kriegschoral* ("German War Choral"), with which he introduced SA poems, like *Schwert und Flamme* ("Sword and Flame") and *Der Freiheit entgegen* ("Toward Freedom"). Heinz Höhne's collection of compositions, *Deutsche Heimat* ("German Homeland"), songs for piano and voice, such as *Feuerspruch* ("Fire Speech") and *Deutschland*, were "rooted in folk culture" and had great appeal to non-SA groups. Specifically, his *Hoch auf dem gelben Wagen* ("High on the Yellow

Wagon") was popular in youth organizations. He also set various Löns poems to music which enjoyed national prestige and popularity. The list of SA songs could be expanded at random. Bajer did not include the Horst Wessel song, "because it deserves special honors"; and, indeed, it was honored, sung and published more frequently than any other Nazi song during the Third Reich and thereafter in media efforts to recapture the aura of National Socialism as one of its most evocative symbols.

The student of SA songs must agree with Bajer that these "songs made history" (the title of yet another article in the June issue of 1939); they were said to have come from the street and found publication in the pages of *Die Musik* which, in the meantime, had become the organ of Rosenberg. Bajer was struck by the "bloodless nature" of the National Socialist revolution; to him, the first of this magnitude in history. The SA had constituted the only military organ of the movement, yet, Bajer said, the land and the people were conquered by their songs, which were constantly on their lips as they marched and fought for fifteen years. "The most effective propaganda means of the SA was the fighting song." Entire villages and city sectors "were spellbound by happy singing brown columns." Notwithstanding other propaganda in print and speeches, people "were most impressed by the new songs, which had entered their ears and hearts like a new creed." Bajer cited as an example, "Already millions look upon the swastika with hope, the day for freedom and for bread has dawned." He added that such words had not been heard for some time and that . . . Horst Wessel, too, had known of the magic quality of the songs. He and his comrades had constantly rehearsed new songs, and people in Berlin knew that "his unit was familiar with the most beautiful fighting songs of the movement." Horst Wessel's unit was the largest and strongest in Berlin, and the song had to take credit for this popularity. "The fighting song was the measuring stick for the forward storming of the movement." It identified the troop, and fellow Germans were told of the "movement of the *Führer*," of "a new creed," and of hope: "Soon Hitler banners will wave over all streets, slavery will not last long." As the traditional "folk song represented the people, the SA represents the nation" in song. "When the SA and their heroism is recalled, people will speak of their fighting and freedom songs. They are forever bound to the memory of the SA." After the assumption of power the nature of the struggle changed. "Also their songs were of a different nature. The fighting songs were replaced by solemn hymns. Although the latter will be taught to the various fighting units of the Reich in systematic manner, the old glorious fighting songs which accompanied the victorious SA through the Brandenburg Gate will survive for centuries."[119]

In 1933 the SA was an important Nazi organization. Its fate is well-known. However, in spite of the elimination of the SA from power, the song literature was valued as a basis for the future culture of the Reich. The new Aryan man was to rise through the spirit embodied in these songs. Perhaps Bajer realized the irony contained in his statement on the survival of the "glorious fighting songs," against the background of suppression of the storm troops. Suppressed was the troop which had sung such verse as:

Sharpen the long knives at the sidewalk!/Let the knives glide into Jewish bodies!/Thick blood must flow,/We shit on the freedom of the Jewish republic./Should the hour of retaliation arrive,/We are prepared for any mass murder./Up with the Hohenzollerns on the lamp-post!/Let the dogs hang until they fall down!/A black pig is hanging in the synagogue,/Throw a hand grenade into parliaments!/Throw the concubine out of princely beds,/smear the guillotine with Jewish fat![120]

The Third Reich may have been pronounced by Nazi ideologists, propagandists, and organizers, but it was also shaped by the existing establishment, the state, the bureaucracy, army, and other institutions. Nonetheless, the songs, their terminology and spirit, remained meaningful. Bajer could not foresee the future, not in 1933, nor in the years of his articles, but the "final solution," the horrors of willful war and the already existing terror within Germany were reflected in the songs.

Segregated Jewish Music

Berta Geissmar observed that social life of music was hardly touched until mid-1934; the opera house *Unter den Linden*, for instance, was run by old, non-Nazi officials[121]—a surprising and revealing statement, in view of the turmoil of the events of 1933, and probably derived from a limited though characteristic perspective. Geissmar attributed the preservation of traditional ways to Göring's moderate version of Nazism. In view of his duplicity in cultural politics throughout the Third Reich and militant stand on the "final solution" later, this assessment is remarkable. Hindsight teaches that Göring had practical motives when he allowed the preservation of some traditionalism in culture at the Prussian State Opera. He also liked to pose as a patron and connoisseur of the arts. Since there were not enough good Nazi musicians around, he came to terms with established ones—including Jews. Geissmar's misjudgment, however, reflected the general reaction to Nazism at the time, although even then numerous musicians were more astute. Or, was this greater understanding due rather to a fundamental pessimism or, even more so, a consequence of direct suffering at the hands of the Nazis, and generally expressed outside the orbit of Nazi power, for example in America? In 1933 many people were deceived by skillful disguises, and, perhaps some of the Nazi culture organizers were not able to realize the consequences of their policies either. It is known that Furtwängler thought all this would pass and that he intended to remain on good terms with the new government. He risked opposition, and numerous people turned to him for help. He was left relatively free to act as he pleased and to exercize his influence in behalf of others. This unique demonstration of independence in music led to the famous open letter, addressed to Dr. Geobbels, April 12, 1933, on "the neutrality of the arts." Referring above all to Jewish artists, he stated that "music was already weakened by the world depression and the radio," and that it "can stand no more experiments... Save the real artists," men like "Klemperer, Reinhardt, Walter." Goebbels wrote that "politics is an art, too, the highest...and, only art which is rooted in the people can be good." He then reassured Furtwängler and the public that good artists would be heard in the new Germany. The tension was eased, Furtwängler's letter was read throughout the world, and German musicians believed in some modus vivendi which would slowly permit the return of normal life.[122]

Deception and self-deception were possible because all Germans appropriated the jargon of the *völkisch* tradition, which, moreover, had roots in all areas of German music before 1933, therewith reflecting genuine sentiment of a large segment of culturally- oriented people. National Socialism was not created by propagandists in a vacuum. Indeed, it accorded with enough popular sentiments to be successful—a fact noted by cultural historians with reference to the intellectual background, but hardly at all by students of totalitarianism. In spite of the priority of organizational matters, political motivation, and propagandistic necessity, the explicit ideology imposed its weight on all activity. Musicians contributed by way of literary analysis of their art form in terms of the official orthodoxy and in the attempts of composition in demonstration of ideological principles. The idealism of this orientation, however, was neutralized by the cynical manipulation of party officials, lending support to the thesis that ideologists and coordinated musicians were opportunistic apologists. Nonetheless, the traditional order appealed to the idealism of the movement, thus attempting to channel its course back to *völkisch* conservatism and creating some room for deviation. Furtwängler and Richard Strauss could attempt to assert their views on German music and its tradition. The anti-Jewish campaign, too, developed rather irregularly, suggesting that it might be tempered. In 1933, the domestic situation did not permit the ultimate measures against Jews which were applied later. Also, international considerations suggested caution, in view of Germany's weak military position. All actions against Jews in the period between 1933 and

1935 were based on special decrees and the Enabling Law, beginning with the government announcement of a boycott of all Jewish business, April 1, 1933. Meanwhile, the foreign press was not aware of the Nazi measures at this stage. On the other hand, Berta Geissmar and Jewish members of the Berlin Philharmonic observed the boycott by leaving Berlin for the day. Jewish stores were guarded and foreign Jews were not molested. Thereafter, the Philharmonic was left untouched. This appearance of normalcy and calm was reinforced by Göring, who feigned shock in interviews conducted by foreign correspondents when questioned over treatment of Jews.[123] An official bulletin of the NSDAP provided a guideline for the execution of the Jewish boycott, calling for "greatest discipline" and for the utmost precaution "not to hurt a Jew physically."[124] The Nazis stood by their idea of segregation— but divorced themselves from the vilest language of the SA songs quoted above. Segregation was even institutionalized with the creation in June 1933 of a now little known, yet then incredibly active, "Jewish Cultural League— *Jüdischer Kulturbund*, the upshot of negotiations between state commissioner Hans Hinkel who, among his many duties, was assigned to supervise non-Aryan artists and a delegation of Jewish cultural dignitaries led by the prominent physician and musician, Dr. Kurt Singer, who became president of the Berlin chapter and of the national federation.[125] Both sides wanted to reduce unemployment among purged Jewish artists—the Nazi policy to pressure Jews into leaving Germany having proved only partially successful. Singer, GMD Joseph Rosenstock and colleagues also wanted to satisfy the cultural needs of the Jewish community—even though and in spite of the fact that Jews were allowed to attend public concerts until 1935—to help prevent the disintegration of communal organizations and combat anti-Semitism. The Nazi state meanwhile was eager to impress the world, the not yet Nazified German bourgeoisie, and the Jews with its version of normalcy by means of this Jewish contribution to the cultural facade and the pretense of Nazi respect for" *völkisch* and Zionist" Jews as a separate people—an effort maintained even beyond the Crystal Night pogrom of November 9-10, 1938 upon express order of Goebbels to Hinkel. In the first year alone the Berlin chapter of 19,000 members with its 125 musicians and actors became a flourishing cultural center which developed a dynamic not intended in all its aspects by the Nazis. Membership in Berlin grew to 20,000 in 1934, to 40,000 by 1937 amidst a national count of 180,000. The JKB produced hundreds of concerts and even operas between 1933 and 1941 in addition to other performances supported by the Jewish communities, special funds for artists and private donations in concert halls and synagogues, and in the homes of wealthy patrons and in private chamber music settings—the latter at times involving Aryan friends, at great risk to all participants. Opera centered in Berlin as a major social and symbolic event, occasionally before audiences of several thousand, under the directorship of Singer himself and GMD Rosenstock, formerly of the distinguished Mannheim stage. Other cities had to make do with concert-form opera due to lack of funds and talent. However, several cities besides Berlin featured JKB orchestras: Frankfurt, Munich, Stuttgart, Mannheim and Breslau, while a traveling ensemble performed extensively throughout the Reich. Personnel everywhere was drawn from the list of victims of the April Laws, including celebrities from the great stages of Germany. Programs ranged from the traditional offerings, reflecting the taste of the cultivated assimilationist and "enlightened" majority, especially in the first year, to the decidedly Jewish liturgical and folk music of, say, a Chemjo Winawer and others which were rooted in the choral traditions of German synagogues, Eastern European folk tradition and associated with Zionism. Winawer, for one, traveled widely with his chorus to many German cities and even abroad. The split within music typified that of the community at large, between the majority organization of German Jews, the *Centralverein* (CV) and the Zionists, for instance over the measures to be employed against anti-Semitism and such fundamentals as ultimate identity and loyalty.[126] By and large the Jewish cultural establishment stayed away from Winawer, although, in time, it learned to appreciate his and other folkloristic contributions to the good fight. Both camps promoted Jewish masters of the past. But Mendelssohn and Mahler seemed too German to the advocates of characteristic Jewish music and corresponding politics. Jewish parochialism also resulted in the rejection of many contemporary Jewish composers who submitted new works by the hundreds which also ranged from a traditional, generally late-Romantic idiom—though some modernist works, like Ernst Toch's Second Piano Concerto, were premiered in Frankfurt by Heide Hermanns under the direction of William Steinberg, while Toch already had emigrated to the U.S.—to that of explicitly Jewish quality and to music which attempted to blend the two. The categories and orientations were reflected in the critiques and commentaries published in the Jewish community papers such as the *Gemeindeblatt der Jüdischen Gemeinde zu Berlin*. Folk songs and liturgical works in Hebrew and even Yiddish were published by the *Jüdischer Verlag Berlin*, for instance, in support of a separate Jewish identity. Julius Sachs published a catalogue of Jewish composers of all orientations, *Der jüdische Musikalien- Katalog* (1936).[127] Finally, the composers were able to negotiate a contract with Stagma, the official German copyright review board which distributed royalties, meager as they were, to the Jewish composers.

Fred Prieberg has noted the irony involved in the founding of the JKB even before the RMK.[128] Ambiguities abounded. Though proud of his organizational achievement, the anti-Semitic SS-*Untersturmführer* Hinkel must have been wary of this flourishing cultural activity of and for Jews, which contradicted several assumptions about the Jews—for instance, their inability to be creative in a non-parasitical capacity. Above all, the musical program itself mirrored that of a traditional society as well as that of the Nazified stages of Germany—a far cry from the music depicted as "degenerate" and identified with Jews by the Nazis. The Jewish cultural leadership and the concert-going public shared taste and standards with their bourgeois German counterparts, while Jewish ethnic music indeed paralleled *völkisch* products. Neither the JKB nor the self-conscious ethnics offered performances of Schönberg's music. Even contemporary efforts yielded "inoffensive" late-romantic and folkloric sounds, and the antipathy to modern music was echoed in the Jewish critical press—*Gleichschaltung*—in the ghetto. To be sure, these theoretical contradictions were kept from the German public as the press and radio were not allowed to attend any JKB events. Nonetheless, one wonders about the impression upon Nazi leaders of this separatist activity which surely reinforced Jewish identity, militancy and resistance. The benefit of appearing as benevolent sponsors of *völkisch* art must have outweighed the perceived threat to the interest of the state by a unified Jewish community which attracted to its events Jews of diverse social, educational, religious and national background and taste. And, of course, Singer also was in a bind, apart from obvious difficulties of organization and having to take orders from committed enemies. Wanting to maintain and revitalize Jewish culture, he stood accused of collaboration and of contributing to the cultural facade of the anti-Semitic state—a position he shared with colleagues and leaders of other Jewish organizations, especially the acknowledged leader of German Jewry, Rabbi Leo Baeck.

Notwithstanding irony, contradiction and ambiguity facing both sides, the flourishing cultural activity was not only tolerated but encouraged by the Nazi state. To be sure, all activity and programs had to clear the censors, were supervised by Hinkel's office and the police (which had to attend each function), and mandatory membership cards were checked. The different Jewish communities were even allowed to pool resources, engage in exchanges and coordinated efforts, culminating in Hinkel's reorganization of the JKB in 1935 into the *Reichsverband der jüdischen Kulturbunde* which he undertook in cooperation with the Gestapo and consistent with the discriminatory Nuremberg Laws of that year. The new *Reichsverband* actually received permission to hold a national congress which convened September 5-7, 1936 in Berlin, at which representatives of the then 125 chapters listened to speakers about the survival of Jewish culture in Germany. Presentations covered "Jewish Liturgical Music and Jewish Folk Songs" (Arno Nadel),

"Jewish Orchestral and Chamber Music" (Dr. Hans Nathan); performances included Winawer's chorus and a few contemporary songs sung by the baritone Wilhelm Guttman, formerly of the Berlin City Opera. The *Reichsverband* also decided to sponsor prizes for different categories of compositorial competition - over one hundred works were submitted. The smiling Hinkel attended, spoke in friendly terms about *völkisch* Jews—suggesting that the entire event paralleled similar ones of the NSKG or the RMK.[129]

The activities continued with opera in Berlin leading the way (194 performances in 1935/36, 89 in 1936/37) with traditional programs before thousands—a fitting feature of the normal conditions the Nazis were trying to convey—past Crystal Night, even after the start of war. Composition also continued, including pointedly Jewish opera, like Jacob Weinberg's "The Chalutzim," with traditional romantic and folkloric sounds and the subject of immigration to Palestine, "Eretz Israel" (premiered September 4, 1938) a classically programmatic work about Jewish vitality within the soil of the old homeland—again, in confirmation of *völkisch* ideology and segregation. Indeed, the experience of the JKB suggested a *völkisch*-segregationist policy in the service of that facade. Although the delusion of normalcy was cultivated until 1941, the quality and quantity of musical life declined due to the rich, famous and young departing from Germany. After the premiere of Weinberg's "Chalutzim" the Winawers left Germany; so did many members of the JKB who could find employment abroad. GMD Rosenstock went to lead the Japanese Philharmonic in Tokyo. Many joined Bronislaw Hubermann's "Palestine Orchestra," under the artistic directorship of the defamed Leo Kestenberg, which also attracted William Steinberg who, in turn, engaged many notable refugee instrumentalists for a concert series founded by the famous anti-fascist conductor Arturo Toscanini. The emigration of Germany's Jewish musicians contributed to the "Sea Change," the transfer of talent from old Europe to the New World, to New York and Los Angeles[130]—securing a base for cultural transformation but also continuity. Like the fox guarding the chicken coop Hinkel observed the comings and goings, the final going of some and the captivity of those who remained for their final demise. Dr. Kurt Singer clung to the JKB even when offered a chair at Yale University while on a visit to New York in 1939. His life ended in the concentration camp at Theresienstadt in 1944.[131]

Until 1941 the Nazis were interested in their version of segregation and the pretense of respect for separate peoples. The "final solution" made the Jewish cultural organization dispensable. Dr. Singer died, but only after he had served a useful function. Notwithstanding the pervasive deception of Geissmar, Furtwängler, Singer, and even some Nazis, the reality of 1933 expressed in the SA song literature amounted to a revolution as depicted by

Nazi commentators. The education structure, above all, contributed its share to the endeavor of raising a new breed of men. Sports and music were joined in special courses at schools and in summer camps.[132] The new man was to integrate all human expression and experience in his person. The singing SA-man was his model. Although the SA was eliminated, its spirit was appropriated by a state which at the same time wanted to appear as civilized, trustworthy and stable in order to allay the fears of a threatened traditional order and the growing alarm of the international community. On a broader basis the ideology was to find implementation. Although "the fighting song was replaced by solemn hymns," the "final solution" by the state was by no stretch of the imagination less radical than the ideology of the less refined SA. Indeed, the SA survived. The only element which was truly suppressed was the democratic-revolutionary, the idealistic and socially offensive feature of a movement which too had fulfilled its purpose. The history of the SA song therefore clearly reflects the history of National Socialism, in addition to which it served as an inspiration for a generation of younger composers. Bajer's reference to the survival of the SA spirit in song suggests the usefulness of the ideology throughout the Third Reich. The rich song literature of the Nazi movement allowed the Nazi elite to maintain its revolutionary pose, even after the fateful days of June and July 1934, in which the revolutionary faction of the movement was sacrificed in favor of a broader power base.

ENDNOTES

[1]See Louis L. Snyder, *The Third Reich, 1933-1945: A Bibliographic Guide to Nationai Sociaiism* (New York and London, 1987) for a brief review of 850 major treatments of the history of National Socialism, arranged with reference to key historiographical controversies—including the question of continuity to which all historians had and have to respond. While Edmond Vermeil in *Doctrinaires de la revolution allemande* (Paris, 1938) and *Essay d'explication* (Paris, 1945), Koppel S. Pinson in his *Modern Germany: Its History and Civilization* (New York, 1954) and many other general histories and monographs locate the roots of Hitler's ideology deep in the German past, others—like Friedrich Meinecke in *The German Catastrophe* (Cambridge, MA, 1950) and Gerhard Ritter in "The Historical Foundation of the Rise of National Socialism," in *The Third Reich*, A Study Published under the Auspices of the Internatinal Council for Philosophy and Humanistic Studies with the Assistance of UNESCO (London, 1955)—argue for discontinuity between mainstream German traditions and National Socialism. Also, Karl Dietrich Bracher in *The German Dictatorship* (New York and Washington, 1970) is critical of those authors—like William L. Shirer in his best seller, *The Rise and Fall of the Third Reich* (London, 1960)—who "treat the antecedents and rise of National Socialism superficially and summarily, as a logical end product of German historical development..."(3) Ernst Nolte in his pioneering *Three Faces of Fascism* (New York, 1966; in German 1963) and Eugen Weber with *The Variety of Fascism* (Princeton, 1964) broadened the examination by comparing the different expressions of European fascism. Students of Nazi thought, ideology and culture have concentrated on Hitler's ideas and intellec-

tual influences on him. Early studies like Peter Viereck's *Roots of the Nazi Mind* and Rohan D'Olier Butler's *Roots of National Socialism* (New York, 1942) have been followed by many other works which confirm continuity in general as well as in select realms of thought and culture. While distinguished artists and intellectual memoir writers and students of serious thought and high culture have rejected National Socialism as alien to the German tradition and thus neglected its study as insignificant, the advocates of continuity have scrutinized the second-rate intellectual progenitors like Langbehn, Lagarde and Moeller van den Bruck—as, for instance, in Fritz Stern's representative study (Introductin, n. 25)—but also notable ones like Darwin, Wagner and Nietzsche who had been appropriated by the Nazis, albeit in distorted form. For confirmation of continuity, see Hans Kohn, *The Mind of Germany: The Education of a Nation* (New York, 1960); William John Bossenbrook, *The German Mind* (Detroit, 1961); Horst von Malnitz, *The Evolution of Hitler's Germany: The Ideology, the Personality, the Moment* (New York, 1973); and George L. Mosse, who in *The Crisis of German Ideology: Intellectual Origins of the Third Reich* (New York, 1964) identifies the intellectual roots of National Socialism in the *völkisch* milieu of the nineteenth and early twentieth centuries when Germany's anti-liberal and anti-democratic ideology was institutionalized in the schools, youth movements, veteran groups and political parties. See also the comprehensive Marxist analysis of George Lukacs, *Die Zerstörung der Vernunft* (rev. ed., Neuwied, 1962); an approach confirmed in the music sociology of the West German Theodor W. Adorno (Introduction, notes 16, 26), especially his *Versuch über Wagner* (rev. ed., Munich and Zurich, 1964) and "Reaktion und Fortschritt," *Moments Musicaux* (Frankfurt a.M., 1958), and the East German Ernst H. Meyer's *Musik im Zeitgeschehen* (Berlin, DDR, 1952). Eberhard Jäckel's *Hitler's Weltanschauung: A Blueprint for Power* (Middletown, 1972) restores the significance of ideology for our understanding of Hitler and the Third Reich, as does Jeffrey Herf (Introduction, n. 27).

[2]The *völkisch* ideology is here understood as that set of ideas developed by nineteenth-century nationalists with reference to the German people (*Volk*) which, according to Mosse in *The Crisis of German Ideology* (4-5) conveyed the union of the German people "with a transcendental essence...fused to man's innermost nature and represented the source of his creativity, his depth of feeling, his individuality, and his unity with other members of the *Volk*." The *völkisch* ideology incorporated the tradition of romantic individualism, irrationalism and anti-modernism in conjunction with a cultural nationalism associated with Herder. It later turned into an activist German and anti-Jewish revoltuion. Although the movement passed out of the hands of cultural critics by 1933, the Nazis were to consider themselves the executors of this mission in the interest of the nation. See Hans Joachim Berbig, "Zur Terminologie von Volk, Nation und Reich in der neueren Geschichte," *Zeitschrift für Religions- und Geistesgeschichte* (1976), 1-15; George L. Mosse (ed.), *Nazi Culture: Intellectual, Cultural and Social Life in the Third Reich* (New York, 1966); and Roderick Stackelberg, *Idealism Debased: From Völkisch Ideology to National Socialism* (Kent, 1981).

[3]Walter Hofer (ed.), *Der Nationalsozialismus: Dokumente 1933-1945* (Frankfurt a.M., 1957), 82.

[4]Prieberg, *Musik*, 113. On May 8, 1933 Goebbels had already spoken of a "stahldurchzitterten, unausgegorenen Romantik," included in Cuno Horkenbach (ed.), *Das Deutsche Reich von 1918 bis heute* (Berlin, 1935), 207; cited in Elke Fröhlich, "Die kulturpolitische Pressekonferenz," *Vierteljahreshefte für Zeitgeschichte* (1974), 357.

[5]Prieberg, *Musik*, 263.

[6]See Introduction, n. 26, for general references; specifically, the Eichenauer quote from *Musik und Rasse*, 302; Rosenberg, *Gestaltung der Idee* (Munich, 1940), 337; on the "degenerate music" exhibit more below. See also Michael H. Kater, "The Jazz Experience in Weimar Germany," *German History* (1988), 154-158; for Pfitzner see more in Prieberg, *Musik*, 34-37. After World War II an anguished Pfitzner explained in a letter to Bruno Walter the crimes of the war and concentration camps as consequences of the treatment Germany received during and after World War I, especially the lies about alleged German atrocities then, and he wanted to have the condemnation of German crimes extended to those of the Russians and Americans—thus anticipating aspects of the article of Ernst Nolte, "Vergangenheit die nicht vergehen will: Eine Rede die geschrieben, aber nicht gehalten werden konnte," *Frankfurter Allgemeine Zeitung*, June 1986, which triggered the *Historikerstreit*. The Pfitzner letter is cited in Gottfried Eberle, "Hans Pfitzner—Präfaschistische Tendenzen in seinem asthetischen und politischen Denken," in Heister and Klein, 140-141.

[7]Peter Raabe, *Die Musik im Dritten Reich* (Regensburg, 1936), 10.

[8]Valentin, 88.

[9]Notice in *Die Musik* (hereafter *DM*), (July 1933), 796.

[10]Berta Geissmar, *The Baton and the Jackboot* (London, 1944), 71.

[11]Bosse, "Führerverantwortlichkeit oder Revolution der Strasse," *Zeitschrift für Musik* (hereafter *ZfM*), (May 1933), 483-485.

[12]These events were covered throughout the German music and feuilleton press—as in the article by Gustav Bosse (above, n. 11). See Prieberg, *Musik*, 41-44; Fritz Busch, *Aus dem Leben eines Musikers* (London, 1949), 188-209. About Trunk see "Erfüllte Anregungen und Wünsche," *ZfM* (May 1933), 486-487.

[13]Wolfgang Langhoff, *Die Moorsoldaten* (Berlin, 1947). Other records indicate that music accompanied labor and beatings at the camps. See Hanns-Werner Heister, "Nachwort: Funktionalisierung und Entpolitisierung," in Heister and Klein, 306-315; Wolfgang Schneider, *Kunst hinter Stacheldraht: Ein Beitrag zur Geschichte des faschistischen Widerstandes* (Leipzig, 1976).

[14]Reichsgesetzblatt (RGBl.), I (1933), 175; Ilse Staff (ed.), *Justiz im Dritten Reich: Eine Dokumentation* (Frankfurt a.M., 1964), 64-65.

[15]*Deutsches Volkstum* (March 1933), 17.

[16]Paul Hübnerfeld, *In Sachen Heidegger* (Hamburg, 1959), 97.

[17]"Was ist Kultur," *Neue Literatur* (July 1933), 380.

[18]Hale, 81. See also Z.A.B. Zeman, *Nazi Propaganda* (2nd. ed., Oxford, 1973), 41-45.

[19]Hale, 79.

[20]Ibid., 244, 246. See also Fröhlich, 348; and Jeremy Noakes and Geoffrey Pridham (eds.),

Documents on Nazism, 1919-1945, (New York, 1974), 334-338. For all matters concerning the Press Conferences, see *Sammlung Sänger*, Bundesarchiv Koblenz (hereafter BA), ZSg 102.

[21]Hale, 86.

[22]Ibid., 120.

[23]Ibid., 218.

[24]Fröhlich, 347-349.

[25]"Neues vom Tage," *Anbruch* (January 1931), 1-3.

[26]*Melos* (December 1932), 397-399.

[27]"Erfüllte Anregungen und Wünsche der *Zeitschrift für Musik*," ZFM (May 1933), 486-487.

[28]Hermann Matzke, "Völkische Kunstpflege," *ZfM* (March 1933), 263.

[29]Kurt Traut (ed.), *Jahrbuch der Musikbibliothek für 1933* (Leipzig, 1934), 5.

[30]See Gurlitt, "Vom Deutschtum in der Musik," *Musik im Zeitbewusstsein* (November 1933), 1-2; his alarm over alien elements in, "Zur gegenwärtigen Orgel-Erneuerungsbewegung," *Musikgeschichte und Gegenwart*, II (1929), 92; reviewed in Eckhard John, "Vom Deutschtum in der Musik," in Albrecht Dümling and Peter Girth (eds.), *Entartete Musik: Eine kommentiert Rekonstruktion—Zur Düsseldorfer Ausstellung von 1938* (Düsseldorf, 1988), 50. See also Josef Müller-Blattau's file, Berlin Document Center (hereafter, BDC).

[31]*Zeitschrift für Musikwissenschaft* (June-July 1933), 385-387, 418.

[32]Arnold Schering, "Zum Beginn des neuen Jahrgangs," *Zeitschrift für Musikwissenschaft* (January 1934), 1.

[33]Hermann W. v. Waltershausen, "Die Wandlungen der Musik Pedagogik seit 1900," *DM* (October 1932), 12-17.

[34]Personalien," *DM* (March 1933), 479. For brief references to musical life in Germany throughout the Third Reich, including descriptive political incidents, governmental proclamations and the reactions of musicians, see the encyclopedic chronology with commentary by Nicolas Slonimsky, *Music Since 1900* (4th ed., New York, 1971), 561-824.

[35]"Personalien," *DM* (April 1933), 560.

[36]"Die Oper und Ihr Publikum," *DM* (April 1933), 481-490.

[37]Otto Steinhagen, "Das Musikleben der Gegenwart," *DM* (May 1933), 620-621.

[38]Ibid; and letter of Barlach to von Schillings, February 23, 1933, at the Prussian Archives at the Akademie der Künste, Berlin (hereafter PadK).

[39]"Was gilt eine Musikkritik?" *Melos* (December 1932), 418-419.

[40]Fritz Stege, "Arbeitsgemeinschaft Deutscher Musikkritiker," *ZfM* (May 1933), 480-481.

[41]"Personalien," *DM* (May 1933), 640.

[42]*DM* (June 1933), 641.

[43]"Aufklang," *DM* (June 1933), 641-643.

[44]"Oper im neuen Zeichen," *DM* (June 1933), 644.

[45]*DM* (June 1933), 649-652.

[46]"Aus dem Berliner Kunstleben Musik," *Völkischer Beobachter* (hereafter *VB*), (February 10, 1933).

[47]"Das Deutsche Konzertleben und seine Erneuerung," *DM* (June 1933), 656.

[48]Wulf, *Musik*, 99-100.

[49]"Ansprache," *DM* (June 1933), 657-659.

[50]Hans Joachim Moser, "Deutscher Musikunterricht und seine Neugestaltung," *DM* (June 1933), 659-669.

[51]Prieberg, *Musik*, 30-32.

[52]Ferdinand Beussel, "Im Zeichen der Wende," *DM* (June 1933), 669-672.

[53]For example, see "Persönliches," *ZfM* (June 1933), 647.

[54]"Im Zeichen der Wende," (above, n. 52). On March 15, 1933, Berlin Radio had issued an absolute ban against the broadcasting of "Negro Jazz." (Slonimsky, 563)

[55]"In 1933: Deutsche Kurzgeschichte des Jazz," *Deutsche Kultur-Wacht* (1933), 14; Wulf, *Musik*, 383.

[56]"Im Zeichen der Wende," (above, n. 52), 673-674.

[57]Ibid., 675.

[58]Letters, PAdK.

[59]Above, n. 11.

[60]Letters; Wulf, *Musik*, 95-96.

[61]For an analysis of Nazi propaganda through its vocabulary, as manifest in Hitler's and especially Goebbels' speeches, see Werner Betz, "The National Socialist Vocabulary, in *The Third Reich*, UNESCO; also Victor Klemperer, *Lingua Tertii Imperii: Die unbewältigte Sprache* (Munich, 1949).

[62]"Berliner Musik," *ZfM* (May 1933), 457-458.

[63]*Berliner Lokal-Anzeiger*, April 27, 1933; Wulf, *Musik*, 23.

[64]*Allgemeine Musikzeitung* (1933), 88; in Henry Bair, "Die Lenkung der Berliner Opernhäuser," in Heister and Klein, 83.

[65]"Um die Deutsche Musik; Ein Bekenntnis," *DM* (July 1933), 727-730.

[66]*Berliner Lokal-Anzeiger*, April 5, 1933; Wulf, *Musik*, 23; Slonimsky, 564.

[67]*Berliner Lokal-Anzeiger*, June 6, 1933. See also Bair, 83-90.

[68]*Deutsche Kultur-Wacht* (1933), 13; Wulf, *Musik*, 24.

[69]*Vossische Zeitung*, February 16, 1933.

[70]Wulf, *Musik*, 25. All information pertaining to the PAdk not otherwise cited is derived from its Archives.

[71]Béla Bartók, *Eigene Schriften und Erinnerungen der Freunde* (Basel and Stuttgart, 1958), 57.

[72]Wulf, *Musik*, 100-101.

[73]Ibid., 58-60.

[74]"Ende der Musikpädagogischen Jugendkonjunktur," *ZfM* (June 1933), 591-592.

[75]Gustav Bosse, "Um Fritz Jöde," *ZfM* (June 1933), 571-591.

[76]Wulf, *Musik*, 25-26.

[77]Hofer, 128.

[78]Ibid., 133.

[79]Ibid., 131-132.

[80]Ibid., 133.

[81]"Erklärung," *ZfM* (June 1933), 599-600.

[82]Loc. cit.

[83]Adolf Strube, *Zum 60. Geburtstag* (1954), 25; Wulf, *Musik*, 66; confirmed to me in interview with Professor Uwe Roehl, Director of Music, Nord-Deutscher Rundfunk in Hamburg, July 5, 1978. Born in 1925, Professor Roehl had studied with Wolfgang Stumme at the Berlin Music Academy for Church and School Music.

[84]Wulf, *Musik*, 68.

[85]*ZfM* (July 1933), 712-717.

[86]"Die Orgelbewegung und ihre gegenwärtige Lage in Deutschland, *ZfM* (June 1933), 594-599.

[87]Letter from Stein to Hinkel, July 1, 1933; Wulf, *Musik*, 69-70.

[88]Letter from Hinkel to Müller, October 7, 1933; Wulf, *Musik*, 71.

[89]"Kleine Mitteilungen—Gesellschaften und Vereine," *ZfM* (May 1934), 561.

[90]Wulf, *Musik*, 32-33.

[91]Ibid., 111.

[92]Ibid., 33.

[93]Ibid., 35-36.

[94]"Musikfeste und Tagungen," *ZfM* (June 1933), 629-631.

[95]"Kleine Mitteilungen," *ZfM* (June 1933), 644-645.

[96]Ibid.

[97]Rita von der Grün, "Funktionen und Formen von Musiksendungen im Rundfunk," in Heister and Klein, 99. See also Heinz Pohle, *Der Rundfunk als Instrument der Politik* (Hamburg, 1955), 257.

[98]Paul Bülow, "Adolf Hitler und der Bayreuther Geistesbezirk," *ZfM* (July 1933), 677-680.

[99]Walter Kühn, *Führung zur Musik* (Lahr i.B., 1939), 33-34.

[100]"Aus neuerschienenen Büchern," *ZfM* (June 1933), 530-534.

[101]*Der Deutsche Almanach für Kunst und Wissenschaft* (1933), 134-135; Wulf, *Musik*, 79-80.

[102]Kurt Huber, "Der Aufbau Deutscher Volksliedforschung und Volksliedpflege," *Deutsche Musikkultur* (June-July 1936), 65.

[103]Wilhelm Ehmann, "Die Liederstunde des Volkes," Ibid., 74-76.

[104]Rudolf Sonner, "Grosstädtische Volksmusik," Ibid., 84-90.

[105]Carl Hannemann, "Volkssingen," *Deutsche Musikkultur* (October-November 1936), 233-238.

[106]See Vernon L. Lidtke, "Songs and Nazis: Political Music and Social Change in Twentieth-Century Germany," in Gary D. Starck and Bede Karl Lackner (eds.), *Essays on Culture and Society in Modern Germany* (Arlington and College Station, 1982), 167-200. Tapes of this extensive song literature are available at several German radio archives, such as Deutsches Rundfunkarchiv Frankfurt a.m. and Sender Freies Berlin; see Reich Rundfunk Gesellschaft also for speeches about culture by the Nazi leaders.

[107]For a detailed secondary account of this success story, see "Musik für Jugend, Volk und Formation," Prieberg, *Musik*, 242-259; for noted musicians at the HJ camps, 247-249.

[108]For a broad review of Nazi-*völkisch* music education, its achievements by 1939 and goals, see Wolfgang Stumme (ed.), *Musik im Volk: Grundfragen der Musikerziehung* (Berlin, 1939) which contains contributions of specialists from many of the organizations identified here.

[109]See Johannes Hodek for a sophisticated review of the magic of the Nazi songs, his own evolution as a student of the subject, and a revealing bibliography in, "'Sie wissen, wenn man Heroin nimmt...'" Von Sangeslust und Gewalt in Naziliedern," in Heister and Klein, 19-35.

[110]Eisler, 339.

[111]Prieberg, *Musik*, 242.

[112]"Das politische Kampflied als Volkslied der Gegenwart," *Mitteldeutsche Blätter für Volkskunde* (1933); Wulf, *Musik*, 264.

[113]"Das politische Kampflied der Gegenwart im Unterricht," *Zeitschrift für Deutschkunde* (1934), 636; Wulf, *Musik*, 264.

[114]Hans Bajer, "Ruhmesblätter in der Geschichte des SA-Liedes," *DM* (December 1936); the song selections (my translation) are taken from this article, 169-176.

[115]The theme of the unknown SA-man was very popular. The uniform integrated the individual into the group, accorded elite status, but took away individuality, too. See Goebbels, "Der unbekannte SA-Mann," *Kampf um Berlin*, 83-105; also *Der unbekannte SA-Mann: Ein guter Kamerad der Hitler-Soldaten* (Munich, 1934).

[116]Hellmuth Langenbucher, *Die Deutsche Gegenwartsdichtung* (Berlin, 1939), 176-178.

[117]Hans Bajer, "Ruhmesblätter in der Geschichte des SA-Liedes," *DM* (January 1937); the following song selections are taken from this article, 257-267.

[118]See also Lidtke, 172-181.

[119]Hans Bajer, "Lieder machen Geschichte," *DM* (June 1939), 586-597.

[120]Wulf, *Musik*, 266.

[121]Geissmar, 102.

[122]Ibid., 78-80.

[123]Ibid., 72.

[124]Hofer, 284.

[125]See Joseph Wulf, *Die Bildenden Künste im Dritten Reich* (Gutersloh, 1963), 147-148; Wulf, *Musik*, 82-83; Prieberg, *Musik*, 78-106.

[126]See Arnold Paucker, *Der jüdische Abwehrkampf gegen Antisemitismus und Nationalsozialismus in den letzten zehn Jahren der Weimarer Republik* (Hamburg, 1968), 39-49.

[127]Prieberg, *Musik*, 94.

[128]Ibid., 97.

[129]Some of the emigre (or refugee) musicians and other JKB members in Los Angeles supplied the information for this examination of the JKB—especially Rudy Brook, who had led a Zionist chorus from Magdeburg, and Richard Dresdner, a singer and voice teacher, who recalled Winawer in Prague—which paralleled the fate of the Jewish Women Association (*Jüdischer Frauenbund*) and that of the general Jewish *Reichsvertretung* under Leo Baeck and confirms Prieberg's assessment.

[130]See H. Stuart Hughes, *The Sea Change: The Migration of Social Thought, 1930-1965* (New York, 1975); Anthony Heilbut, *Exiled in Paradise: German Refugee Artists and Intellectuals in America, from the 1930's to the Present* (Boston, 1983); Eike Middell et al., *Exil in den USA* (Leipzig, 1983), Vol. 3 in *Kunst und Literatur im antifaschistischen Exil, 1933-1945*; and Marion Kaplan, *The Jewish Feminist Movement in Germany: The Campaigns of the Jüdischer Frauenbund, 1904-1938* (Westport, 1979).

[131]Wulf, *Musik*, 82.

[132]"Hochschulen, Konservatorien und Unterrichtswesen," *ZfM* (June 1933), 646.

Music Organization
(1933-1945)

Through the assumption of power and its consolidation in 1933, the Nazi regime deduced from its totalitarian doctrine the right and obligation to regulate the arts. The fulfillment of the *völkisch* promise was the avowed aim and rationale of the revolution. However, this ideology of the "musicalized national community," sung with conviction and articulated in repetitive and accessible manner by music organizers, scholars, journalists and coordinated musicians, was ultimately shaped and guided by an autocratic party organization. It's rigid command structure, from the unquestioned rule of the leader on down, made for unconditional execution of all orders and slavish dependence of lower ranks on their higher manipulators—an unlikely vehicle for the attainment of spiritual goals or musical redemption.

On the other hand, that organization had succeeded in winning over the machinery of the state intact, which it then molded into its own image—the common authoritarian features of party and state helping in that endeavor. By the time of the formal announcement of the one-party state in the summer of 1933, vital state positions had been filled by reliable Nazis. It was time to broaden the appeal of National Socialism by taming the more radical elements of the revolution through stricter party discipline and to reassure the civil service and other traditional and conservative interests, such as the world of culture. The KfdK, for one—the symbol of "the revolution in the streets," of purges, negativism, and "spontaneous" *Gleischschaltung* measures—was soon to be absorbed by the more disciplined and responsible NSKG which, though also noted for its activism and *völkisch* "idealism," characteristically sponsored positive expressions of "German" culture until it, in turn, dissolved within the even less activist "Strength through Joy"— *Kraft durch Freude* (KdF) recreational organizations of the German Labor Front—*Deutsche Arbeitsfront* (DAF).

Having been conditioned to look for state support in the past, musicians especially welcomed state intervention, the musicalization of all party organizations, official declarations of support for the arts, commissions and subsidies. Captivated by Nazi elan, while subject to threats and seduction, they joined the many new musical organizations in the hope of securing employment, professional recognition and prestige. The word was out that Pg's would be hired first, favored for promotion, their compositions performed and aired over the radio.

If their dignity appeared threatened in the shameful scramble for positions left vacant by Jews and other colleagues, who had been declared incompatible with the new order, a combination of motives and circumstances facilitated the relatively harmonious integration of music: 1) zeal of the true believers and beneficiaries who pushed on many fronts for personal gain in the context of national and music's reconstruction; 2) the gloomy background of depression, political uncertainty, unemployment and then the confusion, fear and—even—hope relative to *Gleichschaltung* among the less committed; 3) resignation of those who saw no way out; and 4) Nazi manipulation of all activities and psychological states of those involved as well as deceit and terror. And then there were the shared assumptions and habits—authoritarian, for one, but also the unabashed self-glorification of both Nazi *Herrenmenschen* and musical representatives of "German profundity," and complementary interests—the need for job security and recognition here, for a cultural facade and favorable publicity there—which explain the haste with which musicians collaborated and joined the party. Only the turf fight among prominent Nazi leaders—especially Rosenberg and Goebbels, who vied for cultural supremacy, and between the KfdK and other Nazi cultural institutions, prevented the early creation of a centralized national organization of music. Although the Reich leadership manipulated the process of *Gleichschaltung* at large, Hitler himself had variously encouraged competition within party ranks for the strong and creative to survive and provide the most competent leadership.

The idea of a national music organization had been discussed in Nazi and other circles before 1933. Only thus could music's economic stability be secured and *völkisch* ideals be realized. The Berlin music chapter of the KfdK, for instance, had demanded such a corporate national music representation in 1932 and identified itself as the organizational framework in early 1933. Especially the violinist Gustav Havemann, the conductor and Berlin City Councilman Heinz Ihlert, the musicologist Friedrich Mahling and Karl Stietz agitated in behalf of the KfdK with the support of KfdK founder Rosenberg and KfdK leader and state commissioner Hans Hinkel in this endeavor, until they succeeded in establishing on May 10, 1933 the first organization of and for musicians of national pretension, the *Reichskartell der deutschen Musikerschaft*, in effect, an expansion of the KfdK's music chapter. At its first formal conference on July 4, the *Reichskartell*'s national ambitions were spelled out by President Havemann and his Deputy and Managing Director Heinz Ihlert, who also announced the introduction of a required membership card as a means of purging the profession in accord with the "Aryan Paragraph" of the Professional Civil Service Law and screening members for professional competence and political reliability. It was made clear that the *Reichskartell* pointed in the direction of a German music chamber. Attempts were then made to sign up other professional organizations. By fall, six had enlisted (See Chapter I), notably the prominent organization of educators, the RDTM with its 10,000 members which was reorganized in accordance with standard Nazi procedures of those days: Pg. Havemann had become chairman of its board and Ihlert its deputy managing director, while the ex-chairman Arnold Ebel, a composer, remained as managing director. In spite of this success, the *Reichskartell* was unable to incorporate the largest musicians association, the *Deutscher Musikerverband* with its 20,000 members, organized at that time within the DAF as *Fachschaft Musik*, a powerful rival which also required a membership card and purged its Jewish membership.

Meanwhile, drafts for an all-encompassing Reich Culture Chamber Law (RKKG) were being finalized, signaling not Rust's, Ley's or Rosenberg's victory but, rather the undisputed leadership of Goebbels in all areas of cultural expression and mass communication. Adopted on September 22, 1933, the law instituted a Reich Culture Chamber (RKK), divided into seven separate chambers of literature, radio, theatre, music, films, fine arts, and the press, which the propaganda minister was authorized to organize. An Implementing Ordinance of November 1 designated Goebbels president of the RKK and, in accordance with the leadership principle, instructed him to appoint the presidents of the individual chambers, whose organization and powers were spelled out.

This RKKG clearly confirmed the policy of centralization and the priority of propaganda (Goebbels) over ideology (Rosenberg) in the process of consolidation and broadening of Nazi power, which is not to suggest that the *völkisch* ideals were taken lightly, but that the party recognized the need for control, censorship and reeducation of the nation as a means for their realization. Another central organization might have emerged, but it is a measure of Goebbels' talents and Nazi cynicism that a ministry of propaganda—Goebbels did not like the name—was placed in charge of cultural expression, one that by definition thrived on manipulated appearance rather than substance—a mockery and reversal of German idealist emphasis on essences or of the frequently recited motto, *mehr sein als scheinen.* The members of the KfdK had agitated in earnest against "alien" and "bolshevist" expressions in music, contributed boldly to Nazi success in the early months of power, and gained personal rewards for their front-line efforts. However, the state's fateful commitment of culture to this "impresario" of the Third

Reich reveals clearly, in retrospect, what had been cloaked in the euphemisms of his creation, that not only non-Nazi collaborators but also Fighting Leaguers were manipulated by a regime whose concept of total power in culture had to be broadened beyond the KfdK. Earlier rivalries between musical organizations, though continuing, had become irrelevant in the context of the total reconstruction of cultural life as the *Reichskartell* was transformed into the RMK by the November 1 Implementation Ordinance, and the DAF's *Fachschaft Musik* was officially incorporated. By year's end, the framework of the national music chamber had been instituted corporatively and in law. It managed all branches of music, the establishment of classical music, called *ernste—E Musik*; entertainment, *Unterhaltungs—U Musik*; and the expressly ideological folk, choral and Nazi music; an instrument of power which entertained, edified and indoctrinated.[1]

Propaganda (RMVP) and Culture (RKK)

The RKKG of September 22 assigned culture to the RMVP. The power of manipulation was thus codified in law. The "revolution of the street" was legalized, continuity assured in the eyes of the public between *Gleichschaltung* measures of 1933 and their consolidation in the RMK, while to insiders, the medium had become the message as Goebbels won over Rosenberg as well as Hitler, who also entertained strong views about the purity of art. At the RMVP policies were written into law by a legal division headed by Hans Schmidt-Leonard. For active and otherwise interested musicians and artists the RKK legal expert, Karl Friedrich Schrieber, published a collection of new laws and regulations concerning the cultural professions, official decrees and announcement of the RKK and its single chambers, *Das Recht der Reichskulturkammer* (Berlin, 1935) from which much of the present description is drawn. The same laws were also published in the *Völkischer Beobachter*, chosen by Goebbels as a suitable organ for instructing all cultural professions, the courts and related administrative offices of party and state. This legal chapter in Nazi cultural history extended to music. In 1936 the attorneys Willy Hoffmann and Wilhelm Ritter published a commentary on the new laws, ordinances and orders, *Das Recht der Musik* which addressed copyright regulations in music. Reference works of this sort illustrated the concern of the regime for legality, continuity and legitimacy—reflecting pride in the accomplishments of 1933, a commitment to the Nazi ideals and promises which appeared herewith legally and institutionally realized, and—in the case of the updated copyright law—reassuring composers that the Nazi state would continue to collect fees and disburse royalties. While the wording of copyright regulations generally remained the same, a new body of laws resulted as a consequence of the founding of the RMK, the creation of professional estates of composers, publishers and musicians, and the incorporation of the former Writer's Association into a German Performers' Association, the so-called *Stagma* (*Staatlich genehmigte Gesellschaft zur Verwertung musikalischer Urheberrechte*—Official Copyright Review Board). The decrees of the RMK, professional regulations of all professional estates and Stagma, and the collaboration between musicians and the public lent new content and form to music law.

Furthermore,

According to the present view of the German political leadership, copyright regulations are a socially binding law... The people's community is central to all considerations pertaining to matters of copyright. The creator of a certain work has certain rights, in addition to which he has an obligation to the whole people.[2]

In effect, all musicians learned that the right to practice their craft was a privilege which the regime extended to those it deemed loyal.

The coordinated music journals and the RMK bulletin—*Amtliche Mitteilungen der RMK* (AMRMK) also published the laws and commentaries. Detailed attention was paid to every aspect of music life, beginning with the legal status of the RMVP. In March, 1933, Reich President Hindenburg had announced its creation for the purpose of disseminating among the people the ideas of the government and the national revolution. Given the singular role accorded propaganda, it became the first ministry National Socialist in inception, and created after the seizure of power—its predecessor having been the Reich Propaganda Office of the NSDAP. The new minister—still party propaganda leader—was to take directives only from the Reich Chancellor. He enjoyed this direct access to Hitler throughout the Third Reich.[3]

Soon after the creation of the ministry, Hitler specified the functions of the Reich Minister to include all questions dealing with intellectual, cultural and educational matters, their dissemination at home and abroad, and the administration of these realms. Consequently, the minister encroached upon the jurisdiction of the Foreign Service in the areas of "news and propaganda, the arts, artistic exhibits, film and sports abroad," in addition to taking over former functions of the Interior Ministry such as

general internal political enlightenment, the Academy for Politics, and introduction and observance of national holidays (in cooperation with the Interior), the press (with the Institute for the Science of Journalism), the radio, national anthem, the German library in Leipzig, art, cultivation of music, including the Philharmonic Orchestra, theater, the cinema, and the fight against trash and obscenity.[4]

An exception was made only with regard to the State Opera which remained under the special control of Minister President Göring, administered by Dr. Franz Ulbrichts whose title read, "for special service to the Minister President." Although the priority of Goebbels' ministry in the "culture-political" sector was firmly established, the overlapping of cultural policies with other power centers of the Nazi government, especially those of the Interior, Foreign, Education and Economics Ministries, necessitated difficult negotiations. However, in view of its centrality, the vast Propaganda establishment under the guidance of Goebbels' Ministerial Office, run by his personal *Referent* and administered by his State Secretaries, was empowered to provide direction to the complex network of interrelated governmental agencies. Provincial propaganda offices (*Landesstellen*) were established throughout Germany (13 at first, 42 by the time of the *Anschluss* with 1400 officials), and since the Reich Minister retained his position as Party Propaganda Leader, by delegation and ordinance, the official in charge of a *Landesstelle* also headed the Propaganda *Gaustelle* of the party. After the creation of the RKK under Goebbels' presidency, that same person's authority was extended to local RKK business as *Landeskulturwalter* (supervisor of regional cultural affairs). By the time the *Landesstellen* were renamed *Reichspropagandaämter* (Reich Propaganda Offices) on September 9, 1937, Goebbels had clearly both solidified his power and resolved the state-party conflict within his domain, leaving no doubt that cultural expression served the interest of the state. His power legally defined and the hierarchical organizations in place, the implementation ordinances spelled out the details and ideological justifications; that of November 1 (See above) explained the task of the RKK which, in collaboration with members of all comprised professional branches, but under the leadership of the Reich Minister, was to promote German culture in the interest of people and Reich, to regulate the economic and social affairs of cultural professions, and to harmonize conflicting interests. As President of the RKK, the Minister would be represented by a general assistant and a business manager in each separate chamber. Having the power to appoint the chamber presidents and executive members, to confer special tasks on individual chambers, to sit as highest judge in Personnel matters, he also had the authority to overrule chamber presidents, to announce Culture Chamber ordinances and to submit a budget. Although the chamber presidents formed an advisory council (*Reichskulturrat*) and outstanding personalities in the fields were appointed by chamber presidents to form an honorary senate (Reichskultursenat), real power was vested in Goebbels. Indeed, the presidents were legally representatives of the Culture Chamber and were responsible to it, not to its members. All contact between the chambers and the government had to go through Goebbels, whose jurisdiction extended to the regulation of all activities in the chambers, the making of contracts and the power of public announcement. The police were required to assist the RKK, and the courts and other administrative organizations were asked to cooperate. While real power was vested in the central organization, the chambers carried the expenses of the RKK.[5]

The RKKG was instituted quickly; the RKK was festively inaugurated at the Philharmonic, November 15, 1933, and Goebbels concluded the ceremony with a speech on "A New Beginning of German Culture" and the naming of presidents and board members of the culture chambers. He also decreed that the integration of all artists into the chambers was to be effected by December 15, emphasizing again that membership in a specific chamber was mandatory for professional employment. Stressing the revolutionary nature of this "radical and fundamental reordering" of the entire culture, he insisted on the avowed "respect of the new Germany for artistic genius which, in its new professional organization, is not restricted, but furthered. . .'The RKK does not serve stagnation, but development.' Art cannot be commandeered, and 'political opinion' shall not constitute dilettante license."

Previous legislation, such as the Professional Civil Service Act and its "Aryan Paragraph," was to be applied more systematically at this time in screening all members in accordance with the government's explicit authority—reiterated in the November 1 Implementing Ordinance—to exclude all "dangerous and undesirable elements of the community." This "hard" regulation was "the consequential application of the Nazi ideology, in which personal liberty can only extend so far as not to harm the people's community . . .The goals of the RKK can only be realized in this manner."[6] Yet the general laws and broad organizational structures left much room for interpretation, and personal rivalries, which had characterized 1933 before the announcement of the new organization, were carried on even afterwards between various individuals eligible for membership. While Goebbels continued to fight fellow Reich Leaders Rust, Rosenberg and Ribbentrop, about whose abilities he had serious doubts,[7] among the coordinated musical professionals nasty accusations, race and political past were drawn into the arena of denunciation as before; lower ranks of the cultural establishment continued to rise to fill vacant positions of purged prominence. Nazis still interpreted the comprehensive reordering of culture as the beginning of a complete turnover of existing institutions, with Pg's assuming positions of leadership. The persistent mobility perpetuated a sense of insecurity and confusion in musical circles, in spite of ideological and organizational guidelines and rigid deference to centralized authority. This confusion was often the result of the so-called "revolutionary momentum"—actually an important feature of totalitarianism—according to which the ambitious can and must keep up the attack upon established conservatives under the guise of ideological purity. For instance, Hans Hinkel insisted in 1935 that it was high time for National Socialists to reject those who had not yet proved true conversion to National Socialism in sentiment and action. Only National Socialists could truly understand and realize Nazi principles in the field of cultural politics.[8]

Hinkel, increasingly the key figure in the administration of culture, typified the function of the bureaucrat in the arts in a totalitarian state, unlike those in traditional authoritarian societies. Although traditionalist and *völkisch* musicians controlled coordinated institutions which embodied their sentiments, the totalitarian state did not permit comfort, or a sense of security. Only "healthy people," not "bloodless creatures" can be supporters of Nazi cultural politics.[9] In sum, in spite of the authoritarian command structure of Goebbels' carefully designed organization, the base of which was essentially the traditional—albeit Nazified—musical order, the mobility, insecurity and competition persisted, not really threatening Goebbel's authority, but actually designed and manipulated by him. That is one of the paradoxes of the totalitarian state, containing an authoritarian and a revolutionary mask, the management of which requires great skill, confidence and constant attention.

If mobility, ideological reformulation, and constant affirmation of loyalty constituted the element of German culture which created anxiety and insecurity, the organization of the RKK obviously also represented order and the bureaucratization of cultural life. However, the existence of this organization under the guidance of the Progaganda Ministry was justified on grounds of the revolutionary situation. Indeed, a special propaganda and educational institution is indispensable to a revolution which aims at the total transformation of society, having to overcome not only the various organs of the state, but also those institutions which uphold the moral and spiritual order, namely religion, education and cultural realms. Thus, in principle, the Nazi revolution was unfolding according to plan, and in its structural development it seemed eminently justified, notwithstanding the contradictions, confusion and immediate shortcomings.

In spite of the fundamental inability of a propaganda ministry to pose as authoritarian organ of leadership, it had to function through the RKK for reasons of ideological consistency. The RKK provided form to Nazi cultural policy. It was the crystallization of the "unified propagandistic line" which lives or dies with National Socialism. For this reason members of various professional backgrounds, even of other ministries, held positions in the RMVP. The former economic advisor of Hitler, press chief of the government, and future successor of Schacht as Reich Bank President, Walter Funk—who at one time had wanted to become a musician—also functioned as *Staatssekretär* (undersecretary) in Goebbels' ministry and as vice-president of the RKK. In 1935 he issued a directive to all chamber presidents, which was to be forwarded to all branch organizations and professional departments: "In order to maintain a uniform propagandistic line at all public affairs within the RKK," he decreed in behalf of the minister, "all events of the chambers and their departments may be carried out only after prior consultation with the management of the RKK, Franz Karl Moraller in charge, who had to be informed of all planned events of public consequence and allowed to participate in the preparation and the performance." Specifically, the directive covered

> public demonstrations, propaganda actions, balls, social events, while purely professional or organizational conventions, insofar as they cover only internal business and are not attended by leading personalities of another chamber or organizational association, were excluded. All propagandists of the chambers and departments are responsible to Moraller, who has the authority to deploy them in other fields or to combine them in common action.[10]

The "uniform propagandistic line" reflected cultural centralization, professional coordination, and the specific relationship of all cultural professions with each other through Goebbels' office. The state set standards and supervised the affairs of organizations and its own creation. In practice, Goebbels' office addressed organization and membership, rarely artistic questions. While the RKK was purely political, the professional chambers were both political and artistic. Conflict was inevitable, reflected in the lives of various individuals who represented both aspects.

For example, all chamber presidents were prominent representatives of their profession, as well as political representatives of the state. The Nazis insisted on the dual function of their top administrators. In practice, the function of the chamber and its president raised the question of ultimate loyalty to either the state or the professional community, in spite of ideological definition of synonymity of interests. The many supplementary ordinances to basic organization and legal measures illustrated the need for constant political review throughout the Third Reich. At the same time, art also was defended in numerous articles written by revolutionaries and the artists who warned of bureaucratization. Although Goebbels remained the highest judge in matters of membership disputes, in practice, chamber presidents reviewed membership application. The law and organizational principles were generally spelled out so that presidential review was not even necessary. Moreover, the presidential power of granting exceptional membership status in a chamber—for veterans, for instance—irrespective of the Professional Civil Service Act stipulations, "was to be kept at a minimum and to be applied only in cases which were of no significance to cultural development.. .The return of Jewish influence in literature and the arts of the last decades can only then be prevented."[11] In practice, too, the chambers, as publicly and legally constituted professional estates, exercised the authority of regulating conditions of financial affairs as well as the nature of contractual agreements between the professional groups and individuals belonging to the chambers. The operations of Stagma, pertaining to publishing and performance, were subjected to regulations of the RMK.

All in all, it is evident that without the restrictions imposed on the individual and on the professional chambers, the tasks of the RKK could not have been fulfilled. Its dual function was the dissemination of the Nazi ideology and membership control. The respective chambers gave the impression of artistic self-governance, but in reality all functioned as manipulated instruments of power. The crucial feature of regulations was compulsory membership for the exercise of any artistic profession in Germany. The weight of Goebbels' Propaganda Ministry was uniformly imposed and reinforced through his control of publishing by way of the Reich Chambers of the Press, Literature and Radio, the ministry having bought up all shares of the *Reichsrund-funkgesellschaft* (National Broadcasting Corporation), supervised by the *Reichsrundfunkkammer* (Reich Broadcasting Chamber) which controlled broadcasters and manufacturers of sets, popularly called *Goebbelsschnauzen* ("Goebbels snouts"). The National Broadcasting Company lost its independence, and manufacturers were pressured into producing cheap sets, so that all Germans could afford one. The coordination of the press, all publishing, and the radio provided Goebbels with most extraordinary powers of reaching the people of Germany.

Reich Music Chamber (RMK)

The RKKG of September 22 also created the RMK as a corporate body of public law of and for musicians, which was to promote and administer German music, offer guidance, and regulate economic and social affairs of and for professional musicians, while also providing for the means to purge and control its membership more systematically than before via the notorious questionnaire about ancestry and political reliability. The RMK was to continue the fight against "unsuitable" elements in the professional body and against unemployment—46% of the professions in 1933, it will be recalled—in actuality complementary tasks. While the regulations and laws were formalized and restricted membership lists prepared, a hierarchy was put in place paralleling RMVP offices from Berlin to the local communities. Administrators everywhere were appointed, following the leadership principle.

Economic concerns were addressed as the extensive patronage system took form and assured loyalty within the administrative structure and throughout the professions. Unemployment was reduced from 23,889 in 1933 to 14,547 in 1936, among singers from 1891 to 1392; but it wasn't until war in 1939 that unemployment was nearly eliminated among the then 172,443 professional musicians.[12] Professional musicians were protected from competition of amateurs and the chamber was strengthened by agreements with the Economic Ministry which prohibited membership in more than one chamber.[13] By and large, monopolistic claims of the profession were reinforced by ordinances and agreements with labor and industrial organizations. The Labor Service—Arbeitsdienst (AD) agreed in 1934 that the use of amateur musicians for its musical functions would be restricted in the future.

It was made clear that amateurs as individuals were not allowed to belong to the RMK, whereas membership for professionals was mandatory. At AD functions, professional musicians had to gain permits from the Ortsmusikerschaftsleiter der RMK (local representative of the RMK).[14] Furthermore, the closest cooperation between local representatives of the RMK and local employment offices was encouraged. In order to overcome unemployment in music, the chamber decreed that musicians had to be paid for all public performances. Only the Landesleiter (provincial head) of the chamber could order exceptions to this general provision. Members of amateur groups desiring to earn money as individuals were required to obtain a permit from the local employment office and the local as well as provincial leadership of the RMK. Professional groups were always to have priority. In fact, amateur groups were not permitted to perform at non-internal functions of organizations without a permit of the Landesleiter of the RMK. This applied also to social events. Exceptions would be made twice a year: If the head of the Ortsmusikerschaft was notified two months in advance, amateurs were allowed to perform and charge for their services.[15] Professional musicians were defined in February 1935 by the "Third Ordinance for the Satisfaction of the Economic Situation in German Music Life," as all qualified and reliable persons who were required to belong to the RMK.[16]

The jurisdiction of the RMK extended to every sphere of German music. While the founding of independent organizations was forbidden, the chamber molded existing ones into professional subgroups within the central structure. Indeed, the first step of actual coordination within the chamber was effected through the integration of existing organizations, coordinated by the President's office which was divided into eight fields: general division, finance, economy, law, general cultural questions, propaganda, statistics and archives, and foreign matters. The President was aided by specialist assistants, deputies, a business manager with his assistants, and an executive board of at least two members. The president also appointed prominent representatives of professional subdivisions into an administrative advisory board which he could convene on his own authority. Structurally, the chamber was defined by the RKKG, and Goebbels functioned as supreme authority.[17]

The political powers of the central organization of culture and music were clearly spelled out in the authority to exclude musicians from the organization which was essential for employment. The chamber sent out the questionnaire and provisional membership cards, reviewed the returned information, and researched racial and political reliability in consultation with the Gestapo and other offices. Non-Aryans and otherwise "undesirables" who lacked "reliability" and "professional qualifications" were then formally excluded by letter signed by the RMK president, Richard Strauss first and after 1935 Peter Raabe—all in accordance with the First Implementing Ordinance of the RKKG.

Generally, the retention of the individual under review depended on his compatibility with the interests of the people and the state. Allowances were made for individual error, but every "real public enemy" and "incorrigibly dangerous individual" faced expulsion on grounds of standards which also involved questions of qualification. The chamber reviewed all these matters, the president of the chamber heard appeals, while the president of the RKK was listed as the highest authority in appeals. In order to be able to deal with membership questions efficiently, a *Hauptprüfungsausschuss* (Official Review Board) was instituted at the RMK, functioning as appeal board for membership applications which had been turned down at a lower level. Thus, the review board of the presidium and the administrative advisory board could override the local decision, supervising Nazi law as applied to all public employment in music.[18] By 1939 the RMK announced 341 expulsions. The review process declined at the onset of war, in part due to loss of personnel.

The RMK solidified its position by means of the economic and personnel measures, the patronage this entailed, and the resulting stabilization of musical life. Richard Strauss, the outstanding living composer of the day, was named the chamber's first president for obvious representational reasons. The deputy president, Wilhelm Furtwängler, also served propagandistic ends, suggesting the integration of the old establishment with the new order. The great composer and the great conductor were joined by active Nazis who made up the presidium: Gustav Havemann, Fritz Stein, Paul Graener, Gerd Karnbach, and Heinz Ihlert as managing director. The theatrical manager and musical conductor, Heinz Drewes, who functioned also in various other Nazi organizations, and Paul Graener served as vice presidents. These prestigious posts did not prevent the individuals from maintaining professional or other organizational positions. Drewes, for instance, served in Goebbels' ministry as head of a music department. In 1938 he was asked to organize an official Reich Music Censorship Office which he then headed.

On February 13, 1934, President Strauss delivered the opening address at the first convention of the chamber:

> The RKK—the dream and goal of all German musicians for decades— was created November 15, 1933, thus constituting a most important step in the direction of the reconstruction of our total German musical life. At this point I feel compelled to thank Reich Chancellor Adolf Hitler and Reich Minister Dr. Goebbels in the name of the entire musical profession of Germany for the creation of the RKKG.

Elaborating on the "illustrious history of German music," the "commitment to recreate unity between music and the German people which had been marred in the recent past," "musical taste" and "the poor economic situation of German music," he concluded:

> Since Adolf Hitler's seizure of power has not only resulted in a transformation of the political situation in Germany, but also of its culture, and since the National Socialist government has called to life the RMK, it is evident that the new Germany is not willing to allow artistic life to remain in isolation, but that new ways and means will be explored for the revival of our musical culture.[19]

The *Berliner Lokal-Anzeiger* reported that "prominent German personalities, especially of Berlin's music culture," attended the inauguration ceremonies at the Philharmonic. Havemann conducted the *Landesorchester* Gau Berlin in Beethoven's *Die Weihe des Hauses* and Wagner's *Huldigungsmarsch*, while chamber press chief, Dr. Friedrich Mahling, explained the significance and purpose of the organization to be that of harmonizing economic, legal and cultural interests under the subsuming concept of totality. The RMK was to give expression to "the unified will of the German musical profession, dedicated to the total national construction in the spirit of the new state." The inauguration concluded with a threefold *Sieg-Heil* to the *Führer* as champion and creator of national art and the playing of the Horst-Wessel song.[20]

Strauss participated in an official capacity. He was able to maintain his personal integrity throughout the Third Reich, although he lent himself to the Nazi projection of an integrated culture and its preeminent representatives. A few months after his opening address at the inauguration, he wrote to his long-time associate, the emigre Stefan Zweig, "Who told you that I have ventured so far politically? That I am miming the president of the RMK?"[21] After the Gestapo intercepted other compromising letters to Zweig, thus aggravating an already strained relationship between Strauss and the authorities—he had withheld his signature from the statutes because of the paragraph which excluded Jews from membership, had intervened in behalf of applicants for special consideration for membership, and had a way of making light of Nazis and their measures—he was pressured into resigning in June 1935. The *VB* announced that

the president of the RMK, Dr. Richard Strauss, asked the president of the RKK, Reich Minister Dr. Goebbels, to relieve him of duties as president of the RMK and as president of the professional estate of German composers on grounds of advanced age and poor health. Reich Minister Dr. Goebbels accepted the request and expressed his gratitude for previous services in a personal note. At the same time, Reich Minister Dr. Goebbels appointed GMD Prof. Dr. Peter Raabe as president of the RMK and the composer, Dr. Paul Graener, as president of the professional estate of German composers.[22]

The presidium was also changed in 1935. Heinz Ihlert retained his post as managing director, but Fritz Kaiser, Horst Sander, Franz Adam (official music expert at the national office of the NSDAP, in addition to leading the official Nazi Reich symphony orchestra—NSRSO), Hermann Müller-John (who was the *Leibstandarten-Obermusikmeister*, i.e., Hitler's body guard music maestro), Dr. Friedrich Krebs of the advisory *Staatsrat* (Council of State), and Hermann Stange joined Fritz Stein to form a board of far less representational value than before.[23] However, it was more responsive to Goebbels' ideas. Under Raabe's leadership purification of German music was pursued passionately. He developed into a most suitable representative of the intended symbiosis of National Socialism and music.

In most cases of membership applications, the local commission of the *Landesmusikerschaft*, composed of the president, the expert in the specific profession, the local legal advisor and the head of the professional organization, passed judgment on the basis of the chamber constitution. Individuals who were turned down had a right to appeal the local decision. Raabe presided over the Official Review Board of the chamber, joined by Ihlert as business manager, or his deputy, Kurt Karrasch, the heads of the coordinated professional subdivisions of the chambers or their business managers, and the head of the legal office of the chamber. Conditions of examinations also were carefully spelled out in legal language, covering technical competence and the general area of character, political, social and educational qualifications.[24] Every presidential act was carefully related to the constitutional base and published in the official bulletin of the chamber, the *AMRMK*. Name, residence, birth-place and birthdate were listed to identify the individual under review. Generally the president's signature was affixed to celebrated cases. For instance, he rejected the membership application of the conductor Heinrich Unger, "according to Paragraph 10 of the First Implementing Ordinance of the RKKG of November 1, 1933," inasmuch as "you do not possess the proper qualifications as defined by the RKKG." Hence, Unger lost the right to employment, although an appeal to Goebbels was still possible. Unger was already in London, where Raabe's letter reached him, but he requested membership, nonetheless, because he did not "want to lose his position without a fight."[25]

Raabe's letter was standard. Identical notes were addressed to numerous musicians, copies of which were sometimes forwarded to the Gestapo and other security agencies. The letters corresponded to the published lists in the official chamber bulletins printed in party and music journals and newspapers. The listing in public and the letters were sufficient on the basis of the general line, "since you do not possess the required qualifications as set forth in the the RKKG and as manifest in the practice of the National Socialist order." The Gestapo, other leading offices of state and party, and especially racial authorities pooled expert advice in enabling the president to reach a decision. The composer Wolfgang Stresemann, son of the former Reich Chancellor, was identified as half-Jewish, in addition to being disqualified from membership on the basis of the RKKG. The wording of the letter was the same as that of all others, and he immediately lost the right to employment in the realm of the chamber's jurisdiction.[26] In other cases, those of mixed "racial" background managed to retain positions in German orchestras upon appeal, especially at the Berlin Philharmonic, but elsewhere as well. As indicated above, a review of the racial background of the RMK membership fizzled out after outbreak of World War II in view of reductions in personnel required for the lengthy procedure.

In the eyes of a practicing musician in late-1933, effective coordination had been instituted. The state-created chamber had clearly become an agent of the state. The official bulletin, the *AMRMK* (with its 3,000 circulation) published all government edicts pertaining to music in matters of personnel, organization, policy and ideology, and when in June, 1934, Goebbels designated the

VB the official organ of the RKK, he decreed that henceforth all single culture chambers had to publish their bulletins therein.[27] Thus, bulletins of the RMK leadership reached a wider public. The music journals also printed all official announcements; and legal collections such as Schrieber's and Hoffmann's, handbooks by Schmidt-Leonard and Hinkel, and business manager Heinz Ihlert's publication of the goals, accomplishments and organization of the chamber in *Die Reichsmusikkammer*, 1935, were widely disseminated. The *AMRMK* published chamber directives, advice from superior offices, but also suggestions from the coordinated music community. As sounding board of all parties involved, the bulletin became the vehicle of intrigue and appeals of individuals and organizations which wanted to secure official support. At one time, the chamber was informed that a picture of the persona non grata, Adolf Georg Wilhelm Busch, violinist and composer, who by 1934 was residing in Switzerland, had appeared in the program notes of the Philharmonic, something, wrote Hugo Rasch, "German audiences certainly do not wish to see." Busch was involved again, when a publishing house, Fr. Kistner and C.F. Siegel, apologized for accidentally having sent the recommended score of a new violin concerto to the same Busch and signed the accompanying letter, "*Mit deutschem Gruss Heil Hitler.*" Busch's return of the prospectus and a written protest against the *Heil Hitler*, "an insult to residents of Switzerland," resulted in the public apology to the RMK. All communications were forwarded and published.[28]

Organizational and policy matters transmitted to the chamber via Goebbels' office were printed in the official bulletin and were prone to reach grotesque levels, as in the condemnation of the inclination of certain Germans to prefer foreign to German things and to assume foreign names. "This tendency must be fought with all means, and the musical professions must stand in the front line of battle." The president of the RMK ordered "on the authority vested in me by Paragraph 25 of the First Implementing Ordinance of the RKKG" that members of the corporate music profession were forbidden to assume foreign-sounding names for whatever reason in place of their civil names. This directive also applied to the identification of certain chamber music of other musical groups. German musicians or musical groups known by foreign or foreign-sounding names had to change their names by October 31, 1934 in accordance with this ordinance of September 29, 1934. Violations of this ordinance constituted grounds for expulsion from the music chamber for reason of "unreliability," as specified in Paragraph 10 of the First Amendment of the RKK.[29]

Two ordinances of October 16, 1935, and June 4, 1936, specified that members of the RMK had to inform the chamber of all pseudonyms. It was stressed again that no foreign or foreign-sounding names were permitted, and any name might be rejected by the chamber.[30] Ordinances against "undesirable and dangerous music" were repeatedly published in the bulletin, reprinted in the *VB* and the professional journals. The theme was quite consistent. Raabe availed himself of the power to purge individuals and certain types of music, always on the same authority of the RKKG, amendments, and previous ordinances. In December 1937, he reminded music publishers and dealers of foreign music to present copies of the product before the Official Censorship Office of the RMVP in advance of any distribution in Germany. If certain music had been judged "undesirable," its distribution henceforth would be forbidden. These strictures applied also to free samples, which were not to exceed six hundred copies. The performance of free samples was not permitted.[31]

On the same authority, in the same spirit and in consultation with the Reich Ministers of Propaganda and Economics, Raabe decreed on October 10, 1935, that publishers of and dealers in music materials, members of respective corporate professional subdivisions of the RMK, were ordered to immediately notify the chamber of publishers, dealers and the sale of works of persons who had left the German Reich after the Nazi seizure of power. Noncompliance with the decree would result in the loss of membership in the chamber.[32] The subsequent dismissals became a fundamental feature of the time, publicly announced and executed. Each individual case was placed within the purview of the new legal structure, defended by ideological propaganda and carried out by a coordinated administration.

Directives published in the official bulletins could originate in some higher party office. In addition to Goebbels, other leaders showed their interest in the proper functioning of the RMK. On August 6, 1934, Hess issued a directive to all party organizations to lend their fullest support to the chamber.[33] Even Hitler's special desires were published in the bulletin at the instigation of the Propaganda Ministry. In July 1937, the bulletin stated that the *March of the Nibelung*, performed annually at opening ceremonies of party conventions as accompaniment to those marching in with flags, was no longer to be heard on everyday and profane occasions. The march was to be reserved for party conventions. The administrators throughout the RMK were held responsible for the proper observation of the decree. In another announcement of November 29, 1938, Raabe informed the musical profession of Hitler's desire regarding the *Badenweiler March*, which was to be performed generally only in his presence. Hitler also had decided that the German national anthem was to be played in a solemn manner, giving specific instruction as to tempo, while the Horst-Wessel Song was to have a faster beat in the manner of a revolutionary fighting song.[34]

While the leadership of the RMK issued directives, organizers at all levels participated in national conventions to plan implementation of national policy. The first professional convention of the chamber, in February 1934, was to introduce musicians to the new reality. Fritz Stege reported that the "administrative council" convened for four days, professional departments were introduced by appointed leaders, and various representatives of the professions and provincial administrators became familiarized with the general picture. The inner organization of the chamber was discussed, economic problems were introduced, the legal structure was explained, and the general policy toward musical culture tied all else together.

The general approach of the participants was reminiscent of earlier policy statements. Unemployment was still to be eliminated, education and the HJ were to be coordinated through both national organizations, and a new music culture was to be established in the AD. The comprehensive planning covered new education projects, a new budget "for the revival of music" and elimination of amateurs and part-time musicians from the realm. Concertizing was to be handled in collaboration with the *Deutsche Bühne* (German Stage Association) and the KdF, and conditions for employment at resorts were explained. The relationship to local employment offices was clarified, and copyright regulations were interpreted. The chamber absorbed individuals through existing organizations. Ideological speeches covered every realm of music. It was at this convention that Peter Raabe gave the widely-read and -cited address on the "Reconstruction of German Musical Culture." He referred to Germany's network of stages, orchestras, choral organizations and academies, all of which were now organized on a national level. Generally, the theme of speeches touched on earlier divisiveness, on struggle and competition, "at last" overcome. Indeed, he claimed that the RMK had merged 150 previously independent associations.[35]

The RMK was so structured as to comprise existing professional associations and to continue to absorb more in the future. Traditional institutions, associations, societies, groups and the provisional organizations of Nazi origin thus lost independence or their loosely coordinated status through integration within the all-pervasive and unified system. The structure stood, but the breakdown along professional lines, as published repeatedly in legal publications and throughout the journal literature, underwent some changes. In early 1934 some associations were listed which were renamed in various later forms (1935, 1937) and actually dropped from the organization by 1940, while some additional groupings appeared at the later stage. The following 1934 breakdown will be given here, in its German formulation and in translation: A. *Reichsfachschaft Komponisten (Berufsstand der deutschen Komponisten—* Reich Professional Estate of German Composers), first president Strauss, then Graener; B. *Reichsmusikerschaft* (RMS) (Reich Musicians), president

Havemann, divided again into, 1. *Fachschaft Orchestermusiker* (Orchestra Musicians), II. *Fachschaft Ensemblemusiker, freistehende Instrumentalisten und Sänger* (Ensemble Musicians, Free-lance Instrumentalists, and Singers), III. *Fachschaft Musikerzieher* (Music Educators), IV. *Fachschaft Konzertierende Solisten und Kapellmeister* (Concertizing Soloists and Conductors), V. *Fachschaft Evangelische Kirchenmusiker* (Protestant Church Musicians), IV. *Fachschaft Katholische Kirchenmusiker* (Catholic Church Musicians); C. *Reichsfachschaft Konzertwesen* (Concert Promotion and Management), president Hans Sellschopp and deputy Dr. Otto Benecke, divided again into provisional organizations of 1. *Fachgruppe Ernste Musik* (Serious music), a. *Arbeitsgemeinschaften für Konzertwesen* (Committee . . .), b. *Allgemeiner Deutscher Musikverein* (established concert society), II. *Fachgruppe Unterhaltungsmusik* (Entertainment Music), *Reichskartell der Musikveranstalter Deutschlands* (Entertainment Music Producers), III. *Fachgruppe Konzert-und Vortragskunstvermittlung* (Promotion), *Verband der deutschen Konzertdirektionen* (covers producers, agents, promoters); D. *Reichsfachschaft Chorwesen und Volksmusik* (Choral and Folk Music), in 1934 this section was divided into I. *Chorwesen* (included choral associations) and II. *Volksmusik* (Folk Music); E. *Reichsfachschaft Musikalienverleger* (Music Publishers), first called *Deutscher Musikalien-Verleger Verein* (Association of German Music Publishers); F. *Reichsfachschaft Musikalienhändler* (Music Dealers), first called *Reichsverband der deutschen Musikalienhändler* (Association of German Music Dealers); G. *Arbeitsgemeinschaften zur Förderung des deutschen Instrumentengewerbes* (Promotion of the German Instrument Trade); H. *Phonogilde, Fachverhand für Schallplattenherstellung und - Handel* (Production and Sales of Records).[36]

In the early months of 1934, the music journals published directives of the central organization to the effect of ordering the integration of existing associations. Professionals everywhere were reminded of the necessity to join, through their organizations at first, then as members of the appropriate professional division; meanwhile, appointed leaders organized their domains and presided over professional conventions. Even though the integrated associations maintained some degree of identity and resisted total coordination in 1934, the system increasingly asserted itself.

Composers: Supreme Expectations

The higher priority given to the composers—listed variously between 3500 and 6000 RMK members—in the Nazi scheme was acknowledged by their being listed first. Legally constituted November 15, 1933, composers were highly valued and expected to continue the world-renowned tradition of German creativity and thus provide the substance of Nazi claims to cultural superiority. In its first years in power a confident Nazi state organized its composers around the belief of a musical renaissance, shaped by the Nazi revolution and in the spirit of Goebbels' "romanticism of steel." In early 1933 the KfdK had sponsored the production of new "German" music, particularly of young composers like the teenager Gottfried Müller, the embodiment of the hope for a new genius who would capture the new Germany in music. Other organizations like the NSKG, governmental and party offices at all levels, party officials from Hitler on down to local Gau leaders, and musical institutions followed the KfdK example and sponsored competitions, festivals and commissions for *arteigene* songs, cantatas, oratorios, operas and strictly instrumental works.

Thousands of compositions with *völkisch* and Nazi texts and even musical content and form defined as German were sent to German stages, publishers, and the various party and state sponsors—including the Reich Chancellory which received works with Hitler texts and/or dedications. The overproduction of this "national kitsch" (the term applied in November to the songbooks by Reinhold Zimmermann for schools, the people and the SA) led to a request, published in the *ZfM* (October 1933) by the Chancellory to have unsolicited compositions sent to appropriate publishing houses instead for evaluation and possible publication, and to Goebbels' suggestion at the opening of the RKK on November 15, 1933 that the period of experimentation be over.[37]

The formal organization was to professionalize composition. Nonetheless, the admitted composers were still hurting economically, in spite of the purges of Jews and other inadmissible composers, and they obviously welcomed the opportunity to have their works published and performed as much as possible; they continued to covet state subsidies, fellowships, prizes, commissions, the security of academic positions, bureaucratic posts and honoraria for various services. The elite composers of serious music were especially acclaimed and subsidized by the state by being assured a third of the royalties distributed by Stagma, even though their earnings warranted far less—a commitment which was honored until 1940. By mid-1936 at the latest, Goebbels had lost faith in prospects of a new Nazi music and his increasing support of music's entertainment functions spoke to the interest of *U-musik* (entertainment music), articulated bravely by Norbert Schultze, the celebrated composer of "Bombs over England" and other popular wartime songs especially for propaganda films.

When the war turned against Germany, all music—"some for everyone,"—including classical music—was to entertain, distract and reinforce the will to continue fighting. In the early years of the RMK, however, the composers of serious music received the most benefits and distinctions. They continued to offer their services; they joined the party, formed party organizations—like that of Nazi composers founded in 1934 in Duisburg, for which Paul Graener, Richard Trunk, Hermann Singer and Julius Weissmann were especially active in recruiting young composers—and wrote Nazi music for party and state functions and music festivals. Younger composers were promoted everywhere. Those with proper commitment and especially the Pg's were performed at the established stages, by the numerous party orchestras, at the festivals and were aired over the national radio station under its new musical director, Max Donisch.

Goebbels' realization of the need for continuity thus led him to enlist the further support of Richard Strauss, by also appointing him president of the "corporate profession of German composers. As head of the composers' organization he was aided by three appointees, Hugo Rasch, Gerd Kaernbach, and Julius Kopsch. The so-called *Führerrat* (leadership council) of composers was to deal with problems facing the profession. It included some distinguished German musicians: Max Donisch, Willy Geisler, Paul Graener, Joseph Haas, Siegmund von Haussegger, Paul Hindemith, Eduard Künneke, Hans Pfitzner, E.N. Von Reznicek, Clemens Schmalstich, Georg Schumann, Hermann Unger. A *General Rat* (assembly) was instituted as supervisory organ in special areas: Franz von Blon, Hermann Blume, Hans Bullerian, Siegfried Burgstaller, Carl Ehrenberg, Franz Friedl, Georg Görner, Heinrich Kaminski, I.J. Mraczek, Arno Pardon, Hermann Reutter, Richard Trunk, Georg Vollerthun, Julius Weismann, Felix Woyrsch.[38] This list was published in March of 1934, and included Nazis and several names which were shortly to be anathema.

At the first RMK meeting in March, Strauss proudly announced that the new state had acknowledged the legal status of the corporate profession, that it included distinguished representatives of the German profession, and that "creative artists are in need of the backing of law and corporate organization." But, at the composers' first professional meeting in February before representatives of the international press and foreign composers who were sympathetic to Nazi goals, he had also stressed the composers' responsibilities toward the nation and insisted on proper conduct and solidarity with the policies of the Nazi state. The composers learned that the RMK was an organ of the state and that music had to conform and be affirmative. Meanwhile, the composers' organization spread locally as some *Gau* representatives were appointed already in late-1933: Carl Zander for Berlin and Kurmark, Hermann Unger for the Rhineland and Westfalia, Ludwig Lurmann for the Nordmark, and Dr. Sachse for Munich. Strauss wrote that the leadership principle was to be observed everywhere.[39] The press reported all organizational

developments, that membership in the chamber was compulsory for composers and that all composers who wished to publish their work in Germany
had to apply to Strauss for membership in writing.[40]

On the surface the chamber organization seemed to invest composers with
broad powers of self-governance and administration, but in reality their professional department became a captive organization through which membership, conditions of employment and compositional activity were controlled.
Composers were exclusively represented by the chamber and Stagma. Indeed, a work could be performed in public only if the composer delegated
authority for the box office receipts to Stagma, the only authorized German
concert agency. Earnings were returned to the composer after costs and profit
of Stagma were deducted.[41] In practice, the staggering percentage of
withholding caused much dissatisfaction.[42] This Stagma was no external
agency; its governing board included the president of the corporation of composers, the president of the Reich Writer Chamber, and the president of the
corporation of music publishers, and its business was handled by a manager
who was appointed by the Reich government in consultation with the president of the RMK. Thus, Stagma theoretically functioned as an agent of the
composer's interests;[43] in reality, it functioned as another means of control,
its ordinances not being subject to collective bargaining.

Problems over remuneration and ideology continued, but after each conflict resolution the regime's controls were strengthened. Upon the resignation of Strauss from his dual post, the far less acclaimed but more agreeable
Paul Graener was appointed president of the composer's organization. Hans
Hinkel, who was responsible for Graener's rise in the chamber because of
his "ability to bring a sense of comradery into the profession," addressed the
profession under the presidency of his protege in 1935. Confident that the
leadership of the RMK and its subgroups was now reliable, he reassured the
composers of the state's trust. He added that the RKK would soon cease to
deal directly with matters of the individual profession, thus announcing corporate independence of the Nazified profession—having already given up its
function as publisher of music. Shortly, the dream of National Socialists would
be realized. Music, he announced, would be constituted in two departments,
that of creative music and that of reproductive music. The state would see
to it that "representatives of German music will have no obstacles and that
youth will have the possibility to march forward." Naturally, he was referring to "true inner art of the people, eternally rooted in Germany's soul."
Professional organizations were thus totally integrated, subject to the leadership principle and mindful of their social responsibility. Hinkel concluded that
"no man, no matter what his talent, has the right to give direction to the
politics of culture. Political leadership in cultural affairs is reserved for those

who have experienced National Socialism in its struggle and thus are able to realize its goals."[44]

The Corporate Body of Musicians

Division B, the corporate estate of professional practicing musicians was not only a self-contained subdivision of the chamber, but also the avenue by which musicians obtained membership in the chamber. This function was derived from its earlier status, before the RMK was founded. The earlier *Reichskartell* of German musicians constituted the basis of the chamber and its division B. Again, Gustav Havemann, the old KfdK activist and president of the *Reichskartell*, was appointed president of this new *Reichsmusikerschaft* (RMS) with its more than 80,000 members—the largest division of the entire RKK.[45]

At its sectional convention—Gau Berlin-Brandenburg-Grenzmark in Berlin November 14, 1934—Havemann explained the nature of professional estates within the legal constitution of the new order—a most instructive introduction to conditions in the RMK in general and to totalitarian claims. Through Havemann's and also Heinz Ihlert's reviews before the RMS— published in the December 1934 issue of the *ZfM*—we learn about the dissolution of old associations and how they were reconstituted within the chamber. Compulsory membership was confirmed, but so was a required RMS membership card—somewhat confusing, as commentators referred to the RMK and RMS interchangeably. What is clear is that efforts were made to identify musicians as musicians even when other organizations like the DAF might lay claim to a musician's status as a worker. Early in the year DAF membership had been dropped in favor of the RMK card in the case of musicians employed at German stages—one of those victories of Goebbels over his rivals in the area of cultural life. It had been argued that the RMK, too, was a labor organization and that duplicate membership was unnecessary. Theatre employees had to join their corporate profession, either the theatre chamber or the RMK.[46] The Association of German Stage Employees was officially absorbed by the RMS February 15, 1934.[47]

On May 15, 1934, finally, the government had announced the Theatre Law, under which all performance stages of Germany had been placed within the jurisdiction of the Propaganda Ministry. Stage directors, managers, producers, conductors and performers were required to receive ministerial or delegated permission for employment. Through the RMS, the RMK had indeed emerged as the sole representative body of musicians—Havemann having also led in the fight against private concert agencies. RMS posts were created throughout

Germany, always in touch with the central organization and in harmony with the local authority of the party and civil administrations.[48]

In celebration of national unity, the reiterated accomplishments of the revolution and future prospects of German music, Havemann welcomed members of the RMS of Gau Berlin-Brandenburg-Grenzmark and top officials of party and state, Dr. Walter Funk, as Vice-President of the RKK, the Lord Mayor of Berlin Dr. Heinrich Sahm, representatives of the army, state and city authorities of the NSDAP and its subdivisions, of the *AD* and of the arts and sciences. The presence of these dignitaries was to lend official support to the most numerous cultural estate of the Third Reich, proof of Hitler's commitment to the arts. "The German musician enjoys a privileged position in comparison to musicians in other countries because he is constituted as member of a public and legal corporation in the RMK." Havemann spoke of the traditional musical excellence of even smallest German towns which were now part of a new totality. Every professional musician was to be regarded as an upholder of German culture. Through the RKKG the professional musician had gained his place in the new Germany. "We thank our leader, Adolf Hitler."[49]

While the central RMS represented the practicing musical profession, it also served as administrative unit over several subdivisions which also received administrations, held conventions and organized their domains with respect to member musicians. All professional orchestra musicians, soloists, ensemble musicians and professional conductors were grouped respectively in subdivisions I and II. Conductors who held teaching posts or led amateur choral groups belonged to other divisions. And, again, through membership in the professional chamber, represented by the RMS, professionals had priority in any job situation.[50] Through coordinated stages and other institutions all areas of possible employment were thus secured, both serious and entertainment music having been affected. Managements of resort places also had to consult with the RMK through a special office for such entertainment in order to contract an orchestra.[51] Also, public places of entertainment such as inns, restaurants and cafes had to deal with the chamber directly because only musicians represented by the chamber were allowed to perform in public places. The chamber also issued directives to musicians in the film industry. Film musicians and composers under the age of 25 were required to have permission of the chamber president to be employed.[52]

The conductor Hermann Abendroth organized education within the chamber, structurally listed under RMS, Section III. All areas of music education were included, although jurisdiction was disputed by the Education Ministry of Rust, especially in Prussia. In view of the emphasis on youth and hopes for a new Nazi music culture in the first years of the Third Reich, it is understandable that the RMK tried hard to control professional training. At the first convention of German music educators within the RMS October 13-15, 1934, in Eisenach, Franz Rühlmann of the Music Academy at Berlin spoke on "The Construction of Training Schools for Professional Musicians" as an essential feature for cultural regeneration. The chamber set out to improve the preparation for professional life, delimiting this effort against the areas of general music education in school and through private teachers. Professional musicians were defined, and attention focused on orchestra musicians who were encouraged to attend music academies or conservatories in order to gain the necessary experience of practice in large groups. The state had to set standards throughout music education, so that the children of economically depressed backgrounds would receive equal opportunity. Apparently, the situation was quite out of step with the egalitarian ideals of National Socialism. All in all, Rühlmann concluded, only poor schooling was available for professional orchestra musicians at the time.[53]

Training schools for professionals constituted only one area of the chamber division. The whole education section had developed out of the provisional *Reichsverband Deutscher Tonkünstler und Musiklehrer* (RDTM)—all members of which had joined the RMS, department III collectively—led by Havemann and Arnold Ebel, the latter leading the subsection private music teachers of the education division, i.e., Department III. Schrieber published a whole set of laws governing and standardizing private music lessons. All music teachers were required to become chamber members. A pay scale, subjects to be taught and other teacher-pupil relationships were standardized. For instance, minimum pay for a lesson, if given only once a week, was set at 8 RM.[54] The relationship between teacher and student was to be regulated through a form which had to be filled out by both. First-year music students were not allowed to practice music professionally. In the second year, students at music academies were permitted to become provisional members of the chamber.[55] All heads of music education institutions, as teachers, had to join the chamber, section B, III.[56] The corporate profession of music educators was so regulated as to protect professional interests. The overlapping of authority again caused some confusion, especially in relationship to Rust's domain, but the priority of the RMK was generally upheld in practice. The conventions of section III of the RMS increasingly represented all music instructors of Germany. At Eisenach in October 1934, lectures covered every area of music education. Professional schools, regular schools and private lessons were covered by law and corporate organization on the basis of the general principles which governed all of music.

The integration of Church musicians within the chamber, section RMS, followed the pattern set in 1933. The Civil Service Act with its Aryan paragraph was applied to both Catholic and Protestant musicians. In August 1935, Hinkel informed the SA that "Jews were still playing organ for Germans of Christian faith at their Church services...National Socialism will protect the German people from this sacrilege against Christianity."[57] Indeed, one month after this speech, all "non-Aryan" Church musicians lost their membership in the RMK, obtained originally by means of collective incorporation of the profession.[58] The Church offered no resistance in behalf of its musicians. *Gleichschaltung* assumed radical proportions, even in the domain of most powerful social institutions. Karl Straube, the much-respected Thomaskantor of Leipzig, led the Office of Church musicians which was incorporated in sections V and VI of the RMS. (See Chapter I for detail.) Around this time the final expulsions from the RMS were also affected as a consequence of the procedures set off by the questionnaire about ancestry and reliability.

Concert Management and Promotion

Another comprehensive professional division of the chamber, section C, of concert management and promotion (administered by an *Amt für Konzertwesen*—Office for Concert Management) facilitated and regulated the actual performance of music at places of public entertainment, concert halls and stages throughout Germany. All other aspects of music life related to this important office and its local branches which functioned through a local representative, the *Städtischer Musikbeauftragter* whose honorary position was confirmed by the RMK and the Organization of German Municipalities— *Deutscher Gemeindetag*. In order to revitalize and bring order to German music culture, these local representatives—drawn from local town administrations, party officials and musical life—were appointed generally by mayors, in consultation with the local party office and the local musicians' organization, by early 1935 in 900 to 1,000 towns of over 5,000 population,[59] and by August 1938 in 1,140 towns—approved in each instance by the RMK. These officials who had to possess administrative ability, love music and be politically reliable, regulated and stimulated local music life and were responsible for the season's overall calendar for musicial events; they also functioned as censors, as all programs had to be submitted to them for approval. In conflict situations with the different concert societies, promoters and agencies whose programs they coordinated, the central *Amt* (concert office) at the RMK had to be consulted.[60] Fred Prieberg concedes that by and large the *Musikbeauftragten* played a positive role in bringing order into chaotic conditions, reducing deficits and filling concert halls.[61]

The affairs of this section of the RMK reveal the chamber's well-advertised preoccupation with improving the economic condition of German musicians while simultaneously controlling concert life and programs throughout the country in the service of what RMK business manager Heinz Ihlert acknowledged in a 1935 review of "RMK goals, achievements and organization" as the "cultish" intentions of National Socialism. The central concert office did not dissolve existing concert societies, agencies and promotional enterprises but, instead, under the leadership of Hans Sellschopp and Otto Benecke regulated, integrated and thus benefitted from existing ones—public, private and party institutions, including the distinguished ADMV, which, at its annual festival introduced contemporary music, while also promoting the formation of new societies and programs. At the same time, the office aspired to officially represent soloists and ensembles, signing in their behalf in less than a year in 1935, 1,100 contracts for individuals and finding engagements for 2,139 ensembles. The Nazis claimed the exclusive right to represent subsidized German artists, especially abroad. A foreign office of the section arranged for foreign exchanges with 31 nations between October 1934 and March 31, 1935, in consequence of which, 180 German musicians performed abroad in that period, 113 foreigners in Germany.[62]

Stagma also became a corporate member of this concert office. Its contracts in behalf of its composers with the different concert societies and agencies thus were in-house and saved administrative costs. Founded September 20, 1933, Stagma initially had signed wage agreements with the provisional *Reichskartell* of German Concert Agencies on December 20, 1933. Other contracts followed in behalf of their clients, who by then had also been organized within the RKK: film theatres, choral groups—especially the huge DSB, folk music organizations, the National Broadcasting Company, the League of German Entertainment and Resort Associations, the DAF, HJ, NSKG, KdF, etc. Thus, Stagma functioned as exclusive agent for composers—collecting and distributing revenues but, true to Nazi principles, also negotiating contracts with users of their delegated product with whom it shared common organization and purpose, all under the careful scrutiny of the president of the RKK.[63]

Romanticism of Steel in Choral and Folk Music

Lest the RMK become the exclusive domain of an elite and professional establishment as per narrowly interpreted statute, preoccupied with vested economic interests in consequence of the obvious needs and pretensions of a depressed professional estate and the Nazi state, Goebbels was determined to also include the popular amateur choral and folk music organizations in his empire —the musical *völkisch*-romantic core of National Socialism—the repository of kindred sentiment and a massive vehicle for propaganda. Especially the huge male choral organization, founded back in 1862 in dedication to both the joy of group singing and nationalist causes, the *Deutscher Sängerbund* (DSB) required little ideological adjustment in the Third Reich.

Early on the DSB and its leader Georg Brauner welcomed the new regime. (See Chapter I.) Party membership grew, and in April the party reorganized the DSB as an exclusive Nazi male choral organization. Rival nationalist groups were forced into joining it, while the largest workers' choral association, the Social Democratic *Deutscher Arbeitersängerbund* (DAS) was rejected, even though it had dissolved by its own leadership vote on May 25, 1933 and applied to associate with the DAF, the giant Nazi labor organization. Typically, SA units had disrupted DAS events (as those of communists); DAS properties were confiscated, member groups banned. However, many individuals and some renamed groups were admitted—the best-known being Heinz Thiessen's *Berliner Singegemeinschaft*—Berlin Singing Community (formerly his *Junger Chor*—Young Choir). DSB membership soared close to 800,000 and 22,000-member groups by 1939—an ideological force clearly appreciated by the state for manipulation.

The DSB's genuine *völkisch* spirit also posed several problems for Goebbels. Politically, the organization identified more with the KfdK and Rosenberg, who was even selected its honorary leader in early 1934. It had become caught up in the intra-party struggle against Goebbels, had opposed application for inclusion in the RMK and was even briefly banned before being reconstituted to the satisfaction of Goebbels under new management when Brauner was replaced by the teacher, Pg. and Lord Mayor of Herne, Albert Meister. Ideologically, as well, Goebbels had to assert party prerogative. The songbooks had to be purged of their religious and sentimentally romantic features—not to mention the persistent inclusion of Mendelssohn songs—and replaced by music in the spirit of "romanticism of steel" and explicit Nazi texts; passive sentiment and habits of authoritarian acceptance by political commitment and participation; the single and traditional male chorus by a combative column of National Socialism—a "unified front of the German chorus," in the words of Section D leader Fritz Stein.[64] The singers and especially their leaders and organizers were reschooled at camps, retreats, conventions and festivals; new guidelines were published in the widely circulated *DSB Zeitung* (*DSBZ*), a yearbook and related party organs. Party songs and choral works like the well-known *Feier der neuen Front* ("Celebration of the New Front") of Richard Trunk with text of Baldur von Schirach and hundreds of other nationalist and ritualistic compositions were published, distributed, integrated into the regular songbook repertoire and performed over and over again. The traditional literature was reduced to about a fourth in a DSB Songbook (1934)—purged, focused and made easier. Instructions were issued for simplifying singing, too, to decrease the frequency of performances and of compositions for the traditional four voices, but also to increase offerings for single voice in order to facilitate audience participation.[65]

Lastly, the economic concerns of professionals had to be addressed. While the RMS was apprehensive about the competition of this massive musical army, the *Frankfurter Zeitung* reported on March 23, 1934 that the DSB as an "amateur organization" had refused to apply for membership in the designated section of the RMK because the latter was meant for professionals exclusively. The leader of Section D of the RMK for choral and folk music, Fritz Stein, argued to the contrary that the RMK was intended for all who were active in "the dissemination and creation of music." Moreover, most other choral and music lover societies had already applied in compliance with the law as interpreted by him, beginning with the *Reichsverband für gemischte Chöre Deutschlands* (Reich Association of Mixed Choral Groups of Germany), *Die Vereinigung der Lehrer-Gesangvereine* (League of Teacher Singing Groups), *Der Bund der Lobeda-Chore* (League of Lobeda Choirs) and the *Hamburger Sängerschaft* (Hamburg Singers). Stein added that integration addressed organizations, not individuals. The editors of the *Frankfurter* noted approvingly that negotiations were moving in the right direction subsequent to the resignations of the executive board of the DSB and the new presidency of Albert Meister. The DSB had indeed agreed to consider the needs of professionals by looking for unemployed professional musicians and conductors whenever appropriate and possible and to reduce its role in publishing, a concern of the Publishers Section of the RMK.[66]

Economic concessions—at least on paper, personnel changes in leadership, and fundamental ideological agreement finally resulted in the formal integration of the DSB in March, 1934. The DSB's monopoly was confirmed; regional chapters were tightly reorganized into Gau associations; many smaller choral groups were absorbed by larger ones and the leadership principle was formally instituted at all levels—although frequently disregarded in practice. Integration was actually quite easy once the agreement was finalized. Individuals had no options since they joined through their groups. The "First Ordinance for the Satisfaction of Conditions in German Choral Life" mandated membership by May 15, 1934. Non-member groups were no longer allowed to perform. Membership cards were handed out by the RMS. The organization spread through appointed *Landesleiter* who facilitated the application of new groups and supervised local affairs. Under Stein's direction the Reich associations were dissolved and replaced by professional divisions. Division D guaranteed the uniform treatment of all questions of amateur vocal and instrumental music. In the legal language of Hoffmann and Ritter, 1936, three subordinate groups constituted Division D: I. *Deutscher Sängerbund* as departmental association of all male choral groups; II. Reich association of mixed choral groups; and III. Department of Folk Music.[67] New member groups were joined in one of the subdivisions. Such groups as the League of German Harmonica-Orchestras, for instance, were grouped in section III.[68] The process of integration continued.

In November, 1939 the RMK announced the dissolution of the Protestant Church Choirs and Trombone Choirs, for reasons of "simplified administration." "Insofar as Church and trombone choirs were active outside the Church, they were ordered to apply for membership in one of the three amateur categories of the RMK." The DSB would absorb male choirs, the Reich association of mixed choirs such additional groups, and the department of folk music the "trombone choirs."[69] Under the leadership of Dr. Max Burkhardt the folk music section also expanded greatly, which included no less than 10,647 folk music bands of every variety and predominantly in rural areas.[70] As Department of Folk Music it was the only authorized professional corporation of the RMK for all associations active in the instrumental performance of folk music. Amateurs and professionals were thus joined in the chamber and subjected to the contracts signed corporately with Stagma, October 1, 1934.[71]

Slow to join, the DSB emerged a most reliable embodiment and propagator of National Socialism at its festivals, official state and party functions and in its press. Controls were barely necessary over this association of patriotic singers. Some discord existed as individuals dropped memberships in protest against forced mergers. Others missed traditional local color and the excitement of competitions eliminated by the uniformity of national organizations and ideological themes. Remnants of the transformed workers' groups, too, maintained an awareness of earlier solidarity at their gatherings and rehearsals, as noted in recollections of members.[72] But, generally, the transformation from "the singing people" into a "marching column" enjoyed popular support. Choral groups were able to perform in customary fashion—channeled and manipulated, but also supported and flattered.

The activity and planning culminated in the monumental Twelfth National DSB Festival in Breslau, July 22-August 1, 1937—also the Seventy-Fifth anniversary celebration of the organization (surprisingly, the only such event during the Third Reich), prepared for years by Goebbels who clearly appreciated the propagandistic value of the DSB. Organized like a military parade, 130,000 participants sang, marched, swung flags and Swastika banners in projection of the militant *Volksgemeinschaft*. They performed in concert halls and under the sky. Hermann Behr conducted the Breslau Philharmonic, an enormous chorus and a vast array of soloists in Handel's Festival Oratorium. Offerings ranged from classical music to traditional choral literature, folk music and Nazi works. The spectacle included an address by Hitler praising the DSB and the significance of the German song for Germans within and outside German borders, thus signaling the theme of a return of Germans to the homeland—*heim ins Reich*—which had been a propaganda objective of the DSB all along.

As early as 1933 one of the most notable member groups, the Berlin Teacher Chorus had toured German borderlands. Other groups followed the example as the DSB gained tremendous popularity among Germans in neighboring countries. In March, 1934 it helped found an Association of German Choirs Abroad. Their propagandistic efforts were in accord with the political orientation of the DSB which, as Prieberg has noted, by 1938 boasted a 35 percent party membership, 14 percent membership in the SA and 22 percent involved in Nazi officialdom. DSB Gau leaders then were almost exclusively Pg's.[73] Small wonder that Nazi texts were enthusiastically adopted, performances staged for party and state events and in honor of party officials who liked to be known as DSB promoters, and competitions for performance and composition dedicated to their powerful sponsors. The height of distinction was reached when a group was given permission to sing for Hitler, especially for his birthday, April 20.

Section D of the RMK directed one of the more successful musical activities of the Third Reich in realization of the *völkisch* ideas discussed in Chapter I. The DSB in particular embodied and propagated the ideology in music most effectively. Though generally confirming traditional norms in musical expression, the sheer weight of demand for music, for new Nazi music, yielded contemporary production, an undermining of the traditional *Liedertafel* and even occasional links to the modernist developments in serious music. Indeed, the latter were tolerated within the purified *völkisch* environment.

Music Publishers and Dealers

For purposes of uniformity, completeness, and economic advantage, the publishing, distribution and sales of music materials were also integrated within the comprehensive chamber structure. As contributors to the "dissemination of musical culture," publishers and producers of music materials, sheet-music and other music literature were collectively grouped under Division E of the chamber, the *Deutscher Musikalien-Verleger Verein*. Although the RKKG had provided for the incorporation of the profession into the chamber, an additional specific law was published by the RMK in its official bulletin, September 7, 1934, making the production and distribution of music materials contingent on membership in the chamber, section E. The law was to go into effect by October 1, 1934, by which time membership cards were to be obtained and carried at all times. Retailers, including foreign dealers in Germany, were prohibited from dealing with any publishers or manufacturers who did not possess the membership card.[74] The loosely organized association was to be transformed into the characteristic professional division, although Hoffmann still listed the profession as *Berufsstand der deutschen Musikverleger* (Professional Estate of German Music Publishers).

The final phase of total coordination was effected in 1938 with the official dissolution of the earlier association, reinstituted as the Department of Music Publishers. Its management took directives from the chamber president before and after the latest law.[75] However, coordination was to be accomplished with the aim of total elimination of even the name of former organizations.

Dealers in music materials were organized in the same manner as publishers. This complementary process began with the creation of Division F of the Chamber, as *Reichsverband der deutschen Musikalienhändler*. Again, on July 30, 1934 a supplementary law issued more specific directives. Dealers in music materials on the wholesale and retail level had to belong to the chamber, section F, in order to carry on business. New dealers had to gain the approval of the president of the RMK. Publishers and wholesale business representatives were limited in supplying materials to only those dealers possessing chamber membership cards. Indeed, any dealer in music materials had to be a member of the RMK.[76] As was the case with section E, the association of dealers, section F of the chamber, was dissolved April 1, 1938, being transformed into the *Fachchaft Musikalienhändler* (Profession of Dealers in Music Materials). Again, this professional subdivision retained its basic structure, management and general policy. For the sake of uniformity in terminology and apparent streamlining of the chain of command, the president ordered such changes.[77]

RMK Reality and Achievements

The RMK had indeed become a reality in the lives of German musicians and the organizational and legal measures were implemented in the following years both nationally and locally. Though a captive profession, numerous members happily contributed to the organizational framework of their condition. They not only performed, composed and declared solidarity; they also wrote the directives and did the organizing. Music teachers, instrumentalists, conductors and the occasional GMD like Herbert von Karajan in Aachen were the local *Musikbeauftragten* who regulated and supervised local music programs in cooperation with the RMK and the local town administration. Unemployment was nearly eliminated by 1939, music thrived and played a vital part in the cultural program of the Nazi state, and the RMK took credit for the success. The mechanism of control from Berlin down to the local units in most instances had roots in the manipulated artistic communities, a measure of the regime's real strength. Meanwhile, the party continued to push Pg's into positions of authority to prevent a sliding of the musical profession into complacency and professional aloofness—a potential which gave rise to the postwar claim to "inner emigration." The regime continued to monitor activities and developments, while the relationships between the central administrations, local authorities, other governmental and party offices and the professions were regularized.

The continuing chamber directives concerning membership in the RMS, which precluded membership in the DAF, were issued to local units of the chamber, the *Orts* and *Landes-Musikerschaften.* The local nature of music in practice also was evident in the relationship between the local chamber chapter and the local employment office. By official announcement, musicians gained employment at the employment office through the chamber. An official brown chamber membership card identified the professional musician at the employment office. Part-timers carried white membership cards. Daily working permits could also be issued by the chamber to amateurs, but only in cases of need, that is, in the absence of professional application for a job. Brown cards were to have priority at the employment office. Musicians without identification cards were to be referred to the local office of the RMK.[78] The *Reichsleitung* of the NSDAP, through the directive of Deputy Führer Hess, encouraged close cooperation between national organizations, as well as between the local chapters of the RMK and the employment office, and all formations and local offices of the NSDAP, SS, SA, NSDFB, NSBO, and the DAF. Hess issued an order which was to free professional musicians from party duties, but also members of choral organizations who were active in the NSDAP, SS, SA NSDFP, NSBO and DAF, if bearers of the RMK membership card.[79] Local concert societies, managements, promoters and others concerned with music performance in public were forbidden to stage events without professionals, and professional musicians had to be paid at these performances. Only the *Landesleiter* of the RMK could allow exception. The relationship between amateur musicians and professionals thus contiued to preoccupy local leadership of the chamber.

National policy and local administrations were constantly brought into contact by means of local conventions of the total chamber or of specific professional divisions. Furthermore, national administrators were recruited from the various local administrations. For instance, the successful *Landesleiter* of the Bavarian *Landesmusikerschaft*, Uffinger, joined the Administrative Council of the RMK, while the official Nazi conductor Erich Kloss succeeded to leadership in Bavaria.[80] The faces were thus the same, whether a national or a local convention was called. The conventions contributed to the necessary contact between the administrative structure of the RMS, nationally and locally, with the local musicians organizations. The local administrators of the RMS themselves had to be informed of national policy, while the entire profession had to be indoctrinated. But also the various professions convened to discuss technical matters and political guidelines.

Under the leadership of Hans Sellschopp of the Division of Concert Life, provincial conventions of that Division were held by the local branches in Ludwigshafen and Essen in October and November 1934, respectively. Sellschopp's deputy presided over the same divisions in Breslau, Königsberg, Stettin, Darmstadt, Hamburg, Munich, Stuttgart, Hannover, Dresden, Halle, Cologne and Berlin. These conventions paralleled similar conventions of the total chamber and other divisions, most notably that of Havemann's RMS. The conventions enjoyed the support of city and provincial administrators, party leadership and involved cultural stars as seen above. Funk, Goebbels, Ihlert, Raabe, etc. attended as often as possible to introduce the goals of the RMK and of the various professional subdivisions. The tenor of their speeches followed a basic pattern, noting the accomplishments of previous organizational policy, the slow revival of German culture, the elimination of unemployment, the weeding out of "undesirable elements," the enthusiasm exhibited at the conventions and the gigantic tasks ahead. Political coordination was to be succeeded by a cultural renaissance. Results of the local conventions were then published in the national press and the official bulletins of the chamber.

The organizational efforts and conventioneering publicity culminated in the *Reichsmusiktage*—Reich Music Festival, produced by the RMK, under the instigation and close supervision of Goebbels and his musical advisor Heinz Drewes, in association with the KdF of the DAF, May 22-29, 1938 in Düsseldorf, the city of the Nazi martyr Albert Leo Schlageter and site of national conventions of the NSKG—*"Trutzburg Deutscher Kunst"* (Combat bastion of German Art), in the words of its enthusiastic *Gauleiter* Karl Friedrich Florian. This imposing event, labeled a "musical olympics" and a "military parade of German music," festively presented units of the RMK and outstanding representatives of German music, as well as HJ and NSDSTB musical camps, the Organization of German Municipalities, musical offerings of military and labor units, professional and amateur ensembles and choral groups which performed in formal settings as well as open forums and industrial plants. While the cream of German musicologists convened to assess the state of their art with weighty papers on topics ranging from "the nature of German music" to "the state and music" and "music and race," "degenerate music" was exhibited for the public in the form of defamed books, musical scores, caricatures, photos and models of scenic and stage designs, in addition to musical selections made available through recordings in individual booths. Thus organized by Dr. Hans Severus Ziegler, director of the Weimar National Theatre and head of the Cultural Bureau of Gau Thuringia, Dr. Otto zur Nedden, the dramaturg, musicologist and former leader of the KfdK of Württemberg-Hohenzollern and GMD Paul Sixt, the public was introduced to what Ziegler called a "witch's sabbath" and learned to denounce and avoid in the future the music of Weill, Schönberg, Berg, Hindemith, Stravinsky, Krenek, Schreker, Toch, Sekles, Hauer, Korngold, and many other noted composers and performers, identified by Ziegler in his frequently republished introductory address, "A Settling of Accounts," as "degenerate" and representative of "cultural bolshevism . . . the triumph of *Untermenschentum* (lower human type) and arrogant Jewish insolence." This exhibit of negativity was contrasted with the wide-ranging formal offering of thirty musical programs which included three symphonic performances of traditional and contemporary works by the Düsseldorf City Orchestra under the direction of GMD Hugo Balzer. Three operas were performed: the premiere of *Simplicius Simplicissimus* by Ludwig Maurick, *Don Juan's Last Adventure* by Paul Graener and *Arabella* of Strauss. The musical highlight consisted of Pfitzner's cantata, *Von deutscher Seele*, performed by Balzer and the Düsseldorfers, and Beethoven's Ninth Symphony, played by the Berlin Philharmonic under the direction of Hermann Abendroth—works which were to symbolize German identity and community (in the case of the latter being a distortion of Beethoven's appeal to all humanity, rather than to the nation). The cultural-political and official highlight of the RMT was Goebbels' formal address on May 28, introduced by a "Festival *Vorspiel*," composed for the occasion and conducted by Richard Strauss. The minister reviewed the organizational achievements of music in the Third Reich as a precondition for a musical renaissance of the new Germany, and he explained the event as an effort to bridge the worlds of the RMK and that of the people, thereby to go beyond what the ADMV had represented before its dissolution. The Reich Music Festival was to be repeated annually, but due to the war, the 1939 event—another organizational success—was to be the last one.[81]

Except for the victims of purges and defamation and those few who took a dim view of the vulgarity of the event, like Furtwängler who stayed away or Belá Bartók who protested the absence of his works from the "decadent music" exhibit, the Reich Music Festival underscored the success of music's *Gleichschaltung.*

In numbering more than 80,000, the RMS alone constituted powerful support for Goebbels. Membership stood for the maintenance of a job, and the musicians who communicated through journals and other public information media and who attended the culture-political festivals were ever ready to formulate party principles and compliment their benefactors. Goebbels filled his ministry and subordinate agencies with devoted followers, creating one of the most extensive patronage systems of the Third Reich.[82] In justification of his interference in matters of art he had pointed out on November 26, 1937, that it "occurs in a way that can only work for the benefit of the German artist: through subsidy, the commission of works, and a patronage of the arts, whose generosity is unique today in the whole world."[83] Goebbels astutely emphasized the economic aspects of art, boasting in the same speech of accomplishments in overcoming unemployment and having laid

the cornerstone on which the old-age security program for all art creators must be established. The necessary preliminary work for the attainment of this goal is already in progress. It is a question of finding an oganizational and economic form for every profession in this new field.

Along with this we have also turned our attention, in this year, to the establishment of old-age and recreation homes. Through the magnanimity of the Prussian Minister President not only was a new home for the aged in Weimar bequeathed to German veterans of the stage, but the Marie Seebach Foundation which has been in existence for many years, was given a secure financial basis. In addition, we created a new old-age and recreation home in Oberwisenthal and two new beautiful recreation homes in Arendsee at the Baltic Sea. They are to be opened next spring and will provide accommodations for seventy to eighty German artists seeking rest and recreation. . . Germany marches ahead of all other countries not only in art but also in the care which it showers upon artists, and thus sets an illuminating example.[84]

The program of National Socialism was comprehensive. The music profession was protected by the various decrees "for the satisfaction of economic conditions," and provisions for the aged and retired were planned. Goebbels' arm reached the young and future musicians in party and educational institutions, affecting the shaping of political sentiment of young Germany and indoctrinating all Germans through control of the mass media. He himself referred to this monopoly of public opinion-making in the same speech addressed to the RKK:

The radio broadcasting system has become a real people's institution. Since the National Socialist revolution the number of listeners has increased from four to nine million. The German press, in a rare demonstration of discipline, daily conducts its educational mission among the German people. The way to the nation has been cleared for all cultural efforts and strivings. We have not only sought for talent but have also found talent. In the new state, opportunities have been offered to talented people as never before. They need only reach out for them and make themselves master of them.[85]

Raabe's eulogy of the new state of 1934 was confirmed by Goebbels in 1937, admitting to having fulfilled the dream of the German artist through realization of greater centralized control. Socially secure, economically improved, esteemed by society, he can now serve his great plans in peace and without the bitterest cares for his livelihood.[86] The theme was repeated in 1938 and 1939 at the Reich Music Festivals.

Thus, Goebbels justified the existence of the totalitarian state on the assumption that people want to be and must be guided. Artists were no exception to this rule. The success of coordination of music and the overwhelming support of the centralized system tend to confirm this boast. Certainly the *völkisch* and traditionalist elements in music regarded centralization, security, and conservative guidelines as fulfillment of old demands. In this respect, the principle of centralization and control was shared by the music profession and the party-state. Theoretically, the state saw itself as an agent of the Nazi world view which entailed matters of organization, general principles and culture. In practice, the laws which were introduced in reference to culture could be rationalized in ideological terms. However, in confirming Goebbels' authority, the sum total of policy and organizational measures may be interpreted fundamentally as implementation of that individual's mandate for power.

Totalitarian Controls: Other Power Centers

Those who had envisioned the reconstruction of an authoritarian *Beamtenstaat*, with built-in security and preservation of a traditionalist Germanic ideology with specific reference to music, were reassured by the establishment of the RMK. Ultimately, however, they were to be disappointed.

The means toward the actualization of this reactionary goal, that is to say, the revolution—though also compromised—had become a way of life. Existing institutions were transformed and integrated as planned, but in the process contributed to the potential of a more permanent social revolution, which would bring the technologically and industrially highly modern Germany into the twentieth century in terms of social mobility and public involvement. Idyllic visions of a corporate music community, supported by the state in its effort to recapture the serenity, comforts and security of days long gone, were challenged by the momentum of change and its agent, the RMVP.

The RMK was tainted by its subordination to the RMVP which, as we have seen, embodied too much the principle of expediency and manipulation rather than substance and professional integrity—regardless of the many public reassurances to the contrary—ultimately satisfying neither *völkisch* idealists nor conservative traditionalists. While in practice the profession prospered, fell in line and supported the new order by performing as expected, the totalitarian state also fostered insecurity partly due to the contradictions in the revolutionary situation and partly by design. No one was to take job, station and commission for granted.

Goebbels himself rejected the conservative dream of many supporters. Just as his Radio Chamber tried to reach more people by encouraging them to become listeners as a matter of patriotic duty, he asked individuals to renounce rights and privileges for the benefit of the movement in behalf "of a greater and more comprehensive way of life." He made it clear that "a host of old habits and prejudices to which people had become fondly attached had to be overcome through the organization of the German creative artists in the RKK and their individual chambers."[87]

The totalitarian objectives were indeed institutionalized. The opposition was destroyed, the profession regimented and shaped into an effective propagator of Nazi principles, while conservative-authoritarian tendencies which pointed toward institutional autonomy were checked. Even its own agenices were suspect. No matter how faithful it appeared, the RMK was not left to its own devices. Personnel lists, compositions and programs had to be submitted for approval through the Music (M) Department of the RMVP under Drewes. Goebbels even created new agencies outside RMK controls with authority over music. The much-prized policy of centralization and streamlining of authority was thus violated and conflict resulted even within Goebbels' own jurisdiction. The principle had been invoked during the suppression and *Gleichschaltung* of previously autonomous institutions, but with the RMK in place as virtually a music ministry, the minister would not trust musicians, or so it seemed. His supervisory organs challenged the authorities from within the integrated music community. Although some of these agencies have been mentioned above as part of Goebbels' apparatus of control, their reintroduction here suggests itself as supplement to the presentation of the mass organization of the RMK.

The *Reichsmusikprüfstelle* (Reich Censorship Office of Music) was one such agency of tremendous influence, created by Goebbels on the suggestion of Heinz Drewes, February 1, 1938, which was to determine what constituted "undesirable" and "harmful" music and to guard against it. Under Drewes' leadership this office increased its jurisdictional scope and meddled in RMK areas of performance and publication. On the basis of the *Anordnung zum Schutze Musikalischen Kulturgutes* (Law for the Protection of Music Culture) of March 29, 1939, it emerged as highest judge in areas of dispute within the music community over ideological interpretation of music. Once listed for "contradicting the cultural will of National Socialism," compositions could not appear in print, nor be performed either in Germany or in occupied territory, and individuals who possessed sheet-music listed on this index were required to turn their copies in at the office. The law stressed the priority of this office against any otherwise legally binding interpretation of the RMK and applied to German as well as foreign works distributed in Germany and abroad. Thus, an arm of Goebbels' ministry, section music, extended to an area also under purview of the Foreign Office.[88] As noted above, Drewes combined in his official capacity leadership in the *Reichsmusikprüfstelle* and the RMK. Goebbels placed his men carefully, and the delegated authorities were bound to him.

Goebbels also invaded party organizations, such as the HJ, in his capacity as *Reichspropagandaleiter* (Reich Propaganda Leader). Officials of his *Hauptkulturamt* (Central Culture Office), another office created through the *Reichspropagandaleitung*, entered the administration of the HJ.[89] Education, which had been closely integrated with HJ affairs, was also related to the minister through the music department of the *Hauptschulamt* at the *Reichspropagandaleitung*.[90]

In addition to exercising review of the coordinated music profession through supervisory agencies the minister himself intervened. He formulated policy, issued instructions and supervised. His authority was invoked in serious matters like the adminstration of the questionnaire about racial and political background and affiliations. A notice posted at the City Opera of Berlin— renamed *Deutsches Opernhaus Berlin*—in October 1934 instructed all stage employes to fill out and return the questionnaires and warned that those who failed to comply would have their names forwarded to the Reich Minister.[91] The Propaganda Ministry also served as arbitrator in intra-party rivalries. Organizations sanctioned by the party appealed to Goebbels for defense in various matters, often against the characteristic accusations of other organizations, a favorite device being the reference to Jewish elements which would be held responsible for spreading malicious information about the organization in question. The practice of denunciation, so characteristic of the Third Reich and a consequence of the leadership principle, frequently involved the ministry as originator of a rumor as well as recipient of the complaint.[92] Even the music division of the party headquarters turned to Goebbels in cases involving the dismissal of officials in the music structure, for example when Hess, operating through his culture and music advisors, questioned the political realiability of Fritz Stein.[93]

In principle, the other ministries and agencies were to join Goebbels in mutual subordination to the revolution and its goals, on the understanding, however, that Goebbels' authority was to be supreme in culture. In practice, a process of adjustment and staking out of respective domains ensued, culminating in a maze of jurisdictional confusion which threatened the maintenance of and adherence to one policy. The question of nonmusical personnel dealing with music, suggested already by the overwhelming authority of the nonmusician, Goebbels, in all cultural and artistic affairs, invited other nonmusical powers to extend their domains beyond original limits. As organs of the Nazi state were musicalized—and this state politicized everything—its representatives initiated and supervised music. Hitler, Goebbels, Hess, Göring, Rust, Funk and other leaders, by profession nonmusicians, established themselves as supreme interpreters of music. When the Third Reich was organized enough in music to convene in Düsseldorf in May 1938, Goebbels welcomed German musicians to this grandest of musical festivals. Special attention was reserved for an exhibit of *Entartete Musik* (degenerate music), which was organized and formally introduced by a nonmusician, Staatsrat Dr. Hans Severus Ziegler, who related to music in the capacity of theatrical manager of the German National Theatre in Weimer.[94] He felt competent to offer a comprehensive policy statement toward music in ideological terms. Wolfgang Steinecke, musicologist and music critic, commented in the *Deutsche Allgemeine Zeitung* that the exhibit established "the ideological demand for total power of the Nazi art policy." It left no doubt as to the effect of National Socialism on music in Germany.[95]

The Nazi way of life had affected the leadership and the community alike. Wilhelm Rode, the new director of the German Opera House at Berlin, reminded all male employees in October 1934 to address their *Heil Hitler's* before a lady would do so. "As National Socialists," he decreed, "we have the duty to behave in exemplary fashion also in this respect." Swastikas entered German concert halls. Furtwängler's opposition to the presence of flags and the formal Hitler greeting constituted an exception. The notice this opposition received serves to prove the rule of general compliance. On May 1, 1939, the employees of the German Opera House were asked again by Rode to swear an oath of allegiance to Adolf Hitler.[96] All German artists followed suit in a singular demonstration of solidarity and loyalty.

Through authority of virtually sacrosanct leadership, Hitler functioned as supreme judge in musical affairs. As the apex of the Nazi hierarchy, also in regard to music, he could exercise an immediate influence on musical development and organization. In the face of party rivalry, confusion about jurisdictions of various authorities, and the liberty displayed by rivals in the interpretation of ideological and policy guidelines, his position alone was acknowledged by all as fixed point, an absolute voice. But, being the highest authority in a chain of command explains only part of Hitler's extraordinary power. He also benefited by the people's genuine affection and the carefully cultivated and manipulated impression that he was not aware of the mean streak in National Socialism or of whatever bothered an individual about a particular official measure. The common expression heard then and even still after 1945, "if the *Führer* only knew (or, had known)...."—suggested not only the leadership's conscious deception and the people's self-deception but also the latter's hope for reversal of uncomfortable, criminal and dangerous policies attributed to his evil counsellors like Goebbels.[97]

Inasmuch as the state justified itself on the ideological assumption of serving the community, the official administrative structure of authorities was totally dependent on the supreme leader who, by definition, spoke for the will of the people. Artists were reminded by the commandments of the NSDAP set forth in its organizational handbook of 1943:

> The *Führer* is always right. Never violate principles of discipline. . . Its program be your dogma; it demands total dedication to the movement. You are representative of the party. Act and behave accordingly . . . Right is what benefits the movement and thereby Germany,...your people. If you act according to the commandments, you are a true fighter of your *Führer*.[98]

Hitler served as ceremonial leader in the manner of heads of state of other forms of government. He handed out medals of distinction and prizes for accomplishments in the arts, some of which bore his name. In this official capacity of traditional form he honored musicians by his attendance at concerts and other performances, the frequency of which was greatly applauded. His presence at musical conventions and festivals greatly enhanced the prestige of the new organizers who were in need of support against more established and traditional associations. Hitler personally issued instructions to Franz Adams to found the official Reich Symphony Orchestra (NSRSO), designed the brown tuxedo for the musicians, and subsidized the group's extensive program of tours in Germany and abroad, broadly acclaimed in the national press.[99]

Hitler's position in music symbolized the frustration of the conservative order. If centralization in rigid application of conservative ideas was not even intended by advocates of revolutionary change, it certainly was not possible. In addition to Hitler, the state had other offices whose jurisdictions overlapped with that of the Propaganda Ministry. Naturally, a distinction must also be made between Goebbels' office and the official music structure, inasmuch as Goebbels embodied two realms, speaking not only for himself, his ministry and the subordinated cultural professions, but also for the party and the state. The fact of Goebbels' control of the arts was significant and revealed the importance given to official culture in the Third Reich. Nevertheless, this prominent representative of the party structure was subjected to review. As is evident in all political organizational records and in the language of the coordinated press, Hitler's personal intervention not only affected the music structure, but also the position and influence of its organizational head. Perhaps not too much ought to be made of this situation, since it is difficult to ascertain whether a Führer directive originated truly with him or on suggestion by Goebbels. Goebbels communicated the *Führer's* will in regard to official Nazi music, such as the *Nibelungenmarsch,* the *Badenweilermarsch*, or the Horst-Wessel song. In the official RMK bulletin Goebbels was consulted in ceremonial matters involving the great German masters who were appropriated as Germanic forebears of Nazism, as in the case of the Bruckner affair, when Hitler proclaimed the protection of the Reich over the Bavarian "Walhalla" structure of marble at Regensburg. A Bruckner bust was placed in the "Walhalla," being the only one of two hundred busts decorated by a flag bearing the Swastika symbol. Goebbels gave the opening address at the ceremony, while Hitler received the Bruckner Medal of the Bruckner Society.[100]

Hitler lent himself to what appears to have been Goebbels' design, although he did initiate some moves on his own. Foremost in this latter regard was Bayreuth, which received his special attention and protection. Through him the Reich established its protection over this cultural shrine of Nazi Germany. By executive decree *Parsifal* was to be performed exclusively at Bayreuth. Hitler also offered a 100,000 RM subsidy for the annual festival in February 1934.[101] Berta Geissmar claimed that the interests of Bayreuth were thus safeguarded against the politicking of Goebbels' organizers.[102] Hitler's authority represented the ideological point of view in disputes. The traditionalist musician could count on a fair hearing; Nazi propagandists stressed the impartiality and dedication to ideological principles of their *Führer*. State

Councillor Furtwängler appealed straight to Hitler in his attempts to salvage the tradition, hoping to gain by executive order from the top what seemed subject to an ever-expanding official bureaucracy. Aware of the various rivalries among Nazi leaders, Furtwängler imitated those Nazis who turned directly to Hitler in matters of dispute. Playing on Hitler's weakness for music, he managed to gain numerous concessions which compromised Nazi principles and practices repeatedly. Even Goebbels was subjected to Hitler's rebuke when bankruptcy threatened the Berlin Philharmonic Orchestra. The Party Commissioner of the orchestra in 1933 had spoken for the musicians, and Hitler was furious over the prospect of having Germany's famous orchestra declare bankruptcy.[103] Hitler's independence was also expressed on November 24, 1938 when he appeared at the premiere of Werner Egk's *Peer Gynt* after that opera had been denounced by the party press. Hitler's praise led to further productions and a 10,000 RM gift in prize money for the composer.[104] Thus, Hitler was not only a source of musical inspiration to fanatic followers in the music community, he commented a great deal on music policy, and also intervened even in various technical and jurisdictional disputes. Personal rivalries were often referred to him. As ultimate judge in German life he was powerful enough occasionally to give in to musical demands of the music community against interests of the organization. Such is the nature of absolute power. The apex of the organization can pose as the benevolent protector of the arts against organizational necessity and interests of party and state as upheld by important and petty bureaucrats who, in turn, really sustained his power. Thus, the constant theme of devotion and gratitude in articles and speeches: "The German people thank Adolf Hitler. . ."

Next to Hitler, Göring figured as supreme authority in the Nazi hierarchy, with special interest in matters of culture. His *Reichstag* has been called the "world's best-paid singing society: for its members assembled once or twice a year to listen to Hitler, then stood up lustily to sing 'Deutschland über Alles' and the 'Horst-Wessel Lied' and drew about two hundred and fifty dollars a month year in, year out, for this manifestation of lung power."[105] His Prussian Theatre Commission—under Hinkel's leadership—rivaled the RMVP in the days when ultimate power in the world of cultural expression was not yet determined. While he dissolved the Theatre Commission after the RKKG of November, 1933, he retained control over the State Theatres, including the State Opera in Berlin, thus continuing a rivalry with Goebbels which was symbolized in public in the competition between Berlin's great opera house— Göring's State Theatre projecting an image of stability and continuity in association with Furtwängler and Tietjen; the German Theatre mirroring closely Goebbels' policies, the latter reflected in Wilhelm Rode's contract which specifically bound him to RMVP guidelines.[106]

Göring's concerns spanned the whole spectrum of musical life, from the hallowed halls of the State Opera to matters dealing with such trivia as hit songs. Göring was constantly introduced to the public by his various titles, most frequently as Minister President *Generaloberst* H.G. In regard to a special hit song, the secret police informed the RMK of *Reichjägermeister* ("first hunter of the Reich") Göring's request to forbid the playing of the song *Der Wild- dieb*. The request was issued after consultation with the ministers of the In- terior and Propaganda.[107] His musical interests reflected his pompous per- sonality. He posed as an authority on music, holding forth on the subject in a most expansive manner. Like Hitler, he commented on music aesthetics, attempting to set standards for the community. A traditionalist, he embraced melody "against its destruction by modern trends" while allowing for music's capacity "to establish rapport between hearts where words fail."[108]

This official leader in the Reich government—Prussian Minister President and Interior Minister, *Reichsmarschall* in 1940, and major influence on the chief of the Security Police and the SD, SS-*Gruppenführer* Reinhard Heydrich: titled, bearing medals, and favorite subject of jokes in the Third Reich—was one of the perceptive and shrewd personalities in Hitler's entourage. It was he rather than Goebbels who understood the significance of Furtwängler's demonstrative symphonic rendition of Hindemith's oppositional *Mathis der Maler*, which was branded as *entartet* and placed on the index for its allegorical attack on the Nazi regime, being quite pointed in reference to a public bookburning ceremony, and the thunderous ovation accorded Furtwängler in the presence of the Nazi leadership. Göring realized that Furtwängler constituted a threat to the new regime.[109] As Councillor of State and director of the Berlin State Opera the great conductor engaged in active correspondence with his superior. Göring's clever moves actually contributed to the failure of Furtwängler to reach an agreement with the New York Philharmonic Orchestra when an invitation was extended in 1936. It was also Göring who retained the services of the aged Leo Beck. This noted Jewish conductor at the State Opera had been hired in Imperial Days, and Göring honored this loyalty in spite of Goebbels' open resentment and opposition to this flagrant violation of Nazi principles. Moreover, Furtwängler accepted the directorship at the State Opera on the understanding that other Jews would be retained. Göring agreed in spite of protests of municipal authorities who agitated for the removal of "inadmissible personnel." He judged who was and who was not Aryan.[110] Göring intervened repeatedly to protect Furtwängler's secretary Berta Gissmar from Goebbels who had good reason to destroy all authorities, like Furtwängler, independent of his control. The State Opera under Tietjen, who headed all Prussian State Theatres, was pro- tected by Göring.

In much biographical literature Göring is discussed as a moderate Nazi element in music. He took his role as chief administrator of the Berlin State Opera rather seriously, carving an image of himself as a great patron of the arts,[111] and he consciously protected its members from the grasp of Goebbels. Not only the victims of fascism but also the opportunists within the Nazi realm turned to Göring for protection and support. It is amazing to what degree he became involved in areas seemingly remote from his concerns. When Havemann, the music administrator, was accused of misconduct in his personal as well as in party life, Göring sat as judge at the official party court USCHLA, which was created for purposes of hearing cases involving differences and matters of denunciation within the party.[112] His most immediate influence was felt in the area of education in Prussia. The affairs at the PAdK in 1933 must be related to Göring who, as Prussian Prime Minister, had empowered Rust to supervise the arts in matters of personnel and organization. Interministerial and party-academy communications frequently bore Göring's signature or reference to his name. His activity culminated in a comprehensive reconstitution of the academy. He assumed the title of "Protector" of the academy, while Rust, whom Goebbels, in his diaries, referred to as a "nitwit," was confirmed in his role as supervisory administrator.[113] Rust immediately went to work, suggesting new members, including the musicians Furtwängler, Knab, Kaminski and Reutter, justifying this step as a necessary counter-measure to the dismissals of the past years. The policy was approved by the executive board of the academy, and Amersdorffer thanked Göring officially, July 26, 1937, for having accepted the responsibility for the academy. Nonetheless, the academy suffered and was not satisfied in its request for new members. On March 11, 1940 acting president Schumann complained to Rust that in spite of policy pronouncements no new members had been added since 1932-33. Since then ten musicians had died, four had been dismissed, leaving only nineteen full members. Recommended memberships had to go through complicated screening procedures. On February 2, 1941, Amersdorffer informed Schumann that Göring had decided to postpone the creation of new permanent and full memberships until after the war. All matters pertaining to membership and major policy had to pass by Rust's desk, with supreme authority vested in Göring until a new constitution would be formed. From academy documents it is clear that this new constitution was not about to be completed during the Third Reich. There was much talk about the necessity to create "young blood" on the part of the government, but the academic administration persisted in complaining. The question of new members involved various members of the Nazi elite, until even Hitler heard of the matter, but Rust's refusal to accept new members during the war, a position having Goring's support, carried the day.[114]

On the national level, *Führer* deputy Rudolf Hess also issued policy statements regarding music, as we have seen. He encouraged cooperation between the various official Nazi organizations, SS, SA, and other strictly party organizations, and the membership of the RMK. Hess exemplified party review of organizational matters. He had his hands in the creation of the *Parteiamtliche Prüfungskommission zum Schutze des NS-Schrifttum* (official party censorship office for the protection of Nazi literature), appointing Philipp Bouhler as its head, an active *Reichsleiter* of the NSDAP who, besides his position in the party commission—his capacity in politics and publishing— also was appointed by Hitler personally to head the euthanasia program in 1939.[115] Bouhler's commission was to cooperate with the Propaganda Ministry and with Rosenberg's cultural organization in its review of all written matter which could be related to National Socialism. In October 1936, Bouhler referred specifically to music. Publishers of entertainment music, hit songs and Church music had to obtain special permits from the commission in order to be able to deal with material of the Nazi movement.[116]

Also active in the control of music was the *Hauptkulturamt* of the NSDAP, whose music department initiated musical activity itself, in addition to which its influence was all-pervasive, since it, created by the Propaganda Ministry, cooperated closely with its agencies in all areas affecting music. In 1942 this NSDAP Central Cultural Office dedicated its efforts to the ideological support of the German folk song. Recently created Nazi songs were propagated, and all Nazis were urged to learn them. The office endorsed the general policy of bringing back the folk song to the people. Its views and regulations were published in *Musik in Jugend und Volk* (*MiJV*). Its importance lay in the organization of its own programs, constituting the important ideological step of going beyond coordination of existing institutions to a new Nazi music culture. Nazi intentions were to be realized in organizations of this sort.[117]

The multiplicity of party organizations dealing with music reflected the total commitment of each individual Nazi organ to the general notion of the ideology, according to which a good National Socialist was the incarnation of the *völkisch* dream of the complete personality, that is one who would be both musical and concerned with music. Hence, we understand the involvement of the HJ in music and its dedication to politicizing German youth and educating it specifically to become a future National Socialist community, familiar with its musical tradition and competent to maintain it. HJ leaders never tired of assuring colleagues of other organizations that German youth, or any youth for that matter, had never participated more enthusiastically in the arts than under National Socialism.

In the HJ youth was taught the HJ song literature and to recognize the relationship between art and life, a theme also propagaged in the journal *MiJV*, which also served as organ of the RJF.[118] Many links also existed between the HJ and the RMK. We recall that in April 1934, *Die Musik* had announced that it had become the official organ of the RJF and that youth leader Baldur von Schirach had established himself as authority in music all along and the HJ had officially become an organization exercizing authority in music.[119] Baldur von Schirach had even composed some literature, some of which was published in *Die Fahne der Verfolgten* (Berlin 1933), which was put to music, thus contributing creatively to the image of a singing youth. He was no stranger to music, as his father had been *Generalintendant* (director) at the Weimar stage and was serving in the same capacity since 1934 in Wiesbaden, while his sister, Rosalind von Schirach—employed as coloratura at the Berlin State Opera-Charlottenburg—enjoyed good reviews and was said to represent "an idealized replica of the Nordic-Aryan singer type."[120]

The potential conflict between musicians belonging to the RMK and other mass organizations was legally covered by official support of the professional estate. We have seen that RKK members were not permitted to belong to an industrial, trade or any other professional organization.[121] Nonetheless, the giant labor organization, the DAF, offered a musical program of its own in the Strength Through Joy (KdF) organization which rivaled the choral organization within the professional music chamber. This extensive program of cultural activities was intended to replace similar programs of traditional trade unions and to provide leisure to the worker as incentive to greater productivity. The German worker was encouraged in this manner to participate in organized music on a mass basis. The KdF was modeled after the DAF with its local subdivisions into block and cell chapters. Thus, the German worker was politicized through his place of employment, at work and in the time allotted for leisure.[122] In this area the Nazi ideology could be actualized most meaningfully. Folk music and Nazi fighting songs were introduced and the tradition of male choral singing was upheld. Speakers at RMK conventions realized the potential of these political mass organizations in the service of Nazi ideals. The KdF provided a mass base to the ideologist for the creation of a new singing community.[123]

While the RMK represented professional interests which were supported by law, other mass organizations promoted simpler Nazi ideals. Besides the NSKG, KdF and HJ, the SA and SS also promoted an active music culture. The "political soldier" of the SA and SS was a singing soldier. Yet in this case, too, the RMK was protected by law, as all leaders of SA bands had to be members of the chamber.[124] Under their frequently competent professional leaders, the SA was indeed musicalized. While songs helped shape unit identity, the units also introduced the song literature to the general population. (See Chapter I.) The SA at Breslau was proud of its musical activity; while each brigade had an official song leader who was schooled in music at least once a month, every column had to have singing at least thirty minutes every week. This was to be the model for all SA, SS, and HJ groups.[125]

The HJ, SS, and SA not only participated in a subordinate position at major party or state events, but promoted their own performances. Thus, the Nazi ideology was to be actualized. After one SS concert in Munich, a commentator noted that this "first public and grandiose commitment of the SS to art" was a "demonstration on behalf of the total state to overcome the division between politics and culture." The SS had placed itself in the service of the broad National Socialist community which "comprises everything grown from our people's soil." As a patron of music the SS embodied the Nazi principle of total commitment to all things German.[126]

The SA and SS also aspired to music making of a higher quality, reflecting the symbiosis of music with the party. As we have seen, even before 1933, the party had attracted many professional musicians—music educators, journalists and other music specialists. The attraction increased with the Nazi states' ability to reward its supporters with jobs, promotions, pay increases and positions of authority; it was never wanting in its need for specialists to carry out its music-political program at all levels of state and party organization and to lead its musical organizations. While Pg's also succeeded to jobs and positions of authority at strictly musical institutions, party organizations founded their own musical ensembles and choral groups. In smaller communities local orchestras performed also as local SA ensembles and vice versa. The fact that across Germany, the personnel at musical institutions and big party ensembles—especially in the case of the leaders—became increasingly interchangeable, explains both the quantity and quality of party music-making.[127] Most prominent was the NSRSO under the guidance of Franz Adams, and after 1936, Erich Kloss. This group traveled extensively in Germany and abroad, played for the *Führer* and was supervised specifically by *Führer* Deputy Hess. Party music outfits, such as Havemann's *Landesorchester Gau* Berlin, were subsidized and rewarded by the state to the accompaniment of favorable reviews by the coordinated press. Since music was a most important aspect of German life, the party did not intend to be excluded from it and it managed to perform at a credible level.

Potentially all organizations which carried a music program constituted a threat to Goebbels' authority as culture director in Germany. Particularly the massive organizations, local music establishments under powerful *Gau* leaders, and select party ensembles threatened to be independent of his influence. Less challenging were ceremonial institutions or those honorary institutions which existed for the glory of the new state. The Prussian Council of State, comprising distinguished representatives of various professions, was to advise the government. Its music representative, Furtwängler, had direct access to Göring and Hitler. As State Councillor, he participated in the typical pomp with which Göring liked to introduce the new state to the world. This assemblage of notables could apply itself to influencing decisions in the area of culture.

A *Reichskultursenat* to which Furtwängler also belonged was decorative, too, yet officially instituted with direct access to organs of the party, state and official music. As conductor of the Berlin Philharmonic Orchestra, director of the Berlin State Opera, Vice-President of the RMK and as Prussian Councilor of State Furtwängler combined in his person so many honors that he could pose a potential counter-authority, to which the victims of the new order would flock in desperation. A necessary symbol of coordinated "greatness," Furtwängler could believe himself to be justified in attempting what would appear to be impossible in the face of the overorganization of music in the Third Reich: the maintenance of standards and dignity. Thus, Furtwängler embodied the hopes of Germany's conservative order in music, rising to the occasion as spokesman of tradition and establishment. In terms of intra-party rivalry, however, he did not have much influence.

More obvious threats to Goebbels' authority were posed by fellow ministers. In regard to Germany's youth, Goebbels was not only rivaled by the HJ, but also by Rust's Education Ministry, whose jurisdictions overlapped with that of Propaganda. Goebbels had been assigned "to determine the areas and the tasks of the related ministries, also in cases where the domain of the other ministries were entered." Since questions of culture appeared in so many areas in other ministries, Propaganda had to insist on cooperation and assistance.[128] Although the various ministries were supposed to recognize Goebbels' constitutional authority, in reality the existence of overlapping domains created jurisdictional and personality conflicts. While education as such will not be reviewed here, the influence of Rust must be stressed. He was a radical Nazi who did not require much tutoring from Goebbels about coordination in his domain. Indeed, his position, confirmed by Hitler and Göring (see above in regard to the PAdK), allowed him to extend his authority unhampered by Goebbels' review.

Before the publication of the RKKG, in late 1933, Rust emerged as one of the more powerful Nazi leaders, giving directives, signing executive orders, and pronouncing policy. His office, the Prussian as well as the Reich Education Ministries, harbored some of the more ambitious Nazis who were active also in other ministries, agencies and party organizations. For instance, Wilhelm Stuckart, who had joined the NSDAP in 1922, became Lord Mayor of Stettin in April 1933, until assuming the office of under-secretary in the Prussian Education Ministry in May 1933: he later became under-secretary in both the Propaganda and Interior ministries, in addition to joining Hans Globke in publishing the commentaries to the anti-Jewish Nuremberg Laws. His illustrious career culminated in his activity at the notorious *Reichssicherheitshauptamt* (RSHA). He had good schooling under Rust and was well-qualified for the career in party and administrative affairs.[129] Rust's men demonstrated the interrelationship between ministries. Hans Hinkel was also one of Rust's under-secretaries in the Prussian Education Ministry, before he became more fully involved at the RMVP and the RKK. He was active as a Nazi since 1921, also serving on the *VB*. He was *Blutsordentrager*, SS *Sturmbannführer*, a position to which he rose in 1935, and SS *Gruppenführer* since 1943. Belonging primarily to Rust's structure in the early years of the Third Reich, he was the real Nazi force in the area of education, and specifically music education. As Prussian Prime Minister, Göring appointed him head of the Culture-Political Office of the Prussian Council of State. He also supervised Göring's Prussian Stage Commission in 1933. His colleagues referred to him as RKV, which stands for *Reichskulturwalter* (Reich Culture Supervisor). In addition to all these offices, honors and titles, Hinkel was selected to supervise the cultural life of Jews in Germany (see above), a position which was called *Sonderbeauftragter zur Überwachung der geistigen und kulturellen Tätigkeit der Juden im deutschen Reichsgebiet*. This latter office was placed under the supervision of the Propaganda Ministry for which he increasingly worked as Business Manager of the RKK since 1935, to the satisfaction of the Propaganda Minister.

It was Hinkel who received the countless letters of informers in his capacity as under-secretary and as the authority involving appeals for special consideration relative to the questionnaire and its underlying discriminatory legislation. Intra-party disputes, too, were frequently referred to Hinkel before reaching the desk of Rust, Göring and Goebbels. It is impossible to keep up with the activity of this Nazi dynamo. Every music institution was affected by him through one of the numerous offices connected with his person, whether this would be in the area of pure musical institutions, individuals, the Church, Education, the various ministries, party organizations or agencies and Jewish cultural activities. Wulf's documentation on music in the Third Reich contains no less than fifty-six references to Hinkel. Music in Nazi Germany would not have been the same without this bureaucrat, a telling testimony to the power of his superior, Bernhard Rust, who had an effective organization behind him rooted in party and state structures, and posing a threat to other ministries in this game of filling out one's domain and encroaching on others.

Through vigorous zealots like Hinkel, the Education Ministry established itself as authority in matters of ideology. Questions were sent to this ministry in regards to legal questions and administrative guidelines. Not only Prussian institutions referred to Rust in matters of ideological or technical clarification of policy. In early 1933 the management of the Saxon State Theatre asked whether Paul Graener's opera *Friedemann Bach* would still be performed in view of Graener's allegedly being half-Jewish. In the same note, Hinkel was asked whether it would be advisable to perform Janáček's opera *Jenufa*, inasmuch as it was an excellent piece of art derived from the Czech folk tradition and folk music. Hinkel answered that "our Paul Graener, member of the Fighting League, is Aryan, his librettist Rudolf Lothar, however, is not." In regard to *Jenufa* he had no reservations as such, although the attitude of a foreign country must be considered, given the fact that Czechoslovakia was not on friendly terms with Germany at the time.[130] The issue of *Jenufa* reappeared in later years when such controversies were initiated by Nazi organizations like the NSKG even though the RMVP clearly was in charge.

The Nazi take-over in 1933 did not diminish the power of the Education Ministry. Rust even challenged the SA in April 1934, in regard to local SA academies. He asked the authorities not to monopolize the time of students with party affairs. "In the last two semesters certain problems arose as a result of students suddenly entering the SA in excessively large numbers."[131] Rust held his own in the intra-party struggle. Music education, though in some areas subject to RMK regulation, was kept under control of the Education Ministry within the total structure of the government. The Reich Ministry of Science, Education, and General Enlightenment participated in the creation of the people's community through education. It controlled the conservatories and other music educational institutions. In practice, music education was controlled by Rust and Goebbels jointly, both being interested in the inner development of the new generation which was to be truly Nationalist Socialist.

The Ministry of the Interior under Dr. Wilhelm Frick—a music lover, constituted another authoritative and operational power nexus in close cooperation and competition with Goebbels and all other party organizations. Like Rust, Frick was an old party faithful who had been part of a government in Thuringia before 1933. At that time, he had made a name for himself by purging what remained of the famous Bauhaus in Weimar.[132] A tested Nazi, he was very important in the early phase of the Third Reich, lending himself to the process of Nazifying the machinery of state. At the beginning he played a key role in transferring ultimate authority from the existing civil service to the revolutionary regime. However, in his effort to consolidate his base through strict centralization he created a state-oriented power structure which, notwithstanding its Nazi make-up, ultimately was to represent a conservative bulwark against the party and openly revolutionary organs.[133] Frick's name appears throughout this study on music in connection with denunciations, petty disputes and major rivalries involving both party and state authorities. In general, the Minister was asked to intervene in the affairs of music institutions which had not coordinated themselves in the proper spirit. Until 1935, Frick's Ministry supervised the application of the Professional Civil Service Act, since all officials of public institutions had to prove Aryan ancestry. Frick appointed Dr. Achim Gercke to head an office for race research, assuming the title of *Sachverständiger für Rassenforschung beim Reichsinnenministerium* (Specialist for Race Research at the Interior Ministry). The archives of music institutions contain an immense correspondence from Gercke's office. The PAdK, for instance, divided its correspondence between the three ministries of Propaganda, Education and the Interior. Gercke's office was transformed into the *Reichsstelle für Sippenforschung* (Reich Office for Ancestry Research) in 1935 and, again in 1940, into the *Reichssippenamt* (Office for Genealogical Research), the latter constituting another powerful agency with tremendous influence in the area of music from the time of inception. Thus, Frick supervised the observation of the legal process in Nazi Germany through his office and subsidiary agencies, especially in the delicate area of Nazi racial policy.

In a Ministerial decree of September 1935 the Interior Ministry of Prussia and the Reich reserved to itself the power of reviewing the formation of any cultural association in view of their potential threat to the principle of coordination and the Nazi ideology, the latter category being referred also to the personal review of the *Führer's* special appointee, Alfred Rosenberg, whose authority extended over all matters of Nazi ideology.[134] The driving forces behind Nazi music policy, Hinkel and Havemann constantly asked for Frick's intervention. He enforced music policy in regard to matters of music personnel through his control of the various police commandos. Although the Hinkels and Havemanns also appealed to the strong-arm support of the SA and SS forces, Frick's power and influence, primarily in the early years of the Third Reich, can hardly be overestimated, constituting a functioning and centralized executive power structure of great resources which would have to be considered in any potential struggle between party leaders in the later years of consolidation.

In a more conservative rightist government Frick might have become head of the major power structure. In actuality he was to be demoted as his office became a self-contained ministry which did not cultivate party connections to the degree necessary for survival in the Third Reich. His ministry was maintained, but it was soon superseded by the skillful organizer of police forces, Himmler. Nonetheless, in its relationship to and reliance on the Interior Ministry, music in the Third Reich was seen as an institution under constant review by and subservience to the state.

Both Rust and Frick were Nazis who had cleaned house in their respective domains at an early stage by means of filling positions with Nazis, while at the same time effectively controlling hold-overs from the previous governmental administrations. Partially rooted in conservative administrative structures, these potential rivals to Goebbels' authority in musical matters illustrated the contradictions in a situation which was created by means of revolutionary momentum contained and stabilized in government and its institutions. A different conflict resulted between traditional officials, the hold-overs from the previous government, and the new Nazi elite. In practice, however, the intra-party conflict was of greater consequence, since Nazi-created ministries constituted a more dangerous threat to other elements of the party elite. The sum total of all rivalries between party creations like the the SA and SS, Rosenberg's ideological challenge, or strictly cultural formations like the KfdK or NSKG, on the one hand, and the conservative, though coordinated establishment of party revolutionaries turned bureaucrats, or simply of personalities caught at various levels of this competitive process, on the other hand— vacillating between revolutionary zeal and institutional responsibility—was surprisingly well-managed and reflected the inevitable compromises of the comprehensive ideology translated into the reality of the legal revolution, made possible to no small degree by the mediating position of Hitler. Thus, in spite of revolutionary slogans and the perpetuation of revolutionary momentum, National Socialism became the affair of state. Frick, though Nazi, appealed to the traditionally conservative civil service of Germany to uphold the functioning of the state. Consequently, the purges in the civil service were limited, although the music establishment was affected to a greater degree. Nazification followed the ascent to power. Frick managed to Nazify the Civil Service. His efforts, like those of other Nazi ministers, were geared toward centralization. In music the effort was rather successful, although the inherent conflicts, exemplified in the rivalry of authorities, were never resolved. As it was a necessary consequence of a totalitarian revolution to call upon all elements of society to support the new regime in all areas of life, music was subjected to the review of many authorities. In time, the state structure, headed by Lammer's State Chancellery, had priority over the Party Chancellery, headed by Hess,[135] a consequence of reason of state which stands for the maximization of the exploitation of national resources, thus constituting the necessary negation and consequence of a revolutionary movement. Reason of state would tend to impose itself, especially in time of war, also affecting areas, as seemingly remote from the political and economic sectors like music, which help sustain the war-making capacity of the nation. In Goebbels' ministry the party held its own, inasmuch as party and state were merged in leadership and organization. Indeed, the significance of Goebbels was illustrated in that dual capacity. A Nazi creation, his office set a pattern for totalitarianism in practice.

Musical Foreign Policy

Music has traditionally enhanced Germany's reputation. The whole world resounded to German music, German performers were welcomed the world over and Germany in turn attracted the musical world. The Nazi state demonstrated organizational financial support of this thriving music culture and its reputation at home and abroad. In implementing this commitment, however, the regime revealed its admitted totalitarian and manipulative features so that foreigners asked whether they heard music, pure and simple, or an official agent of Nazi propaganda. After all, music was publicly and legally subsumed under the RMVP—the ministry of thought and image creation, control and dissemination—which was further empowered to absorb the press and cultural functions of the Foreign office.

That much everybody in the world of music knew or, at least, had the opportunity to know. Yet, today's student of the role of music in Nazi foreign policy knows more than even well-informed contemporaries (other than key political leaders and functionaries as well as select members of the press) because of the availability today of privy governmental records which confirm the worst suspicions about thought control and manipulation, personal papers of Nazi leaders like the Goebbels diaries, and the minutes of the confidential RMVP Press Conferences and the Culture-Political Press Conferences (which were among other things strategy sessions in propaganda) were illegally reproduced and kept by Fritz Sänger of the *Frankfurter Zeitung*, as noted above. We also know that news from foreign correspondents was filtered through the DNB (the RMVP monopolized German News Service), was classified there according to grades of confidentiality, and selectively released and revised for standardized publication. Knowledgeable journalists like Fritz Sänger also gained information informally from interviews with political leaders who tended to forget the RMVP's exclusive right to speak for the government and through traditional news networks at home and abroad. Since their privy information was not available to musicians and their agents, it is impossible to simply chart music-political developments relative to foreign policy chronologically. In consideration of the different levels of awareness among all those involved in musical foreign affairs—and since musical foreign policy did not evolve uniformly, recognizably or unidimensionally but rather reactively, subject to various influences and in spurts—the account here will reflect diversity, identify select actors and telling examples, and be marked by digressions.

The assessment of the role of music in foreign affairs is further complicated by the jurisdictional conflicts within the government. Although the RMVP's authority was clearly defined, and Goebbels continued to exercize the strongest influence on propaganda abroad, the regime did not speak with one voice about music abroad, reflecting and reinforcing instead the influences of other Reich leaders and party offices which, too, entered foreign affairs and issued instructions to German musicians. This competition mirrored rivalry at home, which also affected music there. Nevertheless, we have seen that the Nazi state managed to function and music was firmly integrated in its various organizations and contributed to the stability of the new order.

Stability was due to some degree to the Nazis' desire and the need to appear respectable to the outside world. For this reason the traditionally conservative Foreign office, under the accommodating Minister Konstantin von Neurath, maintained a special position in the Nazi state for some time, confident that it was indispensable and that it would be able to tame Hitler, with whom it actually shared many views and objectives, like revision of the Versailles Treaty and even some aspects of Nazi expansionism. Except for the resignation of the Ambassador to the US, Friedrich von Prittwitz und Gaffron, the Foreign Office staff remained largely intact, offering continuity and reassurance to an anxious world. Good foreign relations were the concern of the Nazis while Germany was weak, and music played an important role in this public relations effort.

Exercising restraint and discretion in the early stages of Nazi rule, foreign missions were in no case headed by a Nazi. Much like the Interior Ministry, the Foreign Office relied on old hands, who enjoyed the respect of foreign ministries abroad. The policy of maintaining good relations with the outside world reinforced not only the traditional foreign service but also those in music who had been dealing with German foreign missions, the foreign and cultural ministries of other countries and the various agencies abroad. However, the pragmatists faced increasing ideological pressures which were skillfully manipulated by the party leadership. The impact of these pressures on German music abroad, as on foreign musical groups in Germany, paralleled Nazi encroachments into the domain of the Foreign Office. Respectability was threatened by an organizational and ideological dynamic.

Notwithstanding all official efforts to pose as a responsible government, the world took note of the increasing regimentation of German life, which was not conducive to artistic freedom. The Foreign Office was hard pressed to preserve traditional relationships and the appearance of normalcy, since its efforts were consistently undermined by the coordinated German press which openly expressed the ideology in all its consequences. Music journalism also echoed the hostility to foreigners in music, articulated in consistent segregationist *völkisch* terms which arguably allowed respect for foreign traditions, or on the basis of open anti-Jewish, -Soviet, -Western, -atonal, -jazz, or anti-anti-*völkisch* attitudes. Even distinguished German musicians and commentators lent themselves to this ideological parochialism. As mentioned above, Goebbels and Hinkel set the tone when they insisted that the nationality of a composer mattered a great deal. Thus, Czech music was questioned, famous composers like Tchaikowsky, Thomas, Stravinsky and Bartók were attacked, and Liberia publicly insulted for its "primitive" music. The fighting songs of political formations and compositions by Nazi and collaborating composers in the hundreds expressed nationalistic and anti-foreign sentiments in musical form, and so did the explicitly German programs at party functions, but also on formal stages, like the Berlin *Volksoper* founded by Goebbels for working Germans.[136]

The whole process of *Gleichschaltung* was colored by this wave of narrow-minded nationalism and anti-foreign sentiment. Most seriously, foreign musicians were subjected to the insult of the infamous questionnaire which included questions about race. Foreign compositions, composers, publishers and dealers suffered from restrictive legislation. International festivals, if not abolished (like that at Donaueschingen), were transformed from platforms of modern experiments to events in which the Nazi ideology was imposed on music programs, while the international quality of music itself was scorned in favor of the *völkisch* notion of unique national characteristics of music. *Völkisch* musicians and party organizers transformed the nature of music from the type traditionally exercised in what had been the foremost nation for Western art music.

Hans Pfitzner, a forerunner of National Socialism, was able to gain a great following and state-support for his nativist line, which included well-known anti-foreign and anti-Semitic sentiments. In the summer of 1933 he refused an invitation to participate at the Salzburg Festival because Austria had assumed an anti-German attitude by outlawing the Nazi party in May. His demonstration was widely acclaimed, and other German performers followed his example[137]—upon instructions by the government, as we now know. When Goebbels and Raabe launched their attacks on foreign names in music circles and demanded the removal of foreign works from German stages, and "cheap Western popular music" from places of public entertainment, Pfitzner and his tradition prevailed, while Furtwängler and Kleiber were publicly criticized for maintaining traditional types of programs, and for offering an excessive amount of foreign compositions and atonal works, as if no revolution had taken place.[138]

German diplomats worried over credibility as they attempted to smooth over and rationalize this institutionalized provincialism which led to the renunciation of their traditional modes of thought, which had regarded music as universal art, a medium between the peoples of this earth, an international language. One Nazi commentator denounced this "esperanto of tones" as a feature of a decadent, late-bourgeois, and increasingly internationalist civilization.[139] In this atmosphere Germany eventually established itself as a pariah among nations, embracing a racial policy which set itself willfully apart and a music policy which isolated the German ear. National Socialism was anti-internationalist, and its race doctrine challenged the notion of a common European culture. Mersmann's *Deutsche Muksikgeschichte* was denounced for proposing an understanding of German music in terms of European cultural development.[140]

The consequences of this ideology touch the core of this study, as thousands of German intellectuals, artists and politically or racially defamed members of the community fled Germany in testimony to discrimination and in fear for their lives. Indeed, the Nazis invited "undesirables" to leave in the early phase of the Third Reich. In his 1933 speech at the Party Congress, Hitler had urged all ethnic German artists in foreign countries to identify with Nazi cultural policies and propaganda. Artists were encouraged to present and advocate programs abroad which would be in accord with National Socialism.[141] We have seen how the DSB propagated the Nazi principles in border countries, enticing ethnic Germans to return home to the Reich, and thus caused anxiety among the governments of weaker neighbors, some of which banned the DSB. Even though diverse organizations responded to Hitler's appeal with musical demonstrations, festivals and speeches, intra-governmental records reveal that the RMVP coordinated all such activities in the realms of the press, radio and cultural expression—thus affecting a *Gleichschaltung* of domestic and foreign policy in cultural affairs under its jurisdiction. German music was employed as a medium for concrete political goals, especially directed at ethnic Germans in neighboring countries and coordinated with and by political organizations like the Foreign Countries Organization (*Auslandsorganisation*—AO) of the NSDAP under Gau leader Ernst Wilhelm Bohle and the powerful League of Germans Abroad (*Verein für das Deutschtum im Ausland*—VDA) led by the Carinthian Reich Leader Hans Steinacher. Both of these organizations also sponsored musical performances, radio programs abroad and research. Nazi cultural organizations like Rosenberg's NSKG—more accustomed to its *Gau* and national festivals, also developed contacts with ethnic Germans abroad, and the "German Music Stage" (*Deutsche Musik Bühne*) offered operas and operettas for their ethnic brothers and sisters, in concert with speeches and political demonstrations.

It is not surprising that bordering countries reacted with official measures against the NSDAP and its offensive fighting songs, subversive festivals, select performers, organizers and party formations. First Austria, but then also Czechoslovakia and Poland banned such threatening activities. How were they to understand Hitler's protestations of peace on May 17, 1933—the first in a series of such announced "peace speeches"—when he reassured his neighbors that he would not "Germanize," but neither would he tolerate the suppression of German minorities? He alone would determine the meaning of being a German and what constituted suppression. Astute observers and worried neighbors related these threats to the concrete totalitarian meassures at home, and feared war. The great powers responded with diplomatic maneuvers and assurances of support of weaker countries at an incredible pace in response to the Nazi provocation. As Germany broke off disarmament negotiations in Geneva and left the League of Nations late in 1933, the US and the USSR renewed diplomatic relations. Germany and Poland negotiated a non-aggression pact in early 1934; in mid-year France proposed to Eastern European countries mutual guarantee of borders and non-aggression pacts, etc. Cultural affairs were activated in support of these policies. German emigres reacted against the unprecedented hostility of the "Aryan Paragraph," harassment and then the Nuremberg Laws of 1935—like the well-known music critic and author Paul Bekker who, according to Nazi sources, had battled the Nazis before 1933, fled in that year, was finally stripped of his German citizenshp on orders of the Interior Ministry on March 3, 1936, and fought German interests until the invasion of France terminated his activity there.[142] International artists of note also boycotted Germany. Just as Pfitzner cancelled his engagement at Salzburg, Toscanini would not conduct again at Bayreuth—two key symbols around which fascists and anti-fascists respectively rallied. Articles appeared in the foreign press denouncing current practices in Germany and the destabilizing actions abroad. German diplomatic missions faced increasing pressure from foreign governments to intercede in behalf of well-known victims of the purges. The German Foreign Office shared with music the appearance of autonomy; both were useful, manipulated institutions which depended on the good will of the totalitarian regime and were affected by political events and international relations.

Austro-German relations were especially tense, but musical exchanges and collaboration contributed to the appearance of normalcy in accord with policy objectives. Tours by German artists to neighboring countries were extremely sensitive, moreover, since performing before and alongside German emigres was involved. At the Brahms centennial celebration in Vienna, May 1933, the German Brahms Society collaborated with the Viennese Society of Friends of Music. Artists of the whole world contributed and the Austrian government was officially represented by the Education Minister, Kurt von Schuschnigg, who spoke for Chancellor Dollfuss. The new barriers between Germany and the rest of the world were not yet so evident since musicians were not privy to political plans. The spirit of the festival actually deceived musicians and other participants about the true situation in Germany, precisely because all international affairs of this sort were still largely controlled and operated by old hands in traditional ways. German artists still participated in the opera seasons of New York, London and Paris. In turn, foreigners appeared in Berlin and Bayreuth. In part, the Foreign Office retained its staff, prestige and control through such affairs because the hostile international press, emigres, public opinion abroad and the various pressures of other government could not have been handled by the Nazis as effectively.

But international tension mounted. When Austria banned the Nazi Party in May, 1933 and the German government retaliated with a tax of 1000 Marks on German travel to Austria, the international Salzburg Festival was affected immediately and acquired symbolic significance. Since the festival stood for Austrian independence and was a refuge and platform for German emigres like Walter and Klemperer as conductors in the 1933 season, in addition to the long-anticipated *Faust* production of Max Reinhardt with its emigre actors like Max Pallenberg, the German government ordered a boycott. Pfitzner and major singers like Sigrid Onegin and Wilhelm Rode (soon to be named director of Goebbels' German Opera in Berlin) cancelled. Only Richard Strauss, one of the founders of the festival and premier international star, was given permission to attend. Festival historian Stephen Gallup has written that the festival opened "in a tense atmosphere; German visitors were rare, major artists had cancelled, giant swastikas and fireworks blazed into the night sky from the hills beyond the border near Berchtesgaden, Nazi planes dropped propaganda pamphlets and loudspeakers blared over the border at Freilassing. And then there were the makeshift bomb attacks, which caused no loss of life, but added considerably to the tension. Salzburg became an armed camp "and yet, the festival took place and was a smashing success with "the most eclectic" program ever performed—a mix of much Mozart, Walters' usurpation of Bayreuth with an emotionally received *Tristan*, Clemens Krauss conducting *Die Frau ohne Schatten* and *Rosenkavalier*, the premiere of the Vienna version of Strauss's *Die aegyptische Helena*—and, the hit of the festival, the Reinhardt production of *Faust* with Bernhard Paumgartner's background music conducted by the young Herbert von Karajan who, after brilliant beginnings of his career in the Third Reich would dominate the Salzburg Festival years later. "Caught between excitement and danger," Gallup sums up the momentous event, "between the cacophany of Nazi loudspeakers and sublime singing, the 1933 Festival was an emotional

experience to all who attented. The international press noted Walter's defiance, Strauss's apparent independence, and praised the festival-goers as
friends of Austria."[143]

Yet, the "unexpected" and symbolic success of the festival could not hide
the mortal danger Austria faced. Many Austrians shifted allegiance to the
Third Reich, many left for Germany in open defiance of the Dollfuss government, while some prepared for a coup d'etat. Prophetically, Strauss's collaborator Stefan Zweig, a local celebrity, announced in October that he would
leave Salzburg. He left in early 1934, restlessly moving about in the world
until he put an end to his life in Brazil in 1942; Zweig's autobiographical *Die
Welt von Gestern* (*The World of Yesterday*) captured the atmosphere of this
period in Austrian history, the forboding of disaster but also the persistent
faith in humanity, and introduced a virtual international "who's who" of artists and intellectuals whom he had entertained—a world of "doomed enchant-
ment" in the words of the playwright Carl Zuckmayer.

Salzburg again assumed center stage with the arrival in 1934 of the then
most-sought-after conductor, Arturo Toscanini. That fiery symbol of anti-
fascism who had refused to play the fascist *La Giovinezza* in Bologna in 1930
and had antagonized Mussolini. He had signed a telegram addressed to Hitler
in behalf of German Jews and had turned down that other festival symbol,
Bayreuth, a real conflict for him. Strauss conducted *Parsifal* in his place.
Toscanini had joined the anti-Nazi campaign organized by the great Polish
violinist Bronislaw Hubermann. Toscanini's commitment to Vienna and
Salzburg supported Austrian independence and the victims of fascism, his
stand becoming eminently clear when he conducted Hubermann's Israeli
Philharmonic in 1936.

The preparation for the 1934 Salzburg Festival took place amidst unsettl-
ing rumors about Hitler's Austrian plans. In May the RMVP asked Furtwängler
and Strauss not to participate; the two cancelled their engagements. Then,
the attempted Nazi putsch and assassination of Chancellor Dollfuss on July
25 a few days before the opening of the Festival heightened the tension. But,
again that year, the Festival took place, opening with Clemens Krauss's
memorial performance of the Funeral March from the "Eroica" for the fallen
Chancellor. Walter and Toscanini were lionized in the international press for
the success of the Festival against the background of the Austrian state's severe
crisis.[144] The interplay of politics, art and international relations continued
through the following Salzburg Festival season with Toscanini in charge until the *Anschluss* and Clemens Krauss's increasing unhappiness, resulting in
his betrayal of Vienna and his acceptance of Göring's offer to take over the
Berlin State Opera after Furtwängler's dramatic resignation in late 1934.

Meanwhile, RMVP policy toward Salzburg vacillated between open hostility, permission of Foreign Office "discretion," and even cooperation. Already during the original crisis in May 1933 the German Consul in Salzburg had inquired whether the 1000 Marks tax would apply to German students who had intended to enroll in an international conductor's course at the Mozarteum during the Festival. In answering the Foreign Office request for clarification the RMVP saw no reason for German participation in the course in view of the crisis, but allowed "discretionary" waiver of the tax—which, in fact, became common practice for German travel to Austria until the tax was lifted in 1936.[145] Inconsistent policy permitted von Karajan to conduct at the Salzburg Festival in 1934, while the controversial Hindemith was denied permission to conduct in Vienna that year. Hans Knappertsbusch conducted three concerts in Vienna in 1935, and Karl Böhm, by then a loyal supporter of the regime, was allowed to conduct concerts in early 1936 for the Vienna Concert Society whose musical director, the Nazi activist Leopold Reichwein would play a major role following the *Anschluss* in support of the new order.

Then, in July 1936 an Agreement was worked out between the two countries: Austrian independence was acknowledged, the travel tax rescinded; Austrian Nazis were permitted to display Nazi insignia, and the German press was readmitted to Austria—measures by which Goebbels intended to increase his influence in Austria. Even so, German attendance at the Salzburg Festival remained low that year, and only the actor Werner Krauss and Furtwängler received permission to perform at the 1937 Festival. Nazi policy had shifted to apparent tolerance and neglect, while the Festival prospered under Toscanini's control and conducting (over forty percent of the time), attracting great audiences from all over the world, including famous personages who thus demonstrated their support of a free Austria. Meanwhile, the German representative in Vienna, Franz von Papen—who had already engineered the concordat with the Vatican and had undertaken a special mission to Vienna in 1934—on the surface worked to improve Austro-German relations and attended the Salzburg Festival in 1937,[146] even though it was in this crucial area of Austrian relations that the Nazi party for the first time projected its own initiative, both parallel and in opposition to the Foreign Office.

Power-political developments, particularly during periods of tension, also eclipsed music-political plans. For instance, the long-awaited Reich Music Festival in Düsseldorf, May 22 to May 29, 1938, though intended to constitute the most comprehensive statement on Nazi music policy and RMK achievements to date, did not live up to expectations because of the tense situation internationally. Hitler had marched into Austria, and commentaries attest to the virtual panic pervading Prague in anticipation of Hitler's next moves. Nonetheless, the show went on. German music was introduced to the entire music community, and the special feature of the festival, the exhibition of degenerate music, was praised for its accurate reflection of the previous era of German "shame." While Germany's power political ambitions were demonstrated before the world, German music convened in demonstration of its total coordination with Nazi policy.[147]

Like the Salzburg Festival, the traditional tours of the Berlin Philharmonic Orchestra constituted an element of the familiar in this era of change. As before 1933, these tours throughout Europe were handled in the 1933-1934 and 1934-1935 seasons by the "non-Aryan" Berta Geissmar who, it seems, was indispensable through her connections with foreign agencies, German embassies and foreign cultural ministries, and because of her valuable experience. Her case illustrated early Nazi discretion and the conflict between pressing needs of the moment and ideological considerations. But the foreign legations in Germany, too, appeared to want to perpetuate traditional relations. The French Ambassador M. François-Poncet, for instance, had lent his embassy for concerts throughout his term, and Berta Geissmar assisted in arranging even these events. During the crisis of the Berlin Philharmonic Orchestra over its Jewish members, M. François-Poncet gave a luncheon in honor of the visiting pianist Alfred Cortot, scheduled to appear with the Berlin Orchestra. In what must have appeared as a political demonstration on the one hand and toleration forced by circumstance on the other, the non-Aryan Geissmar was pointedly seated between the French Ambassador and Cortot and opposite the newly appointed musical critic of the *VB*.[148]

German embassies abroad also had traditionally lent support to the tours of the Philharmonic and continued to do so, indeed emphatically in defense of established prerogative. In 1933 the new Interior Ministry had upset the customary pattern through its increasing influence on tours by means of its control of passports. At that time the granting of exit visas to the Jewish members of touring artist groups had become a delicate matter. In view of the careful approach to international relations, however, tours continued to be officially supported. However, the diplomats and German artists abroad had to learn to cope with hostile audiences, frequently incited to active demonstrations by German emigres. In Paris a Union for Combating anti-Semitism interrupted German cultural affairs. This group of angry dissidents was pacified during a stay of the Berlin Philharmonic only by traditional agents and the good records of such people as Furtwängler and Geissmar. Opposing any visitor from Nazi Germany, this group tolerated the concert only out of respect for Furtwängler, his defence of artistic freedom in Germany having received international attention. But during the intermission they insisted on dropping thousands of leaflets among the audience, in the presence of the entire French government and to the applause of the whole house.[149]

These concerts of the Berlin Philharmonic in Paris had highlighted the tours of the orchestra since 1928, and the good relations of the musicians and the French were now tested. The German Ambassador von Hoesch, who had personally supported German artists the past years, and the director of the Paris Opera, M. Jacques Rouché, the dominating force in opera and concert life in France, were both dedicated to upholding the traditional friendship and cultural relations. They were familiar with Furtwängler's attitude in Germany, the famous letter to Goebbels having been reprinted throughout France. Thus, the concerts took place amidst much controversy, the German artist and foreign legations being subjected to scrutiny by Berlin as well as by foreign capitals. German concerts evoked a mixture of protest and enthusiastic response because the musicians not only represented Germany, but also the tradition of a pre-Nazi Germany. The Nazis, meanwhile, tolerated the situation because good music seemed to them a most suitable representative of a culture with which they wanted to be identified.

In addition to the established orchestras, opera companies, conductors and soloist performers, party ensembles like the NSRSO were promoted and sent on tour abroad as representatives of Nazi music making, recording some success—especially in Italy[150]—which was then reported back home, all carefully coordinated by Goebbels with Nazi foreign policy objectives and other interests. Efforts were also exerted to attract foreign artists to Germany to counter foreign policy set-backs and foreign- and emigre-initiated boycotts of German cultural programs.

Particularly noteworthy in 1933 was the acclaim accorded the Japanese conductor, Hidemaro Konoye, a brother of the Japanese Premier, who headed the Nya Symphony Orchestra in Tokyo and the Imperial Music Academy. He was called "the best non-German" Strauss interpreter. Hinkel himself addressed a letter to Heinrich Lammers of the Reich Chancellery in behalf of Konoye, whom he called the "Japanese Furtwängler," asking for an autographed picture of the Führer.[151] The special Japanese-German relationship occasioned no small amount of rationalization by the racist theorists.

But not even the aura of the name of Furtwängler could prevent leading foreign and German emigre musicians from turning down invitations from Germany for the 1934 season. The international reaction to the Aryan-clause of the Career Civil Service Law and the daily harassment of dissidents and Jews was marked by protests and proclamations of solidarity with the victims.

Hubermann's open letter to Furtwängler on August 31, 1933 acknowledged the good efforts of Furtwängler in behalf of human dignity and artistic freedom, while also concluding that the traditional powers which Furtwängler represented were used by the totalitarian state. Hubermann entered the conflict once more after the publication of the Nuremberg legislation, with an article in the *Manchester Guardian*, March 7, 1936 entitled, "Open Letter to the German Intellectual." He noted the "brutalization" of the German population; he would not be able to understand how a girl could have been dragged through the streets of Nuremberg for her associations with Jews. Furtwängler, in turn, deplored the violence but also pleaded that not all Germans should be punished for such deeds. While Hubermann believed in the sincerity of Furtwängler and, perhaps, of the majority's revulsion at such acts in Germany, he insisted that responsible Germans ought not observe such acts in silence.[152] To the emigres, the watchful world and other anti-Nazis abroad, Germany increasingly appeared as a monolith of sentiment. On the other hand, in the eyes of embattled traditionalists, the international boycott of the Berlin season contributed to undermining the position of the traditional influences of diplomats and musicians alike, since the Nazis tended to disregard the advice of the established order when that appeared no longer capable of preventing an international rebuff of the new Germany.

The Foreign Office, governmental and business agents, foreign ministries and musicians clung as long as possible to tradition. Furtwängler conducted at the Wagner Festival in Paris, a regular feature of the Paris Spring season. He engaged an international cast which included such singers as Lauritz Melchior, who would never again set foot in Germany. The governments, German legations and Germany's non-Nazi musicians continued their efforts of goodwill in the face of mounting opposition from the Nazis and the irate public opinion abroad.

The Philharmonic Orchestra itself was restructured and taken over by the Reich in October 1933, thus affecting its international reputation. But the social life around foreign embassies and in the German legations was slow to reflect the political change, at least until the first months of 1934. The refusal of great international soloists to appear with the Berlin Philharmonic in the 1933-1934 season constituted the first major demonstration against that change, thus affecting the relationship between Germany and international music life. Even so, the Nazis themselves continued to cultivate foreign artists. Göring and Goebbels were fond of various international stars in the performing arts. This Nazi penchant for the display of international celebrities contributed to the maintenance of the power of the German Foreign Office and of traditional standards in music and diplomacy. In addition to the appearance of Viscount Konoye in 1933, a large group of Italian artists arrived in Germany, despite Italo-German political tensions. Ottorino Respighi, who was an extraordinary member of the PAdK, Alfredo Cassella, Enrico Mainardi and the Spanish Gaspar Cassado contributed to the success of the Berlin season. German and Italian artists found the Italian embassy in Berlin a congenial place, ever since Ambassador Cerruti and his helpful wife, Donna Elizabeth, had taken up residence there. Artistic events were furthered in a somewhat less lively manner also by the French, Dutch, American and British legations.[153]

If we switch from reading intra-governmental memos and the minutes of the confidential press conferences to the memoir literature of old-hand professionals like Geissmar, the latter's commitment to traditional operations and the belief in their own indispensability stands out. The German Foreign Office was praised for preserving customary professional standards and the cultural exchanges through which excessive Nazification was to be blocked. Department VII of the Foreign Office still regulated cultural activities and exhibitions abroad. The reputation of pre-Hitler officials in the Arts division was intact, and the hopes of the international network of artistic exchanges rested on their security. Yet, in reality Goebbels was in charge, not immediately and totally after the legal mandate and the construction of his bureaucracy, but gradually. The conflict between his RMK and the RMVP Foreign Office under Heinz Drewes, plus the other Nazi offices, like those under the influence of Rosenberg, with Department VII became increasingly apparent, until one day, Geissmar acknowledged, the Department disappeared form the *Wilhelmstrasse* altogether.[154]

Meanwhile, established channels continued to operate in early 1934 when the Berlin Philharmonic, led by Furtwängler and Geissmar, was welcomed on its tour through England, Holland and Belgium by the official ambassadors. Von Hoesch, a non-Nazi, was a most gracious host in London at that time. In England, where violence was a distinct possibility, the integrity of the German ambassador, the good wishes of Sir Thomas Beecham and the music-loving Austrian minister Baron Franckenstein—the latter attending every rehearsal of the touring orchestra—were a source of strength to the traditional powers of diplomacy and music.

Also in The Hague, the German ambassador Count Zech and his wife, née Bethmann-Hollweg, a "charming survival of the ancient regime," were most helpful, although he no longer was allowed to attend emigre concerts by such international celebrities as Bruno Walter and Adolf Busch. The public was hostile and the concerts of Furtwängler were boycotted. The same was true in Belgium, where the old German ambassador Count Lerchenfeld—a long-time supporter of German music, having been ambassador to Austria before assuming his post in Belgium, and an avid chamber music player himself—was already retired by the Nazis. The neighbors of Germany had to be restrained by their governments and police. Thus, it was advisable for the Nazis to preserve the facade of the political, diplomatic grace of the old Foreign Service.[155]

All European nations dragged artistic affairs into the diplomatic cauldron of the 1930s and France was no exception. Commanding a great cultural network throughout Europe and staffed by officials who were sensitive to the arts, French foreign policy involved the arts. It relied on an active Salzburg connection to counter Nazi interests there and under Gabriel Puaux, its Ambassador in Vienna in 1933, intensified French involvement and even attempted to have French music included in the festival program.[156] The French also contributed much to the internationalist facade of German music by performing frequently and attending festivals in Germany.

In France much depended on the Foreign Minister, Barthou, a music lover and Wagner devotee. He and the new German ambassador Dr. Koester—like von Hoesch, not a Nazi—did their best to keep up relations. Geissmar was welcomed by both, receiving much comfort at a time when her position had become unique. She was called "Hitler-Jewess" by a refugee newspaper in Paris. Meanwhile the French, ranging from the President of the Republic to important musicians, attended the Berlin Philharmonia concert in Paris under Furtwängler. Barthou was present on the night before his celebrated departure to Poland.[157] This supporter of the traditional forces in Germany was assassinated in October 1934, thus illustrating the fate of those attempting to stem the Nazi tide by traditional means. Certainly the Nazis put much store in the prestige of Germany's musicians, to the extent of leaning over backward in allowing the Foreign Office its unique position, which indeed gave rise to false hopes in the international community as reflected in the memoir literature. The esprit de corps of the Foreign Service was maintained, it appeared, and Foreign Minister von Neurath—a key symbol of the relatively peaceful and legalistic Germany, though skillfully manipulated by the Nazis, as we know—was assured by Party authority of the importance of his office. The official arrangement at state affairs found the foreign ambassadors seated right behind Hitler, on orders of the Interior. The party assumed the right to receive official state visits—and that is of course crucial—while unofficial visits of musicians were left in the hands of von Neurath's office,[158] according to a government statement in January, 1938.

As the regime became more accustomed to the exercise of power and the discriminatory legislation was implemented in the world of music, the position of the non-Aryan Geissmar became more intolerable to them. Furtwängler's prominence alone protected her from the application of the Aryan-clause. On April 1, 1934, the change-over of the Berlin Philharmonic Orchestra to the Reich Company was completed. The entire staff was retained, although a business manager of the Propaganda Ministry was added in addition to the earlier appointed commissioner. Geissmar was still permitted to handle the foreign affairs of the orchestra, although her name was no longer allowed to appear in transactions with the Reich.[159]

The Foreign legations continued to pursue their own policies. The Italian Ambassador Cerruti phoned Geissmar in February 1934, requesting—at this advanced stage of Nazi subversion of her power—that she arrange an Italian tour of the orchestra under Furtwängler in April. Geissmar was received by Count Ciano at the Palazzo Chigi. She also arranged for a Furtwängler-Mussolini meeting, an act which infuriated Goebbels, since he had had no hand in the affair. Also in Italy the government and the German ambassador von Hassel had to intervene against boycotts by the population. In the end, von Hassel could report to the Foreign Office in Berlin that the tour was successful in spite of the prevalent anti-Nazi sentiments of the Italians and official reservations on the part of the Italian government.[160]

The special position of Geissmar, Furtwängler and the Berlin Philharmonic illustrated the discrepancy between Nazi theory and practice because of expediency. Göring could always be counted on to listen to the manager of the Prussian State Theatres, Heinz Tietjen, who in turn wanted to do everything possible to please Furtwängler. Geissmar was saved from Goebbels by Göring, the man who determined who was and who was not Aryan, while Goebbels himself understood the need for compromise. Nonetheless, this special privilege could not last long. The case of Berta Geissmar illustrated the transition from independence, through a period of uneasy adjustment, to the state of total integration of German music and diplomacy, more or less paralleling the exposure of Nazi intentions internationally. Her part in the Furtwängler-Mussolini meeting offered grounds for Nazi concern. Already in December of 1933, the business manager of a German artist society dealing with German artist relations abroad (*Deutsche Kunstgesellschaft*), Hans Esdras Mutzenbrecher complained about Geissmar to Goebbels' central office. Having personally been under attack from other Nazi agencies, Mutzenbrecher blamed his poor reputation on distorted information which he traced to Geissmar. "I consider it incompatible with the Third Reich for us to be set against one another by a Jewish 'intellectual'. I expect of you (*Ministerialrat* Rüdiger of the Propaganda Ministry), man to man, to undertake steps in my behalf after successful clarification of my case."[161]

Reports against Geissmar and other pressures of this sort mounted as the traditional establishment and methods of international relations regarding music were gradually eroded. While in 1934 German "Aryan" artists were still selectively free to appear abroad, soon the RMK insisted on the right to review each proposed trip abroad, thus facilitating Nazi control over foreign tours.[162] The curtailment of freedom of travel was paralleled by methods and standards imposed on foreign artists in Germany. In reaction to the detailed questionnaire which inquired into his ancestry, Cortot, who had visited Germany the year before, was among those who refused to participate in the 1934-1935 season of the Berlin Philharmonic. Goebbels had instituted the questionnaire without consulting Furtwängler. Upon Furtwängler's complaints in regard to this matter, Goebbels promised to rescind his order. However, he complied only in regard to the Berlin Philharmonic for a while. In general, international tours of foreigners in Germany, like Germans abroad, could no longer be treated separately from official interests. Fading resistance of the Foreign Office against intrusion of the machinery of state, especially of the RMVP, and the struggle of international German music agencies against the RMVP's claim to sole representational rights, were to characterize the prewar years.

The man who had denounced Berta Geissmar, H.E. Mutzenbrecher of the *Deutsche Kuntsgesellschaft*, addressed an interesting and illuminating note to RMK President Strauss in June 1934, taking issue with the proposed dissolution of his organization on orders of the RMVP. The elimination of this independent cultural organization was also deplored by the official Foreign Office, as well as the foreign office of the Party. Mutzenbrecher acknowledged in realistic terms that "camouflaging of our cultural propaganda is of utmost importance in view of anti-German sentiments abroad." His fears reflected not only his personal involvement and interest, but also the actual state of affairs regarding international opinion, the agitation of emigres, and the advice offered by traditional powers in Germany. To him, the undermining of traditional channels for artistic exchanges, including the respected Foreign Office by the RMVP was unfortunate. The anti-Semite Mutzenbrecher, himself a musician, was aware of the inexperience of new official cultural agencies. He foresaw the confusion in the German cultural propaganda effort abroad. What had been possible in Germany would not be so easy with respect to an aroused international community. Mutzenbrecher's advice spanned the entire area of culture as an implement of propaganda. Thus he responded positively to the suggestion of the noted geographer Karl Haushofer, president of the German Academy, who appealed to his friend Rudolf Hess to support the creation of a foreign office as an arm of the German Academy. Deploring the dissolution of his own office, Mutzenbrecher advocated the maintenance of his policy for which the German Academy would be a most suitable agent, inasmuch as it had "earned even greater respect abroad" than his own organization. Thus, "affairs of the Academy would not be associated with clumsy propaganda effort.. .Indeed, propaganda agents must regard themselves fortunate to be able to work under such a perfect facade as that offered by the German Academy.. .In the present Germany we all must learn to operate the extremely difficult mechanism of foreign cultural propaganda."[163]

These revealing communications of a well-connected individual confirm the documented intra-party struggle of agencies and personalities in the realm of foreign affairs. Haushofer was a teacher and friend of *Reichsleiter* Hess, while Mutzenbrecher's activity must be related to his demotion as a result of denunciations. Archival files of Bohle, Funk, Göring, Goebbels, Hess, Rosenberg, and Ribbentrop confirm their competing involvement in cultural representation abroad. The Foreign Office as such was powerless in matters of policy, although its position was formally confirmed. The traditional establishment also suffered greatly when the Goebbels-Furtwängler agreement was announced by the international press in March 1935.[164] After the heroic struggle of resisting what appears in retrospect, as the inevitable, the symbol of the institution of music opposition from within Germany had come to an "arrangement" with the Nazis. No amount of rationalization in terms of exclusive rights of the artist could hide the fact of surrender to the totalitarian state. Furtwängler stayed in Germany on Nazi terms, while his secretary was able to obtain a passport, only, however, through the intervention of the Dutch legation in Berlin. Although the German Foreign Office took orders from Nazi quarters, international pressures still were considered in most cases until the war.

Apart from individual boycotts, the Third Reich had become a reality, and the world collaborated. A number of reasons help explain the readiness of the musical collaborators abroad to continue to serve the interests of the Nazi state, whose motives to some degree resembled those of the German diplomats. Aside from interests in job, pay, international exposure and other career advantages, travel to Germany resulted in many instances from the sympathy of the musician and his/her country for the Third Reich. When the newly organized composers held their first convention February 13-17, 1934, the world press and friendly foreign composers attended, as noted above, including the French Carol-Berard, the Italian Adriano Lualdi, the Swede Kurt Attenberg, and the Austrian Wilhelm Kienzl. Such supporters of the Third Reich were included in a Permanent Council for International Cooperation Among Composers, which was founded to compete with the International Society for New Music. Conservatives, on the other hand, performed in Germany because they shared some Nazi ideals, but they also wanted to support German ideological friends like Furtwängler, to normalize music life, and to steer the country back into traditional patterns. For the sake of normalization, collaborating governments even generally honored the Nazi boycott of Jews who, of course, tended to stay away from Germany anyway.

After the first shocking changes and threats of 1933 and 1934 and further diplomatic crises, additional "peace" protestations by Hitler, and provocations such as the reintroduction of the compulsory draft, the repudiation of the Locarno Treaty, the remilitarization of the Rhineland, and new security arrangements and a major Hitler appeal for world peace while simultaneously declaring war on Jews and communism in early 1936, in that year of the Olympics the Nazi government also engaged in a public relations effort of advertising Berlin as an international music center. The RMK staged an international competition for composers of music, intended to express Olympic and athletic ideals. After national committees selected finalists from a paltry nine (of forty-nine) participating countries, an international jury—stacked with German musicians of clear Nazi persuasion, including by now familiar names like Ihlert, Raabe, Trapp, Havemann, Georg Schumann, Graener and Fritz Stein, as well as two sympathetic foreigners, Yrjo Kilpinen and Francesco Malipiero—awarded gold medals to Paul Höffer for his choral work, "Olympic Oath," and to Werner Eck for his commissioned and well-known "Olympic Festival Music"; silver medals to Kurt Thomas for his "Cantata for the 1936 Olympics" and to the Italian Lino Liviabella for his "The Victor"; and a bronze medal to the Czech Jaroslav Křička for his "To You, Fliers." As in the athletic competition, in music, the Nazi state sported an international look, but, it also wanted to win and overwhelm in demonstration of German superiority.[165]

Music contributed to the Olympic pageantry with performances and hundreds of compositions. And, beyond the Olympics, foreign musicians like the Vienna Boys Choir, the London Philharmonic, established chamber groups and the international stars Fedor Chaliapin, Maria Costes, Claudio Arrau, Alfred Cortot and many more performed in Berlin to justify the claim to the city's internationalism.[166]

The Olympics, international participation in Berlin's concert season and Ambassador Ribbentrop's conciliatory efforts notwithstanding, relations with Great Britain remained strained as Nazi practices became more threatening and offended public opinion, even though the Third Reich tried hard to appeal to that country on racial grounds. In spite of political differences and offensive overtures, artistic exchanges continued, Sir Thomas Beecham, for one, leading the famous London Symphony Orchestra on a Eurpoean tour in 1936 which included Berlin and a concert in Leipzig. The confusion surrounding this affair could not have been greater. The concert in Leipzig was a great success, yet this noted Englishman, who was welcomed by Mayor Goerdeler, a symbol of Conservative resistance to Nazism, became witness to the destruction of the Mendelssohn monument in that great music city. Beecham had wanted to honor Mendelssohn by placing a wreath before the statue, having received Goerdeler's permission and encouragement to do so. Goerdeler had protected the monument until this time on grounds of the international fame of Leipzig as a music city. The Londoners gave their performance while he was out of town and when they went to the *Gewandhaus* the next morning for the placing of the wreath, the statue was gone, having been removed the night before upon orders from acting mayor Haake.[167]

Thus, the Nazis did not hesitate to offend distinguished visitors. Notwithstanding Germany's interest in friendly relations with this member of the Germanic family of nations, the wooing reflected Nazi terms. In September, 1935 *Der Angriff* published an attack on Bosworth and Co.—an English publishing firm founded in Leipzig in 1899, which presented entertainment and coffeehouse music, generally in the form of transcriptions of well-known compositions—for not having kept pace with the elimination of Jewish compositions from its offering. "The latest and comprehensive table of contents of light music at Bosworth simply bypasses the understanding of the new Germany; as we find listed . . . the Jews Mendelssohn-Bartholdy, Meyerbeer, Grünfeld, Offenbach, Weinberger; and even such names which are already as good as forgotten reappear: Schreker, Bloch, Blech, Leo Fall, Stransky (this one even with a ghetto song)."[168] While this attack focused on a firm doing business in Germany, Karl Blessinger wrote in a feature article in *DM*, November 1939, of "England's racial decline as mirrored in its music." He noted the affection of German composers for England—Johann Christian Bach, Haydn and Weber having spent time there. The latter's *Oberon* had premiered in London, an event criticized by Blessinger for its emphasis on staging at the expense of musical context. This was attributed to the influence of the "eternal Jew." Indeed, the London Philharmonic Society was declared to be subject to the influence of the Jew Moscheles (Ignaz Moscheles, the well-known pianist, composer and conductor in the nineteenth century), who also had "attempted to show off with Beethoven." "Through Jewish operations of this sort" German artists had lost favor with the English public, while Mendelssohn was promoted, again by Moscheles, thus contributing to a development in the creative realm of "Mendelssohn-imitations." Blessinger equated Jewish and English practice, apparent in the evaluation of music in purely technical and mechanical terms. "Who ever has attempted to teach the English what we Germans understand as music must agree that soon a point is reached at which mutual understanding is no longer a possibility." Although Blessinger recognized some exceptions, he wrote that the general trend in England had resulted in

an actual internationalization of music which is predicated on the disregard for racial characteristics. It must be noted in this context that one of the most esteemed composers of the nineteenth century in England, Samuel Coleridge-Taylor, was a Negro bastard and that Jewish virtuosos and the few existing modern composers have been well re-

ceived. The influence of these racially alien elements upon this traditionally receptive English people cannot be exaggerated. And if in spite
of all efforts and some happy individual exceptions art music in England
has not been able to flourish, England has contributed most to the contamination of that daily diet of music of the European people.[169]

While the attacks on England were as direct as in the article above, the
offer of friendship was always implied. German ambivalence resulted in am-
biguous signals. On racial grounds, England passed the necessary requirements
for repentance and return to the Germanic community. The clumsy nature
of the ideological formulation had to be reinterpreted for the English by German representatives abroad. However, all the events in Germany, the commentaries and policy statements were reported and made an impression on
opinion in England. When Goebbels cautioned his followers on March 28,
1933 not to harm any Jews physically and not to apply the economic boycott
(announced in the same speech) to foreign Jews, his sensitivity to German
weakness and thus to international attitudes was manifest.

Yet, at the same time the radical policy toward the Jews was openly promoted until, finally, on September 15, 1935 the *Reichsbürgergesetz* was passed,
affirming the principle of citizenship contingent on German or related
blood.[170] Journal editors were instructed at the weekly Culture-Political Press
Conferences to intensify the anti-Semitic campaign and to add anti-Semitic
thrusts to reports about cultural events which, upon review, were not yet
so slanted.[171] The minutes of the press conferences in the summer of 1936,
however, also confirm the manipulation and the opportunistic nature of the
Jewish policy (at least in the limited sphere of cultural politics) which allowed
for taking advantage of the Olympics by informing the international public
about the flourishing cultural activities of Jewish organizations under German auspices. Even though the German press generally was not permitted
to attend and report on the events of the Jewish Cultural League (JKB), in
the year of the Olympics—the very year the weekly Cultural-Political Press
Conferences were instituted, it will be recalled, so that RMVP officials could
instruct feuilleton editors about what and how to report cultural events and
issues—supervisor Hinkel deplored the absence of publicity about the 148,000
JKB members, the forty to fifty weekly JKB events and its annual audience
of about 600,000. He even suggested that ten editors attend JKB events and
interview JKB leaders. The minutes also reveal very clearly his intention to
exploit JKB activites for propaganda purposes. To counter foreign attacks
on Nazi social policy he allowed the famous Rosé Quartet, a member of the
JKB, to appear abroad, and he permitted mention of exceptional Jews in German concert life, like the conductor Leo Blech.

Hinkel also acknowledged and defended the continuing Jewish presence in the business of sheet music, other musical materials and antiquities. For instance, the Graupe Firm was retained for its international reputation, foreign earnings and propagation of German cultural policy. He similarly defended the "Jewish publishers," Peters and Fürstner which were regarded abroad as German firms and whose copyright was not contestable. He responded to complaints about these contradictions by ridiculing ideological purists for "not understanding politics." The minutes of these revealing instruction sessions in which controlled "open" discussion took place attested to Nazi cynicism and reflected the twists and turns of policy relative to developments in international relations.[172] The main point is that in the year of the Olympics, foreigners were assured that segregation allowed for the freedom of both peoples' indigenous talents. Indeed, Jews would benefit from their exclusive organizations, being able to rediscover their roots and character. The Nazis invited the outside world to observe the separate but culturally flourishing activity of Jews in Germany[173]—an ironic twist of Nazi music politics.

In reality, the Hinkel campaign of segregation was exposed as a fraud by other actions. When the burning of undesirable music was suggested back in July 1933—after "the purifying fire of literary poison" in May,[174] the Nazis had already taken a step beyond segregation. And, even though the JKB was protected during Crystal Night, that pogrom was not consistent with Hinkel's protestations to the press. The program of purification by fire, of open terror and murder, coincided with the maintenance and manipulation of a cultural facade that extended beyond the policy of segregation up to the time when the political and international situation forced the hand of Nazi cultural policy makers. Meanwhile, international appeasement coexisted, reflected and reinforced the cultural facade. Indeed, until World War II, the useful Foreign Service of Nazi Germany had to smooth over the obvious contradiction between official ideology and terror, on the one hand, and protestations of international cooperation and goodwill on the other. Again, Furtwängler, Strauss and the entire prestigious music establishment served to project a favorable international profile of the new state. Also, Germany's Jews, marked as victims, were manipulated in behalf of the state which persecuted them. The minority status of Jewish cultural organizations in Germany, guaranteed by the state and upheld by the participation of artistic Jews, was symbolic of the prewar phase of the Third Reich and its international image. Thus, the hostile activities of emigres like Schönberg, Kestenberg, Hubermann and Paul Bekker, could be countered.

In this manner and on many levels of interest and awareness, international relations in music were upheld. Foreign musicians retained their honorary memberships in prestigious institutions, such as the PAdK, and Germans belonged to similar institutions abroad. Even Stravinsky, though much abused by Nazi ideologists, was listed throughout the Third Reich as a member of the PAdK. Indeed, the Academy protested at the office of Rust for the listing of Academy member Stravinsky at the "Degenerate Music" exhibit in Düsseldorf during the Reich Music Festival in 1938. In another note regarding Stravinsky, the Academy noted the political implication in this matter, inasmuch as Stravinsky enjoyed an international reputation of the first order, held French citizenship, was known as a friend of German Music and was not Jewish in spite of the crude reference to him at the exhibit through a gigantic poster which read, "Stravinsky—the Jew." A more acceptable musician on ideological grounds was Sibelius, who also retained his extraordinary membership. The Academy recommended him for the national Goethe prize in October 1935, bestowed on him on Hitler's personal authority through the channels of the Foreign Office, November 29, 1935. The interest in Nordic countries was actually great. The *Allgemeine Musik- Zeitung* reported June 4, 1937 that a reception had been given in honor of the Norwegian composer Christian Sinding, also an extraordinary member of the Academy and present at the Dresden Music Festival. Sinding, too, had received the Goethe medal through personal recommendations of *Reichsleiter* Rosenberg, February 22, 1938, although this had not been a simple matter. Hitler had almost foiled efforts of the Foreign Office and ideological spokesmen when he ordered that no Norwegian may receive the Goethe prize, thus reacting to the overt act of hostility on the part of the Norwegian government which had bestowed the Nobel prize for peace upon the journalist pacifist Carl von Ossietzky, then held in a concentration camp, where he died in 1938. The Foreign Office kept Sinding's case alive, writing letters to Goebbels, encouraging the latter to intercede in behalf of this composer who had openly expressed his sympathy for the Third Reich. Inasmuch as Sinding had received the official prize in Oslo through his King Haakon, it was strongly recommended to follow up by sanctioning the act through official decoration in Germany.[175]

The Sinding case illustrated the complex issues involving artists across national boundaries. A Jugoslavian musician, Dr. Joseph Vlach-Vruticky, a conductor of the Philharmonic orchestra at Ragusa, was recommended for honors through the Academy. Like many musicians of the times, he had dedicated compositions to Nazi leaders: In 1937 a work for Orchestra called *Heldengesang* ("Heroic Song"), dedicated to "the *Führer* and Reich Chancellor," his military marches to "*Generalfeldmarshall* Hermann Göring," a choral work with Jugoslav text to "Minister Dr. Goebbels," and his *Symphonie Poetique* to the Cardinal Archbishop of Vienna, Dr. Innitzer. Advertised as interpreter of classical and modern German music who has furthered

German composers as guest conductor abroad, this author of a work on the *Philosopy of Art*, was styled an "avowed Germanophile". As such, he was recommended for membership in the Academy. Unfortunately, the Academy had to answer that its constitution had been suspended on orders of the government, and that new memberships could not at present be officially reviewed. The consulate in Jugoslavia was informed of the situation and Vlach-Vruticky received official thanks for his dedication of the *Heldengesang* to Hitler. Thus, by May 1939 Göring had not acted in regard to the Academy, and the Foreign Service as well as the Academy had their hands full maintaining normal relations in such otherwise abnormal matters. Indeed, the question was raised whether all foreign members of the Academy had the right to remain members in the Academy, thus questioning the status of Stravinsky, Sibelius, Sinding, etc. On the other hand, German musicians were still honored abroad. The Foreign Office informed the Academy officially (May 27, 1941), of honorary citations received by Professors Schindler, Leschetizky and von Reznicek in Sweden; the Royal Swedish Academy having named the three honorary members. Notwithstanding these activities, the Academy was restricted by the government's indecision. International events dictated policy in regard to musicians, and the fate of the independent Foreign Office too was contingent on developments which were beyond its control.[176]

When the well-known international Donaueschinger festival of modern music was dissolvd after its leading spirits had left Germany, the international festival at Baden-Baden was substituted on the basis of the new principle, which regarded music as expression of nationality. The Foreign Office had to take note of these developments, too, especially in regard to such cultural organizations as the Nordic Ring, styled by the racist author and painter Wolfgang Willrich as "International of those of Nordic Blood" called to defend itself against the "International of Jews and *Untermenschen*" who were poised for a blood bath of Nordic man. Willrich's letter, addressed to Reich Peasant Leader Darré, was dated October 4, 1938, thus making direct reference to the Munich conference, at which the annexation of the *Sudetenland* was decided. He proposed active collaboration with German-Nordic elements in other countries, mentioning specifically the *Action Française* as suitable representative in France.[177] The feasibility of this foreign policy on the basis of racial definition would of course depend on the outcome of the coming great war. Literature and endeavors of this sort foreshadowed the activation of ideology abroad. Until the war, however, the official representatives of Germany compromised their traditional standards at home but allayed foreign fears abroad. They contributed to a confusing and confused world in which normal channels of communications were maintained, denying the reality reported by the world press. In the area of foreign contact the German artist was able to delude himself by believing that the conservative tradition, or at least the genuine *völkisch* ideology, might yet persevere, thus preventing the consequences as recorded by events in the immediate future, precisely because the Nazis were on relatively good behavior in their dealings with music as an international medium.

Apart from encroachments by Goebbels in the areas of culture and public relations, the Foreign Office was undermined directly by the rival party organization under the leadership of the unconventional Ribbentrop, created in 1933 and attached directly to the staff of Hess. Ribbentrop had direct access to Hitler, whose confidence he enjoyed: he became his "Ambassador-at-large," had access to Foreign Office reports other than those specifically addressed to the Minister and State Secretary, and focused on British-German relations to the point of lifting these from Foreign Office jurisdiction—prior to becoming Foreign Minister in fact in 1938. He had been instrumental in extending the invitation to the London Philharmonia Orchestra to tour Germany in 1936, the year he became ambassador to Great Britain. Ironically, he had to deal with Sir Thomas Beecham's new secretary, the emigre Berta Geissmar. Geissmar had made the acquaintance of Beecham while on tour with Furtwängler, at which time the great Englishman offered to help her if ever needed. In 1936 she handled the tours of the Londoners.

Ribbentrop obviously constituted a threat to the Foreign Office, paralleling the general rivalry between the traditional state organizations and those of the party, the latter introducing party functionaries, an array of amateurs, and personal friends of the leader. Berta Geissmar, in dealing with Ribbentrop, who was aristocratic and cultured and whom she found acceptable as a person, but who lacked experience, offered to arrange the tour through friends at the Berlin Philharmonic, thereby greatly relieving Ribbentrop's liaison officer.[178]

Of course, Ribbentrop did not restrict his activities and interests to music. Ulrich von Hassel, German ambassador to Italy, noted after the war that after Ribbentrop's appointment to the Foreign Ministry, February 4, 1938, no member of the service was properly informed about policy. Ribbentrop simply moved his office into the Foreign Ministry, and the transference as such was not noted by von Hassel as a major event. Earlier encroachment had made this move inevitable, although it was not clear whether Ribbentrop rather than Rosenberg would assume open control of the foreign service. As of December 1, 1937, seven of ninety-two staff members had joined the party before entering the diplomatic service, twenty-six had joined since, thirty-seven were still non-members; for twenty-two staff members, no information regarding party membership was listed.[179] By August 1940, seventy-one of one hundred and twenty high-ranking Foreign Service officers were Pg's. In this period after the outbreak of war, new posts in conquered territory were given to party faithfuls. Indeed, Ribbentrop planned a complete reform of the service, an undertaking cut short only by the pressing demands of the war.

The story of the German Foreign Office in the pre-war years was one of various degrees of collaboration and slow subversion of its authority through the rival organizations and ministries of the Nazi state, culminating in the official transfer of power into the hands of Ribbentrop. The Foreign Countries Organization (AO) of the party, notorious for its role in the creation of fifth columns among ethnic Germans abroad, coordinated ethnic German activities, while simultaneously spying on German diplomats. When in 1937 the AO received an official place in the Foreign Office with jurisdiction over all ethnic Germans abroad—its leader Bohle reporting directly to Hess and receiving a cabinet post—the carefully cultivated independence of the Foreign Office under von Neurath's weak leadership and acquiescence was effectively undermined.

In practice, the AO expanded its contacts among ethnic Germans whom it coordinated and manipulated, and played a key role in the dramatic events in pre-*Anschluss* Austria and before and during the Civil War in Spain.[180] It helped arrange German cultural events abroad and was especially active in Latin America, securing radio time for German music and music propaganda aimed at the large ethnic German communities there. A vital role was also played by the long-established and powerful League of Germans Abroad (VDA)—in 1933 under the leadership of the Carinthian propagandist, Reich leader Hans Steinacher, until it was placed under SS leadership to become a major tool of radical ethnic policies which resulted in drawing German ethnics into the Nazi sphere, away from identification with their homelands, in wartime resettlement and post-war expulsion. Historians have noted the central role of the border and ethnic German ideology in "the genesis of National Socialism and later in its foreign policy." K.D. Bracher, for instance, has written that "again and again, it was stressed that leading personalities of the Third Reich by birth belonged in the category of border and ethnic Germans, i.e. Hindenburg (Poznan), Hitler (Braunau), Rosenberg (Riga), Hess (Egypt), Darré (Argentina)."[181] The VDA cultivated the notion of German separatism and superiority. Leading German musicians like Pfitzner (St. Petersberg) shared and helped formulate VDA attitudes, while music was promoted and manipulated as a key expression of ethnic-racist claims.

Thus Nazi practices and expedience were exposed in this area of foreign relations, while sincere ideologists and traditionalist diplomats were repeatedly embarrassed. On the basis of a pro-English policy of the government, Ribbentrop had to compromise official ideology by demonstrating cordiality in his dealings with Berta Geissmar, who had been rejected in Germany. In fact, upon the insistance of Sir Thomas Beecham she accompanied the London orchestra while touring Germany. An official representative of the London orchestra in Germany, she was treated as honored guest, constantly accompanied by leading officials. Ribbentrop assured Beecham that Berta Geissmar had nothing but friends in Germany—an ironic note. While still in Germany, Havemann had added to Mutzenbrecher's denunciation of Geissmar in 1935 in unmistakable and representative terms: "Dr. Geissmar is sabotaging the building of National Socialism through her connections with Jews abroad." In practice, the Nazis themselves were of course utilizing emigre connections abroad. Although contact with refugees in other countries was strictly forbidden by 1934, even the RMK made frequent use of emigre concert agencies in order to form foreign connections which they themselves did not possess.[182]

Notwithstanding the glaring contradictions, Nazi policy abroad imposed itself on traditional organs of international relations. While intellectual ideologists, conservative diplomats, musicians, and fellow-travellers promoted National Socialism as a mass movement internally and as a respectable *völkisch* embodiment of the principle of national self-determination abroad, the Nazis adopted policies which corresponded to their increase in actual political and military power. Music could not remain untouched as Goebbels and Frick extended their controls over musical exchange with foreigners; Ribbentrop successfully rivaled the traditional Foreign Office; Furtwängler attached himself to the new powers, Strauss embarked upon an "inner emigration"; Jews were confirmed in their confined state, and thousands of German intellectuals—especially Jews—left their homeland. This trend, which was marked by increasing agressiveness internationally and culminated in World War II, also helped to accomplish the final elimination of the traditional Foreign Office as a power center. The transition lasted until the war, at which time the Foreign Office emerged as a Nazi-controlled and Nazi-staffed organ of state, executing an imperialistic design contingent on battle events. Before open aggression, however, the process was one of coordination at first, as we have seen, and total integration with organizational and ideological designs later. Symbolic of the transition was Hitler's denunciation of the Nobel Prize in 1935, after which no German national was permitted to receive the international mark of distinction. A "national prize" of 100,000 RM was substituted. The symbolic actions reflected the slow erosion of traditional diplomacy manifested in Hitler's deliberate creation of international crises. The list of incidents in the long chain of German disregard of international agreements continued and was noted by the diplomatic and musical communities. Europe now went through the process experienced by Germans during the first few years of Nazi power. Nazi confidence had at one time grown in proportion to the collapse of republican opposition to coordination internally. Internationally, that same confidence, boldness and aggressiveness were demonstrated in German rearmament, the Saar plebiscite, the remilitarization of the Rhineland and the open discussion of incorporating Austria and the *Sudetenland* into the new Reich, and all of these crises were accompanied by orchestrated music and occasioned hundreds of compositions inciting and commemorating the events. Thus the moderate influence of the Foreign Office was reduced proportionately to the reassertion of a more militant international posture, which was reflected in von Neurath's replacement by von Ribbentrop. At the same time Hitler also created an *Oberkommanda der Wehrmacht* under the leadership of the subservient General Keitel, while old-line military leaders, thus potential oppositionists, War Minister von Blomberg and the Commander-in-Chief von Fritsch were eliminated, thereby giving Hitler absolute control over the generals and diplomats.

Meanwhile, the Third Reich continued to actively subvert the Austrian government, thus complementing the efforts of Austrian Nazis who had been busy sabotaging the attempts of Dollfuss, and then Schuschnigg, to maintain Austria's independence. For Nazis on both sides of the border a legitimate division between Austria and the Third Reich did not exist. Contacts had been upheld across the border by Nazis and non-Nazis alike. Especially in the area of music it was difficult to argue against the existence of a common heritage. Politics activated cultural impulses in the expression of solidarity. The Austrian party acknowledged the position of Hitler, who, after all, was on his way toward fulfilling the historic ambitions of the Austrian Hapsburgs. In the manner of the Nazis before 1933 in Germany, Austrian Nazis identified themselves as patriotic groups, often in the role of martyrs and subjected to governmental persecution. The composer Jaromir Weinberger countered the Nazi offensive with musical means as he dedicated his Czech opera, *Wallenstein*, to the Austrian Chancellor Schuschnigg in allegorical reference to his resistance to encroaching Nazism; the opera was produced in Vienna in German translation, August 1, 1937.[183]

One representative Nazi activist, the composer and conductor Leopold Reichwein, was the subject of an adulatory article in the *ZfM*, March 1936. He had lent himself for such purposes to such an extent that the Austrian police had recently informed the well-known Viennese Concert Society that the appearance of Reichwein was henceforth forbidden. The order was to be understood as a security measure, as a means of forestalling public demonstration and violence. This governmental order reflected the seriousness of the situation in Austria and the government's concern over Nazi activity. Reichwein had taken a political position which threatened the regime. In turn, the Nazi activist was typically cast in the role of martyr, lending himself to party propaganda in Germany. As early as 1920 he had been forced to refrain from conducting by the "all powerful Social Democratic Party of Austria" and the "increasing influence of Jews." At that time, Reichwein had assumed leadership of the newly founded cycle of symphony concerts of the Society of Friends of Music. Upon the death of Ferdinand Löwe the Society had appointed Reichwein its concert director, a position he held until the year of crisis, 1936. This "promoter of young Austrian composers" and embodiment of "upright German sentiment" was well-known in Germany. The September 30, 1933 issue of the *VB* had carried an article by Reichwein entitled "Jews in German Music," in which he took issue with the "Jewish press which alone set standards" in Vienna. Since that time the Viennese "asphalt" press had waged war against Reichwein, a Nazi hero who, as a conductor, had already then dared to reject performances of Mendelssohn and the engagement of Jewish soloists and to publicly stand by "the greatest son of Austrian soil, Adolf Hitler." The Nazi press had referred to Reichwein as the most popular Viennese conductor, who had maintained his rigorous schedule which included speeches at the University of Vienna and other distinguished institutions. Covering the topic of Jews and music, he "had entered the activist line of Adolf Hitler's artists." He had also founded the orchestra of the Vienna chapter of the KfdK, which, however, was restricted to only one performance in consequence of the suppression of the NSDAP in Austria, May 1933. Nonetheless, Reichwein had kept up his fight against the Jewish, as well as against the Christian-Socialist "patriotic" press.[184]

The Austrian music world was integrated within the Nazi design as political events shaped and determined life in music. When Chancellor Schuschnigg visited Hitler on February 12, 1938 and was forced to accept the Nazi Seyss-Inquart into his cabinet as Minister of the Interior, Toscanini vowed not to return to Salzburg or anywhere else in Austria. The Nazis accelerated operations. Seyss-Inquart called for German help, and Germany invaded Austria on March 12, taking it over without opposition. Salzburg, too, fell without resistance. In his last address to the Austrian people Schuschnigg spoke over the radio system which also carried Austrian music. The program came to an abrupt halt after which the Horst-Wessel Song was heard.[185] Schuschnigg was arrested, and the transfer of sovereignty was confirmed by the plebiscite of April 10, accompanied by expressions of loyalty of major musical organizations, including distinguished musicians like the composer Julius Bittner, Siegmund von Hausegger and naturally Reichwein, GMD Karl Böhm, the Society of the Friends of Music, the Vienna Schubert League and more. Self-coordination preceded commands.

The *Anschluss* of Austria marked a convincing demonstration of German strength internationally. German exiles in Vienna, such as Richard Tauber, Artur Schnabel, Jarmila Novotna, Vera Schwarz, Bruno Walter and Erich Kleiber were forced to embark on the characteristic second leg of retreat, either to Prague, London, Paris or New York. Elizabeth Schumann, Lotte Lehmann and the Norwegian contralto Kerstin Thorborg left Austria, never to return. This great German-speaking center of music was now in Nazi hands, as the experience of propaganda and organization in Germany was applied vigorously to the coordination of Austrian music. While German armies marched past enthusiastic crowds to the accompaniment of Prussian martial music, German-Austrian classical sounds, and music composed for the occasion (like lieutenant-colonel Paul Winter's fanfare, *"Grossdeutschland*—April 10, 1938," which commemorated the plebiscite) the true identity of the terror state was revealed, in contrast to the restraints imposed earlier by diplomatic tact which had been contingent on Germany's military weakness. German imperialism provided the base for a dynamic foreign policy toward music, thus contributing to a revival of ideological zeal which might otherwise have stagnated in over-organization, as in Germany, where there were signs of people growing tired of mass demonstrations and ritual expressions of enthusiasm. Moreover, the application of Nazi policy in Austria and Austrian music could be undertaken immediately and with great speed, since Germany was stronger militarily and did not have to consider foreign opinion to the same degree as before.

The *Anschluss* of Austria to the Reich, realizing the principle of national self-determination of Germans in a unified community, provided the Nazi ideologists, music journalists, editors, and organizers with an experimental base of operations on an unprecedented scale and pace. The experience gathered here enabled policy makers in cultural affairs to accompany German armies in their future conquests as practical organizers and propagandists, when the universal principle of national self-determination no longer provided a rationale for cultural expansion.

Goebbels set out to annex all cultural life of Austria, focusing especially on Vienna. Agents of the RMK were dispatched to oversee the coordination of music immediately and commissioners were appointed by State Secretary of the NSAP for Cultural Affairs, Hermann Stuppack, to lead major musical institutions. As in Germany, inadmissable musicians disappeared from small and large institutions alike, the only difference being that the purges took place within a few days in Vienna. Famous men of international standing were immediately affected. Bruno Walter was to have been arrested, but he managed to escape, although his belongings were confiscated and his daughter was temporarily taken into custody. The man who had sent a telegram to Toscanini on February 20, asking him not to desert Salzburg, was again left without a country. He obtained French citizenship through a special decree. At this time, only those who had a "J" identification printed in their passports obtained exit permits legally. The Vienna State Opera was particularly hard hit: Walter left; the venerable Arnold Rosé, leader of the orchestra for fifty-seven years, retired; and the principal cellist, Friedrich Buxbaum, sought refuge in London. Rosé joined Buxbaum and founded the new Rosé Quartet which performed the Kaiser Quartet of Haydn in the presence of the ex-Minister of Austria to London, Baron von Franckenstein, who also had decided against a return to his native land and had asked for English citizenship, which was granted. Franckenstein also was knighted. Meanwhile in Vienna, Mahler and Walter portraits and engravings of Rosé disappeared from the Philharmonia Office. The *Mendelssohngasse* became the *Mestrozzigasse*, the *Gustav-Mahler-Strasse* was renamed *Meistersingerstrasse*, and the famous Mahler-bust by Rodin was removed from the Vienna State Opera. Again, musical commemorations followed the event. An *Ostmark* overture was composed by Otto Besch to celebrate the Nazification and annexation of Austria and was performed at the Reich Music Festival in Düsseldorf, May 22, 1938, where the distinguished musicologist Hans-Joachim Terstappen lectured on "Music in Greater Germany". The composer of popular music, Peter Kreuder captured the moment for "seventy-five million Germans" with the hit song, *Das deutsche Volk am Donaustrand* ("The German people at the bank of the Danube").[186]

On June 11, 1938, the RKKG was officially introduced to Austria, thus subjecting Austrian musicians and their organizations to RMK administration, compulsory membership and the questionnaire. Established norms, legal formulations and precedents, the index and the censorship agencies of Nazi Germany became music law of the new German territory, called the *Ostmark*.[187] After the turmoil, the reality of flight or adjustment, the structure of the RKK finalized the take-over, extending into Austria. This was to become the precedent to be followed in future conquests.

In its May 1939 issue, *DM* recorded the *Anschluss* as it affected the music community. The account of the Austrian musicologist, Professor Alfred Orel, who was appointed to head the Academy of Music, confirmed the general response of the Austrian public, the enthusiastic mass demonstrations, particularly at Hitler's speeches in Linz and Vienna. The musician's reflections complemented the numerous accounts of the emotional response to the historic event, for instance, those contained in the letter of Göring's sister to her brother. She "could not comprehend the wonderful events...being deeply touched...tears rolling down her face, while sitting near the radio."[188] Orel—who had received his PhD under the guidance of the Jewish scholar Guido Adler—wrote that "the overwhelming experience of the fortunate real-

ity which a few weeks earlier had been a distant dream of most painful longing, had also most fundamentally transformed the music life of Vienna." What
appeared as a link in a chain of misfortune to the victims of Nazi aggression
and what amounted to a shock to traditional music, thus constituting what
has here been treated as the imposition of totalitarian authority, was experienced and reviewed as an authentic national regeneration. Especially
music, the characteristic Viennese expression, would be affected by these
events. Orel's account was reminiscent of the articles in Germany in 1933.
He noted the level of Jewish control of the arts in Vienna and the "brutal
suppression of national consciousness" among Austrian artists before, when

> the chains were drawn tighter and tighter, more intolerable, while a
> horde of Jewish parasites sunbathed in the ancient glory of the culture
> center, Vienna...Proportionately to the unfolding of free German art
> beyond the border of the "independent" Austria, the situation in Austria
> deteriorated, as the main stream of "Semigres" (a native pun), if not
> the influence of Paris and London,...flooded Vienna. At the reception
> of Vienna's artists, Minister Dr. Goebbels characterized the situation
> pointedly, "Is there still a sign of native art here?"[189]

Orel recorded that enthusiasm was immediately followed by organizational activity. Existing organizations, such as the Association of Authors,
Publishers and Composers (which had been incorporated in Stagma in Germany), the Association of Music Teachers, Association of Composers, Musicians's Union, Stage Artists Ring, etc., received new administrations, while
the two great Viennese publishing houses, especially the hated Universal-
Edition and the Bühnenverlag J. Weinberger, received supervisory commissioners. All these organizations had to be carefully guided into "the new
times." Orel explained that the state did not intend to liquidate existing institutions, but to maintain flourishing undertakings while "transforming them
into truly cultural organizations." He referred to the great number of music
schools in Jewish hands which now required supervision, citing conditions
at the new Viennese Conservatory of Professor Dr. Josef Reitler, the former
music critic of the Neue Freie Presse, where seventy of one hundred instructors were Jewish. In the wake of reconstruction, Professor Franz Schütz, an
organist, was appointed to the State Academy of Music and Representational
Art as commissioner, to supervise the restructuring of this leading music and
theater institute in Austria, so that it might serve as a model for the entire
music and other educational programs of the land. In addition to expanding
the program in the area of music education, the racial and political legislation of the Reich was to be applied to existing personnel as opponents were

arrested and Jews purged. Austrian music institutions had to "contribute to the rise of the people through their art." The integration of culture policy and Nazi imperialism were blatantly expressed in the appeal to the Vienna State Academy which, as the easternmost Academy of the Reich, "must realize its special obligation to our people. According to the *Führer*, the *Ostmark* was the oldest and the youngest bulwark of *Deutschtum*, and the Academy had to fulfill its mission toward the East.[190]

Public concert life was integrated institutionally through the appointment of Dr. A.C. Hochstetter to the post of Secretary General of the *Konzerthausgesellschaft*. Hochstetter also headed the local RMK. Professor Franz Schütz was appointed commissary leader of the Society of Friends of Music, in addition to his post as director of the Reich Academy of Music at Vienna, while the Vienna Philharmonic Society, that autonomous association of members of the State Opera Orchestra, which had traditionally sponsored its own Philharmonic Concerts, was now supervised by the new commissioner, Wilhelm Jerger, a composer and musicologist. At the State Opera itself, the non-Nazi Dr. Erwin Kerber who had played a vital role at the Salzburg Festival and was placed in the dreadful position of having to hand out dismissal notices, was retained as General Manager "while his artistic advisor, Bruno Walter (Schlesinger), and the conductors, Josef Krips and Karl Alwin (Pinkus) were indeed dismissed." Orel's list of new personalities would not have been complete without mention of the activist leader Reichwein, who was welcomed again at the State Opera. "The previous prevalence of Jews among State Opera soloists necessitated almost total renewal of the ensemble's personnel." Equally noteworthy was the "support to be accorded nationalistic artistic groups, like the Viennese Academic Mozart Society and the famous *Tonkünstler* Orchestra." The organization of music in Austria, especially in Vienna, was undertaken rapidly and thoroughly. Orel reported that the *Führer's* word is borne out in music, "Austria is a pure land." [191]

While the *Anschluss* affected music everywhere in Austria, the impact varied from place to place. Vienna was central and experienced the combination of anxious self-coordination, rapid purges of Jews, old enemies and dissenters, and the construction of an administration based on the RKKG and earlier experiences in Germany. Salzburg, so close to the German border fell to a bloodless coup on March 11, before German troops arrived the next day to confirm the *fait accompli*. The provincial governor and Fatherfront leader Franz Rehrl was replaced by a local Nazi. A few weeks later Göring, Himmler and Hitler passed through the town to the cheers of the crowds. A new musical order was quickly instituted under direct RMVP supervision but, in Salzburg, without major purges—the few Jews and emigres in music life had departed beforehand. Only Bernhard Paumgartner—a non-Jew—lost his position as director of the Mozarteum in exchange for a sinecure. The RMVP and a local Nazi power structure led by the capable Gau leader and later Festival director, Friedrich Rainer, in concert with Kajetan Mühlmann, the new State Secretary for culture in Seyss-Inquart's government, worked with a network of retained officials to preserve a festival of high quality.

The Nazi state had intended to Germanize the festival. Now that the opportunity existed, Göring himself spoke about the celebration of the "German soul." Nevertheless, the minutes of the Culture-Political Press Conferences in Berlin reveal that *Reichsdramaturg* Rainer Schlösser—the director of programming for all German stages—advocated continuity, competence and efforts to retain the festival's international flavor[192]—thereby confirming the RMVP's realistic approach to the assessment of music and to its propagandistic value, as was evident in the minutes of other Culture-Political Press Conferences since their inception in mid-1936.

The 1938 program resembled the successful one of the preceding year as a result of much careful planning—a backhanded tribute to the tradition of the great emigres. An *Egmont* rather than a *Faust* production by a former Reinhardt associate, Böhm in place of Walter and Toscanini, the first Salzburg appearance of the Swiss pianist Edwin Fischer, and several new singers from Berlin joined old hands in a traditional and international program. Under the new management, Salzburg remained competently staffed and attained the credible artistic level useful for Nazi propaganda and cultural facade for the expanding Third Reich, yet in characteristic Nazi form. High art was draped in swastika flags with Goebbels in attendance. Thousands of workers were brought in under the KdF organization to make up for the many foreign cancellations and in demonstration of the romantic-*völkisch*-Nazi people's art concept—at the cost of an enormous subsidy and the ridicule of some foreign journalists, who wrote of a "beer-drinking" and "disinterested" audience. By the time plans were made for 1939, the editors at the Culture-Political Press Conferences had been instructed to deemphasize the Salzburg Festival and to place it on a footing with other music festivals in the Reich; only Bayreuth was to retain special consideration. Regardless of lowered expectations and budget concerns, the festival was overshadowed by the Polish crisis, even though Hitler made two appearances—August 9 and 14—to the delight of the performers, audience and local press. Thereafter the festival reflected the tides of war and propaganda strategies. It retained a remarkably high quality under the capable batons of the Reich's conductors: Böhm, Knappertsbusch, Furtwängler, and especially Clemens Krauss who dominated in the years 1942-44. As the war turned more serious for Germany, Nazi interest in Salzburg waned and the press was instructed to restrict coverage even more, until all festivals were closed as part of Goebbels' total war campaign.[193]

If Salzburg had a celebrated international tradition which was acknowledged and manipulated by Goebbels and, therefore, survived as a musical gem in the care of the Reich's greatest performers and competent and dedicated administrators, another provincial town, Linz, demonstrated an altogether different experience, reported to Fred Prieberg in detailed accounts of key officials of the Nazi period. This expanding industrial city of 150,000 by 1938 had outgrown its cultural establishment due to the pressure of new and upwardly mobile classes which, in addition to the needs of the growing working class, faced severe institutional and financial problems—regardless of the *Anschluss*. Linz had its musical societies, choral associations, an orchestra of only forty contract players and a theatre which offered the typical mix of theatre, concerts, opera and operettas. What makes this capital of upper Austria special in this examination of Nazi music politics is that Hitler's family had moved there in his youth. Young Hitler had attended school in Linz, gone to its theatre, indulged in dreams of becoming an artist or architect there, and had already then developed grandiose plans for rebuilding the city and its cultural centers. As it turned out, the future leader did not forget his home town or architectural projects.

At first, the *Anschluss* in Linz led to the typical application of the RKKG, governmental reconstruction and personnel turnover. But, beyond the formal appointment of officials to the various party and state offices, including those that governed cultural affairs, rational renewal got lost in the maze of conflicting jurisdictions. The newly appointed *Musikbeauftragte*—that official, it will be recalled, responsible for local music programs—Franz Kinzl, an apparently sincere Pg. since 1933, a school teacher and competent composer of some reputation, whose wide-ranging compositional record included "Variations on the Horst-Wessel-Song" and an introduction to another popular Nazi song, *Volk ans Gewehr*, complained to Prieberg in 1963 about the chaotic condition of music in 1938. This was largely due to the number and overlapping of authorities—each party and governmental office at the local, county and provincial level having a cultural section authorized to deal with music. The cultural specialist in Ferry Pohl's Gau Propaganda Office undermined most of Kinzl's plans as well as RMK policies and directives, until Kinzl resigned and joined the army, in spite of some success in staging programs and conducting a concert himself which included his own symphonic poem, *Die Stadt*. His complaints to Berlin had led nowhere. The *Musikbeauftragte* was to possess those qualities which were to help resolve conflict and integrate music life to the satisfaction of music lovers and local and national officialdom. Kinzl's successor, Josef Straub—not a Pg, but the local head of the RMK and of the Linz Concert Society—even consulted with the RMK in Berlin in person—specifically with Dr. Otto Benecke of the RMK Concert Office. His projects:

to expand the entire program, enlarge the orchestra, encourage youth development, enlist more support for a new Concert Society, and engage a young new conductor, Max Kojetinsky, also were undermined by the *Gau* propagandists illustrating the classic features of disorganization due to competing authorities (the theme of this chapter at the national level) and the arbitrariness of local leaders and patronage. The same was demonstrated in the case of the local *Gau* leader August Eigruber's defiance of Goebbels, when he repaid the loyalty of the Jewish pianist Alfred Spitz of the Schuschnigg era by granting him an exceptional RMK membership until finally, in 1942, when pressure against Spitz had resulted in his exclusion from the RMK, Eigruber facilitated Spitz's emigration to America. During the controversy Eigruber allegedly had pointed out that "Goebbels is *Gau*-leader of Berlin; I am *Gau*-leader of the upper Danube and won't take instructions from the *Gau* leader of Berlin."[194]

We learn from the Linz situation that national policy, itself subject to different interpretations and jurisdictional conflicts, depended on local personnel for local implementation. Linz, in this respect, was not unique. However, the city escaped from the common lot because of its relationship to Adolf Hitler, who entered as *deus ex machina* upon the provincial scene. Beginning in early 1939, Hitler intended to turn Linz into a major European cultural center. To this end he had developed elaborate plans and actual designs for urban reconstruction, monumental museums which would store confiscated and captured art resulting from his conquests, a house of art, public buildings and an immense opera. The governmental and party leadership from Bormann, Himmler, Göring and Goebbels down to the *Gau* leader Eigruber became involved in this incredible scheme.[195] Music benefited from this *Führer* project. The incompetent *Gau* Propaganda Chief and his specialist for cultural affairs were forced to resign. Flunkies of local leaders in general were replaced by professionals. For instance, Adolf Trittinger, a prominent organist, was appointed head of the famous Bruckner Conservatory where he had taught the organ while the institution was placed under provincial administration. Meanwhile, three new orchestras were founded and professionally organized under the newly engaged GMD Georg Ludwig Jochum in accordance with the plans of higher authority. Most importantly, Kinzl was recalled to Linz in August 1940—this time combining in his person all the cultural offices that had conspired against the plans of the former *Muzikbeauftragten*. He brought order to music and promoted its various institutions and activities including opera, with the help of Hitler's private fund, and also folk music, music education and especially compositions—all in the interest of his conception of a Nazi society. He had to deal with the Spitz affair which he brought to Berlin's attention, tried to reconcile party with professional interests, and supported local composers, including his own compositions, against Jochum's conservative programming of the classics, and young talent against Jochum's inclination to engage name soloists such as Friedrich Wähler, Ann Konetzni, Georg Kulenkampf, Wilhelm Kempff, Wolfgang Schneiderhahn and Adolf Steiner for the 1940/41 season. He staged an organ improvisation competition which attracted much press coverage and then got Trittinger in trouble. He had asked Trittinger to organize a Hindemith evening which Hitler had learned about since he apparently had a habit of reading the papers of his home town.[196]

The *Anschluss* was affected in music, and music in turn lent itself as an implement of power politics of the dynamic Nazi state. The change from the Vienna waltz to Prussian and Nazi marches on the day of conquest reflected the complicity. By means of the speedy and thorough coordination of Austrian music, the purges of unacceptable musicians and the maintenance and enhancement of institutions and acceptable musicians—including those of international reputation like Furtwängler, who retained his position with the Vienna Philharmonic Orchestra, and Böhm, an enthusiastic supporter of the regime—a pattern for future expansion existed. While Nazi agencies of culture extended their control to the territory conquered by the German state and the integrated cultural life continued to provide a facade for the machinations of the regime, the Foreign Office no longer played a role. International representation was not necessary within the Reich. The diplomats turned their attention to other quarters. For a while longer they invoked the principle of national self-determination and the rights of German minorities elsewhere in Germany—specifically in Czechoslovakia. The manipulated *Sudeten-German* crisis again dictated diplomatic postures as well as musical involvement.

Musicians had participated in Nazi activity in the *Sudetenland* all along, as formerly in Austria. It must be noted, however, that the 3,200,000 *Sudeten* Germans had never been part of the German Reich. Diplomatically, the story of the *Sudetenland* was a replay of events which had led to the *Anschluss* of Austria, also ending with total annexation and the extension of music law, organization and policy. The *Sudeten Deutsche Partei*, led by Konrad Henlein, controlled 70 percent of the *Sudeten* Germans, according to the elections of 1935.[197] Contacts had been maintained across the border with the Reich, and musicians had contributed to the Nazi movement with party songs, such as "We are the Army of the Swastika," by Kleo Pleyer and with festivals of the DSB and the NSKG and other activities, some of which were censored and blocked by the host country. In response to the Austrian *Anschluss*, Nazi agitation increased, and the leadership formulated its Carlsbad program, which was tantamount to a declaration of independence. This activity in

Czechoslovakia paralleled German preparations for an attack, while the German press renewed its interests in the "oppressed" *Sudeten* Germans. Indeed, Hitler signaled open intervention in a speech at the Party Congress in Nuremberg, September 12. After various other critical points, speeches, conferences and threats, the *Sudetenland* was incorporated in October. This major Nazi victory marked the high point of the *völkisch* ideology. In the next crisis in March 1939, Hitler no longer embodied *völkisch* thought; he defended Slovakian rights, summoning to Berlin the Czech president Hacha, who was forced to sign over Bohemia and Moravia as a German Protectorate. Prague was immediately occupied by German forces. Again German refugees had to pack and embark on what was to be for some the third phase of their flight.

The difference between the annexation of Austria and the *Sudetenland* and that of non-German Czechoslovakia was of great importance in the area of music since, heretofore, much of culture policy had been discussed in terms of *völkisch* principles. Undisguised aggression against non-German nationals refuted the rationale of former conquests. Nonetheless, until the war, German minorities still agitated outside the Reich. At Danzig the Nazi success in Czechoslovakia emboldened local Nazis, who gained control of the administration. On April 28, Hitler gave a speech on the Danzig problem. From this moment on, more refugees arrived in Western cities, some of whom had earlier sought refuge in Eastern Europe. German veterans of this migration were joined by other Europeans, especially Czechoslovakians. The Foreign Office and Germany's musicians would no longer credibly uphold their mediating position. Furtwängler was forced to cancel performances scheduled in Paris, although the French soprano Germain Lubin still participated at Bayreuth. However, in mid-1938, international concert life had been permitted to go on. Furtwängler agreed to perform in London, as well as in Salzburg. The premiere of Strauss's *Der Friedenstag*, July 24, attracted music lovers from all over the world to Munich. Increasingly, though, German, Austrian, Czech and Hungarian musicians fled to London, where they were to lend a truly international air to that great music center. When Mussolini adopted Germany's racial laws, "non-Aryan" Germans also had to leave Italy, to seek refuge in London. In Germany and Austria all non-Aryans had to surrender their passports, which would be returned only for purposes of emigration. The stamping of "J" and the names of "Israel" for men and "Sarah" for women had become obligatory. These regulations applied at German consulates abroad, which obviously could no longer uphold a tradition distinct from that of National Socialism.

Crucial in this story of victims and oppressors was the shooting of the German Embassy official von Rath November 7, 1938, by a Polish Jew in

Paris, and the subsequent organized attacks upon the Jewish community, November 9, known as Crystal Night. Nearly one hundred Jews died, 20,000 were taken into custody, hundreds of synagogues and thousands of Jewish stores and homes were demolished. What had been covered by legalism, *völkisch*-segregationist rhetoric, boycotts and denial was now expressed in open terror—despite official attempts to attribute the pogrom to the people's outrage. The terror was in fact centrally planned and executed. Concentration camps for "non-Aryans" were started in Germany and the international community found it difficult to draw a distinction between German and Nazi perpetrators of barbarous acts. Again at this point thousands of "non-Aryans" and even "Aryans"endeavored to leave. By the end of 1938 Paris and London were filled with refugees, and the music communities there had expanded to unprecedented proportions. The concert seasons of 1939 in London, Paris, New York and Switzerland were able to present to an international public an elite of exiles never before encountered in such numbers, while music in Germany was performed as if no international crisis existed.

The war cut short all efforts of the traditional diplomat and representational musician in the countries which rose to meet the German menace, and the Foreign Office was reduced in scope. Yet German musicians continued to perform in allied and neutral nations, and followed German armies into occupied countries. Music life during the war in other nations, though representative of German music culture, cannot be covered here. It has been noted that, indeed, German culture was carried on in exile by the thousands of German refugees, whereas it was suspended in Germany proper. Whatever the merits of this claim, emigre culture constituted such a range of issues and complexity in its own right that mention of its existence must alone suffice in this discussion of music politics in the Third Reich. Central to Nazi music politics, though, was the reality of German music in occupied territories, where Goebbels ruled in competition and cooperation with military commanders, governors and commissioners. The war also eliminated all efforts to consider international opinion in regard to internationalism inside Germany. Musicians were told in 1940 that the performance of entertainment music with foreign texts, especially French and English, was henceforth forbidden.

This bad habit, already incompatible with the feeling of national dignity and cultural responsibility in times of peace, must be condemned twice as severely while we are at war. The Reich minister for General Enlightenment and Propaganda has explicitly decreed, September 2, 1939 (*Amtliche Mitteilingen* 1939, p. 55), that compositions, "which contradict our national sensibility on account of national origin, the composer or the actual content, are no longer to be performed and must be replaced by other works." On the basis of this decree Goebbels prohibited the distribution and the offering of entertainment music which contains or is derived from foreign tongues in the title or text. Composers, practicing musicians, music publishers and distributers will be subjected to regulations of the RKKG if they do not submit to the decree.[198]

Peter Raabe wrote in the same journal, *Die Musik-Woche*, that foreign or entertainment music "will no longer be tolerated."[199] Expressions of national dignity, abuse of foreign music and cultures and threats against German dissidents were discussed at the Culture-Political Press Conferences and confirmed in decrees of Goebbels' ministry and the RMK. Even entertainment music, of increasing importance during wartime in the eyes of Goebbels, was thus integrated with totalitarian policy. The war reinforced the coordination of all musical life, since all efforts of normal international relations with regard to enemy nations had come to an end. Music journalists and authors were again asked to define for the music community, in behalf of the music organization, what constituted truly German music and the definitions had to conform to the latest report on the war situation. With the entry of the United States into the war, the attacks on American music were increased and reprinted throughout the professional journal literature and the popular press. Articles and decrees were formulated especially with reference to music of the American Negro. America was portrayed as a mongrel race whose music reflected a confused culture. For the sake of the "awakening of the healthy racial instinct of Germans" the total state wanted to make sure that alien elements would be removed from German music.[200]

The supression of any real influence of the traditional Foreign Office and the representational musician came to an end with the occupation of foreign lands. Peter Raabe again opened a chapter of Nazi history and music when he identified the fate of German music with that of German armies. Indeed, to him it seemed as if the war were fought in behalf of that great German tradition of music.

Not only musicians participated in the fate of German music, but all Germans, inasmuch as the people of Bach, Beethoven and Bruckner is in no other art as superior to other peoples as in music. To protect this music against all current dangers must be a sacred obligation of all those remaining at home, while the army has left to protect country and the people to which fate has accorded the wonderful and magnificent gift: German music.[201]

Music in Occupied Countries

War in September 1939 reinforced the totalitarian controls established over all areas of cultural expression and public information in Germany. Music and its administration functioned as before—only more so—as tools of propaganda, while the music press reiterated nationalistic and anti-foreign principles in line with wartime objectives. In addition to the existing press conferences, an informal after-hour briefing session, called *Nachbörse*, was instituted in October, at which the "highly intelligent" government spokesman Hans Fritzsche, talked to a select group of around twenty editors about the need for greater flexibility and imagination, to improve ways to affect public opinion in support of the war effort. His successor in 1942, Erich Fischer was less seductive, more prone to instruct in military fashion. Also borrowed from the military in November 1939 was the new *Tagesparole* which went beyond the heretofore instructions, as to what and how to publish in the daily issue of preformulated news. The editors learned about the intense power struggle within the Nazi elite, especially between Goebbels, Dietrich and Ribbentrop, in addition to the issues of war and atrocities in the East.[202]

The war also resulted in the extension of German music culture into occupied countries and its manipulation by the RMVP there. Indeed, music followed all German armies, whose cultural and entertainment needs it was to help satisfy. In western countries like France, Belgium, the Netherlands and Norway, music also was employed to normalize life and reconcile the nations to German domination. The policy enjoyed much support. Self-coordination and collaboration preceded the imposition of German restrictions in the form of censorship of musical programs and Jewish purges; and, finally, the instituting of native organizations similar to and in imitation of the RMK followed the German and Austrian pattern. Under RMVP direction an extensive musical exchange program followed an earlier musical program under military auspices. Integration of the music culture of "Nordic" countries with that of Germany was especially fostered and Nordic music was welcomed on German stages and the radio in confirmation of Nazi ideals and propaganda.

Under occupation, Belgium's music tradition was subjected to typical reviews and purges. While the native and kindred Flemish tradition under the influence of German romanticism was noted, a more recent "international Parisian orientation," was said to have created great confusion. As before in Germany, Austria and Czechoslovakia, the Nazis claimed that the native, the

proponents of a healthy Germanic-Flemish art had been increasingly subjected to political pressures... The imitation of Stravinsky and Ravel was substituted for good taste, while Jewry established itself, and an intellectual Brussels clique applied official and political pressures to supress all efforts of the Reich to further Flemish art...Thus, the performance of a confessional German music was systemically prohibited, while the typical representative of international disintegration was furthered.

As if the war had been fought for the benefit of the occupied countries which, once purged of Jews, would be the deserving beneficiaries of German music, the author Nikolaus Spanuth continued:

The German invasion put an end to this one-sided cultural policy against which the Flemish had been powerless. The removal of racially alien elements necessitated the temporary replacing of all kinds of directionless rubbish to fill the vacuum, until presently the systematic effort of reconstruction has commenced. While the representative French orchestras appropriated German classical music for their programs in order to be able to hold a trump against the Flemish cultural efforts, the *Het Muziekfonds*, a Flemish concert society, coordinated efforts with the Flemish radio to further music of Flemish masters in the country's capital which had been suppressed by the liberalistic system. On the basis of growing consciousness of a Greater Germanic community of blood and fate, German music was appreciated as a national and inexhaustible source of Flemish art which alone contains the necessary reserves, after the elimination of all racially alien influences.[203]

While the prospect of Belgian reconstruction under German domination was intertwined with reference to ethnic strife in Belgium, German policy proceeded carefully in France, the clearest example of using music as a bridge between former adversaries on the basis of a common musical heritage. Not quite so tactful at first, German armies paraded to the sound of Prussian marches—the traditional march of the victor, reminiscent of the historical practice of both nations and immensely pleasing to the conquering army and the folks back home. Permanent German stages were also established, as in Lille which opened in May 1941 and offered rich programs of German classics to German troops. The nationalist Pfitzner appeared throughout Germany's occupied border regions, conducting local and German orchestras which frequently featured his music—thus at Strasbourg in November 1940 and again in 1942, while his "Palestrina" was performed by the Bavarian State Theatre at the Grand Opera in Paris in 1942. But this thrust of the army and nationalism was softened by a flouishing cultural exchange program under the careful guidance of the RMVP.

Music was employed as a means of revitalizing traditional relations—this time as a facade for the new fascist Europe, "fortress Europe." French censors were immediately installed under a civilian administration to purge programs of undesirable music under RMVP direction. Then a "German Institute" at the Foreign Office organized German tours to Paris and elsewhere in France. Karajan came with chorus and orchestra from Aachen, then again with the Berlin State Opera offering "Tristan," a traditional favorite in Paris. In September 1941 the RMVP took charge directly in Paris, installing a musical office under Fritz Piersig of Bremen who continued to censor, sponsor musical exchanges and French-German collaborative performances, and to utilize the same connections in France known to the German Institute and Berta Geissmar in the early years of the Third Reich. Alfred Cortot became head of a kind of RMK for French musicians and Jacques Rouche of the Paris Opera invited German performers, orchestras and opera companies. Paris attracted the top names in German music like Karajan, Clemens Krauss, Eugen Jochum, the Vienna Boys Choir, Wilhelm Kempff and many more. Germans conducted music festivals such as a week of Mozart in late 1941, and made recordings with French musicians, while music journalists wrote program notes, articles and manifestoes jointly with French colleagues in celebration of the new order. Opposition was met head on with purges and arrests, but also by a policy which could be flexible. The RMVP permitted occasional deviation from set standards, for instance by permitting the performance of Russian composers, including contemporary ones, when that was no longer permitted in Germany or compositions of the French avant-garde, although the office of Drewes did not approve a Hindemith performance under Furtwängler.[204]

In general, the relatively liberal policy under Piersig's direction promoted relaxation and normalization through such musical collaboration and other contacts with the French, facilitated also by German personnel who were known to be French-friendly, -speaking and -connected and included people who found Paris safer and more congenial than Nazi Germany. The photo journalist Karl Meyer, who had lost his position at the *Magdeburger Generalanzeiger* in 1935 because of his Jewish wife, wrote serialized novels under a pseudonym, published his photos wherever possible—at the *Frankfurter Illustrierts* and the *Neueste Zeitung*—was protected by Fritz Sänger of the *FZ* and found his way first to occupied Norway and later to Paris.[205] The music journalist Otto Strobel—formerly the defamed editor of the avant-garde music journal *Melos* but nonetheless in possession of a RPK membership due to his veteran status—and his Jewish wife came to Paris. The prominent *Deutsche Allgemeine Zeitung* sent him as its foreign correspondent, while he also still worked for the *Neues Musikblatt* which had replaced *Melos* and for a German paper in Paris, the *Pariser Zeitung*. Piersig cultivated Strobel, a convenient and talented facilitator of collaboration who wrote all kinds of articles consistent with *völkisch* principles. The Nazis could count on journalists who would not dare jeopardize the safety of their Jewish spouses and families—captives who, in the eyes of some, resisted Nazification by their contribution to traditional culture and international relations, as well as holding anti-Nazi views and contacts, but who clearly were tools of manipulation and propaganda.[206]

The other western countries under occupation experienced similar Nazi music policies. German concerts were staged for German troops, while a flexible policy governing cultural collaboration and exchanges were instituted everywhere under RMVP direction, after a period of self-coordination by local fascist leadership and worried professionals—the standard purges, censorship, propaganda, solidarity proclamations, etc. A German Theatre in Oslo was established in early 1941, an outgrowth of an active cultural exchange program. The Netherlands experienced careful guidance under the specialist for all occupied areas, Reich Commissioner Seyss-Inquart, who reinforced self-coordination at such famous institutions as the Concertgebouw Orchestra in Amsterdam. In spite of considerable resistance, a mechanism of control was in place which paralleled the German RMVP and the RKK (by November, 1941), including a *Muziekgilde*—the equivalent of the RMK (by March 1943). Seyss-Inquart was especially keen on promoting German music in the Netherlands organized by a "German-Netherland Cultural Community." In early 1942 a "German Theatre of the Netherlands" in Den Hague was established for the performance of operas, operettas and plays, with mixed though largely German personnel.

Moving to Central Europe, the war also reinforced the demise of the Czech population under occupation, even though *DMW* reported that music life in Prague had prospered in spite of the war. The story here paralleled that in the West. Especially the German Philharmonic Orchestra was said to continue the great tradition of German music in the city. Herbert Zingrosch wrote that this orchestra had been threatened with extinction during the turmoil of September 1938, when the New German Theater had been forced to close its doors and the musicians were dismissed. Thus, the German invasion was said to be justified. "Only the quick action of the Reich Minister for General Enlightenment and Propaganda prevented the disintegration of this orchestra." Reconstituted as the *Sudeten* German Philharmonic Orchestra, it found "a new home in the new *Gau* capital of Reichenberg." The orchestra toured Germany and received rave reviews at the "Day of German Art" ceremonies in Munich in 1939. The transition from German activities in independent Czechoslovakia and the occupation before the war to total establishment of German power during the war was reflected in the experience of the musicians. A few months after the creation of the Protectorate the orchestra moved back to Prague. In April, 1940 it was changed into an institution of the Reich Protector of Bohemia and Moravia, called "German Philharmonic Orchestra of Prague." In September 1940 Goebbels appointed the conductor GMD Joseph Keilberth to lead the orchestra. He was able to mold the eighty musicians into "one of Germany's foremost orchestras" in only one year. The author noted that the beginning of this concert season was of special importance, inasmuch as the Prague *Rudolfinum*, the former German Concert House, again housed the German orchestra, having been the seat of the parliament of the Czech-Slovak Republic. Thus the Germans of Prague recovered their own concert stage.[207]

Germany moved with less circumspection in the East. Even in Czechoslovakia policy was tempered originally compared to Poland where the Nazis extended their power through open warfare upon the population and its culture. Fritz Sänger recalled reports at the *Nachbörse* (December 4, 1940) about the forced resettlement of 200,000 ethnic Germans into the Reich and their integration into the armed forces by means of cultural indoctrination. Minutes of an earlier report (January 16, 1940) reveal the plans for brutality and the policy of "burning bridges that lead backwards." *Gau* leader Greise of Poznan reported on the grisly warfare which resulted in the eradication of the Polish intelligentsia and on the drastic measures taken by him and others—the very *Gau* leader who sponsored music festivals and was known as a promoter of Pfitzner. Greiser also confirmed a policy to prevent the revival of a Polish intelligentsia by limiting schools for children in Poland to the maximum age of eleven and to thus "proletarize" the nation. He also told of plans to institute "the most modern and greatest Jewish expulsion from Lodz—350,000 Jews."[208]

The implementation of these plans are well-known and, indeed, Polish schools, academies, theatres, etc. were closed by the occupation army. On October 31, 1939 Goebbels met with the governor general Hans Frank, Seyss-Inquart and other high functionaries in Lodz to design a policy for the vanquished. Agreement existed over the reduction of cultural activity to a minimum. Poles were to be indoctrinated as to the "hopelessness of their fate as a people." Cultural products such as films were to be censored so that only those of poor quality or those which suggested the greatness and the power of the German Reich could be seen.[209] The best theatres were to be turned over to German artists. Members of the Warsaw Philharmonic Orchestra were not to be permitted in any orchestra of the Reich, while that famous ensemble was confined to perform at a cafe. Indeed, policy restricted musical offerings to entertainment, while all music of higher pretension in addition to national songs, folk music and marches were to be forbidden. Unlike the policy in the West, in Poland culture was to be strictly segregated and maintained at different levels. Poles were not allowed to attend concerts by and for Germans.

The history of this unfortunate country was reflected in the discriminatory policy, and the fate of the large Jewish minority constitutes a most telling document in the story of National Socialism which demonstrated its brutal nature to the fullest in an area apparently removed from the eyes of the population at home. The terror, the atrocities, the uprooting of people and the enslavement of populations—the prelude to actual genocide—formed the background for the extension of music policies from the German base, via the Austrian and Czech experiences, to the cities of Poland.

Yet, the cultivated jurist, art- and music-loving governor general Frank had his own ideas about music in his domain which he wanted to govern without interference from Goebbels. He intended to offer music of highest quality to his German audiences—the native Germans, the new settlers and the military. Thus, it took him only six months to found his own stage in Krakau, the "State Theatre of the General Government" for which he tried to recruit personnel from Germany. The season opened festively September 1, 1940 with Goebbels in attendance, followed by plays, operas, operettas and concerts. He then invited the best possible orchestras of the Reich for guest appearances, and they came from Berlin, Vienna, Leipzig, Munich and elsewhere. He attended many concerts, received the artists and openly discussed his cultural plans with visitors, especially with his friend Pfitzner who repeatedly conducted in Krakau, dedicated a composition to Frank and remained loyal to his patron even through the War Crimes Trial at Nuremberg in 1946.

Again, the ZfM, the journal founded by the humane Robert Schumann, lent its pages to a glorious account of "German music in Krakau," September 1942. The would-be visitor from the Reich was informed that German culture had followed the exodus east of German arms; that Krakau, the capital city of the Generalgouvernement, offered concerts of its Philharmonic (a body of ninety-five musicians under the direction of Rudolf Erb), performances of its State Theatre (founded September 1, 1940, under the supervision of the Main Propaganda Division of the Generalgouvernement, with its director Friedrich Franz Stampe and administrative manager Otto Müller-Hanno), chamber music recitals at the Institute for Eastern Studies (founded April 20, 1940, at the library of Krakau University), solo performances at the theatre of the SS and the police and, in summer, evening serenades at the Gotischen Hof at Krakau, etc.

Upon arrival, the Germans in Krakau were culturally deprived—as the article implied Polish cultural backwardness. For the German newcomers, "Cultural activity of any kind did not exist ....," but then, the Vienna Philharmonic Orchestra offered the "memorable" first German concert at the reopened Krakau Theater—renamed the "German Theatre" December 16, 1939 in the presence of the governor general and other notables, setting off a "cultural awakening" which affected other cities in Poland such as Lemberg (formerly Lodz). This "first German concert at Krakau was credited to the personal initiative of the governor general Dr. Frank, who remained active in his support of German cultural activity." Frank saw to it that distinguished visitors from the Reich would be invited to the concerts of the Philharmonic. "Thus, the encounters with Professor Elly Ney and Wilhelm Kempff and the singers Martha Fuchs and Julius Patzak are well-remembered." Increasingly noted soloists and chamber music ensembles found their way to Krakau. Wherever German music was heard in Krakau, the author enthused, the response was overwhelming. Concerts of the Philharmonic, the State Theatre Orchestra, as of countless other groups were always sold out on the first day. The basis was said to exist for an expansion of German music into the wide Weichsel area and also Galicia.[210]

Frank even violated the earlier agreement with Goebbels that accorded with Hitler's own ideas about Poland. When the governor general found it difficult to attract German musicians for his ensembles he had his conductor Hanns Rohr from Munich hire Polish ones instead—an irony considering Nazi policy and the belief in German musical superiority. Polish musicians—though underpaid—collaborated in the fashioning of the cultural facade behind which the greatest barbarities were performed upon their countrymen. Compromises contributed to the music culture throughout the country, as orchestral and choral organizations were integrated. Gradually Poles were also admitted to concerts. Under Frank's last guest conductor, Hans Swarowsky, a friendlier policy emerged, closer to that of the West in recognition of a common anti-Soviet front, even though mixed groups were denied permission to perform in Germany.

An interesting side note to the conquest of Poland was offered by official attempts to claim Poland's great composer, Francois Frederic Chopin. The people who were to be reduced to slavery and who were considered incapable of cultural achievement had produced this musician who appealed greatly to proponents of German romanticism. While Germans celebrated the defeat of "proud Poland," the accompanying ideologists had to come to terms with the exponent of Polish genius. Thus, in an article of October 28, 1939 Ernst Krienitz, the chief editor of Die Musik-Woche, attributed Chopin's genius to the influence of German-Bohemian teachers, Bach and German romantics and the support of German artists. Nevertheless, in 1943 Frank commissioned a Chopin study which involved the gathering of memorabilia in Poland and the buying of a famous archival collection in Lyon which, among other objectives, continued the attempt to Germanize the great composer[211]—the friend of Heine and other artists and intellectuals in Paris including Jews and French romantics. This kind of distortion says much about *völkisch* apologists turned imperialist. "Social Darwinist" policymakers thus justified conquest, domination and the suppression and distortion of foreign culture.

A description of music in Krakau seems distant from the subsuming topic of rivalries in the Nazi hierarchy of power; yet it is apparent that especially in such remote areas of recent conquest as Poland, personal rivalries would be rekindled as demonstrated in the policies of Hans Frank. The traditional Foreign Service was eliminated from the division of spoils in the conquered territories. However, inasmuch as the diplomats received orders from Ribbentrop, a member of the Nazi elite, as well as from other party noteworthies, even traditional power centers played a role in the transplanted struggles. Certainly Goebbels had extended his organization and influence to a point where his council was heeded—notwithstanding local deviations. The war did not change the fundamental power structure within the party, except for the growing importance of the SS. However, to add to the confusion in the realm of foreign affairs, one other authority attempted to set standards, especially in regard to cultural policy in conquered Eastern territories; and that was the contender for control over all cultural expression in the Reich as well as for von Neurath's portfolio: Alfred Rosenberg. As head of the "Foreign Political Office of the NSDAP," the news of von Ribbentrop's appointment was a severe blow to him. "Exposed and dishonored before the whole world," he wrote to Hitler February 6, 1938, explaining that Göring, to whom he had complained immediately after the announcement of Ribbentrop's appointment on the 4th, understood his hurt, particularly in view of recent assurances received through State Secretary Lammers that his own bureau would be transformed into a more comprehensive commission, dedicated to the "security of the National Socialist *Weltanschauung* and defense against Bolshevism." Since he still headed the official foreign office of the party, which had been scheduled to meet with diplomats in a traditional conference this February 10, he asked Hitler to confirm his promised expanded powers and to admit him to the "secret councils of the cabinet" for which only Reich Ministers were qualified. The creation of this "secret cabinet" changed traditional relations even between party authorities, and Rosenberg insisted on being privy to all information concerning foreign affairs. Göring promised to support his case, since proper ideological schooling and leadership would otherwise not be possible[212]—an interesting example of Göring's duplicity as he later testified that in serious issues of foreign policy Rosenberg was never consulted.[213]

From the very beginning of the Third Reich Rosenberg, an early foreign-affairs advisor of Hitler, had rivaled Goebbels, von Neurath and von Ribbentrop in conducting foreign relations. As such, he did much to undermine traditional elements in the foreign service. At one time he tried to secure control over the next generation by creating a diplomatic school which drew only on young Pg's between the ages of twenty-five and twenty-nine. However, as in other undertakings of this sort, his proteges never distinguished themselves after completing their school terms.[214] His party foreign-affairs office was actually primarily interested in the German communities beyond Germany's frontiers. Rosenberg's influence was therefore great in those territories discussed above, in Germany's attempts to subvert bordering governments and ultimate conquest. Lacking real power, though, he and his organizations busied themselves with cultural affairs abroad, attacking expressions of decadent art, raiding conquered libraries, and evaluating intellectual institutions in the light of National Socialism—always in close contact with other Nazi agencies. Through the situation created by war, the ideologue Rosenberg would tend to lose ground against those forces immediately concerned with conquest. However, he did gain through the attack on the Soviet Union, when a special ministry for Eastern affairs, the *Ostministerium*, was created under his leadership. Thus, his desire, as stated in the letter to Hitler in February 1938, was fulfilled in an unexpected way. He received ministerial status, although his occupation with affairs outside of Germany proper precluded real power in the struggle at home.

Means and Ends: The Goebbels-Rosenberg Rivalry

The Goebbels-Rosenberg rivalry is only now fully addressed at the end of the examination of the Nazi music administration and power centers because it typified and overshadowed all intra-party fighting in cultural life—attested to in masses of documentation—and also because it extended from its domestic origins and base to foreign affairs and the occupation period, thus illustrating the overlapping of the chapter's main topic with that of its end.[215] Both leaders enjoyed the confidence of the supreme leader, Adolf Hitler. Although it is evident that Goebbels deserves the greater attention in a review of music policy and organization, Rosenberg, who had been in contact with Hitler since 1919, was an early editor of the *VB*, head of the party Foreign Affairs Bureau, Reich Leader since 1933 and ultimately Reich Minister of occupied Eastern territories—in addition to having produced the major ideological tract of National Socialism which had sold 950,000 copies by 1941. Rosenberg managed to maintain his position as chief ideologist of the party through his busy office, the Rosenberg bureau, and as such influenced both policy and cultural organization. The two leaders continued to compete throughout the Third Reich since their jurisdictions overlapped and their modes of operation were so different. It appeared that indeed, as Hannah Arendt has pointed out, "for the Nazis the duplication of offices was a matter of principle and not just an expedient for providing jobs for party members."[216] The conscious creation of overlapping authorities despite the officially pronounced policy of streamlining and the unquestioned leadership principle, nourished a rivalry which principally benefitted the supreme leader. Rosenberg rivaled Goebbels, but the clever head of the RMVP threatened the very existence of the "Führer's supervisor of the entire spiritual and ideological education of the NSDAP." Moreover, since Rosenberg criticized all other party leaders, they pressured him in turn. In September, 1935 the Ministry of the Interior actually came to his aid. Frick's order was printed in the press as a warning against the founding of associations, clubs, etc. in the cultural realm and *Weltanschauung* without Rosenberg's consent.[217]

Even though Goebbels held a very low opinion of Rosenberg's mind and organizational ability, he took the ideologist's criticism seriously. Intra-office memoes reveal that he repeatedly warned his organizations against outside intrusion. He specifically advised the RMK not to permit Rosenberg or his NSKG access to its books which contained membership, organizational and budget information, and to reject his rival's bid for an advisory role in his affairs. The president of the RKK cited the leadership principle and the injunction against duplication of offices and functions, the multiple collection of dues and the incorporation of RKK branches in other organizations. Moreover, he wanted to be informed immediately about any interference by Rosenberg.[218] In this campaign he could count on the support of the incorporated musical profession.

Rosenberg continued to interfere nonetheless, through his offices and papers like *Die Musik*. Custodian of Nazi principles, he represented the *völkisch* movement and those disgruntled elements who resented its gradual institutionalization and accommodation. In addition to an uncompromising posture, Rosenberg also carried weight in numbers. As early as March 1933, a demonstration of the NSKG had attracted 16,000 members whose aim it was to "supplement the corporate organization of the cultural profession." Rosenberg was going to keep the movement honest. As an embodiment of the party soul, this ethnic German leader who had found his way home to his Reich enlisted massive musical support at the demonstrations where he lectured on the nineteenth century in familiar *völkisch* terms.

Parallel to the excesses of political democracy and the lack of restraint of its thirty parties, Germany was subjected to impressionism, expressionism, Dadaism and cubism, until finally all form was destroyed and idiocy was celebrated as beauty. Political madness was portrayed artistically, proving again the close relation of *Weltanschauung* and culture as well as lack of *Weltanschauung* and lack of culture.[219]

This speech cannot be distinguished from the ones given before 1933. Indeed, he maintained the ideology against the expediency of the more political Goebbels for years to follow. Yet Rosenberg was not simply a cultural critic, an intellectual of the right. Sixteen thousand demonstrators of a structured organization constituted an important political factor, of which Goebbels was forced to take note. As a party theoretician alone, Rosenberg would not have been too dangerous to Goebbels; but the force of a rival organization with the additional weight of ideological purity and self-proclaimed righteousness were cause for alarm, constituting the grounds for the orders communicated to the RMK. The true power of Rosenberg cannot be readily assessed, but its potential was certainly manifested in the appeal of the mammoth DSB which asked Rosenberg to become its honorary president. When he accepted the position in April 1934, he entered the struggle between that organization and Fritz Stein's sub-section of the RMK (see above).

Goebbels mobilized the organs of propaganda. But his nemesis, too, utilized the journals in attacks on Goebbels' underlings in privy memos and those musicians who had betrayed the movement but appeared to be protected by Goebbels. He also could complain about foul play when he wrote to Goebbels directly in August 1934, in reference to the orchestra of the KfdK and its conductor Gustav Havemann, complaining bitterly of the Minister's attacks on the Fighting League, finding this typical of Goebbels, who slandered it while benefiting from its work. He reminded Goebbels in a personal letter that the KfdK had been able to raise an orchestra under Havemann's guidance "without the support of the Berlin *Gau*—yes, in spite of its opposition. The Fighting League had thereby provided bread and work for good German musicians in the time of struggle. Indeed, gradually the orchestra had been able to demonstrate noteworthy results. At the time of the *Machtübernahme* of the NSDAP," he added pointedly, "you forced Professor Havemann to change the name of *Kampfbundorchester* to *Landesorchester* of *Gau* Berlin, thereby earning the fruits of the work of others.[220]

There was no escaping the fight between the leaders. In a letter of June 15, 1935 to Hess, Rosenberg reproached Goebbels for appointing Hinkel to his managerial position at the RKK after that important official—Rosenberg's erstwhile lieutenant—has had some problems at the NSKG, a complaint which reveals Hinkel's switch to the more powerful organization. On another occasion Rosenberg complained directly to Goebbels in a letter of March 9, 1936 about Moraller's denigration of the NSKG before a gathering of the Reich Propaganda Directorate, February 22, 1936. He harped over difficult access to public radio, negative press and—in private—over the "mephisto's" lack of principle and pernicious influence abroad.

In the most celebrated political cases in the music community, Rosenberg and his NSKG emerged as vociferous advocates against would-be subversives. Hindemith was attacked publicly. The organization also took issue with Furtwängler for having attributed "political denunciation" to "certain circles" (referring to the Nazi authorities). The NSKG commented:

> Dr. Furtwängler take note that an official position of an organization of the National Socialist movement can in no way be identified with political denunciation. The value or lack of value of Paul Hindemith's current products are not the issue in the rejection of the composer by the NSKG. The National Socialist places an evaluation of the personality before that of the work. The fact that Hindemith had consciously projected a non-German posture years before the accession to power...[221]

Rosenberg wrote personally in the *VB*, using Goebbels' official organ for his own ideological formulations. He emerged as the chief ideological opponent of Furtwängler, when the latter established himself as the representative spokesman of traditional forces in the music establishment of coordinated Germany, thus broadening the "Hindemith case" into the "Furtwängler case" and thereby relating the affairs of foremost musicians of a former era to his notions of a generational change which was discussed in terms of the outgoing liberal nineteenth century and the twentieth century of National Socialism consistent with his influential book, *The Myth of the Twentieth Century*.

> Now, if a man like Hindemith...had lived these past fourteen years in the company of Jews... associating almost exclusively with Jews...having received their praise...if he spoiled German music in most shameful fashion, then that is his personal affair. However, all of us have the right to reject him and those subjected to his influence. If through a revolution the entire human, artistic and political surroundings of Mr. Hindemith are eliminated and all areas of life are encompassed by a general regeneration, then we may not escort him into the elevated artistic institutions of the new Reich simply because he happens to be acceptable on the basis of racial considerations.[222]

This "ideological purity" was quite useful to the organizers of more practical persuasion. While Goebbels would compromise himself in his carefully articulated denunciation of Hindemith and Furtwängler, appropriating a language which made sense in the circles of Germany's cultural elite, Rosenberg did not betray any sensitivity to the intellectual impasse of the liberal-conservative establishment of all Western culture as represented by Germany's leading musicians. Overlooking traditional values as a reflection of decadence, he bombarded with ideological fervor. Thus, he lent himself to the elimination of potential enemies of the regime, while simultaneously posing a threat to compromised elements in the new power structure.

The Rosenberg-Goebbels rivalry has rightly received more attention than any other conflict between Nazi leaders in the area of Nazi culture, and it is amply documented in intra-party and governmental communications, their correspondence, diaries as well as publications. By 1936, the conflict was essentially over. Hinkel's move was symptomatic. The RKK had become an effective organization, to the point of legally establishing jurisdiction over Rosenberg's NSKG,[223] and other significant measures were taken then which pointed to Goebbels' widening power, his manipulation of ideology and his compromise with establishment powers in the year of the Olympics. The first Culture-Political Press Conference was instituted in July and, shortly thereafter, the Ministry informed the select assembled editors that the government no longer encouraged the Nazi open air festivals. One year later it officially acknowledged failure in its attempt to foster this unique Nazi art form, known as *Thing-Theater*, which was to have expressed the Nazi revolutionary experience—a significant revision of official policy and a concession to artistic professionalism and competence which could serve the propagandistic needs of the regime to a greater degree than *völkisch* sentiment.[224] To be sure, the latter would continue to be supported and performed, but not in the place of high art. Goebbels also issued his ban on art criticism (including music criticism) late in 1936, to be replaced by art reporting or description. His control of professional music and music reporting was thus complete— formidable tools of propaganda. Rosenberg still operated, complained and was celebrated by his followers; but the council of state was closed to him until foreign conquests required the services again of this ethnic German's special passion, talent and experience. Meanwhile, he meddled in foreign affairs, with emphasis on German minorities in border regions and foreign fascists, and contended for control of the Foreign Office when the facade of the latter's independence was no longer possible.

Rosenberg survived and so did all the other contending authorities and integrated institutions. A significant consequence of the apparent policy of retaining a conservative order amidst well-calculated intimidation of its leaders, general insecurity and timidity, and the multiplicity of administrative agencies, party offices and leaders was the universal public appeal to a generalized ideology—the revenge of Rosenberg in defeat—which in its overwhelming impact hid rivalries at the higher level from the professional musicians. Confusion and slavish dependency benefited the regime.

Some Individual Portraits

Institutionalized confusion, conflicting jurisdictions and internecine warfare also characterized the condition of leading authorities of the music organizations at lower echelons of the Nazi hierarchy—the formulators and victims of Nazi music policies. The leadership principle mandated constant confirmation of loyalty by these second-level leaders who, in turn, expected support from underlings and the professionals they led, represented, and intimidated. If the musicians after 1945 recall terror and fear (thus, Hans Werner Henze in a letter to Hanns-Werner Heister: "the fear to speak about the horror and the fright—that was the terror" of the Nazi period),[225] the prominent artist-bureaucrats who presided over the various music departments, offices and the press also suffered tremendous anxiety. The new men—the purely political Hinkel, as well as the musicians and music journalists-turned-politicians like Graener, Stein, Havemann, Raabe, Stege, Abendroth and even the non-Nazis such as Strauss—battled in a perpetual state of emergency, reflecting and reinforcing the shifts and currents of the higher power structure. The same was true of course for the musical careerists, again exemplified in the life of Strauss, but also in the case of the younger generation of people like Böhm, Karajan, Krauss, Egk and Orff. A normal life was simply not possible. Old habits and moral standards had to be suspended once opposition or emigration were rejected as options and collaboration impacted on career opportunities. In some cases, the regime decided for the individual. Jews and known opponents generally suffered immediately and clearly from discrimination and loss of employment. Emigration removed them from the choices facing former colleagues. For the majority who stayed—for the enthusiastic supporter as well as the "apolitical" professional—the history of the Third Reich taught the impossibility of neutral, apolitical behavior. The regime's flattery and rewards proved irresistible to some, and problematic to others of consequence in all cases.

Richard Strauss was the most prominent and successful living German composer, who had become active in support of the new order beginning in March, 1933 when he signed an anti-Thomas Mann manifesto, substituted for Bruno Walter and Toscanini under controversial circumstances, and continued to collaborate when he accepted the presidency of the RMK November 15—which he took to be an honor and possibly the crowning achievement of his illustrious career. He delivered a ringing endorsement of Nazi music politics in his inaugural address at the first convention of the RMK in February 1934; he wrote music for official events—an Olympic hymn, for instance, for the festive opening ceremony in Berlin, August 1, 1936; and dedicated music to the Nazi elite, for example, a song "in commemoration of November 15, 1933." In place of the German chapter of the anathematic International Society for Contemporary Music, he founded and presided over a new Permanent Council for International Cooperation Among Composers in 1934—a propaganda vehicle led by second-rate composers, who were also well-known friends of the Third Reich, including the Austrian Friedrich Bayer, the Belgian Emil Hullebroeck, Danes Peter Gram and Nils O. Raasted, the Finn Yrjo Kilpinen, the French Carol-Bérard, the English Maurice Besley, the Italian Adriano Lualdi, the Pole Ludomir Rozycki, the Swiss Adolf Streuli, the Czechoslovak Jaroslaw Křička, the Swede Kurt Attenberg and the Islander Jon Leifs, amidst whom Strauss shone as a lone star.[226] He slavishly pledged loyalty, aggressively pursued fame, power and especially royalties; and he was, in turn, officially honored in spite of serious conflicts most of the time—most lavishly for his seventieth birthday, June 11, 1934 when, among other festivities, he received silver-framed autographed portraits of Hitler and Goebbels with dedications to "the venerable great tonemaster with respectful gratitude." Strauss typified the musical facade at the highest level for the regime which manipulated him for its political ends.[227]

Yet, Strauss was no Nazi, and he believed himself capable of affecting politics on the strength of his international reputation, artistic achievement and professional authority. In his mind he retained his integrity and sovereignty as an apolitical artist. Singlemindedly he pursued his self-interest, continued to write music as he saw fit, retained his own point of view—in spite of occasional concessions to the Nazi elite and in tune with the times—as well as his humour, for instance, when he confessed that he was merely passing time when he (who loathed sports) wrote the Olympic hymn for the *Proleten* (the masses).[228] Like others in the early years of the regime he did not grasp the enormity of Nazi racial policy. Deceived by Nazi obfuscation, flattered, pressured, and impressed by the prospective political support of the arts in 1933, he made a pact with Goebbels, opportunistically, naively, and confident that he—the *bon vivant* of massive build, the famous, talented and worldly artist—would overwhelm and dominate his patron and nemesis, the "diminutive doctor" of literary pretension and the manifest handicap of a limp—the subject of fear, hatred and nasty jokes.

Strauss undoubtedly had to compensate for the many liabilities in Nazi eyes as well, as Stefan Zweig among others has pointed out: his Jewish daughter-in-law, his fear for his beloved grandchildren, his Jewish librettists— especially when he continued the association with Zweig after 1933, his Jewish publisher, the many other Jewish associates and friends, his advanced musical style for which piano-player Goebbels whose taste in music was rather pedestrian had no affection, and his frequent indiscretions. The inevitable conflict between the celebrated artist who occasionally referred to Goebbels as that "kid..." or "rogue of a minister" (*Bübchen von Minister*) and his opposite who craved and possessed real power was exacerbated when Goebbels mistook the emigre Arnold Zweig, a Zionist who even abroad continued his campaign against the Nazis, for the less political Stefan Zweig.

In Nazi eyes the party was compromised by the forthcoming performance of the most recent Strauss-Zweig collaboration, the opera *Die Schweigsame Frau* under the baton of Karl Böhm in Dresden. The Saxon Gau leader Mutschmann and the NSKG rebelled, while the latter's leader Rosenberg wrote a clever letter of protest.[229] Hitler approved the performance, nonetheless, and the opera premiered at the Dresden State Opera as planned. While this exceptional tolerance occasioned false hopes among anti-Nazis, Zweig later wrote perceptively that the Nazis had not banned his text because in this case they would have also harmed Germany's most famous living musician, whom they needed for hard currency and prestige in the world. Yet Strauss tried to deemphasize his relationship with his non-Aryan collaborator, whom he asked February 26, 1935 in a letter to write a few books for him, but to keep them secret until a more opportune moment. Zweig's negative reaction prompted Strauss' famous letter of June 17, 1935 which cost him the presidency of the RMK. In the letter he denied belief in Nazi principle and revealed his cupidity by claiming interest in the folk only when it—of whatever nationality—turned into a paying public and, finally, made light of the RMK by claiming to "playact" (*mime*) the role of its president "in order to prevent worse"—an artistic obligation he would have performed under any government.[230]

Having already been placed under Gestapo surveillance, the intercepted letter was turned over to *Gau* leader Mutschmann and from him to a furious Hitler, who ordered suspension of further performances of the opera. Walter Funk was dispatched to Berchtesgaden July 6 to request Strauss's resignation, which followed on July 13 and set off a chain reaction, Peter Raabe became president of the RMK and vacated his post as GMD in Aachen which was assumed by Karajan who thus was launched on his phenomenal career.

At first Strauss took his defeat hard. He wondered why his opera was picked on for its text of a Jewish author, since he knew of performances of other such operas like Paul Graener's "Friedemann Bach." He was clearly shaken by his abrupt removal from office and sheepishly wrote Hitler that very day about his hurt and surprise, his apolitical past and his continuing commitment to German music. Finally he asked for an audience. Politically persona non grata, he did not receive an answer. Goebbels had made his point about the priority of politics, but a modus vivendi emerged by which Strauss retired to his villa to compose music as before—a mild form of "inner emigration," while the regime continued to benefit from his fame and productivity.

The "apolitical" artist recoverd nicely with the incoming royalties. He remained the most performed living opera composer in Germany during the 1935/36 season with the 123 performances of *Rosenkavalier* leading, while his new operas were premiered: *Der Friedenstag* (1937/38), *Daphne* (1938/39), *Capriccio* (1942/43) and, as late as August 1944, *Die Liebe der Danae* at Salzburg under extraordinary wartime circumstances—which reveal to what degree Goebbels was willing to extend himself. The festival had been cancelled as part of Goebbels' decision to shut down all festivals August 1, 1944 in order to marshall resources and concentrate on "total war." But, then, he was persuaded to reopen the festival with Furtwängler conducting the Berlin Philharmonic in Bruckner's Eighth Symphony August 14, and Clemens Krauss and Rudolph Hartmann presenting *Danae* two days later with Strauss in attendance. Strauss, in tears, received a standing ovation.[231]

Withdrawal to his villa notwithstanding, Strauss continued to serve political ends. He retained his position in charge of the Permanent Council for International Cooperation among Composers which propagated German music abroad and the import of "appropriate" foreign music—excluding that of Jews and "culture-bolshevists." The society favored his own works and thus contributed to his income. He continued to write music for official events and was extremely well received. He repeatedly attempted reconciliation with the regime, was a major attraction at the Reich Music Festival in Düsseldorf in 1938, proposed patriotic compositions, wrote a Festival Music for the City of Vienna in commemoration of Hitler's entrance five years earlier, accepted other commissions and composed Japanese Festival Music in honor of Japan's 2600th Anniversary in 1941 in response to a request from the RMVP.

In spite of these gestures and the advantages the Nazi state gained from its foremost musician, the basic mistrust was not overcome. Strauss's authority, energy and ego were not easily harnassed. He retained his independent point of view, made light of ideological narrow-mindedness and issued barbs which offended petty bureaucrats and ideologues who, in turn, further alienated him from Berlin. He was lionized elsewhere—at Salzburg, for instance, where Krauss, who was in charge, featured the works of his friend—and he was drawn to Vienna, in part due to the benign regime of Baldur von Schirach who like Hans Frank in Poland defied central authority and instituted his own music policy. Under von Schirach's patronage a flourishing music culture was maintained. Furtwängler had preserved the status of the Philharmonic. Karl Böhm, upon appointment as Director of the Vienna State Opera and the immediate engaging of Oscar Fritz Schuh and the controversial Caspar Neher from Germany in January 1943, was able to attract talented young singers who were molded into an outstanding ensemble and contributed to the extremely high standards of the institution, which survived the war. The *Gau* leader also protected the family of Strauss, who responded to the city's affection with musical productivity—a number of instrumental works and music for the city. When he offended Hitler once again, in late December 1943, by refusing to offer shelter to refugees and victims of bombing raids, he again provoked a crisis which was only resolved when, upon the special requests of his patrons Frank and von Schirach, as well as Walter Funk and finally Furtwängler, Hitler relented and approved the official celebration of the composer's eightieth birthday.

Thus it went with him. The birthday symbolized his relations with the Third Reich. His friends and fans toasted him heartily. Frank staged a formal celebration in the Krakau State Theatre and forwarded an invitation to the aged musician to conduct in Krakau. His emissaries—two SS officers—are reported by Hans Esdras Mutzenbecher of the already defunct German Artistic Exchange Society to have been asked by Strauss to release some acquaintances from "those silly concentration camps"—and he provided the names.[232] Authentic or not, the incident reveals biographical detail, but also representative behavior. Strauss serves as an example here of the collaboration between art and politics in the Third Reich, magnifying, because of his singular fame, the condition of other (in varying degrees) independent-minded but compromised composers like Werner Egk, Carl Orff, Rudolf Wagner-Regény, Winfried Zillig, and others, including those of popular music like Norbert Schultze. They all were productive and "playacted" their assigned roles, especially Egk who enjoyed much success as a composer of operas, film music, olympic festival music and other commissioned works.

The premiere of Egk's opera, *Die Zaubergeige* (May 22, 1935) elicited much positive press commentary—not surprising in that it was a solid piece by a young and promising composer which confirmed rules of tonality in the voice parts and contained a folk tale subject matter replete with a negative Jewish character—comforting aesthetically, conformist politically and therefore worthy of many performances (198 times in seven seasons) and radio broadcasts. But the dissonances in the orchestral score bothered important opinion shapers in musical matters, the editors Herbert Gerigk of the Rosenberg office and F.W. Herzog of the NSKG. Enthusiasm and controversy carried over to his next opera, *Peer Gynt*—premiered at the Berlin State Opera November 24, 1938. Celebrated as a fresh rendition of Nordic art by the chorus of coordinated criticism, it again was suspect for its disquieting dissonances and jazz elements reminiscent of Stravinsky, which were justified by supporters as intentional reflections of negativity and error, to be overcome and resolved in reassuring tonality—a brilliant mix of traditional and modern expression.[233] The question became the degree to which the impressions of the defamed components overwhelmed positive resolution. Regardless, or precisely because of its illicit sounds, the public loved the work, while many a secret supporter of modern music rejoiced. On the other hand, leading custodians of the Nazi code were again alarmed over the violations and by what some took to be a satire on the regime, an impression unwittingly underscored by Egk at a press conference when he likened a *Troll*, listed in the casting instructions as the embodiment of human depravity, to "a fat guy in a general's uniform" in a possible allusion to Göring, the obese chief of the State Opera and subject of many such jokes throughout the Third Reich.[234]

Hitler's public praise saved the work from possible disaster and resulted in its continuing popularity, further performances—for instance, at the Reich Music Festival in Düsseldorf in May, 1939—followed by increasingly enthusiastic commentary, and access to radio broadcasts. Egk's status and income were assured. His political acceptability had been established by his earlier productivity and explicit essays and speeches about the need for new music that is rooted in the past and the community, his statements of support for the music-political goals of the new order, and commissioned works for the Olympics and other official rituals (*Mein Vaterland* and *Die hohen Zeichen*). These efforts identified him as a competent, popular and reliable representative of the new order who combined his continuing artistic output with official duties which culminated in his appointment to replace Paul Graener as head of the composer section of the RMK in the summer of 1941. He produced a ballet, *Joan von Zarissa*, which premiered in Berlin, January 1940 and was exported to Paris where it premiered July 10, 1942; a revised version of his opera *Columbus* in 1942 which was reviewed in terms of the extension of Western Culture by its hero, but also of the suppression and enslavement of native Aztecs—undoubtedly suggesting a parallel to Hitler's colonization of the East;[235] and collaboratively the music for the propaganda film *Jungens* ("Boys") and its catchy HJ song, "March of the German Youth"— text by Hans Fritz Beckmann. He addressed HJ conferences, wrote music-political essays and was selected delegate for the Permanent Council for the International Cooperation Among Composers in summer 1942.

Werner Egk, a mainly self-taught composer and conductor, embodied the collaboration of music, at its established and promising highest level, with the needs of the Nazi state. The happy coincidence of the interests of music and politics contributed to the cultural facade of the regime but, in the case of Egk, also to the promotion of new music and the younger generation, both of which he successfully defended against the ideologues, party hacks and incompetent beneficiaries of Nazi patronage.

Other composers revealed similar experiences. Musically, all contributed to Nazi culture by their decisions to stay and be productive musicians. Most wrote official and commissioned works, reformulated the values of the music-political order and accepted official positions. However, the more accomplish-ed ones also suffered attacks in the Nazi press for various forms of political unreliability, violations of Nazi musical standards, or personal indiscretions—suggesting that criticism did not cease with Goebbels' formal ban in 1936 and that even authoritative party-journalists engaged in public disputes and disagreed.

The composer, teacher and conductor Carl Orff is well-known for his life-long interest in children's music education and his compositions, especially *Carmina burana*, one of the most frequently performed and recorded choral works of modern times. His career in music education was formally launched in 1924 when he founded the Günther School, which sought to blend move-ment and music. The famous text, the *Schulwerk für Kinder* (*Children's School Compositions*)—the product of publications before and after 1933—had been promoted by Kestenberg and received attention during the Nazi period. Mean-while, Orff continued to compose, scoring triumphs with his *Carmina burana*, not at its premiere in 1936 but after its Dresden production in 1940—Gerigk's early critique might help explain this time lag—*Catulli Carmina* (1943) and a number of operas. His entire oeuvre provoked controversy, marked by sup-port for his distinct forms of expressions: his use of folk dance and song, pro-fane and low-Latin lyrics and rhythmic ostinato, and elemental harmonies; while Orff's detractors misunderstood or disliked those very characteristics as un-German. Among the latter, the "Reich piano auntie," Elly Ney protested against this *Kulturschande* ("cultural outrage").[236]

Orff's music was performed not only on distinguished stages, but also at party functions. The Günther School offered music by its director at the German Dance Festival, which was organized by the *Deutsche Tanzbühne* (German Dance Stage), a part of the RKK since 1934. The School also con-ducted classes for party organizations. Like Egk and Strauss, Orff composed a well-received piece of Olympics music. Unlike Egk, the anti-Semitic Pfitz-ner and the young Nazi sensation Gottfried Müller who refused a request by the NSKG, Orff wrote an Incidental Music for Shakespeare's *A Midsummer Night's Dream* on commission by the City of Frankfurt a.M. for 5000 RM—one of forty-four such efforts documented by Prieberg, aimed at substituting for the Jewish Mendelssohn classic, and the only one whose score survived the war.[237] A dance ensemble of the School was even sent on subsidized tours, including several trips to Paris before and after the start of its German occupation. In view of this collaboration Prieberg, in his generally well-detailed, documented and balanced evaluation, unfairly makes light of Orff's postwar claim regarding his political difficulties during the Third Reich—an unkind accent, it seems, in the case of a musician who maintained his integrity, stuck to his pre-1933 pedagogic and artistic goals and gained worldwide fame. Indeed, Orff exemplified the precarious situation of even music-ideologically acceptable stars—the hope of the Nazi order—who, in this case, was subject to an official investigation by party authorities in May, 1942 on grounds that he was celebrated by ideological enemies of the regime, in addition to reservations about the *Musik- Schulwerk* and his music. The *Gau* Personnel Office, Munich-Upper Bavaria was not able to document anything of concern to the Nazis. The file reveals also that Orff did not belong to the party or to any of its organizations. He lived as privately as possible—largely in the house of a well-to-do mother-in-law, and was inactive politically.[238]

Thus, a pattern was established in which fear and professional ambition prompted accommodation. Another successful and controversial opera composer, Rudolf Wagner-Régeny worked diligently to compensate for his liabilities. He had a half-Jewish wife. Having been born in Romania, he emphasized his ethnic and *Reich*-German heritage. Already suspect as a student of Franz Schreker, an early victim of Nazi purges, he collaborated for his operas, *Der Günstling* (the product of work from 1931 through 1934, premiered 1935), *Die Bürger von Calais* (1939) and *Johanna Balk* (1941) with Caspar Neher, who was notorious for his previous work with Brecht and Weill. Moreover, his musical tendency toward a modernist idiom, including jazz and atonal elements, required a textual and interpretive cover, in addition to the juxtaposition of obvious tonal features—concessions to political as well as market forces.

Through the lenses of Nazi critics, text and music of *Der Günstling* remained within acceptable bounds, except for some American-style song and jazz elements associated with the negative *Günstling* part. The critics praised the work in spite of its musical demands and distant subject matter, which was based on Büchner's treatment of Victor Hugo's *Mary Tudor*, and it enjoyed tremendous success—136 performances in five seasons. While the text of the next opera, *Die Bürger von Calais*, offered more opportunity for positive Nazi identification with the themes of heroic service and sacrifice for the community, even though Gerigk deplored the failure of the opera to succeed in elevating heroic sacrifice above the impression of unheroic and miserable conditions of war in a city under siege,[239] the music emerged even more boldly, free of romantic association, asserting instead an autonomous existence and expression of sensibilities, including atonal features which help explain the fact that the opera was not performed frequently in spite of positive reviews and propagandistic utility in time of war.

Meanwhile, Wagner-Régeny had made explicit accommodationist moves. *DM* (November 1, 1934) had disclosed that the NSKG through its leader Dr. Walter Stang had commissioned from "the impeccably Aryan composers Rudolf Wagner-Régeny and Julius Weismann a new musical setting for Shakespeare's *A Midsummer Night's Dream* to replace the racially tainted Mendelssohn score." Both new works were performed June 6-11, 1935 during the convention of the NSKG in Düsseldorf and Wagner-Régeny's version was premiered on stage in October.[240] By the time of the success of *Die Bürger von Calais* in 1939, the composer had developed powerful contacts within Nazi circles which led to his involvement in intra-party politics. His next and final operatic collaboration with Neher which also involved Oscar Fritz Schuh and Leopold Ludwig, the modernist *Johanna Balk* offended the Viennese audience; but it was protected by *Gau* leader von Schirach who thus, again, demonstrated independent musical policy. Speaking for discussion and freedom of artistic expression as long as national interest was not violated, he explicitly challenged Goebbels' narrow utilitarian wartime policy which promoted simple edification, entertainment and patriotic sentiment. The *Gau* leader even supported select composers like Orff and Wagner-Régeny with stipends.

Wagner-Régeny finally dropped Neher and collaborated with a prominent and successful party author, Eberhard Wolfgang Möller (whose credits included the film *Jud Süss* and who enjoyed von Schirach's support and held party positions in both Schirach's HJ and Goebbels' RMVP), for his next work, *Das Opfer*. This successful Nazi opera was performed at a ceremony inaugurating a Culture Chamber for the Germans in his native Romania and other party events—a shamefully racist work about a woman who dies in order to prevent a *Rassenschande* (racial disgrace), which accorded with other imperialist and anti-Semitic propaganda at the time of "Eastern colonization" and the "Final Solution." The composer was drafted in February 1943, survived the war and resumed a distinguished career in the German Democratic Republic with music marked by the Brecht-Weill and twelve-tone traditions.[241]

The above portraits mirrored those of hundreds of the 6000 composers with membership in the RMK in 1939, particularly those with racial, political and/or musical liabilities who had survived early purges and accommodated themselves to the standards and demands of the Third Reich. They joined the *völkisch* set, the inconspicuous majority and the even younger generation, represented by the Nazi hope for a new genius, Gottfried Müller, who knew no other political framework in the production of an unprecedented volume of music in response to the needs and demands of the Nazi state and society. More musicians made a living in the Third Reich—172,443 at the peak in 1939, according to Prieberg[242]—than before or after and, considering the gap left by the purges in repertoire and personnel, the benefit for survivors was even greater than sheer numbers suggest.

Though compromised, the modernists typically managed to include atonal and jazz elements in their compositions in spite of public apathy and occasional hostility, formal bans and journalistic criticism—contrary to the impression imparted in much secondary literature about Third Reich culture shaped by the reading of governmental intentions and ideological sentiment alone. People were generally purged for personal and political reasons, not for their music. Modernists were criticized but retained, with some notable exceptions. No opera was censored by Reich Dramaturg Schlösser across the board after local acceptance for a premiere.[243] But that does not mean that the threat of censorship, or fear of being purged, were not real. Earlier measures and continuing pressure made for self-coordination and self-censorship. Local stages and party organizations frequently took the initiative in banning new compositions. The overall pattern of collaboration was maintained in the manner revealed in the above cases. Winfried Zillig, for instance, a modernist student of Schönberg and postwar writer on contemporary music, accepted commissions from the NSKG, though he knew to respond to the call for tonality and traditional harmony with pieces like the "Romantic Symphony" for the National Music Festival of the NSKG in 1936 and the attending party dignitaries—a work later performed by the NSRSO. A considerable number of modernists clearly benefited from the RMK's request for contemporary music, and from Schlösser's appeal for new operas, which matched the ambitions of many local conductors, stage directors and concert societies. Thus Zillig, the part-Jewish Boris Blacher, the controversial Hermann Reutter who enjoyed Hinkel's protection, Wolfgang Fortner, Kurt Thomas, Kurt von Wolfurt, Ottmar Gerster who in 1932 had written music for a Socialist festival play, Hugo Distler who produced new and "regressive" church music and committed suicide in 1942, Richard Mohaupt who was expelled from the RMK in 1937 and emigrated with his Jewish wife, and many other controversial composers produced music variously attacked as "degenerate". But they also accepted NSKG commissions and those of other party organizations, governmental agencies, cities, stages and festivals; they competed for these commissions, prizes and stipends; they participated at official, party and professional events; articulated *völkisch* sentiment in behalf of the new order; they wrote what, after the war, were regarded as embarassing dedications, they composed works for Nazi texts and ritualistic use—all in the traditional and appropriate style, approximating the output and behavior of older Nazi colleagues like Paul Graener and Max Trapp and the younger Bernhard Homulka and Gottfried Müller.

The young lion Gottfried Müller, the son of a Dresden preacher and only eighteen years old in 1933, displayd such outstanding promise that he became the great hope of the regime for a Nazi-inspired new music. Rooted in church music—his teachers included the Dresden church music director and organist Bernhard Pfannstiehl, the famous organist Karl Straube and the venerable Frances Donald Tovey at Edinburgh—he was actively promoted by giants of German music—by no means exclusively by the collaborators, but also by people like Fritz Busch and Erich Kleiber, well-known opponents of the regime. Müller's early work raised hope in the revitalization of church music in the tradition of Reger, in opposition to the otherwise moribund establishment, which in early 1933 was dedicated to the reformulation of baroque and pre-baroque styles—dry, out of historical context and lacking development.[244] His identification with the community of the church prepared him for that of National Socialism—an easy transition for "German Christians." Professionally Müller committed himself to the new order by composing a choral work, "Requiem of a German Hero"—dedicated "into the hands of the *Führer*" and premiered by GMD Karl Elmendorff at the *Tonkünstler* festival of the General German Music Society—*Allgemeiner Deutscher Musikverein* (ADMV), in 1934 in Wiesbaden. Herzog raved about the combination of patriotism and religiosity. Even Strobel acknowledged the new talent. The work was performed at distinguished stages and for official occasions, in one instance at the personal request of Hitler. Flush with success and celebrated for his impressive promise, he turned down a church-musical position in search of greater fame and honors. He received a stipend for composition from the city of Dresden and found a new promoter in Karl Elmendorff of Mannheim. But, significantly, Müller also cultivated the direct contact with Hitler's circle and prepared a choral work for the 1939 Party Congress which began with a *Führer* text and was intended to capture the essence of the National Socialist community. When the party instead selected the music of Friedrich Jung, a composer who was promoted by *Reich* leader Robert Ley, Müller had to look elsewhere for the perfomance of his intensely patriotic oratorium.

Müller's fanaticism, ambition, and ultimate failure demonstrated that political accommodation did not always produce desired results. According to the postwar account of Elmendorff's wife, her husband was put off by Müller's increasing Nazi engagement and refused to premiere this musical rendition of Hitler's words at the Dresden State Opera, where Elmendorff had succeeded Karl Böhm, who had moved to Vienna. Incredibly, Müller reacted by denouncing his old friend for alleged treasonable statements, which could have landed him in a concentration camp or worse. Elmendorff was saved from the Gestapo by a friendly functionary who destroyed the accusatory letter.[245] It seems that the insecurity built into the system made even Nazi bureaucrats suspicious of informers. Müller, the young and vindictive ingrate, gained few friends by his behavior. The character flaw produced more cold shoulders, even though Elmendorff finally accepted the oratorio, upon the advice of his bureaucrat friend. The premiere took place in April, 1944, to mixed reviews. Müller became more isolated and had difficulties finding performers for his later compositions.

While Elmendorff survived the deadly denunciations, an exceptionally talented young pianist was not so fortunate. On September 7, 1943 Karlrobert Kreiten, age 27, was executed for his privately-expressed anti-Nazi and defeatist attitudes. His parents received a bill of 639.20 RM for the cost of the execution.[246] One of his teachers, the internationally renowned Claudio Arrau, recalled the tragic victim as the greatest piano talent he had ever met, one capable of continuing in the tradition of Kempff and Gieseking.[247] Kreiten was born in Bonn in 1916 into the bourgeois home of his father Theo—who, though German, was born in Holland. The elder Kreiten was an instructor of composition and piano at the Düsseldorf Music Academy, and a music critic, and his mother, Emmy, was a successful French-speaking singer of Alsacian background. The *Wunderkind* grew up in an enlightened, internationalist and socially alive and connected environment. The family was rooted in that liberal-conservative society which expressed reservation toward National Socialism in 1933. In private, the Nazis were ridiculed and criticized, though not actively resisted. Young Kreiten was influenced sufficiently by his family and friends to resist joining the Nazi student organization.

Accepted into Peter Dahm's master class at the Cologne Conservatory in 1929, Kreiten's exceptional technique, musicality and ability to easily memorize were already—at age 13—recognized. He won a competition in Vienna, in the summer of 1933, before a jury headed by Clemens Krauss, and the Mendelssohn Prize in Berlin later in the year. He also was awarded one of four stipends from the Felix-Mendelssohn-Bartholdy Foundation, whereupon he went to Vienna to begin study with Hedwig Rosenthal-Kanner, which was terminated when the Jewish Rosenthals emigrated to the US in 1938. Their invitation for him to join them was turned down by his family. Upon Furtwängler's recommendation he moved to Berlin to study with Arrau from 1937 to 1940, at which time the Chilean master also left Germany. Kreiten had a reputation for brilliant technique, supreme musicality and a broad repertoire encompassing the classics and new music. His extraordinary career of triumphs at competitions, successful concert and radio performances, recordings and a contract with Telefunken came to an abrupt halt when, unsuspecting, he was arrested by the Gestapo in May 1943, shortly before a concert in Heidelberg.

The Kreiten case illustrates the milieu of terror so often referred to in the memoir literature of survivors, the fear of being overheard— acknowledged by the *deutsche Blick*, the glancing over your shoulder before speaking—as well as the classic condition of bourgeois acquiescence, disdain for the Nazi politicians, and an "apolitical" promotion of career objectives in the context of the police state which, in the final phase of the disastrous and total war, when Himmler became Interior Minister, brought out the worst features of a Nazified population that would inform on its intimidated neighbors. In March, Kreiten had confided to an acquaintance of his mother his reservations about the regime; he predicted that the war was already practically lost and would lead to the total destruction of Germany and its culture.[248] The woman passed on this information to two fanatical members of the Nazi Women's Organization, who denounced Kreiten to the RMK. One of the two informers, Tiny von Passavant, née Debüser—the wife of an army major and a not too successful singer in spite of her membership in various party organizations and performances at Nazi party functions—had known the family in Düsseldorf, and according to friends had envied Emmy Kreiten's and her son's success, was going to get even.[249] The informer had also volunteered her services for the "total war" program at an office assigned to check out all denunciations.

The Kreitens were well-known and respected. Consequently, RMK officials shelved the matter without, however, informing Kreiten of the denunciation. A press notice in late April about a forthcoming engagement of Kreiten in Florence alerted Frau Passavant, who picked up her original letter from the RMK and turned it over to the Gestapo. Still unaware of anything, Kreiten was arrested at that time and taken to Berlin. Again RMK functionaries, especially Fritz von Borries, head of personnel at the RMVP Music Division, and the specialist for cultural affairs at the Rhenish *Gau* office, Wilhelm Raupp, tried to stall; but higher authority intervened and took charge directly. All efforts of family, friends, and sympathetic officials in behalf of the pianist and finally appeals for mercy, like that of the old family friend Furtwängler, proved fruitless. The terror state was intent on issuing a barbaric warning. The notorious People's Tribunal under Roland Freisler convicted the twenty-seven year old musician on September 3, 1943 and he was executed September 7; a press notice followed on the 14th. Called a *Volksschädling*, Karlrobert Kreiten was executed for defeatism, having offered comfort to the enemy, and having undermined the loyalty of his compatriots by incitement, defamation and exaggeration...[250]

While the profession was stunned, some Nazis gloated. For instance, the composer Hermann Unger—Pg since 1931, musical leader of the KfdK, co-founder of the Study Group of Nazi Composers in 1934 and an activist during the purge period himself, whose songs had been performed by Frau Passavant, a relative by marriage—approved the execution before students in Cologne. He was ostracized by colleagues for his anti-Kreiten tirades. The radical measure was also applauded in a comment entitled "Artist—Example and Model," in the Berlin paper, *12-Uhr-Blatt*, attributed to Pg Werner Höfer, the post-war moderator of the popular TV program *Frühschoppen* who, however, denied authorship.[251] In view of his brilliant career, one wonders why Karlrobert Kreiten is not listed in postwar music encyclopedias, as if the memory of him disappeared along with the regime that killed him.

Kreiten's execution was not typical. Others who shared his views were more careful, while those who were brought to trial received only a few years in jail. More typical was his "apolitical" attitude and career, which he shared with thousands, including those who produced and performed entertainment music. Yet entertainment was not innocent—certainly not in times of total manipulation of all music production and reception, including its popular variety of films and hit songs. Entertainment music also was monitored, commissioned, censored and applied. It was variously promoted as "pure entertainment," even though it was cultivated for the political goal of offering distraction from unpleasant realities and war and for revitalizing the citizenry for combat. It reflected and reinforced ideology with its mix of acceptable classical, folk and popular musical forms of expression as well as loaded texts, film images and socio-political content. The same musical craftsmen produced explicit political music: military marches, themes for newsreels and special news bulletins during warfare, other fanfares, party hymns, nationalistic paeans, exhortations to fight, etc.—in tune with entertainment fashion, full of verve and catchiness.

Pop musicians always have to be in step with the times. In 1933 that meant to ride the romantic-sentimental "soft wave" which had replaced jazz and other counter-cultural expressions of the twenties before the official bans of the Third Reich codified the trend—a regressive sound world of reminiscence and denial, against the background of the depression.[252] They also picked up conservative, *völkisch* and Nazi sentiments which they translated into songs about blond and blue-eyed Hitler girls, homeland, comradery, a new spring for the nation, etc. Ex-cabarettists like Ralph Benatzky, Theo Mackensen and Oscar Strauss, who with Bruno Balz and Hans Fritz Beckmann later lent their services for psychological warfare, provided for entertainment, propaganda, and income for themselves.[253] Pop music with ideological messages helped integrate and motivate the nation, its soldiers and youth. But while Goebbels never lost sight of this commitment, he early realized that people cannot march and sing party songs all the time. By mid-1936 his diaries and even public statements reveal a shift to entertainment, traditional modes of cultural expression and propagandistic themes encased in opinions and feelings people already held; for example, an emphasis on more seductive and "apolitical" songs about privacy, dreams and love, capable of creating illusions, mystification and distraction, like Günther Schwenn's *Es geht alles vorüber* ("All will pass") and—after a triumphant and arrogant interlude of *Blitzkrieg* victories and their musical accompaniment, especially the escapist wave during the Stalingrad disaster represented by Bruno Balz's *Es wird einmal ein Wunder geschehen* ("A miracle will happen"), popularized by Zarah Leander, which resulted from a competition for optimistic hit songs sponsored by Goebbels.[254]

Many popular hit songs were originally composed for film, which in Goebbels' scheme was the most important propaganda vehicle, both as a medium of overt indoctrination and even more insidious when ideological themes and political objectives were hidden. Like songs, film gradually performed a distraction function. Earlier it also had suffered KfdK and NSBO intrusion, *Gleichschaltung*, purges, organization in a Reich Film Chamber (RFK) and incorporation into the RKK. A Film Credit Bank financed seventy-three percent of all feature films by 1936. The Reich Cinema Law (February 16, 1934) established censorship and a system of distinction marks, which identified films as to their political worth and offered tax exemptions and a higher share of the profits for those whose films received the higher marks. By March, 1936 all musical film scores and song texts had to be submitted to the censor ten days before shooting could begin. Like the press, the film industry was nationalized, although the facade of familiar company names was retained, and audience reactions were evaluated by means of weekly confidential wartime SD Reports.[255]

Eventually centrally controlled by Goebbels, the Nazi film industry produced 1097 feature films between 1933 and 1945 for a steadily growing audience (8.4 visits per person over age fifteen in 1938 to 14.4 per same age group in 1944). One sixth of these films were devoted to overt propaganda—supplemented by the many documentaries, newsreels and so-called *Tendenzfilme* which contained but did not mention National Socialism—while more than half were of the entertainment variety—the love stories, comedies, crime thrillers and musicals which assumed an increasingly important role in Goebbels' refined understanding of propaganda.[256] During and after Stalingrad, films about perseverance in war and belief in final victory, known as *Durchhaltefilme* paralleled the songs which also reflected historical developments of the regime and the war. Hollywood was not the only great dream factory. Any list of light musicial contributors to the Third Reich would have to include the composer of "Lili Marlene," Norbert Schultze, the man who so boldly had stood up for U-Musik and helped secure its equality in the distribution of royalties in a memorandum to RMK officials and composers before their national meeting at Schloss Burg in October 1940. Born in 1911, a member of a cabaret, then opera conductor in Heidelberg and Darmstadt (1934-1936), director of recording at Telefunken in Berlin and the composer of the successful opera, Der Schwarze Kater (1936) with 724 performances in six seasons, Schultze had mastered the classical and popular idioms of his time and stood ready to serve the Nazi state with compositions upon request. Prieberg concludes that Schultze's extraordinary career was symptomatic of the era, in that it would have taken an altogether different turn without the Nazi state. Schultze confided to Prieberg, in an interview in 1969, that he had made the fateful decision to accept an offer to compose music for a documentary film about the role of the air force in Germany's victory over Poland because his employment by the Tobis studio would secure him a draft deferment. Moreover, the exciting prospect to compose two hours of symphonic music— an extraordinary opportunity for a young man who had two films to his credit, in addition to keeping him out of combat—sealed his commitment to the Nazi state.[257] The resulting music for the film, Feuertaufe ("Baptism by Fire"), directed by Hans Bertram in 1940, and its famous song for the air force, Bomben über Engelland ("Bombs over England") insured Schultze's fame as a composer of catchy marching songs, as well as future contracts. His music became a prototype for this kind of film-music throughout the Third Reich. As the air force song became an indentification mark for the air force, similar songs were written by Schultze and others for other branches of the military, to identify military campaigns, and to create a pop-Wagnerian world of musical motifs which, even out of context, would later recall the service or battle.

This best-known and perhaps most impressive film of German military propaganda, "Batism by Fire," represented and magnified the victorious phase of German armies in romantic, yet terrifying terms, to reassure the nation and intimidate potential enemies. Hitler applauded an early version of the film, which concluded with a military parade following the combat; but he wanted and ordered a different ending which pointed toward the invasion of England—thus, the final song, "Bombs over England."[258] Schultze's music—the air force song, the romantic sweeps, fanfares and other effects— reinforced the moods and action of a film characteristically devoid of dialogue, while a narrator added propagandistic perspectives. Thus, the viewer learned that the depicted destruction of Warsaw was the consequence of "Mr. Chamberlain's doing." Göring was filmed in the end, praising the exploits of his young air force, calling the Poland campaign only a first phase and then threatening the destruction of France and England—followed by trumpet fanfares and the roar of engines. In this manner, propaganda produced an atmosphere of anticipation, of fear and confidence. The film concluded with a stanza of the air force song:

Thus our youngest weapon has been baptized and tempered in the flames. Now the winged host reaches out to the sea, we are ready for battle. Forward against the British lion, for the last, decisive blow. We sit here in judgment of a crumbling Empire—for which purposes German soldiers are fighting.

followed by the famous refrain:

Comrade, comrade, all the girls must wait. Comrade, comrade, the order is clear, we're on our way. Comrade, comrade, the slogan you know; forward at the foe, forward at the enemy—bombs on England! ....

Finally, storm clouds gathered and then disappeared, to reveal a map of Great Britain, followed by an explosion and the map's destruction, the last line of the song sounded: "Bombs, bombs, bombs on England."[259]

The SD Reports confirmed Goebbels' enthusiasm for *Feuertaufe*.[260] In this early phase of the war, before the material deprivation of the Germans, the resolution of conflict by lightning victory—accompanied by smashing fanfares, the variously soothing and happy music designed to soften the harsh realities and severe measures—and the identification of the reaction with its young flier heroes and their new song produced the reaction recorded in the confidential Reports, and committed Goebbels to more of the same. *Feuertaufe* became the basis of Bertram's fictionalized account of the Polish campaign in the film, "Squadron Lützow" (1941) which even borrowed footage and the air force song from the famous documentary model. By that time the war song as an identification mark was well established.[261] A film about "Victory in the West" followed the fall of France. Schultze continued to write songs which chronicled campaigns and identified other military services and political issues: "The Song of the Eastern Campaign"—composed for the invasion of Russia, his "March of the German Grenadiers," "The *Führer* Commands, We Follow," and many others about U-boat men, the air force, navy, tank units, etc.—sung by the soldiers, heard on the radio and praised by Goebbels and reserved for special occasions as "Songs of the Nation."

Norbert Schultze also contributed fanfare introductions for newsreels and special wartime news bulletins which became well-known throughout the war and must be added to that world of musical motifs association with people, places and campaigns—a genre that reflected the *Blitzkrieg* strategy, hitting audiences with identification blasts. The newsreels were a major feature of this media barrage upon the German people during the war, when the coordinated newsreel services were merged into the one *Deutsche Wochenschau* ("German Newsreel") and openly identified as Goebbels' creature. RMVP photograpers supplied the material for the forty-minute newsreels—the product of careful editing and musical additions. They were immensely popular during the early years of war and occasioned much public commentary, according to the SD Reports.[262] Music accompanied these effective implements of propaganda, which were shown in tandem with feature films and thus benefited by the comparison with the fictional entertainment as authentic portrayal of facts.

In preparation for the invasion of the Soviet Union, Goebbels—flushed with military and propagandistic victories—became personally involved in the careful planning of the music which was to introduce and accompany the announcement of the invasion over the radio. Two composers of successful propaganda songs, Herms Niel and Schultze were commissioned to compose the music for the product of an earlier competition for writers, the text of the "Song of the Eastern Campaign," which Goebbels personally had helped edit. Schultze's song was selected, including the well-known "Russian Fanfare" which he had been instructed to add as an introduction or a coda, based on parts of Liszt's *Les Préludes*—a typical example of the Nazi custom of reducing a classical work (in this case one of the literature's most popular symphonic poems) to a fanfare, without development and out of context. Song and fanfare accompanied the news about the Russian invasion on June 22, 1941. Especially the fanfare, also known as the "Victory Fanfare" became one of the most recognized works of music of the Third Reich, announcing special news bulletins and the German newsreel and was applied to other musical works and songs.

Schultze's output, like all propaganda, was affected by the war's development. Just as victories had made Goebbels' job easy, defeat created problems. During and after Stalingrad the entire media shifted from propaganda as an extension and reinforcer of ideology to the psychological management of disillusionment and fear—the latter actually being inculcated and exploited. While newsreels retained their musical identification marks, they lost credibility and popularity according to the increasingly disconcerting SD Reports. Meanwhile the percentage of political films declined from pre-Stalingrad levels, replaced by love stories, operettas and other light entertainment. Simultaneously Goebbels enlisted film and song in his "total war"—songs about fighting to the bitter end and about miracles, and very expensive historical films which portrayed the human qualities necessary for victory in this very real, epic struggle. Frederick the Great in particular was invoked as an example of holding out against overwhelming odds in 1759 in anticipation of another miracle.

In mid-1943, Goebbels commissioned Veit Harlan to produce *Kolberg*—the site of a French siege during the Napoleonic War of 1806-07—an epic about inspired leadership, loyalty and obedience, sacrifice for the fatherland, an indomitable German spirit and, above all, resistance by the people rather than the formal military, in obvious allusion to his *Volkssturm* campaign. A love story was woven into the epic of war, heroism and ultimate defeat, as Kolberg was overrun by superior French forces—a remarkable synthesis of Goebbels' two objectives at this late hour: to offer escapist entertainment and to inspire the will to continue fighting. Norbert Schultze's songs contributed to this final cinematic appeal to national idealism and suicide—classic German romantic themes, explicitly reformulated in Goebbels' diary (March 31,1945) and acted out in the *Götterdämmerung* of the Thousand Year Reich. The film was premiered in Berlin on January 30, 1945, exactly twelve years after what a song then had called "a new spring."[263]

Postwar denazifiers classified Norbert Schultze as a collaborator. Indeed, his career mirrored the history of the Third Reich and the phases of Goebbels' propaganda campaigns. *Der Spiegel* reported in 1968 that he had no regrets about his songs for the Nazi state and total war. He asked, "have not other composers done the same for their country?"[264]

The conductors equaled this record of accommodation. Like other musicans they were taken to task during the postwar denazification proceedings. Once again, Germans had to fill out questionnaires which, indeed, revealed much about collaboration. In Austria, too, the Soviets allowed Clemens Krauss to conduct the Vienna Philharmonic a few weeks after the end of the war, even though Krauss was said to have been Hitler's favorite conductor, had participated at countless official events, never denied his Nazi sympathies and appeared in Veit Harlan's notorious anti-Semitic film *Jud Süss*—but had helped Jews escape from Austria in 1938. Von Karajan, Pg. since 1933, GMD, appointed State Conductor by Hitler upon Goebbels' recommendation on the *Führer's* birthday in 1939—also had conducted at all kinds of official events, including occupied Paris; but his marriage in 1942 to a woman who was one-quarter Jewish may have affected a slow-down of his otherwise meteoric career. He was denazified and given permission to conduct at Salzburg in 1946—an order which was then rescinded; he did not conduct at the Festival that year,[265] but by the next year his postwar career was launched. Böhm had been compromised to an even greater degree. He had demonstrated support for the regime beyond cautionary requirements.

Furtwängler, the most complex case, will be reviewed in Chapter IV. This authoritative representative of the musical order in Nazi Germany had not compromised to the degree of his colleagues; but he suffered from a lengthy denazification proceeding, perhaps for symbolic reasons.[266] By 1947, the musical order of Germany and Austria were again functional.

When Prieberg introduced his devastating expose of collaborations and referred to postwar controversy, denial, mystification and even lawsuits involving not only the notables Egk, Böhm and Karajan, but also the less well-known but also distinguished musicians Johann Nepomuk David, Franz Philipp, Cesar Bresgen, Hermann Heiss and Richard Trunk for their political compositions and associations,[267] he confirmed the condition of thousands of similar musical careers in the totalitarian society. Musicians participated in Nazi culture but, in general, the propagators of high art music (*E-Musik*), no less than those of the entertainment variety, contributed explicit music-political support.

Not only the active musicians experienced the terror and the anguish of compromise; even the leaders suffered from the insecurity they helped create. Peter Raabe would appear as stable and representative of the music-political order as anyone. Known for his pre-1933 *völkisch* sentiments and Kfdk membership and his advocacy of radical measures in 1933, he had written and deliverd inspired and authoritative reflections on the state of the art in the Third Reich and assumed the presidency of the RMK in 1935, when Richard Strauss was no longer deemed suitable. Paul Graener replaced Strauss as head of the corporate composers, and lower echelon personnel changes were effected. The press approved the new music regime. Friedrich W. Herzog praised Raabe for a fine professional record and for having tackled organizational problems with sensitivity to artistic and political concerns.[268]

In charge of the RMK, Raabe administered the purges of the profession via new legislation, the questionnaire and close contacts with the new authorities, to the point of occasionally getting into trouble with the RMVP for too much zeal. At the same time he continued to be active as a conductor and as president of the prestigious *Allgemeiner Deutscher Musikverein* (ADMV) and its annual festival, the *Tonkünstlerfest*. In 1933 and thereafter, he and the new members of the board, the Pg's Max Donisch, Paul Graener, Hugo Rasch, Max Trapp and the publisher/writer Gerhard Tischer coordinated the festival's program with the new spirit in an effort to balance standards with *völkisch* principles—it would seem to be an unassailable enterprise consistent with Goebbels' policy. But other party activists objected to the ADMV and its programs, and Raabe felt obliged to respond to the denunciation of two composers who, in 1936, had charged him with pre-1933 Jewish influence and the favoring of Southern German composers, since Professor Joseph Haas of

Munich tended to favor his own students. Raabe was in fact especially proud of this 1936 program in Weimar in celebration of the organization's seventy-fifth anniversary, which was recognized for its importance by Hitler with a subvention of 15,000 RM and the German National Theatre in Vienna with 10,000 RM. His defense is interesting:

> Before the founding of the Third Reich, all German culture was *verjudet*...Only the *Führer* was able to break the power of Jewry...No organization was able to evade Jewish influence, since each one was dependent on the outcome of elections, rather than the leadership principle...In the music community this was not possible. Like all other governing boards of German cultural societies, this one included Jews.

As to the reference to Jewish participation in the selection of programs, Raabe likened his affairs to those of the Berlin Philharmonic, suggesting that all money would have to be withheld from that distinguished orchestra because it too had been conducted in hundreds of cases by Jews before 1933, employed Jewish musicians, played Jewish compositions and had been, in fact, originally a Jewish organization. Raabe concluded, again, that only the *Führer* managed to break the system. Raabe also defended Professor Haas and other instructors of composition, such as Thuille, Courvoisier and Waltershausen, on the basis of their tremendous popularity. Haas alone has produced seven hundred students in his career. Raabe also quoted from the slander sheet: "...are personages who were responsible for the cultural policies of the ADMV before 1933 morally justified to assume leading positions in the culture of National Socialist Germany?" [269]

More seriously, the festival's program in Weimar was attacked by the powerful, well-connected and singleminded duo of party stalwarts, Dr. Hans Severus Ziegler—State Councillor, director of the Weimar National Theatre and head of the Thuringian *Gau* Cultural Office—and the dramaturg at the Weimar National Theatre, Professor Otto Zur Nedden who, it will be recalled, on their own pursued a singularly radical music policy which took the form at that time of attempting to remove the "cultural bolshevists" Reutter, Knorr, Fortner, Tiessen and Hugo Hermann from the Weimar program. Joined by "degenerate music" expert Heinz Drewes, also an old Weimar hand, the group persuaded the arriving Goebbels to issue bans which were blocked only when Raabe threatened to resign from the RMK presidency.[270] Undeterred, Ziegler turned to the Rosenberg Bureau, where Herbert Gerigk supported him with the organization of the "Degenerate Music" exhibit in 1938. The *Tonkünstlerfest* convened once more, in 1937 in Darmstadt and Frankfurt a.M., highlighting Orff's *Carmina burana*. The RMK then took over functions of the ADMV and replaced the traditional festival with the Reich Music Festival in 1938 in Düsseldorf which included the "Decadent Music" exhibit. Thus the illustrious organization founded by Liszt was dissolved,[271] while Raabe continued in his capacity as RMK president. The traditional *völkisch* moralist, the denunciator and subject of denunciation, bureaucrat and ideologue, managed to accommodate himself, hold his own, contribute to the functioning of the regime and, in the final analysis, to survive. He continued to write and act throughout the Third Reich.

Raabe's position was rather typical. Increasing insecurity inspired greater efforts toward the proving of loyalty and conformity. The party faithful in music was pressed to defend himself, constantly demonstrating the proper sentiments and enthusiasm. Another representative leader in the music community was Professor Fritz Stein, who rose quickly from the beginning of 1933 as commissioner of the State Music Academy at Berlin, 1934 as head of the Chorus and Folk Music division of the RMK—always active in the administration of music and as frequent contributor to the coordinated musical journals. Yet this noted official also suffered from the insecurity so characteristic of Nazi officials. In early 1933 for instance, the student body of the University of Kiel had placed him on a list of twenty-eight so-called "unreliable" professors. The student body of the Berlin Academy, taking note of the proclamation, declared its solidarity with the students of Kiel and asked Stein to resign his post. Supported by powerful connections, Stein turned the matter over to Hans Hinkel and referred to the favorable response of the "national press" to his appointment.[272] In addition to the trouble from below he was subjected to review by highest party circles. It appeared that Stein was not even a party member. He wrote to the party in 1933 that he had always sympathized with Hitler's movement, that he had voted for the party since 1925 and that he had been generous with donations. However, as GMD in the pay of the city of Kiel and as Prussian official he had not been able to join the party. Stein wrote that he was of Aryan descent and that his ancestors could be traced back to... Since May, he was proud to point out, he was a member of the KfdK, serving that organization in the capacity of *Reichsleiter* of the music division. With this commendation he now appealed to the party to accept him as a new member in spite of a momentary ban on new memberships.[273] Rust employed him at the Berlin Academy of Music in April 1933, after a thorough investigation of his character and political sentiment.

The controversy over Stein was kept alive throughout the Third Reich. He was highly praised in the coordinated press. Eberhard Breussner wrote in the *ZfM*, December 1939 that "someone who has demonstrated the ability to lead a male chorus such as the one of the *Leibstandarte Adolf Hitler*

("Hitler's body guard"), has indicated deepest understanding of the nature of the organization and of music politics."[274] With this kind of adulation—it must be taken as such, although it may be taken for a joke—his background in racial and political terms, and his participation in the music structure of the Third Reich, Stein wondered why he was kept from joining the party. Indeed, in July 1935, the *Reichsleitung* NSDAP specifically asked for his removal from the presidium of the RMK in a note to the business manager of the RKK, Franz Karl Moraller. The Director of the Berlin Music Academy obviously offended the ideologists in the party by his loyalty to Hindemith, whom he encouraged to stay at the Academy and in Germany, in spite of all the attacks on him, particularly by the Rosenberg circle.[275] Party machinations were transmitted through organizers who held posts in various party organs. Essentially it was one club which controlled the affairs of musicians, but members of the club were not immune from insinuations, denunciations and ultimate liquidation. Stein cannot be compared to an old party faithful like Moraller. As a musician, originally in the capacity of conductor and critic, he shared the career of Raabe in a situation which had assumed proportions that could hardly have been anticipated either by Nazi moralists or collaborators. Whereas Raabe's moralism led him to roam the night clubs in order to discover alien elements in German entertainment music, Stein lent himself to a journalism of the cheapest kind. He joined the chorus of Hitler admirers after the 1936 plebiscite with a quotation from Handel's *Gelegenheitsoratorium*: "Then the call of God awakens the savior, liberating us from the yoke." He continued,

We are indebted to our *Führer* for fulfilling the thousand-year-old German dream of the united German *Reich*, the true people's community, in which everything happens 'in the framework of the totality and for the benefit of all' who want to produce a renaissance of native German art from the roots of German blood, German feeling and belief. We too, as musicians, regained faith through the historic deed of Adolf Hitler, a faith in eternal values, in the cultural mission of the German soul and German spirit. As German artists in the community of the creative as reconstructed by the National Socialist state, we may again contribute to the building of the sacred temple of German music, according to the parole: 'You are nothing, the *Volk* is everything,' with steadfast faith in our *Führer* and his work of peace, with burning heart and clean hands. For this, we musicians—included are all German chorus singers and amateur musicians—thank the Führer this March 29, with our unanimous oath of allegiance.[276]

Was this a statement of a genuine National Socialist convert, or of a clever opportunist? Regardless, the collaborator was compelled to express his loyalty in a manner suggestive of the insecurity which characterized the musical power structure. Fritz Stein survived the Third Reich. He belonged to the category of survivors who were hard put to demonstrate their innocence. The sadness or the perversity of such a life—from resentment to success and possible compunctions, and after the war to excuses, apologies and certainly this time embarrassment—again illustrate the product of totalitarian rule. Karl Ulrich Schnabel recalled an encounter with Fritz Stein in England after the war. His impression was that of a man who had conservative, even *völkisch* convictions, but also of one who denied his complicity.[277]

One of the most active and decidedly Nazi musical commentators was Fritz Stege, who had been a member of the KfdK since 1929. We owe much of the information contained in the *AMRMK*, specifically those published with commentary in the *ZfM* to his pen. He was also music critic of the *VB* and he wrote for many local papers. In addition, he enjoyed a close relationship with Hans Hinkel.

Fritz Stege's journalism set the pattern for much of the jargon in circulation ever since the Nazi movement addressed music. Unlike Raabe, he was a man of the Nazi movement, lacking Raabe's moral convictions. His numerous articles throughout the Nazi press, ranging from commentaries on musical life in various German cities to official policy statements, document his stature as a Nazi journalist. He touched on every possible aspect of the relationship between music and National Socialism. The language used in describing the music criticism of enemy H.H. Stuckenschmidt has been cited above.

A review of some of these expressions here will illustrate that Stege went beyond the requirement of Nazi journalism. Indeed, he fit the category of those described by Günter Schab, the well-known music critic of the *Düsseldorfer Nachrichten*, as having done more than necessary for survival. Schab acknowledged that all journalists, including anti-Nazis like himself had to be members of the Journalist Association which automatically was transformed into the Reich Press Chamber, but Stege set standards for others in the tendentious music commentary of the day.[278] A sample of Stege's prose makes the point: "Stuckenschmidt produced intellectual fertilizer for the freshly sprouting seeds of Marxist monstrosity." (The German can hardly be translated:...*geistigen Dünger für die munter spriessende Saat marxistischer Sumpfblüten.*) The abusive tone was manifested in threats of this kind: "In the meantime, the National Socialist revolution has proved on whose side is right and wrong."[279] In the *ZfM* he discussed the "serious matter" of race research, ranging from H.F.K. Günther, Schulze-Naumburg, Schemann, Clauss, Brunnhofer, Kurt Gerlach and Darré and its application to music by Richard Eichenauer. Stege introduced the music public to the relationship between race and music, explaining that "atonality, for instance, is incompatible with the Nordic spirit."[280] He wrote at great length about the necessity of coordinating music criticism with National Socialism, a concept which he applied to a new organization under his leadership. His zeal also led to the ludicrous endeavor to evaluate musical instruments in ideological terms. The controversial saxophone, for instance, deserved to be supported, he wrote, although certain methods of performance had to be prevented. The violin, on the other hand, needed to regain its preeminent position as embodiment of ideological conceptions of pure and beautiful sound, and he approved governmental positions along these lines.[281] It was not possible to be more in tune with Nazi principles than this man, whose articles are the evidence about an era which would otherwise be difficult to reconstruct in its enormity.

Stege also fashioned politics from early on in 1933 as an active member of the KfdK. He enjoyed such a reputation that people turned to him with requests for support in the hectic days of denunciations and dismissals—the non-systematized and capricious decisions of those who styled themselves "leaders." In the Stuckenschmidt article, Stege himself suggested the removal of a rival fellow critic. Thus, he wrote, "The *BZ am Mittag* is advised to grant its star critic a leave of absence."[282] Then he became an official. When the Association of German Music Critics was dissolved, KfdK leader and state commissioner Hans Hinkel asked Stege to reorganize the critical profession on the basis of "new considerations." In the *ZfM* Stege responded with an appeal to fellow critics to "practice German *Kulturpolitik*." His temporary organization of German Music Critics, in 1933, became a major expression of his influence and power and was an instrument for purging the music critical profession, upon the request and close contact with KfdK leaders Hinkel and Havemann. Stege's collaboration paid dividends, as he was able to purge rivals and promote friends. In April, 1933 Stege had asked Hinkel for permission to control press cards at the State and City Opera houses. "Those critics (primarily Jewish) who are guilty of grave moral crimes or slander against German works will be taken off the press list and will no longer receive cards."[283]

Nonetheless, Stege also ran into opposition. In response to a rival organization of critics, the Goebbels-sponsored *Reichsverband Deutscher Schriftsteller* (Reich Association of German Writers), as we have seen above, he called a meeting of all local and state representatives of his *Arbeitsgemeinschaft Deutscher Musikkritiker* (Study Group of German Music Critics) to discuss the situation. He followed up with an appeal to the all-powerful

Hans Hinkel to lend his office to the establishment of an independent agency, or some higher authority to sit in judgment between the rival organizations, between his own group of German Music Critics, the ADM, and the music critic division of the writers association, the RDS. He complained that "the RDS has not found it necessary to answer my letters or to maintain contact. Other colleagues who are not qualified are asked to join the new organization." He pointed to his record of which he was proud and asked for support in the name of "cultural political unity." In the name of the leadership principle and the injunction against duplication of offices, he strongly advised against establishing a rival organization since the confusion would cause disunity among critics. Moreover, "what does the writer's association know of the necessity to create a unified cultural policy of criticism in the service of the recreation of our musical culture?"[284]

Political denunciation cut both ways. Stege had experience with the higher authorities, documented in numerous letters to Hinkel, Rust, Havemann, Graener and others, replete with denunciations, slander and the ideological slogans of the day. Principles were applied quite transparently in support of his interest, or on behalf of friends and against his foes. He skillfully utilized his connections in the power structure to denounce opponents who were not all known to be anti-Nazis. In one notorious case, involving the party great Havemann who was accused of collaboration with Professor Georg Schünemann (see above), Stege volunteered his services to testify against Schünemann in order to bring evidence against Pg. Havemann, a one-time friend and associate.[285] In support of his case with the higher authorities, he prided himself, in another letter to Hinkel, on having waged a successful press campaign against the anti-Nazi Felix Weingartner, causing the cancellation of a concert tour of the noted conductor through the Palatinate in 1928. Again in 1933 Stege attacked Weingartner successfully, thus preventing a concert in Hamburg. Having heard of a defense of Weingartner by the musicologist Dr. Friedrich Mahling—an active participant in "the construction of the RKK" who, in the name of the KfdK, had advised against a renewal of attacks on Weingartner for, among other reasons, "having behaved decently these past ten years"—Stege appealed for party unity in "such fundamental cases."[286]

In this manner Stege harrassed opponents and victims, slandered rivals and solidified his position through friends and connections. Nonetheless, he remained vulnerable, like all other officials of the new regime, to denunciations and counter-schemes, especially among organizers of the RDS. Personal rivalries of this sort complicated the establishment of a hierarchy of authority in the new Germany. Stege played a prominent role in the vicious attacks on one of the foremost advocates of "modern music," Hans Heinz

Stuckenschmidt; he used his organization of music critics to involve colleagues in a collective defamation campaign which contributed to the victim's discomfort and ultimate emigration. He also renewed his denunciation of Dr. Friedrich Mahling, who, meanwhile, had become the object of numerous investigations of the Reich Chancellery, the Office of Rosenberg and other Nazi organization over alleged anthroposophic connections. Having joined the party only in 1933, Mahling, nevertheless, had managed to become the press chief of the RMK and remained prominently active in the "culture-political reorganization of the Third Reich" until relieved of his RMK duties and, as chief editor of his journal, *Musik im Zeitbewusstsein,* after an advertisement of the *Moscow Bühnenfestspiele* ("Moscow Stage Festival") had appeared in his journal and caused a monumental controversy.[287] Stege joined a powerful frontal attack on Mahling. While the victim lost party positions, though managing to stay on in an academic capacity at the Music Academy in Berlin, Stege continued on his way. In his own organization, the ADM, he had two members removed, Johannes Günther and Friedrich Wilhelm Herzog, both of whom also belonged to the rival organization of the RDS. When the conflict between the two critic groups became more threatening, Stege wanted to compromise, but the RDS business manager refused to discuss the matter until Stege would reinstate Günther and Herzog. Stege, in turn, appealed to the RKK over this dispute, but also here received no answer. Instead he learned that his position had been undermined rather successfully, since all Berlin music critics meanwhile had received invitations from the RDS to the founding convention of the official Professional Estate of Music Critics as a branch of the broadly based RDS, set for October 26, 1933.[288]

The struggle with the RDS was one thing. In addition, however, Stege's character, as he confided to Hinkel in a letter, was maligned by his enemies. He was accused of having composed a compromising hit song fifteen years earlier which, he agreed, was not quite compatible with the principles of the new state. However, he lamented that he had composed at that time for money in order to support his mother. He insinuated that the rumors about his background were started by "a certain Reinhold Scharnke, editor of the *Funkwoche,* against whom, it turned out, Stege had testified when the former applied for membership in the party. Alas, "my local *Ortsgruppenführer* turned over my testimony to Scharnke without consulting with me first. That *Ortsgruppenführer* was relieved of his duties and censured through the legal procedure before USCHLA (party court)." Nonetheless, having been engaged in a defamation suit, he felt compelled to defend himself:

> I now suffer the consequences...I would not have troubled you with my insignificant concerns, most honored Herr Hinkel, inasmuch as you are

preoccupied with more weighty matters; however, I fear that my silence might have been construed as an admittance of guilt. Although this might sound a bit like boasting I am proud to say that I have maintained an absolutely single-minded and uncompromising political positon these past ten years, already before joining the party (1930), as long-time musical adviser of Reinhold Wulles of the *Deutschvölkische Freiheitsbewegung* (German *völkish* liberation movement) And I will remain true to myself—no matter where fate leads me.[289]

Stege was a Nazi, yet like many other Nazis he was not sure of his position. Herzog and Günther wrote a comprehensive report to the RDS that the ADM lacked official sanction. At one time, indeed, it was to have absorbed the members of the defunct Association of German Music Critics. However, with the founding of the RDS its existence had become no longer necessary. As Stege had accused the RDS of "lack of qualification," his organization was now subject to a similar review; it was said to comprise critics of whom 70 percent were actually practicing musicians, exercising their critical faculties only on a part-time basis, while most trained and acknowledged critics did not belong to ADM. Stege's "personal and moral qualifications for leadership" also were questioned. It is interesting to note that a Nazi organization at this time appealed to traditional names in its behalf against the interest of an alleged temporary organization of Nazis, which had been established in the name of the revolution.

Herzog and Günther attacked Stege on professional and personal grounds. His moral standing was questioned, since abuse of patronage could be proved. Through him the director of the Münster Conservatory, the composer Dr. Richard Gross, had become the local leader of the ADM in Münster. It was obvious that the new appointment in Stege's outfit would favor Gross's works, which were performed largely in Münster. The professions of composer and music critic ought, therefore, not to have been combined in one and the same person, particularly when all effort was concentrated in the local setting. Also, in Düsseldorf Stege had seen to it that a favor was returned to Otto Albert Schneider, a man who had been a "convinced spokesman of Jewish artists before the national revolution, who had favored the Eastern Jew, Jascha Horenstein (the first conductor of the Düsseldorf Opera until his emigration in 1933), over the *kerndeutschen* ("German-to-the-core") Hans Weisbach (the *GMD* in Düsseldorf and since 1933 chief conductor of radio Leipzig), and who had cold-shouldered the National Socialist press." This Schneider, feuilleton editor of the *Düsseldorfer Nachrichten*, had dropped the music critic Richard Wintzer, filling the post with Stege instead. For this favor Stege referred to Schneider in a lecture as "an old fighter for national culture," in addition to placing him in command of the local chapter of the ADM. This report on Stege was rather comprehensive, the details of which have been substantiated to me by Günter Schab, also of the *Düsseldorfer Nachrichten*. Stege, the report went on, had published his hit song quite recently, thus casting doubt on his claim that it had been a practical joke of his student years and due to youthful immaturity. Furthermore, in this connection it was revealed that Stege's mother was presently receiving public assistance, that he was not supporting her and that he had beaten her. Several witnesses testified to these allegations.[290]

In late 1935 Stege lost his press card of the *VB*, thus suffering from a practice that he had so vociferously recommended in 1933. Nonetheless, he kept faith in National Socialism and wrote to Rosenberg: I have much too high an opinion of National Socialism to think that you, most honored *Herr Reichsleiter*, know and sanction this behavior." He then filed a complaint with the party.[291] The fate of Stege again illustrated the insecurity of individuals who contributed to the building of a new society without being privy to the rivalries of major Nazi leaders—in this case Goebbels and Rosenberg—into whose crossfire he had stepped. The crimes cited against him characterized operations of the upper strata of Nazi society. As victim of the system, perhaps an unwitting one—certainly one who was ashamed after the war, according to Günter Schab who recalled an encounter and the timid attempt of a handshake—he continued to write throughout the duration of the Third Reich about such matters as "earlier musical bolshevism," "Nordic music," "music and race," completely in accord with National Socialism. He attacked those who fell into disfavor whenever this seemed opportune. The prominent conductor Erich Kleiber was subjected to an especially vicious attack in January 1935 for his performance in the Philharmonic of the "racially alien music of Stravinsky, the sound-comic who is supported by Jewish circles" and then in the State Opera of a symphonic suite of Alban Berg's opera *Lulu*, "an atonal abomination with saxophone and vibraphone." Stege added that an aroused member of the audience had shouted in indignation, "*Heil* Mozart."[292] Stege wrote, slandered, and maintained his politicking despite setbacks. The Stege case was representative of Nazi music critics and journalists, another category of both accomplices and victims of totalitarianism.

As honored member of the muscial profession and the Nazi establishment was the Pg, composer Paul Graener of the Prussian Academy of Arts, teacher and composer at leading music institutions and Vice-President of the RMK in 1933. Yet Graener, too, was not immune from attack. As noted above, the suspicion of the Saxon State Theatre about an alleged Jewish parent was communicated to party authorities. Hinkel, who had known Graener from the KfdK before 1933, came to his defense, certifying his "Aryan" status.

Graener had led the demonstration against a colleague (noted above) at the Music Academy in Berlin early in 1933. He was committed to the organization of German musicians, believing that composers ought to be in the forefront of the official organization and with their work. Then, too, he wanted his compositions recognized for their national content, thus constituting the culmination of the *völkisch* ideology in the Third Reich in that artistic works were to be subordinated to the national idea. As organizer he was constantly in touch with party authorities; the recipient of the Goethe prize in 1942 through Goebbels on orders of Adolf Hitler, he was forced to pull strings for his own person: in 1944 he appealed to Hinkel for better living accommodations.[293]

Even the Nazi activist Gustav Havemann, who was involved in so many aspects of music organization and purges, in 1933 was subject to personal review and ultimate dismissal from his offices. This foremost member of the KfdK and the RMK, leader of the RMS, division chief in the *Reichsleitung* of the NSDAP, conductor of the KfdK and party orchestras and official in other agencies who entertained connections with all government agencies and ministries, was attacked back in May 1933 before USCHLA, the party court, thereby coming to the attention of even Göring. In characteristic fashion Havemann, a master of intrigue, harassment and denunciations himself, was accused of many crimes: For one, he was said to have wanted "Hinkel rather than Rust as Minister of Education." There was proof of Havemann's statements, in predominantly Jewish company, according to which "Otto Braun (Social Democratic Prussian Minister President, 1920-1932, who emigrated in 1933) was the only qualified dictator for Germany." Furthermore, the testimony continued, he was said to have stated, "Wait until I will take to the barricades, then I will fight for you Jews." Witnesses from the party ranks swore to these written statements. The pianist Wikarsky testified that he had in his possession a photo of Havemann as a member of the "socialist-artistic November group." It was also known that Havemann had been president of the decidedly Jewish *Konzertgeberbund*. In characteristic Nazi fashion the prominent non-Jewish members were omitted, while the Jewish pianist Bertram and Kreutzer, Eisner and Dr. Stern were listed. Havemann had been president for two years, after which he "suddenly joined the NSDAP." He also had compromised himself through closest association with Professor Schünemann, in addition to which he had demonstrated servility in the presence of Leo Kestenberg. The list of alleged friends included many anti-Nazis. Havemann also was said to have wanted the composer Arnold Ebel, Schünemann, Hans Joachim Moser, et al., to join the KfdK, even attempting to prove that Moser was not Jewish. In addition to these weighty offenses against the party line on ideological grounds, his personal life, involving many women, many children, debts and drunkenness, was cited against him.[294] It is ironic that the master Nazi terrorist was criticized for methods which had brought all Nazis to power. Yet Havemann's behavior violated even their standards and he was erratic, as Gottfried Eberle learned in an interview with two of his victims: Havemann's former violin student, Hanning Schröder—who had studied with Julius Weismann and Willibald Gurlitt and was known for his involvement with the Workers Choral Movement and his friendship with Hanns Eisler, Paul Dessau and Heinz Thiessen; and his Jewish wife, Cornelia—the daughter of Max Auerbach, herself a pianist and a Ph.D. in musicology. Pressures on the couple typically intensified in 1933 as jobs were threatened and friends began to avoid them. Hanning Schröder finally was expelled from the RMK in 1934 for his leftist associations and his Jewish wife, although because of his veteran status he managed to obtain a special permit from higher authority (Göring had been approached on his behalf) to continue work as an instrumentalist at a film studio and a theatre stage without RMK membership, and disappearing occasionally in order to avoid raids by local party officials.[295]

The Schröders were close friends of Havemann—in whose house they were married, with whom they had traveled together and played chamber music and whose wife was Cornelia's ex-sister-in-law—until an unfortunate encounter revealed his worst features. As early as 1932, following the excellent showing of the Nazis in an election, Havemann had lectured them on the virtues of National Socialism. Then again, after the Nazi seizure of power, he appeared one day at their apartment, in his self-designed black SA uniform, and threatened "this communist movement." Upon Cornelia's query into the situation of her Social Democratic mother-in-law Havemann flew into a rage over this "insolence," whereupon Cornelia kicked him out. Informed by a friend that he had threatened to denounce them, they were prepared for two Gestapo agents who appeared and searched their apartment.[296]

The Schröders added that they had been aware of Havemann's problems with the party which resulted in his losing his KfdK orchestra and his black uniform. He also had asked repeatedly how he might be of help to them, that he wanted to restore relations. Hanning Schröder concluded that Havemann was essentially apolitical—certainly politically naive—but Cornelia felt he was a sly opportunist and not too clever. While some friends stuck by them, meanwhile, at risk to their own safety, Cornelia also reports on the behavior of Fritz Stein, with whom she had had contact during her studies with Max Reger in Jena in her youth. When in the early period of difficulty she turned to Stein for advice he dismissed her with a reference to *Schicksalsgemeinschaft*, "that's life."[297]

The story of Hanning and Cornelia Schröder documents the condition of countless other victims of the Nazi terror who remained in Germany, barely survived and suffered a variety of indignities. Another victim of Havemann, who emigrated, was Berta Geissmar. She recalled that during a telephone conversation he had insulted and ruthlessly intimidated her. It is noteworthy that at this time Geissmar commented on the exceptional methods of Havemann, referring to the possibility of his punishment if the proper authorities were informed. Thus, an anti-Nazi and Jewish victim of fascism still demonstrated her trust in German authorities, even Nazi authorities, while struggling against such monsters as Havemann. Her testimony would have served well in court against her persecutor; indeed the same content against him was contained in the proceedings before the party court in 1933. An expanded list of accusations against Havemann was forwarded to Göring and Geobbels, an unexpected turn of events in view of the contributions to the cause of National Socialism by the KfdK. While supreme leaders bickered among themselves, individuals struggled for positon and power, not always aware of the intrigues at higher level. Much depended on important connections and alertness to the changing power constellation. Havemann enjoyed his power, relishing his authority and glory. He was not the kind of individual to gain favor with the conservative element of the music society, which had been molded into a collaborating tool of the Nazis. The coordinated art no longer required threats and harassment, like those by the SA. Havemann demonstrated the misfortunes of cultural activists which paralleled the demise of the autonomous SA. Since much depended upon whose favor the individual had secured, e.g., Goebbels, Göring, Rosenberg, Rust, et al. or even Hitler personally—the individual who took his own importance too seriously, relaxing in confidence and a sense of accomplishment, would learn to realize that everyone was expendable.

Havemann was a violinist, conductor, and professor of music, who had entered politics through the KfdK before 1933. His name appears throughout these pages as a significant organizer and party activist whose actions affected individuals immediately and directly. No Nazi organizer could rival his zeal and effort in transforming Germany's music culture at the level of immediate concern to individuals. He had initiated the dismissal of countless German musicians, Jewish and non-Jewish, the disruption of music in many cities and the closing of numerous institutions, having cultivated close connections with important state and party agencies, especially the Interior Ministry and the police. At first he acted as an official of the non-official KfdK, and later as a member of official state organizations, although the Geissmar account revealed an underhandedness which was apparently not condoned, at least in his case, by other authorities. His methods certainly offended Furtwängler.

Early in 1933, Fritz Stege reported that in the take-over of music in Berlin, Professor Havemann had assumed leadership of conquered musical organizations. The *Reichskartell Deutscher Berufsmusiker* was reorganized under him.[298] He was among those responsible for the disruptive demonstration at the Berlin Music Academy in February 1933. Throughout this early phase of Nazism in power, victims and opportunists alike addressed themselves to Havemann, a man of apparently great resources, who was in the confidence of Nazi leadership and enjoying good fortune. Amidst friends and adulation in much of the coordinated press, the attacks on him seemed shocking, symptomatic of the chaotic state of authority under the Nazis and equally ridiculous. The listed points did indeed partially reflect his methods of denunciation and intimidation. The very *Konzertgeberbund* which was listed in association with him at one time had been forced to fight off his vicious threats: "I am forced to ask the leader of the KdfK in Prussia, Hinkel, to close down the *Deutschen Konzertgeberbund*...By your standards it can no longer be tolerated that a club in Germany with a governing board consisting of two-thirds Jews can be called German."[299]

It was Havemann who had initiated proceedings against independent concert agencies early in 1933, requesting that the Association of German Performers (*Bund deutscher Konzert—und Vortragskünstler*) be constituted as the only recognized agency of artists.[300] Geissmar reports that the RMK later aimed to become the sole State Concert Agency in control of all engagements, thus pursuing the earlier goals of Havemann. In early 1934 Havemann had also attacked Geissmar for "sabotaging the building of the National State through her connection with Jews and emigrants abroad, and through her negotiations with foreign countries. It is proposed therefore that she should be taken into protective custody." Geissmar has written in her memoirs:

In order to enforce his denunciation, he had enclosed a copy of a denunciatory letter from abroad to this effect, written on notepaper with the heading of a foreign firm of concert agents, which did not include their names, however. Actually, Havemann was suppressing the fact that this concert agency was run by refugee Germans abroad, who were trying to curry favor with the Party. These agents had spread the story abroad—where people were still badly informed on how these matters were dealt with in Germany—that only the Music Department of the *Reichsmusikkammer* had the right to engage artists for Germany, and that outside Germany all engagements had to be made through their organization, which was the representative of the Music Department. Furtwängler and I, when questioned abroad, had truthfully declared that such a monopoly did not exist, and that everybody could engage his soloists as he wanted. This had been immediately reported to their 'Nazi partner' by the refugees in question, written on their new note-paper, and this document with the foreign letter-heading was sent to the Leaders of the Reich. How could they know that behind the foreign letter-heading were the very people whom they themselves had ex-pelled? The denunciation, very cleverly compiled and apparently from a blameless foreign source, could not but have the desired effect. Not until many years later—when I was already in British service—was I shown the original document. What a perfidious and inglorious fraud.[301]

This incident throws light on Havemann's methods, his character hav-ing been clearly revealed in his betrayal of the Schröders and by Geissmar's account of the telephone conversation. The Schröders survived because of better friends and Furtwängler protected Geissmar in all cases simply by go-ing over Havemann's head, at times appealing even to Hitler directly.[302] The attacks on Havemann, in turn, were as clumsy and fraudulant as his own methods. His personal shortcomings, his dubious character, would under nor-mal circumstances have been sufficient for censure. Perhaps he was never quite comfortable in his role as a Nazi fanatic, as seen in his overtures to the Schröders. He had a son who disapproved of Nazism as well as his father's activities.[303] In Havemann's case, the postwar confrontation of generations took place in the early years of the Third Reich. Generally the role was revers-ed at that time, with the elders having to hold out against an indoctrinated youth. Biographies of these Nazi activists do not seem to attract the contem-porary historian, although it is clear that the lives of these petty leaders reveal the real confusion of culture in the Third Reich.

Organizational Success

The totalitarian system fed on the insecurity of individuals and the rivalries and power struggles among the leaders. Each collaborator, rival and power center within recognized limits publicly contributed to the creation of a mass mood of acceptance and conformity, the sterility and unimaginativeness of which in the world of music were camouflaged by the orchestrated euphoria, organizational business and propaganda. Paul Graener reflected this enthusiasm and the pretension that conflict did not exist within the ranks of coordinated music in a statement which no doubt expressed his "national sentiment," as he had always considered himself a "German artist." This representative Nazi musician wrote in 1934 about the movement, its

success in the arts and the hope it provided for Germany. Notwithstanding
the well-known rivalry between Goebbels and Rosenberg, Graener listed them
side by side in the service of the great ideal:

> Thus, we too joined. The KdfK was created by Alfred Rosenberg and
> Hans Hinkel, its first leaders, and we began to march. Step by step we
> had to clean house... In the meantime the great work of the RKK ex-
> tended itself over all artistic professions, and its opening ceremony in
> November 1933, in Berlin culminated in an unforgettable speech of its
> founder, Minister Goebbels. Thus,...the instrument was created for the
> application of the grand design of corporate reconstruction for the
> benefit of the arts and artists. This refers not only to a renewal of
> organization, inasmuch as the RKK, especially the RMK, will watch over
> the intellectual and artistic life of the nation.

Since no such article could be printed without a quote from the supreme
leader, Graener expressed his "desire and hope in the spirit of the unforget-
table words of Adolf Hitler, "If the artists knew what I will do for them one
day, they would all stand by my side."[304]

Hitler, Goebbels, Rosenberg and Hinkel were listed as a united front, as
they must have appeared to the innocent throughout the Third Reich. The
propagandists, the enthusiasts and the non-suspecting did not worry over
theoretical inconsistency or intra-party rivalry. People like Graener and Raabe
appealed to all top leaders; they would not dare to offend a *Reich* leader.
The common language, the enforced policies, the organization and the top
leadership had become a way of life which overshadowed disruptive tendencies. Did it matter whether Havemann dealt with German refugees abroad
while this was forbidden and subject to punishment when applied to ordinary
Germans, or that the Goebbels-Rosenberg rivalry touched on fundamental
questions of jurisdictional streamlining and the leadership principle? In any
event, authority conflict within official organizations was confined to individual
cases hidden beneath an official jargon of solidarity. The ouster of the victims of discriminatory law, the reality of concentration camps, fear of the
Gestapo, and the practice of denunciation furnished the regime with an air
of consistency, notwithstanding Göring's intervention in behalf of certain Jews
and other exceptional cases, the political compromise of National Socialism
with an established order, and musical developments anathematic to the music
ideology. Of all the loudly proclaimed principles, only the anti-Semitic legislation was applied more or less consistently in the purges of people and their
music—and the exceptions proved the radicalism and singularity of this aspect
of Nazi policy toward music. In practice, inconsistency did not detract from

the momentum toward the approximation of a totalitarian music culture.

The high hopes of people like Graener and Raabe in 1933-34 were realized organizationally, albeit in an unintended form which made Raabe confess shortly before his death in April 1945 that he had always been opposed to the regime.[305] The RMK over which he presided was, in fact, terrorized like the rest of society; it was regimented and received orders from the RKK and increasingly more directly from the RMVP through its Section VI and, after 1937, its music Section (X). The captive music profession prospered nonetheless, or, perhaps precisely because of the clear command structure and the ability of the totalitarian state to organize and manipulate resources efficiently. Control mechanisms, terror, guidelines, subsidies and promotional efforts facilitated an at least quantitatively flourishing music culture and the appearance of unity, integration and common purpose. The economic well-being of music mirrored the stability of the regime and its economy by the mid-thirties. Unemployment in music was reduced considerably, so that by the time of war in 1939 it was no longer an issue, as we have seen: the RMK then reached an all-time high membership of nearly 150,000 full-time and 30,000 part-time professional musicians whose job security, their sense of belonging and the recognition of their contribution to a new social order which included people forgotten in the past, provided the solid motivational base for collaboration. Economic reassurance, flattery and terror produced the accommodation of a profession at peace with the state, serving as cultural facade, propaganda medium, and as an embodiment of social and ideological purpose. Music has traditionally performed an affirmative and supportive social role, and it managed to continue to do so with apparent enthusiasm during the Third Reich.

The regime clearly benefited from its considerable investment in music with funds and personnel, and from its image as music's patron propagated not only in the regimented press at home but also by foreign correspondents who were impressed by the official support of music in Germany, manifested in the number of festivals to which they had been invited. Bayreuth especially served as a symbol of excellence of official patronage—a sincere expression of Hitler's personal devotion, though regulated, funded and exploited for propaganda. Nevertheless, the undeniable success of the regime's organization of music was not so much due to ideology as to Goebbels' and Hinkel's pragmatism and manipulatory skills. The early *völkisch* notion of a genuine new music which would reflect the Nazi experience was abandoned at least by 1936. Instead, the state committed itself to the entire musical establishment as even Rosenberg's NSKG was legally incorporated into an RKK that year and traditional standards were reaffirmed.

While the failure of the revolution in music was thus acknowledged by

Goebbels at the confidential Culture-Political Press Conferences, and in his diaries, private meetings and even some public speeches,[306] the organizational and personnel measures of the period continued to reflect earlier ideological and legal formulations. The institution of the Culture-Political Press Conference in July 1936—that mandatory weekly instruction session for select feuilleton editors, at which directives were issued by RMVP officials and discussed regarding what and how to report on cultural life—confirmed Goebbels' growing disillusionment over the arts in Germany which seemed stagnant and in need of a promotional effort that would stress unity and uniformity—a coverup for failure in the creative realm to produce a high level völkisch art and the ultimate reduction of the music press to the level of propaganda. Here the tendency was institutionalized to stress the positive expression in German art and neglect its negative features—to promote the appearance of a flourishing culture. The minutes of these press conferences[307] reveal the control and standardization of the feuilleton press by the RMVP; the cynicism of the latter; the frank discussion of issues, policies and propaganda strategies which were of course not to be published; and the trend to distract the journalists and their readers from the boredom of artistic uniformity by means of "constructive" commentary which culminated during the war years.[308]

The Culture-Political Press Conference confirmed earlier Gleichschaltung measures, including existing political press conferences, which also regulated the content and method of what was to be reported. Yet, Goebbels had become aware of the need for credibility and repeatedly invited open discussion, creative formulations and the appearance of a free press—an incredible predicament. He also realized the advantage of propagating political messages in a politicized cultural context, and of channeling the freely offered support of artists and intellectuals, without which the enterprise would not have been possible.

The regimentation of the press expressed in the founding of the Culture-Political Press Conference in summer 1936 was most dramatically reinforced by the abolition of art criticism, announced by Goebbels November 27, 1936. In view of the totalitarian theory and practice and the consistent politicization of all art and art criticism it is surprising that the ban came so late, though it made sense in 1936 in light of the above considerations about Goebbels' perception of the state of cultural life and the subsuming political objectives of that year. To the Nazis, art criticism had never been a matter of aesthetics alone. Before 1933, Nazi art criticism had amounted to the defamation of opponents. After the seizure of power, dissidents were effectively silenced and, once the positive Nazi culture was in place, the state could no longer tolerate criticism of official and officially sanctioned art. Suggestions about supportive art commentary and threats against negative and degrading criticisms were issued in the early years of the Third Reich. Consistent with totalitarian principles, the critic was asked

> to overcome the concept of the non-organic and individualist notion of freedom which had had as its aim the elimination of the integrated personality... If National Socialism is truly experienced as total ideology...then standards of art must follow... The experience of a *Weltanschauung* alone creates the precondition and ability for a new cultural criticism and a new cultural organization. The task of education and criticism are thus demonstrated.[309]

In May, 1936 the writing of critical reviews on the evening before the performance (*Nachtkritik*) was banned,[310] followed in November by the sensational circular letter to newspaper reviewers with its injunction to confine themselves to factual accounts of artistic events, eschewing excessive praise or sharp criticism, and establishing a minimum age of thirty to qualify as purveyors of directed opinion in the Third Reich.[311] Henceforth, reviewers had to be licensed by the RKK.

Variously modified, the announcement also known as the "decree for the reconstruction of German cultural life," was published throughout the German press:

> Because this year has not brought an improvement in art criticism, I forbid once and for all the continuation of art criticism in its past form, effective as of today...The critic is to be superseded by the art editor. The reporting of art should not be concerned with values, but should confine itself to description. Such reporting should give the public a chance to make its own judgment, should stimulate it to form an opinion about artistic achievement through its own attitudes and feelings.[312]

Thus, Goebbels appealed to an essentially liberal sentiment of freedom of opinion, in order to eliminate an obstacle to uniformity of opinion. Indeed, he felt compelled to justify his step as not amounting to the suppression of the freedom of opinion, but that he wanted to restrict criticism to those journalists qualified to evaluate art and who appreciated it. A few days after the announcement, RMVP press spokesman, Ministerial Councilor Alfred-Ingemar Berndt elaborated on the decision and announced that select editors under thirty could continue to review art upon proof of their reliability, that the ban did not apply to book reviews, that artists were encouraged to involve reviewers in their creative activities through preliminary discussions in order to promote more interesting feuilletons, and that a negative evaluation on grounds of National Socialist concerns had to be cleared by the Press Office of the RKK beforehand.[313] Other officials reminded editors to reflect the National Socialist viewpoint and the needs of the community in their reviews of art and to regard their commentaries as positive contributions to the reconstruction of German culture.

This prohibition of art criticism has been considered a decisive measure in the history of the Nazis' increasing regimentation of the press and the arts. It provoked much negative commentary and disbelief abroad at the time. Yet Prieberg believes that its significance has been exaggerated; that it betrayed intention, but was not binding. Indeed, after a brief period of hesitation and some violations which elicited no formal reprimands, music critics, then called *Musikbetrachter*, continued to write as before, particularly in the professional journals—which were exempt from the ban anyway. It seems that the Nazi leadership did not mind traditional criticism in the professional press, with its limited readership. More suggestive was the fact that Goebbels did not institute precensorship for routine reviews which would have been necessary for effective regulation. Moreover, his list of reliable art editors licensed to review music included 1410 names by March 1939—a number large enough to suggest the minister's confidence in the profession's voluntary censorship.[314] But that was Goebbels' point, of course. He knew that his ban fell on fertile soil and as such symbolized his manipulative policy which relied not only on collaboration but also on concurrence.

Critics as a group have been controversial in other societies, as in Germany before 1933, and musicians especially have retaliated with caustic witticisms—as those collected by Nicolas Slonimsky in his artful *Dictionary of Musical Invective*. We are reminded of Wagner's Beckmesser caricature of his famous nemesis Hanslick. Many musicians and their audiences have resented the critics' negativism, their alleged display of ignorance, hasty and nasty slander and personal vendettas—all of which were, to the Nazis, reflections of a bygone age. The same people who resented critics were among those who approved Nazi attacks on "decadent" art as Hitler proudly pointed to the 20,000 daily visitors to the "degenerate art exhibit" in Munich in 1937—for him a sign of popular support for his culture-political policy.[315] The party press welcomed the *Musikbetrachter* in place of the critic:

"a word has been removed from the vocabulary and hopefully from the consciousness of the public .... I believe that many misunderstandings, particularly of the creative artist, could have been avoided if this hideous word 'criticism' had been eliminated earlier...having been increasingly associated with excessive individualism, categorical negativism.[316]

The music journalists complied with the decree because many of them, especially in the provinces, agreed with its objective. Criticism was confined to the confidential discussions at the press conference—*en famille*. Yet, even there the minutes reveal that the editors conformed, to the degree that they had to be encouraged to express themselves freely, to ask questions and to be critical.[317] They adopted the standardized language and concepts because these confirmed their image of themselves as art educators with positive values, in the service of national reconstruction.

The new art editors joined educators in educating the nation. While the editors promoted Nazi values encased in music reviews, the pedagogues taught the same values in music courses at the schools, academies and universities under the jurisdiction of the Education Ministry and at the HJ institutions. Music teachers taught mandatory music courses for all youth and the skills required of future professionals. Policy provided for a musicalized nation at an unprecedented level and for prospects of a new Nazi music and a new musician. Success of the policy was measured in the statistics of amateur group singing, professional jobs and performances, organizational jobs and performance, educational activity and student output, the number of compositions and thus income, the expanding radio and recording market, the flourishing and subsidized state network .... Yet, quality at the higher level became an issue after the great purges, censorship, the decreasing international contact, and ultimately the war, as musicians were drafted and their absence affected also quantity—in effect, a stress on an ideological facade to which the musicians, editors and educators contributed.

We have seen that Goebbels became disillusioned over the prospects of a new music at last by 1936, increasingly allocating resources to established institutions and especially to entertainment music. The war reinforced this shift in commitment, exemplified by the first *Wunschkonzert*, the popular radio request concert for the army (October 1, 1939) which featured a potpourri of popular and classical music in an effort to unify the front and the homeland and was the subject of a very successful film in 1940. Nonetheless, the regime hoped to salvage its ideological goal by promoting education and youth from which the new genius might yet emerge—thus, the lionization of Gottfried Müller. Singing schools were established by the RMK. Scholarships and subventions were made available for young composers and performers who were also furthered at the festivals, stages and radio stations. The HJ had access to the radio with regular programs. The coordination of this promotional effort in behalf of German youth was revealed in the instructions to art editors which reached a high point in 1936, declined in the following years and disappeared during the war.[318]

This manipulated cult of the young confirmed basic Nazi principles and was reflected in the pedagogic literature. Peter Raabe, Wolfgang Stumme, and Wolfgang Fortner wrote about music education, reflecting and reinforcing ideology as did the bulk of the educational establishment.[319] Music as an expression of race was stressed by Richard Eichenauer, Karl Blessinger and others who thus looked for a musical renaissance and a "new man"—a topic for the schools and textbooks which, because of its long-range projection, could not be verified and was not addressed at the press conferences.

An interesting consequence of manipulated ideology was the mobilization of the students who occasionally turned against their Nazi mentors, as they did at Kiel and Berlin, where they asked for the dismissal of Fritz Stein. The Reich student leadership asked for the removal of Karl Blessinger in spite of his proven political record.[320] The students upheld ideology against the new bureaucracy and standards against personal and professional shortcomings of people who had advanced their careers due to the purges and denunciations of their victims. While the ultimate authority in music education was contested between Rust and Goebbels, the students who were raised in the HJ and Rust's schools acknowledged only one ideology and structure—a real source of Nazi strength and hope for renewal.

Aside from mass education, the Nazi state instituted elite schools for the leadership of the new society in which music was a subordinated subject as carefully handled as in the projected Platonic society—obviously not quite the diet of a new race of supermen. In all other areas of education, however, as in all Nazi organizations with a musical program, music was advanced as a unifying agent, the companion of drill and leisure and the propagator of ideology; it was public, was appealing and contributed to the feeling of group solidarity and comradery and to the illusion of a wholesome world which distracted from unpleasant realities. The new culture was to be entrusted to the new, Nazi-educated generation. Consequently, the regime even attempted to organize children under the age of ten and then those between ten and fourteen in the *Deutsches Jungvolk*, in addition to the official schooling they received in Rust's schools. Each step in the rearing of children and education was to instill loyalty and a willingness to fight in war; and music was involved in the drills, filled recreational hours and accompanied festivities and important rituals. A high school graduation would typically include a musical program, like the one at Calw in 1937, entitled "Our Youth is Singing: A Young People Rising" with its complement of Nazi compositions.[321] At the age of fourteen, boys enlisted in the HJ and girls in the BDM (compulsory by a law of December 1936), where they still were subjected to music education. The extensive literature on the indoctrination of youth in the Third Reich reveals the singular significance of the program within the general Nazi scheme, its organizational success, but also its contradictions and failures. The rivalry between schools and the HJ threatened the myth of unity, while the official racial and national arrogance, combativeness, and obedience contradicted aspects of traditional humanism, which were also taught. The HJ uniform, a symbol for equality among its bearers, distinguished them from the rest of society and reinforced adolescent rebellion against traditional authorities at home, school and church—desirable to a degree in Nazi eyes, but problematic when the authority was Nazi and official. Girls gained new opportunities which contradicted the traditional female ideal and Nazi hostility to women's emancipation. As the HJ developed into a vast bureaucratized organization and its leadership advanced in age, it began to lose some of its appeal—a serious problem in view of the party's identification with youth. The war also added problems, not the least being the drafting of the older boys who were no longer available as role-models and leaders for the organization. Disenchantment and rebellion resulted in disciplinary measures, surveillance, an increase in regulations and more drills which further alienated hostile youth who developed an oppositional lifestyle and recreational activities like performing and listening to jazz, swing and foreign songs, engaging in sex and sporting alternative dress and grooming which violated HJ and *völkisch* standards. The regime responded with bans, reprimands, jail and even executions.[322]

The Nazis understood that the battle for German youth would have to be won. The way the Nazi-reared youth would go would determine the fate of National Socialism. Because of the brevity of Nazi rule, the experiment hardly allows for conclusions which can be studied by other societies for comparison. The communist experience in the Soviet Union is of greater value in this respect, having stretched over several generations and now being subject to searching analysis in the context of Gorbachev's reforms. In Nazi Germany, people like Peter Raabe had hoped that the radical measures would restore respect for traditional authority and regenerate cultural traditions. Instead, the means became the reality as music educators themselves affected a revolutionary pose that helped undermine the natural order of generational relations in favor of the Nazi claim to having synthesized authority with youth. In that atmosphere of manipulated youthful authority the system hoped for perpetual renewal over one thousand years; but it did not last long enough to be tested under what have to be conditions of normalization and inevitable generational tensions.

Nazi music education helped indoctrinate German youth at a time of national emergency. Sacrifice was demanded and was offered by the millions.

Only the reality of the terrible war shook the faith of many youth in the regime which had ordered the wholesale slaughter. Thus the HJ-bashing working class youth gangs like the "Edelweiss Pirates" and the bourgeois "Swing Youth" rebelled, while the university students organized in the political resistance group known as the White Rose and their spiritual mentor, the professor of philosophy and musicology, Kurt Huber challenged the lies and the brutality of a regime that some of them—like one of their leaders, Hans Scholl—had supported at one time. Music, meanwhile, was but a means, used by collaborators in behalf of the system and by others to demonstrate resistance.

The organization of music in the Third Reich was commemorated in two yearbooks commissioned by the Music Section of the RMVP, the *Jahrbuch der deutschen Musik* of 1943, edited by Hellmuth von Hase, and of 1944, which described the organizational and artistic achievements of the past ten years by identifying names, organizations, offices, functions and policies. A photo of the distinguished composer Siegmund von Hausegger graced the first book followed by Heinz Drewes' introductory survey. Drewes clearly formulated the intention of such a yearbook to reflect the condition of music since the Nazi seizure of power. Ten years offered a perspective, before the projected goals could be institutionalized in a radically new society. By 1943 the Nazi leadership believed that organization had advanced to the point at which the creative and recreative constituents of music had become solid expressions of the Greater German Reich. The editor Hellmuth von Hase then commented on the difficulties involved in this effort, particularly in time of war. Nonetheless, music was kept up in spite of wartime hardships, and musical achievements and the contributors to the yearbook were noted, while all writers looked forward to a bright future of German music. The book was divided into the following sections: A list of the deceased of the year; a review of musical activity in the past year; memorial days and special events; a list of premieres; a list of new organizations and institutions; and then major articles which clearly revealed the nature and accomplishments of the music community: H.J. Moser, "On the Coordination of German Music"; Alfred Morgenroth, "Self-Administration of Professional Estates"; Eberhard von Waltershausen, "Musical Life at the *Hauptkulturamt* of the NSDAP"; Walter Lott, "Important New Works"; *Generalmajor* Paul Winter, "The Singing Army"; Gotthold Frotscher, "HJ Music"; Maria Ottich, "Music of the NS Community of KdF"; Waldemar Rosen, "Germany and the European Music Exchange"; Eugen Schmitz, "German Musicology During the War"; H.J. Moser, "Reich Agency for Music" (created in May 1940 as special musical office of the RMVP under Drewes' supervision with the assistance of the conductors Hans Swarowski and Clemens Krauss): Leo Ritter, "Stagma in Wartime"; Fritz

Chlodwig Lange, "Contemporary Opera"; H.J. Moser, "Mozart in our Time"; Wilhelm Zentner, "Siegmund von Hausegger"; Karl Laux, "Werner Egk"; Karl Holl, "The Musician Elly Ney"; Fritz Oser, "Johann Nepomuk David"; Gerhard Berger, "Helmut Bräutigam"; Fritz Stege, "German Radio in the Third Year of War"; Fritz Heitmann, "The Organ, Instrument of Our Time"; Hellmuth von Hase, "Introduction of New Works to the Concert Stage"; Albert Dreetz, "The Responsibility Toward Art Commentary"; Benno von Arendt, "Realism and Illusions in Staging"; Harald Kreutzberg, "Dancer as Creator of Form"; Herbert Windt, "Why Music for Film?"; followed by accounts of German archives, including articles on publishers, Ed. Bote and G. Bock, the Mozart documents at the archives of Breitkopf and Härtel; the history of music publisher Robert Lienau; and an obituary section, a musical calendar, and general announcements. The second yearbook of 1944 followed the same pattern. This time the front picture of Max Reger reinforced the emphasis on the "German Tradition" in music. Some significant articles follow: Heinz Drewes, "German Music at the Threshold of the Fifth War Year"; Otto Benecke, "Bureau Concert Life"; Fritz von Borries "The *Reichsmusikstelle* and Its Influence"; Hellmuth von Hase, "On the Responsibility of Music Publishers and Dealers in Time of War"; August Martin, "The Musical Instrument in Time of War"; Reinhold Scharnke, "Berlin-World Center of Music"; Hans Reich, "Music in Alsace"; Erich Roeder, "Heinz Drewes"; Albert Dreetz (who was co-editor of this yearbook), "Richard Wetz—Herald of German Soul"; Karl Hasse, "Max Reger and the German Spirit"; Eberhard Breussner, "Edwin Fischer"; Ernst Krause, "Three Composers of Our Time, Hermann Abendroth, Clemens Krauss, Paul von Kemper"; Hans-Felix Husadel, "German Marching Music"; Ferdinand Lorenz, "The Singing Army"; Bruno Aulich, "Radio and Music"; plus some other articles and general lists of performances, upcoming events, memorial announcements, etc. These two books reveal much about music organization and those musicians favored by the regime. However, gone was the ideological fight, the condemnation of alien elements and enemies. These works stood for accomplishment, although the impact of the war on culture also was evident. Indeed, besides several additions to existing offices, change of positions and recent honors, the overwhelming novelty was war. Werner Egk was acknowledged for having been distinguished with the National Prize for Composers in 1939 and the gold medal for his Olympic Festival Music. As a prestigious member of the establishment he had risen to represent the composers of Germany in the estate of composers of the RMK. Others had risen, while still others accompanied German armies and performed abroad. Elly Ney had held classes in Salzburg after the *Anschluss*. Helmuth Bräutigam, a promising young composer, had gone to war and was killed at the eastern front on January 17, 1942. This young man was the product of Nazi music education, having been schooled in part by the composer Johann Nepomuk David and by the HJ. He was active as composer and organizer, meeting his death in a manner advertised by the Nazi state as heroic. The war overshadowed everything. Amidst propaganda about final victory, musicians looked forward to the end in an atmosphere of guilt, shame and uneasy anticipation which was not reflected in these official pages on music. Music was praised as the steady companion of German troops. Keitel himself had written an introduction to an army song book, "At time of combat music is a source of joy, uplifting and inner joy." These words were reprinted in the yearbook of music which concluded with the affirmation of solidarity between the military spirit and German music. "Where we sing, there is Germany."

ENDNOTES

[1]For an introduction to the RMVP, Section R55 at the Bundesarchiv, Koblenz (BA) see Wolfram Werner (ed.), *Reichsministerium für Volksaufklärung und Propaganda* (Koblenz, 1970); for Section R56, RKK including the RMK, see Wolfram Werner (ed.), *Die Reichskulturkammer und Ihre Einzelkammern* (Koblenz, 1987). See also Hans Hinkel (ed.), *Handbuch der Reichskulturkammer* (Berlin, 1937); Heinz Ihlert, *Die Reichsmusikkammer: Ziele, Leistungen und Organisation* (Berlin, 1936); Martin Thrun, "Die Errichtung der Reichsmusikkammer," in Heister-Klein, 75-82; and Volker Dahm, "Anfänge und Ideologie der Reichskulturkammer," *Vierteljahreshefte für Zeitgeschichte* (1986), 53-84. Besides the files on music organization at the BA and the Institut für Zeitgeschichte (hereafter, IfZ), the BDC contains the original files on the music organizers and musicians.

[2]Willy Hoffmann and Wilhelm Ritter, *Das Recht der Musik* (Leipzig, 1936), 2-3 and 12-13.

[3]Gerhard Menz, *Der Aufbau des Kulturstandes* (Munich and Berlin, 1938), 13-17; Wulf, *Die Bildenden Künste*, 99-101. On the founding of the RMVP, its organization and jurisdictional preeminence, see also, BA, R43II/1149 (part of R43, Reichskanzlei, 1919-1945). Compare later jurisdiction after Hitler Decree, August 15, 1943, R55/1435, 1390.

[4]Menz, above, n. 3. See also Zeman, 40. Other ministries published the RKKG in its entirety. For example, see the file of the *Reichsjustizministerium* at the Bayrisches Staatsarchiv.

[5]Hoffmann and Ritter, 102-104 and 248-249; Zeman, 34-38; and BA (above, n. 3).

[6]*Germania*, November 16, 1933; Wulf, *Die Bildenden Künste*, 104-105.

[7]Louis P. Lochner (ed.), *The Goebbels Diaries* (New York, 1948), passim.

[8]*Westfälische Landeszeitung—Rote Erde*, Dortmund, June 7, 1935; Wulf, *Die Bildenden Künste*, 106.

[9]Loc. cit.

[10]Wulf, *Die Bildenden Künste*, 107.

[11]Above, n. 6.

[12]Prieberg, *Musik*, 263. See also Ihlert, *Reichsmusikkammer*, 9, for a listing of legal measures which secured the economic interest of the profession, 20-22. Ihlert repeatedly referred to his contribution to resolving the unemployment crisis in music, as in a testy memo of May 22, 1935 to Hinkel in which he belittled Strauss for organizational incompetence. (BA, R56I/18)

[13]Karl Friedrich Schrieber, *Das Recht der Reichskulturkammer* (Berlin, 1935), 87.

[14]Hoffmann and Ritter, 17.

[15]Schrieber, 16-17 and 92-93.

[16]Hoffmann and Ritter, 36-37. The office of Schmidt-Leonard in a memo of January 25, 1936 to the President of the RMK recommended abolition of this statute in order to counter the RMK's monopolistic claims and restore a friendlier relationship between the organized musicians with other labor and employment offices. (BA, R56I/18) Compare the composers' memo to the RMK president, February 18, 1936, pleading for monopolistic needs.

[17]Hoffmann and Ritter, 104-105.

[18]Ibid., 25-26 and 63.

[19]Printed throughout the press. See in the *Bücherei der Reichsmusikkammer*, I: *Kultur-Wirtschaft-Recht* (Berlin, 1934), 9-10; Wulf, *Musik*, 194-195.

[20]"Neubau des deutschen Musiklebens—Ziele der Musikkammer," *Berliner Lokal-Anzeiger*, February 18, 1934; Wulf, *Musik*, 153.

[21]Richard Strauss and Stefan Zweig, *Briefwechsel* (Frankfurt a.M., 1957), 141-142; Wulf, *Musik*, 195.

[22]*VB*, July 14, 1935; also in Slonimsky, 608.

[23]Wulf, *Musik*, 120.

[24]Schrieber, 103 and 118-122.

[25]Wulf, *Musik*, 131.

[26]Ibid., 132.

[27]Schrieber, 89.

[28]These examples in Wulf, *Musik*, 133-134.

[29]Schrieber, 112-113; Slonimsky, 592.

[30]Hoffmann and Ritter, 44-45.

[31]"Anordnung über unerwünschte und schädliche Musik," *VB*, December 19, 1937.

[32]Wulf, *Musik*, 136.

[33]Schrieber, 100.

[34]Wulf, *Musik*, 134-135. The RMVP had already issued the directive limiting all outdoor performances of Gottfried Sonntag's Nibelungen-Marsch, based on motives from Wagner's Ring cycle, only to important meetings under the aegis of the Nazi party, December 8, 1936. (Slonimsky, 636)

[35]Friedrich Welter, *Musikgeschichte im Umriss* (Leipzig, 1939), 302-303.

[36]"Organisation der Reichsmusikkammer," *DM* (February 1934), 361.

[37]Prieberg, *Musik*, 122-123.

[38]Fritz Stege, "Die erste Arbeitstagung der Reichsmusikkammer," *ZfM* (March 1934), 290.

[39]Ibid., 288-290.

[40]"Meldepflicht für Komponisten," *ZfM* (December 1933), 1269.

[41]Hoffmann and Ritter, 16, 24, 186-187.

[42]Prieberg, *Musik*, 263-264.

[43]Hoffmann and Ritter, 132-135.

[44]*Frankfurter Zeitung*, September 4, 1935; Wulf, *Musik*, 125.

[45]"Einheit des deutschen Musiklebens," *ZfM* (December 1934), 1225. Ihlert listed 89,983 dues-paying members in 1935, *Reichsmusikkammer*, 14.

[46]"buntes Allerlei," *ZfM* (January 1934), 80.

[47]Wulf, *Musik*, 165.

[48]Schrieber, 45-46.

[49]Above, n. 45, 1225-1226.

[50]Fritz Stein, "Chorwesen und Volksmusik im neuen Deutschland," *ZfM* (March 1934), 283.

[51]Hoffmann and Ritter, 26.

[52]Ibid., 53.

[53]"Aufbau von Musikerberufsschulen in Deutschland," *ZfM* (November 1934), 1121-1127.

[54]Schrieber, 101-102.

[55]Hoffmann and Ritter, 85.

[56]Ibid., 16.

[57]*Frankfurter Zeitung*, August 27, 1935; Wulf, *Musik*, 71.

[58]*Deutsche Allgemeine Zeitung*, August 29, 1935; *VB*, September 1, 1935; and *Das Schwarze Korps*, September 5, 1935; Wulf *Musik*, 71.

[59]Wulf, *Musik*, 121. See also Schmidt-Leonard, *Reichskulturkammer*; "Dienstanweisung für Städtische Musikbeauftragte," BA, R561/18.

[60]*AMRMK* (December 12, 1934), 138-140; Wulf, *Musik*, 122-124; also in "Ausländische oder deutsche Konzertprogramme," *ZfM* (November 1934), 1155.

[61]Prieberg, *Musik*, 188.

[62]*Reichsmusikkammer*, 10, 16-17. See also Geissmar, 125.

[63]Hoffmann and Ritter, 15, 38 and 132-135; also *VB*, January 12, 1934.

[64]"Chorwesen und Volksmusik im neuen Deutschland," *Bücherei der Reichsmusikkammer*, 1: *Kultur-Wirtschaft-Recht* (Berlin, 1934), 288-290; Wulf, *Musik*, 126.

[65]Antoinette Hellkuhl, "'Hier sind wir alle versammelt zu loblichen Tun,' Der Deutsche Sängerbund in faschistischer Zeit," in Heister and Klein, 199.

[66]Wulf, *Musik*, 159-160. See also Schrieber, 281-283; and Ihlert, *Reichsmusikkammer*, passim.

[67]Schrieber, 67.

[68]"Kleine Mitteilungen—Gesellschaften und Vereine," *ZfM* (July 1934), 793.

[69]*AMRMK* (November 15, 1939), 5; Wulf, *Musik*, 128.

[70]Prieberg, *Musik*, 201.

[71]Hoffmann and Ritter, 108.

[72]On Thiessen see Dorothea Kolland, "'...in keiner Not uns trennen...,' Arbeitermusikbewegung im Widerstand," in Heister and Klein, 204.

[73]For detail and names, see Prieberg, *Musik*, 198-199.

[74]Schrieber, 107-108.

[75]*AMRMK* (June 6, 1938), 5; Wulf, *Musik*, 128.

[76]Hoffmann and Ritter, 83, 87.

[77]*AMRMK* (April 15, 1938), 3; Wulf, *Musik*, 127.

[78]Schrieber, 95. The RMK's control over work permits was challenged throughout the Third Reich; see, above, n. 16.

[79]"Rudolf Hess schützt die Musiktätigkeit," *ZfM* (November 1934), 1156.

[80]"Kleine Mitteilungen—Gesellschaften und Vereine," *ZfM* (June 1934), 693.

[81]See Dümling and Girth, 105-145, for the program of the Reichsmusiktage: Ziegler's address; Werner Schwerter's report, "Heerschau und Selektion"; and Dümling's comments on Ziegler.

[82]Schoenbaum, 219.

[83]George L. Mosse, *Nazi Culture: Intellectual, Cultural and Social Life in the Third Reich* (New York, 1968), 154.

[84]Ibid., 155-156.

[85]Ibid., 154-155. These boasts are supported by post-war research; see Pohle, 333, passim.

[86]Mosse, *Nazi Culture*, 158.

[87]Ibid., 151-152.

[88]Fritz von Borries, "Die Reichsmusikprüfstelle und ihr Wirken für die Musikkultur," in Hellmuth von Hase and Albert Dreetz (eds.), *Jahrbuch der Deutschen Musik* (commissioned by the RMVP, Leipzig and Berlin, 1944), 49-55.

[89]*Völkische Musikerziehung* (1937), 591; Wulf, *Musik*, 166.

[90]Wulf, *Musik*, 139.

[91]Ibid., 192. For Goebbels' role at Berlin's "German Opera," see Bair, 83-90.

[92]Wulf, *Musik*, 36-37.

[93]Ibid., 105.

[94]Ibid., 472. Wulf mentions Ziegler only as "manager of the exhibit of degenerate music." Otherwise he would not have been included in his documentation because "he was generally neither concerned with music, nor did he write about it.... His few statements serve more as political avowals of National Socialist principles of an old fighter of the party, than as concern for music." Ziegler illustrates the same principle upheld by Goebbels and the other leaders, nonmusical control of the community in behalf of the new state.

[95]"Entartete Musik—Eröffnung der Düsseldorfer Ausstelling," *Deutsche Allgemeine Zeitung*, May 25, 1938.

[96]Wulf, *Musik*, 193.

[97]Eberhard Jäckel, "Hitler und die Deutschen: Versuch einer geschichtlichen Erklärung," in Karl Corino (ed.), *Intellektuelle im Bann des Nationalsocialismus* (Hamburg, 1980), 9.

[98]*Organisationsbuch der NSDAP* (7th ed., 1943), 7; Wulf, *Die Bildenden Künste*, 91.

[99]Max Neuhaus, "Das Nationalsocialistische Reichs-Symphonie-Orchester," *ZfM* (September 1933), 916-919. See Prieberg, *Musik*, 172-177. I have interviewed people who recall the brown suits.

[100]*Hakenkreuzbanner*, Mannheim, June 7, 1937; Wulf, *Musik*, 156-157.

[101]"Kleine Mitteilungen—Gesellschaften und Vereine," *ZfM* (February 1934), 222.

[102]Geissmar, 182.

[103]Ibid., 93-94.

[104]Slonimsky, 681; *Christian Science Monitor*, July 15, 1939; also Prieberg, *Musik*, 319-321.

[105]Lochner, 60.

[106]Bair, passim.

[107]*AMRMK* (May 22, 1935), 47; Wulf, *Musik*, 137-138.

[108]Cited in Hans A. Münster, *Publizistik: Menschen— Mittel—Methoden* (Leipzig, 1939), 74-75; Wulf, *Musik*, 263.

[109]Riess, 175-179.

[110]T.R. Emessen (ed.), *Aus Göring's Schreibtisch: Ein Dokumentenfund* (Berlin, 1947), 46-51.

[111]Ibid., 32-46.

[112]Wulf, *Musik*, 112.

[113]*Rheinisch-Westfälische Zeitung*, Essen, July 15, 1937. The Goebbels remark in Lochner, 432.

[114]PAdK.

[115]Wulf, *Musik*, 159.

[116]Ibid., 141.

[117]Eberhard von Waltershausen, "Die Musikarbeit des Hauptkulturamtes der NSDAP," in von Hase, *Jahrbuch*, 43-44.

[118]See *Musik in Jugend und Volk*, special ed., *Die Orgel in der Gegenwart* (Wolfenbüttel and Berlin, 1939).

[119]"An unsere Leser," *DM* (April 1934), 481. See also Fritz Stege, "Die erste Arbeitstagung der Reichsmusikkammer," *ZfM* (March 1934), 255-256.

[120]"Wir stellen vor: Rosalind von Schirach," *DM* (February 1934), 363.

[121]Hoffmann and Ritter, 63. An extensive correspondence between the Reich leaders Ley, Goebels and Rosenberg attests to the jurisdictional conflict, copies of which are filed in all major archives, eg. BDC, BA, IfZ, but also in local ones, like Bayrisches Staatsarchiv, Munich and the PAdK.

[122]Wulf, *Musik*, 146.

[123]"Kleine Mitteilungen—Gesellschaften und Vereine," *ZfM* (May 1934), 561.

[124]Hoffmann and Ritter, 113-114.

[125]"Die Singende SA," *ZfM* (November 1934), 1151-1152.

[126]Oscar von Pander, "SS-Konzerte," *DM* (December 1934), 205-206.

[127]For names and details, see Prieberg, *Musik*, 170-175.

[128]Wulf, *Die Bildenden Künste*, 99-100.

[129]Wulf, *Musik*, 26.

[130]Ibid., 95-96.

[131]PAdK.

[132]Schoenbaum, 36.

[133]Ibid., 207. Frick's appeal to Hitler to retain control over the Reich Governors, June 4, 1934, in Noakes and Pridham, 243-244. Goebbels, his enemy, contributed to the loss of his office in 1942 when he was appointed Protector of Bohemia-Moravia. (Lochner, 96)

[134]*Berliner Lokal-Anzeiger*, September 11, 1935.

[135]Schoenbaum, 205-206.

[136]Walter Abendroth, "Was die deutschen Opernspielpläne verraten," *Deutsches Volkstum* (1937), 862-865; Wulf, *Musik*, 303.

[137]"Die Jugend bekennt sich zu Hans Pfitzner," *ZfM* (July 1935), 787.

[138]"Ausländische oder deutsche Konzertprogramme,: *ZfM* (November 1934), 1155.

[139]Hans Esdras Mutzenbecher, "Der Opernspielplan in Dritten Reich," *Der Neue Weg—Zeitschrift für das deutsche Theater* (May 1, 1935), 225-226; Wulf, *Musik*, 307.

[140]"Unsere Meinung: Was ist 'deutsche Musikgeschichte?'," *DM* (April 1936), 523-524.

[141]Hermann Killer, *Coburger National-Zeitung*, February 18, 1935; Wulf, *Musik*, 381.

[142]Herbert Gerigk and Theo Stengel (eds.), *Lexikon der Juden in der Musik* (Berlin, 1941), 28.

[143]Steven Gallup, *A History of the Salzburg Festival* (London, 1987), 65-70.

[144]Ibid., 82-86.

[145]Ibid., 65-66.

[146]Ibid., 90-92.

[147]Horst Büttner, "Reichsmusiktage in Düsseldorf," *ZfM*, 736-737. See also Dümling and Girth.

[148]Geissmar, 73.

[149]Ibid., 84.

[150]Erwin Bauer, "Die Italienfahrt des Nationalsozialistischen Reichs-Symphonie-Orchesters," *ZfM* (January 1934), 37-41.

[151]Wulf, *Musik*, 94.

[152]Geissmar, 91-97.

[153]Ibid., 107-109.

[154]Ibid., 109.

[155]Ibid., 110-111.

[156]Gallup, 75.

[157]Geissmar, 117-118.

[158]Schoenbaum, 212.

[159]Geissmar, 115.

[160]Ibid., 118-121.

[161]Wulf, *Musik*, 36-37.

[162]Hoffmann and Ritter, 25.

[163]Wulf, *Musik*, 161-162. See Zeman's analysis along similar lines, 85-110; reflected in Goebbels' diaries: Lochner, passim.

[164]Geissmar, 158.

[165]For additional features of the musical Olympics competition, see Prieberg, *Musik*, 272-274.

[166]Ibid., 379-380.

[167]Wulf, *Musik*, 451-452.

[168]"Unkenntnis oder Absicht," *Der Angriff*, September 9, 1935; Wulf, *Musik*, 454-455.

[169]"England's rassischer Niedergang im Spiegel seiner Musik," *DM*, 37-41.

[170]Hofer, 284.

[171]Fröhlich, 372.

[172]Ibid., 372-374.

[173]Wulf, *Musik*, 82.

[174]Ibid., 83.

[175]PAdK.

[176]Ibid.

[177]Wulf, *Die Bildenden Künste*, 179-180.

[178]Geissmar, 200.

[179]Schoenbaum, 213-214.

[180]See Hans-Adolf Jacobsen, *Nationalsozialistische Aussenpolitik 1933-1938* (Frankfurt a.M., 1968), 90; and Zeman, 77-81.

[181]Bracher, 325.

[182]Geissmar, 127, 135.

[183]Slonimsky, 652.

[184]R. V., "Leopold Reichweins, des Nationalsozialisten, Auftreten in Wien verboten!," ZfM (March 1936), 281-282.

[185]Geissmar, 327. See also Lochner, 70.

[186]Slonimsky, 671; Dümling and Girth, 63, 105.

[187]VB, April 4, 1939.

[188]Görings Schreibtisch, 119.

[189]"Das Wiener Musikleben im Neuaufbau," DM (May 1938), 543-544.

[190]Ibid., 544.

[191]Ibid., 544-545.

[192]Gallup, 108.

[193]Ibid., 108-116.

[194]Prieberg, Musik, 384-391.

[195]Wulf, Die Bildenden Künste, 428-431. Gauleiter Eigruber speeches about the Hitler-Linz relationship have been preserved; Deutsches Rundfunk Archiv, Frankfurt a.M.

[196]Prieberg, Musik, 393-394. Eigruber refers to Hitler's reading the local papers in a recorded speech at St. Florian, May 3, 1944; BA.

[197]Rene Albrecht-Carrie, A Diplomatic History of Europe Since the Congress of Vienna (New York, 1958), 522.

[198]Die Musik-Woche (1940), 28; Wulf, Musik, 288-289.

[199]"Um die Unterhaltungsmusik," Die Musik-Woche (September 7, 1940), 309; Wulf, Musik, 287-288.

[200]DM (December 1942), 68; Wulf, Musik, 291-292.

[201]"Über den Musikbetrieb während des Krieges," ZfM (October 1939), 1030.

[202]Fritz Sänger, Verborgene Fäden: Erinnerungen und Bemerkungen eines Journalisten (Bonn, 1978), 75.

[203]Nikolaus Spanuth, "Deutsche Musik im besetzten Gebiet," ZfM (July 1941), 459-460.

[204]For occupied Paris, see Prieberg, Musik, 397-402; and Lochner, passim.

[205]Unpublished diary in possession of the author. See also, Sänger, 97-99.

[206]Prieberg, *Musik*, 310-317.

[207]"Es sind halt Prager Musikanten," *Die Musik-Woche* (1941), 255-256; Wulf, *Musik*, 324-325.

[208]Sammlung Sänger, BA; also Sänger, *Verborgene Faden*, 71-74.

[209]Wulf, *Musik*, 325.

[210]Alfred Lemke, "Deutsches Musikleben in Krakau," *ZfM* (September 1942), 396-398.

[211]Ernst Krienitz, "Kampf um Chopin," *Die Musik-Woche* (October 28, 1939), 1-2; Wulf, *Musik*, 253.

[212]*Görings Schreibtisch*, 68-70.

[213]Jacobsen, 45.

[214]Schoenbaum, 213.

[215]See Reinhard Bollmus, *Das Amt Rosenberg und seine Gegner: Studium zum Machtkampf im Nationalsozialistischen Herrschaftssystem*; Goebbels-Rosenberg correspondence at BA, IfZ and the BDC; and Zemen, 70-71.

[216]*The Origins of Totalitarianism* (New York, 1960), 397.

[217]*Berliner Lokal-Anzeiger*, September 11, 1935.

[218]Wulf, *Musik*, 142-143; Goebbels-Rosenberg correspondence, BA, passim.

[219]Gustav Cords, "Das grosse Konzert in der Deutschlandhalle—Generalappell der NS-Kulturgemeinde Berlin am 4.3.1933"; Wulf, *Musik*, 144.

[220]Wulf, *Musik*, 20. The "Mephisto" reference in Serge Lange and Ernst von Schenk (eds.), *Memories of Alfred Rosenberg* (New York, 1949), 161; cited in Zeman, 70.

[221]*Frankfurter Zeitung*, November 30, 1934; Wulf, *Musik*, 379.

[222]Alfred Rosenberg, "Ästhetik oder Volkskampf," December 7, 1934.

[223]Fröhlich, 363.

[224]Ibid., 347-348.

[225]In Heister and Klein, 14.

[226]Prieberg, *Musik*, 209.

[227]See Wulf, *Musik*, 194-202; Prieberg, *Musik*, 203-215; and Dietmar Polaczek, "Richard Strauss: Thema und Metamorphosen," in Corino, 61-80.

[228]Strauss-Zweig, 90.

[229]Wulf, *Musik*, 196.

[230]Strauss-Zweig, 141-142. This letter is cited in every treatment of Strauss.

[231]Gallup, 116.

[232]Prieberg, *Musik*, 214. All opera performance statistics are taken from Wilhelm Altmann, *Opern-statistik: Veröffentlicht für die jeweils zurückliegende Spielzeit in den Septemberheften der AMZ*, 60 (1933)-69 (1940). See also Hans Günter Klein, "Viel Konformität und wenig Verweigerung: Zur Komposition neuer Opern 1933-1944," in Heister and Klein, 145-162.

[233]Klein, "Konformität," 152-153.

[234]Prieberg, *Musik*, 320.

[235]Ibid., 323.

[236]Ibid., 326.

[237]Ibid., 158-164.

[238]BDC.

[239]Klein, "Konformität," 149-151.

[240]Slonimsky, 594.

[241]Prieberg, *Musik*, 333-334.

[242]Ibid., 263.

[243]Klein, "Konformität," 156.

[244]See Juan-Allende Blin, "Kirchenmusik unter Hitler," in Heister and Klein, 180-182.

[245]Letter to Prieberg in Prieberg, *Musik*, 239-240.

[246]Ibid., 341-343.

[247]Hartmut Lück, "Ein Exempel wird statuiert; Der Fall Karlrobert Kreiten," in Heister and Klein, 243.

[248]The major source for this biographical sketch is the father's commemoration: Theo Kreiten, *Wen die Götter lieben... Erinnerungen an Karlrobert Kreiten* (Düsseldorf, 1947); specifically here, 50.

[249]Lück, 246.

[250]Ibid., 347; Prieberg, *Musik*, 242.

[251]The Höfer controversy has been covered extensively in the German media. See Lück, 251.

[252]Volker Kühn, "'Man muss das Leben nehmen, wie es eben ist...'—Anmerkungen zum Schlager und seiner Fähigkeit, mit der Zeit zu gehen," in Heister and Klein, 213; and Michael Kater, "Jazz in Weimar Germany," 157.

[253]Kühn, 215.

[254]Ibid., 220-221.

[255]See David Welch, *Propaganda and the German Cinema 1933-1945* (Oxford, 1983), 1-38.

[256]Ibid., 39-46.

[257]Prieberg, *Musik*, 335.

[258]Ibid., 336.

[259]Translation from Welch, 211.

[260]BA, R58/184; Welch, 215.

[261]Welch, 213.

[262]Ibid., 191-203.

[263]See Welch's detailed analysis of "Kolberg," 221-237.

[264]Reported in Kühn, 217.

[265]Gallup, 125.

[266]See Fred Prieberg, *Kraftprobe: Wilhelm Furtwängler im Dritten Reich* (Wiesbaden, 1986) for the most comprehensive and sympathetic analysis.

[267]Prieberg, *Musik*, 9-33.

[268]"Peter Raabe: Prasident der Reichsmusikkammer—Paul Graener: Führer des Berufstandes der deutschen Komponisten," *DM*, August 1935, 850.

[269]Raabe to Goebbels, April 25, 1936; Wulf, *Musik*, 205-208.

[270]Prieberg, *Musik*, 277-278.

[271]In silent protest against *Gleichschaltung*, claimed Slonimsky, 640.

[272]Wulf, *Musik*, 103.

[273]Ibid., 105-106.

[274]"Fritz Stein als Organisator und Musikpolitiker," ZfM (December 1939), 1150.

[275]Moraller combined an extraordinary party career in his person, having joined the party in 1923, been the organizer of the SA in Baden, the editor of the Baden NSDAP-organ, Der Führer, head of the NSDAP news service, 1923-1933, as of 1933 the press chief of the Baden State Ministry and head of the Landesstelle Baden—Württemberg of the RMVP and, finally, the position at hand since October 1934; Wulf, Musik, 105. A leader in Goebbels' offensive against the NSKG, Moraller was threatened by Rosenberg. See Rosenberg to Goebbels, March 9, 1936, BA; above, n. 20.

[276]Die Musik-Woche, March 27, 1936, 6; Wulf, Musik, 331.

[277]Informal conversation with Karl Ulrich Schnabel, February 1970.

[278]Interview with Günter Schab, August 1968.

[279]"Der 'privilegierte Irrtum' H.H. Stuckenschmidt—Eine Abrechnung," Deutsche Kultur-Wacht, 1933, 12; Wulf, Musik, 37-39.

[280]"Zukunftsaufgaben der Musikwissenschaft—Musik und Rassenkunde," ZfM (May 1933), 489-490.

[281]Deutsche Kultur-Wacht (December 16, 1933), 10-11; Wulf, Musik, 294-295.

[282]Above, n. 280.

[283]Wulf, Musik, 211.

[284]Ibid., 216.

[285]Ibid., 113.

[286]Ibid., 209.

[287]Ibid., 179-180. The Mahling scandal also in BA, R561/18; and Prieberg, Musik, 191-192.

[288]Wulf, Musik, 217.

[289]Ibid., 213-214.

[290]Ibid., 217-218; also Schwab interview; August 1968.

[291]Wulf, Musik, 211.

[292]"Berliner Musik," ZfM (January 1935), 41.

[293]Wulf, Musik, 99.

[294]Ibid., 113-114.

[295]Gottfried Eberle, "Als verfehmte überwintern—Zwei Musiker im Dritten Reich: Ein Gesprach mit Cornelia und Hanning Schröder," in Heister and Klein, 253-256.

[296]Ibid., 257-258.

[297]Ibid., 259.

[298]"Berliner Musik," ZfM (May 1933), 457-458.

[299]Wulf, Musik, 111.

[300]Ibid., 109.

[301]Geissmar, 135-136.

[302]Ibid., 121.

[303]Informal conversation with Karl Ulrich Schnabel, February 1970.

[304]"Rückblick und Ausblick," in Ernst Adolf Dreyer (ed.), Deutsche Kultur im Neuen Reich— Wesen, Aufgabe und Ziel der Reichskulturkammer (Berlin, 1934), 55-56; Wulf, Musik, 126-127.

[305]Slonimsky, 798.

[306]Fröhlich, 356-359.

[307]We owe these to Fritz Sänger who kept them illegally. See their analysis in Fröhlich, 347-381.

[308]Ibid., 359.

[309]Hannes Kremer, "Kulturkritik und Weltanschauung," Die Völkische Kunst (1935) 1-2; Wulf, Die Bildenden Kunste, 126-127.

[310]Fröhlich, 363.

[311]Slonimsky, 635.

[312]Mosse, Nazi Culture, 162-163.

[313]Fröhlich, 364.

[314]Prieberg, 284.

[315]VB, September 8, 1937; Fröhlich, 367.

[316]Wilhelm Zentner, "Musikbetrachtung statt Musikkritik," ZfM (March 1937), 260-261.

[317]Fröhlich, 366.

[318]Ibid., 375. On the increase of light entertainment, see Lochner, passim; on *Wunschkonzert*, see also BA, *Sammlung Sänger*, 102/62.

[319]Wulf, *Musik*, 171-178.

[320]Ibid., 475-476.

[321]"Der Soldat ds Dritten Reiches," *Völkische Musikerziehung* (1937), 349; Wulf, *Musik*, 276.

[322]See Detlev Peukert, "Youth in the Third Reich," in Richard Bessel (ed.), *Life in the Third Reich* (New York, 1987), 25-40; also documents in Noakes and Pridham, "Education," 349-353, and "Youth," 353-363; and Friedrich Hossbach, *Zwischen Wehrmacht und Hitler* (Wolfenbüttel, 1949).

Race, Folk Hero and the New German Musician

The more or less successful organization of music and public opinion and the purges of Jews and other undesirable musicians consistent with the ideology and interests of the Nazi state were justified to musicians as preconditions for the reconstruction of a purified national culture to which they would contribute and through which they would be inspired to write a new music. Music politicians, journalists, musicians and musicologists joined in the manipulated attack against representatives and expressions of "cultural bolshevism," especially against jazz and atonality. The previous chapters document a vast, state-sponsored musical enterprise, as thousands of compositions were submitted and performed to fill the gap left by the purges. Aside from the traditional offerings of both the serious and entertainment variety, many new works aspired to reflect the new political order. The theoreticians attempted to identify the positive qualities of these compositions, in search of a definition of what constituted "pure" German music beyond simply cataloguing the variety of music composed by Aryan Germans in Germany for the appreciation and edification of Germans. While the capturing of an inner essence eluded musicologists, composers were not able to get beyond appending Nazi texts to traditional musical forms. Especially during the first three years of the Third Reich, composers produced a tremendous amount of music with Hitler dedications, titles, and appropriate texts (in many instances aplied to old compositions): folk songs, Nazi fighting songs, party cantatas and oratorios, operas, operettas and monumental open air rituals such as the *Thing* Theatre. Serious instrumental works, said to reflect the synthesis of the classical and folk traditions with the Nazi experience and ideas, emerged as expressions of the projected musical renaissance. Titles identified pieces and individual movements, and program notes were added to leave no doubt about the intended association, as in Hansheinrich Dransmann's choral work, *Einer baut einen Dom*, an homage to Hitler, the builder of the Cathedral of the Reich. The state and party organizations supported this creative effort by means of festivals and the encouragement for stages to be receptive to the newly defined contemporary music, especially that of the younger generation, in addition to generous subventions, stipends and prizes.

Out of this strenuous organizational, definitional and creative endeavor and in contradiction to it, a reaction was articulated to what was perceived as a misguided, actually an un-German imposition of extra-musical standards and programs on musical forces, suggesting instead the Nazi revolution as a reference, an experience, and inspiration for a new music. Goebbels' notion of "romanticism of steel" provided an aesthetic-political basis for a new set of definitions and compositional exercises. These were expected to move beyond the crude functionalism of the early years of explicit programs and formulas toward an understanding and expression of a music more consistent with the musical tradition and its assumption of intrinsic tensions, thus allowing a greater variety of compositions to receive the state's approval. Friedrich W. Herzog reformulated Goebbels' slogan in an article, "What is German Music" (August 1934) with reference to the Nazi idea as a kind of vital force—not explicitly imposed, but nonetheless expressed in new musical form which would reflect its German origin (nationalism) and appeal to all members of the community (socialism).[1]

The more flexible and abstract definition appealed to the music establishment. Yet, even this seductive invitation to collaboration proved fruitless, as important musicians, musicologists, journalists and even political leaders gradually acknowledged that creativity of the kind desired would not respond to external command—not in the case of believers in a unique spiritual standard of German music. It is important to recall that not one Nazi opera, i.e. with a Nazi style or explicit text and characters, was performed in National Socialist Germany. Meanwhile, the official exercises in formulation and composition continued, culminating in the Reich Music Festival of 1938, which featured new German music, a meeting of leading German musicologists, and the sensational exhibit of "degenerate music"—the latter two reflecting the Rosenberg faction's continued commitment to defining negative and positive expressions of music, and the ideological search for a new Nazi music which by that time was out of step with the more realistic direction taken by Goebbels back in 1936.

By mid-1936 Goebbels had consolidated his hold over all cultural expressions and the media which were clearly subordinated to the propaganistic needs of the Nazi state. Considerations of power and propaganda had priority over the implementation of völkisch ideas in music. Goebbels' emphasis complemented the reassertions of the formal music organization, after a three-year period of intimidation. Raabe had rejected outside interference in planning for the Tonkünstlerfest of the ADMV in 1936, as we have already seen.

The establishment enjoyed a comeback in the year of the Olympics, to the point of even tolerating atonal compositions at the national festival and various associations of international and modern music, even though these expressions of decadence were severely criticized. Meanwhile, the *Thing* Theatre, other open air rituals and expressions of Nazi kitsch were formally rejected,[2] while the great masters were protected from zealots who probed their racial background, and criticism was regulated. In a revealing article in 1941, Goebbels admitted that the state could not produce art, but had to restrict itself to promote and create the conditions favorable to it.[3] Göring and Hinkel expressed similar opinions about sentiment which, however valuable, was no substitute for good art. This growing realism and accommodation toward the interests of the musical establishment was reflected in Goebbels' growing emphasis on entertainment music, which was to entertain, relax and distract the masses, while classical music was aimed at the bourgeoisie for similar reasons. In 1936 Hinkel supported opera as a form of entertainment, equal in significance to lighter entertainment and recreational works, and in 1939 the Reich dramaturg Schlösser encouraged every opera stage in Germany to premier at least one contemporary work every season.[4] The leadership promoted operettas, hit songs, films and serious music for all Germans.

The restatement here of the conclusions reached in chapters (I) and (II) about Goebbels' priorities offers a perspective and a reminder about manipulation; yet it is not to deny the centrality of ideology in the music politics of the Third Reich. The ideological dynamic was not suppressed, but channeled; it remained a powerful device for capturing the enthusiasm of followers of National Socialism for orientation, manipulation and intimidation. It continued to be propagated and implemented in music by the Nazi politicians and the collaborators who believed it to be policy. The public was not privy to Goebbels' diaries or to the subjects discussed at the Culture-Political Press Conferences. Applied to music, they continued to confirm *völkisch* values, to serve as the reference for the musicological definitions of "German" music and the belief in a musical renaissance and a new Nazi music beyond that of the rejected nationalistic kitsch. However, increasingly after 1936, musical offerings that might qualify as expressions of a new art form emerged from a broader spectrum since the definition had shifted from the single application of Nazi texts and sentiments to the abstract formulation—more in tune with the dynamics of the creative tradition and not so readily verified. The custodians of aesthetic standards continued to search for the new genius at the academies and the HJ, but they did so in line with traditional standards and through consultation with members of the established elite. Traditional criticism in the professional journals attested to standards which prevented false claims. All their hope in Gottfried Müller did not blind the profession to his shortcomings. No opera was performed as "the National Socialist opera," even though 164 new operas were premiered in Nazi Germany. Dransmann's "Cathedral" choral work had received some praise in 1935, but even then was rejected as derivative in musical form.[5] Later, in 1942, a symphony in B-major by Friedrich Jung attempted to synthesize classical forms with Nazi fighting music. This composition of late-romantic dimensions and pomp, some modernistic elements and heroic fanfares and solemn hymns, including a measured Horst-Wessel song, was reviewed more favorably then and even now, by students of Nazi music.[6] Dedicated to Reich Organization Leader Robert Ley, premiered by the NSRSO and officially promoted and aired on the radio, the work with the evocative movement titles of, "1918 Germany," "Heroes Memorial," "Parliamentary Death Dance" and "Germany 1933," represented and glorified the Nazi order and served propaganda, but it was not mistaken for the art work of the future. That projected work and its defini-' tion had become the common objective of the entire manipulated music establishment.

The Musicologist as Myth Maker: Jews and Germans as Ideal Types

Even though the National Socialist ideology was both manipulated and violated by the Nazi leadership, for the community of musicians—as for society at large—it remained very real. Throughout the Third Reich musicians, publicists and musicologists formulated the official guidelines and terms for the redirection of music and music commentary, thus dignifying and legitimizing the Gleichschaltung of the profession.

The musicologists played an especially crucial role in matters of definition and the subsequent rewriting of the musical past, as custodians of which they were qualified to formulate the characteristics of German music and thus to help identify the anticipated new Nazi music and evaluate it after its creation. Trained in an honorable discipline and pressured politically, they assimilated Nazi categories which they then applied to an evaluation of past German musicians for hero status and as possible precursors and prophets, while the words, deeds and musical achievements of the same masters were listed in confirmation of Nazi ideals—a closed circuit. The sum total of this musicological effort amounted to a contribution to Nazi myth-making, both in justification of Nazi power and ideas and in the projection of a new music culture.[7]

Collaboration of this sort was a departure for a profession noted for its lack of political entanglement, an ivory-tower tradition to which it would return after 1945. But even during the Nazi era many musicologists were reluctant to become involved; they withdrew into the distant historical studies of "inner emigration." The politics of music did not follow a grand design but moved instead in trial-and-error fashion. For a while, the profession at large managed to remain sublimely aloof. Very few dissertations addressed political topics: Alfred Bode wrote on "The Culture-Political Tasks of the Administration of German Music" in 1937 at Rostock and Richard Maar on "The Jewish Influence in the Performance of German Violin Music" in 1943 at Erlangen. Even Nazi musicologists stuck to traditional subjects, while the number of dissertations actually declined during the entire period. When the Education Minister offered a prize for the best dissertation written in the spirit of National Socialism, to be presented on the *Führer's* birthday in 1938, the review committee was unable to produce a winner who had conformed to the political specifications, despite pressures on the Nazi Student Organization, the NSDStB.[8]

Gradually, however, the profession adjusted to the new realities. Lectures were offered on German folk songs, on *Deutschtum* and the German qualities of all kinds of musicial expressions. Wagner became a favorite topic. Professional organizations had already been invaded by Nazis in 1933. At its meeting in 1935 at the University of Leipzig, Herbert Gerigk threatened the German Musicological Society, and especially its journal, the *Zeitschrift für Musikwissenschaft*, which he accused of non-involvement. In fact, pressure was hardly necessary by then. The Musicological Society freely accommodated itself; its journal's editor, Max Schneider, publicly welcomed the new order at this important meeting in 1935, even though his colleagues still emphasized the scholarly nature of the organization. Meanwhile, a new State Institute for German Musicological Research was established, under the leadership of Max Seiffert, as a center of politicized musicology. The new institute also published a new journal, the *Archiv für Musikforschung*, which introduced the application of race theory to the categories and methodology of musicology in an article, not by a professor of musicology, but by the teacher and publicist Siegfried Günther in March, 1937.[9] Prieberg argues that this article helped overcome the qualms of many musicologists who henceforth appropriated Nazi terms and sentiment.

By May 1938, the musicological profession was prepared to meet as part of the new Reich Music Festival. Many of Germany's foremost musicologists gathered May 26-28 to deliver around twenty-five papers at five panels on (1) "German Music," chaired by Josef Müller-Blattau, who spoke on the panel topic which reflected the orientation of his book of the same year, *Germanisches Erbe in deutscher Tonkunst* (*The Germanic Heritage in German Music*); (2) "German Masters," chaired by Theodor Kroyer from Cologne, a musicologist otherwise little involved in politics, who spoke about German stylistic qualities in music, while others (Walter Vetter in a paper about "Folk

Characteristics in Mozart's Operas," and Rudolf Gerber on "Folk and Race in the Work and Life of Brahms") more pointedly "Germanized" the masters of the past; (3) "State and Music," led by Heinrich Besseler, a well-known Professor at Heidelberg whose section included papers by Gerhard Pietzsch, Ernst Bücken and Rudolf Steglish who paid tribute to National Socialism for attempting to overcome music's alienation from the community and to restore music's role in the education of the nation as in the ideal Platonic state; (4) "Musicological Research," under Werner Korte who recommended a "subjective" musicology in place of so-called "objective" scholarship; and (5) the major attraction, "Music and Race," chaired by Friedrich Blume, who also delivered a careful analysis of the new musicological methodology relative to biological determinants. Though anxious to remain scholarly, the presenters propagated *völkisch*-racialist values and methodology; they Germanized the masters and music and, in some cases, even lent support to Hitler's imperialism with references to concrete political events such as the *Anschluss* and to the qualities of music which transcend the temporary division of the German people.[10]

Musicology did not differ in its response to the exigencies of the time from that of historical study in general. The craft as a whole was thoroughly integrated into the intellectual mechanism of the state. Dissident historians were purged and universities and professional journals were coordinated. When Friedrich Meinecke resigned the editorship of the *Historische Zeitschrift* in 1936, his place was filled by Karl Alexander von Müller, a confirmed Nazi and anti-Semite. This agent of the new state welcomed the apparent solution to the demise of the intellectual of the previous era:

> This above all we understand, as the winds of the new times breathe upon us; the profound realization of being an inseparable and co-equal part of the folk as a whole: bound to the folk in both life and death; partaking of the terrible will and the mountain-moving faith which, as the old order of things collapsed, arose out of the depths of our Leader: the faith which comes from once more standing within the camp of a struggling people.[11]

The tone of the new scholarship was set, and persons like von Müller produced a new brand of historian with interests in music history. One of von Müller's students, Karl Richard Ganzer, encouraged to study the significance of Richard Wagner, radically reinterpreted music history in two works on *Richard Wagner, the Revolutionary Against the Nineteenth Century* (Munich, 1934) and *Richard Wagner and Jewry*, published in Book 3 of *Jewish Studies* (*Forschungen zur Judenfrage*) (Hamburg, 1938), confirming

Wagner as spiritual forebear of National Socialism[12]—a topic for musicologists and historians alike. The musicologist Robert Pessenlehner was attacked in 1938 by Wolfgang Boetticher for having published "only a few months before the national revolution" his dissertation on the Jewish composer and music critic Hermann Hirschbach, which, to make matters worse, was dedicated to the Jewish music critic Moritz Bauer. With reference to Mahler, Mendelssohn and the composer Friedrich Gernsheim, Pessenlehner had attempted to refute race theories according to which these composers would not have been able to be productive. Boetticher's sarcastic review of Pessenlehner's book also covered his later work, *On the Nature of German Music* (*Vom Wesen der deutschen Musik*), 1937, in which he had not mentioned Bauer. Pessenlehner was attacked for his opportunism and for having jumped on the bandwagon of ideological rhetoric. Indeed, Pessenlehner's change of views illustrated the process of collaboration and the general transformation of scholarship.[13]

Musical performance itself provided the substance of this solemn evocation of Germany's great tradition, as documented in the program notes of the Berlin Philharmonia Orchestra, November 21, 1941, at which Karl Böhm conducted, Gaspar Cassado performed, and Heinrich Sutermeister's *Romeo and Julia* was premiered. Gerhart von Westerman commented on the fine reputation of German music abroad, its classic phase which had evoked universal admiration and the more recent romantic music, as a unique language of the heart, loved and imitated in creative manner elsewhere. While other cultures excelled in some special areas of music, he wrote, the Germans have mastered every aspect of this profoundest of arts. The number of excellent and permanent stages and orchestras were proof of this German preeminence—a claim articulated in numerous musicological articles which also distorted history by alleging exclusive German responsibility for musical developments which had been the product of several cultures, like the suite and the sonata.[14] Musicological cultural imperialism accorded with the policies of the Reich to offer music as an export article.

The Berlin Philharmonic Orchestra—"since the seizure of power, the German Reich Orchestra" and manipulated by the Reich—had engaged in many foreign tours under the most prominent German conductors, most notably Wilhelm Furtwängler. Not even the war had prevented its cultural-political activity; in the two war years the orchestra had traveled to Italy, Hungary, Rumania, Bulgaria, Slovakia, Norway, Denmark, Finland, Holland, Belgium, France, Spain and Portugal, thus encompassing nearly all of Europe. Westerman enthused that Germans allowed time for cultural service while the German people were "engaged in struggle," thereby "documenting the greatness and power of Germany even in its cultural determination."

Culture was promoted in spite and because of hard times but, more significantly, for ideological reasons and for the needs of the Nazi state as we have seen. Musicology and the German stages contributed to the cultural facade by recreating the past and German heroes with which the state identified. This communion with heroic ancestors in the timeless domain of sacred art complemented the music-political program of men like Peter Raabe in reversing the alleged disintegrating, uprooting and alienating features of modern times. The very emphasis on tradition in music and music education, as well as the nostalgic appeal to the individual grandeur of genius, reinforced the understanding of National Socialism in historical and dialectic terms, as old gods were appropriated against the fake values of an age by *völkisch* advocates who offered legitimacy to the epihpany of Adolf Hitler and his representatives in music. Thus, wrote the composer Hans Uldall who also worked for Radio Hamburg, the music academy had to impart knowledge of the past and the technical skills in the context of a sound ideology.[15]

Yet, we have seen that the evocation of the great German tradition encountered difficulty in definition, since especially among other influences the Jewish and Jewish-derivative components of German culture had become an intrinsic part of its hallowed musical realm. While anti-Semitism had always existed in Germany, it had not constituted the exclusive basis of analysis. Even as late as 1934 Hans Mersmann had published his *German Music History* that avoided vicious attacks on anybody and acknowledged the talent of Mendelssohn as part of the German musical tradition which he had enriched with his own masterpieces. Although Mersmann shared various *völkisch* assumptions with Nazi musicology, he was fair and scholarly. Yet, a reviewer in *Die Musik* promptly took issue with this demonstration of a "lack of German sentiment."

To get around the problem of cross-cultural expressions in music and to arrive at a workable definition of pure German music, the musicologist and composer Friedrich Welter in his general music history, *Musikgeschichte im Umriss* (1939) addressed music as an expression of the cultish makeup of all "primitive" cultures and of man's spiritual condition in archaic unity with cult and dance[16]—a useful study for a profession eager to demonstrate its support of the new order. Thus, he promoted awareness of deep cultural roots and fundamental human needs and related these to the present, but he was not able to correlate musical expressions of the prehistoric past with modern styles. Undeterred, the scholar drew parallels between the Germanic past described by Tacitus and Plutarch and the contemporary Nazi state. He compared respective heroes and their music, such as their battle cries. He also recalled the odes for kings and heroic tales sung at court, in addition to characteristic instruments like the harp, performed at the courts of Theodoric and Clovis in evocation of an ancient musical past and a pure state of German music—the latter a questionable proposition, besides having no bearing on the contemporary analysis of style and the definition of a pure German music, which so preoccupied Nazi musicologists and less scholarly publicists. The distinguished Professor Arnold Schering also attempted to identify German music with Germanic forbears in a lecture before the Society for German Education in Berlin, January 1934, even though he acknowledged the absence of compelling data about Germanic music; he jumped from a discussion of *Luren* (bronze age Scandinavian trumpets) to the Sixteenth Century where he claimed to find Germanic elements in the great German music, and then onwards to the Germanic Wagner.[17] The *Luren* cult—one of the more comic expressions of a deadly serious ideological enterprise and thus not supported by Goebbel[18]—attracted other prominent scholars. The instruments were researched, featured in education courses and preserved in museums where, of course, they belonged; they were reconstructed—albeit inauthentically, written into contemporary compositions, performed and heard on radio and recordings.

The assumed pure state of German music then suffered disruption. Welter continued his history dramatically with reference to alien forces; the Roman state and the Church had suppressed some musical practices of the Germans. Nonetheless, the bards had kept alive the national and *völkisch* sentiments in spite of hostility of foreigners. Increasingly, the line between the geographically much larger Germanic world and Germany was blurred, as it had been in Wagner's operas—a kind of mythical blueprint for Hitler's imperialist war. Meanwhile, Welter pursued the conflict between aliens and German music in special chapters on "Jewry in Music" and "Music and its Cultivation in the Third Reich," thus applying Wagner's title and identifying Nazi policy with the insights of the ideological forbear. Like the master, he reviewed not purely Jewish music as used in synagogues, but that music created by Jews in a foreign culture. He noted that Jews had, in fact, contributed little to music in its long history and that they had not existed as musicians in the sixteenth and seventeenth centuries. In spite of some earlier accomplishments in a recreative capacity, the Jewish composer had appeared only in the nineteenth century, first, in the persons of Mendelssohn, Meyerbeer and Offenbach. This cultural and political development, amounting to the "Jewish disintegrating cultural influence," had been so strong that it caused the epochal writing of Wagner's *Jewry in Music* (1850) which underlay H. St. Chamberlain's *Foundations of the Nineteenth Century* (1899), and which, eventually, found its musical-scientific expression in Richard Eichenauer's *Music and Race* (*Musik und Rasse*) (1932). Disregarding documented Jewish friendships and also dedication and veneration of Jews for Wagner, Welter wrote of the failure of Jews to "prevent the victory of Wagner's art form," as if that had been a collective Jewish intention. In the meantime, Jews had managed to gain influence over the people through the daily press and journals and the manipulation of active musicians and liberal Germans. Increasingly, the Jewish composer appeared as "representative of his race," revealing his "way and uprootedness," witness Mahler and Schönberg. Between 1918 and 1933, Welter continued, Jewry and Marxism had invaded all spheres of musical life, furthered by Kestenberg (of the Prussian Education Ministry) and Dr. Seelig. This "ultimate and insolent phase" of Jewry, resulting in the unrestrained undermining of German music, had been represented most notably by Schönberg, Schreker, Weill and Toch, countless Jewish conductors, professional music commentators, government officials, concert agents and music publishers.[19]

The official musicological jargon identified and defined the Jew as a collective concept for all alien and other anathemic developments in music, to be catalogued and purged before the pure and heroic German community could be reestablished. Already atonality and liberalism had been pronounced dead by the Nazi state, but as a means of sustaining the religious fervor of the devoted following, the "music devil" was kept alive in the interplay between positive pronouncements, self-praise, and recognition of achievement— along with the negative, the exhortation to greater effort, and the elevation of the Jew to an almost universal embodiment of evil. German heroes of the past were said to have struggled successfully against the forces of darkness, but the struggle was never-ending. For instance, in spite of official condemnation of foreign music at dance halls, exotic music was still discovered in German places of entertainment in 1939. Jewish demonic qualities and influence were thus demonstrated, and considered self-evident in the persistence of musical forms which had been officially outlawed. Karl Blessinger, the above-mentioned author of the work on *Jewry and Music* (1944), noted that the foreign press reported gleefully that German youth was still dancing to the rhythm of jazz. He described the battle against degenerate music as part of a "gigantic world struggle" which involved even the lowest form of music offered at bars, demonstrating the universal struggle between good and evil, between German and Jew, which reflected and affected everything.[20]

An extensive, manipulated journal literature drew attention to this demonic Jewish force, alerting the German world to the source of general cultural decay. Walter Abendroth wrote in his article "Operatic Ideals of Races and Peoples" that Jews were more akin to the spirit of Romanic peoples than to the German. For that reason, Wagner could praise the Jewish composer of operas, Halévy, as the supreme expression of French opera. The search for effect and grandiose staging of Meyerbeer could not offend the French to the same degree as Germans, since the French tradition of historical opera lent itself more to his talents. Offenbach, too, was hardly to be distinguished from French culture. In France the Jew could present myth as farce, whereas in Germany myth was the source of a national art. The "unscrupulous adaptable talent" of Korngold—Meyerbeer, Puccini and Strauss in one—and the "dirty street song talent" of Weill, were representative of Jewish inroads in Germany. These Jews and others imitated the great masters and distorted them.[21] Jewish artistic adaptability and talent were furthered by Jewish economic and propagandistic interests, which naturally were also controlled by Jews, wrote Friedrich Brand in the above-mentioned article on "Jewish Music Organization of the Music Life of the Nation." Blessinger wrote that the difference between German and Jewish character was clear. "German sorrow becomes Jewish wailing; and German expression of feeling is turned into the Jewish inclination to melancholy and weeping . . . . While the German expression of feeling is always genuine and subjectively honest, that of the Jew is never quite sincere."[22]

Jewish characteristics and the pervasiveness of the "Jewish-destructive spirit" in pre-1933 music had become basic assumptions of musicology in the Third Reich. Comprehensive publications on Jews followed. The "Institute for the Study of the Jewish Question" published *The Jews in Germany* for the interested music public, and especially scholars. As in other publications, the Jew was said to have turned art into an object of financial speculation, a process demonstrated by Meyerbeer and Offenbach and "followed by their learned racial comrades." Especially in the area of entertainment music, this "Jewish business was not controlled by any scruple," and the "effects were catastrophic." The distortion of the operetta into a product of cheap imitation was their work, as well as the epidemic of the modern hit song production which poisoned the musical taste of the people for decades." A few representative names were listed in demonstration of the Jewish preponderance in this one area of music: Bogumil Zepler, Jean Gilbert (who emigrated in 1933), Leo Fall, Oscar Strauss (who also left Germany), Leon Jessel, Emmerich Kalman (who left Austria in 1938), Leo Ascher, Edmund Eysler, Victor and Friedrich Hollaender, Bruno Granichstädten and Paul Abraham. Then followed, "Who did not know them, these monopolists of the international market of light opera? Also the American Jews, Gershwin and Irving Berlin, whose empty hits have flooded German audiences for years, shall not be forgotten here." The "demoralizing impact of Jewry in this area" was allegedly demonstrated when it was recalled that "only a few of these well-known names were trained musicians."[23]

In January 1936, *Die Musik* published a review of another catalogue of Jews in German music, *The Musical ABC of Jews (Das Musikalische Juden-ABC)* which advertised itself as comprehensive and dependable. It is interesting that the critic took issue with several details. He noted real mistakes, surprising in view of the government publication on this subject. Indeed, "honourable Germans, whose ancestry cannot be doubted, are defamed therein." For instance, Hugo Riemann, the founder of German musicology with a world reputation, was erroneously listed as a Jew. The same was true of the Viennese scholar, Robert Haas, while the "full blood Jew," Paul Bekker, was listed as Aryan. "The emigres will enjoy this." Other errors were noted, "Max Bruch, for instance," listed as a Jew,

> has long ago been established as Aryan. Also the Leipzig musicologist Max Steinitzer, has been able to refute the legend of his Jewish ancestry long ago. And the wife of the composer Flick-Steger is Aryan, as far as we are concerned. We are equally surprised to find the excellent dancer Harold Kreutzberg on the Jewish list. Erich Kleiber, whose name is known enough, is listed as Klaiber, Oscar Strauss with SZ, which has been reserved for Aryan names.

The critic pointed out that he favored this kind of compilation, but that this effort did not live up to expectations.[24]

More authoritative and comprehensive was the official publication, intended as a resource for scholars, the *Lexicon of Jews in Music*, commissioned by the Reich Leadership of the NSDAP, on the basis of official documents, edited by Dr. Theo Stengel of the RMK and Dr. Herbert Gerigk of Rosenberg's Bureau. The authors introduced their work in official capacity, noting that

> the purification of German culture, thus German music, of Jewish elements has been accomplished. Clear jurisdictional regulations prevent the Jew from the exercise of his art in Greater Germany. . . . The names of the great from the time of the end of the war to the new order of the Reich are gone. They are so thoroughly forgotten that the accidental appearance of such a name does not always ring familiar, especially among the young. . . . No real relation between German and Jewish spirit is possible. This conclusion causes a clear differentiation, all the more so in recognition of the past years, which showed the trend of a development as soon as Jewish elements were tolerated or even given leading positions. . . . Not the individual Jew but the Jewish question at large is our concern. . . . We measure on the basis of race, we conclude that the Jew is not creative, and that in music he is simply recreative. His parasitic ability to understand the work of others contributes to his virtuosity which, at times, is astounding, although it also

demonstrates his basic emptiness, inasmuch as his Oriental sense must, of necessity, change the content of an occidental musical creation.[25]

The authors claimed to have compiled the first scientific analysis of names in demonstration of the connection between race and music. Indeed, "much time has passed since Richard Wagner's publication on *Jewry in Music* of the nineteenth century had been accepted, Richard Eichenauer's *Music and Race* had been recognized in spite of the controversy it once caused," in addition to which the work of Karl Blessinger had been acknowledged, especially in his major effort on *Mendelssohn, Meyerbeer, Mahler*. Other encyclopedic works had been attempted and were recorded here. However, "this work is more reliable" and it "leaves out names where the question of race has not been answered." The ancestry of the greatest part of recorded Jews and half-Jews (Quarter-Jews and those married to Jews were not listed, "although, especially in the sensitive mentality of artists, an extensive influence of the Aryan part must be assumed.") was alleged to be supported by documents.[26] In the second edition the authors added: "Since the first edition in 1940, new material has enriched the work, especially from the recently occupied territories." The authors acknowledge difficulties in their research. "Jewish sources were not considered reliable since various authors claim certain Aryans as Jews." Thus, Alfred Einstein had listed Hugo Kaun in the *Jüdische Lexikon*. Furthermore, the authors intended to create a "manageable reference work," thus being forced to omit lists of productions and bibliographies "since we did not intend to immortalize Jewish creativity. To the contrary, we want to aid in the quickest elimination of all extant remains from our cultural and spiritual life." Indeed, "as masters of deception, some Jews still escape notice."[27]

This introduction was followed by the alphabetic listing of Jewish musicians, past and present, and a listing of Jewish compositions, some names of which will be presented here:

Achron, Joseph, *Losdseje 5.1.1886, violin virtuoso, pres. of the world executive board of the world center of Jewish music in Palestine—L.A. Attempts to create a Jewish national art-music based on elementary Jewish elements (according to Alfred Einstein—*Das neue Musik-lexikon*.)

Bekker, Paul (H) (the H refers to half-Jew), *Berlin 9.11.1882—New York 1937, music commentator, 1925 Intendant of the State Theatre at Kassel, 1927-32 same at Wiesbaden. Major writer of the *Verfallszeit* ("time of decline"), known as music critic of the *Frankfurter Zeitung* 1911/25, supporter of the disintegrating tendencies of Mahler, Schönberg, Schreker, etc.—Hans Pfitzner wrote against him *Die Ästhetik der musikalischen Impotenz.* . . . Through decree of the Reich Interior Minister, 3.3.1936 Bekker lost his citizenship on the basis of P2 of the law dealing with such matters. The decision read..."Paul Bekker, music commentator, of Jewish descent, lastly, Intendant of the Wiesbaden State Theatre, favored Jewish compatriots there. Through the program and the culture-bolshevist staging of the performances he consciously set himself against German artistic sensibility." After the National Socialist seizure of power he became a worker in the Paris emigre press. In his work he attacks Germany's leaders in lowest manner.

Bloch, Ernst, *Geneva 7.24.1880, also attempted the founding of a Jewish music on the basis of the character and spirit of his race. [This caused positive Nazi response. The same was true in regard to Max Brod, who also used a language similar to the ideological formulators of National Socialism.]

Brod, Max, *Prague 4.27.1884, author and composer. In contrast to most of his racial fellows, Brod attempted to explain the compositions of Jewish composers on the basis of their Jewish mentality. In an essay, "Gustav Mahler's Jewish melodies," he explained that Mahler was most inspired by the chassidic folk song. He ended, "It is more fruitful to regard Mahler on the basis of his Jewish spirit. The tremendous resistance to his music can be explained because his compositions are on the surface quite German, instinctively, however, they appear un-German (and that is so). Through German eyes his compositions appear incoherent, styleless, lacking form, bizarre, cutting, cynical, too soft, mixed with harshness. There is no unity in the German sense. If we attempt to gain access to Mahler's Jewish soul, all falls into place. The same is true of Heine, Mendelssohn, Meyerbeer. . . . In the case of Mahler, the greatest modern Jewish artist is thus perfect . . . At the sound of Eastern Jewish folk songs I understood why his last cycle, the Chinese *Lied von der Erde*, his *Einsamkeiten* are a search for his home, ever, ever, the Orient."

Goldmann, Curt, *Berlin 4.27.1870, thirty pseudonyms, many compositions with leftist titles: "Bolshevik Dance." Then after 1933 a turn to National Socialist titles..."National March: Heil Deutschland Heil"; "Germany Has Awakened"; "SA, Always Ready for Combat"; "SS, the Black Guards"; "HJ is Marching"; "Armed Youth"; "Work Has Liberated Us." He wrote over one thousand compositions.

Hanslick, Eduard (H) *Prague 9.2.1825, + Vienna 8.6.1904, Dr. Phil., 1861/95 Professor at University of Vienna, author critic in the Vienna *Neue Freie Presse*. His 1854 publication of *Vom Musikalisch-Schönen* is generally considered his major work. Richard Wagner recognized the typical Jewish physiognomy of this essay and its tendency which was particularly directed against him and his conception of art. . . . Having once been an admirer of Wagner, he had reversed his opinion after the master's publication of *Das Judentum in der Musik*.

Kestenberg, Leo, *Rosenberg, Hungary 11.27.1882, pianist, since 1918 in charge of music at the Prussian Education Ministry, also since 1921 Professor at the Berlin Music Academy and since 1922 head of the music division of the "Central Institute for Education and Instruction." Kestenberg is considered typical of the time of decay in Germany. After a piano career in Marxist organization, he established himself as specialist in musical affairs at the Prussian Education Ministry immediately after the November-revolution of 1918. . . . He became the Marxist music director of Prussia. A most characteristic gesture was his appointment of Franz Schreker to the position of director of the State Music Academy of Berlin in 1920. He also appointed Arnold Schönberg to a master class for musical composition at the Prussian Academy of Arts in Berlin in 1925. He appointed Paul Bekker as Intendant of the State Theatre at Kassel in 1925, in Wiesbaden in 1927, and Otto Klemperer to the position of Opera director and *Generalmusikdirector* of the Kroll Opera in Berlin. This man was friendly with the Communist Rosa Luxemburg, supporting her in the publication of a last work. [The authors then quoted from an article published in the *Allgemeine Musikerzeitung*, March 1933.] "When he was finally rejected by the people, primarily by German musicians, being forced to vacate the throne in 1932 which he himself had constructed, the musical Germany could breathe again. (The Jews in Germany) However, the cultural ground left behind resembled a harvest field devastated by voracious rodents."

Klemperer, Otto, –Breslau 5.15.1855, conductor, composer, changed religion several times. 1927 Opera Director and *Generalmusikdirektor* of the Kroll Opera which he turned into the Jewish-Marxist experimental stage, ruining it artistically and financially so that it had to close down. He intended to tear down and falsify German master works to such an extent that even his racial compatriots attacked him. Thus, Alfred Einstein's critique of Klemperer's *Figaro*. After the closing of the *Krolloper* he was employed at the State Opera, *Unter den Linden*. His last Berlin abomination was a *Tannhäuser* performance which was reviewed by Alfred-Ingemar Berndt in an article, "Grant Me Four Years" (Munich, 1937): "We simply want to point out that still now, this February 13, 1933, after the seizure of power, the Jewish *Generalmusikdirektor* Klemperer had the audacity to perform the *Tannhäuser* at the occasion of the fiftieth anniversary of Wagner's death which was clearly intended as an insult to the great German master and as a punch in the face of all still healthy-minded persons. According to the *Allgemeine Musikzeitung*, Klemperer managed to prove that the overture sounds terrible and is a mediocre piece of music."

Mahler, certainly one of the most talented composers of his time, also was reviewed in typical manner here as one who had succeeded through "Jewish support, who had praised him as superior musical genius." The Nazis took special note of Jewish attempts to call him an equal to Bruckner. Karl Blessinger was praised for having been the first critic to have attacked him in *Mendelssohn, Meyerbeer, Mahler: Three Chapters of Jewry in Music as Key to Music History of the Nineteenth Century*. Blessinger had identified Mahler with the third stage of falsification of the tradition by Jewry, calling him "the fanatic type of the Eastern Jewish Rabbi." Characteristically, Blessinger had treated music as an expression of racial type; "In all of Mahler's creations the Jew's deep mental anguish is manifest, which has so often been confused with Faustian struggle and the German search for God. Again and again Mahler's music exhibits those features which we have identified as typically Jewish. . . . Jewish cynicism...has been confused with profundity." Gergke and Stengel cited Max Brod's effort to understand Mahler's music as an expression of Jewish nature.

Even Mendelssohn was subjected to racial interpretation. Naturally, his wealth and family connections were emphasized, while the "Mendelssohn cult" was attributed to the influence of his racial comrades. His contributions and accomplishments were belittled and denied, especially his alleged place in the history of German romanticism. German romantics were said to have "cultivated the German *Volkstum*, particularly the German folk song...while Mendelssohn acted as a fanatic enemy against these attempts." He allegedly had commented in 1829 that "'I will tolerate no national music. To the devil with the *Volkstum*.'" Again, Richard Wagner was cited as the first revisionist who had attempted to put a stop to "the contamination of German music." Both Wagner and Schumann were claimed in behalf of the theory which reduced music to an expression of racial characteristics. Blessinger had classified Mendelssohn among "assimilation Jews, thus representing the race which is dedicated to the transformation of inherited culture along Jewish

lines, thereby committing fraud." Also Meyerbeer, born in Berlin, was described as a descendent of a banking family, whose members had become
wealthy "in their capacity as court Jews." He also had been furthered by
"racial comrades." His success had been recorded in opera and popular music,
but Schumann "exposed him," writing in his *Neue Zeitschrift für Musik* about
Meyerbeer's *Die Hugenotten*, "How disgusting I find all of this . . . As a good
Protestant I am furious to see the bloodiest chapter in the history of the religion
reduced to the level of a market-place farce." Schumann had not referred
to this music as a symptom of Jewishness, but the Nazi authors did, referring
to Schumann's description of "'annoying, grumbling and indiscreet rhythm'"
as "expression of typically Jewish traits." Wagner served here in the capacity of moral custodian of the German tradition, which was desecrated by the
likes of Meyerbeer. In the critique of Meyerbeer Wagner had been able to
establish the most characteristic antithetical musical types as rooted in the
nature of each people, inasmuch as Meyerbeer had not aspired to "German
depth of expression." Thus, Wagner, the prototype of what *völkisch* authors
called German profundity, had attacked Meyerbeer for writing music only
for effect. In this catalogue of small and noted musicians, the words of
Schumann, Wagner, and then Blessinger were produced in a progression of
denunciation of undesirable types, reflecting the history of the *völkisch* movement, from the respectable and a national and moral critique of Schumann,
to the aggressive, yet still ideologically sensitive, *völkisch*-Germanic position
of Wagner, and to the pure racism of Blessinger, which characterized the
Nazi dogma toward music. Thus, Blessinger had characterized Meyerbeer
simply as "unscrupulous business Jew and most powerful exponent of the
second phase in the process of forging the appropriated heritage through
Jewry." The authors had nothing really to add to Blessinger's statement.

In each case of a noted musician, the authors wanted to demonstrate the
interconnection of all areas of music life through Jewish elements. No Jewish
composer or performer would have prospered without the financial and propagandistic support offered by racial brothers. Schönberg was furthered by
Mahler; lacking originality he imitated Wagner, and then established his own
twelve-tone music, which constituted "the Jewish principle of reducing
everything to the same level." The musical and social spheres were treated
as an expression of Jewish character in one person. Strictly in musical terms,
Schönberg's innovation amounted to "the total destruction of the natural order
of tones within the tonality principle of our classical music." The words were
again taken from Blessinger. The authors then demonstrated that Schönberg
was admired exclusively by Jewish circles. While the Jewish Alfred Einstein
described Schönberg as "'the most characteristic representative, or, much
rather, exponent, of new music,'" the German Riemann listed Schönberg's

music as "'theoretical regression and hypermodern negation of all theory.'" It was noted that Schönberg's call to the Music Academy at Berlin had been opposed by non-Jewish musicians, and rather characteristically, the authors cited exclusively *völkisch* or Nazi commentators. While it was difficult, perhaps, for Nazi commentators to defame the name of a great musician on the basis of fact and commentary of the past, in the case of Kurt Weill the authors felt most secure in their categoric denunciations: "The name of this composer is inextricably connected with the worst disintegration of our art. In Weill's stage works the Jewish-anarchistic tendency is illustrated in blunt and unrestrained form." Weill allegedly had upheld Marxist notions of class warfare and immoral principles, which in combination constituted the class-warring glorification of the *Untermenschentum* [racially inferior people] and the gutter.

After reading the names cited here alone, the German music public possessed a comprehensive Nazi picture of the Jew in music, the devil who was thus exposed and justified all the measures taken against him in the Third Reich. Long-standing Nazis delighted in calling attention to the opportunism displayed by members of the music establishment, who realized after 1933 that universal categories were binding. Friedrich Herzog wrote that "those music critics who quite recently had still praised Kurt Weill and Ernst Toch as gifted composers, while maliciously treating Hans Pfitzner and Paul Graener as marginal and *teutsch* [old fashioned spelling of *deutsch*, thus referring to the *völkisch* sentiments of the composers], have now decided to celebrate second- and third-rate epigones of romantic descent as great masters."[28] The elimination of the Jews from German music was almost total—the most consistent feature of Nazi music politics. Welter noted that this purge did not eliminate real cultural values, as erroneously suspected by the unfamiliar, but false and alien distortions. He listed three types of Jews in the manner of Blessinger. Mahler represented the third category, being neither international like Meyerbeer and Offenbach, nor assimilated like Mendelssohn, but an imitator of German personalities like Wagner, Bruckner and Strauss, thus demonstrating basic uprootedness to the greatest degree. Being a Jew, thus subject to the laws of his race, Mahler had been incapable of reaching the depth of German feeling and expression. Instead of genuine artistry, he therefore had displayed an astounding level of technical mastery, but produced kitsch, negative expressionism and "narcotic Nirwana."[29] His work was therefore no longer tolerated in the Germany which was engaged in the total transformation of its society. Racial strictures demanded his suppression. The same applied to Mendelssohn, the main target of Nazi criticism, for the reason of having received the greatest acclaim. He also was denied the possibility of ever having reached German depth. Instead of treating him as a German, he was regarded as an intruder who had been celebrated as "substitute of German masters," at times even placed above Beethoven. All his most celebrated works were violently attacked, his violin concerto, the *Midsummer Night's Dream*, his Octet for Strings, all of which "lacked German soul." If he had had soul, he would have composed pure Jewish music.

The imperative to purge the Jewish component of Christianity—reminiscent of the Church's concern in the Middle Ages over Christians' "Judaizing"—was reinforced by the regime's early hostility to religion in general. Yet, in practice, the anti-Christian campaign proved most difficult, suffered reversals, and resulted in serious compromises because of Christianity's deep roots in the German community. Regardless of Jewish taints, church music held too honored a position in Germany to be attacked directly. Instead, the regime strove to confine church music to the church and limit its message to the religious community, while demanding that it not violate the state's totalitarian claims. Ideologically, church music served as a useful model for the state's musical requirements. Its tradition of subordinating music to an extra-musical spiritual program, its conformity to acceptable tonal standards, its authoritarianism and anti-Communism were appreciated and readily appropriated. In return, the churches by and large cooperated with the purges of church music which did not so much affect the music itself as personnel. For various reasons, church leaders declared solidarity with the blood and soil principles of the Third Reich. Consequently, the Church accepted the research of musicologists and claims of Nazi publicists about a *völkisch* musical tradition which encompassed and helped define Christian musical expression; church music was assumed to reflect racial characteristics like any other music.

Yet, there was a problem, inasmuch as Christian music revealed other than native roots. Helmut Schmidt-Garre, a student of Alban Berg and Egon Wellesz, acknowledged this when he wrote an article on the "Racial Style of Nordic Music" in which he, like Welter, suggested that "the spiritual and intellectual capacities of a race may be read in those cultural documents which date back in history to a time not yet subject to racial mixing. . . . It would be most useful, therefore, to study the racial characteristics of our Nordic music" in this early setting. Unfortunately, the oldest examples of Nordic music, he admitted, date back to the time of the Christian conquest of German culture and the Christian choral music evolved from Jewish temple ceremonies which the "people at the time resisted and could not understand," but which, nonetheless, helped shape early German-Christian culture. However, the author posited the existence of an "elementary sound experience of the Nordic race" on the basis of unique instruments uncovered recently in the Scandinavian countries.[35] Other musicologists contributed research into the nature of German music, establishing that melody was Nordic, as were traditional harmony and the preponderance of the major mode.

Not bothered by the apparent contradiction between acknowledged Jewish roots and the claimed Nordic primacy, which in less politicized times would be resolved with reference to synthesis, race expert Eichenauer simply affirmed the priority of the people, which ultimately determine the nature of cultural expression. In 1937 he welcomed what he regarded to be a rich peasant song culture, demonstrated in the publication of a book of peasant songs which included some old chorales that seemed to differ ideologically from the other songs. Eichenauer reasoned that

> the nature of the German choral of its great era during the religious wars contained nothing specifically "Christian," that is in musical terms, but something generally and eternally "German," i.e., that elemental joy in combat, a most characteristic trait of Nordic man . . . Thus, these immortal choral tunes are by no means the personal property of Christian churches. . . inasmuch as all characteristics are derived from the old German folk song.[36]

Thus, the Christian choral, with its Jewish-Christian roots, was simply subsumed under categories of popular culture.

Notwithstanding arbitrary claims about the *völkisch* nature of Christian music, it was regarded enough of a threat to be confined to the Church, and efforts were made to keep it from the concert stage, the radio, and especially from the schools. Even the oratorio and the cantata were thus blocked.

It is clear that the regime was in a bind over a popular musical expression which could not be suppressed, even though it challenged totalitarian claims. Fanatics purged Christian texts, especially those derived from Old Testament sources, from Handel oratorios and even staple Christmas songs like "Silent Night." In wartime also Christian peace messages were censored. Yet, popular resistance and occasional official disapproval of such tampering with cherished tradition resulted instead in the publication and distribution among party, youth and military organizations of new worldly compositions and songs for Christmas, like the well-known *Hohe Nacht der Klaren Sterne* ("Holy Night of Clear Stars"),[37] which captured the sentimental-familiar and mystical-religious spirit without propagating the Christian message.

Musicologists, publicists, and music critics continued to carefully redefine the German nature of music in interaction with new musical offerings. The model, ironically, of the definitional and compositional efforts remained Handel and his oratorios, some of which were purged of Jewish texts and titles. The *Judas Maccabeus* especially suffered repeated alterations, although the most compromising religious texts were simply not performed, while the worldly ones were featured prominently. Also, Bach was celebrated in worldly terms as German prototype, regardless of his Christian setting and orientation. While Eichenauer had found a way to rationalize Christian texts—insisting on purging only Jewish ones, writers busily rewrote so many famous texts that Goebbels issued warnings against defilers of the masters.[38] However, since the threats of Goebbels and other officials did not appear to be binding, the practice of doing violence to select religious music persisted in confirmation of the myth-making enterprise.

In spite of the distortions of many musical expressions of the "Jewish-international conspiracy with its goal of world-domination," as consistently defined by such theoretically inclined fascists as Charles Maurras in France and even Rosenberg, survived in contradiction to the totalitarian doctrine. The other alleged agents of the Jews, frequently referred to as duped, were an array of liberals, Marxists, decadent bourgeois, dishonest capitalists, and cultural proponents of schools and tendencies variously described in ideological terms. In music, the list of Jewish allies was well-known and denounced. It included musicians who were either identified with progressive tendencies, such as Schönberg's student Alban Berg, the foreign representatives of "decadence" like Stravinsky, Ravel, Krenek, or those who had become identified with political oppositionist groups, like Hindemith, people who had joined the emigre class, referred to as internationalist, and who were also increasingy banned from musical programs. Again, Furtwängler was cited for his demonstration of independence as he conducted throughout the Third Reich not only Mendelssohn, but also Ravel, Stravinsky and Hindemith, in the latter case causing the celebrated controversy which involved the high brass of the Nazi elite. To the list of distinguished members of this "international clique" must be added the defamed composers of entertainment music, of the hit songs, jazz and operettas which were identified as manifestations of the "Jewish disintegrating spirit."

The reality of myth-making and identification with mythical types faced difficulties besides those occasioned by the Jewish and Christian components of German music. The Hindemith affair brought out another basic contradiction in both Nazi theory and practice, emphasized in Furtwängler's open-letter defense of the great German composer, inasmuch as Hindemith sybolized the sophisticated conservative solution to problems of modern music. Because of this fact, several Nazi authors came to his defense when he was attacked by officials and party ideologists. Moreover, he was racially acceptable and well-integrated into the musical establishment. Furtwängler referred to him as a great teacher who enjoyed the greatest following of any musician in Germany. Significantly, he pointed out that Hindemith's attempts to synthesize the most advanced levels of musical development with folk music ought not alone to be acceptable to the formulators of Nazi aesthetics, but actually to be celebrated for providing a potential solution to the impasse in modern music and thus the foundation of the much sought-after new Nazi music. Goebbels chose instead to disallow the aesthetic argument against Nazi *Realpolitik*. As a politician, and in this case under advice of Göring, he rejected a theoretical debate on the state of music in its most sensitive area in favor of practical instinct, which warned of a tremendous danger, more serious for the very complexity of the case and because of Hindemith's hold over Germany's brilliant youth.[39]

Support of the traditional and the *völkisch* components of music as the vital basis of the definition of German music encountered additional difficulty, since the Jewish component in German culture had become part of even the folk songs. Heine's *Lorelei*, for instance, long popular and revered as the most characteristic expression of the German soul, was published in songbooks under the listing "author unknown." The *National Socialist Bildungswesen*, organ of the Nazi Socialist Teachers Association, formally asked for the total cessation of singing of those songs known to be composed by Jewish musicians and writers.[40] Handel's name posed the greatest problems because of his choice of Old Testament texts which seemed to support not only the Christian but the Jewish tradition as well. Since people did not get involved in the theoretical rationalization attempted in this regard, the contradiction was never successfully resolved. To a less obvious degree, the status of Bruckner reflected Nazi inconsistency. This composer had subordinated his art to Christian ideals. *Völkisch* apologists pointed to his idealism in demonstration of his truly German nature. He did, indeed, set an example for those who saw an escape from the reality of this world through music, which he had undertaken by way of the Gregorian choral.[41] His otherworldliness, the subject and spirit of his work, and the avowal of a Christian tradition were solace to him as well as to those who still shared his sentiments during the Third Reich. The Nazis, on the other hand, created a real Bruckner cult, claiming him as a nationalist, while disregarding his Christian nature and purpose. At odds with anti-religious fanatics and musicologists who rejected Gregorian chants as Jewish-influenced, Professor Joseph Schmidt-Görg of Bern tried to save this distinguished musical tradition by identifying its Frankish elements. Others tried to claim Schumann as a forerunner of National Socialism who was said to have established what the Nazis called *Musikpolitik*.[42]

The contradictions in Nazi aesthetic theory resulted from the desire to create heroes and villains, not on the basis of serious study of real interests and identification of individuals and classes who reflected real historical development, but through the imposition of a regressive ideology and values derived from cultural resentment and the reactionary and idealistic impulses. The villain was not the exploiter in an establishment which stifled progressive development, but a mythical object, the collective scapegoat which embodied all identifiable ills of modern times. The radical and democratic impulse of the Nazi movement was diverted from social and economic conflict and directed by its reactionary-*völkisch* component into a struggle defined as one between peoples, races, and universal values. All reality and people in history and in present context were reevaluated accordingly. The great masters were treated as past German heroes, in spite of the theoretical proposition that they were shaped by the demands of their race and racist concepts were superimposed on their music. Surprisingly, Beethoven was not considered pure Nordic, although his music was used to demonstrate the essence of Nordic heroism in its highest form. Rosenberg claimed his music as "Eroica of the German people." A dissertation in medicine at Heidelberg—"Were Germany's Most Significant Men of Pure or Mixed Race?"—concluded that Beethoven was racially mixed. Eichenauer also established the mixed heritage of the great musician, and Herbert Gerigk implied membership in the organization of Freemasons, adding politically incriminating evidence against the man who to many fans was Germany's foremost musician of all times. The ludicrous conflict was resolved by Walter Rauschenberg, who allowed for Nordic souls in "dark Germans." He defined

> Nordic as . . . the heroic character of his music which frequently rises to titanic heights. It is significant that in the present time of national regeneration Beethoven's works are most popular, that his music is heard at almost all demonstrations of heroic content. The *Eroica*, the Fifth and Ninth Symphonies, the *Egmont* and *Coriolan Overtures*, have been claimed as typical expression of heroic conviction.[43]

Although the man was suspect, his music reflected the standards by which all music was judged. Notwithstanding the benefits derived from the music in ideological terms, the race experts continued research as they understood it and subjected all German musicians of note to thorough analysis. Richard Eichenauer published his conclusions authoritatively and comprehensively, even though he too was challenged by a large group of younger scholars.

The conflict between physical characteristics of the composer or national and racial ancestry and the musical product, was of course never resolved because it was based on faulty premises. Eichenauer left no doubt as to Beethoven's mixed background, in spite of the pure quality of his music, thus contradicting his correlation theory. In his major work, *Musik und Rasse*, he even detailed the variety of racial types in Beethoven's family as proof of the mixed heritage. Like Friedrich Welter he praised Bach as the supreme Germanic type, both physically and in his music. Wolfgang Stumme also referred to Bach as the foremost inspiration to German youth and folk-conscious composers of the younger generation. On the other hand, Eichenauer attacked Gluck because that cosmopolitan had composed his work to Italian and French texts and aspired to the creation of music which would appeal to all nationalities alike. Thus Eichenauer asked, "Can a man who is so demonstratively uprooted be a Germanic or Nordic artist?" Referring to Gluck's desire to eliminate the boundaries between all nations through music, Eichenauer concluded, "Is not such obliteration of natural divisions the trait of the racial bastard?" Schubert also bothered the ideologists, even though his melodies affirmed set standards of German music. Melody had been praised most consistently as a trademark and foremost element of German music. Indeed, the absence of clearly demonstrable and recognizable melody was considered the most characteristic feature of all decadent and disintegrating forces in a musical work. As an embodiment of what Karl Hasse referred to as German or Nordic cultural sensibilities, Schubert, more than any other German composer, was protected by the *völkisch* ideologists and the Nazi state against disruptive musical agents. However, as a physical type, his eyes, hair color and "a certain softness in the facial expression" compromised his status. Eichenauer claimed the master nonetheless as Nordic.[44]

It is obvious that this entire process of wanting to claim past German masters as embodiments of Germanic principles could not be readily accomplished. Yet the literature dedicated to do just that assumed tremendous proportions. While Beethoven's and Schubert's physical characteristics were questioned, Reger was defended as a German composer, in spite of association with modernistic trends in music.[45] Handel was appreciated as an embodiment of the Nazi hero in spite of Old Testament text and residence in England. Chopin, as reviewed above, was largely Germanized.[46] Liszt was claimed as part of the Germanic tradition, in fact as a forerunner of National Socialism, in spite of Jewish friends and connections, while Franz Lehar, who was called an Aryan and a German in spite of his birth in Hungary, was rejected and barred from German stages for several years because of his association with Jews, possibly a Jewish wife, anti-German sentiment and the trashy content of librettos of his Jewish associates[47]—even though his *Merry Widow* was one of Hitler's favorite compositions. All German composers of the past and present were subjected to this kind of scrutiny and manipulation. Styles of music and instruments were reviewed in relationship to defined categories by polemicists and collaborating musicologists, who researched their subjects with the intention of substantiating basic assumptions. General music histories like that of Welter omitted a significant number of Jewish names from the bibliographies. Genuine conflicts within music were used selectively in demonstration of ideological hypotheses. Brahms's respect for classic form was interpreted as an attempt to sustain the cultural component of music against the technical consequence of the break-up of tonality suggested in the symphonic poem and in Wagner's work. Hence, Welter treated Brahms as a reactionary[48] who nonetheless served the purpose of Nazi cultural policy. Moreover, the presentation of that nineteenth-century conflict in music between the followers of Brahms and Wagner allowed the Nazis to pose as champions of free development. Both Brahms and Wagner were claimed as true German artists.

The trend to purge Jewish and some Christian names, titles, and texts accorded with the major thrust of wiping out all traces of the Jewish presence from German music and consciousness, after the negative features had been established by the scholars and publicists. Meanwhile, the habit of distortion didn't restrict itself to the original target. In spite of official censure, some nasty criticism, and even ridicule, especially from abroad, the purgers, in collaboration with authors of new texts, subjected even the most revered German masters to text alterations. Jewish texts were purged wherever detected, and foreign texts were replaced by German ones. Another favorite distortion involved the replacement of even German historical subjects, lyrics and titles by Nazi counterparts, so that Beethoven's recollection of the Congress of Vienna was turned into the evocation of Hitler's "Day of Potsdam," and a Wagner hymn was enriched by a *Deutschland erwacht* text.[49]

The other side of the purges and alterations, in accordance with Nazi principles and pocket-book needs of Germany's authors and composers, was the promotion of the heroes of the tradition. Naturally, Wagner was the subject par excellence of a Nazi cult . He was viewed as the ideal type who afforded the greatest consistency and harmony between ideological and revolutionary gesture and traditional standards. The press encouraged the people, especially German youth, to look to Bayreuth as a national shrine. The ideal subject for an education in music and for the people in general,[50] as well as of numerous dissertations[51] (with a great deal of justification), the Nazis claimed Wagner as spiritual forebear of their movement, associated with the likes of Constantin Franz, Paul de Lagarde, Gobineau, Chamberlain and Schemann. Indeed, at this time, Wagner was no longer treated exclusively as an artist or as a musician, but as the spiritual and political leader who he had wanted to be in his own day.

The Nazis projected onto Wagner and into his work every aspect of their ideology, their Social Darwinism, imperialism and anti-Semitism, as well as their cultural ideals. As an artist alone he had accomplished what was the dream of *völkisch* thinkers: he had created the *Gesamtkunstwerk*, quite contrary to the German tradition of absolute music, which in other discussions was styled as purest expression of Nordic man, but obviously in fulfillment of the ideological goals of Nazi policymakers in the arts. Here was the model of Nazi cult spectaculars to which all the arts would contribute. The festival meadow of the *Meistersinger* was likened to the Third Reich setting of classlessness and other populist pretensions. In addition to his performance in the arts, Wagner had formulated much of the ideology which in distorted form served as justification of Nazi policy, as well as the projected new music. Wagner's formulation of a new aesthetics, his *völkisch* politics, and the artistic work constituted the most comprehensive legacy of the Germanic past with which National Socialism itself identified. On the other hand, it is assumed here that Wagner was much more complex than his Nazi epigones and admirers, who denied much of his rich oeuvre and the universally human features of a revolutionary who, alive, would have been proscribed in the Third Reich. The SS appropriation did violence to the man and his work. Although Wagner's authoritarianism and his commitment to communal ritual and the reintegration of autonomous arts provided a genuine model for *völkisch* aesthetics and the notion of *Volksgemeinschaft*, the Nazi state was molded on a differeent set of assumptions.

The subject of the most lavish art cult in the Third Reich, Wagner was nonetheless also subjected to the racialist inquiries of specialists and journalists. The issue of his descent never subsided in both *völkisch* and emigre circles. Official spokesmen had to respond. Much research was devoted to proving the Aryan status of the hero, who was said to have begun the fight against Jewry which was won under National Socialism.[52] However, this same Wagner had associated with Jews; he had been furthered by some and had praised others. A most interesting critique was also presented by Walter Abendroth, who attributed such an enormous influence to Wagner in strictly artistic terms that he had stifled all creative impulses for generations. Hence, music degenerated into the various modernistic expressions which the Nazi state had stamped out.[53] Welter had similarly referred to this impact of Wagner. Elsewhere, Abendroth mentioned the fact that Wagner had praised the first Jewish opera composer, Halévy, and his work, *Die Jüdin*. Like Mozart, Wagner had been a Freemason, a fact which had to be rationalized and overlooked.[54]

The new regime benefited from the identification with this hero. In practice, the subject of education and an actively manipulated exegesis, the Wagner cult and the Bayreuth shrine loomed large as symbols of National Socialism as a religion. The *Nibelungenmarsch* was reserved for Party Congresses. The *Meistersinger* inaugurated the Third Reich on the "Day of

Potsdam" in 1933. Wagnerian motifs were sounded at official party gatherings, state functions, Nazi films and newsreels. Bayreuth itself was subsidized and Hitler had himself identified with this foremost artistic shrine of Germany. The *Zeitschrift für Musik* understood the message when it published its July 1933 issue under the heading of "Adolf Hitler and Bayreuth"—setting a trend. Hitler attended as many anniversary celebrations of the master as possible, a fact to which the party press drew attention.[55] Nazi myth-making culminated in the performance and review of Wagner's music dramas, which presented the idealized mythical German past. Journalists and educators described Wagnerian heroes as the embodiment of German virtues, with which the Nazis identified themselves and their offspring. "Which German boy, which German girl cannot find pleasure in Wagner's epic heroes?"— asked Fritz Merseberg in an article in the *Völkische Musikerziehung*, 1938, entitled, "Richard Wagner as Pioneer of National Socialism." Party ideologist Rosenberg, though not really a fan, had written in the *Mythus* that

> the essential quality of Western art has been manifested in Richard
> Wagner, namely that the Nordic soul is not contemplative, nor confined
> to reflect individual psychology, but the willful experience of cosmic-
> spiritual laws and spiritual-architectonic creativity. Richard Wagner is
> the artist in whom the three factors are joined which, each in itself,
> constitutes a part of our total artistic life: the Nordic ideal of beauty,
> physically portrayed by Lohengrin and Siegfried and bound in deepest
> communion with nature, the inner will power of man in *Tristan und
> Isolde*, and the struggle for spiritual height of Nordic-Western man,
> heroic honor, in conjunction with inner veracity. This spiritual ideal of
> beauty is realized in Wotan, in King Mark, and in Hans Sachs.[56]

In addition to these offical comments, *Die Bühne* published the remarks of an anonymous lady:

> The knight Lohengrin is the concretization of the ideal form of the Aryan
> race in its highest state of perfection of manhood. He already embodies
> a condition which rises above the present state of the white race, whose
> purified substance and clarified blood reflect a spiritual being. Along
> with the base content of the blood of lower races other base qualities
> have been discarded, so that the inner contradiction between the higher
> and lower qualities has been resolved; he found peace with himself.
> . . . Elsa appears as untouchable and pure as an angel to us, but she
> has not reached the spiritual height which would make her an equal
> of her hero. She does not yet contain Aryan blood, in that doubt sym-

bolized by Ortrud gains access to her and destroys her secure faith.[57]

Friedrich Baser wrote in a similar way in articles entitled "Richard Wagner as Herald of the Aryan World" and "Race and History in Opera," giving credit to the romantics for having revived an interest in old sagas and epics, but attributing their real "resurrection and the liberation of their deepest content from the ossification process of thousands of years" to Wagner, who was

> guided by his instinctually strong racial sense . . . Already in *Lohengrin* he anticipated the way to the castle of the grail, to the shrine of the Aryan race, which he was to find in all purity only in the *Parsifal*, just as his hero was only able to gain salvation at the second visit to the castle of the grail, mature through struggles and suffering, "through knowing compassion." First he had to overcome the tragedy of individualism, soluble only in the state of Nirvana, by raising it to the level of the people's tragedy of *Tristan und Isolde*, to the communal experience of the Germanic race in the *Ring of the Nibelungen*. Never has a people received a mightier painting of enormous proportions "with confidence in the German spirit.[58]

The harmony between Wagner's theory and his rich artistic achievement raised him to an ideal level above all other forbears. Celebrated as the prophet of his people for allegedly having discovered the connection between race and art fifty years ahead of his time, his *Gesamtkunstwerk*—the musical drama of epic-mythical content—substantively affirmed National Socialism, traditional German values, myths, heroes, and *völkisch* truths. No feature of the art escaped ideological association. Richard Eichenauer determined that race helped explain the preference for certain acoustical ranges in song and instrumental music, even though he admitted that statistical evidence for this thesis did not yet exist. He asked, "do certain voice categories prevail in this or that race?" "If so," he noted, "Wagner's exploitation of the baritone might then be explained."[59] Originator of both theory and source for its substantiation, Wagner served every possible purpose, while contradictory elements of his thought and radical-progressive aspects of his art were denied or explained through dialectic sophistry. Karl Hasse took issue with Wagner's famous word, "To be German, is to do something for its own sake," in this manner. Acknowledging that the sentiment reflected *völkisch* and idealistic seriousness, according to which a critic might deduce the principle of *l'art pour l'art*, Hasse concluded that "in the eyes of National Socialism nothing exists for its own sake because everything serves a public purpose and everything has to happen for Germany and the German people." Inasmuch as Wagner did attempt to create German artwork for the German people, Hasse simply denied the necessary isolation and integrity necessary for artistic work. To him, "Wagner's word . . . was intended in the proper National Socialist sense."[60]

The Wagner myth-making served also as the basis for honoring contemporary musicians as heroes. Thus the *völkisch* radical Hans Pfitzner was celebrated in terms of the aesthetic-ideological categories which he himself had helped establish in a large polemical literature devoted to the assessment of modern music, as we have seen. His career, never smooth, was beset by controversy throughout the Third Reich. An uncomfortable eccentric who had a history of complaining about the lack of income and appropriate recognition, he nonetheless received honors and commissions, in spite of his reluctance to sign solidarity proclamations with the Nazi state and to join the party. *Völkisch* circles appreciated his commitment to national art, his fight against "chaotic" atonality, "primitive" jazz, and bolshevist internationalism before that had become fashionable. He toured Germany's borders as a representative of "German" music before the war and then participated in cultural exchanges during the occupation of conquered neighbors. While some Nazi leaders were annoyed with him, he had access to the elite, which elevated him to the status of an ideological forefighter and prophet. No one had sounded the alarm about music's crisis, articulated the relationship between the arts and the nation, and represented German music and German soul as combatively as this propounder of rooted and otherwise wholesome music of traditional tonality, melody, the "Germanic" triad and human inspiration. Like his idol Wagner, Pfitzner not only polemicized but also created musical masterworks in fulfillment of *völkisch* ideals. While regular stages performed his music, Nazi organizations like the NSKG republished his aesthetics and promoted his music. He was greatly honored at his sixty-fifth birthday in 1934 as herald of German soul and spirit. The National Socialist Student Association invited the public to an evening honoring the composer. The students declared their solidarity with "this greatest German composer, the purest incarnation of the German spirit."[61] And so it went for him throughout the Third Reich. His composition *Von deutscher Seele*—a model of *arteigene* music, was played frequently on official occasions.

The Myth of the Folk-Musical Community

Redefined in *völkisch*-Nazi terms and purged of its "alien" components, the German concert repertoire was performed for its traditional concert-going public. Music's and musicology's accommodation resulted also in the Nazi state compromising some of its militant *völkisch* principles. While the Nazis gained a more credible cultural facade for their political and propagandistic needs, the coordinated musical elite was able to reassert itself and increasingly ward off political intrusion and harassment by the ideological fanatics. The musical establishment had become more valuable to the grand design of the Nazi state. Meanwhile, the *völkisch*-Nazi community continued to believe in a new Nazi music culture by promoting its kind of narrowly defined national music at the NSKG, HJ, KdF and other party music festivals. Organizationally successful, it was able to attract segments of the population not previously exposed to serious music; and through promotion, subsidies, commissions and prizes it gained contributions of prominent composers and promising younger ones who thus reinforced the myth of a viable folk-musical community, even after 1936, when Goebbels and the traditional musical establishment recognized their complementary interests, which were essentially indifferent to higher *völkisch* musical aims.

The *völkisch*-Nazi ideology was very much alive after 1936, albeit in diffused and manipulated forms, as we have seen. Even the traditional repertoire was acceptable only insofar as the old masters were said to have embodied and magnified the simple virtues of the people, of the peasants. An elaborate ritual celebrated these virtues, and music played its part. Prizes, stipends and commissions were offered to German composers who, in addition to artistic achievement, demonstrated rootedness and political reliability. Hence, the creation of the annual German national prize of 100,000 RM for the most deserving artist or scientist. Of special significance in the granting of official prizes in the context of the myth-making enterprise was the City of Hamburg's commemoration of the Nazi saint, Dietrich Eckart, with a prize in his name to the tune of 10,000 RM—to be paid every second year on May 1, the national holiday of the German people. All fellow Germans who had distinguished themselves in the service of the Nazi *Volksgemeinschaft* in the arts and sciences qualified. Hundreds of competitions were also announced just for music.

Corporatively, Goebbels continued to subsidize serious music, even after he abolished the distinction between it and entertainment music as far as the distribution of royalties through Stagma was concerned. Special funds existed for deserving composers who could demonstrate economic hardship and were judged politically reliable. Thus, even the ex-Schönberg student Anton Webern was able to draw from the *Künstlerdank* fund. Large subsidies were also funded by Goebbels for prominent and politically committed composers who helped administer and evaluate these funds and competed for the awards. In 1942 Graener, Pfitzner, and Strauss received 6,000 RM each; Berger, David, Egk, Gerster, Kurt Hessenberg, Höffer, Höller, Joseph Marx,

Pepping, von Reznicek, Trapp, Weissmann and Zilcher each 4,000 RM; Bresgen, Distler, Fortner, Genzmer, Grabner, Knab, Gottfried Müller, Orff, Kurt Rasch, Friedrich Redinger, Georg Schumann, Thiessen and Trunk each 2,000 RM; and von Borck, Chemin-Petit, Frommel and Kornauth each 1,000 RM. Thus, Germany's composer elite was encouraged to express gratitude and contribute creatively to the search for a new Nazi music.[62]

Apart from these RMK administered grants, the cities, *Gaue*, stages, political organizations, festivals and the national leadership announced various kinds of competitions in behalf of the effort to foster compositional enterprise. In August 1933, Fritz Stege had urged the creation of prizes in the cities and towns throughout Germany in order to break the monopoly of the metropolitan centers. The rejuvenation of music had to take placed in the localities within the Reich, he had reasoned, and needed to encompass all forms of musical expression and categories.[63] Düsseldorf offered an annual prize of 5,000 RM for a "native German composition" for which all "German Aryan composers" qualified. Frankfurt subsidized Egk; Dresden, Gottfried Müller; Vienna, Orff; Nuremberg, Hans Grimm; the list is endless. Leipzig established a Bach competition, Vienna instituted prizes in honor of Bruckner, Beethoven, and Schubert, and von Schirach and Hans Frank competed with Goebbels as patrons of creative musicians. The DAF announced competitions for compositions honoring Labor, while the SA, the NSLB, the ASKG and other party organizations vied with Germany's stages with commissions—all designed to satisfy economic needs of the composers, to establish each sponsor's reputation as a patron of "immortal music" and to promote the search for the artwork of the future. Hitler himself offered a national prize for the best folk song composed in Germany, which was to inspire the serious composers and complement the work of the masters of the past. Goebbels kept track of all the awards, and in order to bring order to their proliferation he announced in January, 1939 that his concurrence had to be secured for any award above 2,000 RM. He also sponsored many competitions himself, particularly when he needed a composition for a specific purpose, such as the music to accompany the radio announcement of the Russian invasion (See above), songs for distracting from negative war news, etc. He also asserted his position as a patron when he announced at the Reich Music Festival in Düsseldorf in 1938 a 20,000 RM award for outstanding performers—10,000 RM each for the best pianist and violinist.[64] One year later he established a National Competition for Composers (15,000 RM), after he had announced several commissions at the 1939 Reich Music Festival which went to Egk (10,000 RM) for a new opera, and to Theodor Berger and Paul Höffer 5,000 RM each for instrumental works.

Music festivals like the *Tonkünstlerfest* of the ADMV had been traditional forums for the promotion of new compositions, but, in the Third Reich, around seventy traditional in addition to new festivals of all sorts were drawn into the general Nazi state pageantry. Prizes, for instance, were awarded annually at the "solemn festivities of the Party Congress of the NSDAP." Also, folk festivals and other party celebrations provided popular platforms for appropriate musical experiments. Just as the old masters were said to have expressed national feelings rooted in folk and peasant culture, so the new composers were to give expression to their relationship to the people. Naturally, the Nazis manipulated the so-called "folk festivals" for propagandistic purposes, as each member of the creative community served as medium and celebrated object of propaganda. In turn, the festivals of rooted creativity and group solidarity would reinforce Nazi consciousness. The Central Cultural Office of the Party (Hauptkulturamt) and the Recreation Office at the Rosenberg Bureau collaborated in the publication of "The new Community-Party Archives for National Socialist Festivities and Recreation" and the KdF, Office of Recreation, RMVP, RJF, Reich Nourishment, Women of the DAF, the DAF, the Study Group of German Folk Studies, and Berlin, o.J. jointly produced "Festivals and Celebrations throughout the Year." The collaboration of so many major cultural organizations in Germany testified to the significance attributed to formal folk festivities, at which the myth of a new people's community was concretized. The new German leadership identified itself in these festivals as guardians of people's culture. Commentators noted the revival of singing in public places and the streets and the frequenting of existing theaters and other formal institutions by people who had not previously done so. The party claimed credit for having started a genuine people's movement, which would revive the creation of works equal to those of the great masters[65]—even though such public professions were contradicted by the statements at the confidential Culture-Political Press Conferences at least by mid-1936, as we have seen.

Notwithstanding the crucial reservations about a new Nazi musical art form, the public line was propagated with great enthusiasm. The people were to sing and dance again. All "alien" and "degenerate" features of song and dance were to be purged; ethnic communal and group dancing were promoted instead, while modern dancing in pairs was denounced.[66] All musical activities at the popular and folk level were legally defined by Hoffmann, to whom a "folk festival" epitomized the new order, involving song and dance of, and for, all the people and was to be distinguished from official peasant or patriotic festivities and local religious or class celebrations. A genuine folk festival had to conform to völkisch definition and to exclude not alone "alien" but also serious music, for being incompatible with its gay atmosphere. These folk festivals were also distinguished from national holidays. General holidays addressed by the law of February 27, 1934 (Paragraph 6) were classified as either national or Christian, the latter further broken down between the Reformation festivals of Protestants and the Corpus Christi of the Catholic community. Of the three national holidays, the Day of Hero Commemoration (*Heldengedenktag*) was not defined as a folk festival, but a day of national mourning and concern, while May 1 and the Harvest Thanksgiving (*Erntedankfest*) had to be celebrated in spacious public places. In all cases admission was to be free. Christian festivals also were to be distinguished from all others, thought of as neither national nor of the people, being too serious (even if expressing joyous religious occasions), and they were officially restricted to the Church and family, not to the people. While these official festivals of the people were national affairs, folk music, as such, was actually administered by the RMK under section D. In general, the Nazis organized and manipulated folk music as part of their cult of the peasant, of rootedness and tradition—an essential feature of their officially projected national community.

An important feature of the myth of community was the Hitler cult, which assumed proportions unthinkable in a non-totalitarian society. All myth-making and propagandistic activity contributed to this cult of the leader which, in turn, helped mold the music world, like all of Germany, into a unified body of believers. Embodying the essence of totalitarianism, Hitler aspired to supremacy even in the arts. The symbolic association of politics with music through official tunes—reserved strictly for the leader in the case of the *Badenweiler Marsch*, the National Anthem, and the Horst-Wessel song, which was not allowed to be performed at public coffee houses and other places of entertainment[67]—was concentrated on this one person who commissioned not only the politicians of the realm but also musicians. Music was directly composed for the solemn occasions of Nazi pageantry, rallies and conventions, composers dedicating so-called "consecration fanfares," inauguration fanfares, cantatas, oratorios and flag songs to the *Führer*. Hitler's person assumed an importance formerly reserved for religous leaders and heroes of the past, like those appearing in Wagner's music dramas. That association with Wagner was not lost upon fellow Germans, and the direct allusion to the god-figure of Wagner in Hitler's flight through the clouds in the film *Triumph of the Will*, was addressed to the millions in awe of the god in an airplane. The Hitler cult served the important purpose of assuring common and uniform leadership to all Germans. The creation of the myth attested to the realization of the leadership principle, managed by Goebbels and programmed to check all disintegrating tendencies within the Nazi movement itself and within the great variety of Nazi organizations.

Hitler manipulated and was featured in the all-encompassing cult of the

Third Reich. The music journals, biographies, and musical works portrayed a great man possessed of a gentle side, which found expression in his love for music. Music became sacred through association with him, while he gained the blessing of a tradition of profoundest German spiritual content. Referred to as savior of the art, he was given a free hand in the area of culture. All past efforts of German heroes were redefined as pioneering work. In this manner Hitler was related to past heroes like Bismarck, Frederick the Great and Wagner, only to be elevated above them. Stories were told of his having suffered hunger in order to be able to attend Mozart or Wagner performances. The frequency of his concert attendance also was a matter of record; he was said to have gone to between thirty and forty *Tristan* performances alone in Vienna. What psycho-historians treat as evidence of his infantile traits, evidenced also in the complete reading of Karl May and authors of heroic epics,[68] the Nazi press treated as fanaticism, in that positive sense decreed in offical Nazi language. Even as Chancellor he was said to have crowned a day of hard work with attentive appreciation of chamber music or an evening of lieder.[69] Accounts of Hitler's musicality alone could fill volumes, some of which were at odds with those of unfriendly observers who noted, for instance, that Hitler liked opera, but that he never much cared for symphonic music, and certainly did not attend chamber music performances. His musicality amounted to the humming of melodies, Rauschning recalled.

The reality of the Third Reich did not tolerate accounts of Hitler's infantile traits, monomaniacal and pathological character, and the limits of his interests and capacities. It is, of course, difficult to assess to what degree the uniform propagandistic line was really accepted by German musicians and the music public. But the musical expression of the community was documented, as was the support of the cult of German values, of music defined as German and the evocation of heroes in Wagner's dramas, which were identified with Hitler as inspiration for future German generations and for a new music. Hitler was the bridge between the subjects of German epics and the musical past, and the grandeur which was to be the new Germany of a thousand years. The new musician and the new music were to emerge from the musical expressions of the time and an education which was solidly rooted in the Nazi *Weltanschauung*.[70]

Nowhere was the Hitler cult, the myth of the folk-musical community and Nazi aesthetics as consistently propagated and securely rooted as in the younger generation of musicians who were educated in Rust's schools, the academies, and the HJ by *völkisch* educators, who even in general education featured music as an attractive participatory medium for the propagation of national identity and loyalty to the state. HJ leaders never tired of boasting of HJ group solidarity, devotion to the *Führer* and idealistic commitment to a new Nazi society, including a new music which was rooted in the folk song but was also forward-looking. The HJ sang the national songs, joined in musical groups and produced its own composers. The RJF organized the enthusiasm, attracted excellent teachers, commissioned compositions, which it published in addition to songs and recordings, and secured time on the radio for its programs. It sponsored the publication of *völkisch*-Nazi aesthetics and musicological conclusions drawn from race theory about the characteristics of the German folk song—about tonality, the major mode, the triad and the preeminence of melody—which were to guide the composers of commissioned music: Cesar Bresgen, Georg Blumensaat, Wolfgang Fortner, Gerhard Maasz, Helmut Majewski, Heinrich Spitta and many others. Their marches, songs, festival music, cantatas, soldier songs, secular Christmas songs and folk dances were performed and published in books which included altered pieces of the great masters. This musical product satisfied an immediate need of the Nazi state and conformed to the propagated standards; it also constituted the folk musical basis for a new art music. The higher music culture was to find inspiration in the folk culture of the HJ.

While the HJ marched to its own music, which it believed to conform to music theory, the ideas about music were neither universally taught nor did they lack controversy. The influential music pedagogue, Guido Waldmann, noted in 1937 in *Musik und Volk* that race theory was not yet generally taught, in spite of Hitler's observation that "the blood and race doctrines of the National Socialist movement will cause new insights into the history of the past and the future." He wondered to what extent musicology had responded to the demands of adjusting research to the principles of blood and race, and deplored the apparent infrequent and unenthusiastic response exemplified in the publications these past years, few of which actually dealt with the topic of "race and music," and those which did appear bore the same old names, generally of non-musicians.[71] Notwithstanding Waldmann's criticism, of course, race theory had become part of general music education, but, increasingly, Third Reich commentators insisted on a more technical, scholarly and thorough approach to their subject. The *völkisch* generalizing no longer satisfied the new school of musicology, which demanded thorough research in support of basic Nazi assumptions. One expert, the musicologist Friedrich Blume of the University of Berlin, also criticized the level of race consciousness in music education at the above mentioned Reich Music Festival in 1938, as based on feeling and instinct, although general theory had advanced to the point of being ready for practical application on sound methodological principles. Nonetheless, he admitted that scientifically the relationship between music and race "is not yet fully understood." Race was to be regarded as a fundamental principle, an axiom in the construction of general music theory.

Music education was to prepare for this fundamental understanding and the feeling of German music as the expression of German blood and race, and as the repository of what was referred to as *Heimatgefühl* (feeling for home, country, native setting). He insisted that scientific race research, in combination with traditional methods of musicology, was essential for the creation of a new German musician.[72]

German music instructors espoused their race doctrines in a credible manner, being rooted in their *völkisch* background and in the racial anthropology current before the advent of Nazism. Many teachers seemed to have been devoted to the new science, and the more fanatic encouraged greater effort in research as a means of support for basic assumptions. This concerted effort of education bore one fruit in a *Habilitationsschrift*, presented at the University of Leipzig in 1939 by a student of philosophy on the "Typology of Musical Talent in the German People." Of special interest was the conviction and the total acceptance of the new race science as the author reviewed the general works of race expert Eichenauer and the Bible of racial anthropology, the standard and popular racial anthropology, *Rassenkunde des deutschen Volkes*, by Hans F.K. Günther. While Günther, the recipient of the Science Prize at the Party Congress, 1935, was cited as basic authority, Eichenauer was subjected to attacks on grounds of an overemphasis on intuitive conclusions and a "methodological pessimism" which do not sufficiently allow for an absolute and scientific approach to musical phenomena in racial terms.[73] Other dissertations were published on Bach as German and Mendelssohn as Jew, on the anti-Semitism of German heroes in the past, and on the various racial manifestations in spirit and music. In circles of racial anthropology it was assumed that the science was in its beginning phase, that familiarity with the classic authorities, such as Günther, Clauss and Eichenauer, was a necessity, and that true science would ultimately replace the, at times, intuitive and "instinctual" deductions arrived at on the basis of observation.

Search for the New Music

Actual composition was understood as the acid test of theory: thus, the attention paid to the compositions of Gottfried Müller, whose *Deutsches Heldenrequium* or the latest opera in 1938 of Werner Egk, *Peer Gynt* promised the sought-after Nazi synthesis. From the experimental laboratory of the composer would have to emerge the anticipated new music as an expression of Goebbels' "romanticism of steel"—a kind of Nazi realism, perhaps—beyond the folk and classical forms applied to Nazi texts of the early Nazi period and to the satisfaction of not only party enthusiasts but also of the musical and critical elite. The search for the new music after 1936, which would be rooted and again relate to the community, was no longer restricted to *völkisch* composers but involved the entire spectrum of compositional activity, as everybody had learned to rationalize composition in Nazi terms, either (1) by explicit texts or (2) by reference to the spiritual experience said to be captured in the musical work. While the composers wrote music, the critics formulated theory which continued to evolve in context of the review of musical offerings. Therefore, any assessment of actual musical production, in light of the search for the art work of the future had to reflect both the concrete musical works and accompanying interpretations. While no serious composition escaped ideologically-informed critique, the major ones— especially operas—were evaluated as possible expressions of the new music. The mandate for composers was clear. At the first congress of the corporate profession of the composers of the RMK held at Schloss Burg on the Wupper, in May of 1936, Hinkel had acknowledged accomplishment in organization: "The Reich profession of German composers has been formed and is marching and living as a battalion of creative German musicians. This group must be conscious of its role in the creation of future German music." "Moreover, German composers derive an extra responsibility from the fact that our people are led by a great statesman who is also the first artist of the German nation." In response the composers sent a telegram to their *Führer*, "the first artist of the German nation," whom they were "ever-ready to serve faithfully"—signed by "Paul Graener, in the name of the Reich Professional organization of composers in the RMK."[74]

The state had indeed created the conditions for musical output—6165 works were published in 1936[75]—but, in the context of commission, accommodation, and subordination to culture-political program, the composers had to violate the tradition of musical autonomy and the most recent level of the historically evolved musical material. As the avant-garde was purged, the published and performed music by and large conformed to traditional and *völkisch* standards, which communicated, to be sure, but did not express new forms. Yet, the Nazis also rejected the materialist theory about an inner dynamic of music that compels generational adjustment; they repeated *völkisch* slogans instead, on the priority of experience, and denounced liberals who theorized and defined before experiencing and creating. In reality, of course, the Nazis also began with definitions, as when the composer Hans Uldall wrote in 1937 that "the ideological foundation will give direction and purpose to artistic creativity, guiding it into healthy and practical paths. Through the set delimitations, the creative impulse will receive tremendous encouragement . . . Art in the service of an idea has always been a fruitful undertaking." The collaborating composers willingly accepted Nazi programs in reaction to what they perceived as the impasse of modern music. By an act of will, the acknowledged problems inherent in the development of twentieth-century music were eliminated. An assumed archaic unity, once lost, then seemingly recreated in the Wagnerian art work but out of reach in the contemporary setting, was offered again to an idealistic generation. If traditional conservatives were skeptical about political solutions to system-immanent problems, withdrawing into their music instead in "inner emigration," younger composers like Gottfried Müller had no such compunctions. Yet, the new generation could do no better than reflect the idealist-regressive language of earlier *völkisch* critics, and Uldall conceded that "the idea determines the purpose of the composition, and purpose creates form. We are still looking for new forms which will truly reflect the spirit of our time, but we are aware of something new emerging, in the festive and solemn musicals, open-air and band festivals, mass choruses, youth music festivals and folk instrumental musicals, events in which the young musician can talk to his fellow Germans." The composer concluded that:

> the new attitude toward music will be of decisive significance in its historical development. Polemics concerning melody, harmony, polyphony, tonality and atonality are of comparatively slight importance. Stylistic movements as reflection of value judgment, such as romanticism, new realism, neo-classicism or even new spiritualism, will exist as categories only in the minds of a few anachronistic intellectuals. In the future, German music can be described as either good or bad.[76]

The direction of a potentially new music culture reflected in the above statement was urged upon noted members of the traditional mold. The one-time musical revolutionary Strauss was encouraged to compose a Nazi-realist music drama, in spite of the reservations he had demonstrated in relationship to the new order. We can assume that this talented craftsman could have produced a monumental oratorio closely observing technical specifications and celebrating the dawn of a new civilization. Instead, he produced a comedy, *Arabella*, and *Die schweigsame Frau* in 1933, a one-act opera *Friedenstag*, premiered at the Munich State Opera, and *Daphne* at the Dresden Opera, both in 1938—an output obviously not so useful in the context of the war plans of the time. He did not lend himself to the new spirit, notwithstanding a late trend away from his revolutionary and morally shocking phases. Also, the seasoned Julius Weismann and Ermanno Wolf-Ferrari produced successful operas which neither reflected nor had a bearing on the new age. The new mood of enthusiasm, momentum and regimentation had to find new sources, although traditional concepts of Germanic and naturalistic programs were maintained as a starting point. The young hoped to be able to create something new through adherence to *völkisch* principles, dialectically overcoming the modernistic phase which in Germany had characterized music in the twentieth century up to 1933.

In order to find the way back to the *völkisch* tradition, the state encouraged a revival of composition locally throughout Germany, as we have seen. Again we are reminded of Fritz Stege's suggestion back in 1933, calling for "decentralization," so that

the fate of music will not be decided behind the walls of the metropolis but in the arena of the nature-bound and thus more original countryside. Gone are the times in which locomotives, iron-foundries or other typical products of the metropolis set the standards for actively creative musicians. The generation of future composers will turn to higher, immortal ideals. Its gaze will no longer be focused on select, big-city social strata but on an entire people, the whole nation.[77]

This was the language of the old *völkisch* critic. Modern civilization was rejected, in this case, in favor of the manipulated folk song, which reflected a simpler life, though somehow transformed and updated by Goebbels' slogan of "romanticism of steel"—a *völkisch*-Nazi synthesis. Naturally, serious music, rooted in the great German tradition of symphonic music, opera, music drama, choral works and chamber music, resisted external control. Greatness was the result of a long tradition, sheltered within the system of a benevolent social paternalism and upheld in the historically evolved musical institutions of Germany.

Understanding of this history and the creative process ought to have cautioned against the imposition of a sociopolitical revolutionary program upon the artistic mind, which must insist on the freedom to be responsive to the inherent dynamics of its medium. The pre-1933 dialogue between conservatives and progressive musicians had been the consequence of a variety of tensions in artistic, as well as in social and ideological expression, one of them being the free and immanent unfolding of musical development. Although the functional, tendentious, ornamental or extra-musical program could be created in response to dictation, enforced reactions against modernistic trends alone were not able to resolve crisis and produce a new music. Notwithstanding these reservations, which were indeed expressed in the professional journals, especially after 1936, the serious sector of music was asked to write new music in a traditional idiom for the new society to the point, that is, of cutting out the most recent component which, after all, had become to some degree part of tradition. The heritage of select great masters, from Weber and Wagner to the contemporary Pfitzner and Graener, was to serve as the incentive toward a meaningful symphonia of the people.

Serious music resisted other aspects of National Socialism as well, as it traditionally belonged to the elite of the community. The Nazis, from Hitler down to the *Gauleiter* who shouted during the Richard Wagner Festival in 1935, "Your Nuremberg is our Nuremberg," however, identified with the people and imposed manipulated popular taste and standards upon music. Although a Third Reich, more extended in time, might have allowed for the fulfillment of some theoretical demands, in that the revolutionary period would most likely have been succeeded by normalized conditions, in which conscious imposition of non-musical ideas would have been transformed into subconscious presupposition, in the attempt of immediate wish-fulfillment the musicians and the cultural administration learned that the sublime will not submit, nor can it respond positively to, dictates from below or from above—a view, again, articulated by critics and musicians after 1936 which resulted in ideological compromise and reflected official pragmatism.

If, in the case of serious music—"the profoundest manifestation of the German spirit"—the creative process itself resisted extra-musical pressure, entertainment music posed no such problems, since its composers did not feel bound to difficult and controversial developments and readily utilized proven popular forms of expression. As we have seen above, the hit song industry played a progressively important role in Goebbels' scheme of entertaining and indoctrinating the nation. Hit songs conformed to Nazi demands; their musical forms had evolved away from anathemized jazz and jazz-derivatives to acceptable waltzes, the foxtrot and tango already before 1933, while texts and personnel were purged in 1933 in accordance with policy. The music of operettas also did not require surgery, although the repertoire was purged by more than a half[78] due to the significant Jewish contribution to that field and the fact that the entire genre was suspect as a typical Weimar expression of negativity—which, no matter how innocent and arguably affirmative in its light and good-humoured criticism and satire which confirmed establishment authority and values, offended philistine propounders of *völkisch* principles. The list of dismissals from positions, emigration, and cases of concentration camp internment and murder was a long one for composers and authors of this light venue, including such well-known composers as Paul Abraham, Leo Ascher, Ralph Benatzky, Emmerich Kalman and Oscar Strauss and librettists Robert Gilbert, Fritz Grünbaum and Fritz Löhner. Even Franz Lehar, the composer of Hitler's favorite operetta, *The Merry Widow*, though willing to collaborate, faced opposition during the early years of the regime until his later rehabilitation.

Significantly, operetta had the function to entertain, as was customary, but also to propagate *völkisch*-Nazi characters and values and to inspire the composer and librettist of serious music. This manipulated realm of stylized entertainment reflected Nazi cultural policy, general propaganda, and the realities of musical life like few other cultural media. Ingrid Grünberg focuses her analysis of the operetta in Nazi Germany in the context of significant historical developments on the pace-setting Metropol Theatre in Berlin, where the chief operetta ideologist, director Heinz Hentsche—whose name has become synonymous with the genre of the era—and his star text author, Günter Schwenn, and several composers like Fred Raymond and Will Meisel produced at least one operetta per year which was then performed throughout Germany—a major feature of popular musical activity: *Lauf ins Glück* (1934) celebrated love, athletics and heroic virtues two years before the Olympics; *Auf grosser Fahrt* (1936) focused on the honor of a Nordic girl, on the love of homeland and on other heroic qualities of the representative leading couple. In that pivotal year, on May 10, 1936 the City Stage of Dortmund premiered Hugo Lammerhirt's operetta, *Das glückhafte Schiff*, described by the composer as a "KdF-steamer" which transported fun-loving German vacationers in the manner of the American TV program, "Love Boat"—"the height of Nazi ideology on the music stage," in the words of Prieberg.[79] In the year of the invasion of Poland, *Die oder Keine* (1939) contained themes of racism and colonialism to the accompaniment of light music and in the form of farce; and in the days when Germany was establishing dominion over much of western Europe, *Frauen im Metropol* (1940) celebrated bravery in typically good-humored form and tone. While operettic characters and texts generally conformed to "National Socialist realism" and advertised the military virtues of honor, loyalty, and sacrifice as well as themes of war, struggle and domination—all in good fun—the music of operettas was consistently traditional and appropriately entertaining.[80]

The ideologists wrote much about this and other forms of popular music, which was assumed to be responsive to the very popular taste to which it catered. The public and musical circles were told that the great music of the past had also reflected popular roots and taste which were identified with the folk elements in classical music and thus were dignified, and that an indifference to popular demands would further alienate serious music, which would continue to stagnate—an argument to which not only *völkisch*-Nazi musicians would be responsive. That was the dictatorship's rationale as it undermined the previously autonomous establishment, reflecting and manipulating popular taste in music, to which it then alluded in justifying the purges of "alienated" and alien music and musicians, and imposing rooted

German standards. Confident of popular support in its interpretation of sophisticated art music, the authorities regimented, commissioned, and flattered the composers of light music. This concern for music for immediate consumption and gratification—*Gebrauchsmusik*—was not new, as it reflected music's traditional situation subject to market-manipulating forces in the context of social affirmation and musical reaction, as well as being expressed in the form of socialist realism.

In addition to the popular music performed in public by professionals and heard over the radio, music for the home and amateurs also concerned the regime, as the actively involved people would be rendered even more receptive to indoctrination. Krenek, Weill and Hindemith similarly had attempted to involve the public in music-making. Hindemith especially strove to create functional music and has been rebuked for his violation of the "demand of the historically-evolved musical material" by apologists of the avant-garde, like Theodor W. Adorno. Hindemith appealed to the great German tradition— as he saw it—in which music had always performed a non-musical, social role. His attempt to revive the folk element in modern terms, sensitive to demands of modern musical and social developments and newly conditioned expectations, came close to *völkisch* aesthetics in a nonpoliticized world. It is ironic that Hindemith shared fundamental concerns with Peter Raabe and other Nazi officials, some of whom persecuted him. Hindemith's explicit condemnation of a bookburning in his opera, *Mathis der Maler*—to be performed at the Berlin State Opera, where only months earlier, on May 10, 1933, the actual burning of books had taken place, was an affront which resulted in the ban of a work that, even though conceived in the service of traditional humanist values of artistic integrity and autonomy, might have been appropriated and celebrated by the regime as a version of the desired new musical synthesis.

Advocates of popular music were intimidated by the *völkisch* campaign in the early years of the regime, but increasingly asserted their claims for appropriate consumption and recognition with reference to their entertainment and political functions. They and Goebbels knew that they enjoyed the support of actual rather than the rhetorical proponents of Nazi propaganda. The composer/conductor Siegfried Scheffler further tried to dignify entertainment music by referring to its search for new forms—in distinction to "serious" music which, to him, was rooted in an established tradition. Might the new art music emerge from the workshop of skilled practitioners, who, more than other professionals, know the pulse of their public? Scheffler realized the importance of popular music within the scheme of Nazi populism as well as Goebbels' objectives, and he welcomed its "moral obligation" and its effectiveness.[81]

Naturally, the desirable entertainment music had to correspond to *völkisch* specifications. The HJ joined the other party organizations in giving advice to composers of entertainment music, "enjoining all comrades to contribute to the creation of a new and strictly native type of social music."[82] Also, the official RMK bulletin repeatedly warned composers against the bad habit of including bits of foreign languages in the texts of popular music. Jazz was denounced throughout the Third Reich. Goebbels himself stressed the support of national sentiment in 1940, "particularly in time of war."[83]

Official and professional views were published in a professional journal, *Die Unterhaltungsmusik*, which enjoyed wide circulation, reported on ideological questions, organizational measures and technical details of the broad range of organization of music for cafe, dance, film, bar-room and other sorts of entertainment. The composers of this medium convened occasionally, discussed their affairs and received the latest official version of their function in the new society. Official sentiments were echoed in the SA-journal, *Der SA Mann*, September 18, 1937, in an article taking issue with the "afternoon tea and dance" customs reported in the feuilleton section of the Berlin daily, the *12-Uhr Blatt*. The German reader was told that this particular form of entertainment and recreation of tea and dance must be rejected by all fellow Germans, as it "came to us from England, where it is already a degenerate social form." Dance was to be preserved in the German tradition. As late as 1937 "one dances swing—one hears of the latest hits and learns to recognize all the famous dance orchestras," a sad enough situation, aggravated by the fact that this "choppy, noisy, meaningless squeaking" was described as good music. The artist had to reestablish ties with his people and to be responsive to the folk song and folk dance rhythm of the people. However, the composer of this genre was not to be restricted

> to taking over national and *völkisch* national types; he had to find and develop new forms and melodies in the genre of the folk song and the folk dance. The German people urgently need this light music. One cannot listen to Beethoven, Bach, or Handel every hour of the day. For that one goes to the concert hall, not to the coffeehouse. . . . We, the people of Beethoven, Bach, Mozart, Haydn and Handel, cannot and will no longer allow one of the noblest flowers of cultural life to fall increasingly victim to degeneration and to ultimate degradation to satisfy the demands of big-city night clubs and international bordellos.[84]

Now, in the National Socialist revolution, wrote *Die Musik* on "Social Dance as Expression of German Posture," Germans were about to rediscover themselves in dance, especially in traditional forms in which the "male dances with the sword, staff and other effects," in which

> all movement is characteristically restrained and controlled, the virtuo-
> sity of the individual being transformed in soldiery conformity with the
> movement of the comrades. The clear expression of cultivated German
> dance forms manifests the same force which determines German history
> and ethics, that of planning and organization.

Thus, German nature was to be rediscovered in the richness of its folk-cultural
expression and beauty, as demonstrated in the dance of Munich gymnasts
and leaders of the SS-unit *Deutschland*, appointed by the SS Reich Leader
at the Reich Convention of the NSKG.[85] Young Germany participated and
was to discover new forms. Conscious of the tradition and Nazi standards
and demands, steps were taken to guarantee native dance, in the form of
the "Reich Educational Week for Group Dancing," organized in 1938 by the
recreational department of the NSKG, the KdF, RMVP, RJF, and the
Reichsnährstand ("Reich Agricultural Production"), with participants from all
forty German *Gaue* and strong response in the HJ, the SA and the SS.[86]

Yet, when Peter Raabe visited performers in their bars, cafes and other
amusement centers in 1939, he saw and heard things which did not correspond to "the policies of the *Führer*." He was offended by the sight of "pairs
pushing each other with deadly serious and painful expressions in cramped
rooms." He saw a "man with an instrument unknown to him in grotesque
leaps and contortions." Walter Abendroth commented that "we have to agree
with Peter Raabe: such exotic form of entertainment is not German; and it—
the unmistakable portion of a sick, disappearing time—should no longer be
tolerated in Germany."[87]

All native expressions of light and folk music and dance were to entertain the people, contribute to the shaping of a new national community, and
inspire the serious composer, who would be expected to assimilate these
popular/folk sounds into his new music. The same objectives pertained to
military and band music. Brass bands had previously been associated with
the military, whereas after 1933 countless bands were formed in the HJ, SA,
SS, NSKK and other party formations, fashioned in the image of the German
military musical tradition which, of course, preserved its own musical tradition in active participation. Many young musicians joined military music
organizations, learned their trade, while actively participating in an important area of music life, and prepared for a musical career upon discharge.
In view of the projection of a new society with its own music, the military
tradition must be added to the folk song, popular music, and fighting song
and dance as indispensable features of an active musical life which com-

plemented the existing literature and performance of the prestigious art music, thus constituting the background and source material without which Nazi theory would not have been consistent. In this realm of applied music, Nazi anticipations were not outrageously optimistic.

The National Socialist Masterwork of the Future

Thus we arrive at the creative activities of the composers of serious (classical) music, who faced the extraordinary problem of having to respond to a mandate which was defined on principles external to the musical dynamic itself, and with reference to popular culture. We have already noted that ideologues continued to insist throughout the Third Reich that new music and the music offerred in German concert halls reflect the standards of the Nazi order and, even though the amount of party dedication and overt Nazi works in the realm of serious music declined by 1936—dismissed in part as "national *Kitsch*," the genre survived as an expression of the musicalized nation at the many party and state functions, as well as on German concert stages. However, we have also noted a significant shift in orientation of the musical establishment itself, which by 1936 reasserted itself within bounds and thus complemented Goebbels' growing appreciation of a broader cultural facade than that offered by *völkisch* supporters. The compositional and performance reality, therefore, was a mix of two worlds which coexisted, but also variously overlapped. While both realms were subjected to endless ideological scrutiny and official manipulation, composers of serious music from all factions contributed to the search for new forms, rationalized to varying degrees in terms of official norms.

While the demand for music and musical output in all areas of high art music was enormous during the Third Reich, composers and critics of note acknowledged the problems inherent in the creative enterprise. Ideologues continued to believe that only when all the people participate, when the culture-political goals of National Socialism were realized, would art-music reflect its German nature and tradition. Meanwhile, young composers were to find inspiration at the mass festivals of the new state, which posed as protector of the new mass civilization. At the party conventions over a thousand musicians were used in demonstration of these principles and for obvious propagandistic and acoustic effects. As in all massive Nazi demonstrations, formulators of this version of a new music culture aimed at the elimination of finer sensibilities. Pure and imposing sound was important, and all individual identity was to be submerged in the chorus of massive oneness. It is interesting that even the organizers of the musical program for the party convention of 1938 acknowledged failure in the attempt to integrate the human voice in a chorus of 1,600 members for mass effect. The voice apparently did not lend itself to these massive sound demonstrations as readily as brass instruments, which were more adaptable to the physical and light displays of the day.[88]

If the massive open-air rituals like the *Thing* theatre at the Grünewald, then called Dietrich Eckart-Stage, and other open-air multi-media efforts had not already suffered setbacks and cuts in support by 1936—reflecting top-level policy shift—the war gradually terminated these light-and-sound events, as well as the Party Congress rituals. A victim of the cutbacks also were the electronic musical instruments of Friedrich Trautwein, whose designs of massive loudspeaker towers, tested by Telefunken,[89] were a response to sound limitations experienced at other open-air rituals. Nonetheless, *völkisch* ideologues continued to insist that the people were there to sing and that the classical composer would learn from the experience. "All the people can participate," wrote one enthusiast, "We no longer stand outside of official music, we no longer fight as base competitors, we belong, we are a people also in music. . . We have the folk singing already. The performing folk will be the salvation of the concert stage"[90]—the myth survived to the bitter end.

Thus, the composer received his mandate from the people, in the service of which he was to realize his native creative impulse. He was to cut the roots of his immediate background, the modern situation in music, and find new ways of reflecting the monumental events of the times and charting new forms. "In the beginning stood the deed, not theory, of the musicologist,"[91] uttered one proponent of musical discontinuity. Yet, the purging and uprooting of undesirable music had proceeded under music-external authority. At best, the symptoms of the crisis in music had been removed and the ideologue was hoping for national regeneration as a precondition for a new music. But the possibility that "progressive deviation"—the symptom—which had evolved naturally from within musical development, might take a turn toward a new synthesis was denied. Meanwhile, Germany's leading composers of the "progressive" school were no longer around, nor were they heard in Germany. Schönberg, Hindemith, Bartók, Stravinsky, Křenek, Weill, Toch and others worked abroad and many promising students had followed their masters into exile. "Racially alien" and other ideologically defined elements of degeneracy, materialism, intellectualism, etc., were eliminated as a precondition of the new order and new music. Recent levels of expanded tonal possibilities—termed atonal—were rejected because atonality, Rosenberg said, "contradicts the rhythm of blood and soul of the German people." Thus, "German music is not again to become mere play on sound, a sport of dissonance," which had formerly led to the "prostitution of harmony and chaos of form."

Indicative of the transition, according to Walter Abendroth in his commentary, the various "conscious emanations of the disintegrating spirit" have been conquered by "our *völkisch* awakening." The former, represented at the international music festivals of modern music in Donaueschingen and Baden-Baden, with which Hindemith was associated, had been "dedicated to the destruction of all notions of blood- and folk-dependent art." Abendroth rejected internationalism as a symbol of a "declining *Zeitgeist*." He welcomed instead a reconstituted International Festival of Modern Music at Baden-Baden under new management, at which "representatives of different nationalities emphasized their distinct folk characters." He announced in 1936 that "pure atonality lay buried, appearing as old-fashioned when occasionally still heard."[92] Abendroth would write similarly after 1945, when he noted that National Socialism simply had reinforced the decline of "modernist" music which had begun before 1933.[93]

Internationalism complemented individualism, which also was anathema to *völkisch* theorists and was identified with Schönberg who, to the Church musician Otto Brodde, in 1937, had developed his own esoteric circle in place of the people. Indeed, individualism expressed the alienation of music from the national community. While Brodde still looked forward to a new age of musical creativity, he felt that the political and social revolution under National Socialism had created its precondition.[94]

Notwithstanding totalitarian controls, the seduction, intimidation and indoctrination of a collaborating profession, compositions and even expressions of theory were not uniform. In the search for new music some theorists violated official canons and allowed for the existence of even "atonal music," as long as its creator invented genuine musical themes which were systematically developed. In most cases, however, the efforts were deemed fruitless, since critics declared this music to be generally responsive only to the dictates of the mind, requiring great technical mastery, while leaving the general musical sense empty and the public dissatisfied. One such composition, a "Missa brevis" by Hermann Reutter, op. 33—a chamber music work for voice, violin and cello broadcast by the *Norddeutscher Rundfunk* back in 1933—was typically slandered as "bolshevism in music." The critic in the *Völkischer Beobachter* wrote that "in the field of instrumental music, composers might adhere to certain modern directions, but in the case of the rendition of a text. . . . more than purely musical-technical play is required." The part for voice was judged much too difficult, and much of the remainder of the work "a confusion of tone-sequence in which musical licentiousness celebrates real orgies." The ear was said to be tortured and the listener would finally rebel against the expectation of still recognizing this as music. The critic suspected that "this work intentionally rejected all of the past and that the musical laws of structure, form, melody, harmony and treatment of text were consciously relegated to the junk room."[95]

The philistine voice had found official organs of expression. Yet, Reutter managed to maintain his stature during the Third Reich, enjoyed Hans Hinkel's protection, became director of the Hochsche Conservatory in Frankfurt in 1936 and—continued to compose "atonal" music. In the early years of the Third Reich Erich Kleiber and Furtwängler were denounced for their performance of such "alien" and "decadent" music. Of course Kleiber then emigrated in protest over the Hindemith-Furtwängler affair and Furtwängler withdrew for a while from open confrontation. But, composition in the "modernist" mode continued throughout the Third Reich—marginally and without popular support—as an expression of the establishment's growing reassertion of authority by 1936, which corresponded to Goebbels' own pragmatism and accommodation, and as a result of official promotion of composition in general. Stages were encouraged to include compositions of living composers, and new works were indeed premiered which included, besides Nazi-inspired and ideologically neutral works, compositions in the modern idiom.

Apart from programs dedicated to the propagation of contemporary music at major and provincial stages—Prieberg lists 181 orchestras with 8918 musicians in 1940, of which 132 performed opera[96]—the regular repertoire included modernist experiments, of which we learn through the severe critique they were subjected to. Boris Blacher's orchestral-Capriccio, op. 4, presented by the NSKG in Berlin in 1935, for instance, was denounced by Stege as "un-German" and reminiscent of Stravinsky and Weill.[97] Similarly, Distler, Egk, Fortner, Orff, Ernst Rotter, Wagner-Régeny, Zillig and other innovators were criticized for an idiom held to be incompatible with the goals of the new order. Contemporary music festivals also continued to include previously denounced expressions of "musical bolshevism" in their offerings, even at the famous Baden-Baden festivals, where after 1936 with RMK support, besides German experimentalists Bartók, Stravinsky, Francesco Malipiero, Jean Françaix, Henri Barraud, Arthur Bliss, Marcel Delannoy and other international proponents of the new music were heard. Societies for the promotion of new music became more active again by 1935/36. In Berlin, a Society for Young Musicians organized by the pianist Agathe von Thiedemann, the RMK-sponsored chamber concerts of the Friendship Association of German Artists, and the Study Group of New Music of Hans-Joachim Koellreutter and later Dietrich Erdmann, offered compositions of young experimentalists, including foreign ones. The same commitment survived in Frankfurt, where a Study Group of New Music led by director Hans Meissner, Gerhard Frommel, Alfred Hoehn and the conductors Georg L. Jochum and Bertil Wetzelsberger merged into the Central Office for Contemporary Music under the guidance of Albert Richard Mohr of the Gau office of Hesse-Nassau. Similar societies existed in other cities like Essen, Nuremberg, and in Düsseldorf where a progressive regime promoted new music at the City Stage.[98] German audiences heard their own composers of contemporary music and international modernists. Interesting also was the German-Scandinavian Music Festival of Ernst Rössler and Gustav Scheck which, behind the Nordic label, offered "atonal" works of Fortner, Stravinsky, Hindemith and Rössler's own serialized compositions, which he even defended in print.[99] "Atonal" music was composed, performed—in small circles, to be sure—and criticized by Nazi theorists and provincial critics, while apologists sought to discover symptoms of new music which would be acceptable within the updated and more abstract formulations of Nazi music theory of post-1936.

As atonality survived, so was jazz heard throughout the Third Reich in live performances, over the airwaves, and on German and foreign recordings in various forms of popular expression and as an ingredient of classical music thereby contributing, ironically, to the search for the art work of the future. If atonality was associated with Jews, "Nigger-Jew jazz" was traced to the "blatant race mixing" of America and thus regarded as a major alien component of German music which was frequently confused with other expressions of an avowed "primitivism" in classical music and related types of light music. Jazz offended fascism with its improvisational freedom, its identification with blacks and Jews, its "chaotic" syncopated rhythm and anti-collectivist individualism. This was a genuine antipathy the Nazis shared with broad segments of the public and with Goebbels himself, who cared neither for jazz nor for contemporary classical music, as he confided repeatedly to his diary (on April 7, 1941, for instance) and to his associates. The victim of an incredible amount of polemical invective, jazz was formally banned from the airwaves on orders of the Reich Broadcasting Network, one month after the anti-Semitic Nuremberg Laws were announced in September 1935. Subject to similar prohibitions by local Nazi leaders and harassment by RMK officials appearing unannounced at public places of entertainment, a formal censorship board was instituted which defined and approved acceptable entertainment music for all radio stations. In practice, definitions varied and the regime actually vacillated between repression and toleration—variously even promoting its own version of softened and commercialized jazz performed by popular social band leaders like Barnabas von Géczy, Oskar Joost and, finally, by an official studio German Dance and Entertainment Orchestra under the baton of Franz Grothe.

The ideologues were of course furious over the violation of principle. Herbert Gerigk, for one, complained in 1938 that the German radio had never stopped playing alien jazz, while Peter Raabe was among RMK officials in search of the producers and consumers of the "forbidden fruit"[100] at the night clubs at night, in order to suppress them. Yet, Goebbels had other priorities, as he manipulated jazz for propaganda purposes and realized the necessity for catering to popular demand, in order to prevent German fans from listening to foreign jazz programs on radio, which also aired Allied propaganda.

The survival of jazz and Goebbels' other compromises affected the vision of a new music culture. Jazz had become a significant feature of some contemporary art music, whose distinction from the lighter variety had become blurred, as in Weill's compositions and less obviously in some contemporary offerings of composers like Blacher, Egk and Wagner-Régeny, who also were attracted to rhyhmic and tonal experimentation. The excitement of jazz seemed to echo the sounds of a foreign civilization, out of touch with German order, balance, and control and thus pointed in the direction of a potential musical synthesis other than that envisioned by *völkisch* theorists. While Goebbels' apparent betrayal of the ideologized revolution broadened the range of tonal possibilities, the party ideologues continued the attack on hot jazz as well as its tempered derivatives and substitutes. Nazi authorities throughout the Third Reich confessed that the alien ingredient of music was a complex phenomenon which resisted detection. The racial anthropologists referred to all jazz as Negro-American art which received increasingly hostile attention after American entry into the world war. The young German composer of popular and serious music was asked to relate to his own tradition and *Volk* and to reject such foreign influences. There was no need for jazz, "since we Germans are able to communicate quite adequately in our own musical idiom," wrote Richard Litterscheid in the *National- Zeitung* of Essen.[101]

After all the revolutionary excitement, manifestos, and measures of *Gleichschaltung* and purges, Goebbels' pragmatism legitimated the full range of twentieth-century compositions in the Third Reich which encompassed (l) the diatonic harmony and other standard features of the classic-romantic tradition, (2) occasional expressions of all forms of contemporary experimentalism, including the twelve-tone technique and the incorporation of jazz-elements, (3) the *völkisch*-folkloric emphasis on the folk song and other native elements, and the inclusion of explicit *völkisch*-Nazi programs and texts (actually a subset of the romantic mode), and (4) a mixture of all options.

While Goebbels tolerated jazz and "atonality" for political reasons, however, he strongly supported and identified with traditional and *völkisch* modes of expression. Moreover, he realized that his top priorities—power and war—which had mandated the compromises in the first place, required the loyalty of the party constituency, too. While experimental music existed marginally or constituted only a portion or an aspect of a larger work, traditional and *völkisch* music were an integral part of Nazi ritual. In spite of his manipulatory brilliance and realism, Goebbels was a Nazi who shared fundamental sentiments with his intra-party ideological detractors. He frequently gave his speeches on culture amidst musical spectaculars which encompassed the sounding of fanfares, the brass of official orchestras, and even traditional orchestras, which offered the heroic tradition of the great masters. The contemporary realm was often represented by Pfitzner's music, whose *Von Deutscher Seele* and *Deutschland Erwache* were favorite pieces for official occasions. The audiences would join in massive support of the solemn tones, and readings by professional actors of Hitler's thoughts on art and the people were offered in the absence of the leader. Within this atmosphere the modern composer was to find inspiration.

A major portion of the party composer's output, therefore, continued to consist of the song literature of the movement. The original repertoire was enriched by new compositions—still late in the day—dedicated to Hitler, other party leaders and the Nazi spirit, and commissioned for official occasions. The opera, *Der Erbhof*, by a member of the Wuppertal City Orchestra, captured the blood-and-soil ideology around the theme of a rooted peasant, his land and character[102]—one of numerous such compositions intended to reflect and celebrate the Nazi revolution, which were submitted to German stages but were generally rejected. The world of high art managed to maintain standards in its coexistence with party-inspired work.

In this realm the self-conscious art work of the future was perhaps not even anticipated, since music—regarded as a craft—was clearly subordinated to the communal ritual of the Nazi state. Music was to help mold political consciousness of the national community as defined back in 1933, while musical regeneration was to be realized within this revitalized community; it again had a purpose. Thus, the restoration of traditional forms, the singing of political texts and the experience of community as a means of overcoming modern loneliness and alienation, illustrated the magic—the fascination of fascism. Yet, it might indeed have been in this community-oriented applied music that a new mode, regardless of its regressive form and orientation, might have emerged—at least that is what theorists like Professor Wilhelm Ehmann of the RJF and the University of Innsbruck formulated in 1944 in the second edition of a book on political festival music, wherein he examined the fighting song, the large scale temporal oratorio, the male choral tradition and new festive music of the HJ.[103]

The secular cantata was deemed to be more demanding and was to be reserved for special occasions, but it also was to help shape a sense of community in connection with solemn festivities, and constituted one of the most celebrated and promising forms of music of the Third Reich, according to Richard Eichenauer in 1943 in his review of Heinrich Spitta's popular cantata, *Land, mein Land*,[104] even though the genre had to reach back to Bach for a model, since it had not attracted name composers during the nineteenth century. But that decline was explained away as a manifestation of the deplorable individualism and the search for ever-new compositional forms in the decadent-bourgeois age when the idea of service to the community had become anathema—so reasoned the *völkisch*-Nazi theorists. Eichenauer thus discovered an unfortunate rift between high art and an assumed timeless, eternally valid German festive style—which Wulf Kunold finds to be chimerical since that stylized festive form had never existed as defined by the Nazis, neither in the secular cantata of the seventeenth century, which had been primarily a solo virtuoso piece, nor in the spiritual version, whose complex form had been shaped by the text—a characteristic demonstrated by Kunold by example of the well-known *Saar Kantate* composed by Hermann Erdlen in connection with the Saar plebiscite of January, 1935 (text by Alfred Thieme), which was broadcast over Radio Hamburg one week before the vote and performed repeatedly thereafter. A handwritten score and copies of the original recording were presented to Hitler for his birthday in 1938.

The Saar cantata concluded each of its six parts with a chorale to be sung by the audience (community), in the manner of the Lutheran precedent with which it identified. Although the political text was removed from the current context to a timeless-mythical domain, it clearly had priority over the music which was arranged to simply support general blood-and-soil sentiment and the political objective which was pounded into the audience by means of key words. The one-page text listed the word "German" fifty times, thus emphatically making the point that "the Saar is German"—which was the central line of the incorporated *Saar*-song. The text determined the simple musical structure, which was basically declamatory, homophonic, and included only a few transparent polyphonic parts and simple harmonies. Text and music were competently integrated—the orchestra frequently doubling up with the vocal line—in subordination to the political objective.[105]

This popular cantata served as a model for even simpler works and ambitious efforts, which played a major role in Nazi ritual but, as practiced, amounted to less than a dead-end of musical development in its regressive orientation. Although the communal experience it helped fashion was very real and allowed for theoretical speculation, no new musical forms emerged from this central, and quantitatively the most representative, musical expression of the Nazi ideology—the music of hundreds of composers like Georg Blumensaat, Cesar Bresgen, Gerhard Maase, Johannes Günther, Heinrich Spitta, Helmut Majewski, Richard Trunk, etc. Yet, the theoretical search continued alongside the compositions. When one of the most prolific composers of the RJF, Georg Blumensaat—a student of Hindemith—offered a major new work for the NSKG, the press praised his new compact and internally-compelling form as a model for younger composers. The new intonation of Hitler's words formed one part of an event which presented Rosenberg's lecture on "*Weltanschauung* and Culture" and which closed with the final chorus of Pfitzner's cantata *Von Deutscher Seele*—a typically edifying program.

More important than the simple and the grandiose compositional contributions was the total effect of the presentation, in which the Nazi tradition was commemorated and confirmed. The *Parteitag der Arbeit* ("Party Congress of Labor"), 1937, was recalled by one observer as an imposing picture of the solemn procession of the leaders and the standard-bearers, accompanied by the festive sounds of the NSRSO led by Franz Adam and Erich Kloss. The musical part of the festivities was introduced by Wagner's *Rienzi* overture. Then an appeal was made to all composers in Germany to create solemn music for such occasions. They were asked to take their time, however, so that great music would emerge out of "inner tension and not by use of pathetic means simulating genuine experience, as has been customary in the past." Generally, political demonstrations included such renditions of a musical program of the great masters and contemporary productions written specifically for the occasion. Franz Adams provided "his consecration fanfares of very great distinction and strong polyphonic tension for trumpets and trombones which were played at the moment of the Führer's approach." For the Party Convention of 1937, the *Ordensburg Vogelsang* contributed a "striking flag-raising song." After a ceremony commemorating the dead, a solemn hymn by Franz Adam was sounded as a "life-affirming" high point. The enthusiastic commentator noted that the fanfares may serve as a model in the area of the new sound which affirms a new way of life without destroying the old in the process.[106]

The official Reich Music Festival in Düsseldorf in 1938, important for the display of "degenerate" and "racially alien" music, also offered the new music of the Third Reich, as we have noted. Even the old guard added new compositions written for the occasion to their existing literature of Hitler dedications and political testimonials. A new work of Graener, with the movement entitled "Solemn Hour" of "strict form, rhythmic and hymnlike melody" opened the festivities under the direction of the Düsseldorf GMD, Hugo Balzer, while Strauss composed and conducted a musical introduction to Goebbels' address, the eagerly awaited main culture-political event of the festival. However, Graener pointed out that, in addition to the proven and traditional, "experiment was not to be forgotten insofar as it touches the domain of the soul." Indeed, twenty-five younger contemporaries offered compositions ranging from party hymns to experimental efforts by Egk, Blacher, Joseph Marx, Theodor Berger and others. Egk impressed with a cantata for bass and chamber orchestra, "Nature - Love - Death," while Blacher received critial attention for his "Violin Music in Three Movements." An immense success for the RMK, the festivities closed with a threefold *Sieg Heil* to the Führer and the singing of German hymns.[107] For the repeat of the National Music Festival in 1939 an eager profession submitted 1121 musical scores, including 36 operas and many symphonies, choral works, concertos, chamber music and much festival music.[108]

Most activity in this area of party compositions involved composers of less stature than Graener and Egk. More characteristic were the thousands of *völkisch*-Nazi folk songs, the fanfares of HJ and other youth organizations, and the cantatas. Some songs were more frequently heard than others: Gustav Buchsenschütz's *Märkische Heide*, Arno Pardun's *Volk ans Gewehr*, and those of Hans Baumann, Herbert Napiersky, Gerhard Maasz, Heinrich Spitta, Reinhold Stapelwerk, Hermann Blume, Hansheinrich Dransmann and Hugo Rasch.[109] Compositions were also written for the organ, which was especially suitable for the solemn occasions of party events, national celebrations and choral works. Patriotic programs were also offered over the radio, sometimes for no special occasion, other times for such events as Hitler's birthday, which culminated in 1933 in Richard Trunk's pace-setting chorale, *Du mein Deutschland*. The DAF offered an annual prize for the composition most suitable for mass-choral presentation. The male chorus tradition was kept alive in compositions, for example by Hermann Grabner in the cycle for male chorus, *Der Fackelträger*. The DSB propagated new works—Hermann Simon's *Bauernerde*, Karl Schüler's *Lied der Bauleute*, and songs of Walter Heusel and Konrad Ramrath.[110] The composers of songs were reviewed in groups, whereas the major artists who lent themselves to official ceremonies received individual treatment in the coordinated press and in the *Jahrbücher*, which were compiled toward the end of the Third Reich as we have seen and constituted essential reading for anyone interested in this field of accomplishment in composition, within the broad outlines of Nazi culture.

Nazi music continued to be an important component of musical reality to the very end. It was heard and inspired creative acts which were to be imitated. Nonetheless, the intended classical renaissance was of course not realized in that kind of music. The ideals were set forth universally, and the street, beer halls, the mass meetings, demonstrations in party and composer's organizations, and even the concert stages and festivals responded to the call. However, the artistic evolution within, a necessary ingredient of any meaningful creative output, had been arrested. Talented Nazi sympathizers and non-Nazi professionals alike admitted that the political revolution would be realized in musical creativity only in the future. Werner Egk, who headed the corporate profession of composers within the RMK after 1941, wrote in the *Völkischer Beobachter* as late as 1943 that a future Nazi music culture was at present based on "folk-classical" forms (a somewhat familiar description of Hindemith's tendencies) which marked a necessary reversal of the strict forms of the old, in support of what he called a "recuperation process which, indeed, has been manifested in composition." Egk was hoping for "an alliance of an ideal politics with real art so that all human endeavor would be again directed from its natural roots."[111]

Perhaps Egk was posing a problem which had no solution, inasmuch as the traditional development within the advanced stages of music had been broken off. The anachronism of the *völkisch* and classic as guiding principles in a culture of revolutionary musical development was hardly the key toward the discovery of the roots of life. Fritz Stege ignored the problem altogether. If the new culture was to give rise to new creativity, he wrote in 1936, then this endeavor ought not to be confused with the search for a new form of music. "There is no such thing as National Socialist music" However, he assumed "an art which regarded National Socialism as its source of experience which was indebted to National Socialism for its spiritual stimulation. A symphony, as absolute music in no apparent way related to National Socialism, could demonstrate National Socialism to a greater degree than a work of art bearing Nazi attributes by nonmusical means—insofar as the Nazi sentiment determines the personal construction of the symphony"[112]—a formulation which enabled the entire musical establishment to go about its business in customary manner.

The literature in the late 1930's and the 1940's until the end of the Third Reich reflected the general conclusion that, although organization, policy, program, and even more refined theory were well-established, the creative era in music had not yet dawned. Displays of the past were not followed by comparable products of the new age; this was an era of struggle and intentions. Irrespective of the impact of the Nazis upon music, the traditional establishment had recaptured the field and managed to produce its traditional type of music. Furtwängler continued to compose in a conservative manner and style, following those traditional forms deemed acceptable in the Third Reich and claimed as a form of inner emigration by the composer. A piano concerto of 1942 was to reflect his "tragic figure," he wrote to his friend Ludwig Curtius.[113] To be sure, in preserving much of the old, Furtwängler also encouraged the younger generation. His biographer in the Nazi period, Friedrich Herzfeld, listed an impressive number of contemporary composers who were promoted by him: the well-known old guard of Strauss, Pfitzner and Graener, as well as Joseph Haas, Hermann Zilcher, Paul von Klenau,

Max Trapp, Rudi Stephan, Georg Schumann, Ludwig Thuille, Walter Courvoisier, Julius Weismann, Hermann W. von Waltershausen, Siegmund von Hausegger and August Reuss. The younger generation of Kurt Hessenberg, Hans Brehme, Heinz Schubert, Gottfried Müller, Paul Höffer, Werner Egk, Carl Orff, Johann Nepomuk David, Helmut Bräutigam, and others who were introduced at the German Music Festivals of the ADMV and the Reich Music Festival, also found a place in Furtwängler's program. German concert halls, opera stages, and other institutions, such as the academies and provincial conservatories, continued their support of this traditional form of absolute music, which included some works in the progressive idiom, many of which were applauded, while some were merely tolerated. But none were understood to embody the projected musical component of a new civilization, notwithstanding the appeals and reflections of politicians, commentators and composers, who had announced the end of the "passive and other-worldly oriented *Weltanschauung* of late romanticism with its tendencies toward a boundless individualism and the beginning of a new realism."[114]

The New People's Opera

If absolute music absolutely resisted revitalization in the desired form, the hope for a Nazi-inspired opera appeared more promising. The writing of texts and the casting of roles in accord with *völkisch*-Nazi specifications proved less formidable a task than the definition and composition of a new music. As for the musical part of opera, only the negative was readily identified. In addition to unacceptable texts and works of either defamed authors or composers, atonality, jazz and American song style were also associated with the models of operatic negativity. Berg's *Wozzeck*, Křenek's *Jonny spielt auf* and Weill's *Three Penny Opera* were defined and purged from the repertoire. Composers, authors and opera directors soon learned that native and traditional norms were favored in the form of what was called the *Volksoper* (people's opera) even though an explicit and consistent Nazi theory of opera was never formulated. Texts and the dramatis personae were to be drawn from Germanic mythology or history, or from the realm of the people, though refashioned so as to embody Nazi principles, while the music was to be diatonic and to reflect the melodies and harmonies of the folk song tradition.[115] It appeared that opera was indeed the ideal medium of and for National Socialism, as aesthetic experience and propaganda. It allowed for the presentation of a program, the casting of heroes and villains, and the rendition of an all-encompassing ritual, including a chorus which could be identified with the spirit of community, of National Socialism, as in Wagner's "total work of art." Thus, when Paul Graener's opera, *Der Prinz von Homburg* was performed in 1936 at the State Opera, he asked Hitler to attend because "it took me years to compose this opera as a national work of art."[116]

Yet, in spite of early *völkisch* agitation and eager musical collaboration, the regime, through its Reich dramaturg Schlösser, never committed itself to a narrowly defined Nazi opera, with Nazi characters and identifiable Nazi songs—and not one such explicit Nazi work was staged during the Third Reich. Nazi theorists hoped for something pure instead, reflecting the Nazi spirit, to be sure, but also the standards of the musical tradition. The Dresden musicologist Eugen Schmitz concluded in 1939 that no newly created opera with contemporary subjects had been added to the repertoire; in fact

the stylized form of opera resists such efforts. The person of Horst Wessel might lend himself to spoken drama, but as an opera tenor, in company with baritone and bass SA friends and communist antagonists, this sort of a hero could deteriorate to that form of nationalistic kitsch which has been denounced by the Nazi state and forbidden on cultural grounds.[117]

By 1936, definitional efforts of the new opera accorded with Goebbels' general pragmatism, his concessions to the Nazified and self-coordinating establishment and to public taste and, quite specifically, with his suggestion for new art as an expression of "romanticism of steel." This theoretical basis of what was then termed "National Socialist realism" could ideally be expressed in opera, which to Otto Eckstein-Ehrenegg in 1942

has remained an artistic medium of profound importance, particularly since even in times of extreme crisis the people never ceased to remain faithful to it. If the present music generation replaces the formerly individualistic psychological development of the characters with a supra-individual type given to objective considerations, and if it stresses general community in its music-dramatic experiments—the fate of entire groups of people rather than individual heroes—then the young manifest in artistic form the National Socialist concept of community.[118]

In practice, this useful definition was flexible enough to accommodate the bulk of actual opera production. The reference to "the National Socialist spirit" rather than concrete representation by authors, opera directors and critics led to the identification of many texts and roles of diverse contexts, with the typical Nazi themes of leadership, fidelity, sacrifice, commitment to combat, love of homeland, the community of fate, etc. as expressions of the officially promoted *Volksoper*. As long as an opera did not contradict National Socialism directly it would satisfy the censors. Opera directors generally judged by traditional standards, and Schlösser's office not once withheld approval of an opera already accepted by a stage. Not only did Schlösser not block operas, he actively promoted new works. When, in 1939, he asked each opera house to stage at least one contemporary opera per season, he reinforced a policy that was propagated at least by 1936.

The Nazi state actively supported opera in search of the new *Volksoper*, an idea eagerly picked up by composers, authors and directors. Opera production was booming. Hundreds of operas were composed and submitted; 164 were premiered. While traditional works were most popular—Richard Strauss's *Arabella* (1933) leading all contemporary works with 848 performances in ten seasons[119]—those younger composers most frequently identified as potential creators of the new *Volksoper*—Ottmar Gerster, Werner Egk, Hermann Reutter, Rudolf Wagner-Régeny and later Carl Orff—managed to gain access to the stages: Gerster's *Enoch Arden* (1936) being performed 515 times in six seasons, Egk's *Die Zaubergeige* (1935) enjoyed 198 performances in seven seasons, Wagner-Régeny's *Der Günstling* (1935) 136 performances in five seasons and Reutters' *Doktor Johannes Faust* (1936), although highly controversial for its alleged atonality, 116 performances in seven seasons.[120] The subsidized stage network, led by the great Berlin stages—the State Opera, City Opera and the new People's Opera—and other major opera houses in Vienna, Stuttgart, Dresden, Hamburg, Düsseldorf, etc. responded to the call for new opera by the regime. Provincial stages picked up the works after well-publicized premieres and travelling programs, even though controversial works would occasionally die after being premiered, since the ideological backlash was stronger in the provinces. In general, opera production thrived even during the war years, with nine premieres in the 1939/40 season, fourteen in 1940/41, seventeen in 1941/42, seventeen in 1942/43 and still four in 1943/44.[121] When the Berlin State Opera was destroyed on the night of April 9-10, 1941 by an air attack, Hitler immediately had this most representative institution of the cultural facade reconstructed.[122]

Opera has traditionally been the most public musical event of the season—a social occasion of great ceremonial value, costly, a most important expression of bourgeois culture—which was acknowledged as such by Goebbels in his policy shifts of 1936. No realm of music so much illustrated the theme of the cultural facade for the Nazi state as the world of opera—the expression of high art entertainment par excellence, of its post-1936 atmosphere of business-as-usual and collaboration and, at the same time, of

Nazi accommodation to the cultural habits of German elites. In fact, the regime identified with the ceremonial, as leading state dignitaries attended especially State Opera functions beginning in 1933 on "the day of Potsdam," when Hitler had insisted on Furtwängler conducting *Meistersinger* at the Berlin State Opera, while GMD Karl Böhm conducted *Lohengrin* in Hamburg at a KfdK-sponsored program which featured Alfred Rosenberg as a speaker. While Goebbels relaxed censorship and liberally tolerated expressions of ideologically questionable forms of music, the party press continued to proclaim *völkisch-*Nazi principles in scathing critiques which reflected the anti-modernist attitudes of the public. It might indeed be argued that the occasional success of a modernist piece in Nazi Germany, like Reutter's *Faust*, can in part be attributed to a political gesture of the public in support of the victims of defamation.

However, within the context of relaxed controls and the definitional flexibility of acceptable music, the public favored light opera like Norbert Schultze's *Der Schwarze Peter* (1936) and the non-political works of the old-timers like Strauss, whose *Arabella, Daphne* and *Der Friedenstag* placed among the top ten most performed operas composed during the Third Reich. Julius Weissmann's *Die pfiffige Magd* (1939) placed seventh, while Wolf-Ferrari's works also did well. Among those of the younger generation engaged in the search for the new *Volksoper*, Egk, Wagner-Régeny and Gerster were among the top ten most popular composers; they did well with the audiences and the critics. Otto Eckstein-Ehrenegg claimed that Egk's *Peer Gynt* and Wagner-Régeny's *Bürger von Calais*—both premiered in Berlin in 1939 in response to commissions of the Berlin State Opera director Tietjen—"derived impulses from the contemporary *Zeitgeist* and created new musical and scenic forms." Carl Orff was praised as an innovator when his opera, *Der Mond*, premiered in Munich in 1939. However, the author concluded that the real *Reformator* (creator of a new art form) had not yet emerged[123]—which was a fair assessment.

The claimed innovators did, indeed, produce experimental works that included aspects of the projected *Volksoper*. Egk introduced folk and Nordic settings, enough traditional melody and harmony—termed by him "diatonic of steel"—and Bavarian folk tunes; but key party critics like Herzog and Gerigk also disapproved of his orchestral dissonance, jazz and song-style elements and complicated rhythms, which reminded them of Stravinsky. Gerster addressed Nazi themes, but occasionally he probed beyond basic diatonic patterns and he omitted folk songs. Wagner-Régeny also balanced accommodation with contrariness; while Orff, though increasingly appreciated—in spite of difficulty with the public—was berated for various violations of acceptable standards.[124]

Interestingly, those textual and musical elements which in part elevated the works of these innovators and which related to international developments in modern music, were criticized and did, indeed, raise questions about the norms of the ideal *Volksoper* as commonly understood. Their stature in the Third Reich, however, suggests that ultimately they might have affected a redefinition of the elusive new music, to thus have challenged irritating critics and provided substance to the Nazi claim that change would have to issue from musical practice, not from theory.

Practice, however, also produced opera totally inconsistent with *völkisch* principles. This contradiction was the ultimate consequence of the flexible and expedient policy which looked not to specific Nazi or other conventional forms of musical expression, but to Nazi inspiration which could then be variously claimed. Even atonalists professed to want to create the new *Volksoper*. Critics already deplored the atonal and jazz components in the works of Egk and Wagner-Régeny who, however, rationalized their deviations as expressions of negative themes and characters which were balanced and off-set by tonal and folk musical representations of positive roles and principles. Hermann Reutter, who had been berated for various earlier musical experiments, again appeared to threaten the tonal order in his remarkably successful *Doktor Johannes Faust* (1936)[125] which Nedden and Ziegler, the organizers of the Degenerate Music Exhibit, had wanted to keep from the ADMV festival in 1938. Ottmar Gerster's *Enoch Arden* (1936) and Joseph Haas's *Tobias Wunderlich* (1937) also received mixed reviews for, on the one hand, exemplifying the new *Volksoper* but, on the other, violating basic assumptions about tonality and folk tune qualities.

The "atonal music devil" remained alive in the opera of the Third Reich. While indeed expressed and acknowledged in open reference to the twelve-tone technique on some occasions, it was denied by composers, though discovered by Gerigk, et al., in other cases. There was no doubt about it in the admittedly twelve-tonal operas of the Danish composer Paul von Klenau, who resided in Nazi Germany and promoted Danish-German cooperation. His controversial *Michael Kohlhaas*, premiered in Stuttgart in November, 1933 and performed shortly thereafter at the Berlin City Opera, was claimed by supporters as an expression of "a new folk and human art," while Herzog identified its twelve-tonal technique and its proximity to the model of "cultural bolshevism," Berg's *Wozzek*—a most dangerous association. Undeterred, Klenau justified his "twelve-tone theory as consistent with Nazi insistence on technical competence" which would help overcome "individualistic arbitrariness."[126] He continued to compose in the twelve-tone mode. His next controversial opera, *Rembrandt van Rijn*—based on a preeminent hero in the Nazi mythology of Germanic art—was premiered in Stuttgart and at the

Berlin State Opera in January, 1937. Praised as "the greatest poet composer of our time" in the press, he referred to his twelve-tone scores as a "totalitarian system" and identified this with "Tristan"-harmonies.[127]

These twelve-tonal operas of Klenau were not unique; though rationalized as expressions of new Nazi music, they revealed more about the contradictions of Nazi music. We have seen that Furtwängler performed German "deviationists" as well as questionable foreigners like Debussy, Ravel, Stravinsky, Honegger, Carl Niellsen and Alexander Scriabin. The Schönberg student Winfried Zillig had his operas *Rosse* (1933), *Das Opfer* (1937), and *Die Windsbraut* (1941) premiered which, in part, were appreciated for their innovations in spite of their clear atonality.

Altogether, the avant-garde opera of the Third Reich was a fringe phenomenon which contributed to the search for a new *Volksoper*, in the eyes of a few sympathetic critics. Although it provided some links to the development of modern music since 1945, relative to Nazi music politics it was not of much consequence. On the other hand, opera in general mattered as an important component of Nazi theatre. In spite of all the subsidies and the promotion of new works and the emphasis on the new *Volksoper*, it was the traditional repertoire—especially of the Italians—which remained most popular as an expression of Nazi bourgeois taste.

Nonetheless, the Nazi toleration and promotion of new music continued to secure its support for the Third Reich to its very end. Prieberg has identified more than thirty opera scores composed too late for performance during the war.[128] Composition survived. As composers had adjusted to the new requirements in 1933, they were able to do so again in 1945. But, in spite of official anti-modernist pressures and popular hostility to modern music, basic developments of the art continued. Zillig experimented with "serial forms," by which he attempted to clarify that relationship to tonality which Schönberg had earlier characterized with the prophecy that "one day we may be able to unmask tonality as a special case of the twelve-tone system."[129] Zillig wrote a cycle of songs and other twelve-tone chamber and orchestra pieces, some of which were performed before 1945, others afterwards. The same lines of continuity can be identified in the works of Orff, Egk, Reutter, Fortner, Blacher, Sutermeister, Zimmermann, and especially in the works of the man who had genuinely retired into an inner emigration and composed only for his desk drawer during the Third Reich, Karl Amadeus Hartmann.

Anti-Fascist Music: Karl Amadeus Hartmann

The student of Joseph Haas, Hermann Scherchen and Anton Webern, Karl Amadeus Hartmann expressed the modern idiom under a wide range of influences including Bruckner, Berg, Stravinsky and Blacher, and increasingly understood his music as an anti-fascist medium. He withdrew into "inner emigration" and withheld almost his entire oeuvre from performance during the Third Reich since he did not want to contribute to the "cultural facade of barbarism." The anti-fascist nature of his music—expressed in explicit program notes, titles and choice of subjects, and in dedications to victims and defamed musicians like Hermann Scherchen, Bartók, Berg and Zoltan Kodály—was understood by him to be manifest in its atonality, its themes and stylistic fragments derived from Jewish and Catholic liturgy, and its frequent thematic citations of many so-called "decadent" compositions. At the same time, he was an active member of the "New Beginning" resistance group which supplied food to the victims of the regime.[130] Central to this posture of resistance was his music, rooted in the new music of the twenties, which was cited in all his works and was propagated by him in the Musica Viva Concert Series in Munich shortly after the war—a music which intentionally offered a striking contrast to the music of the Third Reich.

Hartmann's characteristic musical resistance was immediately recorded in his First String Quartet (1933)—referred to as the "Jewish String Quartet" after 1945 because of its Jewish themes and other references to Jewish liturgical practice—by means of which he wished to retain international contact—evident also in clear references to Bartók and other modern composers—and to thus reinforce and objectify his opposition to the new political order. His moving symphonic poem, *Miserae* (1934/35) similarly proclaimed solidarity with the people and music defamed by the regime and expressed his profound grief and anger. Hermann Scherchen—his teacher and a major propagator of new music who lost his job in Germany in 1933—conducted the premiere of *Miserae* at the festival of the International Society for New Music in Prague in 1935—not in Germany, where it was not performed until 1976 as an indictment and as an expression of mourning. It was dedicated to the concentration camp victims: "my friends who had to die hundredfold, who are sleeping for eternity—we won't forget you. Dachau 1933/34."[131] The work in his characteristic tempo—adagio—was punctuated by agitato sections, while he broke through inherited tonal constraints in search of new means to communicate intense emotions and concentrated understanding.[132]

As an exponent of new music it was especially noteworthy that Hartmann turned to opera, which enabled him to dramatize his reaction to the Third Reich in musical as well as textual form. His chamber opera (or scenic oratorium) *Simplicius Simplicissimus* (1934/35) was based on Grimmelshausen's seventeenth-century novelistic account of the Thirty Years War. Anticipating war, Hartmann identified National Socialism with the misery of the Thirty

Years War, although in his finale he went beyond the novel by concluding with the rising of the peasant masses, in allusion to the earlier peasant war of 1525—thus revealing his commitment to the oppressed throughout German history. The anti-fascism of the text was also manifested in the usurpation of typical Nazi music: the folk song which was here Jewish, the fighting song appropriated by peasants and workers, and a chorale proclaimed a Reich of peace rather than the Third Reich. This "epic music-theatre" contained the various expressions of defamed music: alienated *Sprechgesang*, the mixing of tonal and atonal structures, and references not only to Bach, but also to Bartók, Prokofiev and much Stravinsky, and Jewish sections which included themes developed from the First String Quartet.[133]

Hartmann's work continued to evolve in response to the political situation, particularly to the war. He experimented with new, archaic and traditional tonal patterns; he returned to Jewish themes, cited the panorama of defamed music and musicians, repeatedly identified National Socialism with war, misery, terror and fear, yet he also regained a positive outlook, since he believed in the defeat of the Third Reich when war broke out. Though aware of the integrity of music, its own laws, and his obligation to resist extra-musical pressure, he later wrote about his abiding belief in the political nature and purpose of his music.[134]

After the war Hartmann promoted new music at his *Musica Viva* Concert Series and brought out his revised works written during the Third Reich. His eight symphonies especially rank among the major twentieth century expressions of the genre. He also published a collection of essays; reminiscences about Scherchen and Webern; and his assessment of Stravinsky, Schönberg and Honegger. His biography and oeuvre constitute a particularly meaningful anti-fascist commentary on the politics of the Third Reich—expressed revealingly in those characteristic adagio works of anger, mourning and quiet confidence.

The Fraud of a Music Theory

Post-1945 reviewers of the Third Reich will conclude that National Socialism did not fulfill itself in the delicate area of musical composition. The renaissance did not materialize. This is of course not surprising. Ulrich Dibelius, music critic and musical journalist at the Bavarian Radio in Munich, has noted in his post-war publication, *Moderne Musik 1945-1965*, that with the exception of the Viennese school of Schönberg, Webern and Berg, music of the twenties and thirties must be styled "neoclassic." Exaggerating, he also pointed out that during the Third Reich music consisted uniquely of "victory hymns and marching songs," while in reference to modern music he cited Goebbels, who had spoken of "offensive dissonances of musical incompetence." Dibelius maintained that not much good music, qualitatively or quantitatively, had been composed—not even in secret. An excuse had been offered by Eichenauer, who had criticized his party friends for disregarding one basic assumption of National Socialism, that of racial improvement as a precondition of all success. "Significant and enduring renewal," he had argued in *Musik und Rasse*, "may be expected in the cultural-political area only when the biological prerequisites have been established. This work calls for thinking at least in terms of decades, better yet of centuries. . . . National Socialism was engaged in directing the whole people toward something better, but"— and this is the significant point—"National Socialism cannot raise the value of existing individuals. . . . Our *völkisch* renewal" is to be thought of as "an endeavor of generations. If we were asked whether we may look forward to great tone masters in the future, true to our spiritual nature, race research must answer that this is not an artistic question, but simply one which involves the laws of life, i.e., a biological necessity."[135]

Musical creativity had first been redefined in terms of the community. Increasingly, however, the factor of race had become the most characteristic feature of National Socialism in its philosophic attempt to undo the western tradition of transcendence.[136] The question of racial content and determinents became most important in all areas of music, and the theoreticians promoted their "science" with zeal. As Friedrich Blume said at the Reich Music Festival in 1938, the relationship of music and race must be considered fundamental in any evaluation of music. Before music will gain from these insights, however, the science of race in its relation to music must be further explored. At present, the science lags behind, he noted, but the intuitive racial feelings can be applied already.[137] Composition was conceived as a form of expression of the people, the community, the race. On the question of an era of new creativity, the science of race offered the perfect alibi. The brief experience of Nazism in power was of no consequence to the theoretician dealing in generations and centuries, who spoke of a new man. How, then, argue with such a position?

The problems of modern music might not be soluble. Hans Mersmann has offered a telling point of view in his *German Music History*, devoted to the maintenance of musicological standards, yet subjected to the coordinated criticism of colleagues in 1934, since he thought that music was still in the same critical state as before. He granted that the time did not yet allow for meaningful analysis. "The development of subjective individualism, of isolation of the personality from community music, is consequently maintained," he concluded, voicing the same concern as contemporary spokesmen in the non-totalitarian societies. Like his *völkisch* and Nazi colleagues he deplored the rift between modern art and the people. He acknowledged the efforts of the Third Reich to overcome this estrangement, but regretted that this was done through the restoration of past standards. Thus, Wagner's music drama became fundamental, as Bayreuth symbolized the "community-creating power of an idea." Mersman believed that Wagner's aims stood a real chance of realization—a most interesting commentary by a respected musicologist and ex-editor of the progressive *Melos* journal, although official pressure must be taken into account in a true evaluation of these sentiments. Mersmann reflected accurately on the Nazi efforts to relate the productive nineteenth century with the times of National Socialism in a regressive dialectic which denied all recent developments in the art. Yet in distinction to his *völkisch* colleagues, he recognized the self-defeating aim of a movement which was dedicated to winning over the young by means of a past more distant than that remembered by most members of the older generation. He suggested that National Socialism had to find a way into the future by new musical means.[138] Any assessment of musical achievement in the Third Reich must be understood in the context of generally acknowledged crisis; Virgil Thomson, the American composer and one of the foremost advocates of the new music, has noted that "the evolution of our tonal possibilities and grammar was completed by 1914." Since then, only variation of expression is possible, a view implied in the title of Theodor Adorno's *Altern der Neuen Musik*—a departure from his earlier belief in the eternal progress of music and its inexhaustable future possibilities. Dibelius reads an element of "disillusion" into the work of all modern composition. Karlheinz Stockhausen, for instance, demonstrates a music full of contradictions the further he travels, although he is unique, original, and strong, notwithstanding his attempt to subordinate his music to his ideas of a social revolution of the late 1960s and 1970s. Pierre Boulez also wants to expand the old, rather than discover new forms, and after a hopeful beginning Hans Werner Henze fell into the category of *Gesellschaftskunst* (art with social conscience), thereby also reflecting the extra-musical spirit of the public, the patron.[139]

In strictly system-immanent technical terms, indebtedness to the past distinctly characterized the musical world of National Socialism. Uncomfortable, perhaps, in the surroundings of Nazi Germany or fruitlessly attempting to capture the essence of the new Germany in music, the composer of this twelve-year period remained spellbound by the product of its appropriated forbear and romantic prototype (not yet of steel!)—Richard Wagner—as acknowledged by the knowledgable and representative conservative Nazi spokesman in music, Walter Abendroth. The problems of modern music were illustrated in this debt: the artistic product (Wagner's work) preceded Nazi theory which, too, reflected the master's earlier formulations in some of its earlier features. While Wagner's oeuvre—already reactive—had been responsive to the social and artistic developments of his time, the Nazi appropriation of art and idea—out of context—doomed its vision of a new art to failure. Wagner, the craftsman, had created something new out of existing materials and forms; his well-known contribution to the dissolution of the tonal order and thus to the new music of the twentieth century, to the immensely rich tone color of the nineteenth century and, indeed, to the expansion of nearly every element of musical expression, put him in the tradition of the great innovators regardless, and in spite of, his regressive ideology, his vision of reintegrated and all-encompassing ritualistic art which did violence to some aspects of the separate and independently evolved arts, and his nasty polemics.

Wagner, the dramatist, had combined psychology, myth, and music so as to reflect and magnify the consciousness and tensions of the century which had also produced Nietzsche and Freud. The psychological complexities revealed musically in the sacred and erotic qualities of Kundry, in the moving Wotan-Brünnhilde (father-daughter) relationship, in fact, in all the character portraits; and also in the introduction of myth into opera developed from preceding historical opera, the ritual of the hero Siegfried, the story of death and ressurection, the search for identity and the ambition, confidence and authoritarian posturing at Bayreuth—one could go on endlessly to demonstrate his vast range of character traits, interests, artistic themes and an unsurpassed number of talents—stamp Wagner as an expression of the nineteenth century.[140]

Nazi enthusiasm for Wagner was genuine; the *völkisch* tradition had no greater hero for its identification and guidance. Distorted and vulgarized, Wagner's biography served the regime as shrine, doctrine and topic; but it also posed a threat, in that its idiosyncratic lifestyle and artistic vision, progress and autonomy suggested a rejection of totalitarian controls. Wagner was the main intellectual-artistic source and, at the same time, nemesis of National Socialism, to a greater degree even than Nietzsche, simply by virtue of the role of art in Nazi self-understanding and profession.

The conservative and archaic art of music could draw up visions of illusion or deception which were symptomatic of the idealistic framework of the very tradition which underlay National Socialism, not to be confused with the practice of those tough-minded and opportunistic manipulators who dictated music policy in the Third Reich and who acknowledged the impossibility of the Nazi dream by 1936. Wagner could not possibly have been produced in the Third Reich, by which time social conditions had evolved to a point at which musicians could no longer express themselves in the manner which inspired the idealism of epigones. The Wagnerian oeuvre demonstrated the datedness of Nazi ideals in the context of the musical debate of our time and the non-familiarity of Nazi cultural planners—especially Goebbels—with music, while offering a glimpse into a condition of music which might have prospered under National Socialism, if the conservative position had any concrete basis other than its idealistic and regressive ideology. Thus, the relationship between totalitarian ideology and its actual rule was demonstrated, as the revolutionary art and the selected ideals of their historical heroes were appropriated and manipulated, while their lifestyle and historical significance had to be suppressed.

The Nazis inherited the product and the regressive ideology, but not the nineteenth-century pessimism, the conscious cultural despair, which underlay the prodigious creative effort. The fundamental shortcoming of the Nazi music ideology was its dedication to an heroic tradition, symbolized by and in Wagner's work and derived from standards for society of an unreal, an artificial situation of heroes and villains, which in turn was imposed on a very real society. Whereas radical commitment to an artistic vision, and even to be responsive to the demands of the historically-evolved artistic material might be necessary aspects of good art, that same radicalism in the world of politics, with its denial of compromise, moderate solutions, cooperation, and coalitions, could only have resulted in the disaster foretold in Wagner's art. The Nazis inherited the lesson of heroism taught in mythology, self-serving history, and Wagner's art, and applied its standards and possibilities, thereby denying the opportunity to deal with a normalized state of society. The indebtedness to, and the open avowal of, Wagnerian mythical types confirm Nazi notions of endless struggle, war, and the inevitable catastrophe. The real problems of life under normal conditions in a world of reasoned accommodation, which does not readily allow for heroism and villainy, were not even contemplated.

Wagnerian visions had been spelled out. He had insisted that the highest goal of all theater is ritual, referring to himself variously as priest, wizard, magician.[141] Wagner had tried to recreate the assumed archaic unity of artistic expression of both pagan and Christian ritual, and he had chosen the subject of mythology as the most suitable medium. The Nazis applied this artistic program to real life in an essentially fraudulent effort, inasmuch as art is but a mask, a copy of life. The illusion that it can be more than that, and the illusion of unity of the arts cannot be a meaningful substitute for broken reality. Nonetheless, the Nazi leadership benefited from this artistic effort which, in turn, provided the necessary ideological support for its policy toward the arts. The fraud was manifest in the imposed subordination of art to politics. As in the spell cast by the transparent music (in the Venusberg scene, for instance)—the Wagnerian phantasmagoria—time stood still for the musician in the Third Reich. Change, as such, was denied for the artist who was to adorn and mesmerize. In the case of the Wagnerian model—in its timeless projection of reality and the suspension from consciousness by means of the phantasmagoric (spellbinding) device through which all traces of labor were hidden and denied—the work of art was mistaken for reality; that incredible fraud suggested itself. In this drunken state the Wagnerian epic lent itself to the masters of the Third Reich. Yet in the work of art the Wagnerian spell was broken; dreams were brought to their timely end. In its subject matter alone, the *Götterdammerung* contained forebodings of destruction, of universal destruction, again a reminder of the underlying pessimism; even the Wagnerian caricature of the Jew can be interpreted as a reflection of the universal condition of the modern artist, of modern man.

Art, although artificial, has deluded the world into the belief of permanence. But since even the Wagnerian epic has been subjected to critical analysis, artistically understood, both in terms of the human creative process and also ideologically, in terms of its sophisticated and politically utilitarian regressive message, the Nazi's conscious attempt to appropriate that art and its successive imitations, in which a whole society was to act out the phantasmagoria in a mass cult of eternal and universal verities and delusions of grandeur, the Third Reich had to be destroyed as the epic hero, perhaps the last European hero. The creative musician was helpless before the mandate handed him.

The artist can create in the context of a changing reality the kind of circumstances from which Wagner benefited. Spellbound by the master's work, his successors in the twilight of late-romanticism—Mahler, Debussy, Reger, Strauss and the early Schönberg—nonetheless developed their own styles, each in his own way perfecting the delusionary, the fantastic pretension of music that it can hide reality, in fact replace it. The epigones of the Third Reich were commissioned to continue the tradition, but they were forbidden to pursue the most recent expressions of their art. The *cul-de-sac* of the Wagnerian message was manifest in its pretended timelessness, subject only to repetition; but development was hardly possible, save for some technical refinement or, as has been the case more frequently, by means of simplification.

It may appear to be naive to assume that the Nazi leadership believed in the message of the phantasmagoric state. Press Conference Minutes, the diaries and RMVP records reveal Goebbels as the impresario of the Nazi stage who made sure that no non-privy artistic consumer or producer, in the manner of Alice in Wonderland, would uncover the controlling mechanism of the totalitarian state. Wagner was used; so were the musicians who performed and imitated him. Thus, the Nazis believed in the efficacy of art, in the delusionary spell of the phantasmagoric suspension of reality, change, and relative truths; they manipulated art in behalf of an artistically conceived thousand-year empire. There can be no doubt that the Nazi emphasis on the arts reflected a profound understanding of human nature, fears, anticipations, needs and history. Since religion of the day was losing control over human emotions, a secular cult was offered, in whose spell music was to act out its potential. The totalitarian state realized the potential, but not beyond the level of a crude functionalism. Actual musical development could not be commanded at a time of its severe crisis. Then again, that was not really the intention of the Nazi elite. The Nazis simply organized culture as a life-blood for their own cult and as a facade. In terms of history of the art, the period can only be regarded as an external imposition of a regressive message which was no longer relevant to system-immanent impulses.

ENDNOTES

[1]*DM*, 806.

[2]See Klaus Vondung, *Magie und Manipulation, Ideologischer Kult und Politische Religion des Nationalsozialismus* (Göttingen, 1971), 70-74; Fröhlich, 347.

[3]Fröhlich, 358-359.

[4]See Klein, "Konformität," 145.

[5]Fritz Stege, "Berliner Musik," *ZfM* (December 1935), 1364.

[6]See Prieberg, *Musik*, 174-175; Hans-Werner Heister and Jochem Wolff, "Macht und Schicksal: Klassiker, Fanfaren, höhere Durchhaltemusik," in Heister and Klein, 120-121.

[7]See Michael Meyer, "The Nazi Musicologist as Myth Maker in the Third Reich," *Journal of Contemporary History* (October, 1975), 649-666; Eckhard John, "Vom Deutschtum in der Musik," 49-55, and Pamela M. Potter, "Wissentschaftler im Zwiespalt," 62-66, the latter followed by the paper of Friedrich Blume, "Musik und Rasse: Grundfragen einer musikalischen Rassenforschung," 67-76, in Dümling and Girth.

[8]Prieberg, *Musik*, 361-362.

[9]"Musikalische Begabung und Rassenforschung im Schrifttum der Gegenwart." Similarly, scholars cited less than established musicologists like Blessinger and Eichenauer regarding the application of race to music.

[10]The different papers have been published in the professional press. See the review of the Conference in Potter, above, n. 7.

[11]Fritz Stern, *The Varieties of History: From Volaire to the Present* (New York, 1960), 344-345.

[12]*Richard Wagener, der Revolutionär gegen das 19. Jahrhundert* and *Richard Wagner und das Judentum.*

[13]Boetticher, "Deutsch sein heisst unklar scheinen," *DM* (March 1938), 399-404.

[14]See Ernst Bücken, "Aufbruch der Musikwissenschaft," *Westdeutscher Beobachter*, July 6, 1934.

[15]"Weltanschauliche Grundlagen einer neuen Musik," *DM* (May 1937), 674-675.

[16]Welter, *Musikgeschichte*, 7.

[17]See Prieberg, *Musik*, 363. For the definition of German qualities in music by research into the Germanic past, see also the many publications of Josef Maria Müller-Blattau, like his early work, "Die Tonkunst in altgermanischer Zeit: Wandel und Wiederbelebung germanischer Eigenart in der geschichtlichen Entwicklung der deutschen Tonkunst," in Hermann Nollau (ed.), *Germanische Wiedererstehung* (Heidelberg, 1926); *Germanisches Erbe in deutscher Tonkunst* (Berlin, 1938)—featured in the SS publication series, *Deutsches Ahnenerbe*, with an introduction by Himmler.

[18]*Tagebücher* (Zurich, 1948), 357.

[19]Welter, *Musikgeschichte*, 276-278.

[20]*Judentum und Musik* (Berlin, 1944), 155.

[21]*DM* (March 1936), 417-425.

[22]*Judentum und Musik*, 52-53.

[23]*Die Juden in Deutschland* (Munich, 1939), 352. See also Hans Költzsch (ed.), *Handbuch der Judenfrage: Die wichtigsten Tatsachen zur Beurteilung des jüdischen Volkes* (38th ed., Leipzig, 1935); excerpts in Dümling and Girth, 77-86.

[24]"Ein musikalisches Judentum-ABC," *DM* (January 1936), 278-279.

[25]*Lexikon der Juden in der Musik* (Berlin, 1941), 5-6.

[26]Ibid., 7.

[27]*Lexikon der Juden in der Musik* (2nd ed., Berlin, 1943), 8.

[28]"Der Musikkritiker im Dritten Reich," *DM* (January 1935), 244.

[29]Welter, *Musikgeschichte*, 282.

[30]Richard Litterscheid, "Mendelssohn, Mahler und wir," *DM* (March 1936), 413-417.

[31]Eichenauer, *Musik und Rasse*, 289-299.

[32]Fröhlich, 373.

[33]"Um jüdische Musik und das Denkmal eines Juden," *Leipziger Tageszeitung*, September 16, 1936; Wulf, *Musik*, 452.

[34]Friedrich W. Herzog, "Die windgeschützte Ecke," *DM* (March 1937), 416.

[35]*Volksparole*, Düsseldorf, October 24, 1934; Wulf, *Musik*, 236-237.

[36]Richard Eichenauer, "Unser das Land—Gedanken zu dem Liederbuch des deutschen Dorfes," *Odal* (September 1937), 145-147; Wulf, *Musik*, 246.

[37]See *Hohe Nacht der klaren Sterne: Ein Weihnacht- und Wiegenliederbuch* (Wolfenbüttel, 1939).

[38]Fröhlich, 358; also Prieberg, *Musik*, 344-375, for "Korrekturen" and official responses.

[39]Goebbels' speech, *Berliner Lokal-Anzeiger*, December 7, 1934.

[40]*Nationalsozialistisches Bildungswesen* (1937), 627 and "Unzeitgemässe Lieder," *Kölnische Zeitung*, November 24, 1938; Wulf, *Musik*, 423.

[41]Welter, *Musikgeschichte*, 211.

[42]Ibid., 184. The Gregorian Chant was also defended by Müller-Blattau and Blume on several occasions.

[43]*Volk und Rasse* (1934), 189-199; Wulf, *Musik*, 240-241.

[44]Eichenauer, *Musik und Rasse*, 170, 196, 227, 232; Stumme, *Musik in Jugend und Volk* (1939), 3.

[45]Karl Hasse speech at the Reger Festival, Freiburg i.B., *ZfM* (July 1936), 84.

[46]Ernst Krienitz, "Kampf um Chopin," *Die Musik-Woche* (October 1939, 1-2, and Friedrich Herzog (Halle, February 1935); Wulf, *Musik*, 253-255.

[47]Wulf, *Musik*, 437-439.

[48]Welter, *Musikgeschichte*, 216.

[49]See these and many other examples in Prieberg, *Musik*, 352-355.

[50]Walter Engelsmann, "Kunstwerk und Führertum," *DM* (October 1933), 18-19.

[51]Max von Millenkovich-Morold, "Richard Wagner in unserer Zeit," *ZfM* (May 1938), 471.

[52]Otto Tröbes, "Mit Richard Wagner ins Dritte Reich," *Offizieller Bayreuther Festspielführer* (1938), 14-15; Wulf, *Musik*, 319-320.

[53]"Kunstmusik und Volkstümlichkeit," *DM* (March 1934), 414.

[54]"Opernideale der Rassen und Völker," *DM* (March 1936), 424. See also Wulf, *Musik*, 442.

[55]*VB*, February 2, 1933.

[56]Alfred Rosenberg, *Der Mythos des 20. Jahrhunderts* (Munich, 1935), 433-434.

[57]"Beobachtet-festgehalten," *Die Bühne*, November 15, 1936; Wulf, *Musik*, 311.

[58]Cited in Wulf, *Musik*, 311-312.

[59]*Musik und Rasse*, 252-253.

[60]*Nationalsozialistische Grundsätze für die Neugestaltung des Konzerts und Opernbetriebes* (Berlin, 1934); Wulf, *Musik*, 314.

[61]Fritz Stege, "Die Jugend bekennt sich zu Hans Pfitzner," *ZfM* (July 1935), 787.

[62]Prieberg, *Musik*, 267.

[63]"Städtische Musikpreise," *ZfM* (August 1933), 842.

[64]*Theater-Tageblatt*, October 22, 1935, and "Stiftung eines nationalen Musikpreises," *Hannoverscher Anzeiger*, May 5, 1938; Wulf, *Musik*, 190.

[65]Heinrich Guthmann, *Zweierlei Kunst in Deutschland?* (Berlin, 1935), 109; Wulf, *Musik*, 279.

[66]Ludwig Kelbetz, "Vom Gesellschaftstanz in unserer Zeit," *Musik in Jugend und Volk* (1940), 58-59.

[67]Hoffmann and Ritter, 45.

[68]Ernst Nolte, *Der Faschismus in seiner Epoche* (Munich, 1963), 359.

[69]Ernst Lüdtke, "Kanzler und Künstler," *Die Musik-Woche* (February 5, 1938), 81-83.

[70]Raabe, passim.

[71]*Musik und Volk* (June/July 1937), 255-256.

[72]"Musik und Rasse—Grundfragen einer musikalischen Rassenforschung," *DM* (August 1938), 736-737.

[73]Albert Wellek, *Typologie der Musikbegabung im deutschen Volke*, University of Leipzig, 280-281; Wulf, *Musik*, 350-351.

[74]"Die deutschen Komponisten auf Schloss Burg," *Generalanzeiger der Stadt Wuppertal*, May 11, 1936; Wulf, *Musik*, 153-154.

[75]Prieberg, *Musik*, 277.

[76]"Weltanschauliche Grundlagen einer neuen Musik," *DM* (May 1937), 674-675.

[77]*ZfM* (August 1933), 842.

[78]Ingrid Grünberg, "'Wer sich die Welt mit einem Donnerschlag erobern will'...—Zur Situation und Funktion der deutschsprachigen Operette in den Jahren 1933 bis 1945," in Heister and Klein, 228.

[79]*Musik*, 300.

[80]Grünberg, 234-242. See also Otto Schneidereit, *Operette von A-Z*, Berlin (DDR), 1975.

[81]"Deutsche Unterhaltungsmusik," *DM* (April 1941), 229-231.

[82]"Hitlerjugend - Einsatz der Handharmonika in der Musikarbeit," *Völkische Musikerziehung* (1938), 197.

[83]*Die Musik-Woche* (1940), 28.

[84]Mosse, *Nazi Culture*, 49-51.

[85]K. Hennemeyer, *DM* (October 1936), 38-39.

[86]"Swing ist hierfür unpassend," *Westdeutscher Beobachter*, December 7, 1938.

[87]"Würde und Unterhaltung," *Deutsches Volkstum* 1939), 253-254; Wulf, *Musik*, 300.

[88]Helmut Majewski, "Blasmusik auf dem Reichsparteitag 1938," *Musik in Jugend und Volk* (1937-1938), 547-550.

[89]Prieberg, *Musik*, 370-371.

[90]Karl Schüler, "Konzert und Volkstum," *Magdeburger Zeitung*, February 20, 1934; Wulf, *Musik*, 278-279.

[91]"Um die deutsche Musik—Ein Bekenntnis," *DM* (July 1933), 728-730.

[92]"Neue Musik aus neuer Gesinnung," *Deutsches Volkstum* (Hamburg, 1936), 555-556; Wulf, *Musik*, 227-228.

[93]See also Glaser, 200.

[94]Otto Brodde, "Das Volkslied politisch," *Völkische Musikerziehung* (1937), 316-317; Wulf, *Musik*, 229-230.

[95]"Bolschewismus in der Musik," *VB*, February 10, 1933.

[96]*Musik*, 296.

[97]"Berliner Musik," *ZfM* (November 1935), 1246.

[98]Confirmed by Günter Schab; interview, above, Chapter II, n. 278.

[99]Prieberg, *Musik*, 296-299.

[100]Michael Kater, "Forbidden Fruit? Jazz in the Third Reich," *American Historical Review* (February 1989), 11-43; Gerigk, "Was ist mit der Jazzmusik?" *DM* (July 1938), 686. See also Horst H. Lange, "'Artfremde Kunst und Musik unerwünscht'—Jazz im Dritten Reich," in *That's Jazz: Der Sound des 20. Jahrhunderts*, exhibition catalogue (Darmstadt, 1988), for a review of the rich jazz offering in the Third Reich.

[101]Wulf, *Musik*, 386.

[102]Prieberg, *Musik*, 300.

[103]Wilhelm Ehmann, *Musikalische Feiergestaltung*; in Wulf Konold, "Kantaten, Fest- und Feiermusiken," in Heister and Klein, 165.

[104]Richard Eichenauer, *Von den Formen der Musik* (Wolfenbüttel, 1943), 92; Konold, loc cit.

[105]Konold, 165-171

[106]Erwin Bauer, "Musik auf dem Parteitag der Arbeit," *Die Musik-Woche* (October 9, 1937), 6.

[107]*Berliner Lokal-Anzeiger*, May 24, 1938. See also Dümling and Girth, 105-144.

[108]Prieberg, *Musik*, 281.

[109]Alfred Berner, "Das deutsche Volkslied," *Deutsche Musikkultur* (1936-1937), 116.

[110]"Kleine Mitteilungen—Gesellschaften und Vereine," *ZfM* (November 1934), 1173.

[111]"Worum es ging und worum es geht," *VB*, February 14, 1943.

[112]*Völkische Musikerziehung* (1936), 91; Wulf, *Musik*, 247.

[113]Frank Thiess (ed.), *Wilhelm Furtwängler Briefe* (Wiesbaden, 1964), n. 97.

[114]Otto Eckstein-Ehrenegg, "Die tieferen Ursachen der Opernkrise und der Weg ihrer Überwindung," *ZfM* (February 1942), 62-65.

[115]See Klein, 145-148.

[116]Wulf, *Musik*, 96-97.

[117]"Oper im Aufbau," *ZfM* (April 1939), 380-382.

[118]Above, n. 114.

[119]For a complete table of premieres see Klein, 158-162.

[120]Ibid., 149.

[121]Prieberg, *Musik*, 307.

[122]Bair, 89.

[123]Above, n. 114. See also Slonimsky, 681, 686.

[124]Klein, 155. Return to the Egk, Orff and Wagner-Régeny "profiles" in Chapter II for a more detailed examination of these works.

[125]See Albrecht Riethmüller, "Kompositionen im Deutschen Reich von 1936," *Archiv für Musikwissenschaft* (1981), 268-274; Klein, 153.

[126]*ZfM* (April 1934), 402; Prieberg, *Musik*, 303-304. See also Hans Heinz Stuckenschmidt, "Musik unter Hitler," *Forum* (January 1963), 45.

[127]Prieberg, *Musik*, 305.

[128]Ibid., 306.

[129]Winfried Zillig, *Von Wagner bis Strauss: Wegbereiter der neuen Musik* (Munich, 1966), 189-190.

[130]Andreas Jaschinsky, *Karl Amadeus Hartmann—Symphonische Tradition und ihre Auflösung* (Munich and Salzburg, 1982), 18. See also Karl Amadeus Hartmann, *Kleine Schriften*, ed. by Ernst Thomas (Mainz, 1965), 9-16.

[131]Cited in Hans-Werner Heister, "Elend und Befreiung: Karl Amadeus Hartmanns musikalischer Widerstand," in Heister and Klein, 276.

[132]Hartmann, 43.

[133]For his review of his opera see Hartmann, 49-55; also Heister, 279-282.

[134]Hartmann, passim.

[135]Eichenauer, *Musik und Rasse*, 316.

[136]See Nolte, 427-454.

[137]"Musik und Rasse, Grundfragen einer musikalischen Rassenforschung," *DM*, 737.

[138]Mersmann, *Deutsche Musikgeschichte*, 506.

[139]*Spiegel*, December 12, 1966.

[140]Thomas Mann, *Adel des Geistes* (Stockholm, 1945), 404-413.

[141]Ibid., 402-403.

Wilhelm Furtwängler: Collaboration and a Struggle of Authority

The *völkisch* and traditionally conservative factions in the pre-1933 debate on the condition of contemporary music had both contributed to the formulation of Nazi music policy and aesthetics. Due to these shared values, in large part, the traditional order was able to survive and maintain a degree of its standards—in spite of the total Nazi victory in 1933, which resulted in the purges and coordination of organizations and sentiment. But, shared aesthetic norms alone do not explain conservative resurgence. In late 1933, the regime had decided to broaden its revolutionary base in music beyond the KfdK, on political grounds and for propaganda advantages, thus enlisting music in the construction of its cultural facade, and when, by 1936, Nazi cultural leaders, both in private at the culture-political press briefings at the RMVP and in occasional public statements, confessed failure of their earlier hope for a genuine Nazi art music, the concordat between the music establishment and the Nazi state appeared stable. Already in 1933, Goebbels had conceded that political sentiment, though necessary, was no substitute for art—an early presentiment reiterated repeatedly by him and Hans Hinkel from 1936 onwards as party-art was even ridiculed and recent converts to National Socialism were accused of opportunism and dishonesty.

Even though the official *völkisch* propaganda was, of course, still issued massively through all organs of public communication, particularly from the culture-political network of Reich Leader Rosenberg, the traditional music establishment—purged, coordinated and compromised—managed to hold its own, not alone for reasons of its own Nazification but because it was deemed more useful as traditionally constituted. However, this toleration also prompted a fundamental misunderstanding about real power, as some representatives of music mistook the Nazi need for a cultural facade and propaganda vehicle for their own traditional autonomy and authority. Most representative of this misreading on behalf of the conservative, prestigious and authoritarian musical establishment was Germany's great conductor, Wilhelm Furtwängler, whose biography reflected and magnified the fundamental political issue of music in the Third Reich, which took the form of collaboration and an authority struggle between the collaborators, the traditional professional elite, and the totalitarian rulers.[1]

Caution must be taken in evaluating this representative life. The artist of our own market- and consumption-oriented culture envies the dissident artist-intellectual in totalitarian countries on the assumption that the latter is taken seriously and is in a position to speak out as an individual, can question a socio-political order and be suspect, and thus constitute artistic autonomy, integrity and potential power confirmed in the fear and preventive suppression of the repressive agent. Although this envy reflects the artist's misgivings about the status of art in liberal-democratic society, it is also dangerously misguided and out of place for reasons of a basic misunderstanding of the difference between traditional authoritarianism and the dictatorial repression and terror suggested in modern totalitarianism which, ostensibly more responsive to the needs of its community, intends not only to impose absolute rule, but also to establish spiritual-intellectual-artistic uniformity in a never-satisfied need for confirmation and legitimacy. The normal condition in a "free" society, by contrast—understood in appreciation of its relative quality—in which political powers have access to an ubiquitous and most refined information mechanism with which to shape public opinion, tolerates freedom of artistic expression and irritating criticism in context of which "freedom" is confirmed and celebrated in ritualistic piety. Whether the critical artist is taken for a fool or not, the free society allows him to function, protest, irritate and thus contribute to the ideological confirmation of an essentially liberal constitution of that society.

In a totalitarian society, on the other hand, the individualist-anarchist-critical impulse of the artist is suppressed, looming only as potential, and directed by political authority to conform to the manipulated collective will of the community. Under National Socialism the musician faced the guidance and control of an all-embracing power structure—from the supreme party-state leadership and the RMVP on down to the national and local offices of the RMK—which set limits to freedom of expression and performance. Nonetheless, belief in freedom, which is fundamental to honest artistic expression, was sustained even under these conditions, since the musician was promised the satisfaction of participating in the formation of a new society which would eventually allow for a liberalization process, theoretically contained in the vision of future normalization after successful coordination, purges, and reconstruction—and, actually confirmed in the unintended realities of the German Federal Republic after the Nazi experiment. Ralf Dahrendorf's well-known thesis of Hitler's revolution as a necessary first step toward a more liberal society in Germany comes to mind, and also the noted revisionist Austrian Marxist, Ernst Fischer, who has written along these lines about the intellectual partisans in the authoritarian socialist regimes of Eastern Europe in an article on "Power and Impotence of the Intellectual in the Socialist World," *Die Zeit* (March 19, 1968). Reflections on conditions in the 1960s—not to speak of the late-1980s—transcend the scope of the problems of the musician in Nazi Germany, in which immediate reality was more pressing, while liberalization, albeit prospective, appeared doubtful. Nonetheless, some of Fischer's and Dahrendorf's heuristic assumptions can be detected in the commentary of intellectual spokesmen of Germany's coordinated artists under Nazism.

The musician in Nazi Germany was supervized, controlled and restricted through the RMVP, the RMK, and other agencies. The fact of this relationship between politics and music—of the need of the one to regiment the other—nonetheless confirmed the potential power of the musician whose coveted standards also compromised the regime in the eyes of its followers. Uniformity of opinion and musicial offerings were, in fact, violated. Particularly after 1936, a crucial year of change in Nazi policy towards the arts, the musical establishment reasserted itself and produced much music which had been purged earlier, including jazz and atonal serious music. Jews, other purveyors of "degenerate" art, and dissidents were not entirely eliminated. The authorities withdrew demands repeatedly in the face of establishment opposition which, when exercised by Furtwängler, rested on traditional authority and this potential power of the artist. Goebbels' repeated efforts to define the relationship of organization to artistic freedom bear witness to the latent authority of artistic institutions and individuals which cannot simply be regulated through a "profusion of laws," but require "a continuous program of self-help."[2] The potential strength of the artist in Nazi Germany rested on the coincidence of his interest in freedom of expression as ultimate justification of his existence with that of society, which he could thus serve better. Yet, the inherent threat of an art to a political order is contained precisely in this belief in its efficacy in behalf of the state. Totalitarianism must fear any institution, individual authority, or idea employed for propaganda purposes; the greater the value of support, the greater the threat, since any intelligence or creativity demonstrates the capacity of independence and sovereignty over its domain, thus implying a set of universal values derived from the autonomous art, not from principles external to it.

Goebbels clearly understood the predicament when he not only tolerated Furtwängler but honored him with official positions and titles, even though the famous artistic leader of the Berlin Philharmonic Orchestra publicly insisted on his prerogative as an "apolitical" artist and defied the regime—at first naively and ignorant of its true nature and later as a seasoned tactition. In spite of Nazi totalitarian claims and the pressures of the Rosenberg organization for ideological conformity, Goebbels came to an arrangement with this non-party member who, among his many offenses and liabilities in Nazi eyes, withheld the customary Nazi greeting and signature and refused to sign solidarity proclamations. Germany's foremost conductor, Prussian State Councillor, and for a while vice-president of the RMK, refused to conduct any Nazi music and compositions dedicated to the Reich leaders, for to do so offended his sense of dignity; he also would not participate at Nazi functions that might be construed as propaganda for the party, except in a few unavoidable cases, or conduct in German-occupied territories during the war. Most disturbingly to the regime and its followers, he openly interceded in behalf of the victims of persecution in at least eighty documented cases, and he associated with them.[3]

When the Nazis assumed power, Furtwängler, at age 47, was in his prime. His courageous conduct served to preserve the quality and qualified autonomy of the stellar musical institutions entrusted to him at various phases of the Third Reich, including, most notably, the Berlin Philharmonic, but also the Berlin State Opera in the beginning and Vienna's major musical institutions upon the request of the latter's musicians after the *Anschluss*. To Furtwängler the sacred classical music of Germany, which he more than anyone else represented and embodied as its foremost interpreter, reigned sublimely above politics. He argued persuasively—and for tactical reasons, as he confided privately[4]—that music would serve the interests of the Third Reich to a greater degree as a sanctuary and as an expression of German artistic excellence when disassociated from politics and propaganda. His patron and nemesis—Goebbels—agreed. The resulting collaboration pleased neither German emigres who wanted to deprive the Nazis of their cultural facade nor Nazi ideologists who feared the betrayal of their revolution, which had proclaimed the potential of the arts as a social catylist.

In the beginning, Furtwängler was blind to the totalitarian claims and terroristic methods of the regime which came to power legally on January 30, 1933. Its revolutionary style, though offensive to his traditionalist sensibilities, also promised opportunities for music. The regime's commitment to the arts in the service of national regeneration resembled his restorational views. Moreover, as the director of the bankrupt Berlin Philharmonic Orchestra, he welcomed the new sense of urgency regarding music's economic crisis which, like anti-Semitic agitation, was a carry-over from the Republican period. Early interventionist measures were consistent with inherited traditions. He was conditioned to look for state support which, in his mind, did not threaten his authority and music's lofty place above politics, and he would continue to honor his obligation to perform in official capacity. Already in the previous era he had developed a clear conception of autonomy, in spite of final dependency on the public sector. He was well aware of his representational value in Germany and abroad. Before 1933 he had argued for subventions with reference to the diplomatic advantages the state would gain from Germany's foremost orchestra, as he had simultaneously resisted all attempts by non-musical authorities to interfere in matters of musical program and personnel, be it in Berlin or Bayreuth.

While Furtwängler's position was confirmed by the Nazis, his politics were suspect in spite of his traditionalist attitude toward music. Called reactionary for his views on music's autonomy, he was unreliable to the Nazis for his association with Jewish artists and especially his Jewish secretary Berta Geissmar, whom he refused to dismiss. Nonetheless, Goebbels appreciated his value to the regime as well as his affinity with the professed principles underlying Nazi cultural policies. From day one, Goebbels attempted to capture the musician Furtwängler for the regime beyond the level of a pragmatic arrangement. The complex and contradictory relationship between the maestro and the political manipulator, which took the form of mutually compromising collaboration and authority conflict, constituted a main theme with variations within the evolving reality of the politics of music in the Third Reich. While Goebbels appreciated Furtwängler's contribution to the cultural facade even without the latter's identification with National Socialism, the conductor sought to exploit the arrangement and affect the regime's cultural policies. What to Goebbels was a cultural facade meant music as usual to the fighter for autonomy, as he conducted traditional musical programs including Jewish performers and compositions, went on pre-arranged tours, withheld participation at any event deemed by him political and refused to perform Nazi music as compromising and demeaning. Firmly in charge of his orchestra, holder of many other prestigious positions and secure in an international reputation as the outstanding representative of the German symphonic tradition, during the early days of the "revolution" he was also negotiating a contract for the artistic directorship of the Berlin State Opera with the director of Prussian stages, Heinz Tietjen, who reported to Göring, another political authority Furtwängler had to contend with. But the Berlin Philharmonic Orchestra remained central to his concern. Ultimately, the RMVP would assume responsibility for the orchestra and assure its solvency, although for the time being it also suffered from the "revolution of the street." It had to accept members of a disbanded symphonic orchestra, including Pg's who made some trouble. When the RMVP rejected the appeal for special police protection, Bruno Walter cancelled his scheduled subscription concert at the Philharmonic, March 20, after the shocking Leipzig incident. (See above.) Furtwängler refused to substitute, but Strauss jumped in to save the concert and the income for the orchestra, which was in desperate straits. Strauss even donated his 1500

RM salary to the orchestra. The day after, Furtwängler performed *Die Meister-singer* at the State Opera as his formal contribution to the ritualistic inauguration of the new Reich before the world—a first sample of his service to the Nazi state which was consistent with practice during the Republic and with his perception of his duties. The next day he conducted *Elektra*, featuring the "non-Aryan" Rose Pauly, and then he went on tour with his orchestra in demonstration of business as usual.

However, the revolution continued to knock at his door. The Enabling Law established the party dictatorship and thus brought into question his distinction between party and state service. The KfdK invaded concert halls. Havemann wanted to purge his orchestra of its Jewish members, especially Berta Geissmar; he also demanded that it stage a benefit concert for the KfdK. Then he threatened to dissolve the *Deutschen Konzertgeberbund*, the concert agency over which Furtwängler presided, because of its Jewish membership. Furtwängler was able to resist this offensive for a while, but he understood his vulnerability and the need for allies and connections. Then the Reich assigned a commissioner to the orchestra who was to see to its *Gleichschaltung*. Ironically, this cultivated musician, Pg Rudolf von Schmidtseck, shared many assumptions about the orchestra with Furtwängler and collaborated with the management—including Geissmar, in preserving its standards. But, on another front Furtwängler suffered a defeat. At a Board meeting of the Berlin Art Festival in early April, he was unable to prevent the purge of Jewish and other defamed musicians and music from its program. According to Prieberg, these incidents prompted Furtwängler's decision to become the arbiter of music for the whole country and his realization that he needed to cultivate contacts in order to defend the integrity of his domain.[5] Meanwhile, *Gleichschaltuung* proceeded throughout Germany, and the foreign artists who had appealed to Hitler to reverse his racial policy—"we are convinced that such persecutions as take place in Germany at present are not based on your instructions, and that it cannot possibly be your desire to change the high cultural esteem Germany, until now, has been enjoying in the eyes of the whole civilized world..."—were banned from German broadcasting as per an announcement by the Nazi director of Berlin Radio.[6] Furtwängler was furious. The regime's action violated what he assumed to be the arrangement by which he hoped to salvage music, his own authority, international relations and thus to affect cultural policy. Troubled by other alarming developments as well, he resolved to protest to Goebbels.

The Drama of Confrontation

Furtwängler's celebrated letter in defense of music and Jewish artists arrived at the RMVP on April 7, the day the *Reichstag* adopted the Law for the Restoration of the Professional Civil Service. Upon Goebbels' request the letter and Goebbels' reply appeared in the *Vossische Zeitung* on April ll, 1933. The public dispute over music as either sovereign, independent of and superior to politics or as an expression of the people, subject to public support and thus responsible and subordinated to the state, caused a sensation. Furtwängler acknowledged some positive features of the new regime, manifested in the mutual desire for "regeneration of our national honor," and allowing for some of the radical measures in the process of coordination. "If the fight against Jewry is in the main aimed at those artists who demonstrate uprootedness and destruction, who try to impress with kitsch and dry virtuosity, then that is right. The struggle against them and the spirit expressed by them, manifested also by Germanic representatives, cannot be waged too emphatically and with enough consequence." Emphasizing the compatibility and affinity of conservatism in music with the music-ideological platform of Nazism, he repeated that, "Our struggle ought to aim at the uprooted, disintegrating, leveling, and destructive spirit." However, he added a new perspective as he coped with the new reality.

Art and the artist are there to unite, not to separate. I only recognize one line of separation: between good and bad art. At present, the division is drawn between Jew and non-Jew, even in cases in which state-political conviction cannot offer grounds for complaint, with theoretical and relentless severity, while the separation between good and bad music is neglected. The present musical situation, weakened enough by the world crisis, the radio, etc., can tolerate no more experiments. Music cannot simply be allocated and produced upon demand. . . .The question of the quality of music is... a question of life and death. . . .If the struggle aims also at true artists, then it is not in the interest of cultural life, if for no other reason than that artists are rare, wherever it be. No country can do without them without affecting culture adversely.

He then took a bold stand against anti-Semitism and the apparent official encouragement of denunciations and purges, specifying that "men like Walter, Klemperer, Reinhardt, etc. must be able to have a voice in Germany in the future." Goebbels, in turn, welcomed the opportunity to respond to Furtwängler whom he professed to respect, but whose "l'art pour l'art point of view" he identified with a by-gone age. "Art must be good; but beyond this it must be responsible, professional, popular and aggressive." As he lectured on totalitarian virtues he assured the musician that "you will always be able to express your art in Germany..." Indeed, "capable artists whose extra-musical impact does not violate elementary norms of the state, politics and society..." can be certain of the regime's "warmest support."[7]

Having taken his public stand, Furtwängler felt terrific. The international press celebrated him as a defender of art and civilization. Journalists and musicians thanked him, looked to him for leadership against Nazi racism and provincialism, and were lulled into disputes over aesthetics and terminology in view of his accommodationist argumentation. Though clear about the issue of anti-Semitism and musical standards, he had betrayed sympathy for the Nazis' conception of rooted art and their rejection of negative experimentalism. He, as well as his fans and detractors, contributed to the atmosphere of normalcy, as if the issue were aesthetics. In fact, Goebbels' reference to "elementary norms of state..."—a veiled threat—established the priority of politics. By not addressing Jews explicitly in his letter, he managed to broaden the debate about art and thus almost hide key features of policy: its ruthless anti-Semitism and totalitarian controls. Instead, he succeeded in gaining a measure of respect for his willingness to discuss cultural policy. Furthermore, he skilfully bound Furtwängler further to the regime, while at the same time branding him a reactionary defender of vested interests and dated standards.[8]

Furtwängler learned much from the exchange. He understood that the conflict was far from over and that he faced a resourceful adversary who had brilliantly manipulated him. Yet, the fact that Goebbels had publicly debated with him what he took to be cultural policy encouraged him to continue the struggle for autonomy and standards and to press for concrete results. Unfortunately, he soon realized that Goebbels drove a hard bargain. The minister effectively mixed threats with the promise and the withholding of rewards in his relentless drive toward affecting concessions from Furtwängler. Goebbels knew that the musician required his instrument; in the case of Furtwängler it was his orchestra. Furtwängler, in turn, gambled on the minister's appreciation of the benefits the regime would derive from the maintenance of standards and the appearance of independence in artistic matters of Germany's foremost orchestra—thus, this war of nerves. By the time the Berlin Philharmonic Orchestra departed for its major tour beginning April 22, 1933, its financial crisis had not been resolved. On the other hand, the orchestra's management had been asked to submit a list of its Jewish and half-Jewish members in preparation for their eventual dismissal—measures consistent with Nazi policy, but a threat to Furtwängler's authority and the arrangement he thought he was working under. Goebbels would repeatedly link the orchestra's security with the question of its Jewish members as a means of exerting pressure on the conductor known for his intervention for Jews.[9]

Although Furtwängler's public resistance was not typical, his situation was. Through his singular stand the music establishment was forced to confront an official policy which pressed for institutional and social change. The traditionally patronized and obedient musician—the representative and purveyor of the German spirit and of an affirmation of an inner sense of values—was ill-prepared for this revolutionary thrust toward public involvement which amounted to the unwitting impetus toward what Dahrendorf identifies as a necessary ingredient of modernization and liberalization of traditional social and professional relationships. Even the artist was to become a conscious participant in the social and political life of an integrated, egalitarian society. This populist impulse of National Socialism threatened traditional authority. On the other hand, the elitist and authoritarian aspects of the Nazi doctrine undermined the progressive and democratic potential, thereby enabling traditional authority to appeal to inherited liberties and the autonomy of the institution as that of the art, but not to the liberties of the individual, since Furtwängler and other authoritative representatives of the traditional social order did not favor modern democracy either. Thus, Goebbels could again argue that the authoritarian upholders of the autonomy of art and institution were fighting a reactionary battle against the Nazi revolution which in 1933 initiated a political and social program of modernistic implications.

Of course in reality the revolution was compromised, as we have seen. The question of authority, so greatly emphasized, was neither resolved within National Socialism, nor in relationship to coordinated authorities of the professions. Even though Furtwängler publicly questioned and violated Nazi principles and supported Jews, Marxists and avant-guardists, he was promoted and celebrated by the Nazis—albeit in manipulated form. Eager to maintain a high level of music in Germany and at great pains not to antagonize public and international opinion, Göring and Goebbels upheld the facade of independent authority and professional integrity. More dogmatic uniformity and rigidity were still found in Rosenberg's circle and in the provinces among minor officials who resented Furtwängler. At Mannheim his Philharmonic was to perform jointly with the local orchestra whose Nazi leadership had requested that its own section leaders be permitted to replace those of the Berlin group. Furtwängler understood the request as an attempt to remove Jewish section leaders, especially the orchestras' Jewish concert master, Simon Goldberg, from their deserved positions. After the conductor threatened cancellation if the principle of musical excellence were thus violated, the concert took place with the Jews in their customary seats—a scandal in the eyes of local party journalists who threatened action should such an indiscretion be repeated in the future.[10] To aggravate matters, Furtwängler stayed with Jewish friends in Mannheim and refused to attend an official banquet given for members of the local party and the musicians. He was so outraged by the entire incident that he wrote a complaint to Goebbels on April 30 and included a copy of a letter he had written to the management of the Mannheim Orchestra in which he threatened never again to perform with those musicians who would not recognize his and the government's commitment to artistic excellence. He complained about the decline of musical standards in provincial cities and urged a return to the freedom of musical expression and of submitting music to the public judgment in order to prevent further decline of this "most German" art.[11] Meanwhile, provincial voices continued to articulate the party line. The United Music Critics of Silesia joined the chorus against Furtwängler in an article in the ZfM (June, 1933). They supported Goebbels in his public reply to Furtwängler in April and made it plain that Furtwängler's conservative-liberal idea of the autonomous artist was "undesirable." Their defense of Goebbels' definition of "responsible, professional, popular and aggressive art" reflected that of the coordinated profession, as well as the underlying *völkisch* mentality of the greater part of the movement.

After the concerts in Mannheim and a few other German cities, the Berliners arrived in Paris where Jewish and emigre goups almost prevented their performance. The organizers of the boycott finally were persuaded to restrict their activities to the distribution of anti-Nazi leaflets during intermission. This action countered both collaborationist efforts and the Nazis' cultural facade, but it also had the result of strengthening Furtwängler's position with the Nazis who realized his indispensability. He, in turn, though personally distressed by the incident, became more confident about his plans for affecting Nazi policy in favor of music.

Meanwhile, international opinion about his efforts varied, anticipating the post-war Furtwängler controversy. Even though his singular protest was acknowledged abroad—as in the Parisian leaflets—he continued to encounter increasing hostility as the symbol of musical collaboration.[12] While the emigre paper, the *Pariser Tageblatt*, called Geissmar a "Hitler Jewess," Fritz Busch publicly referred to Furtwängler as an opportunist—a charge perhaps occasioned, in part, by their rivalry over the artistic directorship of the Berlin State Opera, which went to Furtwängler and Busch's perception that Furtwängler had schemed against him.[13] *Mitgefangen, mitgehangen*, sounded Busch's accusation, standing for guilt by association. Yet, unbeknownst to him, Furtwängler had actually appealed to the authorities in behalf of his colleague. In fact, ever since his letter exchange with Goebbels, Furtwängler had been beseeched by musicians for help, and he responded passionately. Recently signed to a five-year contract at the Berlin State Opera and appointed official State Conductor by Göring, he utilized his connections, offices and prestige—the advantages, in his mind, of collaboration—for all musicians in need: "Aryans" and Jews, Marxists, atonalists and conservatives alike—including Tietjen, who secretly conspired against him. Like a sovereign, he defended his realm. He wrote letters to the political leadership; thus, to Goebbels on April 30 about declining musical standards in the provinces. In a letter to Rust from Paris while on tour, June 4, 1933, he repeated his concern over declining musical standards and the urgency to reverse racially motivated discriminatory policy, while including appeals in behalf of the Jewish Professor Robert Henried, Arnold Schönberg and Fritz Busch.[14]

The letters, interventions in behalf of victims, additional honors and positions became a pattern. At the end of June his strategy appeared to gain a breakthrough when he was included in a commission appointed by Rust for the supervision of all public concert agencies in Prussia. Standards were to be preserved and contemporary compositions to be promoted. Not significant in the long run, the commission, which also included Max von Schillings, Wilhelm Backhaus and Georg Kulenkampff, reflected jurisdictional confusion and the viability, therefore, of Furtwängler's plans to affect policy.[15] Meanwhile, he continued to perform abroad, where he conducted Jewish musicians and singers and cultivated foreign contacts as his contribution to diplomacy. Whatever the merits of the attacks on Furtwängler therefore, his case was more complex than that of other prominent collaborators or opportunists and less well-known musicians. Some have identified him with "inner emigration"—a term already in use during the Third Reich. Yet, Rudolf Peschel has included Furtwängler in his book on German resistance. Riess likened him to a priest who remained behind to treat the sick, the criminal and the the needy; indeed, he deplored emigre hostility which to him was based on ignorance of his courage and achievement. Whereas emigre hostility actually reinforced his credibility with the Nazis and thus facilitated his efforts in behalf of music and the regime's victims, he has consistently rejected the notion of his political naivete or apolitical escapism as alleged by the otherwise adulatory Geissmar.[16] He has always claimed that he remained in Germany—even as late as shortly before the outbreak of war when the emigre Friedelind Wagner urged him to remain in Paris—in order to resist totalitarianism, preserve music and affect Nazi policy.[17]

His most serious detractors have claimed and still allege that his position was determined by values he shared with the *völkisch* movement—evident, to them, in his consistent support of Pfitzner—including an almost reverential respect for the state which he appeared to have transferred to the new regime, and for German culture, as well as a nineteenth-century style romantic nationalism, which imparted a distinct cultural identity and helps explain his deep mistrust of democratic institutions, his distaste for modernism and intellectualism and his well-bred and selective anti-Semitism—his detractors noting that he defended only talented Jews who enhanced German culture. The harshest critic, Berndt Wessling draws a severe portrait of a ruthless opportunist whose vanity contributed to the silencing and possibly even death of an unfriendly critic, Edwin von der Null—a claim not borne out by the record—and whose jealousy produced sinister plots against rivals like von Karajan. At best, the critics have questioned the advisability of his as well as any expression of collaboration as beneficial to a regime of criminals.

Furtwängler's defenders have stressed his unquestioned musical talent and prestige, his integrity and the heroic struggle against totalitarianism in behalf of music's autonomy, its standards and the victims of persecution—whose collaboration, according to the most recent and detailed apology by Prieberg, reveals a consistent strategy of resistance and even of combating anti-Semitism and thus transcending the arts to encompass politics and engage the Nazis on moral grounds which, like the contrary allegation of Wessling, is not documented, not even in the previously unpublished papers introduced by Prieberg. If Furtwängler's motives remain open to interpretation, his actions confirm the "trial of strength" presented by Prieberg. Whether Furtwängler was seduced by a regime whose cultural policy accorded with some of his own values or was firmly committed to resisting totalitarianism—or whether his collaboration reflected opportunistic impulses or a calling for the defense of music and humanity—he consistently argued that the Third Reich's reputation would benefit by his contribution as a free man and artist, not by one compromised by propaganda and orchestral bodies and programs reduced by purges of its best musicians. Thus, he not only withheld support for the Nazis, but showed more courage in standing up to them than any other artist in the Third Reich, even though he could not resolve the contradiction of having to remain and contribute to their manipulated culture in order to preserve music and challenge their policy.

Furtwängler may indeed have been naive in his belief in his ability to affect policy which he did not even recognize in its essential features, but his political engagement was undeniable; after his appointment to the program commission he continued to plead for dismissed musicians like Bernhard Sekles, Schönberg and the violinist Carl Flesch, whose life he probably saved. On the other hand, to claim escapist music as a form of resistance is another matter. Furtwängler's rendering of great music undoubtedly elevated his audiences above Nazi reality, as his apologists have noted, but it could offer no meaningful political alternative, no matter how high its esteem and its transcending potential. Riess's claiming meaningful opposition for Furtwängler's own compositions during the period of self-imposed exile in 1936 is even less credible. While absolute music is of course an ideal expression of inner emigration and can suggest the withholding of support of a political order, the political significance of this retreat is questionable. Negatively, however, the manifest disapproval on the part of a leading public person can be said to demonstrate the last expression of human autonomy against the totalitarian state. Then again, this autonomous act will reflect the resistance of a privileged social class, propertied to the extent that work is not essential for survival. Thus the act of defiance, liberal in its formulation of principles, reflected the malaise of traditional authority, privilege and social interest, i.e., easily castigated by Goebbels as a reactionary impulse against the potential of egalitarian, centralizing, and public-minded National Socialism. Furtwängler's pouting in the mountain retreat constituted the acknowledgment of initial toleration and collaboration, followed by a period of frustration upon the realization that the modernizing features of National Socialism, which ought not to have been surprising in view of the movement's birth in an industrialized society, were subject to mass-democratic impulses experienced after the catastrophic social consequences of World War I. Nonetheless, the politicly conscious musician, irrespective of the time of conversion to an ideology in defense of either a traditional order, liberal principles or both, finally gained the support of the nonpolitical colleague in flight from social and political involvement through inner emigration. The traditional order was masked by the liberal ideology which became the collective language of conservative and liberal opposition to the totalitarian state. Traditional apathy received converts in the form of motivated withdrawal, as the artistic and nonpolitical German was joined by the political German who chose to withdraw, music offering the illusion that this was, in fact, possible. This escapist feature of Furtwängler's representative position was reminiscent of the prince in Edgar Allan Poe's *The Masque of the Red Death*, who withdraws to a palace with his retinue, while his land is invaded by the pest. The prince locks all doors and celebrates indoors while death celebrates outside. Suddenly, the pest in costume breaks into the fantastic and bizarre masquerade ball and wreaks havoc in the exclusive society. The parallel suggests the interpretation of inner emigration in Germany, dealing with the contemporary aesthete within a world in which lawlessness occurred daily and which ultimately affected the withdrawn. Inner emigration might well have been an impossibility, and having been associated only with exponents of a privileged order it was not able to offer itself as a social model. As Poe concluded that it is impossible to insulate oneself from society, Brecht wrote in a draft of a letter to Hindemith that "music is not an ark upon which one might survive the flood."[18]

Furtwängler's temporary attempt to stay clear of politics proved to be futile. Goebbels' capacity to dictate the terms of public performance overwhelmed him. The faith in the moral superiority of art was no match for the politics of manipulation. Yet, Furtwängler's ambivalent attitude toward the regime, his immense authority and the contradictions inherent in his decision to resist while collaborating, turned him into Germany's most interesting musical case study. He magnified the predicament of the collaborating and captive profession. The biographies of his equals in fame lacked the same drama because he alone appeared to retain both the opportunity and the moral commitment to freedom of choice. Jewish victims like Schönberg, Klemperer and Bruno Walter had no options; they were purged and sent packing—ironic, at best, in the case of Walter, who shared many attitudes with Furtwängler. Like so many other Jewish German artists, Walter chose to go to Austria before the *Anschluss* in order to be as close to German culture as possible. His views and actions differed from those of Furtwängler in no way, the distinctiveness in his biography being based on the Jewish factor. Throughout his career he had also endeavored to keep music clear of politics. Against the Nazi threat, he also attempted at first to preserve music's autonomy by non-political means. In his memoirs he identified his relationship to politics in the manner of a removed historian.[19] Such conservatives clung to an anti-ideological bias, assuming that somehow personal integrity and competence would be respected by an otherwise unscrupulous totalitarian regime. Hindemith might have developed into a complex case because of his acceptability on racial grounds and his music but, after a few years of an ambivalent and controversial relationship with the regime, he took a clear, therefore non-problematic position when he left Germany. While von Karajan collaborated to the point of joining the party in order to promote his career, Strauss decided on a compromise, being too old for experiments but alert enough to maintain personal integrity in his initial period of cooperation in official capacity and later in retreat, illustrating the life of an individual who did not even contemplate meaningful political action. Of all the prominent personalities in music, Furtwängler alone remained and struggled, subject to tremendous pressures and seduction but, due to unique circumstances, exercizing options in relative freedom. He stood as a tragic figure—discredited and celebrated, accused as collaborator and traitor to the best of German tradition, yet also praised as defender of the musical order by millions after the war; despised by some Nazis and admired by others who also manipulated him. In 1946, he commented on his situation in retrospect:

I tried to test myself carefully. I am no better than others, although I did attempt to remain loyal to my basic inclination which motivated me: the love for my homeland and my people, a physical and spiritual concept, and the feeling of responsibility toward the prevention of injustice. Only here could I struggle for the soul of the German people. Outside, people can only protest; anyone can do that.[20]

After the letter exchange with Goebbels and the Mannheim and Paris incidents, Furtwängler continued to solidify his position by accepting an appointment to Göring's ceremonial Prussian State Council on July 20, bringing the Philharmonic's financial plight to the personal attention of Hitler on August 9, and in November becoming Vice-President of the RMK by means of which he was bound organizationally to Goebbels' authority. Most significantly, he announced to the assembled members of the Philharmonic on August 21 that the Führer and the government had committed themselves to the support of the orchestra and to Furtwängler's absolute authority in artistic and personnel matters[21]—in accordance with the Nazi leadership principle which he proceeded to exploit to the fullest. He thus continued to intervene in behalf of several Jewish victims of discriminatory legislation. Meanwhile, he promoted international contacts and exchanges. Most ambitiously, in late June he invited noted Jewish and anti-fascist artists to perform as soloists for his 1933-34 season, including Casals, Cortot, Josef Hofmann, Hubermann, Kreisler, Menuhin, Thibaud, Schnabel and Piatigorsky. In each personal letter he pleaded for the separation of politics and art and for the necessity to maintain Germany's cultural excellence, clearly wishing to undermine the government's anti-Semitic policy and asserting his own authority. While his campaign earned him severe rebuke from the KfdK, the invitees declined. Protesting respect for the friend and colleague and, in several instances, for his objectives, they were unwilling to collaborate with the racist regime, wanting instead to mobilize their prestige against the resources of that state. Yehudi Menuhin immediately declined by cable. Kreisler, Piatigorsky, and Thibaud also declined, even though Kreisler had praised the German revolution in April and urged Toscaninni not to boycott Bayreuth. Casals, of exceptionally strong character and anti-fascist record, declined, while emphasizing his strong. personal friendship with Furtwängler. He understood his friend's desperate position. Cortot refused on the spur of the moment, but later accepted.[22] To all of these artists, politics had intruded into German musical life. They would not perform in Germany as long as equal rights were not accorded to everyone. This position of uncompromising opposition suggested that Furtwängler could not win his battle and that accommodation would ultimately benefit the stronger party.

The letter exchange between Furtwängler and the great violinist Bronislaw Hubermann testifies more than any other document of the period to the confusion and the complexity of the issues facing Furtwängler and the conservative German music establishment. Berta Geissmar, who knew Furtwängler better than any other commentator, attributed the most ambitious conspiratorial motives to him which, of course, could not be revealed. If he wished to remain in Germany in order to soften the impact of the Nazis on music, he needed to cultivate contact with the regime; that, she felt, the emigres and other outsiders had to understand and support, but they chose not to. Their rejections isolated him and undermined his subversive efforts. He

> had written to Huberman out of a strong and sincere conviction. Fighting a brave and lonely battle, he fervently hoped that he might overcome the unnatural measures threatening to strangle Germany's artistic life, if those who shared his feelings would side with him. He reasoned that in all their measures the Nazis always referred to the "Voice of the People." He was convinced that the People would warmly welcome the artists whom they had applauded for many years. He hoped that the great soloists with whom he was linked by so many unforgettable memories would help him to convince the new regime of what the People really wished for.

She then added, however, "What he did not realize was that the new regime did not want to be convinced."[23] In response to his plea for support, Hubermann answered in a letter, written in Vienna and dated August 31, 1933, clearly distinguishing between his and Furtwängler's forms of opposition, yet insisting on his trust in the latter's integrity nonetheless:

> Dear Friend,—
>
> Permit me first of all to express my admiration for the fearlessness, determination, tenacity, and sense of responsibility with which you have conducted your campaign begun in April for rescuing the concert stage from threatening destruction by racial "purifiers." When I place your action—the only one, by the way, that has led to a positive result in the Germany of today—alongside that of Toscanini, Paderewski, and the Busch brothers, all of which sprang from the same feeling of solidarity and concern for the continuation of our culture, I am seized with

a feeling of pride that I, too, may call myself a musician.

Precisely these models of a high sense of duty, however, must prevent all our colleagues from accepting any compromise that might endanger the final goal... You try to convince me by writing, "Someone must make a beginning to break down the wall that keeps us apart."

Yes, if it were only a wall in the concert hall... In reality it is not a question of violin concertos nor even merely of the Jews; the issue is the retention of those things that our fathers achieved by blood and sacrifice, of the elementary preconditions of our European culture, the freedom of personality and its unconditional self-responsibility unhampered by fetters of caste or race...

I cannot close this letter without expressing to you my deep regret at the conditions that have resulted in my being separated for the moment from Germany. I am especially grieved and pained in my relationship as a friend of my German friends and as an interpreter of his German hearers. And nothing could make me happier than to observe a change also outside the realm of concert life which would liberate me from the compulsion of conscience, striking at my very heartstrings, to renounce Germany.[24]

These lines addressed the actual situation of German culture, an uncertain German government, emigre revulsion, conservative hopes, still fair in view of the uncertainty of Nazi policy at this stage and sharing in the political naiveté of Furtwängler, in that the radicalism of the Nazis had not as yet been implemented in all its brutality, thus allowing for hope, yet also the prophetic anticipation of the end of European culture. The next years transformed Germany drastically. Furtwängler had compromised himself to a greater degree under pressures of circumstance, and Hubermann again took to the pen, this time in less friendly and uncertain terms which must have struck the conservative friend in Germany as the enviable expression of men of conscience in freedom. The letter addressed to "German intellectuals" was published in the Manchester Guardian March 7, 1936, in response to the Nuremberg legislation and the destruction of intellectual freedom:

Since the publication of the ordinances regulating the application of the Nuremberg legislation—this document of barbarism—I have been waiting to hear from you one word of consternation or to observe one act of liberation. Some few of you at least certainly must have some comment to make upon what has happened, if your avowals of the past are to endure. But I have been waiting in vain. In the face of this silence I must no longer stand mute. It is two and a half years since my exchange of correspondence with Dr. Wilhelm Furtwängler, one of the most representative leaders of spiritual Germany...

Hubermann then referred to various outrages of the Nazi government, "the brutalization of large sections of the German population," "bestialities of the darkest Middle Ages," as reflected in the story "of a gentle Aryan girl who in punishment of her alleged commerce with a Jew was dragged in a pillory through the principal streets of Nuremberg amid the howl of the mob."

Dr. Furtwängler was profoundly revolted not only at the Nuremberg incidents, which he assured me he and all "real Germans" condemned as indignantly as I,... I am not familiar with Dr. Furtwängler's attitude to these happenings, but he expressed clearly enough his own opinion of all "real Germans" concerning the shamefulness of the so-called race-ravishing pillories; and I have not the slightest doubt of the genuineness of his consternation, and believe firmly that many, perhaps the majority of Germans, share his feelings.

Well, then, what have you, the "real German," done to rid conscience and Germany and humanity of this ignominy... Where are the German Zolas, Clemenceaus, Painlevés, Picquarts, in this monster Dreyfus case against an entire defenseless minority?. . .

Before the whole world I accuse you, German intellectuals, you non-Nazis, as those truly guilty of these Nazi crimes, all this lamentable breakdown of a great people—a destruction which shames the whole white race. It is not the first time in history that the gutter has reached out for power, but it remained for the German intellectuals to assist the gutter to achieve success. It is a horrifying drama which an astonished world is invited to witness; German spiritual leaders with world citizenship and German genius, men called to lead their nation by their precept and example, seemed incapable from the beginning of any other reaction to this assault upon the most sacred possessions of mankind than to coquet, cooperate, and condone. And when, to cap it all, demagogical usurpation and ignorance rob them of their innermost conceptions from their own spiritual workshop, in order thereby to disguise the embodiment of terror, cowardice, immorality, falsification of history in a mantle of freedom, heroism, ethics, German intellectuals reach the pinnacle of their treachery: they bow down and remain silent. . . . Germany, you people of poets and thinkers, the whole world—not only the world of your enemies, but the world of your friends—waits in amazed anxiety for your word of liberation.[25]

Hubermann's sentiments reflected the same cultural standards; rooted in traditional German society as those defended by Furtwängler. The difference, again, lay in their respective circumstances and immediate objectives, predicated on the actual proximity of the one to Nazi power and having to deal with it, and the other's distance from it. The world had indeed been polarized, and the case of Furtwängler illustrated the futile effort of preserving the old world from within. Hubermann spoke for millions throughout the world, adding the voice of a musician to numerous other passionate pleas for liberation of Germany, in a manner which shamed the German intellectual. He went to Palestine and founded a new orchestra in Tel Aviv; he was never again mentioned in Nazi Germany.

In Germany *Gleichschaltung* proceeded and Furtwängler pursued his path of collaboration and resistance while increasingly pressured by Rosenberg and the NSKG (the successor organization of the KfdK) and subject to denunciations by both the local Nazi press and the emigres. On January 16, 1934 he finally signed a five-year contract with Göring for the directorship of the State Opera, thereby strengthening his position at home while arousing concern among emigres and anti-Nazi foreigners. Boycotts of the Berlin Philharmonic took place in England shortly thereafter, limited in scope only by Sir Thomas Beecham's public defense in the *Daily Telegraph* (January 20, 1934) of his German colleague and reference to the Jewish members of the orchestra—the very fact which was simultaneously denounced in the Nazi press. While on tour in Paris that Spring he was castigated in a vicious handout by Hanns Eisler as the "State Councillor by the grace of Göring and Goebbels" who "abetted and provided a facade for Nazi crimes" and "did not protest the expulsion of Germany's best artists"—a reflection of emigre bitterness and militance, but also containing misinformation and distortion of Furtwängler's activities.[26] Evidence to the contrary mounted as Furtwängler defied policy by performing Mendelssohn's *Mid-Summer Night's Dream* music on February 12 of that year in commemoration of the Jewish composer's one-hundred-twenty-fifth birthday, and he continued to schedule Mendelssohn at the Philharmonic, where Kulenkampff performed the romantic's popular violin concerto as late as March 11, 1935. On other occasions he succumbed to pressure, as when he obeyed Hitler's request not to participate at the Salzburg Festival that summer.[27] (See Chapter II.) Meanwhile, he suffered a real loss of power when the new board of directors of his now nationalized Reich Orchestra assumed functional control and designated administrators for business and artistic affairs who were to report to the board of largely RMVP and other government officials rather than to the corporate orchestra; the first conductor, Furtwängler had no vote on the board and Geissmar would no longer be retained as a public official, although he was allowed to keep her as a private secretary.[28] In July the Jewish musicians Simon Goldberg and Joseph Schuster left the orchestra on their own accord; they could no longer tolerate their positions as privileged Jews in the anti-Semitic environment. On the other hand, Furtwängler managed to secure RMVP approval of Hugo Kolberg, who had a Jewish wife, as the new concert master.[29] However, the new contract of July 20, 1934 no longer permitted the engagement of "non-Aryan" soloists.[30]

The pressure on Furtwängler to conform continued when Rosenberg suggested that the Philharmonic perform at the Party Congress called "Triumph of the Will," in September 1934, as a means of tying Germany's foremost orchestra to the party and to thus rid it of its Jewish members and compromise its leader. Geissmar has recorded Furtwängler's anxiety over this matter. Moreover, she blamed foreign dignitaries for their attendance which, she thought, undermined his strategy for music's autonomy and the regime's reform.[31] Hitler actually was persuaded of the orchestra's greater value as an export article—as Furtwängler has consistently argued—and allowed Furtwängler the freedom not to conduct and thereby demonstrate his independence as an artist. However, his case was an isolated one, recalling the early criticism of Hubermann that the fate of a few celebrities, as of the German concert hall, was no longer the issue. The Party Rally was a success and Furtwängler's refusal was of no consequence.

The delicate balance between collaboration and resistance could not be maintained forever in view of the contrary interests of the parties. While the representative and custodian of German music collaborated in order to negotiate for music's integrity and autonomy, the regime manipulated him in its singleminded drive toward an integrated Nazi culture. Meanwhile, the Nazi purists, the Rosenberg faction—undeterred by the apparent protection Furtwängler enjoyed—increased pressures on the conductor's surrogates, Hindemith and Geissmar. While the two victims would eventually emigrate, the conflict over Hindemith took turns which surprised Furtwängler, resulted in his resignation from all offices and thus caused the most serious impasse in relations and his reassessment of his collaboration strategy.

When the Rosenberg press launched a major campaign against Hindemith in Fall, 1934 and a local Saxon authority followed with a ban on a symphonic version of the opera, *Mathis der Maler*, which Furtwängler had already accepted for a premiere at the State opera for May, 1935, the Vice-President of the RMK and State Councillor protested to Goebbels against this invasion of the NSKG into the realm of a properly instituted authority of the state. It is clear that even at this time, Furtwängler still tried to distinguish between the party and the state and to thus deny the party's totalitarian claims. Out of step with clearly formulated Nazi law, he wanted to discuss the issue with

Hitler, and an audience was arranged for November 30. What he also did not know was that Hindemith had been unpopular with the Nazis at least as far back as 1929 and that Hitler personally had called his music degenerate. Now, the composer's new opera appeared to challenge National Socialism with its theme which celebrates art over politics and a public book-burning and thus alerted not only Nazi purists but also the political leadership. Inasmuch as the book-burning scene was but a minute detail in the overall structure, Furtwängler did not at first even realize the political intention of its author; he did not plan to challenge the regime at the time. Indeed, he seemed to be as committed as ever to his balancing act. He had come to the conclusion, he wrote Ludwig Curtius, a prominent archaeologist, that in the foreseeable future the present regime would not collapse. Thus, he advised his friend:

> Inasmuch as the regime has become a reality, every German who relies on employment for means of making a living is asked to decide between maintaining his position or not. In case of a positive decision, he has to come to terms with the dominant party. If you do not want to resign, you have to refrain from provocation . . . as evidenced in the possible reengagement of a Jewish governess for your children. Your position needs you and you need your position. You should not jeopardize it.

Thus he counseled accommodation, although he added that, "quite to the contrary, I am not bound to my position and can afford to act as a free man. (I have a similar matter at hand in the person of Berta Geissmar.) I am fully aware of my actions and of the possibilities of emigration. Remember when writing to me that my mail is read by political police.—dated September 10, 1934."[32]

Furtwängler was rather surprised by the development of the Hindemith affair. Though a "pure Aryan," Hindemith had offended the Nazis as the idol of the young music generation and leading spirit of the prestigious International Festival of Contemporary Music as well as other festivals of modern music on the continent. In addition to his modernism he had shocked the conservative world, for which the Nazis assumed the right to speak, with such works as the opera, *Neues vom Tage*, premiered by Otto Klemperer at the *Krolloper*, in which a nude woman performs the role of the heroine in a bathtub. Then, amidst some controversy, Furtwängler performed the symphonic version of *Mathis der Maler* for the first time in March, 1934.[33] In compiling the program for the State Opera Season, 1934-35, he was informed by Göring in July that Hitler's consent would be necessary for the performance of the new opera. Berta Geissmar confirms that Furtwängler took this questioning of his authority very seriously. The case proved again that "in the Nazi Reich, artistic authority and expert knowledge meant nothing as against the brutal force of dictatorship. For him this was a test case. He was the Musical Director of the Berlin State Opera and no one else. When did the head of a State ever interfere with details of a theater repertoire?"[34]

Yet, the authority conflict in music came to a head against the background of pivotal developments for the Nazis themselves. Geissmar reminds us that "the horrors of June 30th overshadowed the days that followed. The State Opera closed down at the beginning of July. Exhausted by this turmoil, Furtwängler went to stay in Poland. The Nazis' lust for blood seemed to be still unsatiated and I was actually told that when another purge was due Furtwängler would be a victim." These comments are relevant here as illustration of the inter-relationship of all Nazi affairs with those of music. Furtwängler's manifest courage needs to be emphasized in the light of the brutalization of German life and the pervasive sense of personal insecurity. While the Nazis violated all legal precedent during and after the Röhm affair, legitimizing governmental action by a retroactive law, and the creative artist, Hindemith practiced serene inner emigration by simply remaining out of the controversy, Furtwängler resolved to reformulate his position. Geissmar remembers that

> for Furtwängler, however, the decision as to whether he was to be allowed to produce Hindemith's opera was not only an artistic matter, but a vote of confidence and prestige. How could he, the director of Germany's leading Opera House, reconcile with his sense of responsibility the docking of authority which the Nazis were imposing upon him? He declared with great firmness that if this question of principle was not cleared up satisfactorily he would draw his own conclusions.[35]

The liberal-conservative controversy over politics and the progressive-conservative controversy in music had given way to one all-encompassing question of the traditional and autonomous authority of music against the totalitarian demands of National Socialism. Geissmar categorically rejects the possibility of Furtwängler's collaboration for personal gain, and she stresses that, "although he had decided to remain in Germany, he was certainly no Nazi." In the German world, an appointment like Furtwängler's as director of the Berlin State Opera was official, prestigious and authoritative. "These appointments to great musical positions both in Germany and Austria were made for reasons the roots of which lay deep in the German attitude to artistic matters," Geissmar explains to her English readers. "They were positions of unquestioned authority, and were given precisely to those personalities whose absolute authority in their own spheres it was desired to confirm and reinforce by their official character."[36]

Aroused and conscious of prerogative, he had performed the symphonic *Mathis* already in March, while across the country German stages lined up to do likewise. He insisted that not even Göring could interfere with his Philharmonic concerts. Similarly, he had shown independence by performing Mendelssohn's *A Midsummer Night's Dream* music, as we have seen. Since the Nazis were also testing their own jurisdictions and power and had compromised with him before, he obviously misunderstood his authority as leader of an old German order which he thought confirmed in the RMK. Göring had advised him not to take his position too seriously, that, indeed, "this responsibility . . . was borne by the National State and its leaders, and Furtwängler would be well advised not to make a cause célèbre out of the Hindemith matter. . . ."[37] The public saw more in Furtwängler's stand than he himself wished to imply. The performance of the symphonic *Mathis* in March had been applauded as a political demonstration. Indeed, the popularity of the work and the review of the performance were reflected in the worldwide attention in the press. For once, the public had applauded a modern work, the performance and Furtwängler's alleged demonstration, and critics of diverse musical views had joined in the enthusiasm. For instance, the progressive H.H. Stuckenschmidt had viewed the performance of such a work as official sanctioning of modern music, as the toleration of a significant portion of the traditional music culture. "The tremendous success contradicts the contention that modern music is *volksfremd*", he had writtten in the *B.Z. am Mittag* (March 13, 1934). Hans Lyck had agreed in the *Deutsche Zukunft* that "the audience rejoiced when Furtwängler picked up the baton. This was a great deed. We owe him thanks."[38] In reaction to this reception, the party press attacked Hindemith stronger than before. The *VB* declared him to be unacceptable, adding that "Furtwängler had made a regrettable mistake." The Nazis continued to attack progressives and conservatives throughout the year for what they construed as joint resistance to Nazi authority.

The controversy had tremendous consequences. Hindemith suffered breech of contract as the ban on his opera was upheld. He lost his position at the Music Academy at Berlin and went to Turkey in response to a commission of the Turkish government, a project which sustained German interests there and was appreciated by the Nazis.[39] Later he left for America. Yet, more important was the impact on Furtwängler. In the past he had not been subjected to the viciousness of coordinated newspaper attacks directly; his enemies had focused on Geissmar and Hindemith instead. Naively anxious to explain himself to Hitler and the public, he wrote the famous article, "The Hindemith Case" (November 25, 1934), in the widely read *Deutsche*

Allgemeine Zeitung—his second and last attempt to air his conflict with the Nazi regime in the press. Above all, he defended Hindemith against all forms of political attack. The Nazis had rejected Hindemith, in part, because of his Jewish connections and for the recording of music with two refugees, Simon Goldbert (the ex-concert master of Furtwängler's orchestra) and Emanuel Feuermann (ex-teacher at the Berlin Music Academy and member of his orchestra), whom Furtwängler believed to belong to the class of Germany's finest musicians. He deplored the reference to Jewish connections and praised Hindemith as an artist—especially his latest work, *Mathis der Maler*—calling him the most creative musician of the young Germany, who did more for German music in the world than any other member of the younger generation; he concluded that in the Hindemith case fundamental issues of principle were at stake. He asked, "What would happen if vague political denunciations were constantly to be applied to the artist?"—and answered that in the face of the great poverty in creative musicians all over the world, Germany can ill aford to dispense with a man like Hindemith.

Political denunciation had indeed caught up with Furtwängler himself. The reality of the Third Reich had finally been spelled out for him. His article caused a sensation in Germany and abroad. The Sunday issue of the *Deutsche Allgemeine Zeitung* had to print an extra issue. When Furtwängler rehearsed with his orchestra that same Sunday, a large crowd greeted him in the streets leading to the Philharmonic. The applause was greater than ever when Furtwängler finally mounted the platform inside. The political nature of this form of popular demonstration was unmistakable. On the same evening, Furtwängler conducted *Tristan* at the State Opera in the presence of Göring and Goebbels, and again the applause would not cease as Furtwängler appeared. Endless ovations broke out after the performance. Berta Geissmar writes that Göring immediately realized the significance of the demonstration, that indeed Furtwängler's position and authority could no longer be treated in isolation from broader political considerations.[40] His authority, as suggested to him by Hubermann and other emigre critics, had transcended his intention of separating art from politics. Coexistence of the realms seemed no longer possible, not even between the state and a seemingly non-essential and decorative institution. Inasmuch as the public demonstrations were for Furtwängler, they were against the government—that even he now understood.

While the public and the international press celebrated him, the Nazi reaction followed promptly. Hitler immediately cancelled the scheduled meeting with Furtwängler, who learned from Göring, to whom he had turned unbeknownst to the public for a possible reconciliation, that the ban on *Mathis der Maler* would not be lifted. The Minister President blamed his conductor for having created the impasse by his decision to go public with the issue. Goebbels, meanwhile, avoided him altogether. An enraged Hitler demanded an apology if he wished to retain his positions. Finally, the Führer requested his resignation which, when signed by Goebbels on December 5 and by Göring on December 10, included not only his culture-political offices, as he had intended, but his musical posts as well. Shocked and disappointed, he was without his orchestra and had to take note of Clemens Krauss's appointment to the musical directorship at the Berlin State Opera in his stead.

Meanwhile, Rosenberg and the Nazi press were given license to denounce the musician who had publicly challenged the totalitarian claims of the regime. On the other hand, anxious not to suffer further adverse publicity which would have resulted from the courageous conductor's defection, Hitler had him surrender his passport. This restriction prevented his emigration which he had, indeed, contemplated; but in view of his ambivalence toward ever leaving Germany, Hitler's measure probably simply resolved the issue for him and reinforced his deep commitment to his country. The romantic nationalist knew where he belonged and where he could follow what he believed to be his calling—the transmission of German symphonic music in its native environment. Here the public and the musicians understood and adored him. Since the Nazi leaders also wanted him to stay and expressed their gratitude for his previous service and appreciation of his singular artistic powers,[41] a new arrangement was soon worked out which would remain in place in its essential features for the remainder of the Third Reich. While his original strategy of affecting policy by means of high culture-political office had failed, the power of transcendent art would henceforth be tested before a grateful German public, a manipulatory regime and a suspicious world. The second phase of his collaboration, this term as an apolitical guest artist, had begun.

Transcendent Music in Totalitarian Society

The Furtwängler story symbolized the conditions of the musical profession, even though no other musician shared the experience of the representative leader. A tragic hero, he stood alone above the colleagues who, nonetheless, identified with him. Only one musician immediately drew consequences from the resignation. Erich Kleiber cancelled a concert on December 5 at the Philharmonic. Though still bound by contract to the State Opera, he prepared to leave all positions early in 1935 and to return to his native Austria. "If Furtwängler is dropped for political reasons," he protested, "I can no longer remain." When he appeared shortly after this dramatic event of December 5 at the State Opera, the audience rose in tumultuous acclaim, shouting, "Furtwängler, Kleiber." Göring was hissed upon entering his box.[42]

The anti-fascist world, meanwhile, paid tribute to the man decried shortly before as a collaborator. Hubermann wrote a congratulatory letter. No one seemed to care that Furtwängler's resistance had suffered a setback; in fact, most emigres denied the existence of an internal opposition. While they celebrated him as a man of principle at this time, he himself suffered tremendously from what he knew to be defeat and, hence, soon sought a reconciliation with the regime in order to redeem himself and to resume his fight for musical standards and autonomy. For the time being, however, he withdrew and actually hoped to function as a private person—a throwback to his traditionalism which conflicted with his equally strong sense of social responsibility. He now entered a brief period of actual inner emigration, joining those who intended to maintain their personal integrity as best as possible. He withdrew to the Alps where he was harmless and composed in the manner of a nineteenth-century romantic, while Nazi funtionaries in concert with the musical establishment affected further *Gleichschaltung*. He even lost his staff at the Philharmonic, as Schmidtseck was dismissed and Geissmar's contract was allowed to expire by March 1935. Geissmar explains that Furtwängler had tired under the strain of conflict and that he needed the isolation to recover in order to reenter public life and resume his struggle in behalf of music, which to her was inevitable. The Nazis agreed and deplored the fact that he had become the spokesman for all musicians including Jews and others defamed by the regime. His chief enemy, the powerful party ideologist Rosenberg, commented upon the resignation:

> The Hindemith case which, with unexpected suddenness has become the focal point of artistic debate, has been transformed into the Furtwängler case. Two fundamental ideas are aired, displaying the change of generations as the underlying difference between the liberal nineteenth century and the National Socialist twentieth century. . . . It is regrettable that an artist of Furtwängler's stature had to enter the dispute, believing himself to be compelled to identify himself with Hindemith . . . and calling the well-founded National Socialist criticism of Hindemith "political denunciation.". . . Inasmuch as Herr Furtwängler maintained the nineteenth-century mentality and shows no appreciation of the great people's struggle of our time, he drew the proper consequences.[43]

Goebbels addressed the Hindemith-Furtwängler affair in a similar manner on the occasion of the first anniversary of the RKK. Yet it was clear to the pragmatist for that very reason that a next phase of collaboration had to be arranged with the custodian and singular interpreter of the German symphonic tradition who had actually gained in reputation by his courageous public stand and resignation. While job offers came in from abroad, his adoring public made life difficult for his replacements in Berlin, and angry ticket holders demanded their money back—to the tune of close to 180,000 RM. For financial, popular and propagandistic reasons at home and abroad, Goebbels had to deal with his uncomfortable nemesis who insisted on his terms and took comfort in the public outpouring of support which fortified him in the belief in the justice of his cause. His prestige was greater than ever, rooted not in titles, but in moral and artistic authority—a not inconsiderable factor in view of the regime's commitment to a cultural facade and public profession of the heroic qualities which Furtwängler so manifestly embodied.

His decision to remain in Germany actually revitalized him. Assured of the support of the musicians and the public, he clarified his position as that of a free artist who would perform as a guest conductor at home and abroad. Back in Berlin, he cultivated his old connections—especially eager to negotiate with Goebbels—and again began to offer advice regarding music policy in general and the Philharmonic in particular.[44] Like a prophet who had returned from the desert (the mountains), he spoke of eternal German values, though cunningly in the terms of select compatible features of National Socialism—not its narrow and mean definition and application of race theory—naively forgetting, perhaps for tactical reasons, that the regime in practice represented the levelling of values that he and they officially professed to want to eliminate. Speaking for the people and of the necessity of a free press, he neglected the obvious popular support the regime enjoyed and the millions who had joined the party and its organizations. His belief in the transcendental power of music and genius, and, finally, in his own ability and authority—hopelessly out of touch with reality and public morality in the Third Reich—reflected his traditionalist background and authoritarianism which still conflicted with the dictatorial and levelling features of National Socialism.

The Nazi leaders learned that the tenacious conductor had bounced back from humiliation and fervently pursued former objectives. The authorities, in turn, imposed a war of nerves on him; they had been strengthened at home and internationally through the successful Saar plebiscite of January 1935. This new prestige encouraged them also in the Furtwängler affair. He was consciously ignored and slighted, while he added to his own discomfort and their confidence by constantly sending petitions to them. Nobody was available for conferences. Calls and letters went unanswered. Under the stress of this well-calculated policy, he finally offered to conduct in Germany again, on the condition of not having to assume official and representative positions. This was the same proposal which had been rejected before. In a way, the Nazis were caught in a dilemma similar to that of the conductor. They needed him for purposes of the prestige which he would lend to his political masters, in spite of his manifest anti-Nazi sentiments. The significant compromise of Furtwängler consisted in his acknowledgment of Hitler's prerogative to set culture-political policy. He later told Riess that this recognition had the advantage of absolving him from any responsibility regarding Nazi cultural politics, since he embraced the traditional and conservative principle of personal autonomy as an artist. He insisted on practicing his music as a free man, independent of all politics, and that he would not be used for propaganda. Only in this manner could he hope to make music, as he regarded it, in its international and human form. This time Goebbels accepted these proposals, guaranteeing his status as an apolitical artist, an extraordinary concession from the Nazi state.[45]

The official version of the compromise given to the press by Goebbels documents a state close to that of inner emigration. In regard to the Hindemith case, Furtwängler virtually apologized, conceding that Hitler shaped cultural policy and that he had never intended to treat the matter in political terms in the first place, but only from an artistic standpoint, thus forgetting that in this new state nothing could be discussed without bearing political implications. Goebbels concluded that Furtwängler had overlooked the totalization of Nazi demands, but had now recognized his own limitations.[46]

This remarkable development caused confused reactions throughout the world. Furtwängler regarded his statement as a retreat to a position from which he still could perform and save German music without being involved politically with the Nazis. He wrote to his mother that he had agreed to the compromise in order to be able to work abroad as a German. He did not want to become an emigre, though, as he later explained to Friedelind Wagner in Paris. Nonetheless, he emphasized to his mother his decision not to be active in Germany. He believed that it was still possible under National Socialism to exist in musical isolation as under traditional authoritarian governments.[47] However, a more alert outside world, the broad public in Germany and even close associates, regarded the official declaration as capitulation. Berta Geissmar recalled having been surprised by the announcement over the radio while residing in the Baviarian countryside. On February 28, 1934, the broadcast began, "Reich Minister Dr. Goebbels received State Councillor Dr. Furtwängler today." She was so shocked that she did not want to believe her ears, having been subjected to Nazi lies before. "Was this the end of the whole desperate struggle," she wondered, of "this man on whom so many had relied—and who, thanks to his achievements, was as independent of the Nazis as only few Germans were." Thus, she reflected general reaction to this capitulation. Then, however, she noted the most intriguing circumstances underlying the compromise: "Much later I learned the true facts about this matter." Having been subjected to official pressures, pleas of friends and the public, and conversations with associates about possible resumption of activity in Germany, he had drawn up several possible proposals which were typed for him by aides, and "apparently one of them out of zeal or an aptitude for intrigue, deemed it advisable to disclose to high Nazi quarters what was going on within Furtwängler's four walls; a preliminary draft found its way, in this manner, actually to Goebbels' desk." Goebbels used this draft for a comprehensive written statement which he dispatched to Furtwängler for his signature. Furtwängler refused, but "after a long and stubborn fight a compromise was found to serve as the text for publication after Furtwängler's interview with Goebbels. This text, watered down as it was, nevertheless represented a complete surrender of Furtwängler in the eyes of independent observers." The Nazis gained prestige, and a meeting between Furtwängler and Hitler could be arranged.[48] Whatever the merits of this cloak-and-dagger account, nowhere documented by Geissmar, the public certainly knew only of the official announcement, broadcast throughout Germany and published in major newspapers and professional journals. Furtwängler's situation was difficult, certainly more difficult than that of his foreign and emigre critics for whom the Nazis had made decisions—they had no choice—but he ought to have learned through experience that inner emigration in his case was an impossibility. His behavior, especially in view of his intention to continue the struggle on a different level, was most confusing. Through renunciation of offices, he had earlier relinquished the means for resistance which he had, at one time, cited against the accusations of collaboration.

In the context of the overall impact of National Socialism the outcome of the controversy settled the fate of music and Furtwängler, whose rehabilitation resulted in his return in April to his realm of power—the concert hall. The tumultuous ovation occasioned by his first concert with the Berlin Philharmonic Orchestra recalled the demonstrative applause during the Hindemith scandal. This relationship between the maestro and his grateful public constituted a major political theme in itself—which was obvious to the attending party leaders and foreign guests. On May 3, Hitler himself went to a repeat performance of the all-Beethoven concert and witnessed the unprecedented enthusiasm of the audience for the conductor. While the public thus expressed its thanks for the return of this unique artist and symbol of traditional culture, the anti-Fascist world judged it as treason, especially the recorded photo of Hitler shaking Furtwängler's hand after the concert—the token of reconciliation, but actually of the cynical display of the triumph of politics over art. Forgotten were his earlier heroics and continuing resistance. Never mind that he refused to raise his arm in the manner of the day—not even in the presence of the Führer on that staged occasion—and to sign his letters to officials with the customary, "Heil Hitler"; that he continued to resist Aryanization of his orchestra, protect victims and dissidents with whom he retained contact, or that he fired a wind player whose work had deteriorated—an "insignificant" and "not very intelligent person" who tried to hold on to his position by joining the party and appearing in SA uniform.[49]

The public photo of the handshake was followed by other gestures and events which suggested reconciliation. His fiftieth birthday on January 25, 1936 was formally acknowledged with a silver-framed Führer portrait cum dedication and a gift from Goebbels. He also agreed to conduct at Bayreuth in 1936, the year of the Olympics when the regime transformed all Germany into a stage. Yet, not all went smoothly. Furtwängler continued to insist on his apolitical status. He actually made rare appearances—perhaps thereby enhancing his prestige and contributing to the Furtwängler mystique—because he did not want to be used for propaganda. Besides, his ideological opposition continued to irritate the men at the Rosenberg bureau who, in concert with other enemies and rivals, tried to prevent his full rehabilitation. Tietjen felt threatened by his return and Clemens Krauss feared for his position at the State Opera, actively conspiring with the fellow Austrian exile Gauleiter Alfred Frauenfeld against Furtwängler, whom this party activist and business manager of the Reich Theatre Chamber accused in a memo on the Nazification of Austrian culture of undermining Nazi policy in Vienna by associating with emigre Jews, indeed, of ridiculing Nazi principles by having gone out of his way to provide employment at the Vienna State Opera to Herbert Graf, a Jewish emigre noted for his anti-German agitation. The anti-Furtwängler campaign included an anonymous denunciation reported by another Austrian exile and contact of Frauenfeld, the singer and Pg Oskar Jolli, who alleged that Furtwängler had confided his anti-Nazi sentiments to the German-Jewish author Franz Werfel to the extent of suggesting that the Nazi leaders all be shot. Even though some of these surreptitious maneuvers lacked credibility, Furtwängler continued to provoke the Nazi leadership, for instance, when he talked himself out of performing Beethoven's Fifth at the 1935 Party Congress and by still conspicuously intervening in behalf of the victims of discriminatory policy—his constituency regardless of race, ideology or aesthetic position—including the progressive music critic H. H. Stuckenschmidt who had been critical of Furtwängler in the past and assumed erroneously that the collaborating conductor had conspired against him. To the Nazis, this intervention in behalf of an exponent of leftist and avante-garde journalism raised further questions about Furtwängler's reliability.[50]

It is not clear from archival records to what degree he was aware of the denunciations against him which were filed in dangerously bulging dossiers at the offices of Hinkel at the RKK, the Gestapo and by Herbert Gerigk at the Rosenberg bureau with input from petty and famous musicians and a network of conspirators ranging from the names above to an ambitious concert and musicians' agent, Rudolf Vedder, who had connections in the SS which ultimately persecuted him. Confident in the support of his public and musicians and reassured by his international fame, an abundance of offers—including the party-state's request for his services—and the official recognition of his fiftieth birthday, he probably continued to believe in his indispensability and the value of what he represented. He even rejected a sinecure of 40,000 RM per annum, offered by Goebbels at that time, as incompatible with his apolitical status. Quite innocently he signed a new contract with Göring on February 24, 1936 for ten performances at the Berlin State Opera as a guest conductor, which he took to be a further step toward his rehabilitation.

Four days later, while vacationing in Egypt, the American press reported an offer from the New York Philharmonic Society for the most prestigious and best-paid position in international concert life. News of his appointment included biographical reference to his courageous stand against the Nazis and his protection of Jews and half-Jews. The official declaration of the Philharmonic Company read, "We are happy to have engaged this extraordinary conductor . . . who was already celebrated during his first trip to the United States ten years ago." The most remarkable circumstances had led to the appointment, as Furtwängler's old rival, Toscanini, had recommended him, on the assumption that Furtwängler would not occupy a permanent position in Germany, a condition confirmed in earlier declarations of Goebbels and Furtwängler. He would appear in Germany only as guest conductor. Thus, it seemed feasible for him to combine his activities in Germany with those in New York.[51]

The New York offer suggests that Furtwängler had in no way compromised his integrity or his music. New York would not have accepted a Nazi collaborator. Thus, New York was about to gain the most prestigious conductor of Germany, while Furtwängler could maintain his autonomy as foremost musical authority in Germany on the basis of international recognition. On the other hand, realization of the offer would have had a damaging impact on Nazi designs for German concert life. The development which culminated in the offer, the underlying thought behind it, and the various interest groups associated with it dealt a blow to Nazi policy and ideology and to the personal prestige of Goebbels as embodiment of the principle of coordination on ideological grounds, and most specifically to the prestige of the self-proclaimed patron of the arts, Furtwängler's superior at the State

Opera at Berlin, Göring.

One day after the New York announcement on February 29, the German press published his contract at the Berlin State Opera,[52] which was reprinted in America without reference to the fact that he had signed only as a guest conductor. This distorted news item resulted in a wave of protest against the "Nazi" conductor. Meanwhile, an AP bulletin confirmed Furtwängler's position as State Opera Director. According to Geissmar, Göring had decided to forestall developments, announcing Furtwängler's rehabilitation as an artist of the Third Reich without prior consultations with Furtwängler on the matter on the assumption that the statement would outrage the New York press. While indeed protests greeted this news item in New York, Furtwängler had been unaware of Göring's maneuver. The engagement of the opponent of National Socialism had been applauded in New York, but the prospects of the former and future head of the State Opera in Berlin, thus an official representative of the Third Reich, conducting America's foremost orchestra elicited violent opposition. During the controversy over the Furtwängler appointment in America an event took place which overshadowed the dispute: On March 7, 1936 Hitler marched into the Rhineland. The atmosphere was tense, and the proponents of Furtwängler's appointment had to concede defeat. It no longer mattered that Furtwängler proclaimed his innocence in regard to the Göring announcement of an agreement over a new contract concerning the State Opera, that he denied that he was going to be director of that institution, that he intended to conduct there only as guest and that music alone was his profession.[53] Actually, the boycott was organized by a disreputable promoter named Ira Hirschmann who even involved the German-American Bund which, in turn, was subsidized by the Nazis, leading to speculation about the coincidence of the opposition to Furtwängler of American Jews and that of a Nazi organization, most likely Rosenberg's foreign-political bureau.[54] Anti-Nazi sentiment blinded the world into believing Göring in this matter, and gave no attention to Furtwängler's testimony even though the latter was confirmed in the accounts of the German press, which had correctly referred to the conductor's position as a guest only. On other matters the Nazis were not trusted, but in this instance, Göring's statement caused the disavowal of a man who did more to resist the Nazis from within than any other artist in Germany. He told Riess after the war that at the time in Egypt, removed from the turmoil in America and the reality of the Third Reich, he could not imagine that Berlin had committed fraud, had actually lied about him. Having been ignorant of Göring's and Rosenberg's intrigues, he equated the American attacks on his person with anti-German sentiment. Having grown tired of political controversy, he decided to send a telegram to New York from Cairo: "Political controversy is disagreeable to me. I am not a politician, but an exponent of German music which belongs to all humanity regardless of politics. I propose postponement of my appearance in the interest of the Philharmonic Society until the public will realize that music and politics are apart."[55] The publication of these words caused a sensation in New York. The engagement of Furtwängler in America had been blocked by Göring and/or Rosenberg, an unscrupulous businessman, the press in New York, and the pride of the conductor.

Emboldened by the successful remilitarization of the Rhineland and in concert with their plans for the Olympics, the Nazi leaders staged a plebiscite for March 29 for which they asked artists to issue proclamations of solidarity with Hitler. Even though Furtwängler telegraphed his support of a loyalty declaration of the Reich Culture Senate—to his emigre critics an additional token of submission; a tactical move in the eyes of his supporters—Hitler decided to increase political pressure on him by arbitrarily cancelling the opera contract and postponing the actualization of a revised version for a year. When the anxious conductor finally managed to get an audience, the Führer questioned his ideological commitment. On the other hand, Hitler wanted to retain Furtwängler's service—particularly for Bayreuth in this year of the Olympics. Fully aware of an insurmountable conflict, Furtwängler followed the meeting with a letter in which he requested a leave of absence from all conducting responsibilities for a year, except for the Bayreuth Festival, in order to devote himself fully to composing.[56] Upon the appearance of his proposal in the press, his latest phase of internal exile began, based upon his understanding of Hitler's political prerogative. He withdrew to compose and conduct abroad and at Bayreuth, while remaining attentive to political developments—for instance, regarding the increasing pressure on the remaining Jews in Germany, specifically those in music for whom he had become a spokesman, and the ban on art criticism, to which he objected. He appears not to have known of a further denunciation of his ex-secretary Geissmar, submitted by a secretary at the RMVP regarding her alleged conspiracy against the Berlin Philharmonic and Germany and her manipulation of German musicians from her new position in England.[57] Geissmar did indeed maintain her connections in Germany, especially with Furtwängler, and occasionally returned to Germany for business for her new boss, Sir Thomas Beecham, and for vacation. Her activities were monitored and included in the files of Furtwängler's enemies.

On February 10, 1937 Furtwängler returned to the concert hall to conduct a Nazi charity concert (*Winterhilfskonzert*) in the presence of the party leadership and the diplomatic corps—a singular success, which initiated yet another round of involvement with the regime. His popularity with the music public had risen to new heights, and Goebbels again was forced into a chess game, a repeat of the earlier cycle in the complicated relationship. On April 10 there began a Wagner "Ring" cycle at the State Opera; his postponed contract for guest appearances was finally signed to his satisfaction at that time. He also led the Berlin Philharmonic later that month on a tour abroad as an "independent artist." His Bayreuth appearance that year was followed by a disagreeable encounter in Salzburg with Toscanini who argued, "If you conduct in Bayreuth, you can no longer conduct in Salzburg . . . today I think in terms of 'either or'."[58] The lines were drawn between the emigres who continued to cast him as a symbol of collaboration and those like Furtwängler who remained in fascist countries. While the fiery Italian had broken with his own fascist past—though still visiting his native land until the outbreak of war[59]—his German rival maintained his carefully fashioned posture of affecting Nazi policy by associating with the regime. Furtwängler proceeded to contribute to a RMVP-sponsored German cultural week in Paris—as part of the World Exhibit in September—with performances by the Berlin Philharmonic of Beethoven's Ninth and *Walküre* before an enthusiastic audience, French government officials and the diplomatic corps. While the world thus collaborated in the success of the event, Furtwängler dissociated himself from the more overt political features by having Hans von Benda conduct in his place the national anthems, before an audience which rose with raised arms upon the entrance of the French President, appearing after the speeches at an official reception hosted by the German Reich Commissioner for the World Exhibit, and turning down an invitation of an ecstatic Führer, extended to major contributors to the event.[60]

Furtwängler's position vacillated between active interaction with the public authorites and the reliance on transcendent art as an expression of resistance. He concluded 1937 fully immersed in his public activities, but also celebrated as the embodiment of German music, indeed of "old Germany" by a grateful public at home and abroad—as the apolitical artist who maintained his distance from the regime which he acknowledged at the same time. His music—apolitical as such—expressed a tradition in many ways incompatible with National Socialism—one thinks of Beethoven's explicit embrace of humanity—but it was manipulated by Goebbels nonetheless. Furtwängler's own compositions were totally escapist—neither experimental, critical or political nor reflecting international trends. Yet even that kind of music, like its literary counterpart, preserved standards of exclusivity and universality which contradicted Hitler's totalitarian claims and reinforced bourgeois denial of Nazi reality or opposition to it.

The public, which sought comfort in the redemptive powers of Furtwängler's music, also read the literature of inner emigration—an explicit form of withdrawal. Like Furtwängler's music composed in the Alps it sought refuge in some place where no problems existed. Hans Carossa offered such escape in the popular poem of the old well, *Der alte Brunnen*. Also Ernst Wiechert spoke in this manner, addressing, "the poet and youth": "Eternity is silent, noisy is everything ephemeral. Silently God's will glides over earthly strife."[61] His theme was eternal order irrespective of concrete conditions, everything having its proper place, time, and mode of expression. One year before World War II, Carossa spoke about the effects of Goethe on the present, closing with the words, "Let us confess solidarity with those who would not be content with all the world's lands and seas if the realm of the spirit and of the heart were not conquered."[62] Furtwängler's isolation in 1936 and his commitment to the transcendent idiom of music reflected the speeches of Carossa and Wiechert which extolled the virtues of the free spirit, free no matter what the social and political conditions. The autonomous poet and musician offered art as consolation and as refuge, the artist as "quiet and loyal companion" who, no longer sensitive to reality, created within a world of terror a possibility of sublime and socially effective delusion. It was no accident that the reading public of Hans Carossa increased during the Nazi era.[63] Furtwängler's escapist phases were also illustrated in the sentiments of the poet, Eugen Gottlob Winkler, who in 1936 tragically committed suicide at the age of twenty-six. Listed by Rudolf Pechel as a member of "spiritual resistance," Winkler's life and Furtwängler's compositional activity as well revealed only the artists' subjective needs, while betraying political indifference. Regarding himself as an outsider, Winkler was inclined to leave this world to its vices. In his mind, the poet did not belong to society or to the people; he was not even bound by personal human ties.[64] The apotheosis of the artist was as narrow-minded as it was unrealistic. Winkler reacted to the Nazis on aesthetic grounds, with utter contempt which the individual feels for the masses. In a letter he explained, "The approaching novelty will represent the non-spiritual, the proletarian, in disguise. It will contain the smell of the masses, the musty smell of the poor, diluted by the odor of the decaying bourgeois (*Spiessertums*), the smell of the barracks, which will suffocate us. . . . I demand an existence of contemplation which returns to the origin with the means which a culture of two thousand years has conferred upon us."[65] Winkler exemplified the position of conservative inner emigration in extreme form. Ironically, he was tolerated, furthered, and even published in Nazi books in spite of his aristocratic leanings, because he did not analyze his society; he denied it. All he could offer against the profanity of the age was a theology of art in the sublime form of a social anachronism. The decisive events, according to the escapists, occur inside, products of the inner self. The artist of inner emigration could not offer resistance, being preoccupied with the welfare of his soul. However, Berthold Brecht, the outspoken opponent and emigre, offered some understanding which might be applied to the upholders of the romantic and idealistic tradition of conservatism. "Yet I beg you, do not scorn, for all creatures need help from all."[66] That help was offered by Furtwängler whose social sense of responsibility and representative authority did not permit him to succumb for long to the impulse to withdraw which he shared with Winkler.

His withdrawal came to an end in early 1937 as we have seen; in fact, he was never entirely reconciled to an exclusively private existence. How could Germany's most representative and acknowledged leader of music settle for inner emigration? In order to resume his public life and objectives he had to renew his ambivalent relationship with the existing regime that appeared stronger than ever, thus rekindling the controversy that had aroused such passionate reactions before. Hostile to any form of collaboration, even that which involved documented resistance, some anti-fascist emigres and foreigners continued to cast him as a symbol of collaboration and Nazi crimes, even though he did not commit, author or approve any; his restorational commitments were pre- and anti-totalitarian and involved the defense of the victims of persecution, including those who denounced him for his attempted rehabilitation, while the musical establishment at large simply collaborated, lesser musicians who objected to the Nazis withdrew and known enemies of the regime were forced to emigrate. Early decisions proved to be irrevocable for everyone, even though many emigres themselves had only gradually criticized the regime and severed relations consistent with their evolving insights into deteriorating conditions which affected their maintained households in Germany, connections, business interests and the royalties they continued to receive. Furtwängler retained some options and exposed himself to the dangers of an ongoing battle with the brownshirts. Ironically, both the emigres and his overt Nazi enemies like Rosenberg and Himmler rejected his attempt to keep art separate from politics as reactionary representation of the residual *Ständestaat* which confirmed his authority.

Even though the Nazis took a dim view of his corporatist notion of authority, they continued to accept and manipulate him and his romantic idealism which he identified with them as well. Thus, misguidedly—but assuredly also for his own manipulatory reasons—he still played the professed spiritual essence of National Socialism against bureaucratic control and levelling standards. Like many Germans, he appealed to Hitler the idealist, who could be mobilized against the regime of bureaucrats—against powerful people like Heinz Drewes at the RMVP, Hans von Benda at the Berlin Philharmonic and Heinz Tietjen who, in turn, resented his slights and actively conspired against their conductor colleague. He felt so confident about the success of his policy and his indispensability as an artist that he even dared to offend Göring by asking to be relieved of his contractual obligations at the State Opera, adding that conflict in Berlin to his fight with Winifred Wagner whom he had reviled in an incredibly revealing letter—with copies sent to Hitler, Göring and Goebbels—for neglecting to live up to the demands of the Wagnerian legacy by not tolerating a first-rate musician, but relying instead on "the authoritarian state."[67] Thus he confronted the totalitarian leaders with the conviction that his position reflected their own innermost views about art. Surely, Göring would appreciate artistic integrity. In an economizing move at the State Opera the Prussian Prime Minister had elevated Tietjen—a conductor turned manager—to the position of artistic director (in place of the scrapped position of a musical director), thereby putting the returning guest conductor under the authority of a man who by then had become an enemy—an unacceptable situation. Furtwängler wanted out, even though Göring strenuously objected. A testy correspondence reveals Göring's displeasure; he resented having to deal with incidents caused by the difficult conductor on a seasonal basis.[68] Ominously, his search for a new conductor—occasioned by Furtwängler's retirement and the departure of Clemens Krauss—overlapped with the anti-Furtwängler conspiracy which had widened beyond the obvious ideologically-based campaign of Rosenberg, whose office under the administration of Herbert Gerigk compiled a dossier containing the conductor's violations of policy and indiscretions which were shared with other party and security bureaus.[69] The network of opponents included Reich Ministers, hostile culture-political functionaries, artists and the central figure—the music agent, Rudolf Vedder, an implacable enemy of the conductor ever since the latter had rejected an association with him, who had run the Concert Agency of the RMK until July 1935 and whose excellent political connections ranged from Havemann to Göring and influential officers of the SS, an organization he joined in 1941. Among his impressive clientele—a virtual who's who in German music and international soloists who performed in Germany—he represented a rising young star, Herbert von Karajan, the talented and ambitious GMD of Aachen and a Pg., who could offer quality music without the nuisance of his senior colleague. A natural rival of Furtwängler, he was manipulated into the anti-Furtwängler campaign with political overtones.

Oblivious to the surreptitious actions against him, Furtwängler pursued his independent policy which took him to post-*Anschluss* Austria to lead the Vienna Philharmonic upon the request of its leaders who had flown to Berlin to persuade him to take charge and protect it from the furious purges of that period. He introduced this orchestra to Berlin in April and to Nuremberg in September in a performance of the *Meistersinger*, a day before the Party Congress that year before an enthusiastic Hitler, party entourage and diplomatic corps—to his anti-fascist critics again an example of his deplorable collaboration, but to him and his musicians a means of preserving the distinguished institution by preventing rigid application of the Aryan paragraph in a replay of his earlier battles in behalf of the Berlin Philharmonic. During this busy summer he did not forget his Berlin Philharmonic Orchestra, which he took on an international tour.

Meanwhile, the young maestro from Aachen made his fateful debut in Berlin on April 8, 1938. He made enough of an impression for Furtwängler to recommend him in his place to conduct the Berlin Philharmonic at the Pfitzner Festival in Berlin. Karajan's real breakthrough occurred with a *Fideleo* performance at the State Opera, September 30, upon which Vedder's client was signed to a contract by Tietjen. Karajan's conquest of the Berlin public continued with his performance of *Tristan* October 21, followed by a rave review by Edwin v.d. Null in the *BZ am Mittag* (October 22, 1938), entitled, "At the State Opera: The Miraculous Karajan," which included an unseemly comparison with Furtwängler and is documented by Prieberg to be the result of the Vedder-Tietjen-Göring conspiracy against Furtwängler. Null entertained associations in Göring's Air Force Ministry and knew Göring, Tietjen and Vedder personally.[70] Furtwängler retaliated by mobilizing Goebbels, who indeed reprimanded the newspaper for its bombastic review.[71] But the papers and the public loved the controversy which was revived with the reintroduction of the State Opera Concerts for the 1940/41 season under the baton of Karajan which were compared to Furtwängler's Berlin Philharmonic Concert Series, with Göring, Tietjen and Vedder trying to exploit the gains of their client. Even Goebbels benefited from the manipulated rivalry since Furtwängler had to make concessions in order to secure the minister's protection—thus Goebbels' claim that he had broken the resistance of the man he knew to be Germany's preeminent conductor, a feeling shared by Hitler, who apparently did not care for Karajan.[72] On the defensive and not sure about the extent of the conspiracy and the danger to him, Furtwängler looked for allies, cultivated friendlier contact with the bureaucracy and even agreed to play the piano for Hitler at a Christmas reception at the chancellory in 1941.[73] Yet, naively as ever, he provoked SS officials by negatively alluding to the protection the SS offered to Vedder whom he assailed in a memo to the RMVP as an example of the wrong kind of power concentration in the art world at the time.[74]

In spite of the pressures on him, Furtwängler maintained his composure and continued to conduct and pursue his policy in behalf of the musical institutions entrusted to him. He even won a few temporary victories over some of his enemies. Karajan, who had his problems with the regime over his marriage to a woman known to be one-quarter Jewish was not able to dislodge him from his exulted position in Berlin. Vedder's corruption and venality got him expelled from the RMK in 1942—a temporary setback for a man whose career in the SS assured him of rehabilitation and further trouble for the conductor who still was not reconciled to the regime.

His involvement in Vienna set the tone of his work for the remainder of the Third Reich. He remained committed to staying, performing and to preserve institutions, while simultaneously serving as the ultimate facade for the State, which thus continued to tolerate his deviations from Nazi norms— but at a distance from the politics of Berlin. The story of the *Anschluss* has been reviewed above. Music was coordinated with incredible dispatch. The German emigres with whom Furtwängler had still spent some time before these events, Richard Tauber, Artur Schnabel, Bruno Walter, etc., had disappeared. The second phase of their flight took them to non-German parts of Europe and America. In this setting—against the background of Nazi coordination, the desertion of fine talent which included Arnold Rosé, the legendary concert master of the Philharmonic, and the hopes of the existng establishment—Furtwängler reemerged as activist. While the old music establishment again divided into factions of emigres, which formed the bitter opposition abroad, the less fortunate victims, the collaborators and genuine Nazis and the various sub-groups under the category of inner emigration, he once more clarified his position and the prospect of working in behalf of music as an institution by means of his collaboration. In Austria he could start again, assuming the responsibility of protecting the rich tradition of Viennese music, a task which he identified with the necessity of defending European culture as seasoned fighter against National Socialism. On the assumption that Furtwängler was his man, Goebbels inadvertently lent support to the conductor's design by appointing him President of the Bruckner Society, which was to be coordinated as part of the *Gleichschaltung* of Austrian musical life. This replay of an authority struggle coincided with the assertion of autonomy of party elements in Austria. *Gauleiter* Joseph Bürckel, an opponent of Goebbels' intervention in his affairs and in earnest about expert leadership in the culture of his *Gau*, appointed Furtwängler "plenipotentiary" for the entire musical life of Vienna—a power base which Furtwängler had vainly sought in the early years of dealing with the Nazis and now finally acquired in the city which was in desperate need of protection from Nazi purges and levelling designs. Goebbels felt betrayed and tried to intervene and mobilize Bürckel against Furtwängler. At one time he placed the GMD Heinrich K. Strohm from Hamburg at the head of the Vienna Opera—a disastrous appointment which Furtwängler was able to overturn with the support of the new *Gauleiter* Baldur von Schirach, who continued Bürckel's independent policy. (See Chapter II.) Furtwängler also installed his own man,

Karl Böhm as first conductor of the Opera, against the reservations of both Hitler and Goebbels. He undermined coordination efforts of the state in numerous cases, thereby contributing to the maintenance of much of Vienna's independent cultural tradition.[75] At first the Philharmonic had been subjected to the baton of a representative of Goebbels' Ministry but the musicians simply rejected him by playing poorly on purpose. Although the orchestra was integrated into the Nazi cultural administration, through Furtwängler's efforts it managed to survive as a great institution with a degree of autonomy. He had a flag bearing the Swastika removed from the Philharmonic hall, retained the remaining Jewish and half-Jewish musicians and those married to Jews and facilitated emigration and flight of those in danger.

But the overall fight did not cease. When he took the Philharmonic on a guest appearance to Munich in December, 1939, his enemies of old launched an offensive against him which was serious enough to be communicated by the secret police to Bürckel with reference to "known attitudes" and "intimate friends" who might gain influence again.[76] Yet in spite of these pressures, his position in Vienna enabled him to carry on. Moreover, Goebbels continued to value his tours as a major export article of the Reich—at the risk of his emigration which he rejected, however, even when Friedelind Wagner encouraged him to stay in Paris in December 1938 shortly after the November pogrom which affected him deeply, and on later occasions, until finally in early 1945 he escaped. The negative press campaign in New York in 1936 influenced his decision not to stay abroad, even though he continued to receive attractive offers. Meanwhile, his missionary commitment to remaining in Germany also grew. He alone raised a voice in behalf of persecuted musicians in Germany. Carl Flesch and his family were saved by him from deportation to a Polish concentration camp, while the half-Jew Heinrich Wollheim was hired by Furtwängler personally as copyist of music. He continued to be the protector of all musicians, of all shades of political and aesthetic persuasion and the Jews whenever possible. In February 1939 he hid the cabarettist Werner Finck, who was running from the Gestapo.[77] In December of that year he supported Hermann Scherchen, who was identified with left wing political and progressive musical circles, to return to Germany from Switzerland to conduct the Berlin Philharmonic, until he advised him in the summer, 1940 to go to America instead, since he would not be safe in Germany.[78] Against his own aesthetic leanings he promoted modernist composers, also in Vienna where he did so in concert with von Schirach. (See above.) In 1943, in the post-Stalingrad atmosphere, he intervened unsuccessfully in behalf of the denounced Karlrobert Kreiten (See above) whose execution sickened him and was a personal defeat.

The reason for this unique position of the "plenipotentiary" rested on the firm conviction that music was a communal experience which could be upheld against the communal pretensions of the totalitarian state. He explained later that the traditional conservative found new purpose in his art:

> Music originated with the community. As communal experience, it fulfilled another purpose in these dark years. I could offer much to those Germans who were not able to leave, yet who were bound to music—and there were many of those. I could offer the common experience, a substance which released individuals from the state of isolation. I am convinced that it was known in Germany that I remained in Germany not as a Nazi, but as a German. This knowledge provided me with strength. At that time I was told that hundreds of thousands of people regarded my music as a form of protest against the Third Reich . . . that I was something like a last hold. This was confirmed to me by those who participated in an active resistance. Rudolf Pechel, for instance, told me that circles of the resistance acknowledge the fact that I was the only member of the music establishment who really offered resistance, and that I belonged to them.[79]

While Furtwängler's resistance was manifested in individual acts of opposition, the collective expression was symbolic of spiritual resistance as he wanted it to be understood. His music rejected the Nazi spirit. For this reason he later wondered "why the *Fidelio* with its contemporary relevance was never forbidden."[80] This spiritual resistance was acknowledged by the French already before the war when, in recognition of his contribution to their world exhibition in 1937, they bestowed the honorary title of Commander of the Honorary Legion upon him which, to be official, had to be and was approved by Hitler on March 11, 1939.[81] Hitler believed Furtwängler to be Germany's most distinguished conductor and he appreciated his ceremonial value to the point of overriding earlier agreements, when he insisted that Furtwängler conduct at the "Party Congress of Peace" in 1939, announced in Nuremberg on September 1 while German soldiers were invading Poland. Furtwängler was spared from what could have become his unprecedented contribution to the most important annual party event, when Hitler cancelled it because of the war.[82]

The war imposed new strains on Furtwängler. Hitler's total war was the ultimate expression of the total state, and musicians had to lend their support. Furtwängler overcame his well-known resistance to the radio by agreeing to tape concerts at the studio and to have some of these Berlin Philharmonic concerts transmitted over the air beyond the original agreement with the Reich Radio Station which had stipulated transmission of Philharmonic concerts and thereby helped resolve the orchestra's financial crisis in 1933. During the war, the new arrangement brought classical music to new audiences and to the armed forces and earned the musicians exemption from military service. But the conductor insisted on not performing live in occupied countries. Performing abroad had been one of his most cherished activities and one which had enjoyed the support of the Nazi state. During the war he continued to make guest appearances in Italy, Sweden and Switzerland. He compromised himself by performing in Norway one week before German armed forces invaded the country in April 1940. More questionable yet was his contribution to the inauguration of the German State Opera in Prague in November 1940, although he selected Smetana's *Moldau* which the Czechs regard as a national love poem that expressed the soul of their country. When he conducted again in Prague on March 16, 1944 as part of the festivities which commemorated the five-year existence of the Reich Protectorate upon Hitler's personal request, he did so in order to avoid having to play for Hitler's birthday that year. He selected Dvořák's "New World" Symphony which featured a mixture of native Czech and American folk themes and color. The difficulty of maintaining his opposition to objectionable Nazi behavior became evident when he was not able to avoid conducting in occupied Denmark in 1942 and 1943 without jeopardizing the Scandinavian tours of his orchestras which included neutral Sweden. However, even under those compromised circumstances he remained attentive to the needs of the victims of persecution. While on tour with his Vienna Philharmonic in Spring 1943, he helped the Jewish conductor Issay Dobrowen emigrate from occupied Norway to Sweden, where he dined with him in May—an event criticized by the Nazis. The SD and other security police branded his unwillingness to conduct in occupied countries as unpatriotic behavior.[83]

Numerous other issues brought him into conflict with the authorities during the war, especially when he refused services which the state asked of him. At one time Goebbels wanted to film the history of the Berlin Philharmonic, and Furtwängler was to participate. Inasmuch as the projected distortions were unacceptable to him, he refused. He also refused participation in a Beethoven film, a project then dropped. Even in matters of supreme importance, Furtwängler resisted Goebbels' orders, aggravating the bad relations between the two when he refused to conduct at Hitler's birthday celebrations. He recalled to Goebbels that their contract had called for his status as non-political artist. In 1942, however, Goebbels approached him again in regard to Hitler's birthday. This was during the second year of the Russian campaign, and Goebbels had the assignment to drum up popular support for Hitler's leadershp, including that of Furtwängler. Yet, the conductor tried to get out of this compromising and, to him, distasteful ritual. He had prepared an alibi by commitments in Vienna at the time, and engaged Schirach in his behalf. Schirach attempted to mediate, but proved no match for Goebbels. A conference was held, and the youth leader and *Gauleiter* was simply shouted down. Furtwängler had to go to Berlin, marking one of the few times that he conducted against his will. The festivities on April 19 featured Goebbels' rousing "gratitude and loyalty" speech and Furtwängler's rendition of Bach and Beethoven's Ninth—a solemn, though to the conductor a compromising occasion, transmitted by all German radio stations and filmed by UFA. He managed to stay away from the birthday celebrations in the future by pre-arranged medical excuses. Indeed, the state never broke Furtwängler. He even declined the offer of a new house for his newly-acquired family—he married the widow Elizabeth who had four children on June 26, 1943—in order not to have to accept what undoubtedly was expropriated Jewish property, as well as the construction of a private bunker for him—one of the few "indispensable artists"—and his family, at a time when all Germans suffered from the war and the expense would have been excessive.[84] Shortly after the abortive assassination attempt of July 1944, Goebbels intended to publish a brochure entitled *We Stand and Fall with Adolf Hitler*, for which all German artists were to write some appropriate lines suggested by the title and affix their signatures. As mentioned above, Furtwängler was the only noted German artist who did not sign this loyalty declaration. Even though his refusal went unpunished, it was noted and filed by Gerigk at the Culture-Political Archives of the Rosenberg bureau and at the various police and security offices with Himmler in charge. Furtwängler continued to offend the Nazi leaders to the end of their rule. Inquiries were made into his relationship with some of the men involved in the assassination plot. While in Switzerland in 1944, where he participated at the Lucerne Music Festival in association with Jewish artists, Goebbels actually feared that his star conductor might defect. Instead, the controversial musician became the subject of a press war in Switzerland, some papers assailing him for representing the murderous Reich. He returned to Germany. Meanwhile, Martin Bormann had requested access to Rosenberg's files on dissidents and asked for the involvement of Himmler's RSHA in a purge of unreliable artists.[85] Apparently unaware of the mortal danger to him, Furtwängler remained involved in the affairs of his Berlin Philharmonic, and in December argued with representatives of the Reich Broadcasting Network over technical questions. Through his disregard for his personal security, his dedication to artistic standards and his unceasing intervention in behalf of the victims of persecution, he remained committed to the preservation of German music and the humanist tradition and to resistance to the total integration of music into the coordinated structure of National Socialism. He remained in Germany to struggle with the authorities until another trip to

Switzerland February 7, 1945 for a series of concerts. He had learned of the German collapse and the threats to him from his admirer Albert Speer, who had advised him in his conductor's room after the last Philharmonic concert in mid-December, 1944 to go to Switzerland and not to return.[86] Thus, because of Himmler's machinations, he spent the last few months of the war in Switzerland. The outcome of the war no longer in question, he left with the knowledge that his music had survived. When Hitler's death was announced over the radio, a Furtwängler recording of the Funeral March of the *Götterdämmerung* was played.[87]

Rehabilitation

The complex issue of Furtwängler, of inner emigration and collective guilt, was raised immediately after the war. Furtwängler was on an American blacklist of three hundred and twenty-seven persons who were not allowed to exercise their public profession for reasons of being a danger to public security.[88] This was at a time when Goebbels' film of the Berlin Philharmonic was playing in which all German musicians, including Strauss, participated with the exception of Furtwängler. The first clearance of name occurred in March 1946, when his efforts were recognized by an Austrian denazification commission of the Education Ministry, March 9, 1946. The commission declared that Dr. Furtwängler never belonged to the NSDAP or any of its organizations and proved himself an opponent to National Socialism and its policies toward art. It recommended his rehabilitation and reactivation in Austrian music life. The reasons for this verdict were listed as follows: 1) He resigned all posts in 1934; 2) He acted properly during the Hindemith affair; 3) The joint declaration of Furtwängler and Goebbels acknowledged Furtwängler's status as an unpolitical artist; 4) It is documented that Furtwängler supported Jews and "mixtures" in the Philharmonic orchestra; 5) Furtwängler never greeted with raised arm, not even in Hitler's presence, nor did he sign the declaration of support for Hitler, signed by all other German musicians of note; 6) The management of the Vienna Philharmonic declared that the Vienna Philharmonic Orchestra remained an autonomous organization due to efforts of Dr. Furtwängler; 7) Furtwängler refused to conduct in occupied countries; 8) His remaining in Germany contributed to the spiritual resistance and to the defense of Nazi victims. After 1939, he had to fear for his family; 9) He had not entertained intimate relations with the Propaganda Ministry; 10) He refrained from participating at official functions, except under coercion on April 20, 1942. Furthermore, the Commission pointed out that Furtwängler was ready to help rebuild life in Austria and to give benefit concerts for victims of National Socialism.

The American military commission, on the other hand, required more time. Indeed, Furtwängler had to appeal to the Allies for a denazification trial at the denazification commission for artists at the *Schlüterstrasse*. Although General McClure, chief of the Information Service Control, realized that a mistake had been made in the Furtwängler case and that Furtwängler had offered heroic resistance to the Nazis, the American authorities moved slowly in his behalf.[89] In the meantime, famous anti-fascists and victims supported Furtwängler publicly: Bruno Walter, Pablo Casals, Leo Blech, Yehudi Menuhin, Paul Hindemith and many others. On December 12, 1946, his denazification trial finally started in Germany. The chairman of the trial board, Alex Vogel, opened with a question, "You claim to have been an apolitical conductor: Are you not aware of the fact that you were active as a musician?" Furtwängler answered, "Yes, but I did not exercise my art as propaganda for National Socialism, but in order to preserve the good German name. I was active for those who were not Nazis but remained in Germany in spite of everything." The trial was heated, reflecting the violent nature of the controversy which had erupted over the position of all artists, indeed, of all Germany. Furtwängler's rehabilitation ought to have come about automatically. Yet, the issues presented here were reviewed by the various commissions in 1946. During the second meeting with the commission, December 17, favorable witnesses convinced the judges. The Jewish Clemens Herzberg, former business manager of Max Reinhardt and the head custodian of the Philharmonic, Jastrau, were key witnesses. Boleslaw Barlog, manager of the *Schlosspark*-Theatre, Berlin-Steglitz, and a passionate anti-Nazi, took the witness stand in behalf of the conductor, "Furtwängler was the reason for my staying alive throughout the Third Reich. To hear a Furtwängler concert once every four weeks—with such events we did not have to despair totally."[90]

Furtwängler was spoken free, but the opposition to him, especially abroad, did not subside. He also had to deal with the procrastination of the military government which alone had the right to implement the decision of the commission. A series of newspaper articles was published on the Furtwängler case; Erich Reger representing many antifascists when he published his article, *Die guten Willens sind* ("Those of Good Will"), in the Berlin *Tagesspiegel*. He attacked Furtwängler for his insistence that music is independent of politics, concluding that he would play again for a Hitler. Barlog countered in the most memorable defense of Furtwängler in the Berlin paper, *Der Kurier*, in an article, "For Furtwängler":

Furtwängler was one of the few great German artists who offered strong and open resistance to the Nazis. Where were the voices of those now barking so loudly against Furtwängler? . . . Do these people not know that Furtwängler still conducted Mendelssohn in 1935, do they know nothing of his intervention in behalf of Hindemith and those persecuted for racial and political reasons . . . not only musicians. The Propaganda Ministry once declared that "there is no dirty Jew in Germany for whom Herr Furtwängler would not have intervened." Do you not know that Furtwängler threw his *Staatsrat* at Göring's feet, and all his positions and titles, that he returned gifts of Hitler in the form of a monthly pension of 100,000 RM, plus house and estate, on the basis of a plea for the suffering people? . . . that in the end he had to run from Himmler to Switzerland in order to save his life? . . . Max Reinhardt has sent a message from Paris where he had emigrated, thanking Furtwängler for his behavior and declaring that he too would have stayed in Germany if he had been able to do so.[91]

The detail of Barlog's article and official commission findings were also contained in the correspondence of Furtwängler, as he justified his stand during the Third Reich to various friends and public figures.

Meanwhile, Furtwängler received various offers from abroad. The Russians already had invited him to accept a position in East Berlin, and the British wanted to engage him at the old Philharmonic. He also was notified by his friend, Enrico Mainardi, the well-known Italian cellist, that Rome wanted his services. He accepted the latter offer, therewith putting pressure on the *Schlüterstrasse* to speak him free and recommend the same action to all Allies. Finally, he was denazified officially. In May 1947, he gave his first concert in Germany again at the *Titaniaplatz* of Berlin, conducting the *Egmont* Overture, the *Pastorale* and the Fifth Symphony—an all-Beethoven concert. His music was received in the spirit of his statement before the commission: "I could not forsake Germany in its deep need. I do not regret having done this for the German people."[92]

Rehabilitation in America took longer. The issue as presented here was never quite appreciatd in the United States, where public opinion was strongly influenced by emigres who had made their choice, a different choice, by emigrating in 1933. Criticism of the collaborators was reinforced by an American tradition of democratic values and a civic spirit which showed little patience with the argument of inner emigration with which Furtwängler also was erroneously identified. The issue of inner emigration has reemerged in different contexts, for instance, in the debate about American involvement in Vietnam. Zbigniew Brzeinski, for one, has alluded to inner emigration as an option confronting the American people in a state of transition in those difficult days.[93] Although awareness of the difficulties confronting the individual when in conflict with repressive governments has increased in America, proximity to the crimes of the Nazis and the contribution of Americans toward freeing Europe from this dictatorship have contributed to the readiness to treat the affair in categories of right and wrong with not much room for a position in between. The entire realm of inner emigration was rejected by many people immediately after the war, while passions, the horrors of the immediate past, and the sense of righteousness prevailed, and even for some time thereafter—with notable exceptions; Yehudi Menuhin and Bruno Walter stood above the factionalism which still divided the anti-Nazi forces. The entire episode of Furtwängler's rehabilitation after 1945 was reflected in his correspondence—collected and published by Franck Thiess— which testifies to his consistent commitment to his personal and musical principles and his sense of responsibility as the foremost authority in the world of German music in the context of totalitarian controls—a case study of integrity and courage in our time. Most illuminating was his response to accusations of Germany's greatest emigre writer, Thomas Mann, in a letter dated July 4, 1947. He claimed that his case never belonged before a denazification tribunal. "Everybody in Germany knew and knows that I, more than any other German who remained, exerted total effort toward resistance, in spite of Hitler propaganda and photographs." He maintained that lies of American journalism (as in the *New York Times*) had distorted his motives for remaining in Germany. Indeed, he was better informed about resistance than those judging him. Thomas Mann had found distasteful a fifteen-minute ovation greeting Furtwängler, and Furtwängler countered:

Have you forgotten what music means to Germans? . . . A thirty-two minute ovation was accorded artists for a *Tristan* performance in Vienna in 1943, a work which lasted five hours. . . . Fifteen minutes for Berlin—for Beethoven are not extraordinary. . . . Germans find themselves again in Brahms and Beethoven. . . . People who welcomed back a defamed musician did demonstrate, but that is not politics. . . . *Fidelio* stood for Germany; Himmler only ruled it. . . . For you [Thomas Mann], the possibility and responsibility for helping Germany are extraordinary.[94]

Thus, the letter ended with an appeal to the great emigre to join the efforts of reconstruction.

An Apolitical Contrast : Strauss

In order to appreciate Furtwängler's singular stand, other types of inner emigration or collaboration, embodied in the accommodation of those musicians who decided to live within the Nazi system after 1933, must be recalled. For instance, Strauss symbolized the essentially traditional and apolitical group that practiced inner emigration (See Portraits, Chapter II), to the same degree that Furtwängler embodied its political and active option. By contrast, Strauss never opposed the Nazis openly, but signed what had to be signed and accepted public offices and titles imposed on him by the Nazis. Strauss and other apolitical musicians of this category never were Nazis in a positive sense; but they were practical men who looked out for themselves. The classic reaction of Furtwängler in defense of traditional authority and concomitant social relations was foreign to Strauss, who really had nothing to lose except his personal freedom like any other individual in Germany; the most representative German composer of the twentieth century upheld no principle but the one of self-preservation and the interest of his career. As such the Nazis needed and manipulated him, and he became the first president of the RMK, a position he held until the compromising letter to Stefan Zweig was intercepted by the Gestapo, which testified to his clear head as he ridiculed Nazi pretensions in matters of culture. He was removed from office and declared persona non grata. Before he fell into disfavor, however, he had lent himself to Nazi coordination. This inclination had been evident when Bruno Walter was forced to cancel his concert in Leipzig in 1933, whereupon Strauss willingly substituted. Bruno Walter commented in his memoirs that "the composer of the *Heldenleben* did indeed accept the offer to substitute for the colleague who was forcibly removed."[95]

Strauss participated in the official life of German music without registering any form of resistance. Yet, he remained independent, indeed sovereign as an artist, although as a man he was forced to adjust to the situation and compromise some personal standards. Indeed, his activities extended beyond those of the apolitical artist, as demonstrated by Furtwängler in his periods of complete withdrawal, in that he also assumed official functions. We recall his introductory address at the opening session of the RMK on February 2, 1934: "I wish to thank Reich Chancellor Adolf Hitler and Reich Minister Dr. Geobbels for the creation of the Reich Culture Chamber Law in the name of all German musicians," and Hitler's congratulations on his seventieth birthday that same year, "To the great German composer, in sincere admiration." Like Furtwängler, Strauss was of such importance to the Nazis that his opera *Die Schweigsame Frau* was performed in 1934, although the text was written by the Jew Stefan Zweig. As in the story of Furtwängler, the relationship between the Nazis and Strauss also compromised the Nazis. He took advantage of his position and prestige, not as Furtwängler had done in the interest of German music and culture, but for his own freedom as an artist. He maintained connections with victims of the Nazis, protected his Jewish relations and kept up the correspondence with his former librettist Stefan Zweig, whom he continued to ask for additional material—but, he also compromised himself. On December 6, 1934, the day of the first anniversary of the founding of the RMK, Goebbels gave a major policy address which included the denunciation of Hindemith and Furtwängler, at the end of which he read a congratulatory telegram from Richard Strauss. By implication, Strauss supported Goebbels in his denunciations. Although Strauss later disclaimed any knowledge of the telegram when interviewed abroad, the desired effect again testified to the Nazi policy of manipulating prestigious people.[96] If, indeed, the telegram was Goebbels' fabrication, Berta Geissmar still asked herself why he acted as he did. She felt so annoyed with him when she met him in England, after she had emigrated and begun work for Sir Thomas Beecham, that she did not dare ask him directly. She recalled that "he had known my parents' house and myself for many years. Yet," she wondered, "in spite of the fact that he was President of the RMK, he had not made the slightest move to help either Furtwängler or me during all our difficulties in Germany." Therefore,

> it had been out of the question for me to ask him then for even so little as to intervene in order to get my passport back. He himself made use in foreign countries of his Jewish publisher, Herr Fürstner, who had emigrated to London. Stefan Zweig and Hugo von Hoffmannsthal had written wonderful libretti for his operas; but he only remembered these things insofar as they contributed to his own interests. . . . Why had he behaved as he had in the Third Reich? Why had he not, in his position as President of the RMK, supported all of us who were by tradition and merit entrenched within the traditional musical culture of the genuine Germany?[97]

If, as he claimed, he disagreed with Goebbels' denunciation of Furtwängler and Hindemith, "why had he not protected" them, "and also people like myself, against the Government? Why had he not protected the principles vital for Germany's musical life? I burned to express my opinion that had he not played into the hands of the Nazis, many tragedies in the field of music might have been avoided." While thinking of Strauss, she also recalled another German visitor in London, the Dresden stage designer, Professor Fanto, whom everybody believed to be Jewish, although he managed to keep his position without question. Strauss, who loved to play cards wherever he was, had called together a *Skat* party in London, and the following comment was retold to Geissmar. Strauss was questioned about this Fanto, whereupon he answered, "'Well, Fanto, you see—Fanto has been clever, he has simply declared that he was a foundling and does not know anything about his parents. So the Nazis had to leave him where he was.'" Geissmar was outraged. "Considering the agonies which other people had endured on account of just one Jewish great-grandmother—at that time—it must be admitted that this statement direct from the President of the RMK seems a piece of incredible cynicism. What desperate letters addressed to Furtwängler had I seen in the years 1933-34 from people whose private and professional life had depended on the handling of the question of their parentage." Against this background of either cynicism or innocence, the first composer of his day was celebrated by the Nazis and exported by them as representative of the new Germany. At the performance of *Der Rosenkavalier* in London he sat in von Ribbentrop's box. Ribbentrop saw fit to give the Hitler salute while the British National Anthem was played—a piece of effrontery which caused great annoyance."[98]

The contrast between Strauss and Furtwängler was revealing. Furtwängler's moral conviction, his devotion to the humanist tradition and German culture and his open resistance sustained him and others throughout the entire Third Reich. Strauss, on the other hand, was removed from office after his compromising letters to Stefan Zweig were intercepted. Thus ended his significance as a public authority, not living up to the potential rooted in prominence and prestige. After his final resignation he wrote a letter to Hitler in which he insisted again that his life had been devoted to German music and that he was never active politicly. Then he asked for an audience with Hitler so that he might clarify his actions. Hitler never responded to the plea of the musician whom he only recently had honored so greatly, thereby signaling his political end. It is impossible to know what a young Richard Strauss would have done in this situation. He probably would have emigrated. The talented and energetic young musician, opportunistic and consistently anxious to live the good and pleasureful life would have made the clear-cut choice on behalf of his own interest, that of his conscience, and his international prestige. He lacked the stuff of Furtwängler, who lived for a principle, a tradition and authority, in spite of the weight of criticism directed at him from all sides.

Inner emigration in the case of Strauss betrayed weakness. Even a man of Strauss's stature became a victim once the Nazis discovered his reservations about the regime. Rosenberg, the ideological purist, had spoken out against Strauss from the beginning in the belief that the acceptance of honors in the Third Reich implied agreement over fundamentals of National Socialism. After the break, the party declared its boycott of Strauss; he was abused and neglected. Inner emigration, in this case, illustrated forced isolation which ran counter to his nature and intention. The aged composer was aware of his importance and the lack of qualification of the bureaucrats who supervised his affairs. "These are indeed sad times when an artist of my stature has to ask a petty minister what I may compose and perform. I, too, belong to the nation of 'servants and waiters' and I can almost envy my friend Stefan Zweig, who is persecuted on racial grounds."[99]

Ultimately, Strauss was represented by Furtwängler, too, and he shared the latter's authority. The spirit and greatness of Strauss were suspect to the Nazis as reflection of the autonomous music of pre-Nazi days. The importance of the Strauss affair in Nazi eyes was evidenced in the totality of his boycott, supervised by none other than Martin Bormann. All musical journals and the VB were to restrict commentary to a brief statement in regard to any Strauss concert.[100] Hitler ordered that the composer's eightieth birthday in 1944 not be celebrated. It is interesting to note that collaborators like Clemens Krauss and apolitical non-activists like Strauss accepted these instructions, observed also by Strauss admirers. Only Furtwängler protested, intervening on behalf of the grand old man. He appealed to Hitler and Goebbels, basing his argument on the fact that "we" would be regarded as ridiculous were "we" to deal with Strauss in such a way. "Our" cultural policy would not be taken seriously. Hitler agreed and permitted preparations for the performance of Die Liebe der Danae in Salzburg. His birthday was to be celebrated after all.[101] As the greatest composer of his day, Strauss represented music within the Third Reich. Political sensitivity would have turned him into a collaborator of Furtwängler, whom he resembled indirectly only in the latter's moments of withdrawal. His artistic integrity was, of course, never compromised, a fact recognized by Walter Abendroth, who took a dim view of Professor Richard Hagel's eulogy of Strauss, published in the ZfM. Hagel had called Strauss a "singular personality who would require only some slight encouragement . . . to create from the depth of his German nature the National Socialist music drama." Abendroth countered that Strauss's partnerships with Hofmannsthal and Stifter were a genuine and harmonious expression of the master's unacceptable earlier orientation which did not change during the Third Reich.[102] Indeed, Strauss remained Strauss. Because of his eminence he was tolerated, albeit in manipulated form. He looked after himself and his music, but not others, with the exception of personal relations. Emigration would have been catastrophic. Strauss not only represented the apolitical option of German artists; he also was one of many old artists for whom emigration would have introduced a life of dependence and begging. The older members of the group of emigres did not adjust well to their new surroundings. Strauss probably would have conducted once or twice in New York, become the subject of some celebration, and that would have been the end. In Germany, haunted by the Pest, he withdrew to his villa and cultivated his music.

Hitler's Social Revolution

The Nazi impact on music was mixed. While Hitler's "social revolution" was expressed in the Nazification of the musical order, that establishment revealed significant continuities in personnel and musical production—a paradoxical result of Goebbels' manipulatory plicies. Yet, the price for survival under those conditions was high. The dictatorship impeded the free development of music; the related dialogue about music was subsumed instead under the institutional conflict between the totalitarian state and the musical establishment under its conservative leader. Furtwängler represented and defended all music and musicians, the dissidents and victims as well as his traditionalist constituency, and he performed samples of all their music. Although he did not question the moral and political legitimacy of the Nazi state, he violated the substance of Nazi cultural policy and totalitarian claims. The authority struggle he initiated seriously undermined Nazi credibility in the cultural realm and provided for continuities in musical development spanning pre- and post-Nazi trends. Thus, compositions of Strauss and other apolitical musicians assumed political relevance. Their unheroic inner emigration—conditioned by what Thomas Mann contemptuously called *Machtgeschützte Innerlichkeit* (inner virtues protected by the authorities), anachronistic and manipulated to serve propagandistic ends—provided some musical substance for Furtwängler's representative political stand. This music, as that of the modernist collaborators (See Chapter III), may be added to the work of the emigres who carried on the tradition abroad. Furtwängler noted in 1947:

> We must bear in mind that we confront our own German music culture in the persons of Hindemith, but also Křenek, Weill, Toch, in Kreisler, Walter, Klemperer—irrespective of the various reasons for their emigration. And it is equally a fact that Mahler and Schönberg, no less than Mendelssohn of an earlier time, are part of the history of German music and that this music history progressed not only here but had an additional twelve years abroad.[103]

Furtwängler, Strauss, Hindemith and Schönberg contributed to the survival of the tradition—each in his own way—but only Furtwängler was in the position and had the courage to rise in defense of all musicians, the tradition and an embattled social and moral order, vested and institutional interest, and a sense of his own representative authority. Apart from the heroic features of this resistance to dictatorship, amply documented in the recorded sentiments of the actors, the authority conflict also revealed an aspect presented in the Dahrendorf thesis (cited above) which identifies Hitler as a social revolutionary and, by implication, Furtwängler as a defender of privilege, the representative of forces which resisted democratic changes in the past and continued to oppose the threat to elite interests posed by the Nazis. Hitler's social revolution—notwithstanding his pact with established elites which, on the other hand, he undermined, manipulated and selectively destroyed, and the smashing of independent labor organizations—reflected and reinforced long-range social changes which helped shape the post-1945 successor states in Germany.

Notwithstanding the propagandistic intent of all his commentary, Goebbels was quite justified in proclaiming the success of the Nazi revolution, especially with regard to the institutional coordination of music, a revolution rooted in ideological presuppositions which were as credible then to its followers as earlier conservative criticism of institutional and art-immanent aspects of culture had been. We have noted that this ideological consideration reflected the malaise of German society which had become industrialized and modernized materially without the attendant social revolution and the gradual adoption of a liberal democratic character of the political organization of states which have absorbed the move into modern industrialized society elsewhere more gracefully. Liberal and pluralist democracy is a workable modern system, since it balances ideals with stability, universal principles of liberty and equality with the acknowledged interest and mentality of the dominant middle classes. A feature of this working democracy is its strength to absorb and solve its conflicts of interests and assimilate critical thought and art, in addition to guaranteeing equal rights—conditions which were not realized in Imperial Germany and only half-heartedly in the Weimar Republic because of the unresolved contradiction between social development occasioned by rapid industrial and technological change, and the various manifestations of an elite power structure, authoritarian habits and other features of traditionalism which managed to survive.

The Nazi revolution belatedly crystallized the painful process of industrialization and concomitant features of material modernization. Coming late in its distinctly regressive and authoritarian mode and within an anachronistic social structure, the Nazis produced not a liberal democracy but the other twentieth-century answer to political organization in industrial society—the totalitarian state—which effectively challenged not only liberal sentiment, but also traditional authoritarianism.

Thus, Furtwängler's story of heroic self-consecration also revealed the unprecedented challenge to a traditional social order of which he was an authoritative and symbolic representative. This order was reflected in and celebrated institutionalized music which in its emphasis on professionalism and expressions of traditional values—including what Dahrendorf calls the cultivation of "private virtues" as a social value, to be truthful, or to do something for its own sake—ironically was also upheld by the *völkisch* members of Nazi culture. For instance, Peter Raabe attempted to restore self-governance and professional dignity within the corporate organization of the RMK which would facilitate the experience of private virtues, whereas the significance of the Nazi organization of culture lay in manipulation, terror and an emphasis on the display of public loyalty—i.e. Dahrendorf's notion of "public virtues." The musician who had anticipated the institutionalization of *völkisch* culture had to rationalize not only the dictatorial aspects of the regime, its excessive violation of decency, tradition and common standards, but also its policy of centralization, enforced public-mindedness—in short, modernization. The Third Reich did not realize the dreams of the Weimar conservatives and *völkisch* intelligentsia. Having provided the new state with ideological legitimacy, the right-wing intellectuals, *völkisch* critics and conservative aesthetes demonstrated the hopeless advocacy of an anti-political tradition of "private virtues" in the midst of violent political revolution. Hitler shared their bourgeois tastes, their nostalgia for a *völkisch* and heroic music culture, but as a politican he subordinated aesthetics to the will to power. His stand for modernity meant an avowal of those features of our civilization that conservatives and *völkisch* critics despised. In order to gain and maintain power and to implement his imperialistic designs, Hitler—the product and the manipulator of the masses—cultivated technology, bureaucracy, the principles of rationalism, big business and rationalized production in agriculture. Modern states and armies rely on the accumulation of capital, manipulation of the masses, the efficient distribution of resources, and, finally, the pact with the power establishment—necessities which were anathema to *völkisch* visions. The *völkisch* movement had contributed to Hitler's success, having inveighed against massification, rationalism, industrialization and capitalism in its endeavor to recreate a traditional community; it had lent a spiritual and intellectual aura to Nazism; but, in the reality of Nazi power, it survived only to illustrate some fundamental contradictions of the totalitarian creed.

Musicians as a group shared in the general German reverence for the state which they served in exchange for its patronage. Their anti-democratic sentiments reflected the nature of a closed corporation—vestige and accompaniment of the *Ständestaat*, the traditional social order. When the state intervened in musical affairs in 1933, providing full employment and official recognition, the experience of apparent continuity was reassuring. Yet, Nazi totalitarianism developed its own ruthless dynamic and violated traditional norms and values. It also became clear that all independent authority would have to be destroyed for the Nazi state to realize its totalitarian potential. Thus, on political grounds Nazism undermined the very tradition with which it shared many ideological assumptions. The self-conscious and self-respecting traditionalist musician lost, as the Pg's challenged musical standards, ethics, and old authorities—reflected in the hostility to Furtwängler in the provinces. Ideological conformity threatened individuality and dignity as understood by the middle class.

The musical memoir literature takes us back to a realm of the old German middle class which had aspired to share in a common culture with traditional elites, ranging from the great bourgeoisie of the salons to the petty employee of a small orchestra. The fears of this aspiring class prompted a turn to the political right before Hitler denied free elections altogether. Having voted traditionally for the German People's Party, the Democratic Party, the Business Party, or parties of similar middle-class orientation, the conservative musician saw the parties he supported decline to 25 percent in 1928, by 1932 to 5 percent, and in March 1932, to 2.5 percent, while inversely, the vote for the Nazis grew from 2.6 percent in 1928 to the well-known statistic of 43.9 percent in the last relatively free election. Social historians have determined that in addition to the change of voters, the Nazi elite was able to draw on a disproportionate number of civil servants, employees, minor officials, servants and independents, constituting significant sectors of the middle classes. The support and leadership of National Socialism was a middle-class phenomenon with emphasis on its lower social sector.[104] This German middle class fought against being recognized as a class, denied the reality of class struggle and lent itself to the regressive ideology of an embattled order. In view of the Furtwängler story, which more than anything reflects the upper middle-class and traditional elites of German society, it is ironic that this longing for the strong state—the middle-class reaction in all societies to insecurity—resulted in the seizure of power by the radical right.

Hitler's early days in power took the form of a legal revolution which quickly transformed the political structure of Germany. This radical process created the basis for the social revolution that Imperial Germany had missed and the Weimar Republic had held up—that alternate road to modernity. Insofar as the German music establishment was traditionalist, conservative and acceptable to National Socialism in ideological terms, it accepted the legal revolution which was justified on grounds of economic interest and some common ideas. But the social revolution, a consequence of complete Nazi control and the unfolding of the totalitarian state, had not been intended and was not in the interest of the institution. Hence, Furtwängler's stand touched on fundamentals. Even Nazi musicians have repeatedly expressed resentment over excessive centralization and the inevitable process of bureaucratization. Thus, National Socialism was both a blessing and disaster to the apolitical, yet sympathetic music establishment. The concept of equal opportunities of all people, perhaps the most specific characteristic of a modern society, is no necessary consequence of industrialization and will not overcome vested interest and tradition without a fight. The plunge into a modern society, therefore, had always been a painful process—measured in uprootedness, insecurity and human sacrifice; but, the later the break, the more severe the pain. That brutal break with tradition in Germany marked the social consequences of the Nazi revolution.[105]

Hitler had to suppress the social order which had blocked effective democracy before and then stood in the path of his totalitarian ambitions. Total power of the new state was predicated on the destruction of mediating authorities and institutions, inasmuch as institutions generally bind their members in loyalty. Thus, the individual was forced to transfer loyalty from weakened traditional authority and institutions to the state. The RMK became the new home of musicians, structurally part of the centralized authority, controlled and protected by it. The elimination of autonomous institutions and authorities constituted the reality of the social revolution in music, in the context of which the social base of traditional authoritarianism mobilized resistance of German society. Obviously, the state had to assert its prerogative, even though Hitler was forced to fight for modernity against his own bourgeois sentiments in order to survive; he had to centralize his power and pursue the legal revolution. The *Länder* had to lose sovereignty, the bureaucracy and justice had to be centralized, and entrenched social interest had to be undermined. Coordination was the beginning, but total integration was the goal; traditional autonomies, customs and morals had to fall. Surviving authorities of the old order were manipulated in the interest of the broad social revolution. Furtwängler faced the overwhelming power and resources of the mass state, in which traditional autonomy gave way to subordination. Inequalities in organization were theoretically removed, since all administrative functions were subordinated to the central organization, thus constituting the basis for realizing the egalitarian impulse of National Socialism. The totalitarian state differs, therefore, from traditional authoritarian practice of allowing for the existence of other authoritarian institutions and autonomies, and from liberalism which also is posited on the idea of a free play of competing interests. Since totalitarian leadership is threatened by institutions, it has to ask for the elimination of all private spheres. Thus, the contradiction between ideology and practice is not surprising. Nazi power was not based on tradition, nor could the old authoritarian system be recreated. The Nazis were compelled to become totalitarians or transform themselves altogether.

National Socialism was characterized by other paradoxes. It was born of bourgeois insecurity and resentment, while it denied the reality of bourgeois class interest and mentality. It stood for tradition in theory, while in reality it buried tradition. Also the family suffered from a dual Nazi vision. The family existed for the sake of reproduction, as part of the totalitarian principle and imperialistic design, yet also as symbol of the romantic and regressive features of the ideology. Peter Raabe encouraged a return to chamber music, pleading for financial support for the cultivation of music in the home. The state was to support the fundamental social institution which had harbored traditional and therefore anti-revolutionary sentiments. Yet, radical revolutionary thought suggested the elimination of the family. Although the family survived in practice, the state invaded it as well in the endeavor to undermine loyalty even in this smallest social unit. After 1936 all eleven-year-olds had to join the HJ. In its policy of creating a public-minded community, the regime found the family to be an obstacle. Whereas traditional authoritarianism and absolutism have invoked paternal authority and that of God, the totalitarian state fought all potential rivals. The family, the Church and other social groups were not allowed to exist as possible barriers between the individual and the state. Also, professional ties had to be broken since the social reality of a closed professional estate is as hostile to democracy as to totalitariansm. Dahrendorf reminds us that the relocation of populations was no Soviet invention, that the Nazis had already practiced the transference of people out of their native setting, reflecting a fundamental totalitarian policy to which the mass organization of the party lent itself.[106] New organizations such as the giant DAF or the various cultural formations, the army, political armed forces and youth groups absorbed the recently uprooted and contributed to the shaping of a new culture based on uniformity. Traditionalism had always been characterized by its resistance to modernization, thus having provided ideological support to the political right wing which had been poised against progressive political grups that welcomed change. The misalliance between conservatives and Nazis was only understood in the wake of the social revolution which had been imposed by the Nazis in consequence of their legal revolution. The story of music as reviewed in the above pages reflects this same process, beginning with the imposition of a unified administration (legal revolution). Traditional ties, loyalties and identifications were undermined in the work of coordination, relocation, the creation of new organizations and an infusion of the pervasive ideology, and the resistance of an entrenched order, represented by Furtwängler. In social perspective, the *Volksgenosse* constituted the smallest social unit of the Nazi state who, as a musician, contributed to his culture in his specified realm. As a public servant he was forced to participate in the construction of the cultural facade from the heights of the Philharmonic and the State Opera to the village band, from manipulated expressions of high art to political music at party functions. This public orientation of the Nazi musician differed from that of the musician in a liberal democracy. Socially, Germans became public-minded, but they did not influence policy, nor did they care to. They demonstrated in behalf of the state, unless they withdrew into inner emigration. The public function of music was clearly formulated and generally applied in practice, although deviations and violations were not uncommon, as in the perpetuation of the primacy of the private, manifested in inner emigration, but also in the resistance of the churches, various coordinated conservative powers, and above all, the rootedness of most Germans in their localities, professions, surviving institutions and embattled traditions. By 1938, Germany was a totalitarian society of sorts, but also one which reflected its authoritarian tradition. The conservative ally, witness Furtwängler, was not eliminated, but permitted to perform and even to question policy. In the end, it was the war which was the greatest catalyst for change, since it tended to favor social mobility and egalitarianism, but also expediencies which again violated principles. Without a liberal past, the opposition to the Nazis reflected the interests of a traditional social order.

According to Dahrendorf, Hitler's social revolution culminated in the events of July 20, 1944, when the aristocracy and the social-democratic and bourgeois leadership were annihilated. After this date the return of German society to the social constitution of the Empire became impossible. It must be recalled in connection with the story of Furtwängler that resistance to Hitler paradoxically had a regressive dimension. Irrespective of the overwhelming features of decency and heroism, even the realization of resistance in the affair of July 20, 1944, did not constitute a step toward a liberal constitution of German society. In the event of a successful coup, the conspirators envisioned a traditional and authoritarian form of government. By contrast, Hitler's actions pointed toward modernization, thereby providing the basis for the genuine transformation of German society and later the constitution of freedom, whereas the resistance to his regime reflected regressive, if humanist, intention and traditional authoritarianism. Thus, concludes Dahrendorf, the sad course of German history illustrates the unique discrepancy between liberalism and morality, between the free and the good society. The consequences of July 20 signaled the end of a traditional elite.[107] Furtwängler had contact with some of the conspirators and was suspected of having been privy to their plans. Yet, he survived. His authority, rooted in a peripheral activity, was maintained, but obviously in subordination to the interests of the state. When the social consequences of Nazism were realized in their total surrender of traditional values, the concomitant demonstration of faith in victory and the brutal suppression of any form of opposition, Furtwängler had to remove himself from Himmler's clutches.

Within the broad outline of Hitler's social revolution, the struggles in Germany's music establishment—between an established order and the totalitarian organizers, the *völkisch* element of an older generation and the younger Nazis, and ideological purity versus organizational, political and ultimately social consequences of power—assume historic significance. Goebbels' organization carried through its policy in the RMK which met the need for security and molded a sense of social responsibility and public-mindedness in the spirit of National Socialism. Although the *völkisch* elite lent itself to totalitarian design, Raabe's *völkisch* vision, based, as it were, on the primacy of private virtues, also was incompatible with the social implications of the Nazi revolution. The President of the RMK confirmed the legal revolution with his musical policy in order to realize a traditional and idyllic music culture within a conservative social structure. As a Nazi, he rivaled Furtwängler's authority, but as an individual he simply did not possess the stature of an effective opponent. Furtwängler represented the traditional institution and, as such, also spoke for Raabe against the totalitarian regime which violated its own principles as spelled out by its highest music official. The disillusioned moralist of a former era, the politician of cultural despair, participated in the struggle for Germany against the world. In the context of battle, during World War II, differences in the nation were to disappear, rivals were to embrace, and *völkisch* sensibilities were to be suppressed. In tying the fate of music to that of Germany and National Socialism, the *völkisch* musician lost his own tradition. The world which he had denounced had also shaped National Socialism, and the Nazis were sufficiently realistic to liberate themselves from the regressive vision of an ideal *völkisch* community in order to satisfy their will to power which dictated the primacy of politics. The modern world is not run by musicians, notwithstanding the German idealist tradition, the romantic apotheosis of the artist and the false individualism invoked in the Wagnerian music drama. Hitler's success must in large part be attributed to the elites of the old Imperial order which survived the Weimar Republic and accommodated themselves in the belief that their social order could be perpetuated against the reality of modern conditions. Having failed to embrace the principles of liberal democracy, conservative interest and *völkisch* vision had brought to power an alternative agent of modernity, but that was unintentional. Henceforth, music in German had to accommodate itself to modern conditions, similar to those existing in other Western countries— one consequence of Hitler's social revolution.

ENDNOTES

[1]The Furtwängler record in the Third Reich is on file at the BDC and the BA from which much of this chapter is drawn. See also Furtwängler, *Vermächtnis* and Frank Thiess (ed.), *Wilhelm Furtwängler Briefe* (Wiesbaden, 1964), as well as the secondary literature already cited above by Geissmar, Riess and Prieberg, in addition to Bernd W. Wessling, *Furtwängler: Eine kritische Biographie* (Stuttgart, 1985) and Daniel Gillis, *Furtwängler and America* (New York, 1970).

[2]Address at the Annual Congress of the RKK, November 26, 1937; Mosse, *Nazi Culture*, 152.

[3]See a list of names in Prieberg, *Furtwängler*, 443-444.

[4]Ibid.; reference to Wilhelm Furtwängler Archives, Zurich.

[5]Ibid, 74-75. While this objective is clear to Prieberg, it is not to Wessling, who interprets the same conflicts and Furtwängler's political arrangement as a sign of opportunism and the beginning of shameful collaboration. Neither conclusion can be sustantiated convincingly.

[6]*VB*, April 6, 1933; also in Slonimsky, 564-565.

[7]Both letters have been reprinted in Geissmar, Riess, Wessling and, in translation, in Noakes and Pridham, 342-344.

[8]Prieberg, *Furtwängler*, 78-83.

[9]Prieberg denies that Goebbels has made the statement frequently attributed to him that "there is no dirty Jew left in Germany for whom Furtwängler has not pleaded." He traced the same idea in less vulgar terms to a letter of Prof. Dr. Georg Gerullis of Rust's ministry to Hinkel: "Can you name a Jew for whom Furtwängler does not intercede?..." (Ibid., 133-134.) My copy of this letter from the BDC, stamped received July 30, 1933, confirms Prieberg's conclusion.

[10]Editorial, *Hakenkreuzbanner*, April 1933; Prieberg, *Furtwängler*, 91.

[11]BA, R55/1138.

[12]Prieberg even argues that he became a scapegoat for Nazi crimes; in *Furtwängler*, 24-25.

[13]See Grete Busch, *Fritz Busch: Dirigent* (Frankfurt a.M., 1970), 65-66.

[14]The BDC contains this appeal as well as many others by Furtwängler for victims and poten-

tial victims of purges.

[15]Prieberg, *Furtwängler*, 119-120.

[16]*Furtwängler Briefe*, n. 155.

[17]This is also Prieberg's conclusion on hand of his perusal of unpublished papers at the Wilhelm Furtwängler Archives (WFA), passim.

[18]Cited in Jürgen Mainka, "Von innerer zu äusserer Emigration: Eine Szene in Paul Hindemith's Oper *Mathis der Maler*, in Heister and Klein, 271.

[19]Walter, 143.

[20]*Vermächtnis*, 40.

[21]BA, R55/1147.

[22]Geissmar, 91. See Kreisler's appeal in *Berliner Börsenzeitung*, April 6, 1933; Prieberg, *Furtwängler*, 77.

[23]Geismar, 92.

[24]Ibid., 92-94.

[25]Ibid., 95-97.

[26]Eisler, 231.

[27]BA, R55/1184.

[28]Contract development in Furtwängler file, BDC. See memo of v. Keudell of Section VI, RMVP, March 14, 1934.

[29]BA, R55/197.

[30]BDC.

[31]Geissmar, 128.

[32]*Furtwängler Briefe*, n. 77.

[33]Prieberg corrects Geissmar and others who have incorrectly placed the concert in October, 1934; *Furtwängler*, 168-169, 448.

[34]Geissmar, 129-130.

[35]Ibid., 132-134.

[36]Ibid.

[37]Ibid.

[38]Riess, 178.

[39]Hindemith file, BDC: Hindemith report, June 1935; Havemann evaluation, June 18, 1935; various memoranda in Hindemith's behalf by Stein.

[40]Geissmar, 141.

[41]See the detailed account of these dramatic days, an examination of Furtwängler's emotional attachment to Germany and the Nazis' expressions of gratitude to him in Prieberg, Furtwängler, 190-199—based, in part, on the author's thorough analysis of hitherto unpublished materials in the WFA.

[42]Riess, 185.

[43]VB, December 12, 1934.

[44]For example, Furtwängler to Funk, January 3, 1935, BDC.

[45]Riess, 201

[46]"Furtwängler bedauert, DM (March 1935), 437.

[47]Furtwängler Briefe, n. 70.

[48]Geissmar, 158-159.

[49]Ibid., 98.

[50]Frauenfeld to Funk, RKK, July 23, 1935 and RMVP, Section VI to Hinkel at RKK, August 3, 1935; Jolli to Hinkel, September 17, 1935; and Stuckenschmidt to Hinkel, May 3, 1933 and Furtwängler to Hinkel, February 12, 1936; BDC.

[51]Riess, 213.

[52]Berliner Börsen-Zeitung, February 29, 1936; Prieberg, Furtwängler, 255-258.

[53]Riess, 214.

[54]See Prieberg, Furtwängler, 256-258.

[55]Riess, 215.

[56]Furtwängler to Hitler, April 24, 1936, BDC.

[57]Maria Zinkler's denunciation, May 24, 1936 and Berndt to Moraller, May 25, 1936, BDC.

[58]Riess, 226.

[59]Daniel Gillis, 54-57; Prieberg, *Furtwängler*, 457.

[60]Prieberg, *Furtwängler*, 286-288.

[61]Franz Schonauer, *Deutsche Literatur im Dritten Reich* (Olten and Freiburg, 1961), 127.

[62]Hans Carossa, *Wirkung Goethes in der Gegenwart* (Leipzig, 1938), 34.

[63]Schonauer, 129.

[64]Hellmuth Langenbucher, *Dichtung der Jungen Mannschaft* (Hamburg, 1935), 95.

[65]Heinrich Anacker, *Die Trommel: SA-Gedichte* (Munich, 1940), 49.

[66]Berthold Brecht, *Selected Poems* (New York, 1947), 112.

[67]November 15, 1937, WFA; Prieberg, *Furtwängler*, 288-289.

[68]*Görings Schreibtisch*, 37-43.

[69]See the dramatic unfolding of the anti-Furtwängler intrigue revealed in the exhaustive research and compelling arguments of Prieberg in his *Furtwängler*, 290-348.

[70]Ibid., 320.

[71]Bernd Ruland, *Das War Berlin* (Bayreuth, 1972), 280; Prieberg, *Furtwängler*, 315.

[72]Goebbels, *Diary*, May 29, 1943; BA, NL 118/55.

[73]Prieberg, *Furtwängler*, 336.

[74]Ibid., 331-332.

[75]Riess, 235.

[76]BA, R58/375.

[77]Prieberg, *Furtwängler*, 352.

[78]Ibid., 365.

[79]Riess, 241.

[80]Ibid., 243.

[81]BDC.

[82]Bormann to Rosenberg, July 25, 1939; BA, NS 8; Prieberg, *Furtwängler*, 362.

[83]Prieberg cites a draft of a recommendation letter addressed to Luschek, Security Police, Victoria Terrace, Oslo; *Furtwängler*, 390. See also Riess, 254. The SD Reports in BA, NS 15/73; Prieberg, *Furtwängler*, 398-399.

[84]Furtwängler to Hitler, May 21, 1944; BA, R3/1578.

[85]Prieberg, *Furtwängler*, 416-418.

[86]*Erinnerungen* (Frankfurt a.M., 1969), 466.

[87]Riess, 252-268.

[88]*Furtwängler Briefe*, n. 116.

[89]Riess, 19, 278-280.

[90]Ibid., 289-292.

[91]Ibid., 294. See above, n. 9, for the "dirty Jew" reference.

[92]Riess, 29.

[93]*The New Republic*, December 23, 1967.

[94]*Furtwängler Briefe*, n. 163.

[95]Walter, 194.

[96]Geissmar, 145.

[97]Ibid., 229-230.

[98]Ibid., 230-231.

[99]*Strauss-Zwieg Briefwechsel*, 158.

[100]Wulf, *Musik*, 199-200.

[101]Riess, 264.

[102]"Seltsam! Äusserst seltsam!", *DM* (November 1935), 117-120.

[103]*Vermächtnis*, 44.

[104]Dahrendorf, 423-424.

[105]Ibid., 432.

[106]Ibid., 438.

[107]Ibid., 442-444.

INDEX

Index

Illustrations

Rootedness of Music in Village Life (near Magdeburg)

Ich knipste diese Kinderschar,
Als ich in Gutenswegen war.
Sie hatten eine Trommel mit
Und gingen fast im gleichen Schritt.

Ich bremste schnell mein Auto ab.
Mein Apparat, der sagte schnapp
Und schnappte sich die Patrioten.
Hier ist der Anblick, den sie boten.

Children in Gutenswegen, April 8, 1933

Hitler Youth in Hecklingen, May 30, 1935

"Onward with our flag"—text by Hitler Youth leader Baldur von Schirach. Hitler Youth march of the Ufa film, "Hitler boy Quex."

Reich Labor leader Franz Seldte handing to the composer Hermann Blume the first prize in a folk song competition, November 15, 1933.

Hitler Youth playing at a Midsummer Night celebration in Finland, 1936.

I. Lieder der N. S. D. A. P., Vaterlands- und Soldatenlieder

Das Horst Wessel-Lied*)

On everybody's lips: The Horst-Wessel-Song of the SA

The army

The SA Standard "Komotau" on the "Day of the German People," June 1939.

Franz Adam conducting the National Socialist
Symphony Orchestra, 1937.

Hans Hinkel addressing Hans von Benda and the Berlin Chamber Orchestra
before 2000 members of the Waffen-SS, February 7, 1941.

Hitler in the Walhalla near Regensburg before the bust of Anton Bruckner just dedicated by him. June 6, 1937.

Hitler at a window of the Festival House at Bayreuth receiving the "Sieg Heil" of the Wagner community, 1940.

Music Organization

Goebbels addressing the Reich Culture Chamber at the Berlin
Philharmonic, November 15, 1935. Front row: Hitler; to his
right Walter Funk and Max Amann; left: Hermann Göring,
Rudolf Hess, Werner v. Blomberg, Wilhelm Frick.

Richard Strauss (Right) and
Wilhelm Furtwängler at the
opening of the Reich Culture
Chamber, November 15, 1933.

The successor of Strauss as
President of the Reich Music
Chamber, Peter Raabe.

Hitler congratuating Alfred Rosenberg on the Ideology Leader's forty-fifth birthday, January 12, 1938.

Elley Ney in a picture by Walter Rath in a Beethoven Hall program in Bonn, June 27, 1934.

Wilhelm Bruckner-Ruggenberg conducting the Berlin Philharmonic Orchestra at a Recreational Concert, R. Stock & Co., Berlin-Marienfelde, April 9, 1937.

Hitler and company at a concert of Sir Thomas Beecham and the London Philharmonic Orchestra at the Berlin Philharmonic, November 13, 1936.

Wilhelm Furtwängler rehearsing the Berlin Philharmonic Orchestra on tour in London, January 1934.

Culture Supervisor Hans Hinkel addressing the foreign press at the German Foreign Club, April 21, 1941.

Kurt Singer, conducting the chorus and orchestra of the Jewish Culture League in Handel's oratorio, "Israel in Egypt," February 1937.

Caricature of Ernst Krenek's Jonny figure on the "Degenerate Music" exhibit poster and brochure, May 1938.

Arnold Schönberg and Kurt Weill as "degenerate music" exhibit items, May 1938.

Furtwängler before the Berlin Hitler Youth, February 4, 1938.

Furtwängler and Yehudi Menuhin after a concert at the Titania Palast, Berlin, October 1, 1947.

Organization of the Reich Music Chamber (RMK) August 1934

REICH MUSIC CHAMBER
President: Richard Strauss
Deputy: Wilhelm Furtwängler
Council: Wilhelm Furtwängler, Gustav Havemann, Fritz Stein,
       Paul Graener, Heinz Ihlert, Gerd Kernbach
Managing Director: Heinz Ihlert

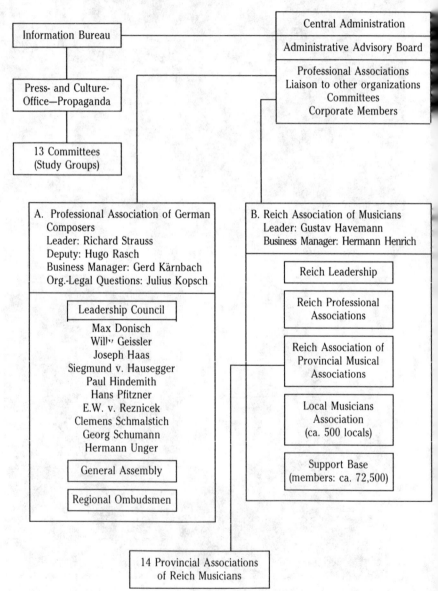

Information Bureau

Central Administration

Administrative Advisory Board

Press- and Culture-
Office—Propaganda

Professional Associations
Liaison to other organizations
Committees
Corporate Members

13 Committees
(Study Groups)

A. Professional Association of German
   Composers
Leader: Richard Strauss
Deputy: Hugo Rasch
Business Manager: Gerd Kärnbach
Org.-Legal Questions: Julius Kopsch

Leadership Council

Max Donisch
Will·ʏ Geissler
Joseph Haas
Siegmund v. Hausegger
Paul Hindemith
Hans Pfitzner
E.W. v. Reznicek
Clemens Schmalstich
Georg Schumann
Hermann Unger

General Assembly

Regional Ombudsmen

B. Reich Association of Musicians
Leader: Gustav Havemann
Business Manager: Hermann Henrich

Reich Leadership

Reich Professional
Associations

Reich Association of
Provincial Musical
Associations

Local Musicians
Association
(ca. 500 locals)

Support Base
(members: ca. 72,500)

14 Provincial Associations
of Reich Musicians

See Chapter II, especially the section on the RMK for detail. Note: The categories at the periphery of the chart, titled "Committees (Study Groups)" at the left side and "Liaisons..." at the right, were not part of the chamber organization as such. The actual structure was divided into 1) the top management which, in turn, was controlled by the RKK, Section VI (theatre, music and art)—and, since 1937, Section X (music) of the RMVP; 2) the central offices which attended to organizational and business matters affecting the whole chamber; and 3) the seven professional divisions (A-G), the core of the chamber which administered actual professional music life. The national organization extended to the provincial and local level as seen at the bottom left of the chart. The divisions A-G had absorbed new and existing music associations whose dissolution was planned. While sections A and B in 1934 included 74,623 "creative" and "recreative" professional musicians, sections E, F and G included representatives of the business side of music (music publishers, dealers and the instrument trade). Concert promoters and the copyright board (STAGMA) were included in division C. Division D included 1.45 million lay members of choral and folk music associations who did not belong to the chambers individually. Increasingly the Music Section of the RMVP affected music-political centralization and manipulated the affairs of the RMK.

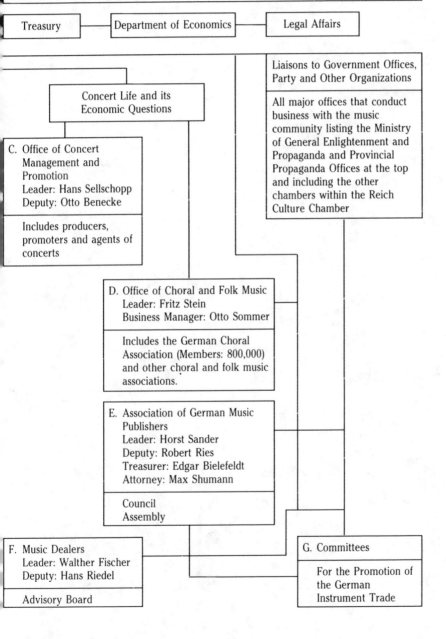

| Treasury | Department of Economics | Legal Affairs |

Liaisons to Government Offices, Party and Other Organizations

All major offices that conduct business with the music community listing the Ministry of General Enlightenment and Propaganda and Provincial Propaganda Offices at the top and including the other chambers within the Reich Culture Chamber

Concert Life and its Economic Questions

C. Office of Concert Management and Promotion
Leader: Hans Sellschopp
Deputy: Otto Benecke

Includes producers, promoters and agents of concerts

D. Office of Choral and Folk Music
Leader: Fritz Stein
Business Manager: Otto Sommer

Includes the German Choral Association (Members: 800,000) and other choral and folk music associations.

E. Association of German Music Publishers
Leader: Horst Sander
Deputy: Robert Ries
Treasurer: Edgar Bielefeldt
Attorney: Max Shumann

Council
Assembly

F. Music Dealers
Leader: Walther Fischer
Deputy: Hans Riedel

Advisory Board

G. Committees

For the Promotion of the German Instrument Trade